ALSO BY PAUL AUSTER

NOVELS

The New York Trilogy

In the Country of Last Things

Moon Palace

The Music of Chance

Leviathan

Mr Vertigo

Timbuktu

The Book of Illusions

Oracle Night

The Brooklyn Follies

Travels in the Scriptorium

Man in the Dark

Invisible

Sunset Park

Collected Novels: Volume One

Collected Novels: Volume Two

Collected Novels: Volume Three

Collected Novels: Volume Four

NONFICTION

The Invention of Solitude

The Art of Hunger

Hand to Mouth

The Red Notebook

Collected Prose

Winter Journal

Here and Now
(with J. M. Coetzee)

Report from the Interior

SCREENPLAYS

Smoke and Blue in the Face

Lulu on the Bridge

The Inner Life of Martin Frost

Collected Screenplays

POETRY

Collected Poems

ILLUSTRATED BOOKS

Auggie Wren's Christmas Story
(with Isol)

City of Glass
(adapted by Paul Karasik
and David Mazzucchelli)

EDITOR

True Tales of American Life

TRANSLATOR

Chronicle of the Guayaki Indians
by Pierre Clastres

4 3 2 1

4 3 2 1

□

PAUL AUSTER

FABER & FABER

First published in the UK in 2017
by Faber & Faber Ltd
Bloomsbury House, 74–77 Great Russell Street,
London, WC1B 3DA

First published in the US in 2017
by Henry Holt and Company, LLC
175 Fifth Avenue, New York, New York 10010

Printed and bound by CPI Group (UK) Ltd, Croydon, CR0 4YY

The right of Paul Auster to be identified as author
of this work has been asserted in accordance with Section 77
of the Copyright, Designs and Patents Act 1988

"Le sourd et l'aveugle," in *Capitale de la douleur*, Paul Eluard
© Editions Gallimard, 1926. Printed by permission of Editions
Gallimard.

"Au bout du monde," in *Fortunes*, Robert Desnos © Editions
Gallimard, 1942. Printed by permission of Editions Gallimard.

*This is a work of fiction. All of the characters, organizations, and events
portrayed in this novel either are products of the author's imagination
or are used fictitiously.*

A CIP record for this book
is available from the British Library

ISBN 978–0–571–32462–0

3 5 7 9 10 8 6 4 2

for Siri Hustvedt

4 3 2 1

1.0

ACCORDING TO FAMILY LEGEND, FERGUSON'S GRANDFATHER departed on foot from his native city of Minsk with one hundred rubles sewn into the lining of his jacket, traveled west to Hamburg through Warsaw and Berlin, and then booked passage on a ship called the *Empress of China,* which crossed the Atlantic in rough winter storms and sailed into New York Harbor on the first day of the twentieth century. While waiting to be interviewed by an immigration official at Ellis Island, he struck up a conversation with a fellow Russian Jew. The man said to him: *Forget the name Reznikoff. It won't do you any good here. You need an American name for your new life in America, something with a good American ring to it.* Since English was still an alien tongue to Isaac Reznikoff in 1900, he asked his older, more experienced compatriot for a suggestion. *Tell them you're Rockefeller,* the man said. *You can't go wrong with that.* An hour passed, then another hour, and by the time the nineteen-year-old Reznikoff sat down to be questioned by the immigration official, he had forgotten the name the man had told him to give. *Your name?* the official asked. Slapping his head in frustration, the weary immigrant blurted out in Yiddish, *Ikh hob fargessen (I've forgotten)!* And so it was that Isaac Reznikoff began his new life in America as Ichabod Ferguson.

He had a hard time of it, especially in the beginning, but even after it was no longer the beginning, nothing ever went as he had imagined it would in his adopted country. It was true that he managed to find a wife for himself just after his twenty-sixth birthday, and it was also true that this wife, Fanny, née Grossman, bore him three robust and healthy sons, but life in America remained a struggle for Ferguson's grandfather from the day he walked off the boat until the night of March 7, 1923, when he met an early, unexpected death at the age of forty-two—gunned down in a holdup at the leather-goods warehouse in Chicago where he had been employed as a night watchman.

No photographs survive of him, but by all accounts he was a large man with a strong back and enormous hands, uneducated, unskilled, the quintessential greenhorn know-nothing. On his first afternoon in New York, he chanced upon a street peddler hawking the reddest, roundest, most perfect apples he had ever seen. Unable to resist, he bought one and eagerly bit into it. Instead of the sweetness he had been anticipating, the taste was bitter and strange. Even worse, the apple was sickeningly soft, and once his teeth had pierced the skin, the insides of the fruit came pouring down the front of his coat in a shower of pale red liquid dotted with scores of pellet-like seeds. Such was his first taste of the New World, his first, never-to-be-forgotten encounter with a Jersey tomato.

Not a Rockefeller, then, but a broad-shouldered roustabout, a Hebrew giant with an absurd name and a pair of restless feet who tried his luck in Manhattan and Brooklyn, in Baltimore and Charleston, in Duluth and Chicago, employed variously as a dockhand, an ordinary seaman on a Great Lakes tanker, an animal handler for a traveling circus, an assembly-line worker in a tin-can factory, a truck driver, a ditchdigger, a night watchman. For all his efforts, he never earned more than nickels and dimes, and therefore the only things poor Ike Ferguson bequeathed to his wife and three boys were the stories he had told them about the vagabond adventures of his youth. In the long run, stories are probably no less valuable than money, but in the short run they have their decided limitations.

The leather-goods company made a small settlement with Fanny to compensate her for her loss, and then she left Chicago with the boys, moving to Newark, New Jersey, at the invitation of her husband's relatives, who gave her the top-floor apartment in their house in the Central Ward for a nominal monthly rent. Her sons were fourteen, twelve, and nine. Louis, the oldest, had long since evolved into Lew. Aaron, the middle child, had taken to calling himself Arnold after one too many schoolyard beatings in Chicago, and Stanley, the nine-year-old, was commonly known as Sonny. To make ends meet, their mother took in laundry and mended clothes, but before long the boys were contributing to the household finances as well, each one with an after-school job, each one turning over every penny he earned to his mother. Times were tough, and the threat of destitution filled the rooms of the apartment like a dense, blinding fog. There was no escape from fear, and bit by bit all three boys absorbed their mother's dark ontological conclusions about the purpose of life. Either work or starve. Either work or lose the roof over your head. Either work or die. For the Fergusons, the weak-minded notion of All-For-One-And-One-For-All did not exist. In their little world, it was All-For-All—or nothing.

Ferguson was not yet two when his grandmother died, which meant that he retained no conscious memories of her, but according to family legend Fanny was a difficult and erratic woman, prone to violent screaming fits and manic bursts of uncontrollable sobbing, who beat her boys with brooms whenever they misbehaved and was barred from entering certain local shops because of her vociferous haggling over prices. No one knew where she had been born, but word was that she had landed in New York as a fourteen-year-old orphan and had spent several years in a windowless loft on the Lower East Side making hats. Ferguson's father, Stanley, rarely talked about his parents to his son, responding to the boy's questions with only the vaguest of brief, guarded answers, and whatever bits of information young Ferguson managed to learn about his paternal grandparents came almost exclusively from his mother, Rose, by many years the youngest of the three second-generation Ferguson sisters-in-law, who in turn had received most of her information from Millie, Lew's wife, a woman with a taste for gossip who was married to a man far less hidden and far more talkative than either Stanley or Arnold. When Ferguson was eighteen, his mother passed on one of Millie's stories to him, which was presented as no more than a rumor, a piece of unsubstantiated conjecture that might have been true—and then again might not. According to what Lew had told Millie, or what Millie said he had told her, there was a fourth Ferguson child, a girl born three or four years after Stanley, during the period when the family had settled in Duluth and Ike was looking for work as an ordinary seaman on a Great Lakes ship, a stretch of months when the family was living in extreme poverty, and because Ike was gone when Fanny gave birth to the child, and because the place was Minnesota and the season was winter, an especially frigid winter in an especially cold place, and because the house they lived in was heated by only a single wood-burning stove, and because there was so little money just then that Fanny and the boys had been reduced to living on one meal a day, the thought of having to take care of another child filled her with such dread that she drowned her newborn daughter in the bathtub.

If Stanley said little about his parents to his son, he didn't say much about himself either. This made it difficult for Ferguson to form a clear picture of what his father had been like as a boy, or as a youth, or as a young man, or as anything at all until he married Rose two months after he turned thirty. From offhand remarks that occasionally crossed his father's lips, Ferguson nevertheless managed to gather this much: that Stanley had often been teased and kicked around by his older brothers, that as the youngest of the three and therefore the one who had spent the smallest part of his childhood with a living father, he was the one most attached to Fanny, that he had been a diligent student and was hands down the best athlete of the three brothers, that he had played end on the football team and had run the quarter mile for the track team at Central High, that his gift for electronics had led him to open a small radio-repair shop the summer after he graduated from high school in 1932 (*a hole in the wall on Academy Street in downtown Newark,* as he put it, *hardly bigger than a shoeshine stand*), that his right eye had been injured during one of his mother's broom-swatting rampages when he was eleven (partially blinding him and thus turning him into a 4-F reject during World War II), that he despised the nickname Sonny and dropped it the instant he left school, that he loved to dance and play tennis, that he never said a word against his brothers no matter how stupidly or contemptuously they treated him, that his childhood after-school job was delivering newspapers, that he seriously considered studying law but abandoned the idea for lack of funds, that he was known as a ladies' man in his twenties and dated scores of young Jewish women with no intention of marrying any of them, that he went on several jaunts to Cuba in the thirties when Havana was the sin capital of the Western Hemisphere, that his greatest ambition in life was to become a millionaire, a man as rich as Rockefeller.

Both Lew and Arnold married in their early twenties, each one determined to break free of Fanny's demented household as quickly as he could, to escape the screaming monarch who had ruled over the Fergusons since their father's death in 1923, but Stanley, still in his teens when his brothers decamped, had no choice but to stay on. He was barely out of high school, after all, but then the years passed, one year after the other for eleven years, and he continued to stay on, unaccountably sharing the same top-floor apartment with Fanny throughout the Depression and the first half of the war, perhaps stuck there through inertia or laziness, perhaps motivated by a sense of duty or guilt toward his mother, or perhaps driven by all of those things, which made it impossible for him to imagine living anywhere else. Both Lew and Arnold fathered children, but Stanley seemed content to go on playing the field, expending the bulk of his energies on building his little business into a bigger business, and because he showed no inclination to marry, even as he danced through his mid-twenties and approached the brink of thirty, there seemed little doubt that he would remain a bachelor for the rest of his life. Then, in October 1943, less than a week after the American Fifth Army captured Naples from the Germans, in the middle of that hopeful period when the war was finally beginning to turn in favor of the Allies, Stanley met the twenty-one-year-old Rose Adler on a blind date in New York City, and the charm of lifelong bachelorhood died a quick and permanent death.

So pretty she was, Ferguson's mother, so fetching with her gray-green eyes and long brown hair, so spontaneous and alert and quick to smile, so deliciously put together throughout the five feet six inches that had been allotted to her person that Stanley, on shaking her hand for the first time, the remote and normally disengaged Stanley, the twenty-nine-year-old Stanley who had never once been burned by the fires of love, felt himself disintegrating in Rose's presence, as if all the air had been vacuumed from his lungs and he would never be able to breathe again.

She, too, was the child of immigrants, a Warsaw-born father and an Odessa-born mother, both of whom had come to America before the age of three. The Adlers were therefore a more assimilated family than the Fergusons, and the voices of Rose's parents had never carried the smallest trace of a foreign accent. They had grown up in Detroit and Hudson, New York, and the Yiddish, Polish, and Russian of their parents had given way to a fluent, idiomatic English, whereas Stanley's father had struggled to master his second tongue until the day he died, and even now, in 1943, close to half a century removed from her origins in Eastern Europe, his mother still read the *Jewish Daily Forward* instead of the American papers and expressed herself in an odd, mashed-up language her sons referred to as Yinglish, a nearly incomprehensible patois that combined Yiddish and English in nearly every sentence that escaped her mouth. That was one essential difference between Rose and Stanley's progenitors, but even more important than how much or how little their parents had adjusted to American life, there was the question of luck. Rose's parents and grandparents had managed to escape the brutal turns of fortune that had been visited upon the hapless Fergusons, and their history included no murders in warehouse holdups, no poverty to the point of starvation and despair, no infants drowned in bathtubs. The Detroit grandfather had been a tailor, the Hudson grandfather had been a barber, and while cutting clothes and cutting hair were not the sorts of jobs that steered you onto a road toward wealth and worldly success, they provided a steady enough income to put food on the table and clothes on your children's backs.

Rose's father, Benjamin, alternately known as Ben and Benjy, left Detroit the day after he graduated from high school in 1911 and headed for New York, where a distant relative had secured a job for him as a clerk in a downtown clothing store, but young Adler gave up on the job within two weeks, knowing that destiny had not meant for him to squander his short time on earth selling men's socks and underwear, and thirty-two years later, after stints as a door-to-door salesman of household cleaning products, a distributor of gramophone records, a soldier in World War I, a car salesman, and the co-owner of a used-car lot in Brooklyn, he now earned his living as one of three minority-share partners in a Manhattan real estate firm, with an income large enough to have moved his family from Crown Heights in Brooklyn to a new building on West Fifty-eighth Street in 1941, six months before America entered the war.

According to what had been passed down to Rose, her parents met at a Sunday picnic in upstate New York, not far from her mother's house in Hudson, and within half a year (November 1919) the two of them were married. As Rose later confessed to her son, this marriage had always puzzled her, for she had rarely seen two people less compatible than her parents, and the fact that the marriage endured for over four decades was no doubt one of the great mysteries in the annals of human coupledom. Benjy Adler was a fast-talking smart aleck, a hustling schemer with a hundred plans in his pockets, a teller of jokes, a man on the make who always hogged the center of attention, and there he was at that Sunday afternoon picnic in upstate New York falling for a shy wallflower of a woman named Emma Bromowitz, a round, large-bosomed girl of twenty-three with the palest of white skins and a crown of voluminous red hair, so virginal, so inexperienced, so Victorian in her affect that one had only to look at her to conclude that her lips had not once been touched by the lips of a man. It made no sense that they should have married, every sign indicated that they were doomed to a life of conflict and misunderstanding, but marry they did, and even though Benjy had trouble staying faithful to Emma after their daughters were born (Mildred in 1920, Rose in 1922), he held fast to her in his heart, and she, though wronged again and again, could never bring herself to turn against him.

Rose adored her older sister, but it can't be said that the opposite was true, for the first-born Mildred had naturally accepted her God-given place as princess of the household, and the small rival who had come upon the scene would have to be taught—again and again if necessary—that there was only one throne in the Adler apartment on Franklin Avenue, one throne and one princess, and any attempt to usurp that throne would be met by a declaration of war. That isn't to say that Mildred was overtly hostile to Rose, but her kindnesses were measured out in teaspoons, no more than so much kindness per minute or hour or month, and always granted with a touch of haughty condescension, as befitted a person of her royal standing. Cold and circumspect Mildred; warm-hearted, sloppy Rose. By the time the girls were twelve and ten, it was already clear that Mildred had an exceptional mind, that her success at school was the result not just of hard work but of superior intellectual gifts, and while Rose was bright enough and earned perfectly respectable grades, she was no more than an also-ran when compared to her sister. Without understanding her motives, without once consciously thinking about it or formulating a plan, Rose gradually stopped competing on Mildred's terms, for she instinctively knew that trying to emulate her sister could only end in failure, and therefore, if there was to be any happiness for her, she would have to strike out on a different path.

She found the solution in work, in trying to establish a place for herself by earning her own money, and once she turned fourteen and was old enough to apply for working papers, she found her first job, which quickly led to a series of other jobs, and by the time she was sixteen she was fully employed by day and going to high school at night. Let Mildred withdraw into the cloister of her book-lined brain, let her float off to college and read every book written in the past two thousand years, but what Rose wanted, and what Rose belonged to, was the real world, the rush and clamor of the New York streets, the sense of standing up for herself and making her own way. Like the plucky, quick-thinking heroines in the films she saw two and three times a week, the endless brigade of studio pictures starring Claudette Colbert, Barbara Stanwyck, Ginger Rogers, Joan Blondell, Rosalind Russell, and Jean Arthur, she took on the role of young, determined career girl and embraced it as if she were living in a film of her own, *The Rose Adler Story*, that long, infinitely complex movie that was still in its first reel but promised great things in the years to come.

When she met Stanley in October 1943, she had been employed for the past two years by a portrait photographer named Emanuel Schneiderman, whose studio was located on West Twenty-seventh Street near Sixth Avenue. Rose had started out as a receptionist-secretary-bookkeeper, but when Schneiderman's photographic assistant joined the army in June 1942, Rose replaced him. Old Schneiderman was in his mid-sixties by then, a German-Jewish immigrant who had come to New York with his wife and two sons after World War I, a moody man given to fits of crankiness and bluntly insulting language, but over time he had conceived a grudging fondness for the beautiful Rose, and because he was aware of how attentively she had been observing him at work since her first days at the studio, he decided to take her on as an apprentice-assistant and teach her what he knew about cameras, lighting, and developing film—the entire art and craft of his business. For Rose, who until then had never quite known where she was headed, who had worked at various office jobs for the wages she earned but little else, that is, without any hope of inner satisfaction, it felt as if she had suddenly chanced upon a calling—not just another job, but a new way of being in the world: looking into the faces of others, every day more faces, every morning and afternoon different faces, each face different from all the other faces, and it wasn't long before Rose understood that she loved this work of looking at others and that she would never, could never, grow tired of it.

Stanley was now working in collaboration with his brothers, both of whom had also been exempted from military service (flat feet and poor eyesight), and after several reinventions and expansions, the small radio-repair shop started in 1932 had grown into a sizable furniture-appliance store on Springfield Avenue that featured all the lures and gimmicks of contemporary American retail: long-term installment plans, buy-two-get-one-free offers, semi-annual blowout sales, a newly-wed consultation service, and Flag Day specials. Arnold had been the first to come in with him, the blundering, not-too-bright middle brother who had lost several jobs in sales and was having a rough go of it trying to support his wife, Joan, and their three kids, and a couple of years after that Lew joined the fold, not because he had any interest in furniture or appliances but because Stanley had just paid off his gambling debts for the second time in five years and had forced him to join the business as a show of good faith and contrition, with the understanding that any reluctance on Lew's part would entail never receiving another penny from him for the rest of his life. Thus was born the enterprise known as 3 Brothers Home World, which was essentially under the direction of one brother, Stanley, the youngest and most ambitious of Fanny's sons, who, from some perverse but unassailable conviction that family loyalty trumped all other human attributes, had willingly taken on the burden of carrying his two failed siblings, who expressed their gratitude to him by repeatedly showing up late for work, filching tens and twenties from the cash register whenever their pockets were empty, and, in the warm months, taking off to play golf after lunch. If Stanley was upset by their actions, he never complained, for the laws of the universe prohibited complaining about one's brothers, and even if Home World's profits were somewhat lower than they would have been without the expense of Lew and Arnold's salaries, the business was well in the black, and once the war ended in another year or two, the picture would be even brighter, for television would be coming in then, and the brothers would be the first boys on the block to sell them. No, Stanley wasn't a rich man yet, but for some time now his income had been growing steadily, and when he met Rose on that October night in 1943, he was certain the best days were still to come.

Unlike Stanley, Rose had already been burned by the fires of a passionate love. If not for the war, which had taken that love from her, the two of them never would have met, for she would already have been married to someone else long before that night in October, but the young man she had been engaged to, David Raskin, the Brooklyn-born future doctor who had entered her life when she was seventeen, had been killed in a freak explosion during a basic training exercise at Fort Benning in Georgia. The news had come in August 1942, and for many months after that Rose had been in mourning, by turns numb and resentful, hollowed out, hopeless, half-mad with sorrow, cursing the war as she shrieked into her pillow at night, unable to come to terms with the fact that David would never touch her again. The only thing that kept her going during those months was her work with Schneiderman, which brought some solace, some pleasure, some reason for getting out of bed in the morning, but she had no appetite for socializing anymore and no interest in meeting other men, reducing her life to a bare routine of job, home, and trips to the movies with her friend Nancy Fein. Bit by bit, however, especially in the past two or three months, Rose had gradually begun to resemble herself again, rediscovering that food had a taste when you put it in your mouth, for example, and that when rain fell on the city it didn't fall only on her, that every man, woman, and child had to jump across the same puddles she did. No, she would never recover from David's death, he would always be the secret ghost who walked beside her as she stumbled into the future, but twenty-one was too young to turn your back on the world, and unless she made an effort to reenter that world, she knew she would crumple up and die.

It was Nancy Fein who set up the blind date for her with Stanley, caustic, wise-cracking Nancy of the big teeth and skinny arms, who had been Rose's best friend since their childhood days together in Crown Heights. Nancy had met Stanley at a weekend dance in the Catskills, one of those crowded bashes at Brown's Hotel for the unattached-but-actively-seeking young Jews from the city, *the kosher meat market*, as Nancy put it, and while Nancy herself was not actively seeking (she was engaged to a soldier stationed in the Pacific who at last word was still among the living), she had gone along with a friend for the fun of it and had wound up dancing a couple of times with *a guy from Newark named*

Stanley. He wanted to see her again, Nancy said, but after she told him she had already promised her virginity to someone else, he smiled, made a neat little comic bow, and was about to walk away when she started telling him about her friend Rose, Rose Adler, *the prettiest girl this side of the Danube River and the nicest person this side of anywhere.* Such were Nancy's genuine feelings about Rose, and when Stanley understood that she meant what she was saying, he let her know he would like to meet this friend of hers. Nancy apologized to Rose for having brought up her name, but Rose merely shrugged, knowing that Nancy had meant no harm, and then she asked: Well, what is he like? In Nancy's words, Stanley Ferguson was about six feet tall, good-looking, a bit old, almost thirty being old to her twenty-one-year-old eyes, in business for himself and apparently doing well, charming, polite, and a very good dancer. Once Rose had absorbed this information, she paused for a few moments, pondering whether she was up to the challenge of a blind date, and then, in the middle of these reflections, it suddenly occurred to her that David had been dead for more than a year. Like it or not, the moment had come to test the waters again. She looked at Nancy and said: I suppose I should see this Stanley Ferguson, don't you think?

Years later, when Rose told her son about the events of that night, she left out the name of the restaurant where she and Stanley met for dinner. Nevertheless, if memory hadn't failed him, Ferguson believed it was somewhere in midtown Manhattan, East Side or West Side unknown, but an elegant place with white tablecloths and bow-tied waiters in short black jackets, which meant that Stanley had consciously set out to impress her, to prove that he could afford extravagances like this one whenever he chose to, and yes, she found him physically attractive, she was struck by how light he was on his feet, by the grace and fluidity of his body in motion, but also his hands, the size and strength of his hands, she noticed that at once, and the placid, unaggressive eyes that never stopped looking at her, brown eyes, neither large nor small, and the thick black brows above them. Unaware of the monumental impact she had made on her stunned dinner companion, the handshake that had led to the utter disintegration of Stanley's inner being, she was a bit thrown by how little he said during the early part of the meal, and therefore she took him to be an inordinately shy person, which wasn't strictly the case. Because she was nervous herself, and because Stanley continued to sit there mostly in silence, she wound up talking for the two of them, which is to say, she talked too much, and as the minutes ticked by she grew more and more appalled with herself for rattling on like a brainless chatterbox, bragging about her sister, for example, and telling him what a brilliant student Mildred was, summa cum laude from Hunter last June and now enrolled in the graduate program at Columbia, the only woman in the English Department, one of only three Jews, imagine how proud the family was, and no sooner did she mention the family than she was on to her Uncle Archie, her father's younger brother, Archie Adler, the keyboard man with the Downtown Quintet, currently playing at Moe's Hideout on Fifty-second Street, and how inspiring it was to have a musician in the family, an artist, a renegade who thought about other things besides making money, yes, she loved her Uncle Archie, he was far and away her favorite relative, and then, inevitably, she began talking about her work with Schneiderman, enumerating all the things he had taught her in the past year and a half, grumpy, foul-mouthed Schneiderman, who would take her to the Bowery on Sunday afternoons to hunt for old winos and bums, broken creatures with their white beards and long white hair, magnificent heads, the heads of ancient prophets and kings, and Schneiderman would give these men money to come to the studio to pose for him, for the most part in costumes, the old men dressed up in turbans and gowns and velvet robes, in the same way Rembrandt had dressed up the down-and-outs of seventeenth-century Amsterdam, and that was the light they used with these men, Rembrandt's light, light and dark together, deep shadow, all shadow with the merest touch of light, and by now Schneiderman had enough faith in her to allow her to set up the lighting on her own, she had made several dozen of these portraits by herself, and then she used the word *chiaroscuro*, and she understood that Stanley had no idea what she was talking about, that she could have been talking Japanese for all the sense it made to him, but still he went on looking at her, listening to her, rapt and silent, thunderstruck.

It was a disgraceful performance, she felt, an embarrassment. Fortunately, the monologue was interrupted by the arrival of the main course, which gave her a few moments to collect her thoughts, and by the time they started in on the food (dishes unknown), she was calm enough to realize that her uncharacteristic rambling had been a screen to protect her from talking about David, for that was the one subject she didn't want to talk about, would refuse to talk about, and therefore she had gone to great and ridiculous lengths to avoid exposing her wound. Stanley Ferguson had nothing to do with it. He seemed to be a decent man, and it wasn't his fault that he had been rejected by the army, that he was sitting in this restaurant dressed in finely tailored civilian clothes rather than tramping through the mud of some distant battlefield or getting himself blown to bits during a basic training exercise. No, it wasn't his fault, and she would be a heartless person to blame him for having been spared, and yet how not to make the comparison, how not to wonder why this man should be alive and David should be dead?

For all that, the dinner went reasonably well. Once Stanley had recovered from his initial shock and was able to breathe again, he proved to be an amiable sort, not full of himself as so many men were, but attentive and well mannered, less than a blazing wit, perhaps, but someone receptive to humor, who laughed when she said something even remotely funny, and when he spoke about his work and his plans for the future, it was clear to Rose that there was something solid about him, dependable. Too bad that he was a businessman with no interest in Rembrandt or photography, but at least he was pro-FDR (essential) and seemed honest enough to admit that he knew little or nothing about many things, including seventeenth-century painting and the art of taking pictures. She liked him. She found him pleasant to be with, but even though he possessed all or most of the qualities of a so-called good catch, she knew she could never fall for him in the way Nancy hoped she would. After the meal in the restaurant, they drifted along the midtown sidewalks for half an hour, stopped in for a drink at Moe's Hideout, where they waved to Uncle Archie as he worked the keys of his piano (he responded with a fat smile and a wink), and then Stanley walked her back to her parents' apartment on West Fifty-eighth Street. He rode upstairs in the elevator with her, but she didn't ask him in. Extending her arm for a good-night handshake (deftly warding off any chance of a preemptive kiss), she thanked him for the lovely evening and then turned around, unlocked the door, and went into the apartment, almost certain she would never see him again.

It was otherwise with Stanley, of course, it had been otherwise with him since the first moment of that first date, and because he knew nothing about David Raskin and Rose's grieving heart, he figured he would have to act quickly, for a girl like Rose was not someone who would remain unattached for long, men were no doubt swarming all around her, she was irresistible, every particle of her cried out grace and beauty and goodness, and for the first time in his life Stanley set out to do the impossible, to defeat the ever-expanding horde of Rose's suitors and win her for himself, since this was the woman he had decided he must marry, and if it wasn't Rose who became his wife, it would be no one.

Over the next four months he called her often, not often enough to become a pest but regularly, persistently, with unabated focus and determination, outflanking his imagined rivals with what he imagined was strategic cunning, but the truth was that there were no serious rivals in the picture, just two or three other men Nancy had fixed her up with after she met Stanley in October, but one by one Rose had found those others wanting, had turned down further invitations from them, and was continuing to bide her time, which meant that Stanley was a knight charging through a vacant field, even as he saw phantom enemies everywhere around him. Rose's feelings about him hadn't changed, but she preferred Stanley's company to the loneliness of her room or listening to the radio with her parents after dinner, and so she seldom refused when he asked her out for the evening, accepting offers to go ice-skating, bowling, dancing (yes, he was a terrific dancer), to attend a Beethoven concert at Carnegie Hall, two Broadway musicals, and several films. She quickly learned that dramas had no effect on Stanley (he dozed off during *The Song of Bernadette* and *For Whom the Bell Tolls*), but his eyes invariably stayed open for comedies, *The More the Merrier,* for example, a tasty little cream puff about the wartime housing shortage in Washington that made them both laugh, starring Joel McCrea (so handsome) and Jean Arthur (one of Rose's favorites), but it was something said by one of the other actors that made the strongest impression on her, a line delivered by Charles Coburn, playing a sort of Cupid figure in the guise of an old American fatso, which he repeated again and again throughout the movie: *a high type, clean-cut, nice young fellow*—as if it were an incantation extolling the virtues of the kind of husband every woman should want. Stanley Ferguson was clean-cut, nice, and still relatively young, and if *high type* meant upstanding, gracious, and law-abiding, he was all of those things as well, but Rose was by no means sure that these were the virtues she was looking for, not after the love she had shared with the intense and volatile David Raskin, which had been an exhausting love at times, but vivid and always unexpected in its continually mutating forms, whereas Stanley seemed so mild and predictable, so safe, and she wondered if such steadiness of character was finally a virtue or a flaw.

On the other hand, he didn't maul her, and he didn't demand kisses from her that he knew she wasn't willing to give, even though it was manifestly clear by now that he was infatuated with her and that each time they were together he had to struggle not to touch her, kiss her, maul her.

On the other hand, when she told him how beautiful she thought Ingrid Bergman was, he responded with a dismissive laugh, looked her in the eye, and said, with the calmest of calm certainties, that Ingrid Bergman couldn't hold a candle to her.

On the other hand, there was the cold day in late November when he showed up unannounced at Schneiderman's studio and asked to have his portrait taken—not by Schneiderman but by her.

On the other hand, her parents approved of him, Schneiderman approved of him, and even Mildred, the Duchess of Snob Hall, expressed her favorable opinion by announcing that Rose could have done a lot worse.

On the other hand, he did have his inspired moments, inexplicable jags of rambunctiousness when something in him was temporarily set free and he turned into a joking, daredevil prankster, as, for example, the night when he showed off for her in the kitchen of her parents' apartment by juggling three raw eggs, keeping them aloft in a dazzle of speed and precision for a good two minutes before one of them went splat on the floor, at which point he let the other two go splat on purpose, apologizing for the mess with a silent comedian's shrug and a one-word declaration: Whoops.

They saw each other once or twice a week over the course of those four months, and even if Rose couldn't give her heart to Stanley in the way he had given his heart to her, she was grateful to him for having picked her up from the ground and set her on her feet again. All things being equal, she would have been content to go on as they were for some time, but just as she was beginning to feel comfortable with him, to enjoy the game they were playing together, Stanley abruptly changed the rules.

It was late January 1944. In Russia, the nine-hundred-day siege of

Leningrad had just ended; in Italy, the Allies were pinned down by the Germans at Monte Cassino; in the Pacific, American troops were about to launch an assault on the Marshall Islands; and on the home front, at the edge of Central Park in New York City, Stanley was proposing marriage to Rose. A bright winter sun was burning overhead, the cloudless sky was a deep and glittering shade of blue, the crystalline blue that engulfs New York only on certain days in January, and on that sun-filled Sunday afternoon thousands of miles from the bloodshed and slaughter of the interminable war, Stanley was telling her that it had to be marriage or nothing, that he worshipped her, that he had never felt this way about anyone, that the entire shape of his future depended on her, and if she turned him down, he would never see her again, the thought of seeing her again would simply be too much for him, and therefore he would disappear from her life for good.

She asked him for a week. It was all so sudden, she said, so unexpected, she needed a little time to think it over. Of course, Stanley said, take a week to think it over, he would call her next Sunday, one week from today, and then, just before they parted, standing at the Fifty-ninth Street entrance to the park, they kissed for the first time, and for the first time since they had met, Rose saw tears glistening in Stanley's eyes.

The outcome, of course, was written long ago. Not only does it appear as an entry in the all-inclusive, authorized edition of *The Book of Terrestrial Life*, but it can also be found in the Manhattan Hall of Records, where the ledger informs us that Rose Adler and Stanley Ferguson were married on April 6, 1944, exactly two months before the Allied invasion of Normandy. We know what Rose decided, then, but how and why she came to her decision was a complex matter. Numerous elements were involved, each one working in concert with and in opposition to the others, and because she was of two minds about all of them, it turned out to be a trying, tormented week for Ferguson's future mother. First: Knowing Stanley to be a man of his word, she recoiled at the thought of never seeing him again. For better or worse, after Nancy he was now her best friend. Second: She was already twenty-one, still young enough to be considered young but not as young as most brides were back then, since it wasn't uncommon for girls to put on wedding gowns at eighteen or nineteen, and the last thing Rose wanted for herself was to remain unmarried. Third: No, she didn't love Stanley, but it was a proven fact that not all love-marriages turned into successful marriages, and according to what she had read somewhere, the arranged marriages prevalent in traditional foreign cultures were no more or less happy than marriages in the West. Fourth: No, she didn't love Stanley, but the truth was that she couldn't love anyone, not with the Big Love she had felt for David, since Big Love comes only once in a person's lifetime, and therefore she would have to accept something less than ideal if she didn't want to spend the rest of her days alone. Fifth: There was nothing about Stanley that annoyed her or disgusted her. The idea of having sex with him did not repel her. Sixth: He loved her madly and treated her with kindness and respect. Seventh: In a hypothetical discussion about marriage with him just two weeks earlier, he had told her that women should be free to pursue their own interests, that their lives should not revolve exclusively around their husbands. Was he talking about work? she asked. Yes, work, he answered—among other things. Which meant that marrying Stanley would not entail giving up Schneiderman, that she could go on with the job of learning how to become a photographer. Eighth: No, she didn't love Stanley. Ninth: There were many things about him that she admired, there was no question that the good in him far outweighed the not-so-good, but why did he keep falling asleep at the movies? Was he tired from working long hours at his store, or did those drooping eyelids suggest some lack of connection to the world of feelings? Tenth: Newark! Would it be possible to live there? Eleventh: Newark was definitely a problem. Twelfth: It was time for her to leave her parents. She was too old to be in that apartment now, and much as she cared for her mother and father, she despised them both for their hypocrisy—her father for his unrepentant skirt chasing, her mother for pretending to ignore it. Just the other day, quite by accident, as she was walking to lunch at the automat near Schneiderman's studio, she had caught sight of her father walking arm in arm with a woman she had never seen before, a woman fifteen or twenty years younger than he was, and she had felt so sickened and angry that she had wanted to run up to her father and punch him in the face. Thirteenth: If she married Stanley, she would finally beat Mildred at something, even if it wasn't clear that Mildred had any interest in marriage. For now, her sister seemed happy enough bouncing from one brief affair to the next. Good for Mildred, but Rose had no interest in living like that. Fourteenth: Stanley made money, and from the way things looked now, he would be making more money as time went on. There was comfort in that thought, but also some anxiety. In order to make money, you had to think about money all the time. Would it be possible to live with a man whose sole preoccupation was his bank account? Fifteenth: Stanley thought she was the most beautiful woman in New York. She knew that wasn't true, but she had no doubt that Stanley honestly believed it. Sixteenth: There was no one else on the horizon. Even if Stanley could never be another David, he was vastly superior to the lot of sniveling whiners Nancy had sent her way. At least Stanley was a grown-up. At least Stanley never complained. Seventeenth: Stanley was a Jew in the same way she was a Jew, a loyal member of the tribe but with no interest in practicing religion or swearing allegiance to God, which would mean a life unencumbered by ritual and superstition, nothing more than presents at Hanukkah, matzo and the four questions once a year in the spring, circumcision for a boy if they ever had a boy, but no prayers, no synagogues, no pretending to believe in what she didn't believe, in what they didn't believe. Eighteenth: No, she didn't love Stanley, but Stanley loved her. Perhaps that would be enough to start with, a first step. After that, who could say?

They spent their honeymoon at a lakeside resort in the Adirondacks, a week-long initiation into the secrets of conjugal life, short but endless, since each moment seemed to have been given the weight of an hour or a day from the sheer newness of everything they were going through, a period of nerves and skittish adjustments, of small victories and intimate revelations, during which Stanley gave Rose her first driving lessons and taught her the rudiments of tennis, and then they returned to Newark and settled into the apartment where they would spend the early years of their marriage, a two-bedroom flat on Van Velsor Place in the Weequahic section of town. Schneiderman's wedding present to her had been a one-month paid vacation, and in the three weeks before she went back to her job, Rose frantically taught herself how to cook, depending exclusively on the sturdy old manual of American kitchen science her mother had given her on her birthday, *The Settlement Cook Book*, which bore the subtitle *The Way to a Man's Heart*, a six-hundred-and-twenty-three-page volume compiled by Mrs. Simon Kander that included "Tested Recipes from the Milwaukee Public School Kitchens, Girls Trades and Technical High School, Authoritative Dieticians, and Experienced Housewives." There were numerous disasters in the beginning, but Rose had always been a fast learner, and whenever she set out to accomplish something she generally wound up doing it with a fair amount of success, but even in those early days of trial and error, of overdone meats and flaccid vegetables, of gooey pies and lumpy mashed potatoes, Stanley never said a negative word to her. No matter how wretched the meal she served him, he would calmly plunge every morsel of it into his mouth, chew with apparent pleasure, and then, every night, every night without fail, look up and tell her how delicious it was. Rose sometimes wondered if Stanley wasn't teasing her, or if he wasn't too distracted to notice what she had given him, but as with the food she cooked, so it was with everything else that concerned their life together, and once Rose began to pay attention, that is, to tote up all the instances of potential discord between them, she came to the startling, altogether unimaginable conclusion that *Stanley never criticized her.* For him, she was a perfect being, a perfect woman, a perfect wife, and therefore, as in a theological proposition that asserted the inevitable existence of God, everything she did and said and thought was necessarily perfect, necessarily had to be perfect. After sharing a bedroom with Mildred for most of her life, the same Mildred who had put locks on her bureau drawers to prevent her younger sister from borrowing her clothes, the same Mildred who had called her *empty-headed* for going to the movies so often, she now got to share a bedroom with a man who thought she was perfect, and that man, moreover, in that same bedroom, was rapidly learning how to maul her in all the ways she liked best.

Newark was a bore, but the apartment was roomier and brighter than her parents' place across the river, and all the furnishings were new (the best that 3 Brothers Home World had to offer, which wasn't the very best, perhaps, but good enough for the time being), and once she started working for Schneiderman again, the city remained a fundamental part of her life, dear, dirty, devouring New York, the capital of human faces, the horizontal Babel of human tongues. The daily commute consisted of a slow bus to the train, a twelve-minute ride from one Penn Station to the other, and then a short walk to Schneiderman's studio, but she didn't mind the travel, not when there were so many people to look at, and she especially loved the moment when the train pulled into New York and stopped, which was always followed by a brief pause, as if the world were holding its breath in silent anticipation, and then the doors would open and everyone would come rushing out, car after car disgorging passengers onto the suddenly crowded platform, and she reveled in the speed and single-mindedness of that crowd, everyone charging off in the same direction, and she a part of it, in the middle of it, on her way to work along with everyone else. It made her feel independent, attached to Stanley but at the same time on her own, which was a new feeling, a good feeling, and as she walked up the ramp and joined yet another crowd in the open air, she would head toward West Twenty-seventh Street imagining the different people who would be coming to the studio that day, the mothers and fathers with their newborn children, the little boys in their baseball uniforms, the ancient couples sitting side by side for their fortieth- or fiftieth-anniversary portrait, the grinning girls in their caps and gowns, the women from the women's clubs, the men from the men's clubs, the rookie policemen in their dress blues, and of course the soldiers, always more and more soldiers, sometimes with their wives or girlfriends or parents, but mostly alone, solitary soldiers on leave in New York, or home from the front, or about to go off somewhere to kill or be killed, and she prayed for them all, prayed they would all return with their limbs attached to still-breathing bodies, prayed, every morning as she walked from Penn Station to West Twenty-seventh Street, that the war would soon be over.

There were no serious regrets, then, no punishing second thoughts about having accepted Stanley's proposal, but the marriage nevertheless came with certain drawbacks, none of which could be directly blamed on Stanley, but still, by marrying him she had also married into his family, and every time she was thrown together with that half-cocked trio of misfits, she wondered how Stanley had managed to survive his boyhood without becoming as crazy as they were. His mother first of all, the still energetic Fanny Ferguson, in her mid- to late sixties by then, who stood no taller than five-two or five-two-and-a-half, a white-haired sourpuss of scowling mien and fidgety watchfulness, muttering to herself as she sat alone on the couch at family gatherings, alone because no one dared go near her, especially her five grandchildren, ages six to eleven, who seemed positively scared to death of her, for Fanny thought nothing of whacking them on the head whenever they stepped out of line (if infractions such as laughing, shrieking, jumping up and down, bumping into furniture, and burping loudly could be considered out of line), and when she couldn't get close enough to deliver a whack, she would yell at them in a voice loud enough to rattle the lampshades. The first time Rose met her, Fanny pinched her cheek (hard enough for it to hurt) and declared her to be a fine-looking girl. Then she proceeded to ignore her for the rest of the visit, as she had continued to do throughout every visit since then, with no more inter-action between them than the blank formalities of saying hello and good-bye, but because Fanny demonstrated the same indifference toward her two other daughters-in-law, Millie and Joan, Rose didn't take it personally. Fanny cared only about her sons, the sons who supported her and dutifully showed up at her house every Friday night for din-ner, but the women her sons had married were no more than shadows to her, and most of the time she had trouble remembering their names. None of this particularly bothered Rose, whose dealings with Fanny were sparse and irregular, but Stanley's brothers were a different story, since they worked for him and he saw them every day, and once she had absorbed the stunning fact that they were two of the most beauti-ful men she had ever seen, male gods who resembled Errol Flynn (Lew) and Cary Grant (Arnold), she began to develop an intense dislike for both of them. They were shallow and dishonest, she felt, the older Lew not unintelligent but crippled by his penchant for gambling on football and baseball games and the younger Arnold all but semi-moronic, a glassy-eyed letch who drank too much and never passed up an oppor-tunity to touch her arms and shoulders, to squeeze her arms and shoul-ders, who called her *Doll* and *Babe* and *Beautiful* and filled her with an ever-deepening revulsion. She hated it that Stanley had given them jobs at the store, and she hated how they made fun of him behind his back and sometimes even to his face, the good Stanley, who was a hundred times the man they were, and yet Stanley pretended not to notice, he put up with their meanness and laziness and mockery without a word of protest, showing such forbearance that Rose wondered if she hadn't inadvertently married a saint, one of those rare souls who never thought ill of anyone, and then again, she reasoned, perhaps he was no more than a pushover, someone who had never learned how to stand up for himself and fight. With little or no help from his brothers, he had built 3 Brothers Home World into a profitable concern, a large, fluorescent-lit emporium of armchairs and radios, of dining tables and iceboxes, of bedroom suites and Waring blenders, a high-volume, mid-quality operation that served a clientele with mid-level and low incomes, a wondrous, twentieth-century agora in its way, but after several visits in the weeks following the honeymoon, Rose had stopped going to the store—not just because she was working again, but because she felt uneasy there, unhappy, entirely out of place among Stanley's brothers.

Still, her disappointment in the family was softened somewhat by the brothers' wives and children, the Fergusons who were not really Fergusons, the ones who had not lived through the calamities that had befallen Ike and Fanny and their offspring, and Rose quickly found herself with two new friends in Millie and Joan. Both women were years older than she was (thirty-four and thirty-two), but they welcomed her into the tribe as an equal member, according her full status on the day of her wedding, which meant, among other things, that she had been given the right to be let in on all sister-in-law secrets. Rose was particularly impressed by the fast-talking, chain-smoking Millie, a woman so slender that she seemed to have wires under her skin rather than bones, a smart and opinionated person who understood what kind of man she had married in Lew, but no matter how loyal she remained to her scheming, profligate husband, that didn't prevent her from issuing a steady flow of ironic cracks about him, such clever, acerbic asides that Rose sometimes had to leave the room for fear of laughing too hard. Next to Millie, Joan was something of a simpleton, but so warm-hearted and generous that it still hadn't occurred to her that she was married to a dunce, and yet, what a good mother she was, Rose felt, so tender and patient and caring, whereas Millie's sharp tongue often led her into tangles with her kids, who were less well behaved than Joan's. Millie's two were eleven-year-old Andrew and nine-year-old Alice, Joan's three were ten-year-old Jack, eight-year-old Francie, and six-year-old Ruth. They all appealed to Rose in their different ways, except for Andrew perhaps, who seemed to have a rough and belligerent side to him, which led to frequent scoldings from Millie for punching his little sister, but the one Rose liked best was Francie, unmistakably it was Francie, she simply couldn't help herself, the child was so beautiful, so exceptionally alive, and when they met it was as if they fell in love with each other at first sight, with the tall, auburn-haired Francie rushing into Rose's arms and saying, Aunt Rose, my new Aunt Rose, you're so pretty, so pretty, so very pretty, and now we get to be friends forever. So it began, and so it continued afterward, each one enthralled with the other, and there were few things better in this world, Rose felt, than to have Francie crawl into her lap when they were all sitting around the table and start talking to her about school, or the last book she had read, or the friend who had said something nasty to her, or the dress her mother was going to buy for her birthday. The little girl would relax into the cushioning softness of Rose's body, and as she talked Rose would stroke her head or her cheek or her back, and before long Rose would feel she was floating, that the two of them had left the room and the house and the street and were floating through the sky together. Yes, those family gatherings could be gruesome affairs, but there were compensations as well, unexpected little miracles that occurred at the unlikeliest moments, for the gods were irrational, Rose decided, and they bestowed their gifts on us when and where they would.

Rose wanted to be a mother, to give birth to a child, to be carrying a child, to have a second heart beating inside her. Nothing counted as much as that, not even her work with Schneiderman, not even the long-range and as yet ill-defined plan of one day striking out on her own as a photographer, of opening a studio with her name on the sign above the front door. Those ambitions meant nothing when she compared them to the simple desire to bring a new person into the world, her own son or daughter, her own baby, and to be a mother to that person for the rest of her life. Stanley did his part, making love to her without protection and impregnating her three times in the first eighteen months of their marriage, but three times Rose miscarried, three times in her third month of pregnancy, and when they celebrated their second wedding anniversary in April 1946, they were still childless.

The doctors said there was nothing wrong with her, that she was in good health and would eventually carry a child to term, but these losses weighed heavily on Rose, and as one unborn baby succeeded another, as one failure led to the next, she began to feel that her very womanhood was being stolen from her. She wept for days after each debacle, wept as she hadn't wept since the months that had followed David's death, and the normally optimistic Rose, the ever-resilient and clear-eyed Rose, would tumble into a despond of morbid self-pity and grief. If not for Stanley, there was no telling how far she might have fallen, but he remained steadfast and composed, unflustered by her

tears, and after each lost baby he would assure her it was only a temporary setback and all would come out right in the end. She felt so close
to him when he talked to her like that, so grateful to him for his
kindness, so enormously well loved. She didn't believe a word he said,
of course—how could she believe him when all the evidence declared
he was wrong?—but it soothed her to be told such comforting lies. Still,
she was puzzled by how calmly he accepted the announcement of each
miscarriage, by how untormented he was by the brutal, bloody expul-
sions of his unborn children from her body. Was it possible, she wondered, that Stanley didn't share her desire to have children? Perhaps he
didn't even know he felt that way, but what if he secretly wanted things
to go on as they were and continue to have her all to himself, a wife with
no divided loyalties, no split in her affections between child and father?
She never dared voice these thoughts to Stanley, would never have
dreamed of insulting him with such unfounded suspicions, but the
doubt persisted in her, and she asked herself if Stanley hadn't been too
good at fulfilling his roles as son, brother, and husband, and if that
were the case, perhaps there was no room left in him for fatherhood.

On May 5, 1945, three days before the war in Europe ended, Uncle
Archie dropped dead of a heart attack. He was forty-nine years old, a
grotesquely young age for anyone to die, and to make the circumstances
even more grotesque, the funeral was held on V-E Day, which meant that
after the benumbed Adler family left the cemetery and returned to
Archie's apartment on Flatbush Avenue in Brooklyn, people were dancing in the streets of the neighborhood, blasting the horns of their cars,
and shouting in raucous merriment to celebrate the end of one half of
the war. The noise went on for hours as Archie's wife, Pearl, and their
twin nineteen-year-old daughters, Betty and Charlotte, and Rose's
parents and sister, and Rose and Stanley, and the four surviving members of the Downtown Quintet, and a dozen or more friends, relatives,
and neighbors sat and stood in the silent apartment with the shades
drawn. The good news they had all been looking forward to for so long
seemed to mock the horror of Archie's death, and the jubilant, singing
voices outside felt like a heartless desecration, as if the entire borough of
Brooklyn were dancing on Archie's grave. It was an afternoon Rose
would never forget. Not just because of her own sorrow, which was
memorable enough, but because Mildred grew so distraught that she
drank seven scotches and passed out on the sofa, and because it was

the first time in her life that she saw her father break down and cry. It was also the afternoon when Rose told herself that if she was ever lucky enough to have a son, she would name him after Archie.

The big bombs fell on Hiroshima and Nagasaki in August, the other half of the war came to an end, and in mid-1946, two months after Rose's second wedding anniversary, Schneiderman told her that he planned to retire soon and was looking for someone to buy his business. Given the progress she had made in their years together, he said, given that she had turned herself into a skilled and competent photographer by now, he wondered if she had any interest in taking over for him. It was the highest compliment he had ever paid her. Flattered as she was, however, Rose knew the timing was wrong, for she and Stanley had been putting aside all their extra money for the past year in order to buy a house in the suburbs, a one-family house with a backyard and trees and a two-car garage, and they couldn't afford to buy both the house and the studio. She told Schneiderman she would have to talk it over with her husband, which she promptly did that evening after dinner, fully expecting Stanley to tell her it was out of the question, but he ambushed her by saying the choice was hers, that if she was willing to give up the idea of the house, she could have the studio as long as the cost was something they could manage. Rose was flabbergasted. She knew that Stanley had set his heart on buying the house, and suddenly he was telling her the apartment was perfectly all right, that he wouldn't mind living there for another few years, all of which was untrue, and because he was lying to her like this, lying because he adored her and wanted her to have whatever she wanted, something changed in Rose that evening, and she understood she was beginning to love Stanley, truly love him, and if life continued to go on in this way much longer, it might even be possible for her to fall in love with him, to be struck down by an impossible second Big Love.

Let's not be rash, she said. I've been dreaming about that house, too, and jumping from assistant to boss is a big step. I'm not sure I'm ready to handle it. Can we think it over for a while?

Stanley agreed to think it over for a while. When she saw Schneiderman at work the next morning, he, too, agreed to let her think it over for a while, and ten days after she started thinking, she discovered she was pregnant again.

For the past several months, she had been seeing a new doctor, a man she trusted named Seymour Jacobs, a good and intelligent doctor, she felt, who listened to her carefully and didn't rush to conclusions, and because of her past history with the three spontaneous miscarriages, Jacobs urged her to stop commuting to New York every day, to stop working for the length of her pregnancy, and to confine herself to her apartment with as much bed rest as possible. He understood that these measures sounded drastic and a touch old-fashioned, but he was worried about her, and this might be her last good chance to have a child. *My last chance*, Rose said to herself, as she went on listening to the forty-two-year-old doctor with the large nose and compassionate brown eyes tell her how to succeed at becoming a mother. No more smoking and drinking, he added. A strict, high-protein diet, daily vitamin supplements, and a routine of special exercises. He would stop by to see her every other week, and the instant she felt the slightest twinge or pain, she should pick up the phone and dial his number. Was all that clear?

Yes, it was all clear. And so ended the dilemma of whether to buy a house or the studio, which in turn put an end to her days with Schneiderman, not to speak of interrupting her work as a photographer and turning her life upside down.

Rose was both elated and confused. Elated to know she still had a chance; confused by how she was going to cope with what amounted to seven months of house arrest. An infinite number of adjustments would have to be made, not just by her but by Stanley as well, since he would have to do the shopping and the bulk of the cooking now, poor Stanley, who worked so hard and put in such long hours as it was, and then there would be the added expense of hiring a woman to clean the apartment and do the laundry once or twice a week, nearly every aspect of daily life would be altered, her waking hours would henceforth be governed by a multitude of interdictions and restraints, no lifting of heavy objects, no moving the furniture around, no struggling to open a stuck window during a summer hot spell, she would have to keep a vigilant watch over herself, become conscious of the thousands of small and large things she had always done unconsciously, and of course there would be no more tennis (which she had grown to love) and no more swimming (which she had loved since earliest girlhood). In other words, the vigorous, athletic, perpetually moving Rose, who felt most fully herself whenever she was engaged in a rush of high-speed, all-consuming activity, would have to learn how to sit still.

Of all people, it was Mildred who saved her from the prospect of terminal boredom, who stepped in and transformed those months of immobility into what Rose would later describe to her son as *a grand adventure*.

You can't sit around the apartment all day listening to the radio and watching that nonsense on television, Mildred said. Why not get your brain working for once and do some catching up?

Catching up? Rose said, not understanding what Mildred was talking about.

You might not realize it, her sister said, but your doctor has given you an extraordinary gift. He's turned you into a prisoner, and the one thing prisoners have that other people don't is time, endless amounts of time. Read books, Rose. Start educating yourself. This is your chance, and if you want my help, I'll be happy to give it.

Mildred's help came in the form of a reading list, of several reading lists over the months that followed, and with movie theaters temporarily off-limits, for the first time in her life Rose satisfied her hunger for stories with novels, good novels, not the crime novels and bestsellers she might have gravitated to on her own but the books that Mildred recommended, classics to be sure, but always selected with Rose in mind, books that Mildred felt Rose would enjoy, which meant that *Moby-Dick* and *Ulysses* and *The Magic Mountain* were never on any of the lists, since those books would have been too daunting for the meagerly trained Rose, but how many others there were to choose from, and as the months passed and her baby grew inside her, Rose spent her days swimming in the pages of books, and although there were a few disappointments among the dozens she read (*The Sun Also Rises*, for example, which struck her as fake and shallow), nearly all the others lured her in and kept her engrossed from first to last, among them *Tender Is the Night, Pride and Prejudice, The House of Mirth, Moll Flanders, Vanity Fair, Wuthering Heights, Madame Bovary, The Charterhouse of Parma, First Love, Dubliners, Light in August, David Copperfield, Middlemarch, Washington Square, The Scarlet Letter, Main Street, Jane Eyre*, and numerous others, but of all the writers she discovered during her confinement, it was Tolstoy who said the most to her, demon Tolstoy, who understood all of life, it seemed to her, everything there was to know about the human heart and the human mind, no matter if the heart or mind belonged to a man or a woman, and how was it possible, she wondered, for a man to know what Tolstoy knew about women, it made no sense that one man could be all men and all women, and therefore she marched through most of what Tolstoy had written, not just the big novels like *War and Peace, Anna Karenina,* and *Resurrection,* but the shorter works as well, the novellas and stories, none more powerful to her than the one-hundred-page *Family Happiness,* the story of a young bride and her gradual disillusionment, a work that hit so close to home that she wept at the end, and when Stanley returned to the apartment that evening, he was alarmed to see her in such a state, for even though she had finished the story at three in the afternoon, her eyes were still wet with tears.

The baby was due on March 16, 1947, but at ten in the morning on March second, a couple of hours after Stanley had left for work, Rose, still in her nightgown and propped up in bed with *A Tale of Two Cities* leaning against the northern slope of her enormous belly, felt a sudden pressure in her bladder. Assuming she had to pee, she slowly extricated herself from the covering sheet and blankets, inched her mountainous bulk to the edge of the bed, put her feet on the floor, and stood up. Before she could take a step toward the bathroom, she felt a rush of warm liquid flowing down the inner halves of her thighs. Rose didn't move. She was facing the window, and when she looked outside she saw that a light, misty snow was falling from the sky. How still everything seemed at that moment, she said to herself, as if nothing in the world were moving but the snow. She sat down on the bed again and called 3 Brothers Home World, but the person who answered the phone told her Stanley was out on an errand and wouldn't be back until after lunch. Then she called Dr. Jacobs, whose secretary informed her that he had just left the office on a house call. Feeling some panic now, Rose told the secretary to tell the doctor she was on her way to the hospital, and then she dialed Millie's number. Her sister-in-law picked up on the third ring, and thus it was Millie who came to fetch her. During the short ride to the maternity ward at Beth Israel, Rose told her that she and Stanley had already chosen names for the child who was about to be born. If it was a girl, they were going to call her Esther Ann Ferguson. If it was a boy, he would go through life as Archibald Isaac Ferguson.

Millie looked into the rearview mirror and studied Rose, who was sprawled out on the backseat. Archibald, she said. Are you sure about that one?

Yes, we're sure, Rose answered. Because of my Uncle Archie. And Isaac because of Stanley's father.

Let's just hope he's a tough kid, Millie said. She was about to go on, but before she could get another word out of her mouth, they had reached the hospital entrance.

Millie rounded up the troops, and when Rose gave birth to her son at 2:07 the following morning, everyone was there: Stanley and her parents, Mildred and Joan, and even Stanley's mother. Thus Ferguson was born, and for several seconds after he emerged from his mother's body, he was the youngest human being on the face of the earth.

1.1

HIS MOTHER'S NAME WAS ROSE, AND WHEN HE WAS BIG ENOUGH to tie his shoes and stop wetting the bed, he was going to marry her. Ferguson knew that Rose was already married to his father, but his father was an old man, and it wouldn't be long now before he was dead. Once that happened, Ferguson would marry his mother, and from then on her husband's name would be Archie, not Stanley. He would be sad when his father died, but not too sad, not sad enough to shed any tears. Tears were for babies, and he wasn't a baby anymore. There were moments when tears still came out of him, of course, but only when he fell down and hurt himself, and hurting yourself didn't count.

The best things in the world were vanilla ice cream and jumping up and down on his parents' bed. The worst things in the world were stomach aches and fevers.

He knew now that sourballs were dangerous. No matter how much he liked them, he understood that he mustn't put them in his mouth anymore. They were too slippery, and he couldn't help swallowing them, and because they were too big to go all the way down, they would get stuck in his windpipe and make it hard to breathe. He would never forget how bad it felt the day he started to choke, but then his mother rushed into the room, lifted him off the ground, turned him upside down, and with one hand holding him by the feet, pounded him on the back with the other hand until the sourball popped out of his mouth and clattered onto the floor. His mother said: *No more sourballs, Archie.*

They're too dangerous. After that, she asked him to help her carry the bowl
of sourballs into the kitchen, and one by one they took turns dropping
the red, yellow, and green candies into the garbage. Then his mother
said: *Adios, sourballs.* Such a funny word: *adios.*

That happened in Newark, in the long-ago days when they lived in
the apartment on the third floor. Now they lived in a house in a place
called Montclair. The house was bigger than the apartment, but the truth
was that he had trouble remembering much about the apartment anymore. Except for the sourballs. Except for the venetian blinds in his
room, which rattled whenever the window was open. Except for the day
when his mother folded up his crib and he slept alone in a bed for the
first time.

His father left the house early in the morning, often before Ferguson was awake. Sometimes his father would come home for dinner, and
sometimes he wouldn't come home until after Ferguson had been put
to bed. His father worked. That was what grown men did. They left
the house every day and worked, and because they worked they made
money, and because they made money they could buy things for their
wives and children. That was how his mother explained it to him one
morning as he watched his father's blue car drive away from the house.
It seemed to be a good arrangement, Ferguson thought, but the money
part was a little confusing. Money was so small and dirty, and how
could those small, dirty pieces of paper get you something as big as a
car or a house?

His parents had two cars, his father's blue DeSoto and his mother's
green Chevrolet, but Ferguson had thirty-six cars, and on gloomy days
when it was too wet to go outside, he would take them out of their box
and line up his miniature fleet on the living room floor. There were two-
door cars and four-door cars, convertibles and dump trucks, police
cars and ambulances, taxis and buses, fire trucks and cement mixers,
delivery trucks and station wagons, Fords and Chryslers, Pontiacs and
Studebakers, Buicks and Nash Ramblers, each one different from the
others, no two even remotely alike, and whenever Ferguson began to
push one of them across the floor, he would bend down and look inside
at the empty driver's seat, and because every car needed a driver in order
to move, he would imagine he was the person sitting behind the wheel,
a tiny person, a man so tiny he was no bigger than the top joint of his
thumb.

His mother smoked cigarettes, but his father smoked nothing, not even a pipe or cigars. Old Golds. Such a good-sounding name, Ferguson thought, and how hard he laughed when his mother blew smoke rings for him. Sometimes his father would say to her, *Rose, you smoke too much*, and his mother would nod her head and agree with him, but still she went on smoking as much as before. Whenever he and his mother climbed into the green car to go out on errands, they would stop for lunch in a little restaurant called Al's Diner, and as soon as he finished his chocolate milk and grilled-cheese sandwich, his mother would hand him a quarter and ask him to buy her a pack of Old Golds from the cigarette machine. It made him feel like a big person to be given that quarter, which was about the best feeling there was, and off he would march to the back of the diner where the machine stood against the wall between the two restrooms. Once there, he would reach up on his toes to put the coin in the slot, pull the knob under the pillar of stacked-up Old Golds, and then listen to the sound of the pack as it tumbled out of the bulky machine and landed in the silver trough below the knobs. In those days, cigarettes didn't cost twenty-five cents but twenty-three cents, and each pack came with two freshly minted copper pennies tucked inside the cellophane wrapper. Ferguson's mother always let him keep those two pennies, and as she smoked her post-lunch cigarette and finished her coffee, he would hold them in his open palm and study the embossed profile of the man on the face of the two coins. Abraham Lincoln. Or, as his mother sometimes said: *Honest Abe*.

Beyond the little family of Ferguson and his parents, there were two other families to think about, his father's family and his mother's family, the New Jersey Fergusons and the New York Adlers, the big family with two aunts, two uncles, and five cousins and the small family with his grandparents and Aunt Mildred, which sometimes included his Great-aunt Pearl and his grown-up twin cousins, Betty and Charlotte. Uncle Lew had a thin mustache and wore wire-rimmed glasses, Uncle Arnold smoked Camels and had reddish hair, Aunt Joan was short and round, Aunt Millie was a little taller but very thin, and the cousins mostly ignored him because he was so much younger than they were, except for Francie, who sometimes babysat for him when his parents went to the movies or to someone's house for a party. Francie was far and away his favorite person in the New Jersey family. She made beautiful, complicated drawings of castles and knights on horses for him, let him eat as much vanilla ice cream as he wanted, told funny jokes, and was ever so pretty to look at, with long hair that seemed both brown and red at the same time. Aunt Mildred was pretty as well, but her hair was blond, unlike his mother's hair, which was dark brown, and even though his mother kept telling him that Mildred was her sister, he sometimes forgot because the two of them looked so different. He called his grandfather Papa and his grandmother Nana. Papa smoked Chesterfields and had lost most of his hair. Nana was on the fat side and laughed in the most interesting way, as if there were birds trapped inside her throat. It was better to visit the Adler apartment in New York than the Ferguson houses in Union and Maplewood, not least because the drive through the Holland Tunnel was something he relished, the curious sensation of traveling through an underwater tube lined with millions of identical square tiles, and each time he made that subaquatic journey, he would marvel at how neatly the tiles fit together and wonder how many men it had taken to finish such a colossal task. The apartment was smaller than the houses in New Jersey, but it had the advantage of being high up, on the sixth floor of the building, and Ferguson never tired of looking out the window in the living room and watching the traffic move around Columbus Circle, and then, on Thanksgiving, there was the further advantage of being able to watch the annual parade pass in front of that window, with the gigantic balloon of Mickey Mouse almost smack against his face. Another good thing about going to New York was that there were always presents when he arrived, boxed candies from his grandmother, books and records from Aunt Mildred, and all kinds of special things from his grandfather: balsa-wood airplanes, a game called Parcheesi (another excellent word), decks of playing cards, magic tricks, a red cowboy hat, and a pair of six-shooters in genuine leather holsters. The New Jersey houses offered no such bounties, and therefore Ferguson decided that New York was the place to be. When he asked his mother why they couldn't live there all the time, she broke into a big smile and said: *Ask your father.* When he asked his father, his father said: *Ask your mother.* Apparently, there were some questions that had no answer.

He wanted a brother, preferably an older brother, but since that wasn't possible anymore, he would settle for a younger brother, and if he couldn't have a brother, he would make do with a sister, even a younger sister. It was often lonely having no one to play with or talk to, and experience had taught him that every child had a brother or a sister, or several brothers and sisters, and as far as he could tell, he was the only exception to that rule anywhere in the world. Francie had Jack and Ruth, Andrew and Alice had each other, his friend Bobby down the street had a brother and two sisters, and even his own parents had spent their childhoods in the company of other children, two brothers for his father and one sister for his mother, and it didn't seem fair that he should be the only person among the billions of people on earth who had to spend his life alone. He had no clear knowledge of how babies were produced, but he had learned enough to know they started inside the bodies of their mothers, and therefore mothers were essential to the operation, which meant that he would have to talk to his own mother about changing his status from only child to brother. The next morning, he brought up the subject by bluntly asking her if she could please get busy with the work of manufacturing a new baby for him. His mother stood there in silence for a couple of seconds, then lowered herself to her knees, looked him in the eyes, and began stroking his head. This was strange, he thought, not at all what he was expecting, and for a moment or two his mother looked sad, so sad that Ferguson instantly regretted having asked the question. Oh, Archie, she said. Of course you want a brother or a sister, and I'd love for you to have one, but it seems I'm done making babies and can't have any more. I felt sorry for you when the doctor told me that, but then I thought, Maybe it's not such a bad thing, after all. Do you know why? (*Ferguson shook his head.*) Because I love my little Archie so much, and how could I love another child when all the love I have in me is just for you?

It wasn't just a temporary problem, he now realized, it was eternal. No siblings ever, and because that struck Ferguson as an intolerable state of affairs, he worked his way around the impasse by inventing an imaginary brother for himself. It was an act of desperation, perhaps, but surely something was better than nothing, and even if he couldn't see or touch or smell that something, what other choice did he have? He called his newborn brother John. Since the laws of reality no longer applied, John was older than he was, older by four years, which meant that he was taller and stronger and smarter than Ferguson, and unlike Bobby George who lived down the street, chubby, big-boned Bobby, who breathed through his mouth because his nose was always clogged with wet green snot, John could read and write and was a champion

baseball and football player. Ferguson made sure never to talk out loud
to him when other people were in the room, for John was his secret,
and he didn't want anyone to know about him, not even his father
and mother. He slipped up only once, but it turned out all right because
the flub occurred when he happened to be with Francie. She had come
to babysit that evening, and when she walked out into the backyard
and heard him telling John about the horse he wanted for his next
birthday, she asked him who he was talking to. Ferguson liked Francie
so much that he told her the truth. He thought she might laugh at him,
but Francie merely nodded, as if expressing her approval of the concept
of imaginary brothers, and so Ferguson allowed her to talk to John as
well. For months afterward, every time he saw Francie, she would first
say hello to him in her normal voice and then bend down, put her mouth
against his ear, and whisper: Hello, John. Ferguson was not yet five
years old, but he already understood that the world consisted of two
realms, the visible and the invisible, and that the things he couldn't see
were often more real than the things he could.

Two of the best places to visit were his grandfather's office in New
York and his father's store in Newark. The office was on West Fifty-
seventh Street, just one block from where his grandparents lived, and
the first good thing about it was that it was on the eleventh floor, even
higher than the apartment, which made looking out the window even
more interesting than on West Fifty-eighth Street, for his gaze could
travel far more deeply into the surrounding distance and take in many
more buildings, not to speak of most of Central Park, and down on the
street below the cars and taxis were so small that they resembled
the toy cars he played with at home. The next good thing about the office
was the big desks with the typewriters and adding machines on them.
The sound of the typewriters sometimes made him think of music, especially when the bell rang at the end of a line, but it also made him think
of hard rain falling on the roof of the house in Montclair and the sound
of pebbles being thrown against a glass window. His grandfather's secretary was a bony woman named Doris who had black hairs on her forearms and smelled of breath mints, but he liked it that she called him
Master Ferguson and let him use her typewriter, which she referred to
as Sir Underwood, and now that he was beginning to learn the letters
of the alphabet, there was the satisfaction of being able to put his fingers
on the keys of that heavy instrument and tap out a line of *a*'s and *y*'s,

for example, or, if Doris wasn't too busy, of asking her to help him write his name. The store in Newark was much bigger than the office in New York, and there were many more things in it, not just a typewriter and three adding machines in the back room, but row after row of small gadgets and large appliances and a whole area on the second floor for beds and tables and chairs, numberless numbers of beds and tables and chairs. Ferguson wasn't supposed to touch them, but when his father and uncles were out of sight or had their backs turned to him, he would occasionally sneak open a refrigerator door to smell the peculiar smell inside or hoist himself onto a bed to test the bounce of the mattress, and even when he was caught doing those things, no one was terribly angry, except Uncle Arnold sometimes, who would snap at him and growl: Hands off the merchandise, sonny. He didn't like being talked to in that way, and he especially didn't like it when his uncle swatted him on the back of the head one Saturday afternoon because the sting had hurt so much he had cried, but now that he had overheard his mother say to his father that Uncle Arnold was a dope, Ferguson didn't really care anymore. In any case, the beds and refrigerators never held his attention for long, not when there were the televisions to look at, the newly built Philcos and Emersons that reigned over all the other goods on display: twelve or fifteen models standing side by side against the wall to the left of the front door, all of them turned on with the sound off, and Ferguson liked nothing better than to switch the channels on the sets so that seven different programs were playing simultaneously, what a delirious swirl of mayhem that set in motion, with a cartoon on the first screen and a Western on the second screen and a soap opera on the third and a church service on the fourth and a commercial on the fifth and a newscaster on the sixth and a football game on the seventh. Ferguson would run back and forth from one screen to another, then spin around in a circle until he was almost dizzy, gradually moving away from the screens as he spun so that when he stopped he would be in a position to watch all seven of them at once, and seeing so many different things happen at the same time never failed to make him laugh. Funny, so funny it was, and his father let him do it because his father thought it was funny, too.

Most of the time, his father wasn't funny. He worked long hours six days a week, the longest days being Wednesday and Friday, when the store didn't close until nine o'clock, and on Sunday he slept until ten or ten-thirty and played tennis in the afternoon. His favorite command was: *Listen to your mother.* His favorite question was: *Have you been a good boy?* Ferguson tried to be a good boy and listen to his mother, although he sometimes fell down on the job and forgot to be good or to listen, but the lucky thing about those failures was that his father never seemed to notice. He was probably too busy to notice, and Ferguson was grateful for that, since his mother rarely punished him, even when he forgot to listen or be good, and because his father never yelled at him in the way Aunt Millie yelled at her children and never swatted him in the way Uncle Arnold sometimes swatted cousin Jack, Ferguson concluded that his branch of the Ferguson family was the best one, even if it was too small. Still, there were times when his father made him laugh, and because those times were few and far between, Ferguson laughed even harder than he might have laughed if they had happened more often. One funny thing was being thrown up in the air, and because his father was so strong and had such hard, bulging muscles, Ferguson flew up almost to the ceiling when they were indoors and even higher than that when they were in the backyard, and not once did it cross his mind that his father would drop him, which meant that he felt safe enough to open his mouth as wide as he could and fill the air with loud bellyfuls of laughter. Another funny thing was watching his father juggle oranges in the kitchen, and a third funny thing was hearing him fart, not just because farts were funny in themselves but because each time his father let out a fart in his presence, he would say: Whoops, there goes Hoppy— meaning Hopalong Cassidy, the cowboy on TV that Ferguson liked so much. Why his father would say that after he farted was one of the world's great mysteries, but Ferguson loved it anyway, and he always laughed when his father said those words. Such an odd, interesting idea: to turn a fart into a cowboy named Hopalong Cassidy.

Not long after Ferguson's fifth birthday, his Aunt Mildred married Henry Ross, a tall man with thinning hair who worked as a college professor, as did Mildred, who had finished her studies in English literature four years earlier and was teaching at a college called Vassar. Ferguson's new uncle smoked Pall Malls (*Outstanding—and they are mild*) and seemed highly nervous, since he smoked more cigarettes in one afternoon than his mother did in an entire day, but what intrigued Ferguson most about Mildred's husband was that he talked so quickly and used such long, complicated words that it was impossible to understand more than a fraction of what he was saying. Still, he struck Ferguson as a good-hearted fellow, with a jolly boom in his laugh and a bright glow in his eyes, and it was clear to him that his mother was happy with Mildred's choice, since she never referred to Uncle Henry without using the word *brilliant* and repeatedly said that he reminded her of someone named Rex Harrison. Ferguson hoped his aunt and uncle would get cracking in the baby department and rapidly spew forth a little cousin for him. Imaginary brothers could take you just so far, after all, and perhaps an Adler cousin could turn into something like an almost-brother or, in a pinch, an almost-sister. For several months, he waited for the announcement, every morning expecting his mother to come into his room and tell him that Aunt Mildred was going to have a child, but then something happened, an unforeseen calamity that overturned all of Ferguson's carefully worked-out plans. His aunt and uncle were moving to Berkeley, California. They were going to teach there and live there and were never coming back, which meant that even if they did produce a cousin for him, that cousin could never be turned into an almost-brother, since brothers and almost-brothers had to live nearby, preferably in one's very house. When his mother took out a map of the United States and showed him where California was, he was so disheartened that he pounded his fist on Ohio, Kansas, Utah, and every other state between New Jersey and the Pacific Ocean. Three thousand miles. An impossible distance, so far away that it could have been in another country, another world.

It was one of the strongest memories he carried away from his boyhood: the trip to the airport in the green Chevrolet with his mother and Aunt Mildred on the day his aunt left for California. Uncle Henry had flown out there two weeks earlier, so it was just Aunt Mildred who was with them on that hot, humid day in mid-August, Ferguson riding in the back dressed in short pants, his scalp moist with sweat and his bare legs sticking to the imitation-leather seat, and although it was the first time he had been to an airport, the first time he had seen planes up close and could savor the immensity and beauty of those machines, the morning remained inside him because of the two women, his mother and her sister, the one dark and the other blond, the one with long hair and the other with short hair, each so different from the other that you had to study their faces for a while to understand they had come from the same two parents, his mother, who was so affectionate and warm, always touching and hugging you, and Mildred, who was so guarded and held back, rarely touching anyone, and yet there they were together at the gate for the Pan Am flight to San Francisco, and when the number of the flight was announced over the loudspeaker and the moment came to say good-bye, suddenly, as if by some hidden, predetermined signal, the two of them began to weep, tears were cascading from their eyes and dropping to the floor, and then their arms were around each other and they were hugging, weeping and hugging at the same time. His mother had never cried in front of him before, and until he saw it with his own eyes, he hadn't even known that Mildred was capable of crying, but there they were weeping in front of him as they said good-bye to each other, both of them understanding that it could be months or years before they saw each other again, and Ferguson saw it as he stood below them in his five-year-old's body, looking up at his mother and his aunt, stunned by the excess of emotion pouring out of them, and the image traveled to a place so deep inside him that he never forgot it.

In November of the following year, two months after Ferguson entered the first grade, his mother opened a photography studio in downtown Montclair. The sign above the front door said Roseland Photo, and life among the Fergusons suddenly took on a new, accelerated rhythm, beginning with the daily morning scramble to get one of them off to school on time and the other two into their separate cars to drive off to work, and with his mother now gone from the house five days a week (Tuesday through Saturday) there was a woman named Cassie who did the chores, cleaning and making beds and shopping for food and sometimes even making dinner for Ferguson when his parents worked late. He saw much less of his mother now, but the truth was that he needed her less. He could tie his own shoes, after all, and whenever he thought about the person he wanted to marry, he would hesitate between two potential candidates: Cathy Gold, the short girl with the blue eyes and long blond ponytail, and Margie Fitzpatrick, the towering redhead who was so strong and fearless that she could lift two boys off the ground at once.

The first person to sit for a portrait at Roseland Photo was the proprietor's son. Ferguson's mother had been aiming her camera at him for as long as he could remember, but those earlier pictures had been snapshots, and the camera she had used was small and light and portable, whereas the camera in the studio was much bigger and had to be mounted on a three-legged stand called a tripod. He liked the word *tripod*, which made him think of peas, his favorite vegetable, as in the expression *two peas in a pod*, and he was also impressed by how carefully his mother adjusted the lights before she began taking the pictures, which seemed to indicate she was in full command of what she was doing, and to see her working with such skill and assurance gave Ferguson a good feeling about his mother, who was suddenly no longer just his mother but someone who did important things out in the world. She made him wear nice clothes for the picture, which meant putting on his tweed sports jacket and his white shirt with the broad collar and no top button, and because Ferguson found it so enjoyable to be sitting there as his mother went about the business of getting the pose just right, he had no trouble smiling when she asked him to. His mother's friend from Brooklyn was with them that day, Nancy Solomon, who had once been Nancy Fein and now lived in West Orange, funny Nancy with the buck teeth and the two little boys, his mother's bosom buddy and therefore a person he had known all his life. His mother explained that after the photos were developed, one of them would be blown up to a very large size and transferred to canvas, which Nancy would then paint over, turning the photograph into a color portrait in oils. That was one of the services Roseland Photo was planning to offer its customers: not just black-and-white portraits, but oil paintings as well. Ferguson had trouble imagining how this could be done, but he figured Nancy would have to be an awfully good painter to pull off such a difficult transformation. Two Saturdays later, he and his mother left the house at eight o'clock in the morning and drove to downtown Montclair. The street was nearly deserted, which meant there was a free parking space directly in front of Roseland Photo, but twenty or thirty yards before they came to a stop, his mother told Ferguson to shut his eyes. He wanted to ask her why, but just as he was about to open his mouth and speak, she said: No questions, Archie. So he shut his eyes, and when they pulled up in front of the studio, she helped him out of the car and led him by the hand to the place where she wanted him to be. All right, she said, you can open them now. Ferguson opened his eyes and found himself looking into the display window of his mother's new establishment, and what he saw there were two large images of himself, each one measuring about twenty-four inches by thirty-six inches, the first one a black-and-white photograph and the second one an exact replica of the first only in color, with his sandy hair and gray-green eyes and red-flecked brown jacket looking much as they did in the real world. Nancy's brushwork was so precise, so perfect in its execution, that he couldn't tell if he was looking at a photograph or a painting. Some weeks passed, and with the pictures now on permanent display, strangers began to recognize him, stopping him on the street to ask if he wasn't the little guy in the window of Roseland Photo. He had become the most famous six-year-old in Montclair, the poster boy for his mother's studio, a legend.

On September 29, 1954, Ferguson stayed home from school. He had a fever of 101.6 and had spent the previous night throwing up into an aluminum stew pot his mother had put on the floor beside his bed. When she left for work in the morning, she told him to stay in his pajamas and sleep as much as he could. If he couldn't sleep, he was to remain in bed with his comic books, and whenever he had to go to the bathroom, he should remember to put on his slippers. By one o'clock, however, the fever had dropped to 99 and he was feeling well enough to go downstairs and ask Cassie if he could have something to eat. She made him scrambled eggs and dry toast, which went down without disturbing his stomach, and so rather than go upstairs and return to his bed, he shuffled into the small room next to the kitchen that his parents alternately referred to as the den and the little living room and turned on the television. Cassie followed him in, sat down on the sofa beside him, and announced that the first game of the World Series would be starting in a few minutes. The World Series. He knew what that was, but he had never watched any of the games, and only once or twice had he watched any regular-season games, not because he didn't like baseball, which in fact he enjoyed playing very much, but simply because he was always outside with his friends when the day games were on, and by the time the night games started he had already been put to bed. He recognized the names of some of the important players—Williams, Musial, Feller, Robinson, Berra—but he didn't follow any particular team, didn't read the sports pages in the *Newark Star-Ledger* or the *Newark Evening News*, and had no idea what it meant to be a fan. By contrast, the thirty-eight-year-old Cassie Burton was an ardent follower of the Brooklyn Dodgers, chiefly because Jackie Robinson played for them, number 42, the second baseman she always called *my man Jackie*, the first person with dark skin to wear a major league uniform, a fact that Ferguson had learned from both his mother and Cassie, but Cassie had more to say on the subject because she was a person with dark skin herself, a woman who had spent the first eighteen years of her life in Georgia and spoke with a heavy southern accent, which Ferguson found both strange and marvelous, so languid in its musicality that he never tired of listening to Cassie talk. The Dodgers weren't in it this year, she told him, they had been beaten out by the Giants, but the Giants were a local team as well, and therefore she was rooting for them to win the Series. They had some good colored players, she said (that was the word she used, *colored*, even though Ferguson's mother had instructed him to say the word *Negro* when talking about people with black or brown skin, and how odd it was, he thought, that a Negro should not say *Negro* but *colored*, which proved—yet again—just how confounding the world could be), but in spite of the presence of Willie Mays and Hank Thompson and Monte Irvin on the Giants' roster, no one was giving them a chance against the Cleveland Indians, who had set a record for the most wins by an American League team. We'll see about that, Cassie said, not willing to concede anything to the oddsmakers, and then she and Ferguson settled in to watch the broadcast from the Polo Grounds, which started out badly when Cleveland scored twice in the top of the first inning, but the Giants got those runs back in the bottom of the third, and then the game evolved into one of those tense, well-pitched struggles (Maglie versus Lemon) in which no one does much of anything and all can hinge on a single at-bat, which elevates the importance and drama of every pitch as the game wears on. Four consecutive innings with no one crossing the plate for either team, and then, suddenly, in the top of the eighth, the Indians put two runners on base, and up stepped Vic Wertz, a power-hitting left-handed batter, who tore into a fastball from Giants' reliever Don Liddle and sent it flying deep to center field, so deep that Ferguson thought it was a sure home run, but he was still a novice at that point and didn't know that the Polo Grounds was an oddly configured ballpark, with the deepest center field in all of baseball, 483 feet from home plate to the fence, which meant that Wertz's monumental fly ball, which would have been a home run anywhere else, was not going to make it to the bleachers, but still, it was a thunderous blast, and there was every certainty it would sail over the head of the Giants' center fielder and bounce all the way to the wall, good enough for a triple, perhaps even an inside-the-park home run, which would give the Indians at least two if not three more runs, but then Ferguson saw something that defied all probability, a feat of athletic prowess that dwarfed every other human accomplishment he had witnessed in his short life, for there was the young Willie Mays running after the ball with his back turned to the infield, running in a way Ferguson had never seen a man run, sprinting from the second the ball left Wertz's bat, as if the sound of the ball colliding with the wood had told him exactly where the ball was going to land, Willie Mays not looking up or back as he sprinted toward the ball, knowing where the ball was throughout its entire trajectory even if he couldn't see it, as if he had eyes in the back of his head, and then the ball reached the top of its arc and was descending to a spot some 440 feet from home plate, and there was Willie Mays extending his arms in front of him, and there was the ball coming down over his left shoulder and landing in the pocket of his open glove. The moment Mays caught the ball, Cassie jumped up from the sofa and started shrieking, *Hot damn! Hot damn! Hot damn!*, but there was more to the play than just the catch, for the instant the men on base had seen the ball leave Wertz's bat, they had started running, running with the conviction that they were going to score, that they had to score because no center fielder could possibly catch such a ball, and so right after Mays caught the ball, he spun around and threw it to the infield, an impossibly long throw that was thrown so hard that he lost his cap and fell to the ground after the ball left his hand, and not only was Wertz out, but the lead runner was prevented from scoring on the fly ball. The score was still tied. It seemed inevitable that the Giants would win in the bottom of the eighth or ninth, but they didn't. The game went into extra innings. Marv Grissom, the new relief pitcher for the Giants, held the Indians scoreless in the top of the tenth, and then the Giants put two men on in the bottom of the inning, prompting manager Leo Durocher to send in Dusty Rhodes as a pinch hitter. What a good-sounding name that was, Ferguson said to himself, Dusty Rhodes, which was almost like calling someone Wet Sidewalks or Snowy Streets, but when Cassie saw the thick-browed Alabaman take his warm-up swings, she said: *Look at that old cracker with the stubble on his chin. If he ain't drunk, Archie, then I'm the queen of England.* Drunk or not, Rhodes's eyesight was in excellent form that day, and a split second after the arm-weary Bob Lemon delivered a not-so-fast fastball over the middle of the plate, Rhodes turned on it and pulled it over the right-field wall. Game over.

Giants 5, Indians 2. Cassie whooped. Ferguson whooped. They hugged, they jumped up and down, they danced around the room together, and from that day forth, baseball was Ferguson's game.

The Giants went on to sweep the Indians by winning the second, third, and fourth games as well, a miraculous upset that brought much happiness to the seven-year-old Ferguson, but no one was happier with the results of the 1954 World Series than Uncle Lew. His father's oldest brother had suffered his ups and downs as a gambler over the years, consistently losing more than he won but winning just enough to keep himself from drowning, and now, with the smart money all on Cleveland, it would have made sense for him to follow the herd, but the Giants were his team, he had been pulling for them through good seasons and bad since the early twenties, and for once he decided to ignore the odds and bet with his heart rather than his brain. Not only did he put his money on the underdogs but he wagered they would win four in a row, a hunch so preposterous and delusional that his bookie gave him odds of 300 to 1, which meant that for the modest sum of two hundred dollars, the sharp-dressing Lew Ferguson walked off with a pot of gold, *sixty grand*, an enormous amount back in those days, a fortune. The haul was so spectacular, so startling in its ramifications, that Uncle Lew and Aunt Millie invited everyone to their house for a party, a celebratory blowout with champagne, lobster, and thick porterhouse steaks that featured a viewing of Millie's new mink coat and a spin around the block in Lew's new white Cadillac. Ferguson was out of sorts that day (Francie wasn't there, his stomach hurt, and his other cousins barely talked to him), but he assumed that everyone else was having a good time. After the festivities ended, however, as he and his parents were on their way home in the blue car, he was caught by surprise when his mother started bad-mouthing Uncle Lew to his father. He couldn't follow everything she said, but the anger in her voice was unusually harsh, a bitter harangue that seemed to have something to do with his uncle owing his father money, and how dare Lew splurge on Cadillacs and mink coats before paying his father back. His father took it calmly at first, but then he raised his voice, which was something that almost never happened, and suddenly he was barking at Ferguson's mother to stop, telling her that Lew didn't owe him anything, that it was his brother's money and he could do anything he goddamned pleased with it. Ferguson knew his parents sometimes argued (he could hear their voices through the wall of their bedroom), but this was the first time they had fought a battle in front of him, and because it was the first time, he couldn't help feeling that something fundamental about the world had changed.

Just after Thanksgiving the following year, his father's warehouse was emptied out in a nighttime burglary. The warehouse was the one-story cinder-block building that stood behind 3 Brothers Home World, and Ferguson had visited it several times over the years, a vast, dank-smelling room with row upon row of cardboard boxes containing televisions, refrigerators, washing machines, and all the other things the brothers sold in their store. The stuff on display in the showrooms was merely for the customers to look at, but whenever someone wanted to buy something, it would be taken out of the warehouse by a man named Ed, a big fellow with a mermaid tattooed onto his right forearm who had served on an aircraft carrier during the war. If it was a small thing like a toaster or a lamp or a coffeepot, Ed would hand it to the customer, who could drive it home in his or her own car, but if it was a big thing like a washing machine or a refrigerator, Ed and another large-muscled vet named Phil would load it into the back of the delivery truck and drive it to the customer's house. That was how business was conducted at 3 Brothers Home World, and Ferguson was familiar with the system, old enough to understand that the warehouse was the heart of the operation, and so when his mother woke him up on the Sunday morning after Thanksgiving and told him that the warehouse had been robbed, he immediately grasped the dreadful significance of the crime. An empty warehouse meant no business; no business meant no money; no money meant trouble: the poorhouse! starvation! death! His mother pointed out that the situation wasn't quite that desperate because all the stolen goods were insured, but yes, it was a tough blow, especially with the Christmas shopping season about to begin, and since it would probably be weeks or months before the insurance company paid up, the store wouldn't be able to survive without an emergency loan from the bank. Meanwhile, his father was in Newark talking to the police, she said, and because every article had a serial number on it, maybe there was a chance, a small chance, that the robbers would be hunted down and caught.

Time passed, and no robbers were found, but his father managed to get the loan from the bank, which meant that Ferguson and his family were spared the dishonor of having to relocate to the poorhouse. Life went on, then, more or less as it had been going for the past several years, but Ferguson sensed a new atmosphere in the household, something grim and sullen and mysterious hovering in the air around him. It took a while before he could identify the source of that barometric shift, but by observing his mother and father whenever he was with them, both singly and in tandem, he concluded that his mother was essentially the same, still full of stories about her work at the studio, still producing her daily quotient of smiles and laughter, still looking him directly in the eye whenever she spoke to him, still up for fierce games of ping-pong in the winterized back porch, still listening to him intently whenever he came to her with a problem. It was his father who was different, his normally untalkative father who now said almost nothing at the break-fast table in the morning, who seemed distracted and barely present, as if his mind were concentrating on some dark, grievous thing he wasn't willing to share with anyone. Sometime after the beginning of the new year, when 1955 had turned into 1956, Ferguson summoned up the cour-age to approach his mother and ask her what was wrong, to explain why his father looked so sad and distant. It was the burglary, she said, the burglary was *eating him alive*, and the more he thought about it, the less he could think about anything else. Ferguson didn't understand. The warehouse had been broken into six or seven weeks ago, the insur-ance company was going to pay for the lost goods, the bank had come through with the loan, and the store was still on its feet. Why would his father worry when there was nothing to worry about? He saw his mother hesitate, as if struggling to decide whether to take him into her confidence, not sure if he was old enough to handle the facts of the story, doubt flickering in her eyes for no more than an instant, but palpable for all that, and then, as she stroked his head and studied his not-yet-nine-year-old face, she took the plunge, opening up to him in a way she had never done before, and let him in on the secret that was tearing his father apart. The police and the insurance company were still working on the case, she said, and they had both come to the conclusion that it was an *inside job*, meaning the burglary had not been committed by strangers but by someone who worked at the store. Ferguson, who knew everyone on the staff of 3 Brothers Home World, from the warehouse men Ed and Phil to the bookkeeper Adelle Rosen to the repairman Char-lie Sykes to the janitor Bob Dawkins, felt the muscles in his stomach clench into a small fist of pain. It wasn't possible that any of those good people could have done such an evil thing to his father, not a single one of them was capable of such treachery, and therefore the police and the insurance company must be wrong. No, Archie, his mother said, I don't think they're wrong. But the person who did it wasn't any of the people you just mentioned.

What did she mean by that? Ferguson wondered. The only other people connected to the store were Uncle Lew and Uncle Arnold, his father's brothers, and brothers didn't rob one another, did they? Things like that simply didn't happen.

Your father had a terrible decision to make, his mother said. Either drop the charges and the insurance claim or send Arnold to prison. What do you think he did?

He dropped the charges and didn't send Arnold to prison.

Of course not. He never would have dreamed of it. But you understand now why he's been so upset.

A week after Ferguson had this conversation with his mother, she told him that Uncle Arnold and Aunt Joan were moving to Los Angeles. She would miss Joan, his mother said, but it was probably better this way, since the damage that had been done was beyond repair. Two months after Arnold and Joan left for California, Uncle Lew smashed up his white Cadillac on the Garden State Parkway and died in an ambulance on the way to the hospital, and before anyone could comprehend how swiftly the gods accomplished their work when they had nothing better to do, the Ferguson clan had been blown to bits.

1.2

WHEN FERGUSON WAS SIX, HIS MOTHER TOLD THE STORY OF HOW
she had nearly lost him. Not lost in the sense of not knowing
where he was but lost in the sense of being dead, of exiting this world
and floating up to heaven as a bodiless spirit. He wasn't yet a year and
a half old, she said, and one night he began running a fever, a low fever
that rapidly shot up to a high fever, just over 106, an alarming temperature even for a small child, and so she and his father bundled him
up and drove him to the hospital, where he started going into convul-
sions, which easily could have done him in, for even the doctor who
removed his tonsils that night said it was touch-and-go, meaning that
he couldn't be certain whether Ferguson would live or die, that it was
all in God's hands now, and his mother was so scared, she told him, so
horribly scared she would lose her little boy that she nearly went *out of
her mind.*

That was the worst moment, she said, the one time when she believed
the world could actually come to an end, but there were other rough
spots as well, a whole list of unforeseen jolts and mishaps, and then she
began enumerating the various accidents that had befallen him as a
young child, several of which could have killed him or maimed him,
choking on an unchewed sliver of steak, for example, or the piece of
broken glass that went through the bottom of his foot and required
fourteen stitches, or the time he tripped and fell on a rock, which tore
open his left cheek and required eleven stitches, or the bee sting that
swelled his eyes shut, or the day last summer when he was learning how

to swim and nearly drowned when his cousin Andrew pushed him
under the water, and each time his mother recounted one of these
events, she would pause for a moment and ask Ferguson if he remembered, and the fact was that he did remember, remembered nearly all of
them as if they had happened only yesterday.

It was mid-June when they had this conversation, three days after
Ferguson had fallen out of the oak tree in the backyard and broken his
left leg, and what his mother was trying to demonstrate by going
through this litany of small catastrophes was that whenever he had
hurt himself in the past he had always gotten better, that his body
had hurt for a while and then had stopped hurting, and that was precisely what was going to happen with his leg. Too bad he had to be in
a cast, of course, but eventually the cast would come off and he would
be as good as new. Ferguson wanted to know how long it would take
before that happened, and his mother said a month or so, which was
an extremely vague and unsatisfactory answer, he felt, a month being
one cycle of the moon, which might be tolerable if the weather didn't
become too hot, but *or so* meant even longer than that, an indefinite and
therefore unbearable length of time. Before he could get himself fully
worked up over the injustice of it all, however, his mother asked him a
question, a strange question, perhaps the strangest question anyone
had ever asked him.

Are you angry at yourself, Archie, or angry at the tree?

What a perplexing thing to throw at a boy who hadn't even finished kindergarten. Angry? Why should he be angry at anything?
Why couldn't he just feel sad?

His mother smiled. She was happy he didn't hold it against the tree,
she said, because she loved that tree, she and his father both loved that
tree, and they had bought this house in West Orange mostly because of
the big backyard, and the best and most beautiful thing about the backyard was the towering oak that stood in the center of it. Three and a
half years ago, when she and his father had decided to leave the apartment in Newark and buy a house in the suburbs, they had looked in
several towns, Montclair and Maplewood, Millburn and South Orange,
but none of those places had the right house for them, they felt weary
and discouraged from looking at so many wrong houses, and then they
came to this house and knew it was the one for them. She was glad he
wasn't angry at the tree, she said, because if he had been angry she

would have been forced to chop it down. Why chop it down? Ferguson asked, beginning to laugh now at the thought of his mother chopping down such a large tree, his beautiful mother dressed in work clothes as she assaulted the oak with an enormous, gleaming axe. Because I'm on your side, Archie, she said, and any enemy of yours is an enemy of mine.

The next day, his father returned from 3 Brothers Home World with an air conditioner for Ferguson's room. It's getting hot out there, his father said, meaning he wanted his son to be comfortable as he languished on the bed in his cast, and it would also help with his hay fever, his father continued, preventing pollen from entering the room, for Ferguson's nose was highly sensitive to the airborne irritants that emanated from grass and dust and flowers, and the less he sneezed during his convalescence, the less his broken bone would hurt, since a sneeze was a powerful force, and a big one could resonate throughout your entire body, from the top of your whiplashed head to the tips of your toes. The six-year-old Ferguson watched his father go about the business of installing the air conditioner in the window to the right of the desk, a far more elaborate operation than he would have imagined, which began with the removal of the screen window and called upon such things as a tape measure, a pencil, a drill, a caulking gun, two strips of unpainted wood, a screwdriver, and several screws, and Ferguson was impressed by how quickly and carefully his father worked, as if his hands understood what to do without any instructions from his mind, autonomous hands, as it were, endowed with their own special knowledge, and then came the moment to hoist the large metallic cube off the ground and mount it in the window, such a heavy object to lift, Ferguson thought, but his father managed it without any apparent strain, and as he completed the job with the screwdriver and the caulking gun, his father hummed the song he always hummed when he fixed things around the house, an old Al Jolson number called *Sonny Boy—You've no way of knowing / There's no way of showing / What you mean to me Sonny*. His father bent down to pick up an extra screw that had fallen on the floor, and when he stood up straight again he suddenly grabbed the small of his back with his right hand. *Och un vai*, he said, I think I've strained a muscle. The cure for strained muscles was to lie flat on your back for several minutes, his father told him, preferably on a hard surface, and since the hardest surface in the room was the floor, his father promptly lay down on the floor next to Ferguson's bed. What an unusual vantage that was, to be looking down at his father stretched out on the floor below him, and as Ferguson leaned over the edge of the bed and studied his father's grimacing face, he decided to ask a question, a question he had thought of several times in the past month but had never found the proper moment to ask: What had his father done before he became the boss of 3 Brothers Home World? He saw his father's eyes roam across the ceiling, as if searching for an answer to the question, and then Ferguson noticed the muscles around his father's mouth pulling downward, which was a familiar gesture to him, an indication that his father was struggling to suppress a smile, which in turn meant that something unexpected was about to happen. *I was a big-game hunter*, his father said, calmly and flatly, betraying no sign that he was about to launch into the most egregious load of nonsense he had ever imparted to his son, and for the next twenty or thirty minutes he reminisced about lions, tigers, and elephants, the *sweltering heat of Africa*, hacking his way through dense jungles, crossing the Sahara on foot, scaling Mount Kilimanjaro, the time when he was nearly swallowed whole by a giant snake, and the other time when he was captured by cannibals and was about to be thrown into a pot of boiling water, but at the last minute he managed to wriggle out of the vines that were strapped around his wrists and ankles, outran his murderous captors, and disappeared into the thick of the jungle, and the other time when he was on his last safari before coming home to marry Ferguson's mother and was lost in the darkest heart of Africa, which was known as *the dark continent*, and wandered onto a broad, endless savanna where he saw a herd of grazing dinosaurs, the last dinosaurs left on earth. Ferguson was old enough to know that dinosaurs had been extinct for millions of years, but the other stories seemed plausible to him, not necessarily true, perhaps, but possibly true, and therefore worthy of being believed— perhaps. Then his mother walked into the room, and when she saw Ferguson's father lying on the floor, she asked him if anything was wrong with his back. No, no, he said, I'm just resting, and then he stood up as if his back were indeed fine, walked over to the window, and turned on the air conditioner.

Yes, the air conditioner cooled off the room and cut down on sneezes, and because it was cooler his leg didn't itch as much under the plaster cast, but there were drawbacks to living in a refrigerated chamber as well, the noise first of all, which was a queer and confusing noise, since there were times when he heard it and times when he didn't, but when he did hear it he found it monotonous and unpleasant, but worse than that there was the matter of the windows, which had to remain shut in order to keep the cool air in, and because they were permanently closed and the motor was perpetually running, he couldn't hear the birds singing outside, and the only good thing about being cooped up in his room with a cast on his leg was listening to the birds in the trees just beyond his window, the twittering, chanting, warbling birds who made what Ferguson felt were the most beautiful sounds in the world. The air-conditioning had its pluses and minuses, then, its benefits and hardships, and as with so many other things the world doled out to him in the course of his life, it was, as his mother often put it, *a mixed blessing*.

What bothered him most about falling out of the tree was that it needn't have happened. Ferguson could accept pain and suffering when he felt they were necessary, such as throwing up when he was sick or letting Dr. Guston jab a needle into his arm for a shot of penicillin, but unnecessary pain violated the principles of good sense, which made it both stupid and intolerable. A part of him was tempted to blame Chuckie Brower for the accident, but in the end Ferguson realized that was no more than a feeble excuse, for what difference did it make that Chuckie had dared him to climb the tree? Ferguson had accepted the dare, which meant he had wanted to climb the tree, had chosen to climb the tree, and therefore he himself was responsible for what had happened. Never mind that Chuckie had promised to follow Ferguson up if Ferguson went first and then had backed down from his promise, claiming he was scared, that the branches were too far apart and he wasn't tall enough to reach them, but the fact that Chuckie hadn't followed him up was immaterial, for even if he had been there, how could he have prevented Ferguson from falling? So Ferguson fell, he lost his grip while reaching for a branch that was at most one quarter of an inch beyond the point where he would have been able to grasp it securely, lost his grip and fell, and now he was lying in bed with his left leg imprisoned by a plaster cast that would remain a part of his body for *a month or so*, meaning more than a month, and there was no one to blame for this misfortune but himself.

He accepted the blame, understood that his present condition was entirely his own fault, but that was a far cry from saying the accident couldn't have been avoided. Stupid, that's what it was, just plain stupid to have forged on with his climbing when he couldn't fully reach the next branch, but if the branch had been one particle of an inch closer to him, it wouldn't have been stupid. If Chuckie hadn't rung his doorbell that morning and asked him to come outside and play, it wouldn't have been stupid. If his parents had moved to one of the other towns where they had been looking for the right house, he wouldn't even know Chuckie Brower, wouldn't even know that Chuckie Brower existed, and it wouldn't have been stupid, for the tree he had climbed wouldn't have been in his backyard. Such an interesting thought, Ferguson said to himself: to imagine how things could be different for him even though he was the same. The same boy in a different house with a different tree. The same boy with different parents. The same boy with the same parents who didn't do the same things they did now. What if his father was still a big-game hunter, for example, and they all lived in Africa? What if his mother was a famous movie actress and they all lived in Hollywood? What if he had a brother or a sister? What if his Great-uncle Archie hadn't died and his own name wasn't Archie? What if he had fallen out of the same tree and had broken two legs instead of one? What if he had broken both arms and both legs? What if he had been killed? Yes, anything was possible, and just because things happened in one way didn't mean they couldn't happen in another. Everything could be different. The world could be the same world, and yet if he hadn't fallen out of the tree, it would be a different world for him, and if he had fallen out of the tree and hadn't just broken his leg but had wound up killing himself, not only would the world be different for him, there would be no world for him to live in anymore, and how sad his mother and father would be when they carried him to the graveyard and buried his body in the ground, so sad that they would go on weeping for forty days and forty nights, for forty months, for four hundred and forty years.

There was a week and a half to go before the end of school and the beginning of summer vacation, which meant he wouldn't miss enough time to flunk kindergarten because of too many absences. That was something to be thankful for, his mother said, and surely she was right, but Ferguson wasn't in a thankful mood during those first days after the accident, with no friends to talk to except in the late afternoon when Chuckie Brower would stop by with his little brother to look at the cast, with his father gone from morning to night because he was at work, with his mother driving off for several hours a day in search of a vacant shop to house the photography studio she was planning to open in the fall, with the housekeeper Wanda mostly busy with her washing and cleaning except when she brought lunch up to Ferguson at noon and helped him empty his bladder by holding the milk bottle he was supposed to pee into instead of doing his business in the bathroom, such indignities he had to bear, all for the stupid mistake of having fallen out of a tree, and to add to his frustration there was the fact that he hadn't yet learned to read, which would have been a good way to pass the time, and with the television downstairs in the living room, inaccessible, temporarily out of bounds, Ferguson spent his days musing on the imponderable questions of the universe, drawing pictures of airplanes and cowboys, and practicing how to write by copying the sheet of letters his mother had made for him.

Then things began to brighten somewhat. His cousin Francie finished her junior year of high school, and for several days before she left to work as a counselor at a summer camp in the Berkshires, she came to the house to keep him company, sometimes for just an hour, sometimes for three or four, and the time he spent with her was always the most enjoyable part of the day, no doubt the only enjoyable part, for Francie was the cousin he liked best, liked more than anyone else in either one of his two families, and how grown-up she was now, Ferguson thought, with bosoms and curves and a body similar to his mother's, and just like his mother she had a way of talking to him that made him feel calm and comfortable, as if nothing could ever go wrong when he was with her, and sometimes it was even better to be with Francie than his mother, for no matter what he did or said, she never got angry at him, not even when he lost control of himself and became *rambunctious*. Clever Francie was the one who came up with the idea to decorate his cast, a job that took three and a half hours, such careful brushstrokes as she covered the white plaster with an array of brilliant blues and reds and yellows, an abstract, swirling pattern that made him think of riding on an exceedingly fast merry-go-round, and as she applied the acrylics to his new and detested body part, she talked about her boyfriend, Gary, big Gary who used to play fullback on the high school football team but was now in college, Williams College in the Berkshires, not far from the camp where the two of them were going to work together that summer, she was looking forward to it so much, she said,

and then she announced that she was *pinned*, a term not familiar to
Ferguson at the time, so Francie explained that Gary had given her his
fraternity pin, but *fraternity* was a word that eluded Ferguson's understanding as well, so Francie explained again, and then she broke into a
big smile and said never mind, the important thing was that being
pinned was the first step toward getting engaged, and the plan was
that she and Gary were going to announce their engagement in the fall,
and next summer, after she had turned eighteen and was finished with
high school, she and Gary were going to be married. The reason why
she was telling him all this, she said, was that she had an important job
for him, and she wanted to know if he was willing to do it. Do what?
Ferguson asked. To be the ring bearer at the wedding, she said. Once
again, Ferguson had no idea what she was talking about, so Francie
explained once again, and when he listened to her tell him that he
would walk down the aisle with the wedding ring perched on top of a
blue velvet pillow and that Gary would take it from him and then put
it on the fourth finger of her left hand to conclude the marriage ceremony, Ferguson agreed that it was an important job, perhaps the most
important job he had ever been given. With a solemn nod of the head,
he promised he would do it. It would probably make him nervous to
walk down the aisle with so many people looking at him, of course, and
there was always the chance that his hands would tremble and the
ring would fall to the ground, but he had to do it because Francie had
asked him to, because Francie was the one person in the world he
couldn't ever let down.

When Francie came to the house the following afternoon, Ferguson
immediately understood that she had been crying. Reddened nose,
foggy, pink-tinged traces around both her left and right irises, a handkerchief balled up in her fist—even a six-year-old could figure out the
truth from that evidence. Ferguson wondered if Francie had been quar-
relling with Gary, if suddenly and unexpectedly she was no longer
pinned, which would mean the marriage was off and he wouldn't be
called upon to carry the ring on a velvet pillow. He asked her why she
was upset, but rather than pronounce the name *Gary* as he imagined
she would, Francie started talking about a man and a woman named
Rosenberg, who had been put to death yesterday, *fried in the electric chair*,
she said, speaking those words with what sounded like both horror and
disgust, and it was wrong, wrong, wrong, she went on, because they

were probably innocent, they had always said they were innocent, and why would they let themselves be executed when they could have spared their lives by saying they were guilty? Two sons, Francie said, two little boys, and what parents would willingly turn their children into orphans by refusing to declare their guilt if they were guilty, which meant they must have been innocent and had died for nothing. Ferguson had never heard such outrage in Francie's voice, had never known anyone to be so distraught over an injustice committed against people who qualified as strangers, for it was clear to him that Francie had never met the Rosenbergs in person, and therefore it was something deadly serious and important that she was talking about, so serious that those people had been *fried* for it, what a dreadful thought that was, to be fried like a piece of chicken submerged in a pan of hot, bubbling oil. He asked his cousin what the Rosenbergs had supposedly done to deserve such a punishment, and Francie explained that they had been accused of passing secrets to the Russians, vital secrets concerning the construction of atomic bombs, and since the Russians were communists, which made them our mortal enemies, the Rosenbergs had been convicted of treason, a ghastly crime that meant you had betrayed your country and should be put to death, but in this case the crime had been committed by America, the American government had slaughtered two innocent people, and then, quoting her boyfriend and future husband, Francie said: *Gary thinks America has gone mad.*

This conversation hit Ferguson like a blow to the stomach, and he felt as lost and afraid as he had been when his fingers slipped off the branch and he started falling out of the tree, that gruesome sensation of helplessness, nothing but air around him and below him, no mother or father, no God, no nothing but the emptiness of pure nothing, and his body on its way to the ground with nothing in his head but the fear of what would happen to him when he got there. His parents never talked to him about things like the Rosenbergs' execution, they protected him from atomic bombs and mortal enemies and false verdicts and orphaned children and fried grown-ups, and to hear Francie tell him about all that in one grand gush of emotion and indignation caught Ferguson by complete surprise, not like a punch to the stomach, exactly, but more like something from one of the cartoons he watched on television: a cast-iron safe falling from a tenth-floor window and landing on his head. Splat. A five-minute conversation with his cousin Francie, and everything had gone splat. There was a big world out there, a world of bombs and wars and electric chairs, and he knew little or nothing about it. He was dumb, so perfectly dumb and hopeless that he found it embarrassing to be himself, an idiot child, present but not accounted for, a body occupying space in the same way a chair or a bed occupied space, nothing more than a witless zero, and if he meant to change that, he would have to get started now. Miss Lundquist had told his kindergarten class that they would learn how to read and write in the first grade, that there was no sense in rushing things and that they would all be mentally ready to begin next year, but Ferguson couldn't wait until next year, he had to begin now or else condemn himself to another summer of ignorance, for reading and writing were the first step, he concluded, the only step he was in a position to take as a person of no account, and if there was any justice in the world, which he was seriously beginning to question, then someone would come along and offer to help him.

By the end of that week, help appeared in the form of his grandmother, who drove out to West Orange with his grandfather on Sunday and settled into the bedroom next to his for a visit that lasted well into July. He had acquired a pair of crutches the day before she showed up, which allowed him to move around freely on the second floor and eliminated the humiliations of the milk bottle, but descending to the first floor on his own was still out of the question, the journey down the stairs was far too perilous, and so he had to be carried by someone, yet one more insult to be endured in silence and smoldering resentment, and because his grandmother was too weak and Wanda was too small, the carrying had to be done by his father or mother, which made it necessary to go down early in the morning, since his father left for work at a little past seven A.M. and his mother was still searching for the right place to set up her studio, but no matter, he didn't care about sleeping late, and it was preferable to spend the mornings and afternoons on the screened-in porch than to languish in the chilly tomb upstairs, and while the weather was often hot and humid, the birds were back in the picture now, and they more than compensated for any discomfort. The porch was where he finally conquered the mysteries of letters, words, and punctuation marks, where he struggled under the tutelage of his grandmother to master such oddities as *where* and *wear*, *whether* and *weather*, *rough* and *stuff*, *ocean* and *motion*, and the daunting conundrum of *to, too,* and *two.* Until then, he had never felt particularly close to the woman whom fate had chosen to serve as his grandmother, his nebulous Nana from midtown Manhattan, a benign and affectionate person, he supposed, but so quiet and self-contained that it was difficult to establish a connection with her, and whenever he was with his grandparents, his boisterous, madly entertaining grandfather seemed to take up all the room, which left his grandmother in the shadows, almost entirely effaced. With her squat, round body and thick legs, with her dowdy, old-fashioned clothes and stolid shoes with the fat, low heels, she had always struck Ferguson as someone who belonged to another world, an inhabitant of another time and place, and consequently she could never feel at home in this world, could live in the present only as a kind of tourist, as if she were just passing through, longing to go back to where she had come from. Nevertheless, she knew everything there was to know about reading and writing, and when Ferguson asked her if she would be willing to help him, she patted him on the shoulder and said of course she would, it would be an honor. Emma Adler, wife of Benjy, mother of Mildred and Rose, proved to be a patient if plodding teacher, and she went about the business of instructing her grandson with systematic thoroughness, beginning with an examination of Ferguson's knowledge on the first day, needing to know exactly how much he had learned so far before she devised an appropriate course of action. She was heartened by the fact that he could already recognize the letters of the alphabet, all twenty-six of them, most of the small letters and all of the capitals, and because he was so advanced, she said, it was going to make her job much less complicated than she had thought it would be. The lessons she subsequently gave him were divided into three parts, writing for ninety minutes in the morning, followed by a lunch break, reading for ninety minutes in the afternoon, and then, after another pause (for lemonade, plums, and cookies), forty-five minutes of reading out loud to him as they sat together on the porch sofa and she pointed to the words she thought would be hard for him to understand, her chubby right index finger tapping the page below such tricky spellings as *intrigue, melancholy,* and *thorough,* and as Ferguson sat there beside her, breathing in the grandmother smells of hand lotion and rosewater perfume, he imagined the day when all of this would become automatic for him, when he would be able to read and write as well as any other person who had ever lived. Ferguson was not a dexterous child, as his fall from the oak had proved, not to speak of the other spills and stumbles that had dogged his early life, and the writing part caused more difficulty for him than the reading part. His grandmother would say, Watch how I do this, Archie, and then she would slowly write out a letter six or seven times in a row, capital B's, for example, or lowercase f's, after which Ferguson would try to imitate her, sometimes succeeding at the first go, other times failing to get it just right, and whenever he continued to fail after the fifth or sixth attempt, his grandmother would place her hand on top of his hand, wrap her fingers around his fingers, and then guide the pencil over the page as their two hands executed the letter in the proper way. This skin-on-skin approach helped quicken his progress, for it removed the exercise from the realm of abstract forms and made it tactile and concrete, as if the muscles in his hand were being trained to perform the particular task required by the contour of each letter, and by repeating the exercise again and again, every day going over the letters he had already learned and adding four or five new ones, Ferguson eventually took control of the situation and stopped making errors. With the reading part, the lessons advanced smoothly, since there were no pencils involved and he could fly along at a rapid pace, encountering few barriers as he moved from three- and four-word sentences to ten- and fifteen-word sentences in the course of two weeks, and such was his determination to become a full-fledged reader before his grandmother's visit came to an end, it was almost as if he were willing himself to understand, forcing his mind into a state of such receptiveness that once a new fact was learned, it stayed there and wasn't forgotten. One by one, his grandmother would print out sentences for him, and one by one he would read them back to her, beginning with *My name is Archie* and moving on to *Look at Ted run* to *It's so hot this morning* to *When will your cast come off?* to *I think it's going to rain tomorrow* to *How interesting that the little birds sing more beautifully than the big birds* to *I'm an old woman and can't remember learning how to read, but I doubt I caught on as quickly as you have,* and then he graduated to his first book, *The Tale of Two Bad Mice,* a story about a pair of housebound rodents named Tom Thumb and Hunca Munca who smash up a little girl's dollhouse because the food in there isn't real but made of plaster, and how thoroughly Ferguson savored the violence of their destructive fury, the rampage that followed the shock of their disappointed, unsatisfied hunger, and as he read the book out loud to his grandmother, he faltered over just a few words, difficult words whose meanings escaped him, such as *perambulator, oilcloth, hearth-rug,* and *cheesemonger.* A good story, he said to his grandmother after he had finished, and very funny, too. Yes, she agreed, a highly amusing story, and then, as she kissed him on the top of his head, she added: I couldn't have read it better myself.

The next day, his grandmother helped him write a letter to Aunt Mildred, whom he hadn't seen in almost a year. She was living in Chicago now, where she worked as a professor and taught large college students like Gary, although Gary was at a different college from hers, Williams College in Massachusetts, whereas her college was called the University of Something. In thinking about Gary, he naturally started thinking about Francie as well, and it struck him as peculiar that his cousin was already talking about marriage at seventeen when Aunt Mildred, who was two years older than his mother, which made her many years older than Francie, still wasn't married to anyone. He asked his grandmother why Aunt Mildred had no husband, but apparently there was no answer to that question, for his grandmother shook her head and admitted that she didn't know, speculating that it could be because Mildred was so busy with her work or else because she simply hadn't found the right man yet. Then his grandmother handed him a pencil and a small sheet of lined paper, explaining that this was the best kind of paper for writing letters, but before he began he should think carefully about what he wanted to tell his aunt, and on top of that he should remember to keep his sentences short, not because he wasn't capable of reading long sentences now, but writing was a different story, and since printing the letters was a slow process, she didn't want him to run out of steam and stop before the end.

Dear Aunt Mildred, Ferguson wrote, as his grandmother spelled out the words for him in her high, undulating voice, drawing out the sound of each letter as if it were a little song, the melody rising and falling as his hand inched across the page. *I fell out of a tree and broke my leg. Nana is here. She is teaching me how to read and write. Francie painted my cast blue, red, and yellow. She is mad about those people who fried in the chair. The birds are singing in the yard. Today I counted eleven kinds of birds. The yellow finches are my favorites. I read The Tale of Two Bad Mice and Peewee the Circus Dog. What do you like better, vanilla or chocolate ice cream? I hope you will visit soon. Love, Archie.*

There was some disagreement over the use of the word *fried*, which his grandmother thought was an excessively vulgar way to talk about a tragic event, but Ferguson insisted there was no choice, the language couldn't be changed because that was how Francie had presented the matter to him, and he found it a good word precisely because it was so vivid and disgusting. Anyway, it was his letter, wasn't it, and he could write anything he wanted to. Once again, his grandmother shook her head. *You never back down, do you, Archie?* To which her grandson answered: *Why should I back down when I'm right?*

Not long after they sealed up the letter, Ferguson's mother unexpectedly came home, chugging down the street in the red, two-door Pontiac she had been driving since the family moved to West Orange three years ago, the car that Ferguson and his parents referred to as *the Jersey Tomato,* and when she had finished putting it away in the garage, she came striding across the lawn in the direction of the porch, moving at a faster pace than she normally did, an accelerated clip that fell somewhere between walking and jogging, and once she was close enough for Ferguson to distinguish her features, he saw that she was smiling, a big smile, an unusually big and brilliant smile, and then she lifted her arm and waved to her mother and son, a warm salutation, a sign that she was in excellent spirits, and even before she walked up the steps and joined them on the porch, Ferguson knew exactly what she was going to say, for it was clear from her early return and the buoyant expression on her face that her long search was finally over, that the site for her photography studio had been found.

It was in Montclair, she told them, just a short jump from West Orange, and not only was the place large enough to fit in everything she would need, it was plop in the middle of the main drag. There was work to be done, of course, but the lease wouldn't start until September first, which would give her enough time to draw up the plans and start construction on day one. What a relief, she said, good news at last, but there was still a problem. She had to come up with a name for the studio, and she didn't like any of her ideas so far. Ferguson Photo was no good because of the double-*f* sound. Montclair Photo was too bland. Portraits by Rose was too pretentious. Rose Photo didn't work because of the double-*o* sound. Suburban Portraits made her think of a sociology textbook. Modern Image wasn't bad, but it made her think of a magazine about photography rather than a flesh-and-blood studio. Ferguson

Portraiture. Camera Central. F-Stop Photo. Darkroom Village. Light-house Square. Rembrandt Photo. Vermeer Photo. Rubens Photo. Essex Photo. No good, she said, they all stank, and her brain had gone numb.

Ferguson chimed in with a question. What was the name of the place where his father had taken her dancing, he asked, something with the word *rose* in it, the place where they'd gone before they were married? He remembered that she'd told him about it once because they'd had such a good time there, that they'd *danced their heads off*.

Roseland, his mother said.

Then Ferguson's mother turned to her own mother and asked her what she thought of *Roseland Photo*.

I like it, her mother said.

And you, Archie? his mother asked. What do you think?

I like it, too, he said.

So do I, his mother said. It might not be the best name ever invented, but it has a nice ring to it. Let's sleep on it. If we still like it in the morning, maybe the problem is solved.

That night, as Ferguson and his parents and his grandmother lay asleep in their beds on the second floor of the house, 3 Brothers Home World burned to the ground. The telephone rang at a quarter past five in the morning, and within minutes Ferguson's father was in his bottle-green Plymouth driving to Newark to inspect the damage. Since the air conditioner was going at full blast in Ferguson's room, he slept through the telephone call and the commotion of his father's hasty, pre-dawn departure, and it wasn't until he woke at seven that he found out what had happened. His mother looked agitated, more confused and distraught than Ferguson had ever seen her, no longer acting as the rock of composure and wisdom he had always thought she was but someone just like himself, a fragile being prey to sadness and tears and hopelessness, and when she put her arms around him he felt frightened, not just because his father's store had burned down and there would be no more money for them to live on, which meant they would have to move to the poorhouse and subsist on porridge and dried-out pieces of bread for the rest of their days, no, that was bad enough, but the truly frightening thing was to learn that his mother was no stronger than he was, that the blows of the world hurt her just as much as they hurt him and that except for the fact that she was older, there was no difference between them.

Your poor father, his mother said. He's spent his whole life building up that store, he's worked and worked and worked, and now it all comes to nothing. A person lights a match, an electric wire short-circuits in a wall, and twenty years of hard work turn into a pile of ashes. God is cruel, Archie. He should protect the good people of this world, but he doesn't. He makes them suffer just as much as the bad ones. He kills David Raskin, he burns down your father's store, he lets innocent people die in concentration camps, and they say he's a kind and merciful God. What a joke.

His mother paused. Small tears were glistening in her eyes, Ferguson noticed, and she was chewing on her lower lip, as if she were trying to prevent more words from coming out of her mouth, as if she understood she had already gone too far, that she had no right to express such bitterness in front of a six-year-old child.

Don't worry, she said. I'm just upset, that's all. Your father has fire insurance, and nothing is going to happen to us. A nasty bit of bad luck is what it is, but it's only temporary, and in the end we'll all be fine. You know that, Archie, don't you?

Ferguson nodded, but only because he didn't want his mother to be upset anymore. Yes, maybe they would be fine, he thought, but then again, if God was as cruel as she said he was, maybe they wouldn't. Nothing was certain. For the first time since he'd come into the world two thousand three hundred and twenty-five days ago, all bets were off.

Not only that—but who on earth was David Raskin?

1.3

His cousin Andrew was dead. *Shot down in action was* how Ferguson's father explained it to him, the action being a night patrol in the frigid mountains that stood between North and South Korea, a single bullet fired by a Chinese Communist soldier, his father said, which entered cousin Andrew's heart and killed him at the age of nineteen. It was 1952, and the five-year-old Ferguson supposed he should feel as wretched as everyone else in the room, Aunt Millie and cousin Alice to begin with, who couldn't go longer than ten minutes without breaking down and crying again, and sad Uncle Lew, who smoked cigarette after cigarette and kept looking down at the floor, but Ferguson couldn't muster the grief he felt was required of him, there was something false and unnatural about trying to be sad when he wasn't, for the fact was that he had never liked cousin Andrew, who had called him *pipsqueak* and *runt* and *little shithead*, who had bossed him around at family gatherings and had once locked him in a closet *to see if he was tough enough to take it,* and even when he left Ferguson alone, there were the things he said to his sister, Alice, the cutting epithets such as *pig-face* and *dog-brain* and *pencil-legs*, which made Ferguson cringe with disgust, not to speak of the pleasure Andrew seemed to take in tripping and punching cousin Jack, who was only one year younger than Andrew but half a head shorter. Even Ferguson's parents admitted that Andrew was a *troubled boy,* and for as long as Ferguson could remember he had been overhearing stories about his cousin's antics at school, talking back to the teachers, setting trash cans on fire,

breaking windows, flunking classes, so many misdeeds that the principal finally kicked him out in the middle of his junior year, and then,
after he was caught stealing a car, the judge offered him a choice, either
jail or the army, so Andrew joined the army, and six weeks after they
shipped him to Korea, he was dead.

   It would be years before Ferguson understood the full impact of
this death on his family, for he was too young at the time to grasp anything but the ultimate effect it had on him, which wasn't made mani-
fest until he was seven and a half, and therefore the two years between
Andrew's funeral and the event that cracked apart their little world
passed in a blur of present-tense childhood, the mundane affairs
of school, sports and games, friendships, television programs, comic
books, storybooks, illnesses, scraped knees and banged-up limbs, occasional fistfights, moral dilemmas, and countless questions about the
nature of reality, and through it all he continued to love his parents
and feel loved by them in return, most of all by his high-spirited,
affectionate mother, Rose Ferguson, who owned and operated Roseland Photo on the main street in Millburn, the town where they lived,
and, to a lesser, more precarious degree by his father, the enigmatic
Stanley Ferguson, who said little and often seemed only dimly aware
of his son's existence, but Ferguson understood that his father had
much on his mind, that running 3 Brothers Home World was an all-
out, round-the-clock job, which necessarily meant he was distracted,
but at those rare moments when he wasn't distracted and could focus
his eyes on his son, Ferguson felt confident that his father knew who
he was, that he hadn't confused him with someone else. In other words,
Ferguson lived on safe ground, his material needs were taken care of
in a consistent, conscientious manner, a roof over his head, three meals
a day, freshly laundered clothes, with no physical hardships to be
endured, no emotional torments to arrest his progress, and in those
years between the ages of five and a half and seven and a half, he was
developing into what educators would have called a healthy, normal
child of above-average intelligence, a fine specimen of midcentury
American boyhood. But he was too caught up in the tumult of his own
life to pay attention to what was happening outside the circle of his
immediate concerns, and because his parents weren't the sort of
people who shared their worries with small children, there was no
way to prepare himself for the disaster that struck on November 3,

1954, which expelled him from his youthful Eden and turned his life into an entirely different life.

Among the many things Ferguson knew nothing about prior to that fateful moment were the following:

1) The extent of Lew and Millie's grief over the death of their son, compounded by the fact that they saw themselves as failed parents, having brought up what they considered to be *a damaged person*, a delinquent child with no conscience or moral foundation, a mocker of rules and authority who exulted in stirring up havoc wherever he could, a liar, a cheat from start to finish, a bad egg, and Lew and Millie tortured themselves over this failure, wondering if they had been too hard on him or too soft on him, wondering what they could have done differently to prevent him from stealing that car, which proved to be his death sentence, and how torn up they felt for having encouraged him to join the army, which they thought might help straighten him out but instead had put him in a wooden box six feet under the ground, and therefore they felt responsible for his death as well, not just his fractious, angry, misspent life but also his death on that frozen mountaintop in godforsaken Korea.

2) Lew and Millie had a taste for alcohol. They were one of those couples who drank as both a sport and a compulsion, a bibulous, insouciant pair of theatrical charmers whenever they were lubricated within the scope of their capacities, which were substantial, but oddly enough it was the pin-thin Millie who seemed the steadier of the two, who rarely ever wobbled or slurred, whereas her much larger husband sometimes went overboard, and even before Andrew's death, Ferguson could remember the time when he saw his uncle passed out on the couch and snoring in the middle of a loud family party, which everyone had found so funny when it happened, but now, in the aftermath of that death, Lew's drinking had increased, spreading beyond the parties, the cocktail hours, and the post-dinner nightcaps into high-noon lunchtime sloshes and secret tipples from the flask he carried around in the inside pocket of his jacket, which no doubt helped numb the pain twisting through his guilt-ridden, ravaged heart, but the booze began to affect his work at the store, sometimes rendering him incoherent when he talked to customers about the relative merits of Whirlpool and Maytag washing machines, and when he wasn't incoherent, he was occasionally irritable, and when he was irritable, he often took pleasure

in insulting people, which was no way to conduct business at 3 Brothers Home World, and so Ferguson's father would have to step in, pull Lew away from the offended customer, and tell him to go home and sleep it off.

3) A known fact about Lew was his penchant for gambling. If not for Millie's job as a buyer for Bamberger's department store in downtown Newark, the family would have gone broke many years earlier, since most of what Lew earned at 3 Brothers Home World tended to wind up in his bookie's pocket. Now, as his drinking burgeoned out of control, so too did his taste for long-odds hunches, the dream of the spectacular, once-in-a-lifetime killing, the kind of legendary bet gamblers would go on talking about for decades, and the more erratic his guesswork became, the more his losses grew. By August 1954, he was thirty-six thousand dollars in the hole, and Ira Bernstein, the man who had been handling his bets for the past dozen years, was running out of patience. Lew needed cash, no less than ten or twelve thousand, a hefty lump to prove his good intentions, or else the boys with the baseball bats and the brass knuckles would be coming around to pay him a visit, and because he couldn't ask Stanley for the money, knowing his kid brother had been serious when he'd sworn never to bail him out again, he stole it from Stanley instead—by putting a stop order on a check to 3 Brothers' G.E. supplier and transferring the amount of the check over to himself. He knew he would be found out eventually, but it would take some time for the discrepancy to come to light, since the flow of cash for goods between the store and its suppliers ran on a system of mutual trust and the bookkeeping lagged months behind the actual exchanges, and those months would give him the time he needed to put things right again. In late September, Ferguson's uncle saw his chance. It would mean putting a stop order on another check, but if all went well, the embezzled nine thousand dollars would be turned into a haul worth ten times that amount, which would be more than enough to make good on the two stopped checks, pay off Bernstein in full, and walk away with a nifty bundle for himself. The World Series was about to begin, with the Indians heavily favored over the Giants, so much a sure thing that betting on Cleveland was hardly worth the effort, but then Lew thought: If the Indians were that powerful a club, what was to stop them from winning four in a row? The odds on such a bet were far more enticing. Ten to one for a sweep, whereas putting his money on

Cleveland one game at a time would yield only pennies. So Lew found himself another bookmaker, that is, someone whose name wasn't Bernstein, and put the nine thousand two hundred dollars he had stolen from his brother on the Indians, betting they would run the table without a single loss to the Giants. No one knew where Ferguson's uncle watched the first game, but as Stanley and Arnold and the rest of the staff at 3 Brothers Home World gathered around the television sets in the store to follow the action with fifty or sixty walk-in customers, who weren't real customers but Giants' fans with no televisions of their own, Lew slipped out to watch the game by himself, perhaps in a local bar or some other place, an unknown spot where no one saw him live through the horror of watching Mays run down Wertz's fly ball in the top of the eighth inning, and then, even more terrible, the soul-crushing devastation that followed some minutes later when he saw Rhodes turn on Lemon's pitch and send the ball into the right-field stands. One swing of a man's bat, and another man's life was in ruins.

4) In mid-October, the G.E. supplier informed Stanley that they had no record of payment for a truckload of freezers, air conditioners, fans, and refrigerators that had been delivered in early August. Mystified, Stanley went to the 3 Brothers bookkeeper, Adelle Rosen, a plump widow of fifty-six who kept a yellow pencil in her hair and believed in the virtues of precise penmanship and rigidly aligned columns, and once Stanley explained the problem to her, Mrs. Rosen pulled out the company checkbook from her desk drawer and found the stub for August tenth, which verified that payment had been made in full for the amount they owed, $14,237.16. Stanley shrugged. The check must have been lost in the mail, he said, and then he asked Mrs. Rosen to put a stop order on the August check and issue a new one to the G.E. supplier. The next day, a deeply puzzled Mrs. Rosen reported to Stanley that a stop order had already been put on that check as far back as August eleventh. What could that possibly mean? For the briefest of brief instants, Stanley wondered if Mrs. Rosen hadn't betrayed him, if his heretofore steadfast employee, who was widely known to have been secretly in love with him for the past eleven years, wasn't guilty of cooking the books, but then he looked into Mrs. Rosen's troubled, adoring eyes and dismissed the thought as nonsense. He called Arnold into the back office and asked him what he knew about the missing fourteen thousand dollars, but Arnold, who looked no less shocked

and confused than Mrs. Rosen had looked when confronted by this same mystery, said he couldn't even begin to imagine what was going on, and Stanley believed him. Then he called in Lew. The oldest member of the clan denied everything at first, but Stanley didn't like the way his brother kept looking past him at the wall behind his shoulder while they were talking, so he pressed on, grilling Lew about the stop order on the August check, insisting that he was the only one who could have done it, the only possible candidate, since Mrs. Rosen was in the clear, as were Arnold and himself, and therefore it had to be Lew, and then Stanley began to bore in on the question of Lew's recent gambling activities, the exact amounts he had wagered, the total extent of his losses, what baseball games, what football games, what boxing matches, and the harder Stanley pushed, the more Lew's body appeared to weaken, as if the two of them were slugging it out in a ring and each word was another punch, another blow to the gut, to the head, and bit by bit Lew began to stagger, as if his knees were about to buckle, and suddenly he was sitting in a chair with his face in his hands, sobbing out a chopped-up, barely audible confession. Stanley was appalled by what he heard, for in point of fact Lew wasn't the least bit sorry about what he had done, and if he was sorry about anything it was only that his plan hadn't worked, his beautiful, flawless plan, but the Indians had let him down and lost the first game of Series, and fuck Willie Mays, he said, fuck Dusty Rhodes, and Stanley finally understood that his brother was beyond hope, that for a full-grown man to point his finger at a couple of ballplayers and think they were the cause of his troubles meant his mind was no more developed than a child's, an idiot child at that, someone as impoverished and handicapped as Lew's own son, the dead and buried Private Andrew Ferguson. Stanley was tempted to tell his brother to leave the store and never come back, but he couldn't do that, it would have been too sudden, too harsh, and as he pondered what to say next, knowing he couldn't say anything until his anger had subsided somewhat, at least down to a level that wouldn't make him regret his words, Lew began to talk again, and what he was telling Stanley was that they were all up to their necks in it and that the store was finished. Ferguson's father had no idea what Lew was talking about, so he held his tongue a bit longer, beginning to feel that perhaps his brother had actually lost his mind, and then Lew was talking about Bernstein and how much money he owed him, more than twenty-five thousand now, but that was only the tip of the iceberg, for Bernstein had begun charging interest, and every day the amount was going up, up, up, and in the past two weeks there had been half a dozen phone calls, a voice on the other end of the line threatening him to pay what he owed or else suffer the consequences, which variously meant that a team of men would jump him in the dark and break every bone in his body, or else blind him with acid, or else cut up Millie's face, or else kidnap Alice, or else kill both Millie and Alice, and he was scared, Lew told his brother, so scared that he couldn't sleep anymore, and how was he going to raise the cash when his house was carrying two mortgages and he had already borrowed twenty-three thousand dollars from the store? Now Stanley's knees were beginning to buckle as well, he felt disoriented and dizzy, no longer quite himself, no longer fully encased in his own skin, and so he sat down in a chair on the other side of the desk from Lew, wondering how fourteen thousand dollars had suddenly turned into twenty-three thousand dollars, and as the two brothers looked at each other across the surface of the gray metal desk, Lew told Stanley that Bernstein had come up with a proposal, and as far as he was concerned it was the only way out of it, the only possible solution, and whether Stanley liked it or not, it had to be done. What are you talking about? Stanley said, speaking for the first time in the past seven minutes. They're going to burn down the store for us, Lew said, and once we collect on the insurance, everyone takes a cut. Stanley said nothing. He said nothing because he had to say nothing, because the only thought in his head at that moment was how much he wanted to kill his brother, and if he ever dared to speak those words out loud, to tell Lew how much he wanted to put his hands around his throat and strangle him to death, his mother would curse him from her grave and go on torturing him for the rest of his life. At long last Stanley rose from the chair and began walking toward the door, and once he had opened the door, he paused on the threshold and said: I don't believe you. Then he left the room, and with his back to his brother he heard Lew say: Believe me, Stanley. It has to be done.

5) Stanley's first impulse was to talk to Rose, to unburden himself to his wife and ask for her help in stopping Lew, but again and again he struggled to get the words out of his mouth, and again and again he failed, each time backing down at the last minute because he couldn't bear the thought of listening to what she would say to him, what he

knew she would say to him. He couldn't go to the police. No crime had been committed yet, and what sort of a man accuses his brother of plotting a potential crime when he has no hard evidence to substantiate proof of a conspiracy? On the other hand, even if Bernstein and his brother eventually went through with it, would he have it in him to go to the police and have his brother arrested? Lew was in danger. They were threatening to blind him, to kill his wife and daughter, and if Stanley stepped forward now, he would be responsible for that maiming, for those deaths, which meant that he was a part of it, too, an unwilling co-conspirator in spite of himself, and if things went wrong and Bernstein and Lew were caught, he had no doubt that his brother wouldn't hesitate to name him as an accomplice. Yes, he despised Lew, he was sickened by the mere thought of him, and yet how deeply he despised himself for feeling that hatred, which was sinful and grotesque and only further increased his inability to act, for by failing to talk to Rose he understood that he had chosen the past over the present, had renounced his place as husband and father to go back to the dark world of son and brother, a place where he had no wish to be anymore, but he couldn't escape, he had been sucked back into it, and for the next two weeks he walked around in a demented state of dread and fury, walled off from everyone by his unbroken silence, seething with frustration, wondering when the bomb inside his head would finally explode.

6) As he saw it, there was no alternative but to play along—or pretend to play along. He needed to know what Bernstein and company were planning, to be kept abreast of the details, and in order to learn those things he had to trick Lew into believing he was with him, so the next morning, just twenty-four hours after their last conversation, the chilling dialogue that had ended with the words *It has to be done*, Stanley told Lew that he had changed his mind, that against his better judgment and with infinite disgust in his heart, he understood there was no other way. This falsehood produced the desired results. Thinking Stanley was now on board, a grateful, trembling, all but unhinged Lew began to treat his brother as his cherished ally and most trusted confidant, and not once did he suspect that Stanley was acting as a double agent whose sole intention was to gum up the works and prevent the fire from happening.

7) There would be two men, Lew informed him, a seasoned arsonist with no criminal record working in tandem with a lookout, and the

date was set for next Tuesday, the night of November second/third, as long as it turned out to be a dry night with no rain in the forecast. Lew's job was to dismantle the burglar alarm and provide the men with keys to the store. He would spend the night at home and suggested Stanley do the same, but Stanley had other plans for that night, or just a single plan, which was to park himself in the unlit store and chase off the firebug before he could start his work. Stanley wanted to know if the men would be carrying guns, but Lew wasn't certain, Bernstein had neglected to touch on that point with him, but what difference did it make, he asked, why worry about something that didn't concern them? Because someone might choose the wrong moment to go walking past the store, Stanley said, a cop, a man out with his dog, a woman on her way home from a party, and he didn't want anyone to get hurt. Burning down a business for three hundred thousand dollars in insurance money was bad enough, but if some innocent bystander happened to be shot and killed in the process, they could go to jail for the rest of their lives. Lew hadn't thought of that. Maybe he should bring it up with Bernstein, he said, but Stanley told him not to bother, since Bernstein's men were going to do exactly as they pleased, regardless of what Lew wanted. That put an end to the discussion, and as Stanley walked away from his brother and entered the downstairs showroom, he realized that this question of guns or no guns was the great unknown variable, the one factor that could destroy his plan. It would make sense for him to buy a gun before Tuesday, he told himself, but something in him balked at the idea, a lifetime of revulsion toward guns, so much so that he had never fired one or even held one in his hand. His father had been killed by a gun, and what good had it done him to be carrying his own revolver in that Chicago warehouse thirty-one years ago, he had been shot down anyway, killed with an unfired thirty-eight in his right hand, and who knew if he hadn't been killed because he'd gone for his gun first, leaving his killer no choice but to shoot him in order to save his own life? No, guns were a complicated business, and once you pointed a weapon at someone, especially someone with a weapon of his own, the thing you were counting on to protect you was just as likely to turn you into a corpse. Besides, the man Bernstein had dug up to incinerate 3 Brothers Home World wasn't a contract killer but an arsonist, an ex-firefighter according to Lew, that was a good one, a man who once made his living putting out fires now setting them for fun and profit, and why would he need a gun to do that? The lookout was another matter, no doubt some broad-chested thug who would come to the store fully armed, but Stanley figured he would be waiting outside while the ex-fireman went about his job, and since Stanley would already be inside before the two of them showed up, he concluded that a gun wouldn't be necessary. That didn't mean he would go there empty-handed, but a baseball bat would serve his purpose just as well, he felt, a thirty-six-inch Louisville Slugger would scare off the torch just as effectively as a thirty-two-caliber pistol, and given Stanley's state of mind in the two weeks leading up to November second, the demonic, half-mad, out-of-control roar of thoughts that had been raging in his head since the morning of Lew's confession, he found the idea of a baseball bat deeply and perversely funny, so funny that he laughed out loud when the idea came to him, a brief yelp of a laugh that rose up from the bottom of his lungs and burst out of him like a splatter of buckshot bouncing off a wall, for the whole gruesome comedy had started with a baseball bat, the bat used by Dusty Rhodes at the Polo Grounds on September twenty-ninth, and what better way to end the farce than by taking hold of another bat and threatening to bash in the head of the man who wanted to burn down his store?

8) On the afternoon of the second, Stanley called Rose to tell her he wouldn't be coming home for dinner that evening. He would be working late with Adelle, he said, going over the books in preparation for an audit that was scheduled for Friday, and chances were it would keep them busy until around midnight, so Rose shouldn't bother to wait up for him. The store closed at five on Tuesdays, and by five-thirty everyone but Stanley was gone—Arnold, Mrs. Rosen, Ed and Phil, Charlie Sykes, Bob Dawkins, and the absent Lew, who had been too frightened to come to work that morning and had spent the day at home with a pretend fever. Bernstein's men wouldn't be turning up until one or two in the morning, and with several blank hours in front of him, Stanley decided to go out to dinner, indulging himself with a visit to his favorite Newark restaurant, Moishe's, which specialized in Eastern European Jewish cuisine, the same food Stanley's mother had cooked for him in the old days, boiled beef with horseradish, potato pirogen, gefilte fish, and matzo ball soup, the peasant delicacies of another time, another world, and Stanley had only to walk into the dining room at Moishe's to be thrown back into his vanished childhood, for the restau-

rant itself was a throwback, a threadbare, inelegant place with cheap, plastic-laminated tablecloths and dusty light fixtures hanging from the ceiling, but each table was adorned with a blue-tinted or green-tinted seltzer bottle, a sight that for some reason never failed to provoke a small surge of happiness in him, and when he heard the grouchy, ill-mannered waiters talking in their Yiddish-inflected voices, that brought comfort to him as well, although he would have been hard-pressed to explain why. So Stanley dined on the dishes of his youth that night, starting with borscht and a dollop of sour cream, followed by a plate of pickled herring, and then on to a main course of flank steak (well-done) with cucumbers and potato pancakes on the side, and as he squirted jets of seltzer water into his clear ribbed glass and worked his way through the meal, he thought about his dead parents and his two impossible brothers, who had caused him so much heartache over the years, and also about his beautiful Rose, the person he loved most but not well enough, never well enough, a fact he had understood for some time now, and it pained him to admit there was something blocked and stifled about him, a flaw in his makeup that prevented him from giving her as much of himself as she deserved, and then there was the little boy, Archie, a pure conundrum that one, no doubt a lively, quick-thinking fellow, a boy above most other boys, but he had been his mother's child from the start, so attached to her that Stanley had never managed to find a way in, and after seven and a half years he was still flummoxed by his inability to read what the boy was thinking, whereas Rose always seemed to know, as if by some inborn knowledge, some inexplicable power that burned in women but was rarely granted to men. It was unusual for Stanley to dwell on such matters, to drive his thoughts into himself and seek out his failings and sorrows, the torn threads of his patched-together life, but this was not a usual moment for him, and after two long weeks of silence and inner struggle, he was exhausted, barely capable of standing up anymore, and even when he could stand up, too unsteady to walk in a straight line, and once he had paid for his dinner and was driving back to 3 Brothers Home World, he wondered if his plan made any sense at all, if he hadn't deluded himself into thinking it would work simply because he was right and Lew and the others were wrong, and if that was the case, perhaps he should just drive on home and let the store burn to the ground.

9) He returned to the store a few minutes past eight. All dark, all

still—the nightly nothingness of mute televisions and dozing Frigi-
daires, a cemetery of shadows. He had little doubt he would live to
regret what he was doing, that his calculations were bound to go wrong,
but he had no other ideas, and it was too late to think of another one
now. He had started the business when he was eighteen, and for the
past twenty-two years it had been his life, his one and only life, and
he couldn't let Lew and his band of crooks get away with destroying it,
because there was more to this place than just a business, it was a man's
life, and that man's life was the store, the store and the man were one,
and if they set fire to the store, they would be setting fire to the man as
well. A few minutes past eight. How many hours to go? At least four,
perhaps as many as five or six, a long time to sit there doing nothing,
waiting in a pitch-black room for a man to show up with his cans of
gasoline and his book of killer matches, but there was no choice except
to wait there in silence and hope the baseball bat was as strong as it
looked. He settled into a chair in the back office, Mrs. Rosen's chair, the
one that belonged to the desk in the far corner, which had the best view
through the narrow, rectangular window set in the wall between the
office and the showroom, and from where he was sitting, he could
see all the way to the front entrance, or would have been able to see it if
the store hadn't been in total darkness, but the gasoline man would
surely be carrying a flashlight in his pocket, and once Stanley heard
the front door open, the light would be turned on, even if only for a
second or two, and then he would know where the man was. Immediately after that: throw on the overhead lights, burst out of the back
room clutching the bat in his upraised hand, shout at the top of his voice,
and order the man out of there. Such was the plan. Cross your fingers,
Stanley, he said to himself, and if luck isn't with you, then cross your
heart and hope to die. Meanwhile, he went on sitting in Mrs. Rosen's
chair, which was mounted on wheels and could swivel from side to
side and tip back and forth, a standard office chair, comfortable enough
to sit in for a little while, but hardly a good spot for the long haul, long
being the four or five hours that were still in front of him, and yet the
more uncomfortable the better, Stanley reasoned, since a state of mild
discomfort would help to keep him alert. Or so he thought, but as he sat
there behind the gray metal desk, rocking back and forth in Mrs. Rosen's
chair, telling himself that this was the worst moment of his life, that he
had never felt unhappier or more lonely than he did now, that even if he

managed to get through the night in one piece, everything else had been smashed, hammered into dust by Lew's betrayal, and after this night nothing would ever be the same, for now that he was betraying Lew, Bernstein would resort to his old threats, which would put Lew and Millie in danger again, and if anything happened to them it would be on Stanley's head, he would have to live with it and die with it, and yet how could he not do what he was doing, how could he let himself get caught up in an insurance scam and risk going to jail, no, he couldn't let them burn down the store, they had to be stopped, and as Stanley continued to think about these things, which were the same things he had been thinking about and thinking about for the past two weeks, he understood that he couldn't take it anymore, that he had come to the limit of what was possible for him, that he was worn out, weary beyond all measure, so tired that he couldn't bear to be in the world anymore, and little by little his eyes began to close, and before long he had stopped fighting to keep them open and had put his head down on his folded arms, which were lying on the desk in front of him, and two or three minutes after that he was asleep.

10) He slept through the break-in and the subsequent dousing of the store with twelve gallons of gasoline, and because the man who had come to do the job had no idea that Stanley was sleeping in the back room, he lit the match that ignited 3 Brothers Home World with a guiltless conscience, knowing he was about to commit an act of arson but not that he would later be charged with manslaughter as well. As for Ferguson's father, he never had a chance. By the time he opened his eyes, he was no more than half conscious, unable to move because of the vast clouds of smoke he had already inhaled, and as he struggled to lift his head and breathe some air into his scalded lungs, the fire was burning its way through the door of the back room, and once it had entered the room, it rushed over to the desk where Stanley was sitting and ate him alive.

THESE WERE THE things Ferguson did not know, the things he could not have known during the two years that separated his cousin's death in the Korean War from his father's death in the Newark fire. By spring of the following year, his Uncle Lew was in prison, along with the gasoline man Eddie Schultz, his lookout accomplice George Ionello, and

the mastermind of the operation, Ira Bernstein, but by then Ferguson
and his mother had left the New Jersey suburbs and were living in
New York, occupants of a three-bedroom apartment on Central Park
West between Eighty-third and Eighty-fourth Streets. The photography studio in Millburn had been sold, and because his father's life
insurance policy had provided his mother with two hundred thousand
tax-free dollars, there were no financial burdens, which meant that
even in death, the loyal, pragmatic, ever-responsible Stanley Ferguson
was continuing to support them.

First, the shock of November third, and with it the spectacle of his
mother's tears, the onslaught of intense, smothering embraces, her
gasping, shuddering body pressed against him, and then, some hours
later, the arrival of his grandparents from New York, and the day after
that the appearance of Aunt Mildred and her husband, Paul Sandler,
and through it all the comings and goings of countless Fergusons, the
two weeping aunts, Millie and Joan, the stone-faced Uncle Arnold, and
even the treacherous, not-yet-exposed Uncle Lew, so much chaos and
noise, a house with too many people in it, and Ferguson sat in a corner
and watched, not knowing what to say or think, still too stunned to
cry. It was unimaginable that his father should be dead. He had been
alive the previous morning, sitting at the breakfast table with a copy of
the *Newark Star-Ledger* in his hands, telling Ferguson it was going to be
a cold day and he should remember to wear his scarf to school, and it
made no sense that those were the last words his father would ever
speak to him. Days passed. He stood in the rain beside his mother as
they lowered his father into the ground and the rabbi intoned a dirge
in incomprehensible Hebrew, such awful-sounding words that Ferguson wanted to cover his ears, and two days after that he returned to
school, to fat Mrs. Costello and his second-grade class, but everyone
seemed afraid of him, too embarrassed to talk to him anymore, as if an
X had been stamped on his forehead to warn them not to come near,
and even though Mrs. Costello kindly offered to let him skip the group
lessons and sit at his desk reading whatever book he wanted, that only
made things worse somehow, for he found it difficult to keep his mind
on the books, which normally gave him so much pleasure, since his
thoughts would invariably drift off from the words on the page to
his father, not the father who was buried in the ground but the father
who had gone to heaven, if there was such a place as heaven, and if

his father was indeed there, was it possible that he was looking down on him now, watching him sit at his desk pretending to read? It would be nice to think that, Ferguson said to himself, but at the same time, what good would it do? His father would be glad to see him, yes, which would probably make the fact of being dead a bit less unbearable, but how could it help Ferguson to be seen if he himself couldn't see the person who was looking at him? Most of all, he wanted to hear his father talk. That was what he missed above everything else, and even though his father had been a man of few words, a master in the art of giving short answers to long questions, Ferguson had always liked the sound of his voice, which had been a tuneful, gentle voice, and the thought that he would never hear it again filled him with an immense sadness, a sorrow so deep and so wide that it could have contained the Pacific Ocean, which was the largest ocean in the world. *It's going to be a cold day, Archie. Remember to wear your scarf to school.*

The world wasn't real anymore. Everything in it was a fraudulent copy of what it should have been, and everything that happened in it shouldn't have been happening. For a long time afterward, Ferguson lived under the spell of this illusion, sleepwalking through his days and struggling to fall asleep at night, sick of a world he had stopped believing in, doubting everything that presented itself to his eyes. Mrs. Costello asked him to pay attention, but he didn't have to listen to her now, since she was only an actress trying to impersonate his teacher, and when his friend Jeff Balsoni made the extraordinary, uncalled-for sacrifice of giving Ferguson his Ted Williams baseball card, the rarest card among the hundreds in the Topps collection, Ferguson thanked him for the gift, put the card in his pocket, and then tore it up at home. It was possible to do such things now. Before November third, they would have been inconceivable to him, but an unreal world was much bigger than a real world, and there was more than enough room in it to be yourself and not yourself at the same time.

According to what his mother later told him, she hadn't been planning such a quick departure from New Jersey, but then the scandal broke, and suddenly there was no choice but to get out of there. Eleven days before Christmas, the Newark police announced that they had cracked the 3 Brothers Home World case, and by the next morning the ugly particulars were front-page news in every paper across Essex and Union Counties. Fratricide. Gambling Kingpin Arrested. Ex-Fireman

Turned Firebug Held Without Bail. Louis Ferguson Indicted On Multiple Charges. His mother kept him home from school that day, and then the day after that, and the day after that, and every day until the school closed for Christmas vacation. It's for your own good, Archie, she said to him, and because he couldn't have cared less about not going to school, he didn't bother to ask her why. Much later, when he was old enough to grasp the full horror of the word *fratricide*, he understood that she was trying to protect him from the vicious talk circulating around town, for his name was now a notorious name, and to be a Ferguson meant you belonged to a family that was damned. So the soon-to-be-eight-year-old Ferguson stayed at home with his grandmother as his mother went about the business of putting the family house on the market and searching for a photographer to buy her studio, and because the newspapers never stopped calling, asking, begging, harassing her to open up and give *her side of the story*, the latter-day Jacobean drama now known as the Ferguson Affair, his mother decided that enough was enough, and two days after Christmas, she packed up some suitcases, loaded them into the trunk of her blue Chevy, and the three of them drove to New York.

For the next two months, he and his mother lived in his grandparents' apartment on West Fifty-eighth Street, his mother back in the old bedroom she had once shared with her sister, Mildred, and Ferguson camped out in the living room on a small fold-up cot. The most interesting part of this temporary arrangement was that he didn't have to go to school, an unexpected liberation caused by their lack of a fixed address, and until they found a place of their own, he would be a free man. Aunt Mildred opposed the idea of no school for him, but Ferguson's mother calmly brushed her off. Don't worry, she said. Archie is a bright kid, and a little time off won't hurt him. Once we know where we'll be living, we'll start looking for a school. First things first, Mildred.

It was a strange time, then, unconnected to anything he had known in the past, utterly separate from the way things would be for him after they moved into their apartment, *a curious interregnum*, as his grandfather put it, a short span of hollowed-out time in which he spent every waking moment with his mother, the two beaten comrades who trekked up and down the West Side looking at apartments together, conferring about the pluses and minuses of each place, mutually deciding that the one on Central Park West would be just about ideal for them, and then his mother's surprising declaration that the house in Millburn was being sold with the furniture, all the furniture, and that they would be starting again from zero, just the two of them, so after they found the apartment they spent their days shopping for furniture, looking at beds and tables and lamps and rugs, never buying anything unless they both agreed on it, and one afternoon, as they were examining chairs and sofas at Macy's, the bow-tied clerk looked down at Ferguson and said to his mother, Why isn't this little boy in school?, to which his mother replied, with a hard stare into the nosy man's face: *None of your business*. That was the best moment of those strange two months, or one of the best moments, unforgettable because of the sudden feeling of happiness that rose up in him when his mother said those words, happier than at any time in weeks, and the sense of solidarity those words implied, the two of them against the world, struggling to put themselves together again, and *none of your business* was the credo of that double effort, a sign of how much they were depending on each other now. After shopping for furniture, they would go to the movies, escaping the cold winter streets for a couple of hours in the dark, watching whatever happened to be playing just then, always in the balcony because his mother could smoke up there, Chesterfields, one Chesterfield after another as they sat through movies with Alan Ladd, Marilyn Monroe, Kirk Douglas, Gary Cooper, Grace Kelly, and William Holden, Westerns, musicals, science fiction, it didn't matter what was showing that day, they would walk in blindly and hope for the best from *Drum Beat, Vera Cruz, There's No Business Like Show Business, 20,000 Leagues Under the Sea, Bad Day at Black Rock, The Bridges at Toko-Ri,* and *Young at Heart,* and once, just before the strange two months came to an end, the woman in the glass booth who sold them their tickets asked his mother why the little boy wasn't in school, and his mother answered: *Butt out, lady. Just give me my change.*

$$\boxed{1.4}$$

Fɪʀsᴛ, ᴛʜᴇʀᴇ ᴡᴀs ᴛʜᴇ ᴀᴘᴀʀᴛᴍᴇɴᴛ ɪɴ Nᴇᴡᴀʀᴋ, ᴀʙᴏᴜᴛ ᴡʜɪᴄʜ ʜᴇ remembered nothing, and then there was the house in Maplewood that his parents bought when he was three, and now, six years later, they were moving again, to a much larger house on the other side of town. Ferguson couldn't understand it. The house they had been living in was a perfectly good house, a more than adequate house for a family with just three people in it, and why would his parents want to go to the trouble of packing up all their things to move such a short distance—especially when they didn't have to? It would have made sense if they were going to another city or another state, as Uncle Lew and Aunt Millie had done four years ago when they'd moved to Los Angeles, or as Uncle Arnold and Aunt Joan had done the next year when they'd moved to California as well, but why bother to change houses when they weren't even going to another town?

Because they could afford it, his mother said. His father's business was doing well, and they were in a position to live on a grander scale now. The words *grander scale* made Ferguson think of an eighteenth-century European palace, a marble hall filled with dukes and duchesses in white powdered wigs, two dozen ladies and gentlemen dressed in opulent silk costumes standing around with lace hankies and laughing at one another's jokes. Then, as he embellished the scene a bit further, he tried to imagine his parents in that crowd, but the costumes made them look ridiculous, laughable, grotesque. He said: Just because we can afford something doesn't mean we should buy it. I like our house and think we should stay. If we have more money than we need, then we should give it to someone who needs it more than we do. A starving person, a crippled old man, someone with no money at all. Spending it on ourselves isn't right. It's selfish.

Don't be difficult, Archie, his mother replied. Your father works harder than any two men in this town. He deserves every penny he's made, and if he wants to show off a little with a new house, that's his business.

I don't like show-offs, Ferguson said. It's not a good way to act.

Well, like it or not, little man, we're moving, and I'm sure you'll be happy about it once we settle in. A bigger room, a bigger backyard, and a finished basement. We'll put a ping-pong table down there, and then we'll see if you can finally get good enough to beat me.

But we already play ping-pong in the backyard.

When it isn't too cold outside. And just think, Archie, in the new house we won't be bothered by the wind.

He knew that some of the family's money came from his mother's work as a portrait photographer, but a much larger share of it, nearly all of it in fact, was produced by his father's business, a chain of three appliance stores called Ferguson's, one of them in Union, another in Westfield, and the third in Livingston. Long ago, there had been a store in Newark called 3 Brothers Home World, but that was gone now, sold off when Ferguson was three and a half or four, and if not for the framed black-and-white photograph that hung on a wall in the den, the 1941 snapshot that showed his smiling father standing between his two smiling uncles in front of 3 Brothers Home World on the day it opened for business, all memories of that store would have been expunged from his mind forever. It was unclear to him why his father no longer worked with his brothers, and on top of that there was the even greater puzzle of why Uncle Lew and Uncle Arnold had both left New Jersey to *start new lives in California* (his father's words). Six or seven months ago, in a fit of longing for his absent cousin Francie, he had asked his mother to explain their reasons for moving so far away, but she had simply said, *Your father bought them out*, which wasn't much of an answer, at least not one he could understand. Now, with this unpleasant development about a new and bigger house, Ferguson was beginning to grasp something that had previously escaped his attention. His father was rich. He had more money than he knew what to do with, and from the look of how things seemed to be going, that could only mean he was becoming richer and richer by the day.

This was both a good thing and a bad thing, Ferguson decided. Good because money was a necessary evil, as his grandmother had once told him, and since everyone needed money in order to live, it was surely better to have too much of it than too little. On the other hand, in order to earn too much, a person had to devote an excessive amount of time to the pursuit of money, far more time than was necessary or reasonable, which happened to be the case with his father, who worked so hard at running his empire of appliance stores that the hours he spent at home had been diminishing steadily for years, so much so that Ferguson rarely saw him anymore, since his father had fallen into the habit of leaving the house at six-thirty, so early in the morning that he was inevitably gone before Ferguson had woken up, and because each store stayed open late two nights a week, Monday and Thursday in Union, Tuesday and Friday in Westfield, Wednesday and Saturday in Livingston, there were many nights when his father failed to come home for dinner, returning to the house at ten or ten-thirty, a good hour after Ferguson had been put to bed. The only day when he could count on seeing his father was therefore Sunday, but Sundays were complicated as well, with several hours in the late morning and early afternoon given over to tennis, and that meant tagging along with his parents to the town courts and waiting around until his mother and father had played a set together before he got a chance to bat the ball around with his mother while his father played his weekly match with Sam Brownstein, his tennis friend since boyhood. Ferguson didn't despise tennis, but he found it boring compared to baseball and football, which were the best games as far as he was concerned, and even ping-pong trumped tennis when it came to sports that involved nets and bouncing balls, so it was always with mixed feelings that he trudged off to the outdoor courts in spring, summer, and fall, and every Saturday night he would climb into bed hoping for rain in the morning.

When it didn't rain, tennis was followed by a drive to South Orange Village and lunch at Gruning's, where Ferguson would scarf down a medium-rare hamburger and a bowl of mint-chip ice cream, a much-anticipated Sunday treat, not just because Gruning's made the best hamburgers for miles around and produced their own ice cream but because it smelled so good in there, a mixture of warm coffee and grilling meat and the sugary emanations of manifold desserts, such good smells that Ferguson would dissolve in a kind of delirious contentment as he breathed them into his lungs, and then, once they were back in his father's two-toned Oldsmobile sedan (gray and white), they would return to the house in Maplewood to wash up and change their clothes. On a typical Sunday, one of four things would happen after that. They would stay at home and *putter around,* as his mother called it, which generally meant that Ferguson would follow his father from room to room as he repaired things that needed mending, broken toilet flushers, faulty electrical connections, squeaking doors, while his mother sat on the sofa reading *Life* magazine or went downstairs into her basement darkroom and developed pictures. A second option was going to the movies, something he and his mother enjoyed above all other Sunday pastimes, but his father was often reluctant to indulge their cinematic fervor, since movies were of scant interest to him, as were all other forms of what he called *sit-down entertainment* (plays, concerts, musicals), as if being trapped in a chair for a couple of hours and passively taking in *a bunch of silly make-believe* was one of life's worst tortures, but his mother usually won the argument by threatening to go without him, and so the three Fergusons would climb back into the car and drive off to see the latest Jimmy Stewart Western or Martin-and-Lewis comedy (Newark's own Jerry Lewis!), and it never failed to astonish Ferguson how quickly his father would fall asleep in the darkness of the theater, the oblivions that would engulf him even as the opening credits were rolling across the screen, head tilted back, lips slightly parted, drowned in the deepest slumber as guns blasted, music swelled, and a hundred dishes crashed to the floor. Since Ferguson always sat between his parents, he would tap his mother on the arm whenever his father drifted off like that, and once he had her attention, he would point to his father by jerking back his thumb, as if to say, Look, he's at it again, and depending on his mother's mood, she would either nod her head and smile or shake her head and frown, sometimes emitting a brief, muffled laugh and sometimes exhaling a wordless *mmmm.* By the time Ferguson was eight, his father's dark-theater swoons had become so common that his mother began referring to their Sunday film excursions as *the two-hour rest cure.* No longer did she ask her husband if he wanted to go to the movies. Instead, she would say to him: *How about a knockout pill, Stanley, so you can catch up on your sleep?* Ferguson always laughed when she delivered that line. Sometimes his father laughed along with him, but most of the time he didn't.

When they weren't puttering around or going to the movies, Sunday afternoons were spent paying visits to other people or having other people pay visits to them. With the rest of the Fergusons on the other side of the country now, there were no more family get-togethers in New Jersey, but there were several friends who lived nearby, that is, friends of Ferguson's parents, in particular his mother's childhood friend from Brooklyn, Nancy Solomon, who lived in West Orange and did the oil paintings for Roseland Photo, and his father's childhood friend from Newark, Sam Brownstein, who lived in Maplewood and played tennis with his father every Sunday morning, and on Sunday afternoons Ferguson and his parents sometimes visited Brownstein and his wife, Peggy, who had three children, a girl and two boys, all of whom were older than Ferguson by at least four years, and sometimes the Brownsteins came to visit them at their house, which was soon to be their house no more, and when it wasn't the Brownsteins it tended to be the Solomons, Nancy and her husband, Max, who had two boys, Stewie and Ralph, both of whom were younger than Ferguson by at least three years, which made these back-and-forth New Jersey visits with the Brownsteins and the Solomons something of a trial for Ferguson, who was too old to enjoy playing with the Solomon children and too young to enjoy playing with the Brownstein children, who in fact were too old to be considered children anymore, and so Ferguson often found himself stranded in the middle at these gatherings, not quite certain where he should go or what he should do, since he quickly lost patience with the antics of the three- and six-year-old Stewie and Ralph and was out of his depth with the talk that went on between the fifteen- and seventeen-year-old Brownstein boys, which left him with no recourse but to spend the Brownstein visits in the company of thirteen-year-old Anna Brownstein, who taught him how to play gin rummy and a board game called Careers, but she was already endowed with breasts and had a metallurgy works clamped onto her teeth, which made it hard for him to look at her, since bits of food were perpetually lodged in the silvery network of her braces, tiny particles of unchewed tomatoes, soggy bread crusts, disintegrating blobs of chopped meat, and whenever she smiled, which was often, Ferguson was gripped by a sudden, involuntary rush of queasiness and had to turn his head away.

Still, now that they were on the verge of moving, which had led to important new information about his father (the problem of too much money, too much time spent on making money, so much time that his father had become all but invisible to him for six days of the week, which Ferguson now understood was something he resented, or at least felt bad about, or that frustrated him, or made him angry, or some other word he hadn't thought of yet), and with the question of his father now on his mind, Ferguson found it instructive to look back on those tedious visits with the Brownsteins and Solomons as a way of studying man-hood in action, of comparing his father's behavior with that of Sam Brownstein and Max Solomon. If the size of the houses they lived in was any measure of how much money they earned, then his father was richer than both of them, for even their house, the Ferguson house, the one that was supposedly too small and needed to be replaced by something better, was larger and more attractive than the Brownstein and Solomon houses. His father drove a 1955 Oldsmobile and was talking about trad-ing it in for a new Cadillac in September, while Sam Brownstein drove a 1952 Rambler and Max Solomon a 1950 Chevrolet. Solomon was a claims adjuster for an insurance company (whatever that meant, since Ferguson had no idea what a claims adjuster did), and Brownstein owned a sporting goods store in downtown Newark, not three stores as Ferguson's father did but one store, which nevertheless brought in enough money for him to support his wife and three children, whereas Ferguson's father's three stores supported just one child and a wife, who happened to work as well, which Peggy Brownstein did not. Like Fer-guson's father, Brownstein and Solomon went to work every day in order to earn money, but neither one of them left the house at six-thirty in the morning or worked so late into the night that his children were already in bed by the time he came home. The quiet, stolid Max Solomon, who had been wounded as a soldier in the Pacific and walked with a slight limp, and the loud-mouthed, expansive Sam Brownstein, brimming with jokes and back-slapping bonhomie, each so different from the other in their outward bearing and yet, at their core, different from Ferguson's father in remarkably similar ways, for both of those men worked in order to live, whereas his father seemed to live in order to work, which meant that his parents' friends were defined more by their enthusi-asms than their burdens or responsibilities, Solomon by his passion for classical music (vast record collection, hand-built hi-fi system), Brownstein by his love of sport in all of its many incarnations, from basketball to horse racing, from track and field to boxing, but the only thing Ferguson's father cared about beyond his work was tennis, which was a meager, restrictive sort of hobby, Ferguson felt, and whenever Brownstein switched on the television to a baseball game or football game during one of their Sunday visits, the boys and men in both families would gather in the living room to watch, and nine times out of eleven, just as he did at the movies, his father would struggle to keep his eyes open, struggle for five or ten or fifteen minutes, and then he would lose the struggle and fall asleep.

On other Sundays, there were the family visits with the Adlers, both in New York and Maplewood, which provided Ferguson with additional subjects to examine in his laboratory of masculine behavior, in particular his grandfather and Aunt Mildred's husband, Donald Marx, although perhaps his grandfather didn't count, since he came from an older generation and was so unlike Ferguson's father that it felt odd even to put their names in the same sentence. Sixty-three years old and still going strong, still working at his real estate business and still making money, but not as much as his father, Ferguson thought, since the apartment on West Fifty-eighth Street was rather cramped, with a minuscule kitchen and a living room only half the size of the one in Maplewood, and the car his grandfather drove, an odd purple Plymouth with pushbutton gear controls, looked like a circus car next to his father's sleek Oldsmobile sedan. Yes, there was something buffoonish about Benjy Adler, Ferguson supposed, with his card tricks and handshake buzzers and high wheezing laugh, but his grandson loved him just the same, loved him for the way he seemed to love being alive, and whenever he was in one of his storytelling moods, the narratives were delivered so swiftly and pungently that the world seemed to collapse into a pure outrush of language, funny stories mostly, stories about Adlers of the past and sundry close and distant relatives, his grandfather's mother's cousin, for example, a woman with the delicious name of Fagela Flegelman, who was apparently so brilliant that she had mastered nine foreign languages before she turned twenty, and when her family left Poland and arrived in New York in 1891, the officials at Ellis Island were so impressed by her linguistic skills that they hired her on the spot, and for the next thirty-plus years Fagela Flegelman worked as an interpreter for the Department of Immigration, interviewing thousands upon thousands of fresh-off-the-boat future Americans until the facility closed in 1924. A long pause, followed by one of his grandfather's enigmatic grins, and then another story about Fagela Flegelman's four husbands and how she outlived them all, ending up as a rich widow in Paris with an apartment on the Champs-Élysées. Could such stories have been true? Did it matter if they were true?

No, his grandfather didn't count because he was off the charts, *disqualified by reason of inanity*, as the old man might have put it in one of his dreadful puns, but Uncle Don was only a couple of years younger than Ferguson's father, and therefore he was a fit candidate for scrutiny, perhaps even a better one than Sam Brownstein or Max Solomon, for like his father those two men lived in the New Jersey suburbs and were members of the striving middle class, a merchant and a white-collar worker, but Don Marx was a creature of the city, born and bred in New York, educated at Columbia, and by some miracle he had no job, at least not one with an employer and a regular paycheck, spending his days at home with a typewriter that produced books and magazine articles, a man unto himself, the first such man Ferguson had ever known. He had moved in with Aunt Mildred three years ago, leaving his wife and son in his old apartment on the Upper West Side, which was another first for Ferguson, a divorced man, a man embarked on a second marriage as of one year ago, having *lived in sin* with Ferguson's aunt for the first two years of their cohabitation (something his father and grandparents and Great-aunt Pearl had all frowned upon but had made his mother laugh), and the small apartment Don Marx shared with Aunt Mildred on Perry Street in Greenwich Village was filled with more books than Ferguson had ever seen in a place that was not a bookstore or a library, books everywhere, on shelves lining the walls of the three rooms, on tables and chairs, on the floor, on the tops of cabinets, and not only was Ferguson bewitched by this fantastical clutter, but the mere fact that such an apartment existed served to demonstrate that there were other ways of living in this world than the one he knew, that his parents' way was not the only way. Aunt Mildred was an associate professor of English at Brooklyn College, Uncle Don was a writer, and although they must have made money from those jobs, enough money to live on in any case, it was clear to Ferguson that they lived for other things besides making money.

Unfortunately, he didn't get a chance to go to that apartment often, only three times so far in those three years, once for a dinner with his parents and twice alone with his mother for afternoon visits. Ferguson had warm feelings toward his aunt and new uncle, but for some reason his mother and her sister weren't close, and the sad but ever more apparent truth was that his father and Don Marx had nothing to say to each other. He had always sensed that his father and aunt got along well, and now that his aunt was no longer single, he was convinced the same held true for his mother and uncle. The problem was the woman-woman connection and the man-man connection, for his mother, as the younger of the two sisters, had always looked up to Mildred, and Mildred, as the older of the two sisters, had always looked down on his mother, and with the men there was the utter indifference each one had toward the other's work and outlook on life, dollars on the one hand, words on the other, compounded further perhaps by Uncle Don having fought in Europe during the war and his father having stayed home, but that was probably a groundless supposition, since Max Solomon had been a soldier as well, and he and his father were always able to talk, at least to the extent that his father was able to talk to anyone.

Still, there were the mutual visits to his grandparents' apartment for Thanksgiving, Passover, and occasional Sunday gatherings, as well as the other Sundays when Aunt Mildred and Uncle Don would climb into the backseat of the purple Plymouth and accompany his grandparents on day trips to New Jersey. Ferguson therefore had ample opportunities to observe his Uncle Don, and the startling conclusion he came to was that in spite of the vast difference between his father and his uncle regarding their backgrounds, their educations, their work, and their manner of living, they were more the same than not the same, more similar to each other than his father was to Sam Brownstein or Max Solomon, for whether they were in the business of making dollars or making words, each man was driven by his work to the exclusion of all other things, which made them both tense and distracted when they weren't working, obtuse and self-involved, semi-blind. There was no question that Uncle Don could be more loquacious than his father, funnier than his father, more interesting than his father, *but only when he wanted to be,* and now that Ferguson had come to know him as well as he did, he saw how often he seemed to look straight through Aunt Mildred when she talked to him, as if he were searching for something behind her back, not able to hear her because he was thinking about something else, which was not unlike how his father often looked at his mother now, more and more often now, the glazed-over look of a man unable to see anything but the thoughts inside his own head, a man who was there but not there, gone.

That was the real difference, Ferguson concluded. Not too little money or too much money, not what a person did or failed to do, not buying a larger house or a more expensive car, but ambition. That explained why Brownstein and Solomon managed to float through their lives in relative peace—because they weren't tormented by the curse of ambition. By contrast, his father and Uncle Don were consumed by their ambitions, which paradoxically made their worlds smaller and less comfortable than those who weren't afflicted by the curse, for ambition meant never being satisfied, to be always hungering for something more, constantly pushing forward because no success could ever be big enough to quell the need for new and even bigger successes, the compulsion to turn one store into two stores, then two stores into three stores, to be talking now about building a fourth store and even a fifth store, just as one book was merely a step on the way to another book, a lifetime of more and more books, which required the same concentration and singleness of purpose that a businessman needed in order to become rich. Alexander the Great conquers the world, and then what? He builds a rocket ship and invades Mars.

Ferguson was in the first decade of his life, which meant that the books he read were still confined to the realm of children's literature, Hardy Boys mysteries, novels about high school football players and intergalactic travelers, collections of adventure stories, simplified biographies of famous men and women such as Abraham Lincoln and Joan of Arc, but now that he had begun his investigation into the workings of Uncle Don's soul, he felt it might be a good idea to read something he had written, or try to read something, and so one day he asked his mother if they had any of his uncle's books in the house. Yes, she said, they had both of them.

F: Both of them? You mean he's written only two?

F's mother: They're long books, Archie. Each one took years to write.

F: What are they about?

F's mother: They're biographies.

F: Good. I like biographies. Who are the people?

F's mother: People from long ago. A German writer from the early nineteenth century called Kleist. And a French philosopher and scientist from the seventeenth century called Pascal.

F: Never heard of them.

F's mother: To tell the truth, I hadn't either.

F: Are they good books?

F's mother: I think so. People say they're very good.

F: You mean you haven't read them?

F's mother: A few pages here and there, but not all the way through. I'm afraid they're not my cup of tea.

F: But other people think they're good. That must mean Uncle Don makes a lot of money.

F's mother: Not really. They're books for scholars, and they don't have a big audience. That's why Uncle Don writes so many articles and reviews. To pad his income while he does the research for his books.

F: I think I should read one.

F's mother (*smiling*): If you want to, Archie. But don't be disappointed if you find it hard going.

So Ferguson's mother gave him the two books, each one over four hundred pages long, two heavy volumes with small print and no illustrations published by Oxford University Press, and because Ferguson liked the cover of the Pascal book better than the Kleist cover, with its stark photograph of the Frenchman's white death mask hovering against a pure black background, he decided to tackle that one first. One paragraph in, he understood that it wasn't merely hard going, it was no going at all. I'm not ready for this, he said to himself. I'll have to wait until I'm older.

If Ferguson couldn't read his uncle's books, he could nevertheless study how he behaved with his son, which was a topic of great interest to Ferguson, no doubt the essential topic, the one that had launched him into his systematic examination of contemporary American manhood, for his growing disillusionment with his own father had made him more attentive to how other fathers treated their sons, and he had to gather evidence in order to judge whether his problem was uniquely his own or a universal problem common to all boys. With Brownstein and Solomon, he had been exposed to two different expressions of paternal conduct. Brownstein was jocular and chummy with his offspring, Solomon was grave and tender; Brownstein chattered and praised, Solomon listened and wiped away tears; Brownstein could lose his temper and scold in public, Solomon kept his thoughts to himself and let Nancy discipline their boys. Two modes, two philosophies, two personalities, one altogether unlike Ferguson's father, the other somewhat like, but with this fundamental exception: Solomon never fell asleep.

Uncle Don couldn't fall asleep because he no longer lived with his son and saw him only rarely, one weekend every month, two weeks in the summer, just thirty-eight days a year, but when Ferguson did the calculations in his head, he realized that while he saw his father more often than that—fifty-two Sundays a year to begin with, along with family dinners on the nights when his father didn't come home late from work, more or less half the nights of the week, which would tally up to about a hundred and fifty Monday-through-Saturday dinners per year, far more contact than Uncle Don's son had with his father—there was nevertheless a hitch, for Ferguson's new cousin-by-marriage always saw his father alone on those thirty-eight yearly get-togethers, whereas Ferguson was never alone with his father anymore, and when he searched his memory for the last time they had been together with no one else in the room or the car, he had to go back more than a year and a half, to a rain-filled Sunday morning that had washed out the weekly ritual of tennis and Gruning's, when he and his father had climbed into the old Buick and driven off to buy the makings of brunch, standing in line at Tabachnik's with their numbered ticket as they waited their turn in that crowded, good-smelling store to stock up on whitefish, herring, lox, bagels, and a tub of cream cheese. A distinct, luminous memory—but that had been the last time, October 1954, one-sixth of his life ago, and when you subtracted the first three years of his life, which he could no longer actively remember, close to one-quarter of his life ago, the equivalent of ten years for a forty-three-year-old man, for at this point in the story Ferguson was nine.

The boy's name was Noah, and he was three and a half months younger than Ferguson. Much to Ferguson's regret, the two of them had been kept apart during the years of sinful cohabitation, since Uncle Don's ex-wife, justifiably angry at having been dumped in favor of Aunt Mildred, had refused to allow her son to be tainted by contact with the home-wrecker and her family, which extended beyond the Adlers to the

Fergusons as well. When Uncle Don and Aunt Mildred decided to get married, however, the injunction had been lifted, since everything was legal now, and the ex-wife was no longer in a position to make those demands on her ex-husband. Ferguson and Noah Marx therefore met at the wedding, which took place in December 1954, a small affair held at Ferguson's grandparents' apartment with no more than twenty guests, family members from both sides along with a few intimate friends. Ferguson and Noah were the only children present, and the two boys hit it off from the start, each one being an only child who had always yearned for a brother or sister, and the fact that they were the same age and would henceforth be first cousins, stepcousins by marriage, perhaps, but nevertheless bound together in the same family, turned that initial encounter at the wedding into a kind of auxiliary wedding, or ceremonial alliance, or blood-brother initiation, since they both knew they would be involved with each other for the rest of their lives.

They saw each other infrequently, of course, since one lived in New York and the other in New Jersey, and because Noah was potentially available only thirty-eight days a year, they had been together only six or seven times in the eighteen months since the wedding. Ferguson wished it could have been more, but it was enough to have reached some conclusions about Uncle Don's performance as a father, which was nothing like his own father's, and yet different from Brownstein's and Solomon's as well. Then again, Noah was a special case, a scrawny, snaggle-toothed rascal who bore no resemblance to the children of those other men, and handling him required a special touch. Noah was the first cynic Ferguson had ever met, a subversive prankster and wise-ass motormouth, smart, ever so smart, both smart and funny at the same time, a far more nimble and sophisticated thinker than Ferguson was at that point and consequently a delight to be with if you were his friend, which Ferguson most definitely was by now, but Noah lived with his mother and saw his father only thirty-eight days a year, and he was forever testing his father's patience during the time they spent together, and yet why wouldn't he be against his father, Ferguson thought, since Uncle Don had essentially abandoned him when he was five and a half years old. Ferguson had developed a great fondness for Noah, but he also knew his cousin could be impossible, a belligerent, irritating pest, and so his affections were somewhat divided between father and son, solidarity with the abandoned boy but also some sympathy for the

put-upon father, and before long Ferguson understood that Uncle
Don wanted him to come along on his father-son outings with Noah in
order to serve as a buffer between them, a moderating presence, a distraction. So off the three of them went to Ebbets Field to watch the
Dodgers play the Phillies, off they went to the Museum of Natural History to look at dinosaur bones, off they went to a double bill of Marx
Brothers movies in a rerun house near Carnegie Hall, and Noah would
always start the afternoon with a series of bitter cracks, taunting his
father for dragging him out to Brooklyn because that was what fathers
were supposed to do, wasn't it, shove their boys into hot subway cars
and take them to baseball games, even though the father couldn't have
cared less about baseball, or: See the caveman in the diorama, Dad? At
first I thought I was looking at you, or: The Marx Brothers! Do you
think they're related to us? Maybe I should write to Groucho and ask
him if he's my real father. The truth was that Noah loved baseball, and
even if he was miserably inept at playing it, he knew the batting average of every Dodger and carried around an autograph (which his father
had given him) from Jackie Robinson in his front pocket. The truth
was that Noah was absorbed by every display at the Museum of
Natural History and didn't want to leave the building when his father
said it was time to go. The truth was that Noah laughed his head off
through *Duck Soup* and *Monkey Business* and left the theater shouting,
What a family! Karl Marx! Groucho Marx! Noah Marx! The Marxes
rule the world!

Through all these tempests and confrontations, these sudden lulls
and bursts of manic gaiety, these alternating fits of laughter and aggression, Noah's father persevered with a strange and steadfast calm, never
responding to his son's insults, refusing to be provoked, weathering
each assault in silence until the wind changed direction again. A mysterious, unprecedented form of paternal conduct, Ferguson felt, less
to do with a man controlling his temper than with allowing his boy to
punish him for crimes he had committed, with subjecting himself to
these flagellations as a way of doing penance. What a curious pair they
were—a wounded boy screaming love with each act of hostility toward
his father and a wounded father emanating love by not slapping him
down, by letting himself be punched. When the waters were still, however, when combat had temporarily ceased and father and son were
drifting along in their boat together, there was one remarkable thing

that Ferguson had noted: Uncle Don talked to Noah as if he were an adult. No condescension, no fatherly pats on the head, no setting down of rules. When the boy talked, the father would listen. When the boy asked a question, the father would answer him as if he were a colleague, and as Ferguson listened to them talk, he couldn't help feeling some envy, for at no time had his father ever talked to him in that way, not with that respect, that curiosity, that look of pleasure in his eyes. All in all, then, he concluded that Uncle Don was a good father—a flawed father, perhaps, even a failed father—but nevertheless a good father. And cousin Noah was a most excellent friend, even if he could be a bit crazy at times.

On a Monday morning in mid-June, Ferguson's mother informed him at breakfast that they would be moving into the new house by the end of the summer. She and his father were about to *close on it* next week, and when Ferguson asked her what that meant, she explained that a closing was real estate jargon for buying a house, and once they had given the money and signed the papers, the new house would be theirs. That was grim enough, but then she went on to say something that struck Ferguson as both outrageous and wrong. *As luck would have it,* his mother continued, *we've also found a buyer for the old house.* Old house! What was she talking about? They were eating breakfast in that house now, they were living in that house now, and until they packed up and left for the other side of town, she had no right to talk about it in the past tense.

Why so glum, Archie? his mother said. This is good news, not bad news. You look like someone who's about to march off to war.

He couldn't tell her he had been hoping that no one would buy the house, that no one would want it because they would all see that it suited the Fergusons better than anyone else, and if his mother and father weren't able to sell the house, then they wouldn't be able to afford the new one, which would force them to stay where they were. He couldn't tell her because his mother looked so happy, happier than he had seen her in a long time, and few things were better than seeing his mother look happy, and yet, and yet, his last hope was gone now, and *it had all happened behind his back.* A buyer! Who was that unknown person, and where had he come from? No one ever shared anything with him until after it had happened, things were always being worked out behind his back, and he never had a say in any of it. He wanted a vote! He was sick of being a child, sick of being pushed around and told what to do. America was supposed to be a democracy, but he lived in a dictatorship, and he was fed up, fed up, fed up.

When did it happen? he asked.

Just yesterday, his mother said. When you were in New York with Uncle Don and Noah. It's quite an amazing story.

How so?

Do you remember Mr. Schneiderman, the photographer I used to work for when I was young?

Ferguson nodded. Of course he remembered Mr. Schneiderman, that grumpy old geezer who came to dinner about once a year, the one with the white goatee who slurped his soup and once had farted at the table without even noticing it.

Well, his mother said, Mr. Schneiderman has two grown sons, Daniel and Gilbert, both of them around your father's age, and yesterday Daniel and his wife came here for lunch, and guess what?

You don't have to tell me.

Quite amazing, don't you think?

I suppose.

They have two children, a thirteen-year-old boy and a nine-year-old girl, and that girl, Amy, is about the prettiest little girl I've ever seen. A real heartthrob, Archie.

Good for her.

Okay, sourpuss, but what happens if she winds up living in your room? Would you care?

It'll be her room then, not mine, so why would I care?

The school year ended, and the following weekend Ferguson was sent off to a sleepaway camp in New York State. It was the first time he had left home, but he went without dread or compunction because Noah was going with him, and the fact was that he was sick of home just then, weary of all the talk about old houses that weren't old and pretty girls who would be stealing his room, and eight weeks in the country would surely take his mind off those aggravations. Camp Paradise was situated in the northeastern quadrant of Columbia County, not far from the Massachusetts border and the foothills of the Berkshires, and his parents had chosen to send him there because Nancy Solomon knew someone who knew someone whose children had been going to that camp for years and had nothing but good things to say about it, and once Ferguson was signed up, his mother spoke to her sister, who then spoke to her husband, and Noah was signed up as well. Ferguson and his cousin left from Grand Central Station with a large contingent of fellow campers, close to two hundred boys and girls between the ages of seven and fifteen, and a couple of minutes before they boarded the train, Uncle Don took Ferguson aside and asked him to watch out for Noah, to see that he stayed out of trouble and wasn't picked on by the other boys, and because Uncle Don had that much confidence in him, which implied that he saw something strong and trustworthy about Ferguson, Ferguson promised Uncle Don he would do everything he could to make sure Noah was protected.

Fortunately, Camp Paradise wasn't a rough sort of place, and it didn't take long before Ferguson understood that he could let down his guard. Discipline was lax, and unlike Boy Scout camps or religious camps, whose objective was to *build character in the young,* the directors of Camp Paradise held to the less exalted aim of making life as enjoyable as possible. In his first days there, as Ferguson began to adjust to the new environment, he made several interesting discoveries, among them the fact that he was the only boy in his group who lived in the suburbs. Everyone else came from New York, and he was surrounded by a multitude of city kids who had grown up in neighborhoods such as Flatbush, Midwood, Boro Park, Washington Heights, Forest Hills, and the Grand Concourse, Brooklyn boys, Manhattan boys, Queens boys, Bronx boys, the sons of middle-class and lower-middle-class schoolteachers, accountants, civil servants, bartenders, and traveling salesmen. Until then, Ferguson had assumed that private summer camps were exclusively for the children of rich bankers and lawyers, but apparently he had been wrong, and then, as the days passed and he learned the names of scores of boys and girls, first names and last names both, he understood that everyone in the camp was Jewish, from the husband and wife owners (Irving and Edna Katz) to the head counselor (Jack Feldman) to the counselor and junior counselor in his own cabin (Harvey Rabinowitz and Bob Greenberg) to every last one of the two hundred and twenty-four campers who were there for the summer. The public school he attended in Maplewood was populated by a mixture of Protestants, Catholics, and Jews, but now it was all Jews and only Jews, and for the first time in his life Ferguson had been thrust into an ethnic enclave, a ghetto of sorts, but in this case a fresh-air ghetto with trees and grass and birds darting across the blue sky above him, and once he had absorbed the newness of the situation, it ceased to have any importance to him.

What counted most was that his days were spent in a round of pleasurable activities, not just ones he already knew, such as baseball, swimming, and ping-pong, but assorted novelties that included archery, volleyball, tug-of-war, rowing, broad-jumping, and, best of all, the miraculous sensation of paddling a canoe. He was a sturdy, athletic boy who was naturally drawn to these physical pursuits, but the good thing about Camp Paradise was that one could choose between activities, and for those not athletically inclined there was art, pottery, music, and theater instead of rugged competition with bats and balls. The only mandatory activity was swimming, two thirty-minute swim sessions per day, one before lunch and one before dinner, but everyone liked to cool off in the water, and if you weren't an accomplished swimmer, you could splash around in the shallow end of the lake. Therefore, when Ferguson was fielding grounders at one end of the camp, Noah was drawing in the art shack at the other end of the camp, and when Ferguson was gliding across the water in his beloved canoe, Noah was busy rehearsing a play. The runty, odd-looking Noah had clung to Ferguson during the first week, nervous and unsure of himself, no doubt expecting someone to trip him or call him names, but the attack never materialized, and soon he began to settle in, making friends with some of the other boys, putting his cabinmates in stitches with his Alfred E. Neuman impersonations, and even (Ferguson was flabbergasted) acquiring a suntan in the process.

Of course there were disputes and conflicts and occasional brawls, for this was Camp Paradise and not paradise itself, but nothing out of the ordinary as far as Ferguson could tell, and the one time he came close to exchanging blows with another boy, the cause of the disagreement was so laughable that he couldn't muster the enthusiasm to fight. It was 1956, a year in a string of many years when New York stood at the center of the baseball universe, with three teams that had dominated the sport through a decade-long run, the Yankees, Dodgers, and Giants, and except for 1948, at least one of those teams and often two of them had played in the World Series every year since the first year of Ferguson's life. No one was neutral. Every man, woman, and child in New York and its surrounding suburbs rooted for a team, for the most part with intense devotion, and the supporters of the Yankees, Dodgers, and Giants all despised one another, which led to many useless arguments, an occasional punch in the face, and once, notoriously, a barroom shooting death. For the boys and girls of Ferguson's generation, the longest-running argument revolved around the question of which team had the best center fielder, since all three of them were superb players, the best ones at that position anywhere in baseball, among the finest in the history of the game, and many hours were squandered by those young people in debating the virtues of Duke Snider (Dodgers), Mickey Mantle (Yankees), and Willie Mays (Giants), and so fervent were the supporters of each team that most of them would blindly defend the center fielder on his or her ball club out of pure, unflinching loyalty. Ferguson was a Dodger fan because his mother had grown up in Brooklyn as a Dodger fan and had inculcated him with a love of underdogs and hopeless causes, since the Dodgers of his mother's childhood had been a bumbling, often pathetic team, but now they were a powerhouse, the reigning world champions, on a par with the almighty Yankees, and of the eight boys who bunked in his cabin that summer, three were for the Yankees, two were for the Giants, and three were for the Dodgers, among them Ferguson, Noah, and a boy named Mark Dubinsky. One afternoon, during the forty-five-minute rest period that followed lunch, which was usually spent reading Superman comic books, writing letters, and studying two-day-old box scores in the *New York Post*, Dubinsky, whose bed stood to the left of Ferguson's (Noah's was to the right), brought up the old question once again, telling Ferguson how staunchly he had argued for Snider over Mantle in a discussion with two Yankee fans that morning, fully expecting Dodger-fan Ferguson to take his side, but Ferguson didn't do that, for much as he worshipped the Duke, he said, Mantle was a better player, and on top of that Mays was even better than Mantle, only by a whisker, perhaps, but clearly better, and why would Dubinsky persist in deluding himself about the facts? Ferguson's answer was so unexpected, so tranquil in its assertions, so thorough in its demolition of Dubinsky's belief in the power of faith over reason that Dubinsky took offense, violent offense, and a moment later he was standing over Ferguson's bed and yelling at the top of his voice, calling Ferguson a traitor, an atheist, a communist, and a two-timing fraud, and maybe he should bash him in the gut to teach him a lesson. As Dubinsky clenched his fists, preparing to pounce on Ferguson, Ferguson sat up and told him to take it easy. You can think what you want, Mark, he said, but I'm entitled to my opinion, too. No, you're not, Dubinsky answered, still beside himself, not if you're a Dodger-man you're not. Ferguson had no interest in fighting Dubinsky, who was not normally prone to such hotheaded behavior, but that afternoon it seemed he was longing for a fight, that something about Ferguson had gotten under his skin and he wanted to break their friendship to pieces, and as Ferguson sat on his bed, pondering whether he could talk his way out of it or whether he would indeed be compelled to stand up and fight, Noah suddenly butted in. Boys, boys, he said, speaking in a deep, darkly funny Father-knows-best voice, stop this senseless quarreling at once. We all know who the best center fielder is, don't we? Ferguson and Dubinsky both turned and looked at Noah, who was lying on his bed with his elbow on the pillow and his head propped up in his hand. Dubinsky said: All right, Harpo, let's hear it— but it better be the right answer. Now that he had their attention, Noah paused for a moment and smiled, a goofy yet inordinately beatific smile that lodged itself in Ferguson's memory and was never lost, recalled again and again as he passed from childhood to adolescence and into his adulthood, a lightning bolt of pure, wild-eyed whimsy that revealed the true heart of the nine-year-old Noah Marx for the second or two it lasted, and then Noah ended the confrontation by saying: I am.

For the first month, Ferguson never thought about how happy he was in that place. He was too immersed in what he was doing to stop and reflect on his feelings, too caught up in the now to be able to see past it or behind it, *living in the moment*, as his counselor Harvey had said about performing well in sports, which was perhaps the real definition of happiness, not knowing you were happy, not caring about anything except being alive in the now, but then parents' visiting day was suddenly looming, the Sunday that marked the midpoint of the eight-week session, and in the days before that Sunday arrived, Ferguson was startled to discover that he wasn't looking forward to seeing his parents again, not even his mother, whom he had thought he would miss terribly but hadn't, had missed only in some intermittent and painful flashes, and especially not his father, who had been erased from his mind for the past month and no longer seemed to count for him. Camp was better than home, he realized. Life among friends was richer and more fulfilling than life with parents, which meant that parents were less important than he had previously supposed, a heretical, even revolutionary idea that gave Ferguson much to think about as he lay in his bed at night, and then visiting day was upon him, and when he saw his mother step out of the car and begin walking in his direction, he unexpectedly found himself fighting back tears. How ridiculous. How perfectly embarrassing to behave like that, he thought, and yet what could he do about it except run into her arms and let her kiss him?

Something was wrong, however. Uncle Don was supposed to have driven up to the camp with Ferguson's parents, but he wasn't with them, and when Ferguson asked his mother why Noah's father wasn't there, she gave him a tense look and said she would explain later. Later occurred about an hour after that, when his parents drove him across the Massachusetts border for lunch at a Friendly's restaurant in Great Barrington. As usual, it was his mother who did the talking, but for once his father looked attentive and engaged, following her words as closely as Ferguson did, and given what she had to say, what the circumstances demanded she say, it didn't surprise Ferguson that his mother looked more rattled than at any time in recent memory, her voice quavering as she spoke, wanting to spare her son the worst of it but at the same time unable to soften the blow without distorting the truth, for the truth was what mattered now, and even if Ferguson was only nine years old, it was imperative that he hear the whole story, with nothing left out.

This is it, Archie, she said, lighting an unfiltered Chesterfield and blowing a bluish-gray cloud of smoke across the Formica table. Don and Mildred have split up. Their marriage is over. I wish I could give you the reason, but Mildred won't tell me. She's so ravaged, she hasn't stopped crying for the past ten days. I don't know if Don has fallen for someone else or if things just cracked up on their own, but Don is out of the picture now, and there's no chance they'll get back together. I've talked to him a couple of times, but he won't tell me anything either. Just that he and Mildred are finished, that he never should have married her in the first place, that everything was wrong from the start. No, he's not going back to Noah's mother. What he's planning to do is move to Paris. He's already cleared out his stuff from the Perry Street apartment, and he's set to leave before the end of the month. Which brings me to Noah. Don wants to spend some time with him before he takes off, so his ex-wife, and by that I mean his first ex-wife, his ex-wife

Gwendolyn, has come to the camp today to fetch Noah and drive him back to New York. That's right, Archie, Noah is leaving. I know how close the two of you have become, what good friends you are now, but there's nothing I can do about it. I called that woman, Gwendolyn Marx, and told her that no matter what's happened between Don and Mildred, I wanted our boys to stay in touch, that it would be a pity if their friendship suffered because of it, but she's a hard person that one, Archie, bitter and angry, with a heart made of ice, and she said she wouldn't consider it. And after his father leaves for Paris, I asked, will Noah be coming back to camp? Out of the question, she said. Well, at least give the boys a chance to say good-bye to each other on Sunday, I said, and she said, get this, she said: What for? I was burning by then, about as angry as I've ever been in my life, and I shouted at her: How can you ask that question? And she calmly answered: I need to protect Noah from emotional scenes; his life is hard enough as it is. I don't know what to tell you, Archie. The woman is out of her mind. And there's my sister doped up on tranquilizers, weeping her heart out on the bed. And Don has walked out on her, and Noah has been taken from you, and frankly, kid, it's one hell of a beautiful mess, isn't it?

The second month at Camp Paradise was the month of the empty bed. The bare mattress on the metal springs to the right of where Ferguson continued to sleep, the bed of the now absent Noah, and every day Ferguson asked himself if they would ever see each other again. Cousins for a year and a half, and now cousins no more. An aunt who had married an uncle, and now married no more, with the uncle living on the other side of the Atlantic Ocean, where he could no longer be with his boy. Everything solid for a time, and then the sun comes up one morning and the world begins to melt.

Ferguson went home to Maplewood at the end of August, said good-bye to his room, said good-bye to the ping-pong table in the backyard, said good-bye to the broken screen door in the kitchen, and the following week he and his parents moved into their new house on the other side of town. The era of life on a grander scale had begun.

2.1

F OR AS LONG AS HE COULD REMEMBER, FERGUSON HAD BEEN LOOKING AT the drawing of the girl on the White Rock bottle. That was the brand of seltzer his mother bought on her twice-weekly trips to the A&P, and since his father was a firm believer in the virtues of seltzer water, there had always been a bottle of White Rock sitting on the table at dinner. Ferguson had therefore studied the girl hundreds of times, keeping the bottle near him in order to look at the black-and-white image of her half-naked body on the label, that enticing, serenely elegant girl with the small bare breasts and the white loincloth draped around her hips falling open to reveal the entire length of her right leg, the fore-grounded leg that was curled under her as she leaned forward on her hands and knees and gazed into a pool of water from her perch on the jutting rock, which fittingly bore the words *White Rock,* and the curi-ous, altogether unlikely thing about the girl was that two diaphanous wings were protruding from her back, which meant that she was more than human, a goddess or an enchanted being of some sort, and because her limbs were so slender and she gave the impression of being so small, she still qualified as a girl and not yet a full-grown woman, regardless of her breasts, which were the tiny, budding breasts of a twelve- or thirteen-year-old, and with her neatly pinned-up hair expos-ing the bare, luminous skin of her neck and shoulders, she was just the kind of girl a boy could entertain serious thoughts about, and when that boy turned a little older, say twelve or thirteen, the White Rock girl could easily evolve into a full-blown erotic charm, a summons to a world of fleshly passion and fully awakened desires, and once that happened to Ferguson, he made sure that his parents weren't looking at him when he looked at the bottle.

There was also the kneeling Indian girl on the box of Land O'Lakes butter, the adolescent beauty with her long black braids and the two colorful feathers sticking out of her beaded headband, but the problem with this potential rival to the White Rock nymph was that she was fully clothed, which greatly lessened her allure, not to speak of the further problem of her elbows, which were thrust out stiffly from her sides because she was holding up a box of Land O'Lakes butter, identical to the one sitting in front of Ferguson, the same box but smaller, with the same picture of the Indian girl holding up another, smaller box of Land O'Lakes butter, which was an intriguing if perplexing notion, Ferguson felt, an infinite regress of ever-shrinking Indian girls holding up ever-shrinking boxes of butter, which was similar to the effect produced by the Quaker Oats box, with the smiling Quaker in the black hat receding to some distant vanishing point beyond the grasp of human vision, a world inside a world, which was inside another world, which was inside another world, which was inside another world, until the world had been reduced to the size of a single atom and yet was still somehow managing to grow smaller. Interesting in its way, but hardly the stuff to inspire dreams, so the Indian butter maiden continued to run a distant second to the White Rock princess. Not long after he turned twelve, however, Ferguson was let in on a secret. He had gone down the block to visit his friend Bobby George, and as the two boys sat in the kitchen eating tuna fish sandwiches, in walked Bobby's fourteen-year-old brother, Carl, a tall, chunky fellow with a good head for math and a face spotted with pimples, who sometimes bullied his younger brother and sometimes talked to him as an almost-equal, but on that rainy Saturday afternoon in mid-March the unpredictable Carl was in a generous mood, and as the boys sat at the table chewing their sandwiches and drinking their milk, he told them that he had made an astonishing discovery. Without mentioning what the discovery was, he opened the refrigerator and pulled out a box of Land O'Lakes butter, extracted a pair of scissors and a roll of Scotch tape from a drawer by the sink, and then carried the three items over to the table. Look at this, he said, and the two boys watched as he cut apart the six-paneled box and set aside the two large panels with the picture of the Indian girl on them.

He cut into one of the pictures, removing the girl's knees and the bare skin just above the knees, which were sticking out from under the edge of her skirt, and then taped the knees over the butter box in the other picture, and lo and behold, the knees had been turned into breasts, a pair of large, naked breasts, each one with a red dot in the center of it that for all the world could have passed as a perfectly drawn nipple. The prim Lakota squaw had been transformed into a luscious sexpot, and as Carl grinned and Bobby squealed with laughter, Ferguson looked on without making a sound. What a clever bit of business, he thought. A few swipes from the scissors, a single strip of transparent tape, and the butter girl had been undressed.

There were photographs of naked women in *National Geographic*, a magazine Bobby's parents subscribed to and for some reason never threw away, and every so often during the spring of 1959, Ferguson and Bobby would come home from school and head straight for the Georges' garage, where they would comb through stacks of the yellow magazines searching for images of bare-breasted women, anthropological specimens from primitive tribes in Africa and South America, the black-skinned and brown-skinned women from warm-weather places who walked around with little or no clothing on their bodies and weren't ashamed to be seen like that, who displayed their breasts with the same indifference an American woman would feel in exposing her hands or ears. The photographs were distinctly unerotic, and except for a rare young beauty who popped up in every seventh or tenth issue, most of the women were not attractive to Ferguson's eyes, but still, it was exciting and instructive to look at those pictures, which if nothing else demonstrated the infinite variety of the female form, in particular the multitudinous differences to be found in the size and shape of breasts, from the large to the small and everything in between, from buoyant, surging breasts to flattened, sagging breasts, from proud breasts to defeated breasts, from symmetrical breasts to oddly matched breasts, from laughing breasts to crying breasts, from the thinned-out dugs of ancient crones to the bulging enormities of nursing mothers. Bobby snickered a lot during these foraging expeditions through the pages of *National Geographic*, laughing to cover up the embarrassment he felt for wanting to look at what he called *dirty pictures*, but Ferguson never thought of the pictures as dirty and never felt embarrassed by his desire to look at them. Breasts were important because they were the most prominent and visible feature that distinguished women from men, and women were a subject of great interest to him now, for even if he was still just a prepubescent boy of twelve, enough was stirring inside him for Ferguson to know that the days of his boyhood were numbered.

CIRCUMSTANCES HAD CHANGED. The warehouse robbery of November 1955, followed by the car crash of February 1956, had removed both of Ferguson's uncles from the family circle. The disgraced Uncle Arnold now lived in far-off California, the deceased Uncle Lew had left this earth for good, and 3 Brothers Home World was no more. For the better part of a year, his father had struggled to keep the business going, but the police never managed to recover the stolen appliances, and because he had forfeited his claim to the insurance money by refusing to press charges against his brother, the losses incurred by this act of mercy were too great to be overcome. Rather than go further into debt, he paid off the emergency loan from the bank with help from Ferguson's grandfather and sold out, unburdening himself of the building, the warehouse, and whatever stock remained, fleeing the ghosts of his brothers and the ruined enterprise that had been his life for more than twenty years. The building was still there, of course, standing in its old spot on Springfield Avenue, but now it was called Newman's Discount Furniture.

Ferguson's father returned his father-in-law's loan with proceeds from the sale and then opened up a new, significantly smaller store in Montclair, Stanley's TV & Radio. From Ferguson's point of view, this was a much better arrangement than the old one, for his father's new business happened to be on the same block as Roseland Photo, and now it was possible for him to drop in on either one of his parents anytime he wished. Stanley's TV & Radio was cramped, yes, but it had a nice, cozy feel to it, and Ferguson enjoyed visiting his father there after school, sitting down beside him at his workbench in the back room as his father repaired televisions, radios, and all manner of other things as well, taking apart and then putting back together dysfunctional toasters, fans, air conditioners, lamps, record players, blenders, electric juicers, and vacuum cleaners, for word had quickly spread that Ferguson's father was a man who could fix anything, and as the young clerk Mike Antonelli stood in the front room of the shop selling radios and televisions to Montclair residents, Stanley Ferguson spent most of his time in the back, tinkering in silence, patiently dissecting broken machines in order to make them work again. Ferguson understood that something in his father had been crushed by Arnold's betrayal, that this reduced incarnation of his former business represented a profound personal defeat for him, and yet something in him had also changed for the better, and the principal beneficiaries of that change were his wife and son. Ferguson's parents argued far less than they had before. The tension in the household had dissipated, in fact often seemed to have disappeared altogether, and Ferguson found it reassuring that his mother and father now had lunch together every day, just the two of them in their corner booth at Al's Diner, and again and again, in a variety of different ways, and yet always in the same way, Ferguson's mother would make remarks to him that essentially meant this: *Your father is a good man, Archie, the best man anywhere.* A good man, and a still largely silent man, but now that he had given up his old dream of becoming the next Rockefeller, Ferguson felt more comfortable in his presence. They could talk a little now, and most of the time Ferguson felt reasonably certain that his father was listening to him. And even when they didn't talk, Ferguson took pleasure in sitting beside his father at the workbench after school, doing his homework at one end of the table as his father went about his business at the other, slowly taking apart yet another damaged machine and putting it back together.

Money was less plentiful than it had been in the days of 3 Brothers Home World. Instead of two cars, Ferguson's parents now owned one car—his mother's 1954 powder-blue Pontiac—and a red Chevrolet delivery van with the name of his father's business printed on each of the side doors. In the past, his parents had sometimes gone away together on weekend excursions, mostly to the Catskills for a couple of days of tennis and dancing at Grossinger's or the Concord, but they had stopped doing that after Stanley's TV & Radio opened in 1957. In 1958, when Ferguson was in need of a new baseball glove, his father drove him all the way to Sam Brownstein's store in downtown Newark to buy one *at cost* instead of giving him the money to buy the same glove at Gallagher's, the sporting goods shop in Montclair. The difference amounted to twelve and a half dollars, an even twenty as opposed to thirty-two-fifty, not a large difference in the grand scheme of things but a crucial savings nevertheless, enough to alert Ferguson to the fact that life had changed and that from now on he would have to think carefully before he asked his parents for anything beyond what was strictly essential. Not long after that, Cassie Burton stopped working for them, and in much the same way that his mother and Aunt Mildred had wept in each other's arms at the airport in 1952, Cassie and his mother both wept on the morning Cassie was told the family could no longer afford to keep her. Yesterday, it had been steaks, today it was hamburgers. The family had slipped a notch or two, but who in his right mind would lose any sleep over a little belt-tightening? A book from the public library was the same book you bought in a store, tennis was still tennis whether you played at the municipal courts or a private club, and steaks and hamburgers were cut from the same cow, and even if steaks were supposed to represent the pinnacle of the good life, the truth was that Ferguson had always loved hamburgers, especially with ketchup on them—which was the same ketchup he had once smeared over the plump, medium-rare sirloins his father had liked so much.

Sunday was still the best day of the week, particularly when it was a Sunday that didn't include visits to or from other people, a day that Ferguson could spend alone with his parents, and now that he was bigger and stronger and had turned into an agile, sports-crazed twelve-year-old, he relished the morning tennis matches with his parents, the singles matches with his father, the two-against-one matches between mother-son and husband/father, the doubles matches that paired him with his father against Sam Brownstein and his younger son, and after tennis there was lunch at Al's Diner, along with the inevitable chocolate milkshake, and after lunch there were the movies, and after the movies there was Chinese food at the Green Dragon in Glen Ridge or fried chicken at the Little House in Millburn or hot open turkey sandwiches at Pal's Cabin in West Orange or pot roast and cheese blintzes at the Claremont Diner in Montclair, the crowded, inexpensive dining spots of the New Jersey suburbs, noisy and unsophisticated, perhaps, but the food was good, and it was Sunday night, and the three of them were together, and even if Ferguson was starting to pull away from his parents by then, that one day a week helped maintain the illusion that the gods could be merciful when they chose to be.

AUNT MILDRED AND Uncle Henry had failed to produce the Adler cousin he had longed for as a small boy. The reasons were unknown to him, whether sterility or infertility or a conscious refusal to add to the world's population, but in spite of Ferguson's disappointment, the no-cousin vacuum on the West Coast had ultimately worked to his advantage. Aunt Mildred might not have been close to her sister, but with no children of her own, and with no other nephews or nieces anywhere in sight, whatever maternal impulses she had in her were showered upon her one and only Archie. After her removal to California when Ferguson was five, she and Uncle Henry had returned to New York several times for extended summer visits, and even when she was back in Berkeley during the rest of the year, she kept in touch with her nephew by writing letters and occasionally calling him on the phone. Ferguson understood that there was something glacial about his aunt, that she could be harsh and opinionated and even rude with other people, but with him, her one and only Archie, she was another person, full of praise and good humor and curiosity about what her boy was doing and thinking and reading. From his earliest childhood, she had been in the habit of buying him gifts, an abundance of gifts that had usually come in the form of books and records, and now that he was older and his mental capacities had increased, the number of books and records she shipped to him from California had also increased. Perhaps she didn't trust his mother and father to give him the proper intellectual guidance, perhaps she thought his parents were a couple of uneducated bourgeois nobodies, perhaps she believed it was her duty to rescue Ferguson from the wasteland of ignorance he dwelled in, thinking that she and she alone could offer him the help necessary to scale the exalted slopes of enlightenment. It was no doubt possible that she was (as he had once overheard his father say to his mother) an *intellectual snob*, but there was no arguing against the fact that, snob or not, she was a genuine intellectual, a person of vast erudition who earned her living as a university professor, and the works she exposed her nephew to were indeed a great blessing to him.

No other boy in his circle of acquaintances had read what he had read, and because Aunt Mildred chose carefully for him, just as she had chosen carefully for her sister during the period of her confinement thirteen years earlier, Ferguson read the books she sent to him with an avidity that resembled physical hunger, for his aunt understood what books would satisfy the cravings of a rapidly developing boy as he moved from six years old to eight years old, from eight years old to ten years old, from ten years old to twelve years old—and beyond that to the end of high school. Fairy tales to start with, the Brothers Grimm and the many-colored books compiled by the Scotsman Lang, then the wondrous, fantastical novels by Lewis Carroll, George MacDonald, and E. Nesbit, followed by Bulfinch's retelling of Greek and Roman myths, a child's version of *The Odyssey, Charlotte's Web,* a book culled from *The Thousand and One Nights* and reassembled as *The Seven Voyages of Sinbad the Sailor,* and then, some months after that, a six-hundred-page selection from the whole of *The Thousand and One Nights,* and the next year *Dr. Jekyll and Mr. Hyde,* horror and mystery stories by Poe, *The Prince and the Pauper, Kidnapped, A Christmas Carol, Tom Sawyer,* and *A Study in Scarlet,* and so strong was Ferguson's response to the book by Conan Doyle that the present he received from Aunt Mildred for his eleventh birthday was an enormously fat, profusely illustrated edition of *The Complete Sherlock Holmes.* Those were some of the books, but there were the records as well, which were no less important to Ferguson than the books, and especially now, in the past two or three years, starting when he was nine or ten, they had been coming in at regular three- and four-month intervals. Jazz, classical music, folk music, rhythm and blues, and even some rock and roll. Again, as with the books, Aunt Mildred's approach was a strictly pedagogical one, and she led Ferguson along by stages, knowing that Louis Armstrong had to come before Charlie Parker, who had to come before Miles Davis, that Tchaikovsky, Ravel, and Gershwin had to precede Beethoven, Mozart, and Bach, that the Weavers had to be listened to before Lead Belly, that Ella Fitzgerald singing Cole Porter was a necessary first step before one graduated to Billie Holiday singing *Strange Fruit.* Much to his regret, Ferguson had discovered that he possessed not one jot of talent for playing music himself. He had tried the piano at seven and had quit in frustration a year later; he had tried the cornet at nine and had quit; he had tried the drums at ten and had quit. For some reason, he had trouble reading music, couldn't fully absorb the symbols on the page, the empty and filled-in circles sitting on the lines or nestled between them, the flats and sharps, the key signatures, the treble clefs and bass clefs, the notations refused to go into him and become automatically recognizable as letters and numbers once had, and therefore he was compelled to think about each note before he played it, which slowed his progress through the bars and measures of any given piece and, in effect, made it impossible for him to play anything. It was a sad defeat. His normally quick and

efficient mind was handicapped when it came to decoding those recal-
citrant marks, and rather than persist in beating his head against the
wall, he had abandoned the struggle. A sad defeat because his love of
music was so strong and he could hear it so well when others played it,
for his ear was sensitive and finely tuned to the subtleties of composition and performance, but he was hopeless as a musician himself, an
utter washout, which meant that he was now resigned to being a listener, an ardent, devoted listener, and his Aunt Mildred was clever
enough to know how to feed that devotion, which surely counted as
one of the essential reasons for being alive.

That summer, on one of her visits back east with Uncle Henry,
Aunt Mildred helped illuminate Ferguson on another matter of great
concern to him, something unrelated to books or music but equally
significant to his mind, if not more so. She had come out to Montclair
to spend some days with her one and only and his parents, and when
the two of them sat down to lunch together on the first afternoon (his
mother and father were off at work, which meant that Ferguson and
his aunt were alone in the house), he pointed to the bottle of White
Rock seltzer water sitting on the table and asked her why the girl had
wings sprouting from her back. He couldn't understand it, he said.
They weren't angel wings or bird wings, which were the kinds of wings
you might expect to see on a mythological creature, but fragile insect
wings, the wings of a dragonfly or a butterfly, and he found that deeply
perplexing.

Don't you know who she is, Archie? his aunt said.

No, he replied. Of course I don't. If I did know, why would I be
asking the question?

I thought you read the Bulfinch I gave you a couple of years ago.

I did.

All of it?

I think so. I might have missed a chapter or two. I can't remember.

Never mind. You can look it up later. (*Lifting the bottle off the table,
tapping her finger against the drawing of the girl.*) It's not a very good
picture, but it's supposed to be Psyche. Do you remember her now?

Cupid and Psyche. I did read that chapter, but they never said anything about Psyche having wings. Cupid has wings, wings and a quiver
of arrows, but Cupid is a god, and Psyche is just a mortal. A beautiful
girl, but still a human girl, a person like us. No, wait. Now I remember.

After she marries Cupid, she becomes immortal, too. That's right, isn't it? But I still don't understand why she has those wings.

The word *psyche* means two things in Greek, his aunt said. Two very different but interesting things. *Butterfly* and *soul*. But when you stop and think about it carefully, *butterfly* and *soul* aren't so different, after all, are they? A butterfly starts out as a caterpillar, an ugly sort of earth-bound, wormy nothing, and then one day the caterpillar builds a cocoon, and after a certain amount of time the cocoon opens and out comes the butterfly, the most beautiful creature in the world. That's what happens to souls as well, Archie. They struggle in the depths of darkness and ignorance, they suffer through trials and misfortunes, and bit by bit they become purified by those sufferings, strengthened by the hard things that happen to them, and one day, if the soul in question is a worthy soul, it will break out of its cocoon and soar through the air like a magnificent butterfly.

No TALENT FOR music, then, none for drawing or painting, and gruesomely inept at singing, dancing, and acting, but one thing he had a gift for was playing games, physical games, sports in all their seasonal varieties, baseball in the warm weather, football in the chilly weather, basketball in the cold weather, and by the time he was twelve he belonged to teams in all of those sports and was playing year-round without interruption. Ever since that late September afternoon in 1954, the never to be forgotten afternoon he had spent with Cassie watching Mays and Rhodes defeat the Indians, baseball had been a core obsession, and once he began playing in earnest the next year, he proved to be surprisingly good at it, as good as the best players around him, strong in the field, strong at bat, with an innate feel for the nuances of any given situation during the course of a game, and when a person discovers he can do something well, he tends to want to keep doing it, to do it as often as he possibly can. Countless weekend mornings, countless weekday afternoons, countless early evenings throughout the week playing pickup games with his friends in public parks, not to mention the multiple home-grown offshoots of the game, among them stickball, wiffleball, stoopball, punch ball, wall ball, kickball, and roofball, and then, at nine, Little League, and with it the chance to belong to an organized team and wear a uniform with a number on the back, number 9, he was always number 9 for that team and all the others that followed it, 9 for the nine players and the nine innings, 9 as the pure numerical essence of the game itself, and on his head the dark blue cap with the white *G* sewn onto the crown, *G* for Gallagher's Sporting Goods, the sponsor of the team, which was a team with a full-time, volunteer coach, Mr. Baldassari, who drilled the players in fundamentals during the weekly practice sessions and clapped his hands and shouted insults, orders, and encouragement during the twice-weekly games, one on Saturday morning or afternoon and the other on Tuesday or Thursday evening, and there was Ferguson standing at his position in the field, growing from a puny stick of a thing to a robust boy during the four years he spent on that team, second baseman and number eight hitter at nine, shortstop and number two hitter at ten, shortstop and cleanup hitter at eleven and twelve, and the added pleasure of playing before a crowd, fifty to a hundred people on average, parents and siblings of the players, assorted friends, cousins, grandparents, and stray onlookers, cheers and boos, yelling, clapping, and stomping from the bleachers that started with the first pitch thrown and lasted until the final out, and during those four years his mother seldom missed a game, he would watch for her as he was warming up with his teammates, and suddenly she would be there, waving to him from her spot in the bleachers, and he could always hear her voice cutting through the others when he came up to bat, *Let's go, Archie, Nice and easy, Archie, Sock it out of here, Archie,* and then, after the demise of 3 Brothers Home World and the birth of Stanley's TV & Radio, his father started coming to the games as well, and although he didn't shout in the way Ferguson's mother did, at least not forcefully enough to be heard above the crowd, he was the one who kept track of Ferguson's batting average, which rose steadily as the years advanced, ending in an absurdly high .532 for the last season, the last game of which had been played two weeks before Ferguson and Aunt Mildred had their conversation about Psyche, but he was the best player on the team by then, one of the two or three best in the league, and that was the kind of average one expected from a top twelve-year-old player.

Young children didn't play basketball in the fifties because they were seen as too small, too weak to launch shots at ten-foot-high rims, so Ferguson's education in the science of hoops didn't start until the year he turned twelve, but he had been playing football steadily from the age of six, tackle football with helmets and shoulder pads, halfback mostly, since he was a determined if not especially fast runner, but once his hands grew large enough to grip the ball firmly, his position changed, since Ferguson and his friends discovered that he had a crazy talent for throwing passes, that the spirals he flung with his right hand had more speed, more accuracy, and went much farther than anyone else's, fifty, fifty-five yards down the field by the time he was fourteen, and although Ferguson didn't love the game with the same thoroughness and ardor that he loved baseball, he exulted in playing quarterback, for few sensations felt better than completing a long pass to a receiver running full-tilt toward the end zone thirty or forty yards from the line of scrimmage, the uncanny sense of an invisible connection through empty space was similar to the experience of sinking a twenty-foot jump shot, but even more satisfying somehow, the connection being with another person as opposed to an inanimate object made of twine and steel, and so he endured the less appealing aspects of the sport (the rough tackles, the murderous blocks, the bruising collisions) in order to repeat the never less than thrilling sensation of throwing the ball to his teammates. Then, in November 1961, as a fourteen-and-a-half-year-old ninth grader, he was sacked by a two-hundred-and-fifteen-pound defensive lineman named Dennis Murphy and wound up in the hospital with a broken left arm. He had been planning to try out for the high school team next fall, but the problem with football was that you needed your parents' permission in order to play it, and when he came home from his first day of high school and presented the form to his mother, she refused to sign. He pleaded with her, he denounced her, he cursed her for behaving like a hysterical, overprotective mother, but Rose wouldn't budge, and that was the end of Ferguson's career as a football player.

I know you think I'm an idiot, his mother said, but one day you'll thank me for this, Archie. You're a strong boy, but you'll never be strong enough or big enough to turn into a lummox, and that's what you have to be to play football—a thick-bodied lummox, a lunkhead who enjoys smashing other people, a human animal. Your father and I were so upset when you broke your arm last year, but now I see it as a blessing in disguise, a warning, and I'm not about to let my son crack up his body in high school so he can hobble around on a pair of damaged knees for the rest of his life. Stick to baseball, Archie. It's a beautiful sport, and you're so good at it, so exciting to watch, and why risk losing baseball by injuring yourself in a meaningless football game? If you want to go on throwing those passes of yours, play touch football. I mean, look at the Kennedys. That's what they do, isn't it? The whole family up there in Cape Cod romping around on the lawn, flinging footballs left and right, laughing their heads off. It sure looks like a lot of fun to me.

THE KENNEDYS. EVEN now, as an independent, free-thinking, occasionally rebellious fifteen-year-old boy, he marveled at how well his mother continued to understand him, how deftly she could pierce through to his heart when the situation demanded it, his ever blundering and conflicted heart, for even though he was unwilling to admit it to her or anyone else, he knew she was right about football, that he was temperamentally unsuited to the protocols of blood combat and would be better served by concentrating on his cherished baseball, but then she had turned the crank another notch and brought up the Kennedys, which she knew was a subject of real importance to him, far more important than the ephemeral issue of football or no football, and by deflecting the conversation from scholastic sports to the American president, the conversation had become a different conversation, and suddenly there was nothing more to be said.

Ferguson had been following Kennedy for more than two and a half years by then, beginning with the announcement of his candidacy for the Democratic nomination on January 3, 1960, precisely two months before Ferguson's thirteenth birthday and three days after the start of the new decade, which for some reason Ferguson had been looking forward to as a sign of ecstatic renewal, the whole of his conscious life having been spent in the fifties with an old man as president, the heart attack–prone, golf-playing ex-general, and Kennedy struck him as something new and altogether remarkable, a vigorous young man out to change the world, the unjust world of racial oppression, the idiotic world of the Cold War, the perilous world of the nuclear arms race, the complacent world of mindless American materialism, and with no other candidate addressing those problems to his satisfaction, Ferguson decided Kennedy was the man of the future. He was still too young at that point to understand that politics is always politics, but at the same time he was old enough to understand that something had to give, for those early days of 1960 were filled with news about the lunch-counter sit-in staged by four black students in North Carolina as a protest against

segregation, the disarmament conference in Geneva, the downing of
the U-2 spy plane in Soviet territory and the arrest of pilot Gary Powers, which led Khrushchev to walk out of a summit meeting in Paris
and ended the Geneva disarmament talks with no progress made on
halting the spread of nuclear weapons, followed by growing hostility
between Castro and the United States, which cut its imports of Cuban
sugar by ninety-five percent, and then, seven days after that, on the evening of July thirteenth, Kennedy won the nomination on the first ballot
at the Democratic convention in Los Angeles. That was the first of three
consecutive summers Ferguson spent at home in New Jersey playing
American Legion baseball with the Montclair Mudhens, four games a
week as leadoff hitter and second baseman that first year, since he was
the youngest player on the team now and was starting from the bottom
again, the lone thirteen-year-old on a team of fourteen- and fifteen-year-
olds, and all through those hot months of July and August, as Ferguson
read newspapers and books such as *Animal Farm*, *1984*, and *Candide*,
listened closely to Beethoven's Third, Fifth, and Seventh Symphonies for
the first time, loyally kept up with each new issue of *Mad* magazine,
and played and replayed the *Porgy and Bess* album by Miles Davis, he
continued to stop in at his mother's studio and his father's store for
impromptu visits, and after those brief hellos he would walk to the local
Democratic Party headquarters a block and a half down the street, where
he would help the adult volunteers lick stamps and envelopes in
exchange for an endless supply of campaign buttons, bumper stickers,
and posters, which he affixed with Scotch tape to every vacant spot on
the four walls of his bedroom, so that by the end of the summer his
room had been transformed into a shrine to Kennedy.

Years later, when he was old enough to know better, he would look
back on that period of youthful hero worship and cringe, but that was
how things stood for him in 1960, and how could he possibly have
known any better when he had been living on this earth for only thirteen years? So Ferguson rooted for Kennedy to win, in the same way
he had once pulled for the Giants to win the World Series, for a political campaign was no different from a sporting event, he realized, words
instead of blows, perhaps, but no less rough than the bloodiest boxing
match, and when it came to the office of president, the struggle was
fought on a scale so grand and so spectacular that there was no better
show anywhere in America. Glamorous Kennedy versus dour Nixon,

King Arthur versus Gloomy Gus, charm versus resentment, hope versus bitterness, day versus night. Four times the two men squared off on
television, four times Ferguson and his parents watched the debates in
the little living room, and four times they were convinced that Kennedy
had gotten the better of Nixon, even though people said Nixon had
trumped him on the radio broadcasts, but television was all that
mattered now, television was everywhere and would soon be everything, just as Ferguson's father had predicted during the war, and the
first television president had clearly won the battle on the home screen.

The victory of November eighth, the narrow victory by a hundred
thousand popular votes, one of the smallest margins in history, and the
more substantial victory in the electoral college by eighty-four votes, and
when Ferguson went to school the next morning and celebrated with
his pro-Kennedy friends, some of those figures were still not known,
and talk was already circulating about why nothing had been heard
from Illinois, there were rumors that Mayor Daley of Chicago had stolen voting machines from Republican districts and dumped them in
Lake Michigan, and when that accusation reached Ferguson's ears, he
had trouble accepting it, the idea was too reprehensible, too nauseating,
for a trick like that would have turned the election into a bad joke, a trav-
esty of devious manipulations and lies, but then, just as Ferguson was
about to give full vent to his outrage, he abruptly reversed the direction
of his thoughts, realizing that he had to stop with the Boy Scout stuff
and admit that anything was possible. Corrupt men were everywhere,
and the more powerful the man, the greater the potential for corruption,
but even if the story was true, there was nothing to suggest that Kennedy had anything to do with it. Daley and his band of crooks from
Cook County—perhaps. But not Kennedy, never Kennedy.

Still, in spite of his unbroken confidence in the man of the future,
Ferguson spent the rest of the day walking around with an image in
his head of those submerged voting machines lying at the bottom of
Lake Michigan, and even after the final numbers proved that Kennedy
would have won the election with or without Illinois, Ferguson continued to think about the machines, continued to think about them for
years.

On the morning of January 20, 1961, he told his parents he wasn't
feeling well and asked if he could stay home from school. Since Ferguson was a conscientious boy and not known for inventing imaginary

ailments, his wish was granted. That was how he came to watch Kennedy's inauguration speech, sitting in front of the television set while his mother and father worked at their jobs downtown, alone in the little living room just off the kitchen, watching the ceremony take place in the cold and blustery Washington weather, so frigid and windswept that when the ancient, rheumy-eyed Robert Frost stood up to read the poem he had been asked to write for the occasion, the same Robert Frost who was responsible for the one line of poetry Ferguson knew by heart, *Two roads diverged in a yellow wood*, the wind gave a fierce, sudden kick just after he arrived at the lectern, wrenching the one-page manuscript from his hands and gusting it high into the air, which left the frail, white-haired bard with nothing to read, but he pulled himself together with admirable poise and alacrity, Ferguson felt, and with his new poem flying out over the crowd, he recited an old poem from memory, turning what could have been a disaster into an odd sort of triumph, impressive but somehow comical as well, or, as Ferguson put it to his parents that evening, both funny and not funny at the same time.

Then came the newly sworn-in president, and the moment he began to deliver his speech, the notes emanating from that tightly strung rhetorical instrument felt so natural to Ferguson, so comfortably joined to his inner expectations, that he found himself listening to it in the same way he listened to a piece of music. Man holds in his mortal hands. Let the word go forth. Pay any price, bear any burden. The power to abolish all forms of human poverty and all forms of human life. Let every nation know. The torch has been passed. Meet any hardship, support any friend, oppose any foe. A new generation of Americans. That uncertain balance of terror that stays the hand of mankind's final war. Now the trumpet summons us again. A call to bear the burden of a long twilight struggle. But let us begin. Born in this century, tempered by war, disciplined by a hard and bitter peace. Let us explore the stars. Ask. Ask not. A struggle against the common enemies of man: tyranny, poverty, disease, and war itself. A new generation. Ask. Ask not. But let us begin.

For the next twenty months, Ferguson watched closely as the man of the future stumbled forward, launching his administration with the birth of the Peace Corps and then nearly destroying it with the Bay of Pigs debacle on April seventeenth. Three weeks after that, a human-sized football named Alan Shepard was punted into space by NASA and

Kennedy declared that an American would walk on the moon before the end of the sixties, which Ferguson found difficult to believe but hoped would happen, for he wanted his man to be proven right, and then Jack and Jackie were off to Paris to meet de Gaulle, followed by two days of talks with Khrushchev in Vienna, and one blink of the eyes later, as Ferguson read his first book about contemporary American politics, *The Making of the President, 1960*, the Berlin Wall had gone up and the Eichmann trial in Jerusalem had begun, that dolorous spectacle of the half-bald, twitching murderer sitting alone in the glass box, which Ferguson watched on television every day after school, engulfed by the horror of it and yet keeping his eyes fixed on the screen, unable to stop looking, and by the time the trial was over, he had worked his way through all 1,245 pages of *The Rise and Fall of the Third Reich*, the immense tome by blacklisted former journalist William Shirer, which won the National Book Award in 1961 and was the longest book Ferguson had ever read. The next year began with another extraterrestrial exploit: John Glenn catapulted beyond the edge of the troposphere and circling the earth three times in February, which Scott Carpenter repeated in the spring, and then, just two days after James Meredith became the first black student admitted to the University of Mississippi (another spectacle Ferguson watched on television, praying the poor man wouldn't be stoned to death), Wally Schirra outdid Glenn and Carpenter by looping around the globe six times in early October. Ferguson was in the tenth grade by then, his first year at Montclair High School, and because his mother had refused to sign the form in September, the football season had started without him. He was largely over that disappointment by the time of Schirra's journey, however, having found a new interest in the person of Anne-Marie Dumartin, a fellow sophomore who had come to America from Belgium two years earlier and was in his geometry and history classes, and so absorbed was he by this object of his rapidly growing affections that there was little time to think about the man of the future just then, and so, on the night of October twenty-second, when Kennedy addressed the American people and told them about Russian missile bases in Cuba and the naval blockade he was about to put in force, Ferguson was not at home with his parents watching the broadcast. Instead, he was sitting on a bench in a public park with Anne-Marie Dumartin, wrapping his arms around her body and kissing her for the first time. For once, the normally attentive Ferguson was not paying attention, and the greatest international crisis since the end of the Second World War, the threat of nuclear conflict and the possible end of the human race, did not register with him until the following morning, after which he began paying attention again, but within a week his man Kennedy had outmaneuvered the Russians, and the crisis was over. It had looked as if the world was about to end—and then it didn't.

By THANKSGIVING, THERE was no question in his mind that it was love. He had lived through numerous infatuations in the past, starting with the kindergarten crushes on Cathy Gold and Margie Fitzpatrick when he was six, succeeded by a furious whirl of dalliances with Carol, Jane, Nancy, Susan, Mimi, Linda, and Connie at twelve and thirteen, the weekend dancing parties, the kissing sessions in moonlit backyards and basement alcoves, the first tentative advances toward sexual knowledge, the mysteries of skin and saliva-coated tongues, the taste of lipstick, the smell of perfume, the sound of nylon stockings rubbing together, and then the breakthrough at fourteen, the sudden jump from boyhood into adolescence, and with it a new life in an alien, ever mutating body, unbidden erections, wet dreams, masturbation, erotic longings, nightly lust dramas performed by shadows in the sex theater now lodged in his skull, the somatic cataclysms of youth, but all those physical changes and upheavals aside, the fundamental quest both before and after his new life began had always been a spiritual one, the dream of an enduring connection, a reciprocal love between compatible souls, souls endowed with bodies, of course, mercifully endowed with bodies, but the soul came first, would always come first, and in spite of his flirtations with Carol, Jane, Nancy, Susan, Mimi, Linda, and Connie, he soon learned that none of those girls possessed the soul he was looking for, and one by one he had lost interest in them and allowed them to disappear from his heart.

With Anne-Marie Dumartin, the story was playing itself out in reverse. The others had all begun as intense physical attractions, but the better he had come to know them, the more disenchanted he had felt, whereas he had barely noticed Anne-Marie in the beginning, had not exchanged more than a few words with her throughout the month of September, but then their European History teacher arbitrarily paired them to work on a project together, and once Ferguson began to know her a little, he discovered that he wanted to know her more, and the more he came to know her, the higher she rose in his estimation, and after three weeks of daily meetings about the decline and fall of Napoleon (the subject of their joint paper), the once plain-looking Belgian girl with the slight French accent had been transformed into an exotic beauty, and Ferguson's heart was entirely filled up with her, bursting with her, and he meant to keep her there for as long as he could. A sudden, unforeseen conquest. A fifteen-year-old boy caught with his guard down, and then Cupid lost his way and accidentally wound up in Montclair, New Jersey, and before Psyche's husband could buy a new ticket and head back to New York or Athens or wherever he was going, he shot off an arrow for the sport of it, and thus began the agonizing adventure of Ferguson's first great love.

Small but not uncommonly small, a shade under five-five with no shoes on, dark, medium-length hair, round face with symmetrical features and a sturdy, unbashful nose, full lips, slender neck, dark brows crowning gray-blue eyes, vivid eyes, illuminated eyes, slender arms and fingers, breasts fuller than might have been expected, narrow hips, thin legs and delicate ankles, a beauty that did not declare itself at first glance, or even at second glance, but one that emerged with growing familiarity, gradually boring itself into the eye and thereafter indelible, a face difficult to turn away from, a face to dream on. A smart and serious girl, an often somber girl, not prone to outbursts of laughter, parsimonious with her smiles, but when she did smile, her whole body turned into a knife of radiance, a gleaming sword. A newcomer, and therefore friendless, with little desire to ingratiate herself or fit in, a stubborn self-possession that appealed to Ferguson and made her different from any other girl he had known, the laughing teenage girls of northern New Jersey in all their splendid frivolity, for Anne-Marie was determined to remain an outsider, a girl uprooted from her house in Brussels and forced to live in vulgar, money-obsessed America, sticking fast to her European style of dressing, the ever-present black beret, the belted trench coat, the plaid jumpers, the white shirts with men's ties, and even though she would sometimes admit that Belgium was a dismal country, a gray and dreary patch of land wedged between the Frogs and the Huns, she would also defend it whenever she was challenged, claiming that small, almost invisible Belgium had the best beer, the best chocolate, and the best *frites* anywhere in the world. Early on, during one of their first meetings, before Psyche's husband had strayed into Montclair and loosed his arrow on his unsuspecting victim, Ferguson brought up the subject of the Congo and Belgium's responsibility for the slaughter of hundreds of thousands of oppressed black people, and Anne-Marie fixed her eyes on his and nodded. You're a clever boy, Archie, she said. You know ten times more than any ten of these idiot Americans put together. When I started this school last month, I decided I would stick to myself and not make any friends. Now I think I was wrong. Everyone needs a friend, and you can be that friend if you want to be.

By the night of their first kiss on October twenty-second, Ferguson had learned just a few scant facts about Anne-Marie's family. He knew that her father worked as an economist for the Belgian delegation to the U.N., that her mother had died when Anne-Marie was eleven, that her father had remarried when she was twelve, and that her two older brothers, Georges and Patrice, were university students in Brussels, but that was the extent of it, along with the micro-detail of her having lived in London between the ages of seven and nine, which accounted for the fluency of her English. Before that night, however, not a single word about the stepmother, not a word about the cause of the mother's death, not a word about the father except for the job that had brought the Dumartins to America, and because Ferguson understood that Anne-Marie was reluctant to talk about those matters, he didn't press her to open up to him, but little by little, over the weeks and months that followed, more information came out, the grisly story of her mother's cancer to begin with, cervical cancer metastasizing to levels of such pain and hopelessness that her mother ultimately killed herself with an overdose of pills, which was the official story, in any case, but Anne-Marie suspected her father had started his affair with her future stepmother months before her mother's death, and who knew if the widowed Fabienne Corday, a so-called family friend of long standing, for three years now the second wife of Anne-Marie's blind and adoring father, the wretched woman who was now her stepmother, hadn't forced those death pills down her mother's throat in order to accelerate the transition from clandestine affair to marriage sanctified by the Catholic church? An outrageous slander, no doubt entirely untrue, but Anne-Marie couldn't help herself, the possibility continued to eat away at her thoughts, and yet even if Fabienne was innocent, that wouldn't have

made her any less despicable, any less worthy of the hatred and contempt Anne-Marie felt for her. Ferguson listened to these revelations
with mounting sympathy for his beloved. Fate had wounded her, and
now she was stuck inside a troubled household, at war with an odious
stepmother, disappointed by a selfish, inattentive father, still mourning
her dead mother, bereft at having been exiled to a harsh, unwelcoming
America, angry, angry at everything, but rather than scare Ferguson off,
the operatic scale of Anne-Marie's difficulties only drew him closer to
her, for now she had been turned into a tragic figure in his eyes, a noble,
suffering character hounded by the blows of fortune, and with all the
fervor of an inexperienced fifteen-year-old boy, his new mission in
life was to rescue her from the clutches of her unhappiness.

It never occurred to him that she might have been exaggerating, that
the grief she felt over losing her mother had distorted her vision, that
she had pushed away her stepmother without giving her a chance, turning her into an enemy for no other reason than the fact that she was not
her mother and never would be, that her overworked father was doing
the best he could for his enraged and obstinate daughter, that there
was, as there always is, another side to the story. Adolescence feeds on
drama, it is most happy when living *in extremis*, and Ferguson was no
less vulnerable to the lure of high emotion and extravagant unreason
than any other boy his age, which meant that the appeal of a girl like
Anne-Marie was fueled precisely by her unhappiness, and the greater
the storms she engulfed him in, the more intensely he wanted her.

Arranging to be alone with her was difficult, since they were both
too young to drive and had to depend on their feet for transportation,
which necessarily limited the range of their movements, but one dependable recourse was the empty Ferguson house after the end of the school
day, the two hours before his parents came home from work when he
and Anne-Marie could go upstairs to his room and shut the door. Ferguson gladly would have taken the plunge with her, but he knew Anne-
Marie wasn't ready for it, and so the subject of losing their virginity
was never openly discussed, which was the way such matters were
handled in 1962, at least for properly raised fifteen-year-olds from the
middle and upper middle classes of Montclair and Brussels, but if neither one of them had the courage to defy the conventions of the era, that
didn't mean they neglected to make use of the bed, which fortunately
was a double bed, with ample room on its surface for the two of them

to stretch out side by side and take part in sex that wasn't fully sex but which nevertheless had the taste and feel of love.

Until then, it had all been about kissing, prolonged excursions of tongues wandering through the insides of mouths, wet lips, napes and the backs of ears, hands clutching faces, hands traveling through heads of hair, arms enfolding torsos, shoulders, waists, arms wrapped around other arms, and then with Connie the previous spring the first hesitant move to put hands on breasts, well-guarded breasts to be sure, safely covered by both blouse and bra, but he wasn't shoved or swatted away, which represented a further advance in his education, and now, with Anne-Marie, the blouse had come off, and a month after that the bra had come off, which coincided with the removal of his shirt, and even that partial nakedness was an undreamt-of pleasure that surpassed all other pleasures, and as the weeks went on it was only by pure force of will that Ferguson restrained himself from taking hold of her hand and thrusting it onto the bulge inside his pants. Sharply remembered afternoons, not just because of what they did on that bed together but because it all happened in broad daylight and was visible, as opposed to the blind fumbles in the dark with Connie, Linda, and the others, the sun was in the room with them and he could see her body, their two bodies, which meant that each act of touching was also an image of that touching, and on top of that there was a constant undercurrent of fear in the room, a dread that they would lose track of the time and one of his parents would knock on the door while they were still embracing or, even worse, barge into the room without remembering to knock, and while neither of those things ever happened, there was always a chance they would, which filled those afternoon hours with a sense of urgency, danger, and outlaw daring.

She was the first person he allowed into the inner chambers of his secret music palace, and when they weren't rolling around on the bed or talking about their lives (mostly Anne-Marie's life), they would listen to records on the small, two-speaker machine that sat on a table in the southern corner of the room, a present from Ferguson's parents for his twelfth birthday. Now, three years later, 1962 had become the year of J. S. Bach, the year when Ferguson listened to Bach more than any other composer, in particular Glenn Gould's Bach, with an emphasis on the *Preludes and Fugues* and the *Goldberg Variations*, and Pablo Casals's Bach, which included endless playings of the six pieces for unaccompanied cello, and Hermann Scherchen conducting the *Suites for Orchestra* and the *Saint Matthew Passion*, which Ferguson had concluded was the finest piece Bach had ever written, hence the finest piece ever written by anyone, but he and Anne-Marie also listened to Mozart (the *Mass in C Minor*), Schubert (piano works performed by Sviatoslav Richter), Beethoven (symphonies, quartets, sonatas), and numerous others as well, nearly all of them gifts from Ferguson's Aunt Mildred, not to speak of Muddy Waters, Fats Waller, Bessie Smith, and John Coltrane, which was not to speak of all sorts of other twentieth-century souls, both living and dead, and the best thing about listening to music with Anne-Marie was watching her face, studying her eyes and looking at her mouth as tears gathered or smiles formed, how deeply she felt the emotional resonances of any given piece, for unlike Ferguson she had been trained since earliest childhood and could play the piano well and had an excellent soprano voice, so excellent that she broke her vow not to participate in high school activities and joined the chorus midway through the first semester, and that was perhaps their greatest bond, the need for music that ran through their bodies, which at that point in their lives was no different from the need to find a way to exist in the world.

There was so much to admire about her, he felt, so much to love in her, but Ferguson never deluded himself into thinking he would be able to hold on to her, at least not past another few months or weeks or days. Right from the start, in the earliest moments of his budding infatuation, he could sense that her feelings were not as strong as his, and much as she seemed to like him, much as she seemed to enjoy his body and his record albums and his way of talking to her, he was destined to love more than he was loved in return, and within a month of their first kiss, he understood that he would have to play by her rules or else risk not being with her at all. What maddened him most was her inconsistency, how often she broke promises, how often she forgot things he said to her, how often she backed out of dates at the last minute, telling him that she wasn't feeling well or that there was trouble at home or that she thought they were supposed to meet on Saturday, not Friday. He sometimes wondered if there was another boy, or several boys, or a boy back in Belgium, but it was impossible to know from observation, since the first rule she demanded he adhere to was an injunction against any public displays of affection, meaning that Montclair High was off-limits, that even when they crossed paths in the classrooms, corridors, and cafeteria they would have to pretend not to be involved with each other, that they could nod, say hello, and talk as if they were passing acquaintances, but at no time were they allowed to kiss or hold hands, which was normal conduct for every other steady couple in the school, and if that was the game she wanted to play with him, who knew if she wasn't also playing it with someone else? Ferguson felt foolish for having agreed to such an absurd bargain, but he was living under a deranged sort of enchantment just then, and the thought of losing her was far worse than the humiliation of pretending to be someone he was not. Still, they went on seeing each other, and the times they spent together always seemed to go smoothly, he always felt happiest and most fully alive when he was with her, and whatever conflicts or disagreements they had invariably seemed to take place on the telephone, that strange instrument of disembodied voices, each invisible to the other as they talked through the wires that ran from his house to hers, and if and when he caught her at a bad moment, he often found himself listening to a cranky, pigheaded, impossible kind of person, someone altogether different from the Anne-Marie he thought he knew. The saddest, most demoralizing of these conversations came in the middle of March. After a month of tryouts for the high school baseball team, of living through the weekly postings of names on the locker room bulletin board, the anxious search for his own name on the slowly shrinking list of players who had survived the latest cut, he called to tell her that the final list had gone up and that he was one of only two sophomores who had made the varsity. A long silence on the other end of the line, which Ferguson broke by saying: I just wanted to share the good news with you. Another pause. And then her response, delivered in a flat, cold voice: Good news? Why should I think it's good news? I hate sports. Especially baseball, which must be the dumbest game ever invented. It's empty and childish and boring, and why would a smart person like you want to waste your time running around a field with a pack of morons? Grow up, Archie. You're not a kid anymore.

What Ferguson didn't know was that Anne-Marie was drunk when she said those words, as she had been several other times during their recent talks on the phone, that for some months she had been smuggling bottles of vodka into her room and drinking whenever her parents were out, long solo binges that freed the devils inside her and turned her tongue into a weapon of cruelty. The sober, well-mannered, intelligent girl of the daylight hours vanished when she was alone in her room at night, and because Ferguson never set eyes on that other person, only talked to her and listened to her angry, half-baked pronouncements, he had no idea what was going on, no idea that the first love of his life was headed for a crack-up.

That last conversation took place on a Thursday, and Ferguson was so peeved and bewildered by her hostile denunciations that he was almost glad when she failed to show up at school the following morning. He needed time to think things through, he said to himself, and not having to see her that day would make it less difficult to recover from the hurt she had caused him. Struggling against the impulse to call her after school on Friday, he left the house the instant he dropped off his books and went down the block to see Bobby George, who was the other sophomore who had made the varsity team, bulky, broad-necked Bobby, now a first-rate catcher and champion goofball, one of the morons from the pack of morons Ferguson would soon be playing with. He and Bobby wound up spending the evening with some of the other baseball morons, fellow sophomores who had made the J.V. team, and when Ferguson walked into his house a few minutes before midnight, it was too late to call Anne-Marie. He restrained himself on Saturday and Sunday as well, fighting off the temptation to dial her number by keeping his distance from telephones, determined not to give in, aching to give in, desperate to hear her voice again. He woke up on Monday morning fully cured, the rancor purged from his heart, prepared to forgive her for Thursday's unaccountable outburst, but then he went to school, and once again Anne-Marie was absent. He figured it was a cold or the flu, nothing of any consequence, but now that he had granted himself the right to talk to her, he called her house at lunchtime from the pay phone next to the cafeteria entrance. No answer. Ten rings, and no answer. Hoping he had dialed the wrong number, he hung up the receiver and tried again. Twenty rings, but no answer.

He called steadily for two days, panic mounting with each failed attempt to get hold of her, ever more confused by what appeared to be an inexplicably empty house, a telephone that rang and rang and was never picked up, what in the world was happening, he asked himself, where had everyone gone, and so early on Thursday morning, a good hour and a half before the first bell at school, he walked to the Dumartins' house on the other side of town, a large gabled house with an immense front lawn on one of Montclair's most elegant streets, the Street of Mansions, as Ferguson had called it when he was a small child, and even though Anne-Marie had insisted he stay away from there because she didn't want him to meet her parents, he had no choice but to go there now in order to solve the mystery of the unanswered phone, which in turn might help him solve the mystery of what had happened to her.

He rang the doorbell and waited, waited long enough to conclude that no one was at home, then rang the doorbell again, and just as he was about to turn around and leave, the door opened. A man was standing in front of him, a man who was clearly Anne-Marie's father—the same round face, the same jaw, the same gray-blue eyes—and even though it was just seven-twenty in the morning, he was already fully dressed, smartly outfitted in his dark blue diplomat's suit and his starched white shirt and his striped red tie, cheeks smooth from his early morning shave, a hint of cologne hovering around his head, which was a rather good-looking head, Ferguson thought, but somewhat weary around the eyes, perhaps, or else in the eyes, a fretful, distracted, melancholic sort of gaze, which Ferguson found moving somehow, no, not moving exactly, *compelling*, no doubt because this was the face that belonged to Anne-Marie's father.

Yes?

I'm sorry, Ferguson said, I realize it's quite early, but I'm a friend of Anne-Marie's from school, and I've been calling the house for the past few days, wanting to know if she's all right, but no one ever answers, so I got worried and walked over here to find out.

And you are?

Archie. Archie Ferguson.

There's a simple explanation, Mr. Ferguson. The telephone has been out of order. A terrible inconvenience for all of us, but I've been assured the repairmen will be coming today.

And Anne-Marie?

She hasn't been well.

Nothing serious, I hope.

No, I'm certain everything will be fine, but for now she needs to rest.

Would it be possible for me to visit her?

I'm sorry. If you give me your number, I'll have her call you as soon as she's feeling a little better.

Thank you. She already has the number.

4 3 2 1

Good. I'll tell her to contact you. *(A brief pause.)* Just give me your name again. It seems to have slipped my mind.

Ferguson. Archie Ferguson.

Ferguson.

That's right. And please tell Anne-Marie that I'm thinking about her.

So ended Ferguson's one and only encounter with Anne-Marie's father, and as the door closed and he began walking toward the street, he wondered if Mr. Dumartin would forget his name again, or if he would simply forget to tell Anne-Marie to call him, or if he would not tell her to call him on purpose, even if he remembered his name, since that was the job of all fathers everywhere on earth—to protect their daughters from boys *who were thinking about them.*

After that, silence, and four long days of nothing. Ferguson felt as if someone had tied him up and pushed him off a boat, and after sinking to the bottom of a lake, which was necessarily a large lake, no less broad and profound than Lake Michigan, he had been holding his breath underwater, four long days among the dead bodies and rusted voting machines without drawing a breath, and by Sunday night, his lungs about to burst, his head about to burst, he finally found the courage to pick up the phone, and an instant after he dialed the Dumartins' number, there she was. So happy, she said, so glad to hear from him, sounding as if she meant it, explaining that she had called him three times that morning (which could have been true, since he had been out with his parents playing tennis), and then she began to tell him about the vodka, the months of secret drinking in her room, culminating in the final binge on Thursday night, the last night they had spoken to each other, which ended with her passing out on the floor, and when her father and stepmother came home from their New York dinner party at eleven-thirty, they saw that her bedroom door was open and the light was on, so they went in and found her, and because they couldn't wake her, and because the bottle was empty, they called an ambulance to transport her to the hospital, where her stomach was pumped and she regained consciousness, but rather than send her home the next morning, they transferred her to the psychiatric ward, where she was given tests and interviewed by doctors for three days, and now that she had been diagnosed as a manic-depressive in need of long-term psychotherapy, her father had decided she should return to Belgium as soon as possible, which was all she had ever wanted, a chance to escape her horrid stepmother, to put an end to her exile in horrid America, which no doubt had caused her to start drinking in the first place, and now that she would be living with her mother's sister in Brussels, her beloved Aunt Christine, which meant that she would be with her brothers and cousins and old friends again, she was feeling happy, happier than she had felt in a long, long time.

He saw her only once after that, a farewell date on Wednesday, an exceptional school-night outing that his mother allowed because she knew how important it was to him, even giving him extra money for cab fare (the first and only time it ever happened), so that he and his *Belgian girl* would not have to endure the humiliation of being chauffeured around by one of his parents, which would only have underscored how young he was, and since when had anyone that young ever been seriously in love? Yes, his mother continued to understand him, at least many of the important things about him, and he was grateful to her for that, but still, that last evening with Anne-Marie turned out to be a miserable and awkward business for Ferguson, a futile exercise in trying to maintain his dignity, reining in his sorrow so as not to beg or cry or say something harsh to her out of bitterness or disappointment, but how not to remember throughout the evening that this was the end, the last time he would ever see her, and to make matters worse, she was at her very best that night, so warm, so effusive in what she said about him, *my wonderful Archie, my beautiful Archie, my brilliant Archie,* each kind word seemed to be describing someone who wasn't there, a dead person, they were words that belonged in a funeral oration, and even worse than that was her unaccustomed cheerfulness, the joy he could see in her eyes when she talked about going away, not once stopping to think that going away meant leaving him behind *the day after tomorrow,* but suddenly she was laughing and telling him not to worry, they would see each other again soon, he could come to Brussels and spend the summer with her, as if his parents could afford to fly him to Europe, they who had not once gone to California to visit Aunt Mildred and Uncle Henry in all the years they had been there, and then she was saying something even more incomprehensible and wounding to him, sitting on the bench in the park where they had first kissed in October and were now kissing again on their last night together in March, saying that maybe it was a lucky thing for him that she was going, that she was so messed up and he was so normal, and he deserved to be with a healthy, normal girl, not a sick, crazy girl like her, and from that moment until he dropped her off at her house twenty minutes later, he felt as sad as he had ever been in his whole disgustingly normal life.

A week later, he wrote her a nine-page letter and sent it to her aunt's address in Brussels. A week after that, a six-page letter. Three weeks after that, a two-page letter. A month after that, a postcard. She didn't answer any of them, and by the time school let out for the summer, he understood that he was never going to write to her again.

THE TRUTH WAS that healthy, normal girls didn't interest him. Life in the suburbs was dull enough, and the problem with healthy, normal girls was that they reminded him of the suburbs, which had become far too predictable for his taste, and the last thing he wanted was to be with a predictable girl. Whatever her shortcomings, whatever anguish she had caused him, at least Anne-Marie had been full of surprises, at least she had kept his heart pounding in a state of prolonged suspense, and now that she was gone, everything had become dull and predictable again, even more oppressive than it had been before she walked into his life. He knew it wasn't her fault, but he couldn't help feeling betrayed. She had abandoned him, and from now on it was either make do with the morons or live in solitary confinement for the next two years, at which point he would flee this place and never come back.

He was sixteen now, and he spent the summer working for his father and playing baseball in the evenings, always baseball, still and always baseball, which was no doubt a mindless pursuit but continued to give too much pleasure for him to think of abandoning it, this time in a league for high school and college players from around the county, a stiff and competitive league, but he had done well in his first year on the Montclair varsity, starting third baseman and number five hitter, a .312 batting average for a good team, the best team in the Big Ten Conference, and he was hitting for more power now as he continued to grow, five-eleven at the last measurement, 174 pounds the last time he stepped on the scales, and so he played that summer in order to keep his hand in and spent the mornings and afternoons working for his father, mostly driving around town in the van delivering and installing air conditioners with a guy named Ed, and when there was nothing to deliver, he would help Mike Antonelli up front with sales or fill in for Mike while he took one of his frequent coffee breaks at Al's Diner, and when there were no customers in the store, he would go into the back room and sit with his father until someone else showed up, his almost fifty-year-old father, still lean and fit, still anchored to his work table and repairing broken machines, his walled-off and silent father, almost serene now after six years in the quiet of that back room, and while Ferguson consistently offered to help with the repair work, even though he was clumsy and unskilled in all that pertained to machines, his father always shrugged him off, saying his son shouldn't be wasting his time on broken toasters, he was traveling a road that would lead to far greater things than that, and if he wanted to make himself useful, he should bring in some of those poetry books he had at home and read out loud while his old man took care of the broken toasters, and so it was that Ferguson, who had been ingesting vast amounts of poetry in the past year and a half, spent a portion of that summer reading to his father in the back room of Stanley's TV & Radio, Dickinson, Hopkins, Poe, Whitman, Frost, Eliot, Cummings, Pound, Stevens, Williams, and others, but the poem his father seemed to like best, the one that seemed to make the strongest impression on him, was *The Love Song of J. Alfred Prufrock*, which startled Ferguson, and because he was unprepared for that reaction, he understood that he had missed something, had been missing something for a long time now, which meant that he would have to rethink everything he had previously assumed about his father, for once he had finished the last line, *Till human voices wake us, and we drown*, his father turned to him and looked into his eyes, looked at him with an intensity Ferguson had never seen in all the years he had known him, and after a long pause he said: Oh, Archie. What a magnificent thing. Thank you. Thank you so much. And then his father shook his head back and forth three times and spoke the last words again: *Till human voices wake us, and we drown*.

The last week of summer. August twenty-eighth, and the March on Washington, the speeches at the Mall, the immense crowds, tens of thousands, hundreds of thousands, and then the speech that schoolchildren would later have to memorize, the speech of speeches, as important on that day as the Gettysburg Address had been on its day, a big American moment, a public moment for all to see and hear, even more essential than the words spoken at Kennedy's inauguration thirty-two

months earlier, and everyone at Stanley's TV & Radio stood in the front
room and watched the broadcast, Ferguson and his father, big-bellied
Mike and shrimpy Ed, and then Ferguson's mother came in as well,
along with five or six pedestrians who happened to be walking by, but
before the big speech there were several other speeches, among them
an address delivered by a local New Jersey man, Rabbi Joachim Prinz,
the most admired Jew in Ferguson's part of the world, a hero to his
parents, even if they did not practice their religion or belong to a synagogue, but all three Fergusons had seen him and heard him talk at
weddings, funerals, and bar mitzvahs at the temple he presided over in
Newark, the famous Joachim Prinz, who as a young rabbi in Berlin had
denounced Hitler even before the Nazis took power in 1933, who saw
the future more clearly than anyone else and urged Jews to quit Germany, which led to repeated arrests by the Gestapo and his own expulsion in 1937, and of course he was active in the American civil rights
movement, and of course he had been chosen to represent the Jews that
day because of his eloquence and well-documented courage, and of
course Ferguson's parents were proud of him, they who had shaken his
hand and talked to him, the person who was now standing before the
camera and addressing the nation, the entire world, and then King
stepped to the podium, and thirty or forty seconds after the speech
began, Ferguson looked over at his mother and saw that her eyes were
glistening with tears, which amused him greatly, not because he felt it
was inappropriate for her to respond in that way but precisely because
he didn't, because this was yet one more instance of how she engaged
with the world, her excessive, often sentimental reading of events, the
gushes of feeling that made her so susceptible to tearing up at bad
Hollywood movies, the good-hearted optimism that sometimes led to
muddled thinking and crushing disappointment, and then he looked
over at his father, a man almost entirely indifferent to politics, who
seemed to demand so much less from life than his mother did, and
what he saw in his father's eyes was a combination of vague curiosity
and boredom, the same man who had been so moved by the dreary
resignation of Eliot's poem was having a hard time swallowing the
hopeful idealism of Martin Luther King, and as Ferguson listened to
the mounting emotion in the minister's voice, the drum-roll repetitions
of the word *dream*, he wondered how two such oddly matched souls

could have married and stayed married for so many years, and how he himself could have been born from such a couple as Rose Adler and Stanley Ferguson, and how strange, how deeply strange it was to be alive.

ON LABOR DAY, about twenty people came to the house for an end-of-summer barbecue. His parents rarely organized such large gatherings, but two weeks earlier his mother had won a photography competition sponsored by the governor's new arts council in Trenton. The award came with a commission to produce a book of portraits of one hundred *outstanding New Jersey citizens*, a project that would be sending her around the state to photograph mayors, college presidents, scientists, businessmen, artists, writers, musicians, and athletes, and because the job would be well paid and Ferguson's parents were feeling flush for the first time in several years, they decided to celebrate with a grilled-meat blowout in the backyard. The usual crowd was there—the Solomons, the Brownsteins, the Georges from down the block, Ferguson's grandparents and his Great-aunt Pearl—but some other people turned up as well, among them a family from New York called the Schneidermans, which consisted of a forty-five-year-old commercial artist named Daniel, the younger son of Ferguson's mother's old boss, Emanuel Schneiderman, who was now living in a retirement home in the Bronx, and Daniel's wife, Liz, and their sixteen-year-old daughter, Amy. On the morning of the Labor Day fête, as Ferguson and his parents chopped vegetables and prepared barbecue sauce in the kitchen, his mother told him that he and Amy had known each other as small children and had played together a few times, but somehow she had fallen out of touch with the Schneidermans, twelve years had fluttered off the calendar, and then, just a couple of weeks ago, on a visit to see her parents in New York, she had bumped into Dan and Liz on Central Park South. Hence the invitation. Hence the Schneidermans' first-ever visit to Montclair.

His mother continued: From the look in your eyes, Archie, I gather you've forgotten about Amy, but back when you were three and four, you had quite a crush on her. Once, when we all went to the Schneidermans' apartment for a late-afternoon Sunday dinner, you and Amy went into her room, closed the door, and took off all your clothes. You can't even remember that, can you? The adults were still sitting around the table, but then we heard you giggling in there, shrieking with laughter, making those wild, out-of-control sounds only little children can make, and so we all got up to see what the commotion was about. Dan opened the door, and there you were, the two of you, just three and a half or four years old, jumping up and down on the bed, stark naked, shrieking your heads off like a pair of crazy people. Liz was mortified, but I found it hilarious. That ecstatic look on your face, Archie, the sight of your two little bodies bouncing up and down, a savage joy filling the room, nutty human children acting like chimpanzees—it was impossible not to burst out laughing. Your father and Daniel both laughed, too, I remember, but Liz charged into the room and ordered you and Amy to get dressed. At once. You know that angry mother's voice. *At once!* But before you could get your clothes on, Amy said one of the funniest things I've ever heard. Mommy, she asked, all serious now and very thoughtful, pointing her finger directly at your privates and then at her own, Mommy, why is Archie so fancy and I'm so plain?

Ferguson's mother laughed, laughed hard and long at the memory of those words, but Ferguson only smiled, a weak excuse of a smile that quickly vanished from his face, for few things gave him less pleasure than hearing about the idiotic shenanigans of his early childhood. He said to his still laughing mother: You like to tease me, don't you?

Only sometimes, she said. Not so often, Archie, but sometimes I just can't resist.

An hour later, Ferguson went out into the yard with his book of the moment, *Journey to the End of the Night*, and sat down in one of the Adirondack chairs he and his father had repainted earlier in the summer, dark green, dark, dark green, but rather than open the book and learn more about Ferdinand's adventures at the Ford Motor plant in Detroit, he just sat there and thought as he waited for the first guests to arrive, marveling at the fact that he had once romped on a bed with a naked girl, had once been naked himself as he romped with the naked girl, and how perfectly comical it was that he should have no memory of having done that, whereas now he would give almost anything to be with a naked girl, to be naked in bed with a naked girl was the single most important aspiration of his lonely, loveless life, not one kiss or embrace in more than five months, he said to himself, a full spring and almost an entire summer of mourning for the absent, half-naked

Anne-Marie Dumartin, and now he was about to meet the unremem-
bered naked girl from his distant past, Amy Schneiderman, who no
doubt had developed into a normal, healthy girl, boring and predictable as most girls were, as most boys were, as most men and women
were, but that couldn't be helped, and given that he hadn't even met
her yet, he would just have to see what he would see.

What he saw that afternoon was the person who became the *next
one*, the successor to the crown of his desires, a girl who was neither normal nor not normal but burning, unafraid, aware of the exceptional
self she had been born with, and some weeks after their first encounter,
as summer dissolved into autumn and the world around them suddenly
turned dark, she became the *first one* as well, meaning that naked Amy
Schneiderman and naked Archie Ferguson were no longer jumping on
the bed but lying in the bed, rolling around under the covers, and for
years after that she would continue to bring him the greatest joys and
the greatest torments of his young life, to be the indispensable other who
dwelled inside his skin.

But back to that Monday afternoon in September 1963, the Labor
Day barbecue in the Fergusons' backyard, and the first glimpse he had
of her as she stepped out of her parents' blue Chevrolet, the head of dirty
blond hair emerging from the backseat, and then the surprising fact of
how tall she was, at least five-eight, perhaps five-nine, a big girl with
an impressively handsome face, not pretty or beautiful but handsome,
solid nose, forthright chin, large eyes of still undetermined color, neither heavy nor slight of build, smallish breasts under a blue short-sleeved
blouse, long legs, round ass encased in a pair of tight-fitting tan slacks,
and an odd sort of galumphing walk, torso pitched forward ever so
slightly, as if impatient to be barreling forward, a tomboy's walk, he supposed, but fetching and unusual, signaling that she was someone to be
reckoned with, a girl different from most sixteen-year-old girls because
she carried herself without the slightest trace of self-consciousness. His
mother presided over the introductions, a handshake with the mother
(slightly tense, a brief smile), a handshake with the father (relaxed, amiable), and even before he shook hands with Amy, he could sense that
Liz Schneiderman didn't like his mother because she suspected her husband was half in love with her, which might have been true, considering the protracted hug of greeting Schneiderman gave the still beautiful
forty-one-year-old Rose, and then Ferguson was shaking Amy's hand,

her long and remarkably slender hand, determining that her eyes were dark green with some flecks of brown in them, observing when she smiled that her teeth were a bit too big for her mouth, a fraction too big and therefore arresting, and then he heard her voice for the first time, *Hello, Archie*, and at that moment he knew, knew beyond any doubt that they were destined to be friends, which was a ridiculous assumption to make, of course, since how could he have known anything at that point, but there it was, a feeling, an intuition, a certainty that something important was happening and that he and Amy Schneiderman were about to set off on a long journey together.

Bobby George was there that day along with his brother, Carl, who was about to begin his sophomore year at Dartmouth, but Ferguson had no desire to talk to either one of them, not to the swift-thinking Carl nor to the bird-brained, ever-joking Bobby. What he wanted was to be with Amy, the only other young person at the party, and so within forty-five seconds of shaking her hand, as a strategy to avoid having to share her with the others, he invited her up to his room. It was a somewhat impetuous thing to do, perhaps, but she accepted with a willing nod of the head, saying *Good idea, let's go*, and up they went to Ferguson's second-floor refuge, which was no longer a shrine to Kennedy but a place crammed with books and records, so many books and records that the overcrowded shelves could no longer contain the collection, which was continuing to grow in piles stacked up against the wall nearest to the bed, and it pleased him to watch Amy nod again as she entered the room, as if telling him that she approved of what she saw, the scores of sanctified names and hallowed works, which she then proceeded to examine more closely, pointing to this one and saying, *A hell of a good book*, pointing to that one and saying, *I still haven't read it*, pointing to a third and saying, *Never heard of him*, but before long she sat down on the floor at the foot of the bed, which prompted Ferguson to sit down on the floor as well, face to face with her from a distance of three feet, leaning his back against the drawers of his desk, and for the next hour and a half they talked, stopping only when someone knocked on the door and announced that food was being served in the backyard, which propelled them downstairs to join the others for a while as they ate hamburgers and drank forbidden beer in front of their parents, all four of whom failed to blink at this flouting of the law, and then Amy reached into her bag, pulled out a pack of Luckys, and lit up in front of her parents—who again failed to blink—explaining that she didn't smoke much but loved the taste of tobacco after a meal, and once the meal and the cigarette had been taken care of, Ferguson and Amy excused themselves and took a slow walk around the neighborhood as the sun began to go down, eventually landing on a bench in the same small park where he had kissed Anne-Marie for the last time before she disappeared, and not long after Ferguson and Amy arranged to see each other again in New York on a Saturday later that month, they too began to kiss, an unplanned, spontaneous leap as one mouth latched onto the other, a delicious slobber of flailing tongues and clanking teeth, instant arousal in the rambunctious nether zones of their postpubescent bodies, kissing with such abandon that they might have eaten each other up if Amy hadn't suddenly pulled away from him and started to laugh, a spurt of breathless, astonished laughter that soon had Ferguson laughing as well. Good grief, Archie, she said. If we don't stop now, we'll be ripping off our clothes in a couple of minutes. She stood up and extended her right arm to him. Come on, crazy man, let's go back to the house.

They were the same age, or very nearly the same age, two hundred months old as opposed to a hundred and ninety-eight months old, but because Amy had been born at the end of 1946 (December 29) and Ferguson at the beginning of 1947 (March 3), she was a full year ahead of him in school, which meant that she was about to start her senior year at Hunter while he was still stuck in the trenches as a lowly junior. College was no more than a nebulous anywhere to him at that point, a far-flung destination that had yet to be given a name, whereas she had been studying maps for the better part of a year and was almost ready to begin packing her bags. She would be applying to several schools, she said. Everyone had told her she would need backups, second and third options, but Barnard was her first choice, her only choice, really, because it was the best college in New York, the all-girl twin of all-boy Columbia, and objective number one was to stay in New York.

But you've been in New York all your life, Ferguson said. Wouldn't you like to try some other place?

I've been to other places, she said, lots of other places, and every one of them is called Yawn City. Have you ever been to Boston or Chicago?

No.

Yawn City One and Yawn City Two. L.A.?

No.

Yawn City Three.

Fine. But what about a school in the country? Cornell, Smith, one of those places. Green lawns and echoing quads, the pursuit of knowledge in a rustic setting.

Joseph Cornell is a genius, the Smith Brothers make excellent cough drops, but freezing my ass off for four years at Wilderness U. isn't my idea of a fun time. No, Archie, New York is *it*. There's no other place.

He had known her for approximately ten minutes when they exchanged these words, and as Ferguson listened to Amy defend New York, declare her love of New York, it occurred to him that she herself was somehow an embodiment of her city, not only in her confidence and quickness of mind but also and especially in her voice, which was the voice of brainy Jewish girls from Brooklyn, Queens, and the Upper West Side, the third-generation New York Jewish voice, meaning the second generation of Jews born in America, which had a slightly different music from the New York Irish voice, for example, or the New York Italian voice, at once earthy, sophisticated, and brash, with a similar aversion to hard *r*'s but more precise and emphatic in its articulations, and the more he accustomed himself to those articulations, the more he wanted to go on hearing them, for the Schneiderman voice represented everything that was not the suburbs, not his life as it existed now, and therefore the promise of an escape into a possible future, or at least a present inhabited by that possible future, and as he sat in the room with Amy and later walked through the streets with her, they talked about any number of things, mostly about the roller-coaster summer that had started with the killing of Medgar Evers and ended with Martin Luther King's speech, the endless tangle of horror and hope that seemed to define the American landscape, and also about the books and records on the shelves and floor of Ferguson's room, not to mention schoolwork, SATs, and even baseball, but the one question he did not ask her, was determined at all costs to refrain from asking, was whether she had a boyfriend, for he had already decided he was going to do everything in his power to make her the *next one*, and he had no interest in learning how many rivals were standing in his way.

On September fifteenth, less than two weeks after the Labor Day barbecue, which was exactly six days before they were supposed to get together again in New York, she called him, and because he was the one she called and no one else, he understood that there was no boyfriend in the picture, no rival to be afraid of, and that she was with him now in the same way he was with her. He knew that because he was the person she chose to call when she heard the news about the bombing of a black church in Birmingham, Alabama, and the murder of four little girls inside, another American horror, another battle in the race war spreading across the South, as if the March on Washington two and a half weeks earlier had to be avenged with bombs and murder, and Amy was crying into the phone, struggling not to cry as she told him the news, and bit by bit, as she slowly pulled herself together, she began to talk about what could be done, about what she felt had to be done, not just laws passed by politicians but an army of people to go down there and fight the bigots, and she would be the first one to join up, the day after she graduated from high school she would hitchhike to Alabama and work for the cause, bleed for the cause, make the cause the central purpose of her life. It's our country, she said, and we can't let the bastards steal it from us.

They saw each other the following Saturday and every other Saturday throughout the fall, Ferguson riding the bus from New Jersey to the Port Authority terminal and then taking the IRT express train to West Seventy-second Street, where he would get off and walk three blocks north and two blocks west to the Schneidermans' apartment on Riverside Drive and Seventy-fifth Street, Apartment 4B, which was now the most important address in New York City. Outings of various sorts, nearly always just the two of them together, occasionally with some of Amy's friends, foreign films at the Thalia on Broadway and Ninety-fifth Street, Godard, Kurosawa, Fellini, visits to the Met, the Frick, the Museum of Modern Art, the Knicks at the Garden, Bach at Carnegie Hall, Beckett, Pinter, and Ionesco at small theaters in the Village, everything so close and available, and Amy always knew where to go and what to do, the warrior-princess of Manhattan was teaching him how to find his way around her city, which had rapidly become his city as well. Nevertheless, for all the things they did and all the things they saw, the best part of those Saturdays was sitting in coffee shops and talking, the first rounds of the ongoing dialogue that would continue for years, conversations that sometimes turned into fierce spats when their opinions differed, the good or bad film they had just seen, the good or bad political idea one of them had just expressed, but Ferguson didn't mind arguing with her, he had no interest in pushovers, the pouting, nincompoop girls who wanted only what they imagined to be the formalities of love, this was real love, complex and deep and pliable enough to allow for passionate discord, and how could he not love this girl, with her relentless, probing gaze and immense, booming laugh, the high-strung and fearless Amy Schneiderman, who one day was going to be a war correspondent or a revolutionary or a doctor who worked among the poor. She was sixteen years old, pushing toward seventeen. The blank slate was no longer entirely blank, but she was still young enough to know she could rub out the words she had already written, rub them out and start again whenever the spirit moved her.

Kisses, of course. Embraces, of course. Along with the irksome fact that Amy's parents tended to stay at home on Saturday afternoons and evenings, which limited the opportunities for being alone in the apartment and led to much chilly-weather necking on benches in Riverside Park, some furtive, back-bedroom makeout splurges at parties given by Amy's friends, and twice, just twice, on the two occasions when her homebody parents stepped out for the evening, a chance to indulge in earnest, half-naked tumbles on the bed in Amy's room, marked by the old fear that the door would be flung open at the worst possible moment. The frustrations of not being fully in control of their lives, hormonal frenzies thwarted again and again by circumstances, the two of them growing ever more desperate as the weeks passed. Then, on a Tuesday night in mid-November, Amy called with good news. Her parents would be going out of town the weekend after next, three full days in distant Chicago to visit her mother's ailing mother, and with her big brother Jim not scheduled to fly in from Boston until the day before Thanksgiving, she would have the apartment to herself while her parents were gone. A whole weekend, she said. Just think of it, Archie. A whole weekend with no one in the apartment but us.

He told his parents that he and a couple of his friends had been invited to another friend's house on the Jersey shore, a lie so ornate and nonsensical that neither one of them saw through it, and when he left for school on the Friday in question, it seemed altogether appropriate that he should be carrying a small overnight bag with him. The plan was to leave for New York the instant school let out, and if he was lucky enough to catch the first bus, he would be at Amy's apartment by four-thirty or a quarter to five, and if he missed the first bus and had to take the second, by five-thirty or a quarter to six. Another dull day in the corridors and classrooms of Montclair High School, concentrating on the clock as if he could will time forward by the sheer power of his thoughts, counting the minutes, counting the hours, and then, in the early afternoon, the announcement over the public address system that the president had been shot in Dallas, followed by another announcement sometime later that President Kennedy was dead.

Within minutes, all activities at the school came to a halt. Handkerchiefs and tissues appeared in a thousand pairs of hands, mascara was running down the cheeks of sobbing girls, boys walked around shaking their heads or punching the air with their fists, girls were hugging, boys and girls were hugging, teachers were sobbing and hugging while others looked blankly at walls and doorknobs, and before long students were massing in the gym and cafeteria, no one had any idea what to do, no one was in charge, all feuds and animosities had stopped, there were no enemies anymore, and then the principal's voice came over the public address system again and announced that school was dismissed, that everyone could go home.

The man of the future was dead.

Unreal city.

Everyone was going home, but Ferguson was carrying his overnight bag and walking to the Montclair bus stop to wait for the New York bus. He would call his parents later, but he wasn't going home. He needed to be by himself for a while, and then he needed to be with Amy, and he would stay with her as planned throughout the weekend.

Two roads diverged in an unreal city, and the future was dead.

Waiting for the bus, then mounting the steps of the bus and looking for a seat, sitting down in the fifth row and then listening to the gears shift as the bus pulled away and headed for New York, then riding through the tunnel as a woman sobbed in the seat behind him and the driver talked to a passenger up front, *I can't believe it, I can't fucking believe it*, but Ferguson believed it, even though he felt entirely removed from himself, floating somewhere just outside his body, but at the same time clear in his head, altogether lucid, with no inclination to break down and cry, no, all this was too big for that, let the woman behind him sob her heart out, it probably made her feel better, but he would never feel better and therefore he didn't have the right to cry, he only had the right to think, to try to understand what was happening, this big thing that resembled nothing else that had ever happened to him. The man talking to the driver said: *It reminds me of Pearl Harbor. You know, everything all calm and quiet, a lazy Sunday morning, people hanging around the house in their pajamas, and then BANG, the world explodes, and suddenly we're at war.* Not a bad comparison, Ferguson thought. The big event that rips through the heart of things and changes life for everyone, the unforgettable moment when something ends and something else begins. Was that what this was, he asked himself, a moment similar to the outbreak of war? No, not quite. War announces the beginning of a new reality, but nothing had begun today, a reality had ended, that was all, something had been subtracted from the world, and now there was a hole, a nothing where there had once been a something, as if every tree in the world had vanished, as if the very concept of tree or mountain or moon had been erased from the human mind.

A sky without a moon.

A world without trees.

The bus pulled into the terminal at Fortieth Street and Eighth Avenue. Rather than walk through the underground passageways to Seventh Avenue as he normally did on his trips to New York, Ferguson climbed the stairs and went out into the late November twilight, walking east along Forty-second Street as he headed toward his subway stop at Times Square, one more body in the early rush-hour crowd, the dead faces of people going about their business, everything the same, everything different, and then he found himself pushing his way through clusters of motionless pedestrians gathered on the pavement, all of them looking up at the stream of illuminated type circling the tall building in front of them, JFK SHOT AND KILLED IN DALLAS—JOHNSON SWORN IN AS PRESIDENT, and just before he reached the steps that would take him down to the IRT subway platform, he heard a woman say to another woman, *I can't believe it, Dorothy, I just can't believe what my eyes are seeing.*

Unreal.

A city without trees. A world without trees.

He hadn't called Amy to find out if she had come home from school. It was possible that she was still with her friends, swept up in the confusion of the moment, overwrought, too shaken to have remembered that he was coming, and so when he pushed the buzzer of Apartment

4B, it was unclear to him whether anyone would answer. Five seconds of doubt, ten seconds of doubt, and then he heard her voice talking to him through the intercom, *Archie, is that you, Archie?*, and a moment later she buzzed him in.

They spent several hours watching the coverage of the assassination on TV, and then, with their arms wrapped around each other in a tight embrace, they stumbled into Amy's room, lowered themselves onto the bed, and made love for the first time.

THE FIRST ISSUE OF THE *COBBLE ROAD CRUSADER* APPEARED ON January 13, 1958. A. Ferguson, the founder and publisher of the infant newspaper, announced in a front-page editorial that the *Crusader* would "report the facts to the best of our ability and tell the truth no matter what the cost." The printing of the inaugural edition of fifty copies was overseen by production manager Rose Ferguson, who took the original handwritten dummy to Myerson's Print Shop in West Orange to execute the task of reproducing both sides of the twenty-four-by-thirty-six-inch sheet and turning out facsimiles on paper thin enough to be folded in half, and because of that fold, the *Crusader* entered the world looking more like a genuine news organ (almost) than some homemade, typewritten, mimeographed newsletter. Five cents a copy. No photographs or drawings, some breathing room up top for the stenciled masthead, but otherwise nothing beyond two large rectangles filled with eight columns of densely packed hand-printed words, the penmanship of an almost-eleven-year-old boy who had always struggled to form his letters neatly, but in spite of some wobbles and misalignments, the results were legible enough, with an overall design that came across as a sincere if somewhat demented version of an eighteenth-century broadsheet.

The twenty-one articles ranged from four-line squibs to two three-column features, the first of which was the lead story on the front page, with a headline that read, A HUMAN TRAGEDY. DODGERS AND GIANTS LEAVE N.Y. FOR WEST COAST, and included extracts from interviews Ferguson had conducted with various family members and friends, the most dramatic response coming from fellow fifth-grader Tommy Fuchs: "I feel like killing myself. The only team left is the Yankees, and I hate the Yankees. What am I supposed to do?" The feature on the back explored a developing scandal at Ferguson's elementary school. Four times in the past six weeks, students had crashed into one of two brick walls in the gym during dodgeball games, causing an outbreak of black eyes, concussions, and bleeding scalps and foreheads, and Ferguson was agitating for pads to be installed to prevent further injuries. After eliciting comments from the recent victims ("I was going after the ball," said one, "and before I knew it I was bouncing off the bricks with a bashed-in head"), Ferguson spoke to the principal, Mr. Jameson, who agreed that the situation was out of control. "I have spoken to the Board of Education," he said, "and they've promised to pad the walls by the end of the month. Until then—no more dodgeball."

Vanishing baseball teams and preventable head injuries, but also stories about missing pets, storm-damaged utility poles, traffic accidents, spitball contests, *Sputnik,* and the state of the president's health, as well as brief notices about the current doings of the Ferguson and Adler clans, such as STORK BEATS DEADLINE!: "For the first time in human history, a baby was born on its due date. At 11:53 P.M. on December 29, just seven minutes before the clock ran out on her, Mrs. Frances Hollander, 22, of New York City, gave birth to her first child, a 7 pound, 3 ounce boy named Stephen. Congratulations, cousin Francie!" Or, A BIG STEP UP: "Mildred Adler was recently promoted from associate professor to full professor by the English Department at the University of Chicago. She is one of the world's leading authorities on the Victorian novel and has published books about George Eliot and Charles Dickens." And then, not to be overlooked, there was a boxed-in rectangle in the lower right-hand quadrant of the back page that bore the title *Adler's Joke Corner,* which Ferguson planned to include as a regular feature in all issues of the *Crusader,* for how could he neglect a resource as valuable as his grandfather, the king of the bad joke, who had told so many bad jokes to Ferguson over the years that the young editor in chief would have felt remiss if he hadn't used some of them. The first example went as follows: "Mr. and Mrs. Hooper were on their way to Hawaii. Just before the plane landed, Mr. Hooper asked his wife if the correct pronunciation of the word *Hawaii* was Hawaii—with a *w* sound—or Ha*v*aii—with a *v* sound. 'I don't know,' Mrs. Hooper said. 'Let's ask someone when we get there.' In the airport, they spotted a little old man walking by in a Hawaiian shirt. 'Excuse me, sir,' Mr. Hooper said. 'Can you tell us if we're in Hawaii or Ha*v*aii?' Without a blink of hesitation, the old man said, 'Ha*v*aii.' 'Thank you,' said Mr. and Mrs. Hooper. To which the old man replied: 'You're *v*elcome.' "

Subsequent issues were published in April and September of that year, each one an improvement on the last, or so Ferguson was told by his parents and relatives, but with his school friends it was a different story, for after the success of the first issue, which had taken his class by storm, a number of resentments and animosities began to surface. The closed-in world of fifth- and sixth-grade life was bound by a strict set of rules and social hierarchies, and by taking the initiative to launch the *Cobble Road Crusader*, that is, by daring to create something out of nothing, Ferguson had inadvertently overstepped those bounds. Inside those bounds boys could win status in one of two ways: by excelling at sports or by proving themselves to be masters of mischief-making. Good marks in school were of little importance, and even exceptional talent in art or music counted for almost nothing, since those talents were seen as inborn gifts, biological traits similar to the color of one's hair or the size of one's feet, and therefore not fully connected to the person who possessed them, mere facts of nature independent of human will. Ferguson had always been reasonably good at sports, which had allowed him to fit in with the other boys and avoid the dreaded fate of outcast. Mischief-making bored him, but his anarchic sense of humor had helped to cement his reputation as a decent fellow, even if he kept his distance from the wild, strutting boys who spent their weekends dropping cherry bombs into mailboxes, shattering lampposts, and making obscene phone calls to the prettiest girls in the grade above them. In other words, Ferguson had breezed along so far without running into excessive difficulties, his good grades considered neither a plus nor a minus, his tactful, unaggressive approach to interpersonal relations having buffered him against the angers of other boys, which meant that he had been in few fistfights and seemed to have made no permanent enemies, but then, in the months before he turned eleven, he decided he wanted to make a splash, which expressed itself in the form of a self-published, one-sheet newspaper, and suddenly his classmates understood that there was more to Ferguson than they had suspected, that he was really quite a clever young man, a crackerjack boy with the strength of mind to pull off an intricate stunt like the *Crusader,* and therefore all twenty-two fellow members of his fifth-grade class coughed up their nickels for a copy of the first issue, congratulating him on his fine work, laughing at the funny turns of phrase that dotted his articles, and then the weekend came and by Monday morning everyone had stopped talking about it. If the *Crusader* had ended after that first issue, Ferguson would have spared himself the grief that ultimately fell upon his head, but how could he have known there was a difference between being clever and too clever, that a second issue in the spring would start turning some of the class against him because it would prove that he was working too hard, too hard as opposed to their not hard enough, meaning that Ferguson was an industrious go-getter and they were little more than lazy, good-for-nothing louts? The girls were still with him, every one of the girls, but the girls weren't competing with him, it was the boys who were beginning to feel the pressure of Ferguson's diligence, three or four of them in any case, but Ferguson was too filled with his own happiness to notice, too flush with the triumph of completing another issue to question why Ronny Krolik and his band of hoodlums refused to buy the new edition of the *Crusader* when he brought it to school in April, thinking, if he thought about it at all, that they simply didn't have enough money.

In Ferguson's opinion, newspapers were one of mankind's greatest inventions, and he had loved them ever since he had learned how to read. Early in the morning, seven days a week, a copy of the *Newark Star-Ledger* would appear on the front steps of the house, landing with a pleasant thump just as he was climbing out of bed, thrown by some nameless, invisible person who never missed his mark, and by the time he was six and a half Ferguson had already begun to take part in the morning ritual of reading the paper while he ate his breakfast, he who had willed himself to read during the summer of the broken leg, who had fought his way out of the prison of his childish stupidity and turned into a young citizen of the world, now advanced enough to comprehend everything, or almost everything but abstruse matters of economic policy and the notion that building more nuclear weapons would ensure a lasting peace, and every morning he would sit at the breakfast table with his parents as each one of them tackled a different section of the paper, reading in silence because talking was so difficult that early in the morning, and then passing around completed sections from one to the other in a kitchen filled with the smells of coffee and scrambled eggs, of bread warming and browning in the toaster, of butter melting into hot slabs of toast. For Ferguson, it was always the funnies and sports to begin with, the oddly appealing Nancy and her friend Sluggo, Jiggs and his wife Maggie, Blondie and Dagwood, Beetle Bailey, followed by the latest from Mantle and Ford, from Conerly and Gifford, and then on to the local news, the national and international news, articles about movies and plays, so-called human interest stories about the seventeen college boys who crammed into a telephone booth or the thirty-six hot dogs consumed by the winner of the Essex County eating contest, and when all those had been exhausted and there were still a few minutes to spare before he set off to school, the classified ads and personals. *Darling, I love you. Please come home.*

The appeal of newspapers was altogether different from the appeal of books. Books were solid and permanent, and newspapers were flimsy, ephemeral throwaways, discarded the instant after they had been read, to be replaced by another one the next morning, every morning a fresh paper for the new day. Books moved forward in a straight line from beginning to end, whereas newspapers were always in several places at once, a hodgepodge of simultaneity and contradiction, with multiple stories coexisting on the same page, each one exposing a different aspect of the world, each one asserting an idea or a fact that had nothing to do with the one that stood beside it, a war on the right, an egg-and-spoon race on the left, a burning building at the top, a Girl Scout reunion at the bottom, big things and small things mixed together, tragic things on page 1 and frivolous things on page 4, winter floods and police investigations, scientific discoveries and dessert recipes, deaths and births, advice to the lovelorn and crossword puzzles, touchdown passes and debates in Congress, cyclones and symphonies, labor strikes and transatlantic balloon voyages, the morning paper necessarily had to include each one of those events in its columns of black, smudgy ink, and every morning Ferguson exulted in the messiness of it all, for that was what the world was, he felt, a big, churning mess, with millions of different things happening in it at the same time.

That was what the *Crusader* represented for him: a chance to create his own mess of a world in something that looked like a legitimate paper. Not truly legitimate, of course, no more than a rough approximation at

best, but his young boy's amateur version of the real thing was close
enough in spirit to make an impression on his friends. Ferguson had
been hoping for that kind of response, he had wanted to turn heads and
make the class notice him, and now that his wish had been granted, he
plunged into the second issue with an ever-growing sense of confidence,
a new faith in the power of his own genius, and so blind had that faith
become that not even the partial boycott by Krolik and his pals could
make him see what was happening. It wasn't until the next morning that
his eyes began to open somewhat. Michael Timmerman was one of his
closest friends, a smart and popular boy whose grades were even
better than Ferguson's, a quasi-heroic figure who towered over evil
midgets like Ronny Krolik in the way an oak towered over a patch of
poison ivy, and when Michael Timmerman pulled you aside on the
playground before school and said he wanted to talk, you were more
than happy to listen to him. His first words were all about how good
he thought the *Crusader* was, which pleased Ferguson enormously,
since the opinion of the top athlete and scholar in the class weighed
more than anyone else's opinion, but then Timmerman went on to say
he would like to work with Ferguson, that he wanted to join the staff of
the *Crusader* and contribute articles himself, which would make a good
publication even better, he felt, for who had ever heard of a one-man
newspaper, there was something weird and rinky-dink about having
one reporter write all the articles, and if Ferguson gave him a chance
and things worked out well, maybe there could eventually be three or
four or five reporters, and if everyone chipped in some money to help
with the printing costs, maybe the *Crusader* could expand to four
pages or eight pages, with everything set in type instead of depending
on Ferguson's atrocious handwriting, and just like that it would start to
look like a real paper.

Ferguson was not prepared for any of this. The *Crusader* had always
been intended as a one-man show, his show, for better or worse his show
and no one else's, and the idea of sharing the stage with another boy,
much less several other boys, made him ill with unhappiness. Timmerman was smothering him with his comments and suggestions, trying
to strong-arm him into ceding control of his rinky-dink rag with its atrocious hand-printed letters, but didn't Timmerman realize that he had
already thought about those things, that even if he had known how to
type he wouldn't have used a typewriter because the look would have

been wrong, and because he couldn't afford to pay a printer, owing to the fact that he was eleven years old, he had opted for handwriting instead, and what did Timmerman know about his mother's deal with Myerson to give a discount on portraits of his three children in exchange for the use of his printing equipment to run off the facsimiles, that was how things worked, he wanted to tell Timmerman, you bartered to cut down costs and did the best with what you had, and forget about chipping in to produce a so-called real paper, no five boys could ever raise enough money to afford that expense, and if Timmerman had been anyone other than his most admired friend, Ferguson would have told him to butt out of his business and start his own paper if he had so many bright ideas, but he respected Timmerman too much to speak his mind, he didn't want to risk insulting his friend, and so he took the coward's way out and hedged his bets, saying *Let me think about it* instead of giving a clear yes or no, hoping time would dull Timmerman's newfound passion for journalism and that the matter would be forgotten in a couple of days.

Like most successful boys, however, Timmerman was not someone who gave up easily or forgot. Every morning for the rest of the week, he approached Ferguson on the playground and asked if he had come to a decision, and every morning Ferguson tried to put him off. Maybe, he said, maybe it's a good idea, but it's spring now, and there won't be enough time to put out another issue before the end of the school year. We're both busy with Little League these days, and you can't imagine how much work goes into it. Weeks of work, months of work. So much work that I'm not even sure I want to do it anymore. Give it a rest for a while, and maybe we can talk about it again over the summer.

But Timmerman would be away at camp over the summer, and he wanted to resolve the question now. Even if the next issue wouldn't be coming out until the fall, he needed to know if he could count on it or not, and why in the world was Ferguson having so much trouble deciding what to do? What was the big deal?

Ferguson understood that he was cornered. Four straight days of badgering, and he knew it wouldn't stop until he gave an answer. But what was the right answer? If he told Timmerman he didn't want him, he would probably lose a friend. If he agreed to let Timmerman join the paper, he would despise himself for buckling in. A part of him was flattered by Timmerman's enthusiasm for the *Crusader*, and another part of him was beginning to dislike his friend, who was no longer acting like a friend but a smooth-talking bully. No, not quite a bully, but a manipulator, and because the manipulator was the most powerful and influential person in the class, Ferguson was loath to do anything that would offend him, for if Timmerman felt wronged by Ferguson, he could turn the entire class against him, and Ferguson's life would become an unrelenting misery for the rest of the school year. And yet, he couldn't allow the *Crusader* to be destroyed just for the sake of preserving the peace. No matter what happened, he would still be trapped inside his own skin, and better to be turned into an outcast than to lose all respect for himself. On the other hand, even better not to be turned into an outcast if he could help it.

Both yes and no were out of the question. What Ferguson needed was a maybe that would offer some hope without pinning him down to a lasting commitment, a delaying tactic camouflaged as a step forward, which in truth would be a step backward and a chance to buy more time. He proposed that Timmerman take on a test assignment to see if he enjoyed the work, and once he had written up the story, they would look at it together and decide if it belonged in the *Crusader*. Timmerman seemed to balk at first, looking none too pleased at the thought of having to be judged by Ferguson, but that was to be expected from a straight-A student with absolute confidence in his intellectual gifts, and so Ferguson was compelled to explain that the test was necessary because the *Crusader* was his thing and not Timmerman's, and if Timmerman wanted to be a part of his thing, he would have to prove that his work fit in with the spirit of the enterprise, which was snappy, funny, and quick. It didn't matter how smart he was, Ferguson said, he had yet to write a single newspaper article, he had no experience at all, and how could they join forces unless they knew what his stuff sounded like? Fair enough, Timmerman said. He would write a sample piece and prove how good he was, and that would be that.

This is what I'm thinking, Ferguson said. *Who is your favorite movie actress—and why?* Talk to everyone in the class, every girl and every boy, and ask them all that one question: Who is your favorite movie actress—and why? Be sure to write down every word they say, word for word the exact answers they give you, and then go home and turn the results into a one-column story that will make people laugh when they read it, and if you can't make them laugh, at least make them smile. Okay?

Okay, Timmerman said. But why not favorite actor, too?

Because contests with one winner are better than contests with two winners. The actors can wait until the next issue.

So Ferguson bought himself some time by sending Timmerman off on this useless, make-work errand, and all was calm for the next ten days as the rookie reporter gathered his data and set about to write the article. As Ferguson had suspected, Marilyn Monroe received the most votes from the boys, six out of eleven, with the other five going to Elizabeth Taylor (two), Grace Kelly (two), and Audrey Hepburn (one), but the girls gave Monroe only two of their twelve votes, with the other ten distributed among Hepburn (three), Taylor (three), and one each to Kelly, Leslie Caron, Cyd Charisse, and Deborah Kerr. Ferguson himself hadn't been able to decide between Taylor and Kelly, so he'd flipped a coin and wound up giving his vote to Taylor, while Timmerman, faced with a similar dilemma between Kelly and Hepburn, had flipped the same coin and wound up going for Kelly. Complete nonsense, of course, but there was something amusing about it as well, and Ferguson noted how conscientiously Timmerman went about the business of interviewing the kids and jotting down their comments in his small, spiral-bound reporter's notebook. Top marks for legwork and industry, then, but that was only the beginning, the foundation of the house, as it were, and it was still unclear what kind of structure Timmerman would be capable of building. There was no doubt that the boy had a good brain, but that didn't mean he could write well.

During that ten-day period of watching and waiting, Ferguson lapsed into an odd state of ambivalence, becoming less and less sure of how he felt about Timmerman, uncertain whether he should go on resenting him or begin to show some gratitude for his hard work, one minute hoping he would fail with the article and the next moment hoping he would succeed, wondering if it might not be a good idea to have another reporter share the load with him after all, realizing now that there was a certain satisfaction in assigning tasks to other people, that being the boss was not without its pleasures, for Timmerman had followed his orders without complaint, and that was a new feeling, the sense of being in charge, and if all went well with Timmerman's article, perhaps he should consider letting him in, not as a partner, of course, no, not that, never that, but as a contributing writer, the first of what could be several contributing writers, which could end up making it possible to expand the *Crusader* from two pages to four. Perhaps. And then again, perhaps not, for Timmerman had yet to hand in the article, even though he had finished the interviews in five days, and now that another five days had gone by, Ferguson could only conclude that he was struggling with it, and if Timmerman was having a hard time, that probably meant the piece was no good, and anything less than good would be unacceptable. He would have to tell that to Timmerman's face. Imagine looking into the eyes of hotshot Michael Timmerman, he said to himself, the one person who had never failed at anything, and telling him he had failed. By the morning of the tenth day, Ferguson's hopes for the future had collapsed into a single wish: that Timmerman was writing a masterpiece.

As it turned out, the article wasn't bad. Not horribly bad, in any case, but it lacked the bounce Ferguson had been hoping for, the touch of humor that would have turned its trivial subject into something worth reading about. If there was any consolation in this letdown, it came from the fact that Timmerman seemed to think it was bad as well, or so Ferguson surmised from the author's self-deprecatory shrug when he handed him the finished manuscript on the playground that morning, accompanied by an apology for having taken so long to do the job, but it hadn't been as easy as he was expecting it to be, Timmerman said, he had rewritten the article four times, and if he had learned anything from the experience, it was that writing was *a pretty tough business.*

Good, Ferguson said to himself. A little humility from Mr. Perfect. An admission of doubt, perhaps even an admission of defeat, and therefore the confrontation he had been dreading most likely would not be taking place, which was a good thing, a most excellent and reassuring thing, since Ferguson had spent the past days imagining fists flying into his stomach and summary banishments to the outer realms of the scorned. Still, he realized, if he wanted to keep their friendship intact, he would have to tread cautiously around Timmerman and make sure he didn't step on his toes. They were big toes, and the person they belonged to was a big boy, and amiable as that boy could be; he also had a temper, which Ferguson had witnessed several times over the years, most recently when Timmerman had decked Tommy Fuchs for calling him *a stuck-up shit*, the same Tommy Fuchs who was known to his detractors as Tommy Fucks, and Ferguson had no wish to be fucked around by Timmerman as Tommy Fucks had been.

He asked Timmerman to give him a few minutes, and then he withdrew to a corner of the playground to read the article alone:

"The question was: Who is your favorite movie actress—and why? A poll of the twenty-three students in Miss Van Horn's fifth-grade class has given us the answer—Marilyn Monroe, who garnered eight votes, winning out over Elizabeth Taylor, who came in second with five votes . . ."

Timmerman had done a creditable job of reporting the facts, but his language was bland, stiff to the point of lifelessness, and he had concentrated on the least interesting part of the story, the numbers, which were profoundly boring when compared to what the students had said about their choices, comments Timmerman had shared with Ferguson and then had largely neglected to work into the piece, and as Ferguson recalled some of those statements now, he found himself beginning to rewrite the article in his head:

" 'Va va voom,' said Kevin Lassiter, needing just three short words to explain why Marilyn Monroe was his favorite movie actress.

" 'She seems like such a kind and intelligent person, I wish I knew her and could be her friend,' said Peggy Goldstein, defending her choice of Deborah Kerr.

" 'So elegant, so beautiful—I just can't tear my eyes away from her,' said Gloria Dolan about her number one, Grace Kelly.

" 'Some dish,' said Alex Botello, referring to his top star, Elizabeth Taylor. 'I mean, get a load of that body of hers. It makes a boy want to grow up real fast.' "

Impossible to ask Timmerman to go back to the beginning and write the article for a fifth time. Useless to tell him that his work had produced neither a laugh nor a smile and that he might be better served by focusing on the why instead of the who. It was too late to get into any of that now, and the last thing Ferguson wanted was to lord it over Timmerman and start lecturing him on what he should or shouldn't write. He walked back to where Mr. Big Toes was standing and returned the article to him.

Well? Timmerman said.

Not bad, Ferguson replied.

You mean not good.

No, not *not good*. Not bad. Which means pretty good.

And what about the next issue?

I don't know. I haven't even thought about it yet.

But you're planning to do one, right?

Maybe. Maybe not. It's too soon to tell.

Don't give up. You've started something good, Archie, and you've got to keep it going.

Not if I don't feel like it I don't. Anyway, why should you care? I still don't get why the *Crusader* is suddenly so important to you.

Because it's exciting, that's why, and I want to be part of something exciting. I think it would be a lot of fun.

Okay. I'll tell you what. If I decide to do another issue, I'll let you know.

And give me a chance to write something?

Sure, why not?

You promise?

To give you a chance? Yes, I promise.

Even as he spoke those words, Ferguson knew that his promise meant nothing, since he had already made up his mind to shut down the *Crusader* for good. The fourteen-day battle with Timmerman had worn him out, and he was feeling depleted and uninspired, disgusted with himself for his weak-minded changes of heart, demoralized by his reluctance to stand up for himself and fight for his position, which was a one-man paper or nothing, and now that he had made his splash and done what he had set out to do, perhaps it was better that it should be nothing, better that he should get out of the pool, dry himself off, and call it quits. Besides, it was baseball season now, and he was busy playing for the West Orange Chamber of Commerce Pirates, and when he wasn't playing baseball he was busy reading *The Count of Monte Cristo*, the immense book that Aunt Mildred had sent him last month for his eleventh birthday, which he had finally started after the second issue of the *Crusader* had been put to bed, and now that he was in it he was fully in it, for it was without question the most absorbing novel that had ever fallen into his hands, and how pleasant it was to be following the adventures of Edmond Dantès every night after dinner instead of counting the words in his articles in order to fit them into the narrow columns of his broadsheet, so much labor, so many late nights squinting under his one-bulb lamp, forging on in the near-black while his parents thought he was asleep, so many false starts and corrections, so many silent thanks to the man who had invented erasers, knowing now that the job of writing was as much about removing words as adding them, and then the tedious work of going over every penciled letter with ink to make sure the words would be dark enough to be legible in the facsimiles, exhausting, yes, that was the word for it, and after his prolonged and harrowing standoff with Timmerman, he was exhausted, and as any doctor would have told him, the only cure for exhaustion was rest.

He rested for a month, finished the Dumas with a heavy heart, afraid that years might go by before he came across another novel as good as that one, and then, in the three days following his completion of the book, three things happened that changed his thinking and brought him out of retirement. He simply couldn't help himself. The words of a new headline had popped into his head, and so delightful were those words to him, so vivid was the rhyming jangle of their clattering consonants, so tricky was the way their apparent nonsense was in fact not nonsense but sense, that he longed to see those words in print, and so, reneging on his vow to leave the newspaper business, he started planning a third issue of the *Crusader*, which would carry his one-two punch of a headline in large letters across the front page: FRACAS IN CARACAS.

It began on May thirteenth, when Richard Nixon was attacked by a mob of Venezuelan protesters on the final stop of a three-country goodwill tour of South America. The vice president had just landed at the airport, and as his motorcade drove through the streets of downtown Caracas, the crowds lining the sidewalks chanted *Death to Nixon!*, *Nixon Go Home!*, and before long Nixon's car was surrounded by scores of people, mostly young men, who began spitting on the car and smashing the windows, and a few moments after that they were tipping the car from side to side, jostling it back and forth with such fury that it looked as if the car was about to turn over, and if not for the sudden appearance of Venezuelan soldiers, who dispersed the mob and cleared a path for Nixon's car to get away, things might have ended badly, quite badly for everyone concerned, especially for the almost murdered Nixon and his wife.

Ferguson read about it in the paper the next morning, saw footage of the incident on the TV news that evening, and late the following afternoon cousin Francie, her husband Gary, and their five-month-old baby stopped by the house for a visit. They lived in New York now, where Gary was about to finish his first year of law school at Columbia, and ever since Ferguson's performance as ring bearer at the wedding ceremony four years earlier, Gary had treated his young cousin-in-law as a kind of protégé, an up-and-coming fellow traveler in the world of ideas and manly pursuits, which had led to some long conversations about books and sports, but also about politics, which were something of an obsession for Gary (who subscribed to *Dissent*, *I. F. Stone's Weekly*, and the *Partisan Review*), and because Francie's husband was an intelligent young man, surely the best thinker Ferguson knew besides his Aunt Mildred, it was only natural that he should ask Gary what he thought about Nixon's run-in with the mob in Venezuela. They were outside in the backyard together, walking under the oak tree that Ferguson had fallen out of when he was six, the tall, heavyset Gary puffing on a Parliament as Ferguson's mother and Francie sat on the porch with baby Stephen, that plump little novice human being, as young in relation to Ferguson as Ferguson had once been to Francie, and as the two women laughed together and took turns holding the baby, the didactic, ever-solemn Gary Hollander was talking to him about the Cold War, the blacklist, the Red Scare, and the unhinged anti-communism that drove American foreign policy, which had led the State Department into supporting vicious, right-wing dictatorships all around the world, especially in Central and South America, and that was why Nixon had been attacked, he said, not because he was Nixon but because he represented the government of the United States, and that government was despised by vast numbers of people in those countries, justly despised for backing the tyrants who oppressed them.

Gary paused to light another Parliament. Then he said: You follow what I'm saying, Archie?

Ferguson nodded. I get it, he said. We're so scared of communism, we'll do anything to stop it. Even if it means helping people who are worse than communists.

The next morning, while reading the sports pages over breakfast, Ferguson stumbled across the word *fracas* for the first time. A Detroit pitcher had thrown a ball at a Chicago batter's head, the batter had dropped his bat, run to the mound, and punched the pitcher, and then the players from both teams had charged out onto the field and taken slugs at one another for the next twelve minutes. *Once the fracas subsided,* the reporter wrote, *six players were ejected from the game.*

Ferguson looked over at his mother and said: What does the word *fracas* mean?

A big fight, she answered. A commotion.

That's what I thought, he said. I just needed to make sure.

Months passed. The school year ended with no further trouble from Krolik, Timmerman, or anyone else, and then Miss Van Horn's twenty-three ex-pupils parted company for the summer vacation. Ferguson went off to Camp Paradise for his second eight-week stint there, and although most of his time was spent running around on ball fields and splashing in the lake, there were enough free hours during the post-lunch rest periods and the post-dinner lulls for him to write the articles and map out the design for the third issue of the *Crusader.* He finished the job at home during the two-week gap between the end of camp and the start of school, working every morning, afternoon, and most evenings in order to meet his self-imposed deadline of September first, which would give his mother enough time to run off the facsimiles at Myerson's to have the issue ready by the first day of school. It would be a good way to begin the year, he felt, a little jolt to get things off to a fast start, and after that he would see what he wanted to do, decide whether there should be more *Crusader*s or if this was in fact the last one.

He had promised Timmerman he would let him know if there was going to be another issue, but all the articles had been written before he had a chance to contact him. He called Timmerman's house the day after he came home from camp, but the housekeeper told him that Michael and his parents and two brothers were on a fishing trip in the Adirondacks and wouldn't be returning until the day before school started. Earlier in the summer, Ferguson had considered writing the funny, va-va-voom version of the movie actress story and putting it in the issue, but he had killed the idea out of deference to Timmerman's feelings, understanding how cruel it would have been to run it, how hurt Timmerman would have been by such a witty demolition of his own dull effort. If he had kept Timmerman's version of the story, he might have considered publishing it as a courtesy, but he had given it back to him on the playground in April, and therefore it wasn't possible. A new issue of the *Cobble Road Crusader* was about to hit the jungle gyms and classrooms of Ferguson's elementary school, and Michael Timmerman knew nothing about it.

That was his first mistake.

His second mistake was that he remembered too much from his conversation with Gary in the backyard.

The fracas in Caracas was old news by then, but Ferguson couldn't let go of the phrase, it had been rattling in his head for months, so rather than use the headline for a report on what had happened to Nixon, he turned the piece into a boxed editorial in the middle of the front page, with FRACAS IN CARACAS appearing just above the fold and the rest of the article just below it. Inspired by his talk with Gary, he argued that America should stop worrying about communism so much and listen to what people in other countries had to say. "It was wrong to try to overturn the vice president's car," he wrote, "but the men who did that were angry, and they were angry for a reason. They don't like America because they feel America is against them. That doesn't mean they're communists. It only means that they want to be free."

First came the punch, the angry punch to his stomach as Timmerman yelled the word *liar* and knocked him to the ground. The last twenty-one copies of the *Crusader* flew out of Ferguson's hands, and then they began to scatter across the schoolyard in the stiff morning wind, shooting past the other children like an army of stringless kites. Ferguson stood up and tried to deliver a punch of his own, but Timmerman, who seemed to have grown three or four inches over the summer, swatted it away and countered with another blow to the gut, which landed with far greater force than the first one had, not only knocking Ferguson to the ground again but knocking the breath clear out of him. By then, Krolik, Tommy Fucks, and several other boys were standing over Ferguson and laughing at him, taunting him with words that sounded like *pus-bucket*, *faggot*, and *cunt-brain*, and when Ferguson managed to stand up again, Timmerman pushed him to the ground for the third time, pushed him hard, which sent Ferguson crashing down on his left elbow, and within seconds the horrible funny-bone pain had all but immobilized him, which gave Krolik and Fucks enough time to start kicking dirt in his face. He closed his eyes. Somewhere in the distance a girl was screaming.

Then came the reprimands and punishments, the after-school detention, the idiot task of writing the words *I will not fight in school* two hundred times, the ceremonial, bury-the-hatchet handshake with Timmerman, who refused to look into Ferguson's eyes, who would never look into his eyes again, who would go on hating Ferguson for the rest of his life, and then, just as they were about to be dismissed by their new sixth-grade teacher, Mr. Blasi, the principal's secretary walked into the classroom and told Ferguson that he was wanted downstairs in Mr. Jameson's office. What about Michael? Mr. Blasi asked. No, not Michael, Miss O'Hara replied. Just Archie.

Ferguson found Mr. Jameson sitting behind his desk with a copy of the *Cobble Road Crusader* in his hands. He had been in charge of the school for the past five years, and every year he seemed to grow a little shorter and rounder and to have a little less hair on his head. Brown hair to begin with, Ferguson remembered, but the thinning strands that were left had now turned gray. The principal didn't invite Ferguson to sit down, so Ferguson remained on his feet.

You understand that you're in serious trouble, don't you? Mr. Jameson said.

Trouble? Ferguson said. I've just been punished. How can I still be in trouble?

You and Timmerman were punished for fighting. I'm talking about this.

Mr. Jameson tossed the *Crusader* onto his desk.

Tell me, Ferguson, the principal continued, are you responsible for every article in this issue?

Yes, sir. Every word of every article.

No one helped you write anything?

No one.

And your mother and father. Did they read it in advance?

My mother did. She helps me with the printing, so she gets to see it before anyone else. My father didn't read it until yesterday.

And what did they say to you about it?

Nothing much. Nice job, Archie. Keep up the good work. Something like that.

So you're telling me that the editorial on the front page was your idea.

Fracas in Caracas. Yes, my idea.

Tell the truth, Ferguson. Who's been poisoning your mind with communist propaganda?

What?

Tell me, or else I'm going to have to suspend you for printing these lies.

I didn't lie.

You've just started the sixth grade. That means you're eleven years old, right?

Eleven and a half.

And you expect me to believe that a boy your age can come up with a political argument like this one? You're too young to be a traitor, Ferguson. It just isn't possible. Some older person must be feeding you this garbage, and I'm guessing it's your mother or father.

They're not traitors, Mr. Jameson. They love their country.

Then who's been talking to you?

No one.

When you started your paper last year, I went along with it, didn't I? I even let you interview me for one of the articles. I found it charming, just the sort of thing a bright young boy should be doing. No controversy, no politics, and then you go away for the summer and come back a Red. What am I supposed to do with you?

If it's the *Crusader* that's causing the problem, Mr. Jameson, you don't have to worry about it anymore. There were only fifty copies of the back-to-school issue, and half of them blew away when the fight started. I've been on the fence about whether I should keep going with it, but after the fight this morning, my mind is made up. The *Cobble Road Crusader* is dead.

Is that a promise, Ferguson?

So help me God.

Stick to that promise, and maybe I'll try to forget that you deserve to be suspended.

No, don't forget. I want to be suspended. Every boy in the sixth grade is against me now, and school is about the last place I want to be anymore. Suspend me for a long time, Mr. Jameson.

Don't make jokes, Ferguson.

I'm not joking. I'm the odd man out, and the longer I can stay away from here, the better off I'll be.

His FATHER WAS in a different line of work now. No more 3 Brothers Home World, but a vast weatherproof bubble that sat on the West Orange–South Orange border and was called the South Mountain

Tennis Center, six indoor courts that allowed the tennis enthusiasts of the area to indulge their passion for the sport twelve months a year, to play during rainstorms and blizzards, to play at night, to play before the sun rose on winter mornings, half a dozen green, hard-surface courts, a pair of locker rooms equipped with sinks, toilets, and showers, and a pro shop that sold rackets, balls, sneakers, and tennis whites for men and women. The 1953 fire had been ruled an accident, the insurance company had paid up in full, and rather than rebuild or open another store in a new location, Ferguson's father had gener-ously given his employee-brothers a share of the money (sixty thou-sand dollars each) and had used the remaining one hundred and eighty thousand to put his tennis project into motion. Lew and Millie took off for southern Florida, where Lew became a promoter of dog races and jai alai matches, and Arnold opened a store in Morristown that specialized in children's birthday parties, stocking his shelves with bags of balloons, crepe-paper streamers, candles, noisemakers, funny hats, and pin-the-tail-on-the-donkey posters, but New Jersey wasn't ready for such a novel concept, and when the store went out of business two and a half years later, Arnold turned to Stanley for help and was given a job in the pro shop at the Tennis Center. As for Fer-guson's father, every day of the two and a half years it had taken Arnold to run his store into the ground had been spent in raising capital to augment the money he had invested on his own, searching for and eventually buying land, consulting with architects and con-tractors, and then, finally, erecting the South Mountain Tennis Cen-ter, which opened its doors in March 1956, one week after his son's ninth birthday.

Ferguson liked the weatherproof bubble and the eerie, echoing sounds of tennis balls flying around in that cavernous space, the pop-pop-pop medley of rackets colliding with balls when several courts were in use at the same time, the intermittent squeaks of rubber soles jam-ming against the hard surfaces, the grunts and gasps, the long stretches when not a single word was spoken by anyone, the hushed solemnity of white-clad people batting white balls over white nets, a small, self-enclosed world that looked like no other place in the big world outside the dome. He felt that his father had done the right thing in changing jobs, that television sets and refrigerators and box-spring mattresses can speak to you for just so long and then a moment comes when you should jump ship and try something else, and because his father was so fond of tennis, why not earn his living from the game he loved? All the way back in 1953, in the spooky days after 3 Brothers Home World burned to the ground, when his father was beginning to formulate his plan for the South Mountain center, his mother had warned him of the risks involved in such a venture, the enormous gamble his father would be taking, and indeed there had been many ups and downs along the way, and even after the center had been built, it had taken some time before the membership ranks grew large enough for the incoming fees to sur-pass the monthly costs of running such a large operation, which meant that for most of the three-plus years between late 1953 and mid-1957 the Ferguson family had depended on the earnings of Roseland Photo to keep its head above water. Things had improved since then, the center and the studio were both running well in the black, generating enough income to provide for such extravagances as a new Buick for his father, a fresh paint job for the house, a mink stole for his mother, and two con-secutive summers at sleepaway camp for Ferguson, but even though their circumstances were more comfortable now, Ferguson understood how hard his parents worked to maintain that comfort, how consuming their jobs were and how little time they had for anything else, especially his father, who kept the tennis center open seven days a week, from six in the morning until ten at night, and while he had a staff of employees to help him, Chuck O'Shea and Bill Abramavitz, for example, who could more or less run things on their own, and John Robinson, an ex–Pullman porter who watched over the courts and locker rooms, and deadbeat Uncle Arnold, who ground out his hours in the pro shop smoking Camels and flipping through newspapers and racing forms, and the three young assistants, Roger Nyles, Ned Fortunato, and Richie Siegel, who rotated in six- and seven-hour shifts, and half a dozen high school part-timers, Ferguson's father rarely took any days off dur-ing the cold-weather months, and not many during the warm-weather months either.

Because his parents were so preoccupied, Ferguson tended to keep his troubles to himself. In the case of a dire emergency, he knew he could count on his mother to stand with him, but the fact was that there hadn't been any emergencies in the past couple of years, at least none bad enough to send him rushing to her for help, and now that he was eleven and a half, most of the situations that had once seemed dire to him had been reduced to a set of smaller problems he could solve on his own. Getting beaten up on the playground before the first day of school was no doubt a big problem. Being accused of spreading communist propaganda by the principal was unquestionably a big problem as well. But was either one of those problems grave enough to be considered dire? Forget that he had been close to tears after the smackdown in Mr. Jameson's office, forget that he had gone on fighting back those tears during the entire walk home from school. It had been a wretched day, probably the worst day of his life since the day he fell out of the tree and fractured his leg, and there was every reason in the world for him to want to break down and cry. Punched by his friend, insulted by his other friends, with nothing but more punches and more insults to look forward to, and then the final indignity of being called a traitor by his dumb coward of a principal, who didn't even have the nerve to suspend him. Yes, Ferguson was feeling blue, Ferguson was struggling not to cry, Ferguson was in a tough spot, but what good would it do to tell his parents about it? His mother would be all sympathy, of course, she would want to hug him and take him in her arms, she would gladly turn him into a little boy again and hold him on her lap as he bawled forth his tearful lamentations, and then she would become angry on his behalf, she would threaten to call Mr. Jameson and give him a piece of her mind, a meeting would be arranged, the adults would argue about him, everyone would be shouting about the pinko subversive and his pinko parents, and what good would that do, how could anything his mother said to him or did for him stop the next punch from coming? His father would be more practical about it. He would take out the boxing gloves and give Ferguson another lesson in the art of fisticuffs, *the sweet science*, as his father liked to call it, surely the worst misnomer in human history, and for twenty minutes he would demonstrate how to keep your guard up and defend yourself against a taller opponent, but what use were boxing gloves on a playground where people fought with bare knuckles and didn't follow the rules, where it wasn't always one against one but often two against one or three against one and even four against one? Dire. Yes, perhaps it was dire, but Father didn't know best, Mother didn't know best, and therefore he would have to keep it to himself. No cries for help. Not a word to either one of them. Just stick it out, stay clear of the playground, and hope he wasn't dead before Christmas.

He lived in hell for the entire school year, but the nature of that hell, and the laws that governed that hell, kept shifting from month to month. He had assumed it would largely be a matter of punches, of being punched and then punching back as hard as he could, but big battles in the open air were off the agenda, and although he was often punched during the first weeks of school, he never had a chance to punch back, for the punches he received were delivered without warning—a boy rushing up to him out of nowhere, belting him in the arm or the back or the shoulder, and then running away before Ferguson could respond. Punches that hurt, one-blow sneak attacks when no one was looking, always a different boy, nine different boys from the eleven other boys in his class, as if they had all conferred with one another and worked out their strategy in advance, and once Ferguson had received those nine punches from the nine different boys, the punches stopped. After that it was the cold shoulder, those same nine boys refusing to talk to him, pretending not to hear Ferguson when he opened his mouth and said something, looking at him with blank, indifferent faces, acting as if he were invisible, a drop of nothingness dissolving into the empty air. Then came the period of pushing him to the ground, the old trick of one boy getting down on his hands and knees behind him while another boy pushed from the front, a quick shove to make him lose his balance, and then Ferguson would find himself tumbling over the crouching boy's back, and more than once his head hit the ground first, and not only was there the dishonor of being caught with his guard down once again, there was the pain. So much fun, so much laughter at his expense, and the boys were so cunning and efficient that Mr. Blasi never seemed to notice a thing. The defaced drawings, the scribbled-over math assignments, the missing lunch bags, the garbage in his cubby, the cut-off jacket sleeve, the snow in his galoshes, the dog turd in his desk. Winter was the time of pranks, the bitter season of indoor nastiness and ever-deepening despair, and then the ice thawed a couple of weeks after his twelfth birthday, and a new round of punches began.

If not for the girls, Ferguson surely would have crumbled to pieces, but none of the twelve girls in the class turned against him, and on top of that there were the two boys who refused to take part in the savagery, the fat and slightly moronic Anthony DeLucca, variously known as Chubs, Blubs, and Squish, who had always looked up to Ferguson and had often been victimized by Krolik and company in the past, and the new boy, Howard Small, a quiet, intelligent kid who had moved to West

Orange from Manhattan over the summer and was still feeling his way as a neophyte in the suburban hinterlands. In effect, the majority of the students were in Ferguson's camp, and because he wasn't alone, at least not altogether alone, he managed to tough it out by adhering to his three central principles: never let them see you cry, never lash back in frustration or anger, and never breathe a word about it to anyone in authority, especially not his parents. It was a brutal and demoralizing business, of course, with countless tears shed into his pillow at night, ferocious, ever more elaborate dreams of revenge, prolonged descents into the rocky chasms of melancholia, a grotesque mental fugue in which he saw himself jumping off the top of the Empire State Building, silent harangues against the injustice of what was happening to him, accompanied by a fitful, frantic drumbeat of self-contempt, the secret conviction that he deserved to be punished because he had brought this horror upon himself. But that was in private. In public he forced himself to be hard, to take the punches without emitting a single yelp of pain, ignoring them in the way you ignored ants on the ground or the weather in China, walking away from each new humiliation as if he were the victor in some cosmic struggle between good and evil, reining in any expression of sorrow or defeat because he knew the girls were watching, and the more bravely he stood up to his attackers, the more the girls would be on his side.

It was all so complicated. They were twelve years old now, or on the cusp of turning twelve, and some of the boys and girls were beginning to pair off, the old divide between the sexes had narrowed to a point where male and female stood on almost common ground, suddenly there was talk about boyfriends and girlfriends, about going steady, nearly every weekend there were parties with dancing and spin-the-bottle games, and the same boys who just a year ago had tormented girls by pulling their hair and pinching their arms were now in favor of kissing them. Still the number one boy, Timmerman had forged a romantic alliance with the number one girl, Susie Krauss, and the two of them reigned over the class as a kind of royal couple, Mr. and Miss Popularity 1959. It helped Ferguson that he and Susie had been friends since kindergarten and that she was the leader of the anti-bully forces. When she and Timmerman became an item at the end of March, the atmosphere began to change somewhat, and before long Ferguson noticed that he was being attacked less often and that fewer boys were attacking him. Nothing was ever said. Ferguson suspected that Susie had given her new beau an ultimatum—stop torturing Archie or I'm gone—and because Timmerman was more interested in courting Susie than in hating Ferguson, he had backed off. He still treated Ferguson with contempt, but he stopped using his fists on him and no longer vandalized his belongings, and once Timmerman withdrew from the Gang of Nine, several other boys dropped out as well, since Timmerman was their leader and they followed him in all things, so that for the last two and a half months of school there were only four tormentors left, Krolik and his band of imbeciles, and while it was hardly pleasant to be given the treatment by those four, it was far better than being worked over by nine. Susie wouldn't tell him whether she had spoken to Timmerman or not (protocol demanded that she remain silent on the subject out of loyalty to her love), but Ferguson was almost certain she had, and so grateful was he to Susie Krauss and her noble fighter's heart that he began to long for the day when she would eventually dump Timmerman and the field would open for him to try his luck with her. He thought about it continually throughout the early weeks of spring, deciding that it would probably be best to begin by asking her to spend a Saturday afternoon with him at his father's tennis center, where he could show her around and demonstrate how knowledgeable he was about the inner workings of the place, which would no doubt impress her and put her in the right mood for a kiss, or perhaps several kisses, and if not a kiss, then at least holding hands. Given the volatility of preteen romances in that corner of the New Jersey suburbs, where the average alliance lasted just two or three weeks and two months of couplehood was the equivalent of a ten-year marriage, it was not unreasonable for Ferguson to hope that his opportunity would come before school let out for the summer.

In the meantime, he had his eye on Gloria Dolan, who was prettier than Susie Krauss but not as exciting to be with, a gentle, plodding soul when compared to the sprinting, spitfire Susie, and yet Ferguson had his eye on her because he had discovered that Gloria had her eye on him, quite literally she was looking at him when she thought he wasn't looking at her, and how many times in the past month had he caught her staring at him in class, sitting at her desk as Mr. Blasi turned his back to the students and worked out another math problem on the blackboard, no longer paying attention to the white chalk numerals but studying Ferguson instead, as if Ferguson had become a subject of intense interest to her, and now that Ferguson had become aware of that interest, he too began turning his head away from the blackboard to look at her, and more and more often now their eyes would meet, and every time that happened they would smile at each other. At that point in his journey through life, Ferguson was still waiting for his first kiss, his first kiss from a girl, a true kiss as opposed to the fraudulent kisses from mothers, grandmothers, and female first cousins, an ardent kiss, an erotic kiss, a kiss that would go beyond the mere pressing of lips upon lips and send him flying into hitherto unexplored territory. He was ready for that kiss, he had been thinking about it since before his birthday, in the past few months he and Howard Small had discussed the matter repeatedly and at length, and now that he and Gloria Dolan were exchanging secret smiles in class, Ferguson decided that Gloria should be the first one, for every signal pointed to the inevitability of her being the first one, and so it was, on a Friday night at the end of April, during the course of a gathering at Peggy Goldstein's house on Merrywood Drive, that Ferguson took Gloria into the backyard and kissed her, and because she kissed him back, they went on kissing for a good long while, far longer than he had imagined they would, perhaps ten or twelve minutes, and when Gloria slipped her tongue into his mouth after the fourth or fifth minute, everything suddenly changed, and Ferguson understood that he was living in a new world and would never set foot in the old one again.

BEYOND THOSE LIFE-ALTERING kisses with Gloria Dolan, the other good thing about that dismal year was his deepening friendship with the new boy, Howard Small. It helped that Howard had come from somewhere else, that he had entered the scene on the first fateful morning of the new school year without prejudices or preconceptions about who was who or who was supposed to be what, that he had bought the third issue of the *Cobble Road Crusader* within minutes of reaching the playground and was happily scanning its contents when he saw the boy who had just sold it to him being attacked by Timmerman and the others, and because he was a person who knew right from wrong, he immediately took Ferguson's side and then stuck with Ferguson from that day forward, and because he too occasionally came under attack for the crime of being Ferguson's friend, the two boys grew close, since each would have been entirely alone if not for the existence of the other. Sixth-grade pariahs—and therefore friends, within a month the best of friends.

Howard, not Howie, emphatically not Howie. Small by name but not in size, just a fraction of an inch shorter than Ferguson and already beginning to fill out, no longer a scrawny child but an ever more robust preteen, solid and strong, physically unafraid, a kamikaze sportsman who compensated for his mediocre abilities with relentless enthusiasm and effort. Wit and kindness, a fast learner with a talent for performing well under pressure, surpassing even Timmerman in one hundred percent test scores, a reader of books, as Ferguson was, a developing student of politics, as Ferguson was, and a boy with a wondrous gift for drawing. The pencil he carried around in his pocket churned out landscapes, portraits, and still lifes of near-photographic precision, but also cartoons and comics, which largely derived their humor from unlikely puns, words yanked out of their familiar roles because their sounds were congruent with the sounds of other, unrelated words, such as the drawing entitled *He Flies Through the Air with the Greatest of Ease*, which showed a boy propelling himself across the sky with a large capital *E* in his outstretched hands, while other boys in the background struggled along with diminutive lowercase *e*'s, or else Ferguson's favorite, the one in which Howard turned the word *toiletries* into a new form of vegetation, a drawing that bore the title *Pinsky's Fruit Farm*, with a row of cherry trees on top, neatly labeled *Cherry Trees*, and a row of orange trees in the middle, neatly labeled *Orange Trees*, and a row of toilet trees on the bottom, neatly labeled *Toilet Trees*. What a fine and funny idea, Ferguson thought, and what a good ear to have broken apart the original word and changed it into two words, but even more than the ear it was the eye that counted, the eye in conjunction with the hand, since the result wouldn't have been half as effective if the toilets hanging from the branches hadn't been drawn so well, for Howard's toilets were nothing less than sublime, the most faithful and accurately rendered toilets Ferguson had ever seen.

Howard's father was a math professor who had moved the Smalls to New Jersey because he had been offered a new post as dean of students at Montclair State Teachers College. Howard's mother worked as an editor for a women's magazine called *Hearth & Home*, which meant that she commuted to New York five days a week and seldom returned to West Orange before nightfall, and because Howard had a twenty-year-old brother and an eighteen-year-old sister (who were both off at college), his circumstances were remarkably similar to Ferguson's—a de facto only child who mostly came home to an empty house after school. Few suburban women had jobs in 1959, but Ferguson and his friend both had mothers who were more than just housewives, and consequently they had been forced to become more independent and self-reliant than the bulk of their classmates, and now that they were twelve and careening toward the gate of adolescence, the fact that they had large swaths of unsupervised time to themselves was proving to be an advantage, since at that stage of life parents were surely the least interesting people in the world, and the less one had to do with them the better. They could therefore go to Ferguson's house after school and turn on the television to watch *American Bandstand* or *Million Dollar Movie* without fear of being reprimanded for squandering the last precious hours of daylight by sitting indoors *on such a beautiful afternoon*. Twice that spring they even managed to talk Gloria Dolan and Peggy Goldstein into going back to the house with them for four-person dance parties in the living room, and because Ferguson and Gloria were old hands at kissing by then, their example inspired Howard and Peggy to attempt their own initiation into the complex art of tongue-bussing. On other afternoons, they would go to the Smalls' place instead, secure in the knowledge that they would not be interrupted or spied upon as they opened the bottom drawer of Howard's brother's desk and pulled out the pile of girlie magazines he kept stashed in there under the innocuous decoy of a high school chemistry book. Long conversations would follow about which naked woman had the prettiest face or the most attractive body, comparisons would be made between the models in *Playboy* and the ones in *Gent* and *Swank*, the slick, well-lit color photos of the quasi-unreal-looking *Playboy* women as opposed to the cruder, grainier images in the cheaper magazines, the glossified all-American young beauties and the older, more lascivious tramps with their harsh faces and bleached-blond hair, the point of the discussion always being which one was the most arousing to you and which woman would you most like to make love to when your body was ready to engage in real sex, something that for the moment was still not possible for either one of them, but it wouldn't be long now, maybe another six months, maybe a year, and finally they would go to sleep one night and wake up the next morning to discover they were men.

Ferguson had been tracking the changes in his body since the first sign of impending manhood appeared in the form of a single hair sprouting from his left armpit when he was ten and a half. He knew what it meant and was surprised, since it seemed to have come too early, and at that point he was not prepared to say good-bye to the boy-self that had belonged to him since birth. He found the hair ugly and ridiculous, an intruder sent by some alien force to mar his previously unblemished person, and therefore he plucked it out. Within days it had returned, however, along with an identical twin that arrived the following week, and then the right armpit swung into action as well, and before long the isolate strands were no longer distinguishable, the hairs were turning into nests of hair, and by the time he was twelve they had become a permanent fact of life. Ferguson watched with horror and fascination as other zones of his body were transformed as well, the almost invisible blondish down on his legs and forearms turning darker, thicker, and more abundant, the emergence of pubic hair on his once smooth lower belly, and then, just after he turned thirteen, the odious black fuzz that began germinating between his nose and upper lip, so disgusting and disfiguring that he shaved it off one morning with his father's electric razor, and when it grew back a couple of weeks later, he shaved it off again. The horror was not being in control of what was happening to him, of feeling that his body had been turned into the site of an experiment conducted by some mad, prankster scientist, and as new hair continued to proliferate over greater and greater areas of his skin, he couldn't help thinking about the Wolfman, the hero of that gruesome film he had seen with Howard on television one night back in the fall, the metamorphosis of a normal man into a woolly-faced monster, which Ferguson now understood was a parable about the helplessness one experiences during puberty, for you are doomed to become whatever your genes have decided you will be, and until the process is finished, you have no idea what the next day will bring. That was the horror of it. But along with the horror there was fascination, the knowledge that however long and difficult the journey might be, it would eventually lead to the kingdom of erotic bliss.

The problem was that Ferguson still knew nothing about the nature of that bliss, and struggle as he did to imagine what his body would feel in the throes of an orgasm, Ferguson's imagination continually failed him. His early double-digit years were filled with rumors and hearsay but no hard facts, mysterious, unconfirmed stories from boys with older, adolescent brothers that alluded to the unlikely spasms involved in the attainment of erotic bliss, the pulsing streams of milky white fluid that spurted out of your penis, for example, which some-times traveled several feet or even yards through the air, the so-called ejaculation, which was always accompanied by that much sought after blissful feeling, which Howard's brother Tom described as the best feel-ing in the world, but when Ferguson pressed him to be more specific and describe what that feeling was, Tom said he wouldn't know where to begin, it was too hard to put into words and Ferguson would simply have to wait until the time came for him to feel it himself, a frustrating answer that did nothing to alleviate Ferguson's ignorance, and while some of the technical terms were now familiar to him, such as the word *semen*, which was the sticky stuff that shot out of you and carried the sperm that were essential for creating babies, Ferguson invariably thought of a shipful of sailors whenever someone used that word in his presence, merchant seamen dressed in milky white uniforms coming ashore and heading for honky-tonk bars along the docks to flirt with half-naked women and join the old salts in drunken sea chanteys as a one-legged man in a striped shirt blasted out the tune on his ancient concertina. Poor Ferguson. His mind was in a muddle, and because he still couldn't imagine what any of the words really meant, his thoughts tended to dart out in several directions at once. Sea-man would soon become see-man, and an instant later he would imagine he was blind, tapping his way into the noisy bar with a white cane in his hand.

It was clear that the central actor in this drama was his groin. Or, to hark back to the terminology of the ancient Hebrews, his loins. That is to say, his privates, which in the medical literature were commonly referred to as genitalia. For as long as he could remember being him-self, it had always felt good to touch himself down there, to fiddle with his penis when no one was looking, in bed at night or early in the morn-ing, for example, manipulating that fleshy extrusion until it rose up stiffly in the air, doubling or tripling or even quadrupling in size, and with that startling mutation an inchoate sort of pleasure would begin to spread through his body, particularly the lower half of his body, a formless rush of feeling that was not yet bliss but suggested that bliss

would one day be achieved by a similar kind of friction. He was growing steadily now, every morning his body seemed to be a little larger
than it had been the day before, and the growth of his penis was keeping pace with the rest of him, no longer the nubby dickey bird of pre-
hair childhood but an ever more substantial appendage, which now
seemed to possess a mind of its own, lengthening and hardening at the
least provocation, especially on those afternoons when he and Howard
studied Tom's nudie magazines. They were in junior high school now,
and one day Howard repeated a joke he had been told by his brother:

A science teacher asks his students: What part of the body can
expand to six times its normal size? He points his finger at Miss
McGillacuddy, but instead of answering the question, the girl begins to
blush and covers her face with her hands. The teacher then points at
Mr. MacDonald, who quickly responds: The pupils of the eyes. Correct,
says the teacher, and then he turns back to the blushing Miss McGillacuddy and addresses her with an irritation bordering on contempt. I
have three things to tell you, young lady, he says. One: You haven't been
doing your homework. Two: You have a dirty, filthy mind. And three:
You're in for a life of bitter disappointment.

Not six times, then, not even after he was fully grown. There were
limits to what he could expect from the future, but whatever the exact
measurements were, whatever the proportions between soft repose and
hard readiness, the increase would be sufficient unto the day, and the
night of that day, and all the nights and days that followed.

Junior high was unquestionably superior to the grammar school
that had held him prisoner for the past seven years, and with more than
a thousand students charging through the halls at the end of each fifty-
minute period, he no longer had to endure the suffocating intimacy of
being trapped in a room with the same twenty-three or twenty-four
people every Monday through Friday from the beginning of September to the end of June. The Gang of Nine was a thing of the past, and
even Krolik and his three toadies had essentially disappeared from
view, since Ferguson rarely crossed paths with them anymore. Timmerman was still present, a fellow class member in four of Ferguson's academic subjects, but the two boys coexisted by going out of their way to
ignore each other, a less than happy standoff but not an unbearable one.
Better yet, Timmerman and Susie Krauss had parted ways, just as Ferguson had hoped they would, and because Ferguson himself had lost

contact with Gloria Dolan over the summer, his first kissing mate had now cast her eyes on handsome Mark Connelly, which disappointed Ferguson but didn't entirely crush him, since a path had been opened for him to go after Susie Krauss, the girl of his sixth-grade dreams, and he jumped at his chance by calling her one evening during the first week of school, which led to a Saturday afternoon visit to his father's tennis center, which in turn led to their first kiss the following Saturday and many other kisses on subsequent Fridays and Saturdays over the next few months, and then they too parted ways, with Susie falling into the arms of the aforementioned Mark Connelly, who had lost Gloria Dolan to a boy named Rick Bassini, and Ferguson pining for an ever more attractive Peggy Goldstein, who had broken off with Howard sometime ago, but Ferguson's best friend had recovered with his heart intact and was now offering that same heart to the bright and bubbly Edie Cantor.

So it went throughout that year of ephemeral crushes and round-robin loves, which was also the year when more and more of his friends turned up at school with braces on their teeth, and the year when everyone began to worry about outbreaks of bad skin. Ferguson felt lucky. So far, his face had been attacked by just three or four modest volcanoes, which he had popped at the first opportunity, and his parents had decided his teeth were straight enough to spare him the ordeals of orthodontia. More than that, they had insisted he go back to Camp Paradise for another summer. He had assumed that thirteen was perhaps a bit too old for camp and had therefore asked his father over the Christmas holidays if he could spend July and August working at the tennis center, but his father had laughed, saying there would be plenty of time for work later. You need to be out in the air, Archie, his father told him, running around with boys your own age. Besides, you can't get your working papers until you're fourteen. Not in New Jersey you can't, and you wouldn't want to get me into trouble for breaking the law, would you?

FERGUSON WAS HAPPY at camp. He had always been happy there, and it was good to be reunited with his New York summer friends, the half dozen city boys who kept going back year after year as he did. He took pleasure in the eternal sarcasm and humor of their fast-talking, high-spirited selves, which often reminded him of the way American soldiers spoke to one another in movies about World War II, the jocular, wise-cracking banter, the compulsion never to take anything seriously, to turn every situation into an excuse for yet another joke or mocking aside. No doubt there was something admirable about attacking life with such wit and irreverence, but it could also become wearisome at times, and whenever Ferguson had his fill of his cabinmates' verbal antics, he would find himself missing Howard, his close friend of the past two years, the closest friend he had ever had, and with Howard far away at his aunt and uncle's dairy farm in Vermont, where he spent all his summers, Ferguson began writing letters to him during the one-hour rest period after lunch, numerous short and long letters in which he set down whatever he happened to be thinking about at the moment, for Howard was the one person in the world he could unburden himself to, the one person he was not afraid to trust or confide in, the singular, unimpeachable friend with whom he could share everything, from criticisms of other people to comments about books he had read to musings about the difficulty of suppressing farts in public to thoughts about God.

There were sixteen letters in all, and Howard kept them in a square wooden box, holding on to them even after he had grown up and begun his life as an adult because the thirteen-year-old Ferguson, his friend of the straight teeth and shining countenance, the founder of the long defunct but never forgotten *Cobble Road Crusader*, the boy who had broken his leg at six and gashed his foot at three and nearly drowned at five, who had weathered the depredations of the Gang of Nine and the Band of Four, who had kissed Gloria Dolan and Susie Krauss and Peggy Goldstein, who had been counting the days until he entered the kingdom of erotic bliss, who had assumed and expected and entirely taken for granted that there were many years of life still in front of him, did not live to the end of the summer. That was why Howard Small saved those sixteen letters—because they were the last traces of Ferguson's presence on this earth.

"I don't believe in God anymore," he wrote in one of them. "At least not the God of Judaism, Christianity, or any other religion. The Bible says that God created man in his own image. But men wrote the Bible, didn't they? Which means that man created God in *his* image. Which also means that God doesn't watch over us, and he certainly doesn't give a damn about what men think or do or feel. If he cared about us at all, he wouldn't have made a world with so many terrible things in it. Men wouldn't fight wars and kill each other and build concentration camps. They wouldn't lie and cheat and steal. I'm not saying that God didn't create the world (no man did that!), but once the job was done he disappeared into the atoms and molecules of the universe and left us to fight it out among ourselves."

"I'm glad Kennedy won the nomination," he wrote in another letter. "I liked him better than the other candidates, and I'm sure he'll beat Nixon in the fall. I don't know why I'm sure, but it's hard to imagine Americans wanting a man called Tricky Dick to be their president."

"There are six other boys in my cabin," he wrote in yet another letter, "and three of them are old enough to 'do it' now. They jerk off in their beds at night and tell the rest of us how good it feels. Two days ago, they did what they call a circle jerk and let us watch, so I finally saw what the stuff looks like and how far it spurts. It's not milky white but a sort of creamy white, a bit like mayonnaise or hair tonic. Then one of the three jerk-off kings, a big guy named Andy, got another boner and did something that amazed me and everyone else. He bent over and sucked his own dick! I didn't know it was humanly possible to do that. I mean, how could anyone be flexible enough to twist his body into that position? I tried to do it myself in the bathroom yesterday morning, but I couldn't get my mouth anywhere near my dick. Just as well, I suppose. I wouldn't want to walk around thinking of myself as a cocksucker, would I? But still, what a strange thing it was to see."

"I've read three books since I've been here," he wrote in the last letter, which was dated August ninth, "and I thought they were all terrific. Two of them were sent to me by my Aunt Mildred, a little one by Franz Kafka called *The Metamorphosis* and a bigger one by J. D. Salinger called *The Catcher in the Rye*. The other one was given to me by my cousin Francie's husband, Gary—*Candide*, by Voltaire. The Kafka book is by far the weirdest and most difficult to read, but I loved it. A man wakes up one morning and discovers that he's been turned into an enormous insect! It sounds like science fiction or a horror story, but it isn't. It's about the man's soul. *The Catcher in the Rye* is about a high school boy wandering around New York. Nothing much happens in it, but the way Holden talks (he's the hero) is very realistic and true, and you can't help liking him and wishing you could be his friend. *Candide* is an old book from the 18th century, but it's wild and funny, and I laughed out loud on almost every page. Gary called it a political satire. I call it great stuff!

You must read it—and the other ones too. Now that I've finished them all, what strikes me is how different these three books are. They're all written in their own way, and they're all very good, which means that there isn't just one way to write a good book. Last year, Mr. Dempsey kept telling us there was a right way and a wrong way—remember? Maybe with math and science there are, but not with books. You do them in your own way, and if your way is a good way, you can write a good book. The interesting thing is that I can't decide which one I liked best. You'd think I would know, but I don't. I loved them all. Which means, I guess, that any good way is the right way. It makes me happy to think about all the books I still haven't read—hundreds of them, thousands of them. So much to look forward to!"

The last day of Ferguson's life, August 10, 1960, began with a brief rain shower just after dawn, but by the time reveille sounded at seven-thirty, the clouds had blown off to the east and the sky was blue. Ferguson and his six cabinmates headed to the mess hall with their counselor, Bill Kaufman, who had finished his sophomore year at Brooklyn College in June, and during the thirty or forty minutes it took them to eat their oatmeal and scrambled eggs, the clouds returned, and as the boys walked back to the cabin for cleanup and inspection, rain was beginning to fall again, a rain so fine and inconsequential that it hardly seemed to matter that no one was wearing a poncho or carrying an umbrella. Their T-shirts were covered with dark specks of moisture, but that was the extent of it—the mildest of mild dousings, water in such small quantities that it didn't even make them wet. As they started in on the morning ritual of making their beds and sweeping the floor, however, the sky continued to darken, and before long the rain began to fall in earnest, hitting the roof of the cabin with larger, ever more accelerated drops. For a minute or two, there was a lovely sort of off-key syncopation to the sound, Ferguson felt, but then the intensity of the rain increased, and the effect was lost. The rain wasn't making music anymore. It had turned into a mass of dense, undifferentiated sound, a percussive blur. Bill told them that a new weather system was heading in from the south, and with a cold front simultaneously coming down from the north, they could expect a long, hard soak. Get comfortable, boys, he said. It's going to be a big storm, and we'll be sitting in this cabin for most of the day.

The dark sky grew even darker, and inside the cabin it was becoming difficult to see. Bill switched on the overhead light, but even after the light came on it still felt dark in there, for the seventy-five-watt bulb was too high up in the rafters to illuminate much of anything down below. Ferguson was on his bed, flipping through a back issue of *Mad* magazine that had been circulating around the cabin, reading with the aid of his flashlight and wondering if any morning had ever been as dark as this one. The rain was battering the roof now, a full-bore assault, pounding on the shingles as if the liquid drops had turned to stone, millions of stones were falling from the sky and hammering down on them, and then, far off in the distance, Ferguson heard a dull basso rumbling, a thick, congested noise that made him think of someone clearing his throat, thunder that must have been many miles away from them, somewhere in the mountains, perhaps, and this struck Ferguson as odd, since in his experience the thunder and lightning of electric storms had always come in tandem with the rain, but in this instance it was already raining, raining as hard as it could possibly rain, and the thunder was still nowhere near them, which led Ferguson to speculate that perhaps there were two storms going on at once, not just a storm and a cold front, as Bill had said, but two separate storms, one directly overhead and the other approaching from the north, and if the first storm didn't play itself out before the second storm arrived, the two storms would crash into each other and merge, and that would create one hell of a mighty storm, Ferguson said to himself, a monumental storm, the storm to end all storms.

The bed to the right of Ferguson's was occupied by a boy named Hal Krasner. Since the beginning of the summer, the two of them had kept up a running gag in which they impersonated smart George and stupid Lennie, the drifters from *Of Mice and Men*, a book they had both read earlier in the year and found ripe with comic possibilities. Ferguson was George and Krasner was Lennie, and nearly every day they would spend a few minutes improvising crackpot dialogues for their chosen characters, a steady round of nonsense that would begin with Lennie asking George to tell him what it was going to be like when they got to heaven, for example, or George reminding Lennie not to pick his nose in public, idiotic exchanges that probably owed more to Laurel and Hardy than to Steinbeck, but it amused the boys to indulge in these shenanigans, and with rain now pouring down on the camp and everyone stuck inside, Krasner was in the mood to have another go at it.

Please, George, he said. Please make it stop. I can't stand it no more.

Make what stop, Lennie? Ferguson asked.

The rain, George. The noise of the rain. It's too loud, and it's beginning to drive me crazy.

You've always been crazy, Lennie. You know that.

Not crazy, George. Just stupid.

Stupid, yes. But also crazy.

I can't help it, George. I was born that way.

No one's saying it's your fault, Lennie.

Well?

Well what?

Are you going to stop the rain for me?

Only the boss can do that.

But you're the boss, George. You've always been the boss.

I mean the big boss. The one and only.

I don't know no one and only. I only know you, George.

It would take a miracle to pull off a thing like that.

That's all right. You can do anything.

Can I?

The noise is making me sick, George. I think I'll die if you don't do it.

Krasner put his hands over his ears and moaned. He was Lennie telling George that he had come to the limit of his strength, and Ferguson-as-George nodded in sad commiseration, knowing that no man could stop the rain from falling, that miracles were beyond the scope of mankind's power, but Ferguson-as-Ferguson was having trouble keeping up his end of the act, Krasner's sick-cow moans were simply too funny, and after listening to them for another few seconds, Ferguson burst out laughing, which broke the spell of the charade for him although not for Krasner, who assumed that Ferguson was laughing as George, and therefore, still posing as Lennie, Krasner removed his hands from his ears and said:

It ain't nice to laugh at a man like that, George. I might not be the smartest guy in the county, but I got a soul, just like you and everyone else, and if you don't wipe that grin off your face, I'll snap your neck in two, just like I done to them rabbits.

Now that Krasner-as-Lennie had delivered such an earnest and effective speech, Ferguson felt obliged to force himself back into character, to become George again for Krasner's sake and the sake of the other boys who were listening to them, but just as he was about to open his lungs and shout out an order for the rain to stop—*Enough with the waterworks, boss!*—the sky blasted forth a piercing clap of thunder, a noise so loud and so explosive that it shook the floor of the cabin and rattled the window frames, which went on humming and vibrating until the next burst of thunder rattled them again. Half of the boys jumped, jerked forward, twitched involuntarily in response to the sounds, while others called out by pure reflex, the air shooting from their lungs in short, startled exclamations that seemed to be words but were in fact instinctive grunts in the form of words—*wow, whoa, waw.* The rain was still coming down hard, lashing against the windows and making it difficult to see anything through them—nothing more than a wavy, watery darkness lit up by sudden spears of lightning, all black for ten or twenty heartbeats and then a moment or two of blinding white light. The storm that Ferguson had imagined, the vast double storm that would fuse into one storm when the air from the north and the air from the south collided, was upon them now, and it was even bigger and better than he had hoped it would be. A grand tempest. An axe of fury tearing apart the heavens. An exhilaration.

Don't worry, Lennie, he said to Krasner. There's no need to be scared. I'm going to put an end to this noise right now.

Without pausing to tell anyone what he was about to do, Ferguson leapt off his bed and ran for the door, which he yanked open with a hard, two-handed tug, and even though he could hear Bill's voice shouting behind him—*What the hell, Archie! Are you crazy!*—he didn't stop. He understood that it was indeed a crazy thing to be doing, but the fact was that he wanted to be crazy just then, and he wanted to be out in the storm, to taste the storm, to be part of the storm, to be inside the storm for as long as it took for the storm to be inside him.

The rain was superb. Once Ferguson crossed the threshold and stepped out onto the ground, he realized that no rain had ever fallen harder, that the drops of this rain were thicker and traveling faster than any other drops he had known, that they were rushing down from the sky with the force of lead pellets and were heavy enough to bruise his skin and perhaps even dent his skull. A magnificent rain, an all-powerful rain, but in order to savor it to the fullest, he figured he should run to the cluster of oaks that stood about twenty yards in front of him, for the leaves and branches would protect his body from those falling bullets, and so Ferguson made a break for it, dashing across the soggy, slippery ground toward the trees, splashing through ankle-deep puddles as thunder boomed above him and around him and bolts of lightning shot down within yards of his feet. He was thoroughly soaked by the time he got there, but it felt good to be soaked, it was the best of all good feelings to be soaked like that, and Ferguson felt happy, happier than he had been at any time that summer or any other summer or any other time of his life, for surely this was the greatest thing he had ever done.

There was little or no wind. The storm wasn't a hurricane or a typhoon, it was a raging downpour with thunder to stir up his bones and lightning to dazzle his eyes, and Ferguson wasn't the least bit afraid of that lightning, since he was wearing sneakers and had no metal objects with him, not even a wristwatch or a belt with a silver buckle, and therefore he felt safe and exultant under the shelter of the trees, looking out at the gray wall of water that stood between him and the cabin, watching the dim, almost entirely obscured figure of his counselor Bill, who was standing in the open doorway and seemed to be shouting to him, or shouting at him as he gestured for Ferguson to come back to the cabin, but Ferguson couldn't hear a word he was saying, not with the noise of the rain and the thunder, and especially not when Ferguson himself began to howl, no longer George on his mission to save Lennie but simply Ferguson himself, a thirteen-year-old boy wailing in exaltation at the thought of being alive in such a world as the one he had been given that morning, and even when a shaft of lightning struck the top branch of one of the trees, Ferguson paid no attention to it, for he knew he was safe, and then he saw that Bill had left the cabin and was running toward him, why in the world would he do that, Ferguson asked himself, but before he could answer the question, the branch had broken off from the tree and was falling toward Ferguson's head. He felt the impact, felt the wood crack down on him as if someone had clubbed him from behind, and then he felt nothing, nothing at all or ever again, and as his inert body lay on the water-soaked ground, the rain continued to pour down on him and the thunder continued to crack, and from one end of the earth to the other, the gods were silent.

HIS GRANDFATHER CALLED IT A *CURIOUS INTERREGNUM*, MEANING A time that stood between two other times, a time of no time when all the rules about how you were supposed to live had been thrown out the window, and even though the fatherless boy understood that it couldn't last forever, he wished it could have gone on longer than the two months he had been given, another two months on top of the first two, perhaps, or another six months, or maybe even a year. It had been good to live in that time of no school, that curious gap between one life and the next when his mother was with him from the second he opened his eyes in the morning until the second he closed them at night, for she was the only person who felt real to him anymore, the only real person left in the world, and how good it had been to share those days and weeks with her, those strange two months of eating out in restaurants and visiting empty apartments and going to the movies nearly every afternoon, so many movies watched together in the darkness of the balcony, where they could cry whenever they wanted to and not have to explain themselves to anyone. His mother called it *wallowing in the mud*, and by that Ferguson supposed she meant the mud of their unhappiness, but sinking into that unhappiness could be eerily satisfying, he discovered, as long as you sank into it as far as you could and weren't afraid to drown, and because the tears kept pushing them back into the past, they had protected them from having to think about the future, but then one day his mother said it was time to start thinking about it, and the crying came to an end.

Unfortunately, school was inevitable. Much as Ferguson would have wished to prolong his freedom, it was not in his power to control such things, and once he and his mother decided to rent the apartment on Central Park West, the next order of business was to place him in a good private school. Public school was out of the question. Aunt Mildred was emphatic about that point, and in a rare instance of accord between the sisters, Ferguson's mother followed her advice, knowing that Mildred was better informed on matters of education than she was, and why throw Archie onto the rugged asphalt of a public school playground when she could afford the expense of private school tuition? She only wanted what was best for her boy, and New York had turned into a grimmer, more dangerous city than the one she had left in 1944, with youth gangs roaming the streets of the Upper West Side armed with switchblades and deadly zip guns, just twenty-five blocks north of where her parents lived and yet another universe, a neighborhood that had been transformed by the influx of Puerto Rican immigrants in the past few years, a dirtier, poorer, more colorful place than it had been during the war, the air now charged with unfamiliar smells and sounds, a different sort of energy animating the sidewalks on Columbus and Amsterdam Avenues, one had only to step outdoors to feel an undercurrent of menace and confusion, and Ferguson's mother, who had always felt so comfortable in New York as a child and young woman, worried about her son's safety. The second half of the curious interregnum was consequently devoted to more than just shopping for furniture and going to the movies, there were also the half dozen private schools on Mildred's list to be looked at and discussed, the tours of classrooms and facilities, the interviews with headmasters and admissions directors, the I.Q. tests and entrance exams, and when Ferguson was accepted by Mildred's number one choice, the Hilliard School for Boys, there was such rejoicing in the family, such a wave of warmth and enthusiasm washing over him from his grandparents and his mother and his aunt and uncle and his Great-aunt Pearl that the nearly eight-year-old fatherless boy figured school might not be such a bad way to pass the time, after all. It wasn't going to be easy to fit in, of course, not when it was late February and the school year was almost two-thirds finished, and it wasn't going to be fun having to wear a jacket and tie every day, but perhaps it wouldn't be a problem, and perhaps he would begin to get used to the clothes, but even if it was a problem and he didn't get used to the clothes, it wasn't going to make any difference, for he was on his way to the Hilliard School for Boys whether he liked it or not.

He went there because Aunt Mildred had convinced his mother that Hilliard was one of the best schools in the city, with *a long-standing reputation for academic excellence,* but no one had told Ferguson that his fellow students would be among the richest children in America, the scions of privileged, old-money New York, or that he would be the only boy in his class who lived on the West Side and one of only eleven non-Christians in a school with a K-through-12 enrollment of nearly six hundred. At first, no one suspected he was anything other than a Scottish Presbyterian, an understandable error in light of the name his grandfather had been given after the Rockefeller bungle of 1900, but then one of the teachers noticed that Ferguson's lips weren't moving when he was supposed to be saying *Jesus Christ, our Lord* at morning chapel, and word eventually got out that he was one of the eleven and not one of the five hundred and seventy-six. Add in the fact that he entered the school as a latecomer, a mostly silent boy with no ties to anyone in the class, and it would appear that Ferguson's tenure at Hilliard was doomed from the start, doomed before he even set foot in the building on his first day.

It wasn't that anyone was unkind to him, or that anyone harassed him, or that he was made to feel unwelcome. As with every other school, there were friendly boys and neutral boys and nasty boys, but not even the nastiest among them ever taunted Ferguson for being a Jew. Hilliard might have been a stuffy, jacket-and-tie sort of place, but it also preached tolerance and the virtues of gentlemanly self-control, and any act of overt prejudice would have been dealt with harshly by the authorities. More subtly, and more confusingly, what Ferguson had to contend with was a guileless sort of ignorance that seemed to have been injected into his classmates at birth. Even Doug Hayes, the ever amiable and good-hearted Dougie Hayes, who had made a point of befriending Ferguson from the moment he arrived at Hilliard, who had been the first boy to invite him to a birthday party and had subsequently asked him over to his parents' townhouse on East Seventy-eighth Street no fewer than a dozen times, could still ask, after having known Ferguson for nine months, what he was planning to do on Thanksgiving.

Eat turkey, Ferguson said. That's what we do every year. My mother and I go to my grandparents' apartment and eat turkey with stuffing and gravy.

Oh, Dougie said. I had no idea.

Why not? Ferguson answered. Isn't that what you do?

Of course. I just didn't know your people celebrated Thanksgiving.

My people?

You know. Jewish people.

Why wouldn't we celebrate Thanksgiving?

Because it's kind of an American thing, I guess. The Pilgrims. Plymouth Rock. All those English guys with the funny black hats who came over on the *Mayflower.*

Ferguson was so bewildered by Dougie's comment that he didn't know what to say. Until that moment, it had never occurred to him that he might not be an American, or, more precisely, that his way of being an American was any less authentic than the way Dougie and the other boys were American, but that was what his friend seemed to be asserting: that there was a difference between them, an elusive, indefinable quality that had to do with black-hatted English ancestors and the length of time spent on this side of the ocean and the money to live in four-story townhouses on the Upper East Side that made some families more American than others, and in the end the difference was so great that the less American families could barely be considered American at all.

No doubt his mother had chosen the wrong school for him, but in spite of that perplexing conversation about Jewish dining habits on national feast days, not to mention other perplexing moments both before and after his talk with Dougie H., Ferguson never felt any desire to leave Hilliard. Even if he failed to grasp the peculiar customs and beliefs of the world he had entered, he did his best to comply with them, and not once did he blame his mother or Aunt Mildred for having sent him there. He had to be somewhere, after all. The law said that every child under the age of sixteen had to go to school, and as far as he was concerned, Hilliard was no better or no worse than any other penitentiary for the young. It wasn't the school's fault that he did so badly there. In those bleak early days following Stanley Ferguson's death, young Ferguson had concluded that he was living in an upside-down universe of infinitely reversible propositions (day = night, hope = despair, power = weakness), which meant that when it came to the question of school he was now obliged to fail rather than succeed, and given how good it felt not to care anymore, to court failure as a matter of principle and will himself into the comforting arms of humiliation and defeat, it was all but certain that he would have failed just as gloriously anywhere else.

His teachers found him *lazy and unmotivated, indifferent to authority, distracted, stubborn, shockingly undisciplined, a human puzzle.* The boy who had answered every question on the entrance exam correctly, who had won over the admissions director with his sweet nature and precocious insights, the late-in-the-year add-on who was supposed to bring home top marks in every subject earned only one Excellent on his first report card, which was issued in April of his second-grade year. The subject was gym. A grade of Good for reading, writing, and penmanship (he had tried to do worse, but he was still a beginner at masking his talents), Satisfactory in music (he couldn't resist belting out the Negro spirituals and Irish folk songs that Mr. Bowles taught them, even though he struggled to stay in tune), and Poor in everything else, which included math, science, art, social studies, comportment, citizenship, and attitude. The next and final report card, which was issued in June, was almost identical to the first, the only difference being his grade in math, which descended from Poor to Fail (he had perfected the art of giving wrong answers to arithmetic questions by then, three out of every five on average, but he still couldn't bring himself to misspell more than a tenth of his words). Under normal circumstances, Ferguson would not have been asked back for the following year. His work had been so hideously subpar as to suggest profound psychological trouble, and a school like Hilliard was not accustomed to carrying dead weight, at least not when the flunker came from a non-legacy family, *legacy* meaning a third- or fourth- or fifth-generation boy whose father wrote out a check every year or sat on the board of trustees. They were willing to give Ferguson another chance, however, for they understood that his circumstances were anything but normal. Mr. Ferguson had died in the middle of the school year, a sudden, violent death that had sent the boy spinning into the nether zones of grief and disintegration, and surely he deserved a little more time to pull himself together. He had too much potential for them to give up on him after just three and a half months, and therefore they informed Ferguson's mother that her son would have one more year to prove himself. If he could turn it around by then, he would no longer be on probation. If not, well, that would be that, and good luck to him wherever he happened to land.

Ferguson hated himself for having disappointed his mother, whose life was hard enough without having to fret about his rotten performance at school, but there were more important issues at stake than trying to please her or bending over backward to impress the family with a report card full of Excellents and Very Goods. He knew that life would have been simpler for him and everyone else if he had toed the line and done what was expected of him. How easy and thoroughly uncomplicated it would have been to stop giving wrong answers on purpose, to begin paying attention again and make everyone proud of him for being such a conscientious boy, but Ferguson had embarked on a grand experiment, a secret investigation into the most fundamental matters concerning life and death, and he couldn't turn back now, he was traveling down a rough and perilous road, alone among the rocks and twisting mountain paths, in danger of falling off the precipice at any moment, but until enough information had been gathered to provide him with conclusive results, he would have to go on putting himself at risk—even if it meant being expelled from the Hilliard School for Boys, even if it meant turning himself into a disgrace.

The question was: Why had God stopped talking to him? And if God was silent now, did that mean He would be silent forever or eventually start talking to him again? And if He never talked again, could it mean that Ferguson had deluded himself and God had never been there in the first place?

For as long as he could remember, the voice had been in his head, talking to him whenever he was alone, a quiet, measured voice that was at once reassuring and commanding, a baritone murmur bearing the verbal emanations of the great invisible spirit who ruled the world, and Ferguson had always felt comforted by that voice, protected by that voice, which told him that as long as he kept up his end of the bargain all would go well for him, his end being an eternal promise to be good, to treat others with kindness and generosity, and to obey the holy commandments, which meant never lying or stealing or succumbing to envy, which meant loving his parents and working hard at school and staying out of trouble, and Ferguson believed in the voice and did his best to follow its instructions at all times, and since God seemed to be keeping up His end of the bargain by making things go well for him, Ferguson felt loved and happy, secure in the knowledge that God believed in him just as much as he believed in God. So it went until he was seven and a half, and then one morning in early November, a morning that felt no different from any other morning, his mother walked into his room and told him his father was dead, and everything suddenly changed. God had lied to him. The great invisible spirit could no longer be trusted, and even though He went on talking to Ferguson for the next several days, asking for another chance to prove Himself, beseeching the fatherless boy to stay with him *through this dark time of death and mourning,* Ferguson was so angry at Him that he refused to listen. Then, four days after the funeral, the voice abruptly went silent, and since that day it hadn't spoken again.

That was the challenge now: to figure out whether God was still with him in the silence or whether He had vanished from his life for good. Ferguson didn't have the heart to commit a knowing act of cruelty, he couldn't bring himself to lie or cheat or steal, he had no inclination to hurt or offend his mother, but within the narrow scope of misdeeds he was capable of, he understood that the only way to answer the question was to break his end of the bargain as often as he could, to defy the injunction to follow the holy commandments and then wait for God to do something bad to him, something nasty and personal that would serve as a clear sign of intended retribution—a broken arm, an attack of boils on his face, a rabid dog biting off a chunk of his leg. If God failed to punish him, that would prove He had indeed disappeared when the voice stopped talking, and since God was supposedly everywhere, in every tree and blade of grass, in every gust of wind and human feeling, it made no sense that He could disappear from one place and still be everywhere else. He necessarily had to be with Ferguson because He was in all places at the same time, and if He was absent from the place where Ferguson happened to be, that could only mean that He was in no place and had never been in any place at all, that He in fact had never existed and the voice Ferguson had taken for the voice of God had been none other than his own voice speaking to him in an inner conversation with himself.

The first act of revolt had been tearing up the Ted Williams baseball card, the precious card that Jeff Balsoni had slipped into his hand a couple of days after he returned to school as a gesture of undying friendship and commiseration. How disgusting it had been to destroy that gift, and how shameful it had been to turn his eyes away from Mrs. Costello and pretend she hadn't been there, and now that he was at Hilliard, how unconscionable it was for him to be pursuing his campaign of willful self-sabotage, building on his efforts of the first year to establish a new pattern of maddeningly inconsistent results, a far more effective strategy than one of pure failure, he decided, a hundred percent on two math tests in a row, for example, and then twenty-five percent on the next, forty percent on the one after that, and then ninety percent followed by a dead-last zero, how mystified they all were by him, his teachers and classmates alike, not to mention his poor mother and the rest of his family, and yet even though Ferguson continued to spit on the rules of responsible human behavior, no dog had jumped up to bite him on the leg, no boulder had dropped on his foot, no slamming door had crushed his nose, and it seemed that God had no interest in punishing him, for Ferguson had been engaged in a life of crime for almost a year now, and still there wasn't a single scratch on him.

That should have settled the matter once and for all, but it didn't. If God wouldn't punish him, that meant He couldn't punish him, and therefore He didn't exist. Or so Ferguson had assumed, but now that God was on the verge of being lost to him forever, he asked himself: What if he had already been punished enough? What if the killing of his father had been punishment on such a grand scale, a tragedy with such monstrous, everlasting effects, that God had decided to spare him from any other punishments in the future? That seemed possible to him, by no means certain but possible, yet with the voice still silent after so many months, Ferguson had no way of confirming his intuition. God had wronged him, and now He was struggling to make it up to Ferguson by treating him with divine gentleness and mercy. If the voice could no longer tell him what he needed to know, perhaps God could communicate with him in some other way, through some inaudible sign that would prove He was still listening to his thoughts, and so began the final stage of Ferguson's long theological inquiry, the months of silent prayer when he begged God to reveal Himself to him or else lose the right to bear the name of God. Ferguson wasn't asking for some grand, biblical revelation, a mighty clap of thunder or a sudden parting of the seas, no, he would have been content with something small, an infinitesimal miracle that only he himself would have been aware of: for the wind to blow hard enough to push an errant scrap of paper across the street before the traffic light changed color, for his watch to stop ticking for ten seconds and then start again, for a single drop of rain to fall from a cloudless sky and land on his finger, for his mother to say the word *mysterious* within the next thirty seconds, for the radio to turn on by itself, for seventeen people to pass in front of the window within the next minute and a half, for the robin on the grass in Central Park to pull out a worm before the next plane passed overhead, for three cars to honk their horns at the same time, for the book in his hand to fall open to page 97, for the wrong date to appear on the front page of the morning paper, for a quarter to be lying next to his foot when he looked down at the sidewalk, for the Dodgers to score three runs in the bottom of the ninth and win the game, for his Great-aunt Pearl's cat to wink at him, for everyone in the room to yawn at the same time, for everyone in the room to laugh at the same time, for no one in the room to make a sound for the next thirty-three and a third seconds. One by one, Ferguson wished for those things to happen, those things and many others as well, and when none of them happened over six months of wordless supplication, he stopped wishing for anything and turned his thoughts away from God.

YEARS LATER, HIS mother confessed to him that for her too the beginning had been less difficult than what came next. The curious interregnum had been almost bearable, she said, with so many urgent, practical decisions to be made, the matter of selling her house and business in New Jersey, of finding a place to live in New York, of furnishing that place while she went about the job of putting Ferguson in a proper school, the sudden onslaught of obligations that fell down on her during the early days of her widowhood had not been a burden so much as a welcome distraction, a way of not having to think about the Newark fire every minute of her waking life, and thank God for all those movies, she added, and the darkness of the theaters on those cold winter days, and the chance to disappear into the make-believe of those dumb stories, and thank God for you too, Archie, she told him, my brave little man, my rock, my anchor, for the longest time you were the only real person left in the world for me, and without you what would I have done, Archie, what would I have lived for, and how on earth would I have been able to go on?

No doubt she had been half-crazed during those months, she said, a madwoman fueled by cigarettes, coffee, and steady bursts of adrenaline, but once the questions of home and school had been answered, the whirlwind subsided and then stopped altogether, and she sank into a long period of thought and reflection, horrible days, horrible nights, a time of numbness and indecision when she weighed one possibility against another and struggled to imagine where she wanted the future to take her. She was lucky in that regard, she said, lucky to be in a position to choose between alternatives, but the fact was that she had money now, more money than she had ever dreamed of having, two hundred thousand dollars from the life insurance alone, not to mention the money she had collected from the sale of the Millburn house and Roseland Photo, which included the additional sums she had earned from selling the furniture in the house and the equipment in the studio, and even after she deducted the thousands she had spent on the new furniture and the annual cost of sending Ferguson to private school and the monthly cost of renting the apartment, she had more than enough left over to do nothing for the next twelve or fifteen years, to go on living off her dead husband until the day her son graduated from college— and far beyond that if she found herself a clever stocks-and-bonds man and invested in the market. She was thirty-three years old. No longer a beginner in life, but hardly what one would call a has-been, and though it comforted her to muse on the blessings of her good fortune, to know that it was within her power to live a life of leisure well into her old age if she was of a mind to do that, as the months passed and she continued to meditate and do nothing, her time mostly given over to traveling through Central Park four times a day on the crosstown bus, taking Ferguson to school in the morning and then returning home, picking up Ferguson in the afternoon and again returning home, and on the mornings when she couldn't bring herself to jump back on the bus and return to the West Side, she would spend the six and a half hours Ferguson was in school wandering around the East Side, browsing alone in shops, lunching alone in restaurants, going to movies alone, going to museums alone, and after three and a half months of that routine, followed by a strange, empty summer holed up in a rented house on the Jersey shore with her son, where they spent the bulk of their time indoors watching television together, she discovered she was growing restless, itching to work again. It had taken her the better part of a year to reach that point, but once she got there, the Leica and the Rolleiflex finally came out of the closet, and before long Ferguson's mother was sailing on a ship headed back to the land of photography.

She went about it differently this time, throwing herself out into the world rather than inviting the world to come to her, no longer interested in maintaining a studio at a fixed address, which she now felt was an outmoded way of doing photography, needlessly cumbersome in a time of rapid transformations, with new high-speed film stocks and ever more efficient lightweight cameras overturning the field, making it possible to rethink her old ideas about light and composition, to reinvent herself and move beyond the limits of classical portraiture, and by the time Ferguson began his second year at Hilliard, his mother was already casting about for work, stumbling onto her first job in late September when the man who had been hired to take pictures at her cousin Charlotte's wedding fell down a flight of stairs and broke his leg, and because there was only a week to go before the day of the wedding, she volunteered to fill in for him at no charge. The synagogue was out somewhere in the Flatbush section of Brooklyn, the old neighborhood of the first Archie and Great-aunt Pearl, and between the marriage ceremony and the removal of the wedding party to a catering hall two blocks to the south, Ferguson's mother used her tripod to take formal black-and-white portraits of all the family members in attendance, the bride and groom to begin with, twenty-nine-year-old Charlotte, who had seemed destined never to marry anyone after her fiancé was killed in the Korean War, and thirty-six-year-old widower dentist Nathan Birnbaum, followed by Great-aunt Pearl, Ferguson's Nana and Papa, Charlotte's twin sister, Betty, and her accountant husband, Seymour Graf, Aunt Mildred (who was now teaching at Sarah Lawrence) and her husband, Paul Sandler (who worked as an editor at Random House), and finally Ferguson himself in a picture with his two second cousins (Betty and Seymour's children), five-year-old Eric and three-year-old Judy. Once the party began at the catering hall, Ferguson's mother abandoned her tripod and spent the next three and a half hours wandering among the guests, taking hundreds of pictures of the ninety-six people who were there, unposed, spontaneous shots of old men in quiet conversation with one another, of young women laughing as they drank wine and shoveled food into their mouths, of children dancing with grown-ups and grown-ups dancing together after the meal was done, all the faces of all those people captured in the natural light of that bare, unglamorous setting, the musicians perched on their small stage as they clanged forth their tired, corny songs, Great-aunt Pearl smiling as she kissed her granddaughter's cheek, Benjy Adler whooping it up on the dance floor with a twenty-year-old distant cousin from Canada, a frowning nine-year-old girl sitting alone at a table with a half-eaten piece of cake in front of her, and at one point during the festivities, Uncle Paul walked up to his sister-in-law and remarked that she seemed to be enjoying herself, that he hadn't seen her so happy and animated since she'd moved to New York, and Ferguson's mother simply said, I have to do this, Paul, I'll go nuts if I don't start working again, to which Mildred's husband replied: I think I can help you, Rose.

Help came in the form of a commission to go to New Orleans and photograph Henry Wilmot for the dust jacket of his forthcoming novel, a much anticipated work by the past winner of the Pulitzer Prize, and when the sixty-two-year-old Wilmot told his editor how pleased he was with the results, that is, called Paul Sandler and informed him that from now on no one but that *beautiful woman* would be allowed to take his picture, more commissions for author photos came in from Random House, which led to work for other New York publishers as well, which in turn led to magazine assignments for feature stories about writers, film directors, Broadway actors, musicians, and artists in *Town & Country*, *Vogue, Look, Ladies' Home Journal*, the *New York Times Magazine*, and other weeklies and monthlies over the years that followed. Ferguson's mother always photographed her subjects in their own environments, traveling to the places where they lived and worked with her portable light stands, fold-up screens, and collapsible umbrellas, shooting writers in their book-filled studies or sitting behind their desks, painters in the tumult and splatter of their studios, pianists sitting behind or standing next to their gleaming black Steinways, actors looking into their dressing room mirrors or sitting alone on bare stages, and for some reason her black-and-white portraits seemed to capture more about the inner lives of those people than most photographers were able to extract from shooting those same well-known figures, a quality that had less to do with technical skill, perhaps, than with something about Ferguson's mother herself, who always prepared for her assignments by reading the books and listening to the records and looking at the paintings of her subjects, which gave her something to talk about with them during their long sessions together, and because she talked easily and was ever so charming and attractive, ever so not a person to talk about herself, those vain and difficult artists would find themselves relaxing in her presence, feeling that she was genuinely interested in who and what they were, which was in fact true, or mostly true most of the time, and once the seduction had taken effect and their guard had come down, the masks they wore on their faces would gradually slip off and a different sort of light would begin to emerge from their eyes.

On top of this commercial work for magazines and book publishers, Ferguson's mother kept busy with her own projects, what she called her *wandering-eye explorations*, which abandoned the meticulous control required to produce first-rate portraits for a *come-what-may openness to chance encounters with the unexpected*. She had discovered this contrary impulse in herself at her cousin Charlotte's wedding, that unpaid job from 1955 that had turned into an exuberant, three-and-a-half-hour binge of manic picture taking as she spun her way through the crowd, freed from the restraints of laborious preparation and plunged into a whirl of rapid-fire compositions, one picture succeeding the next, ephemeral instants that had to be caught precisely then or not at all, pause for half a second and the picture would be gone, and the ferocity of concentration called for under the circumstances had thrown her into a kind of emotional fever, as if every face and body in the room had been rushing in on her at once, as if every person there were breathing inside her eyes, no longer on the other side of the camera but within her, an inseparable part of who she was.

Predictably enough, Charlotte and her husband hated those photographs. Not the others, they said, not the portraits that had been shot at the synagogue after the marriage ceremony, which were truly marvelous, pictures they would cherish for years to come, but the stuff from the wedding party was incomprehensible, so dark and raw, so unflattering, everyone looked so sinister and unhappy, even the laughing people looked vaguely demonic, and why were the shots so off-kilter, why was everything so severely underlit? Miffed by the rebuke, Ferguson's mother sent the newlyweds copies of the portraits with a short accompanying note that read, *Glad you liked these*, sent another batch to Aunt Pearl, another batch to her parents, and a last one to Mildred and Paul. After receiving his package, her brother-in-law called to ask why she hadn't included anything from the wedding party. Because those pictures stink, she said. All artists are revolted by their own work, her new supporter and advocate replied, and eventually Ferguson's mother was persuaded to develop thirty prints from the more than five hundred images she had shot that afternoon and mail them to Paul's office at Random House. Three days later, he called back to say that not only did they not stink but that he found them remarkable. With her permission, he was going to give them to Minor White at *Aperture* magazine. They deserved to be published, he said, to be seen by people who cared about photography, and since he knew White a little bit, why not start at the top? Ferguson's mother wasn't sure if Paul meant what he was saying or if he merely felt sorry for her. She thought: Kind man steps in to help lost and grieving relative in her time of trouble, man with connections seeks to connect unconnected widow-photographer to a new life. Then she thought: Pity or no pity, Paul was the one who had sent her down to New Orleans, and while he could have been acting on a whim, or on blind intuition, or on some long-shot hunch, now that the grumpy, alcoholic Wilmot had lauded her for doing *one hell of a damned fine job*, perhaps her brother-in-law believed he had put his money on the right horse.

Whether Paul influenced their decision or not, the editorial board at *Aperture* accepted her pictures for publication, a portfolio of twenty-one prints that appeared six months later under the title *Jewish Wedding, Brooklyn*. That triumph, and the jolt of exaltation that shot through her when the letter from *Aperture* showed up in the mail, were soon tempered by frustration, however, and then nearly destroyed by anger, since she couldn't publish the photos without securing releases from the people who were in them, and Ferguson's mother made the mistake of contacting Charlotte first, who stubbornly refused to allow those *grotesque snapshots* of herself and Nathan to be published in *Aperture* or any other *cruddy magazine*. Over the next three days, Ferguson's mother spoke to all the other participants, among them Charlotte's mother and her twin sister, Betty, and when no one else raised any objections, she called Charlotte back and asked her to reconsider. *Out of the question. Go to hell. Who do you think you are?* Aunt Pearl tried to reason with her, Ferguson's grandfather scolded her for what he called a *selfish disregard of others*, Betty called her a pinhead and a priss, but the new Mrs. Birnbaum wouldn't budge. The three pictures with Charlotte and Nathan in them were therefore scrapped, three others were chosen to take their place, and a photo story about a wedding was published with no bride or groom anywhere in sight.

Nevertheless, it was a start, a first step toward living in the only future that made sense to her, and Ferguson's mother forged on, emboldened by the publication of those photos to pursue other noncommissioned projects, *her own work*, as she called it, which continued to be found in the pages of *Aperture* and sometimes between the covers of books or on the walls of galleries, and the most important element of that transformation was perhaps the last-minute decision she made before the appearance of *Jewish Wedding*, all the way back in the spring of 1956, when she got down on her knees before her bed and asked Stanley to forgive her for what she was about to do, but it had to be this way, she said to him, any other way would force her to go on living in the ashes of the Newark fire until she too burned up into nothing, and so it was, and so it continued to be for all the years of her future life, that she signed her work *Rose Adler*.

IN THE BEGINNING, the eight-year-old Ferguson was only dimly aware of what his mother was up to. He understood that she was busier than she had been, out and about on most days working at various photography jobs, or else locked up in what had once been the spare bedroom, which she had turned into a place for developing pictures and which was always sealed shut because of the fumes from the chemicals, and though it was good to see that she was smiling more and laughing more than she had during the spring and summer, the rest of what was happening was not good, not at all good as far as he was concerned. The spare bedroom had been his room for more than eight months, his own private retreat where he could sort through his baseball cards and knock down plastic pins with his plastic bowling ball and throw beanbags through the holes in the wooden target and aim darts at the small red bull's-eye, and now it was gone, which could hardly be called a good thing, and then, sometime in late October, not long after his bright room had been transformed into an out-of-bounds darkroom, another not-good thing occurred when his mother told him it would no longer be possible for her to pick him up after school. She would continue to take him there in the morning, but she couldn't count on being free in the afternoon anymore, and so his grandmother would be the one to meet him at the front steps and escort him back to the apartment. Ferguson didn't like it, since he was opposed to any and all change as a matter of strict moral doctrine, but he wasn't in a position to protest, he had to do what he was told, and what had once been the best part of the day—seeing his mother again after six and a half hours of boredom, reprimands, and bitter struggles with the Almighty—was turned into a dull plod westward with his fat, waddling Nana, an old woman so shy and so withheld that she never knew what to say to him, which meant that more often than not they rode back home in silence.

He couldn't help it. His mother was the only person he cared about or felt comfortable with, and everyone else grated on his nerves. The people in his family had their good points, he supposed, in that they all seemed to like him, but his grandfather was too loud, his grandmother was too quiet, Aunt Mildred was too bossy, Uncle Paul was too fond of listening to his own voice, Great-aunt Pearl was too smothering in her affections, cousin Betty was too brash, cousin Charlotte was too stupid, little cousin Eric was too rambunctious, little cousin Judy was too much of a crybaby, and the one relative he would have given anything to see again, his cousin Francie, was a college student in faraway California. As for his classmates at Hilliard, he had no real friends, only acquaintances, and even Dougie Hayes, the boy he saw more than anyone else, laughed at things that weren't funny and never understood a joke when he heard one. Except for his mother, it was hard for Ferguson to attach himself to any of the people he knew, since he always felt alone when he was with them, although being alone with others was probably a little less terrible than being alone with himself, which invariably seemed to push his thoughts back to the same old obsessions, as with his constant begging of God to produce a miracle that would finally put his mind at rest, or, even more insistently, with the photograph in the *Newark Star-Ledger* that he wasn't supposed to have looked at but did, studying it for three or four minutes while his mother left the room to fetch a pack of cigarettes, the picture with the caption that read *The scorched remains of Stanley Ferguson*, and there was his dead father in the burned-down building that had once been 3 Brothers Home World, his body stiff and black and no longer human, as if the fire had turned him into a mummy, a man with no face and no eyes and a mouth wide open as if locked in the middle of a scream, and that charred, mummified corpse had been put in a coffin and buried in the ground, and whenever Ferguson thought about his father now, that was the first thing he saw in his mind, the scorched remains of the black, half-incinerated body with the open mouth still screaming from the bowels of the earth.

It's going to be a cold day, Archie. Remember to wear your scarf to school.

Morbid ruminations were among the not-good things that belonged to that rough year of being eight and turning nine, but there were some good things as well, even things that happened every day, such as the after-school television program that ran from four o'clock to five-thirty on Channel 11, ninety straight minutes (with commercial interruptions) of old Laurel and Hardy movies, which turned out to be the finest, funniest, most satisfying movies ever made. It was a new show that had been launched in the fall, and until Ferguson accidentally turned it on one afternoon in October, he had known nothing about that ancient comedy team, since Laurel and Hardy had been mostly forgotten by 1955, their films from the twenties and thirties were never shown in theaters anymore, and it was only because of television that they were starting to make a comeback among the little people of the greater metropolitan area. How Ferguson came to adore those two idiots, those grown men with the minds of six-year-olds, brimming with eagerness and goodwill and yet always quarreling and tormenting each other, always falling into the most improbable and dangerous predicaments, nearly drowned, nearly blown to bits, nearly brained into oblivion, and yet always managing to survive, hapless husbands, bumbling schemers, losers to the last, and yet in spite of all their punching and pinching and kicking, what good friends they were, bound together more tightly than any other pair in *The Book of Terrestrial Life*, each one an inseparable half of a single, two-part human organism. Mr. Laurel and Mr. Hardy. It pleased Ferguson immensely that those were the names of the real men who played the make-believe characters of Laurel and Hardy in the films, for Laurel and Hardy were always Laurel and Hardy no matter what circumstances they happened to find themselves in, whether they lived in America or another country, whether they lived in the past or the present, whether they were furniture movers or fishmongers or Christmas-tree salesman or soldiers or sailors or convicts or carpenters or street musicians or stable hands or prospectors in the Wild West, and the fact that they were always the same even when they were different seemed to make them more real than any other characters in movies, for if Laurel and Hardy were always Laurel and Hardy, Ferguson reasoned, that must have meant they were eternal.

They were his steadiest, most reliable companions all during that year and well into the next, Stanley and Oliver, a.k.a. Stan and Ollie, the thin one and the fat one, the feebleminded innocent and the puffed-up fool, who in the end was no less feebleminded than the first, and while it meant something to Ferguson that Laurel's first name was the same as his father's, it didn't mean that much, and surely it had little or nothing to do with his growing fondness for his new friends, who in no time at all had become his best friends, if not his only friends. What he loved most about them were the bedrock elements that never varied from film to film, beginning with the *Cuckoos* theme song in the opening credits, which announced that the boys were back for another adventure and *What would they think of next?*, the familiar turns that never grew tiresome to him, Ollie's tie twiddles and exasperated looks into the camera, Stan's dumbfounded blinks and sudden tears, the gags that revolved around their bowler hats, the too-big one on Laurel's head, the too-small one on Hardy's head, the smashed-in hats and burning hats, the hats yanked down over the ears and the hats stomped underfoot, their propensity for falling down manholes and crashing through broken floorboards, for stepping into muddy bogs and neck-high puddles, their bad luck with automobiles, ladders, gas ovens, and electric sockets, Ollie's blowhard gentility when talking to strangers, *This is my friend Mr. Laurel*, Stan's nonsensical gift for igniting his thumb and puffing on nonexistent but functioning pipes, their out-of-control laughing jags, their penchant for breaking into spontaneous dance routines (both so light on their feet), their unanimity of purpose when confronting their adversaries, all bickering and discord forgotten as they pulled together to destroy a man's house or wreck a man's car, but also the variations on who they were and how their identities sometimes overlapped and even merged, as when Ollie rubbed Stan's foot thinking it was his own foot and sighed with pleasure and relief, or the ingenious ways in which they sometimes duplicated themselves, as when big Stanley and big Oliver babysat their toddler sons, little Stan and little Ollie, who were miniature replicas of their fathers, since Laurel and Hardy played both sets of roles, or when Stan was married to a female Ollie and Ollie to a female Stan, or when they met their long-lost twin brothers, close friends whose names were of course Laurel and Hardy, or, best of all, when a blood transfusion went wrong at the end of a film and Stan wound up with Ollie's mustache and voice and the smooth-faced Hardy collapsed into a Laurel crying fit.

Yes, they were ever so droll and inventive, and yes, Ferguson's stomach sometimes ached from laughing so hard at their buffoonery, but why he found them laughable, and why his love for them began to flower beyond all reason, had less to do with their clownish antics than their persistence, with the fact that they reminded Ferguson of himself. Strip away the comic exaggerations and slapstick violence, and Laurel and Hardy's struggles were no different from his own. They, too, blundered from one ill-conceived plan to the next, they, too, suffered through countless setbacks and frustrations, and whenever misfortune brought them to the snapping point, Hardy's angers would become his angers, Laurel's befuddlements would mirror his befuddlements, and the best thing about the botches they made for themselves was that Stan and Ollie were even more incompetent than he was, more stupid, more asinine, more helpless, and that was funny, so funny that he couldn't stop laughing at them, even as he pitied them and embraced them as brothers, kindred spirits forever smacked down by the world and forever standing up to try again—by hatching another one of their harebrained plans, which, inevitably, would knock them to the ground once more.

Most of the time, he watched the films alone, sitting on the floor in the living room about a yard from the television set, which his mother and grandmother both considered to be too close, since the rays emitted by the cathode tube would *ruin his eyes,* and whenever one of them caught him in that position, he would have to remove himself to the more distant sofa. On the days when his mother was still out working when he returned home from school, his grandmother would stay with him in the apartment until his mother came back from her *daily duties* (as the nursemaid put it in *The Music Box,* complaining to a policeman after Stan had planted his shoe in her rear end: *He kicked me right in the middle of my daily duties*), but Ferguson's grandmother had no interest in Laurel and Hardy, her passion was for cleanliness and domestic order, and once she had given her grandson his post-school snack, generally two chocolate chip cookies and a glass of milk, but sometimes a plum or an orange or a stack of saltines that Ferguson would coat with dabs of grape jelly, he would go off to the living room to turn on his program and she would busy herself with scrubbing down kitchen counters or scouring off crud from the stove burners or cleaning the sinks and toilets in the two bathrooms, a dedicated destroyer of filth and germs who never grumbled about her daughter's shortcomings as a housekeeper but nevertheless sighed often as she went about these tasks, no doubt chagrined that her own flesh and blood did not adhere to her rigorous standards of sanitary living. On the days when Ferguson's mother was already at home when he returned from school, his grandmother would simply drop him off and leave, exchanging a kiss and a few words with her daughter but rarely pausing long enough to go to the trouble of taking off her coat, and when his mother wasn't developing pictures in her darkroom or preparing dinner in the kitchen, she would occasionally join her son on the sofa and watch Laurel and Hardy with him, now and then laughing as hard as he did (at the *daily duties* line in *The Music Box*, for example, which became a private joke between them, a term that eventually replaced the old words they had used to refer to the human posterior, a long list that had included such dependable idioms as backside, *tuchas*, keister, heinie, rear end, fanny, and rump, as with the question his mother would sometimes ask when they were in different rooms, calling out, *What are you up to, Archie?*, and if he wasn't standing or walking or lying down somewhere in the apartment, he would respond, *I'm sitting on my daily duties, Ma*), but most often she would merely chuckle at Stan and Ollie's pranks and pratfalls, or give a little smile, and when things started to get out of hand, with whacks and thwacks and painful blows, she would wince or else shake her head and say, *Oh, Archie, that's just awful*, not meaning that the film was awful but that the roughhousing was too excessive for her. Ferguson didn't agree, of course, but he was old enough to understand that it was possible for someone not to like Laurel and Hardy as much as he did, and he felt she was a good sport for sitting there with him, since he knew that Stan and Ollie were too dumb and childish for her and that even if she watched them every day for a year, she would never become a fan.

Only one person in the family shared his enthusiasm, just one grown-up had the acuity to recognize the genius of his beloved imbeciles, and that was his grandfather, the elusive Benjy Adler, who had always been something of a mystery to Ferguson, a man who seemed to possess two or three different personalities, effusive and generous on some days, shut down and distracted on other days, at times nervous,

even jittery and short-tempered, at times calm and expansive, by turns
warmly attentive to his grandson and almost indifferent to him, but on
his good days, the days when he was in one of his spirited moods and
the jokes were flying out of his mouth, he was a sterling companion, a
co-conspirator in what Ferguson thought of as the Bore War (his scrambled incarnation of the misheard and misunderstood Boer War), which
he took to be a militant assault against the dullness of life. In late November, Uncle Paul sent Ferguson's mother on another trip, this time all the
way out to New Mexico to photograph Millicent Cunningham, an
eighty-year-old poet who was about to publish her *Collected Essays* with
Random House, and during her absence Ferguson holed up at his
grandparents' apartment near Columbus Circle. He had been living in
Laurel-and-Hardy Land for more than a month by then, entirely dug in
with his new infatuation and nearly bereft when weekends rolled
around now, since the program was off the air on Saturday and Sunday, but the first night he spent at West Fifty-eighth Street happened to
be a Monday, which gave him five straight afternoons of Mr. Fat and
Mr. Thin, and when his grandfather came home early from work on the
first afternoon, explaining that it had been *a slow day at the office,* he
plunked himself down on the sofa next to Ferguson to watch the program, which seemed to affect his sixty-two-year-old mind in the same
way it affected Ferguson's eight-year-old mind, and before long he was
shuddering with laughter, at one point so excessively that he began to
wheeze and cough and turn red in the face, and so thorough was his
delight that he came home early from the office every day that week to
catch the show with his grandson.

    Then came the surprise, the Sunday visit in early December when
Ferguson's grandparents walked into the apartment on Central Park
West loaded down with packages, some of them so heavy that Arthur,
the superintendent of the building, had to wheel them in on a hand
truck, which earned him a five-dollar tip from Ferguson's grandfather
(five dollars!), and another one in an exceedingly long cardboard box
that his grandparents carried in together, each one grasping an end with
two hands, and so long was the box that it nearly didn't make it into the
apartment, and when he saw his grandmother smile (how rarely she
smiled) and heard his grandfather laugh and felt his mother's hand
settle onto his right shoulder, he knew that something exceptional was
about to happen, but he had no idea what that thing could be until the

packages were unwrapped and he discovered that he now owned a sixteen-millimeter movie projector, a roll-up movie screen with a collapsible tripod base, and copies of ten Laurel-and-Hardy shorts: *The Finishing Touch, Two Tars, Wrong Again, Big Business, Perfect Day, Blotto, Below Zero, Another Fine Mess, Helpmates,* and *Towed in a Hole.*

Little matter that the projector had been bought secondhand—it worked. Little matter that the prints were scratched and the sound sometimes seemed to be coming from the bottom of a bathtub—the films were watchable. And with the films came a whole new set of words for him to master—*sprocket,* for example, which turned out to be a far better word to think about than *scorched.*

ON THE WEEKENDS when his mother wasn't out of town on an assignment—and the weather wasn't too cold or too wet or too windy— most Saturday mornings and afternoons were spent prowling the streets in search of good photographs, Ferguson trotting along beside his mother as she strode down the sidewalks of Manhattan or mounted the steps of municipal buildings or scaled rocks or crossed bridges in Central Park, and then, for no reason that was ever apparent to him, she would come to a sudden halt, aim her camera at something, press the shutter release, and click, click-click, click-click-click, which wasn't the most absorbing activity in the world, perhaps, but it belonged to the pleasure of being with his mother, of having her all to himself again, and how not to enjoy the lunches they ate together in coffee shops along Broadway and on Sixth Avenue in the Village, where ten times out of ten he would order a hamburger and a chocolate milkshake, always the same meal at the midpoint of those Saturday excursions, a hamburger, please, yes, a hamburger, please, as if it were part of a sacred ritual, which meant it could never vary in any way down to the smallest detail, and then the Saturday evenings and/or Sunday afternoons when they went to the movies together, sitting in the balcony where his mother could smoke her Chesterfields, movies that were never Laurel and Hardy movies but new productions from Hollywood such as *It's Always Fair Weather, The Tall Men, Picnic, Guys and Dolls, Artists and Models, The Court Jester, Invasion of the Body Snatchers, The Searchers, Forbidden Planet, The Man in the Gray Flannel Suit, Our Miss Brooks, Bhowani Junction, Trapeze, Moby Dick, The Solid Gold Cadillac, The*

Ten Commandments, Around the World in Eighty Days, Funny Face, The Incredible Shrinking Man, Fear Strikes Out, and *12 Angry Men,* the good and bad films of 1955, 1956, and 1957 that carried them through his time at Hilliard and on into his first year at the next school he attended, the Riverside Academy, on West End Avenue between Eighty-fourth and Eighty-fifth Streets, a coed institution of so-called progressive tendencies that had been founded twenty-nine years earlier, exactly one hundred years after the founding of Hilliard.

No more blazers and ties, no more morning chapel, no more bus trips through Central Park, no more days trapped in a building without girls, all of which were decided improvements, but the biggest difference between the third and fourth grades was not so much the leap to another school as the end of Ferguson's duel with God. God had been defeated, exposed as a powerless nonentity who could no longer punish or inspire fear, and with the celestial overman now cut out of the picture, Ferguson could give up playing the old game of Intentional Screw-up, or, as he sometimes called it in later years, *Ontological Chicken.* He had succeeded so well at failure that he had grown tired of his gift for subterfuge and self-immolation. No one at Hilliard had ever suspected what he'd been up to, he had fooled them all, not only his teachers and fellow students but his mother and Aunt Mildred as well, not one of them ever figured out that he had done it on purpose, that his wildly erratic performance in the third grade had been nothing but an act, a cannily devised effort to prove that nothing he did could ever matter if no divine force were watching over him. He had won the argument with himself by getting thrown out of Hilliard—not expelled, exactly, since they allowed him to stay until the end of the year, but they had seen enough of Ferguson to want no more of him after that. The headmaster told his mother that Archie was the most daunting enigma he had ever come across in all his years at the school. He was both the best student and the worst student in his class, he said, at times brilliant and at other times utterly moronic, and they no longer knew what to do with him. Were they looking at a latent schizophrenic, he asked, or was Archie just another lost boy who would eventually find himself? Since Ferguson's mother knew her son was neither a moron nor a future mental case, she thanked the headmaster for his time and set about looking for another school.

He received his first report card from the Riverside Academy on a

Friday in mid-November. After an entire year of Poors and Fails from Hilliard, Ferguson's mother was expecting better results from the new school, but nothing close to the seven Excellents and two Very Goods Ferguson brought home that day. Stunned by the magnitude of the reversal, she walked into the living room at five-thirty, just as *The Laurel and Hardy Show* was ending, and sat down beside her son on the floor.

Good work, Archie, she said, holding up the packet of grades in her right hand as she tapped it with her left. I'm very proud of you.

Thanks, Ma, Ferguson replied.

You must be enjoying your new school.

It's pretty good. All things considered.

What does that mean?

School is school, which means it's not something anyone enjoys that much. You go because you have to go.

But some schools are better than others, aren't they?

I suppose.

For instance, Riverside is better than Hilliard.

Hilliard wasn't bad. For a school, that is.

But you prefer not having to travel so far every day, don't you? And not having to wear a uniform. And having girls and boys together instead of just boys. It makes life a little better, doesn't it?

Much better. But the school itself isn't that different. Reading, writing, arithmetic, social studies, gym, art, music, and science. I do the same things at Riverside that I did at Hilliard.

What about the teachers?

About the same.

I thought they were less strict at Riverside.

Not really. Miss Donne, the music teacher, yells at us sometimes. But Mr. Bowles, the music teacher at Hilliard, never raised his voice. He's the best teacher I've had anywhere—and the nicest.

But you have more friends at Riverside. Tommy Snyder, Peter Baskin, Mike Goldman, and Alan Lewis—all such fine boys—and that cutie-pie, Isabel Kraft, and her cousin Alice Abrams, beautiful children, real winners. In two months, you've made as many friends as you ever had in New Jersey.

They're fun to be with. Some of the other kids, not so much. Billy Nathanson is about the meanest toad I've ever met—much worse than anyone at Hilliard.

But you didn't have any friends at Hilliard, Archie. Sweet Doug Hayes, I guess, but no one else I can think of.

It was my fault. I didn't want any friends there.

Oh? And why is that?

It's hard to explain. I just didn't want any.

No friends and bad grades at one school. Lots of friends and good grades at another school. There has to be a reason for that. Do you have any idea what it is?

Yes.

And?

I can't tell you.

Don't be ridiculous, Archie.

You'll be mad at me if I tell.

Why on earth would I be mad at you? Hilliard's in the past now. It makes no difference anymore.

Maybe not. But you'll still be mad at me.

And what if I promise not to be mad?

It won't do any good.

Ferguson was looking down at the floor by then, pretending to examine a loose thread in the carpet as a way to avoid his mother's eyes, for he knew he would be lost if he dared to look into them now, her eyes had always been too strong for him, they were charged with a power that could decipher his thoughts and extract confessions from him and overwhelm his puny will even as he fought to resist her, and now, horribly and inevitably, she was reaching out and touching his jaw with the tips of her fingers, gently prodding him to lift his face and look into her eyes again, and the moment he felt her hand make contact with his skin, he knew that all hope was gone, tears were gathering in his eyes, the first tears that had been there in months, and how humiliating it was to feel the invisible faucet turn on again without warning, no better than stupid, weepy Stan, he said to himself, a nine-year-old infant with faulty plumbing in his brain, and by the time he found the courage to fix his eyes on his mother's eyes, two waterfalls were trickling down his cheeks and his mouth was moving, words were tumbling out of him, the story of Hilliard was being told, the battle with God and the reason for the bad grades, the silenced voice and the murder of his father, breaking the rules in order to be punished and then hating God for not punishing him, hating God for not being God, and Ferguson had no idea if his mother understood what he was telling her, her eyes looked pained and confused and almost tearful, and after he had been talking for two or three or four minutes, she leaned over, put her arms around him, and told him to stop. Enough, Archie, she said, let it go, and then the two of them were crying together, a marathon sobfest that lasted for close to ten minutes, which was the last time either one of them broke down in the presence of the other, almost two years to the day since Stanley Ferguson's body had been put in the ground, and once the crying slowly came to an end, they washed their faces, put on their overcoats, and went out to the movies, where they gorged themselves on hot dogs in the balcony instead of eating dinner and then shared a large box of popcorn, which they washed down with fizzless, watery Cokes. The title of the movie they saw that evening was: *The Man Who Knew Too Much.*

YEARS PASSED. FERGUSON was ten, eleven, and twelve, he was thirteen and fourteen, and among the family events that occurred during those five years, the most important was no doubt his mother's marriage to a man named Gilbert Schneiderman, which happened when Ferguson was twelve and a half. A year before that, the Adler clan had lived through its first divorce, the inexplicable breakup between Aunt Mildred and Uncle Paul, a couple who had always seemed so right for each other, two chattering bookworms who had been married for nine years with no apparent conflicts or betrayals, and then it was all over, Aunt Mildred was moving to California to join the English Department at Stanford and Uncle Paul was no longer Ferguson's Uncle Paul. Then his grandfather disappeared—a heart attack in 1960—and not long after that his grandmother was gone as well—a stroke in 1961—and within a month of that second funeral, Great-aunt Pearl was diagnosed with terminal cancer. The Adlers were diminishing. They had begun to look like one of those families in which no one got to be very old.

Schneiderman was the first-born son of his mother's former boss, the man with the German accent who had taught her photography during the early days of the war, and since Ferguson understood that his mother was bound to remarry at some point, he was not opposed to her choice, which struck him as the best choice among the several that had been available to her. Schneiderman was forty-five, eight years older than Ferguson's mother, and the two of them had first crossed paths on the morning she started working at his father's studio in November 1941, which somehow comforted Ferguson, knowing that his mother had met his stepfather even before she met his father, 1941 as opposed to 1943, a date that had previously marked the beginning of the world for him, but now the world had become even older than that, and it was reassuring to know there was already an accumulated past between them and therefore she wasn't rushing into the marriage blindly, which had always been Ferguson's greatest fear, watching his mother get swept off her feet by some smooth-talking clown and then waking up in the morning to discover she had committed the mistake of her life. No, Schneiderman seemed to be a solid sort, someone you could trust. Married to a woman for seventeen years, father of two kids, and then a call from a state trooper summoning him to a Dutchess County morgue to identify a woman's body, the body of his wife, who had been killed in a car accident, followed by four years alone, which was almost as long as Ferguson's mother had been alone since his father's death. His grandparents were still alive in September 1959, and the wedding was held in their apartment on West Fifty-eighth Street, where the five-foot-two-inch Ferguson served as best man. Among the guests were his new stepsisters, twenty-one-year-old Margaret and nineteen-year-old Ella, both college students, doddering Emanuel Schneiderman, the foul-mouthed goat whom Ferguson had already met three or four times and would never consider a grandfather, not even after his own grandfather died, Gil's brother, Daniel, his sister-in-law, Liz, his sixteen-year-old nephew Jim and twelve-year-old niece Amy (all arms and legs, that girl, with braces on her teeth and a row of zits on her forehead), and Paul Sandler, Ferguson's ex-uncle, who remained his mother's champion in spite of the divorce from Mildred, the editor of her first two books, the full-length *Jewish Wedding* and the recently published *Toughs*, ninety black-and-white portraits of Puerto Rican street gang members and their girlfriends, but Aunt Mildred wasn't there, she had written that she was too busy with her courses at Stanford to make the trip, and as Ferguson looked at his ex-uncle Paul looking at his mother, he wondered if he hadn't been a contender for his mother's hand and had lost out to Gil Schneiderman, which could have meant that his breakup with Aunt Mildred had something to do with his belated understanding that he had fallen for the wrong sister. Impossible to know, but perhaps that explained why Mildred was in

California that afternoon and not in New York, which also might have accounted for why she seemed to have broken off contact with Ferguson's mother, for no one said a word about her absence at the wedding party, at least not within earshot of Ferguson, and because he couldn't bring himself to ask his ex-uncle Paul or his grandparents why no one had mentioned it, the questions forming in his head that afternoon remained unanswered. Yet one more story that would never be told, he said to himself, and then he took the ring out of his pocket and handed it to the burly man with the high forehead and large ears who was about to become his stepfather.

His mother called it a new beginning, and in the beginning of that beginning there were many things to adjust to, a multitude of big things and small things that were suddenly and forever different now, starting with the big fact of living in a household made up of three people instead of two and the novelty of having that third person spend every night in his mother's bed, a five-foot-ten-inch man with hair on his chest who walked around in the morning wearing old-fashioned boxer shorts and peed loudly into the toilet and hugged and kissed his mother every time she looked at him, a new breed of masculinity for Ferguson to contend with, broad-shouldered but unathletic, elegant in an old-fashioned, distracted sort of way, with his heavy tweed suits and vests, his sturdy shoes and longer than average hair, a bit awkward socially, not given to jokes or breezy chatter, tea in the morning instead of coffee, schnapps, cognac, and a nightly cigar, a steady, stolid, Germanic approach to the business of living, with occasional lapses into grumpiness and fits of distemper (a genetic gift from his father, no doubt) but mostly kind, often exceedingly kind, a stepfather who never showed the slightest ambition to become a substitute father and was happy to be addressed as Gil rather than Dad. For the first six months, the three of them lived together in the apartment on Central Park West, but then they moved to a larger place on Riverside Drive between Eighty-eighth and Eighty-ninth Streets, with a fourth bedroom that was turned into a study for Gil, a change that Ferguson welcomed because he now lived closer to his school and could sleep a little later in the morning, and although he missed the old apartment's third-floor view of Central Park, he now had a seventh-floor view of the Hudson River, which turned out to be more stimulating because of the constant procession of boats and ships that moved back and forth across the water, and beyond the water there was the land on the other side, the New Jersey side, and whenever Ferguson looked at it he would think about his old life there and try to remember himself as a small boy, but that time was becoming so distant now, it was almost gone.

Schneiderman was the chief music critic at the *New York Herald Tribune*, a demanding position that forced him to be out most evenings attending concerts, recitals, and operas, and then the deadline rush to type up the review and deliver it to the arts editor that same evening, which seemed an almost impossible task to Ferguson, a mere two or two and a half hours to marshal his thoughts about the performance he had just seen and heard and write something coherent about it, but Schneiderman was an old hand at working under pressure, on most nights he finished his articles without once lifting his hands off the keyboard, and when Ferguson asked him how he could crank out the words so quickly, he answered his stepson by saying, I'm really quite a lazy fellow, Archie, and if I didn't have deadlines bearing down on me, I'd never get anything done, and Ferguson was impressed that his stepfather could make fun of himself in that way, since it was clear to him that the man was anything but lazy.

Schneiderman had stories to tell, unlike Ferguson's father, who had rarely told stories except for far-fetched ones about prospecting for gold in the Andes or shooting elephants in Africa, but these were true stories, and as the adjustment period gradually turned into something that resembled everyday life, Ferguson began to feel comfortable enough to press his mother's husband to talk to him about his past, for Ferguson's mind was no longer strictly a child's mind, and he enjoyed hearing what it had been like to grow up in Berlin, to be listening to someone who had spent the first seven years of his life in that far-off city, which in Ferguson's imagination was first and foremost the capital of Hitler's Hell, the most evil city on the face of the earth, but not then, Schneiderman informed him, not for someone who left there in 1921, and even if his life started just after the beginning of the First World War, what people had once called the Great War, he remembered nothing about it, the entire cataclysm was a blank to him, and the first event in his life that he could recall with any certainty was sitting at the kitchen table in his family's apartment in Charlottenburg with a piece of bread in front of him and covering the bread with spoonfuls of black currant jam as he watched his baby brother Daniel in his high chair, who was all of

six or eight months old at the time, which meant the war was about to
end or was already over, and the reason why that scene remained so
vivid to him was perhaps because Daniel was spewing forth a mass of
clotted milk all over his bib without noticing it, smiling through the
onslaught as he banged his hands against the table, and Schneiderman
had marveled at the fact that someone could be so brainless and incompetent as to throw up on himself without being aware of what he was
doing. No Hitler, then, but a momentous time for all that, the seeds of
future disaster already being planted at Versailles, armed struggle in
Berlin as the Spartacist rebellion surged up briefly and was crushed, followed by the arrests of Rosa Luxemburg and Karl Liebknecht, whose
murdered bodies were later found in the Landwehr Canal, not to mention the outbreak of the Russian Civil War, the Reds against the Whites,
the Bolsheviks against the world, and because Russia was so close to
Germany, the sudden influx of refugees and émigrés who streamed into
Berlin, unstable, tottering Berlin, heart of the ragged Weimar Republic
in which a loaf of bread would eventually cost twenty million marks. It
was essential that Schneiderman give the boy this rudimentary history
lesson so he would understand why the family had left for America,
why Schneiderman's father had concluded that Germany was a dead-
end place and had gotten them out of there as quickly as possible, which
proved to be just in time, since America put a stop to immigration in
1924 and barred the gates thereafter, but it was 1921 now, late summer,
with Schneiderman about to turn seven and his brother a month past
three, and off they sailed with their parents and a trunkful of German
books, leaving from Hamburg on a ship called the S.S. *Passage to India*,
bound for the mountainous territory of Washington Heights, or so
Schneiderman had assumed, but his English was less than good at that
point, almost nonexistent, in fact, and what did a seven-year-old boy
know about anything except what his parents had told him? The language was the toughest obstacle, his stepfather said, the difficulty of
speaking English without a German accent, which made him stick out
as a foreigner and led to taunts and frequent punches from the boys
in his school, for he wasn't just any foreigner but a German, the lowest,
most despised form of humanity in those years after the war, a good-
for-nothing Kraut or Hun or Boche or Heinie, take your pick, and even
as his understanding of English grew to a point of deepest familiarity,
even as his vocabulary expanded and he conquered the nuances of

English syntax and grammar, he still took his lumps because of that unseemly accent. *Vee go schvimming in dee zummer, yah Archie?*, Schneiderman said, by way of demonstration, and because Schneiderman rarely tried to be funny, Ferguson appreciated this little stab at humor, which in fact was quite funny, and he laughed, and an instant later they were both laughing.

The thing of it is, Schneiderman said, knowing German probably saved my life.

When Ferguson asked him to explain, his stepfather started talking about the war, about enlisting in the army just after Pearl Harbor because he wanted to go back to Europe and kill Nazis, but because he was a little older than most of the boys, and because he'd gone to college and was fluent in both German and French, he was kept out of combat and thrown into an intelligence unit instead. Ergo, no duty on the front lines. And because of that, no bullets or bombs to put him in an early grave. Ferguson was of course eager to know what he had done in the intelligence unit, but like most men who had come home from the war, Schneiderman didn't want to talk about it. He simply said, Interrogating German prisoners, interviewing Nazi officials, putting my German to good use. When Ferguson asked him to elaborate, Schneiderman smiled, patted his stepson on the shoulder, and said, Some other time, Archie.

If there was any drawback to the new arrangement, it was that Schneiderman had no interest in sports—not in baseball or football, not in basketball or tennis, not in golf or bowling or badminton. Not just that he didn't play any of those games himself but that he never even glanced at the sports pages, which meant that he paid no attention to the ups and downs of the local professional teams, not to speak of the college teams and high school teams, and ignored the exploits of every sprinter, shot-putter, high jumper, broad jumper, long-distance runner, golfer, skier, bowler, and tennis player in the world. One of the reasons why Ferguson had not been opposed to the idea of his mother getting married again was that he had assumed her second husband would necessarily be a sportsman, since she herself was so fond of swimming and tennis and ping pong and even bowling, and he had been looking forward to having a grown man in the house with whom he could share some sporting activities, whether throwing around a baseball or a football or shooting baskets or playing tennis (it didn't matter which one), and if this hypothetical stepfather turned out not to be an athletic sort of person, there was an excellent chance that he would be a fan of at least one sport, since most men were, as his grandfather had been, for example, whose sport had been baseball, and when the two of them hadn't been talking about Laurel and Hardy and asking themselves if the shorts weren't better than the features or vice versa, most of their conversations had been about analyzing the relative merits of Mantle, Snider, and Mays, dissecting Alvin Dark's talent for smacking the ball to right-center when the hit-and-run was on, debating who had the stronger arm, Furillo or Clemente, or if there was any truth to the story that Yogi Berra kept a razor blade in his right shin guard in order to nick up the ball before he threw it back to Whitey Ford. Every year from the age of six to ten Ferguson had gone to at least three games with his grandfather, their annual tour of the New York City ballparks, the Polo Grounds in Manhattan, Yankee Stadium in the Bronx, and Ebbets Field in Brooklyn, where they saw their one World Series game together in 1955, but three was the minimum, and after Ferguson's father died and the Dodgers and Giants left town, the total per season was usually six or seven trips to Yankee Stadium, *the house that Ruth built*, and how Ferguson had savored those outings in the blistering, sunlit afternoons of July and August, eyes fixed on the field with its immaculate green grass and smooth brown soil, a formal garden tucked inside the great stone city, pastoral pleasures amid the raucous shouts and whistles from the crowd, thirty thousand voices booing in unison, what a sound that was, and through it all his grandfather would patiently keep score with his stubby pencil, predicting whether the batter would wind up on base or not according to what he called *the law of averages*, meaning that a slumping batter was bound to get a hit because *he was due*, and no matter how many times he got it wrong, his grandfather never abandoned faith in his law, his flawed law of guesswork nonsense. All those games with his bizarre, incomprehensible Papa, who on the warmest days would protect himself from the sun by spreading a white handkerchief over his bald head because it was *too hot for hats*, and now that he was gone Ferguson understood that no one could ever take his place, least of all Schneiderman, who was probably the one New Yorker in any of the five boroughs whose heart hadn't been broken when the Dodgers and Giants decamped to California after the 1957 season.

It was a drawback, then, perhaps even a disappointment to have fallen in with a man who had no feeling for the dramas and delights of physical competition, but in all fairness to Schneiderman, the opposite was no doubt also true, for Ferguson's inability to play a musical instrument must have come as a disappointment to his stepfather, who was skilled at both the piano and the violin, not at the highest professional level, perhaps, but to Ferguson's untrained ear his renditions of Bach, Mozart, Beethoven, and Schubert were flat-out marvels of beauty and precision, as good as anything to be heard on the hundreds of L.P. records Schneiderman had brought with him to Central Park West. It wasn't that Ferguson hadn't tried, but his struggle to master the rudiments of keyboard proficiency had ended in failure, at least according to his teacher, old frizzy-haired Miss Muggeridge, who probably freelanced as a witch when she wasn't breaking the spirits of young children forced to study the piano. After nine months of lessons when he was in the first grade, his mother was told he was *a heavy-handed clod of a boy*, which led her to conclude that she had started him too early (forget about Mozart composing symphonies when he was six and seven—he didn't count!), and when she suggested to her failed pianist that he take a year off before making a fresh start with another teacher, Ferguson was relieved that he would never have to see Miss Muggeridge again. The year off was of course the year of the Newark fire, and once they moved to New York and got past the curious interregnum, the little one was at Hilliard, the big one was in disarray, and the piano was forgotten.

So Schneiderman had disappointed Ferguson, and Ferguson had disappointed Schneiderman, but since neither one of them ever spoke about it to the other, each one remained unaware of the other's disappointment. Eventually, when Ferguson became a starting forward on his freshman basketball team, Schneiderman began to show some interest in sports, at least to the extent of going to several games with Ferguson's mother, where he cheered on his stepson from the stands, but Ferguson never learned how to play a musical instrument. Still and all, it can safely be said that Ferguson profited more from his stepfather's involvement with music than Schneiderman did from his stepson's talent for putting balls in hoops and boxing out opponents for rebounds. At twelve and a half, Ferguson knew nothing about any kind of music except rock and roll, which he and his friends unanimously adored. His head was filled with the lyrics and melodies of Chuck Berry, Buddy Holly, Del Shannon, Fats Domino, and dozens of other pop singers, but when it came to classical music he was a virgin, not to mention jazz, blues, and the nascent folk revival, about which he was utterly ignorant as well, barring some comic ballads by the Kingston Trio, who were having their moment then. Knowing Schneiderman changed all that. For a boy who had been to only two concerts in his life (a performance of Handel's *Messiah* at Carnegie Hall with Aunt Mildred and Uncle Paul; a matinee of *Peter and the Wolf*, which he saw with his lower school classmates during his first month at Hilliard), a boy who owned not a single record of classical music, whose mother owned not a single record of any kind and listened only to ancient standards and big-band stuff on the radio, for such a boy, who lacked even the smallest glimmer of knowledge about string quartets or symphonies or cantatas, just listening to his stepfather play the piano or the violin was a revelation, and beyond that there was the further revelation of listening to his stepfather's record collection and discovering that music could actually reconfigure the atoms in a person's brain, and beyond what happened in the apartments on Central Park West and Riverside Drive, there were the excursions with his mother and Schneiderman to Carnegie Hall and Town Hall and the Metropolitan Opera House that began just weeks after the three of them settled in together. Schneiderman wasn't on a pedagogical mission, there was no plan to give the boy or his mother a formal education in music, he merely wanted to expose them to works he thought they would respond to, which meant not starting off with Mahler or Schoenberg or Webern but with booming, joyful works such as the *1812 Overture* (Ferguson gasped when he heard the cannon for the first time) or histrionic pieces such as the *Symphonie Fantastique* or the vibrant program music of *Pictures at an Exhibition*, but bit by bit he lured them in, and before long they were accompanying him to Mozart operas and Bach cello recitals, and for the twelve- and thirteen-year-old Ferguson, who continued to adore the rock and roll he had always adored, those nights out in the concert halls were nothing less than a revelation about the workings of his own heart, for music was the heart, he realized, the fullest expression of the human heart, and now that he had heard what he had heard, he was beginning to hear better, and the better he heard, the more deeply he felt—sometimes so deeply that his body shook.

□ □ □

THE ADLERS WERE shrinking. One after the other they were dying their too-early deaths and disappearing from the world, and with Aunt Mildred's removal to California and ex-uncle Paul's expulsion from the family, combined with the relocation to southern Florida by cousin Betty and her husband Seymour (along with Ferguson's two second cousins, Eric and Judy) and the fact that Betty's sister Charlotte was still not talking to her cousin Rose because of the Wedding-Pictures War of 1955 and 1956, Ferguson and his mother were the only Adlers left in New York, the only ones still above ground who hadn't absconded or smashed their links to the clan. In spite of these losses, however, new blood had entered their lives in the form of various Schneidermans, a collection of stepsisters and stepcousins and a stepaunt, a stepuncle, and a step-grandfather for Ferguson, which for his mother was translated into two stepdaughters, a stepniece and stepnephew, a sister-in-law, a brother-in-law, and a father-in-law, and those Schneidermans now constituted the bulk of the family they belonged to because a city clerk had signed and stamped a marriage certificate declaring Gil and his mother to be lawfully wedded husband and wife. It was a *strange change*, as Ferguson's grandfather had put it in one of their last talks together, and indeed it was strange to have been given two sisters because of a wedding, two unknown women who had suddenly become his closest relatives because a man who was equally unknown to him had signed his name on a piece of paper. None of that would have mattered if Ferguson had liked Margaret and Ella Schneiderman, but after several encounters with his new stepsiblings, he had concluded that those fat, ugly, stuck-up girls didn't deserve to be liked, for it soon became clear that they resented his mother for marrying their father and were disgusted with their father for having betrayed the memory of their mother, who had become a sanctified being after her terrible death in that crackup on the Taconic State Parkway. Well, Ferguson's father had died a terrible death, too, which theoretically should have put all of them in the same boat, but the Schneiderman sisters weren't interested in their new stepbrother, they barely deigned to talk to the twelve-year-old nobody, the big college girls from Boston University had no use for the son of the riffraff woman who had stolen their father from them, and even though Ferguson had been puzzled by their behavior at the wedding—the two of them standing off to the side and talking to no one but each other, mostly in whispers, mostly with their backs turned toward the bride and groom—it wasn't until two weeks later, when they were invited to dinner at the New York apartment, that Ferguson understood how nasty and ungenerous they were, particularly Margaret, the older one, although the younger, less obnoxious Ella invariably followed her sister's lead, which was probably even worse, and there the five of them were at that never to be forgotten dinner, which had taken his mother so many hours to prepare, wanting to prove her solidarity with Gil by putting herself out for his daughters, those vicious, snotty girls who pretended not to hear his mother when she asked them questions about their life in Boston and what they were planning to do after college, who snidely grilled her about her knowledge of music, which was next to zero, of course, as if to prove to their father that he had married an uncultured imbecile, and when Margaret asked her new stepmother whether she preferred listening to Bach keyboard pieces on the harpsichord, as played by Wanda Landowska, for example, or on the pianoforte by someone like Glenn Gould (not piano, pianoforte), Gil finally exploded and told her to shut up. An open palm slammed down on the dinner table, rattling the silverware and tipping over a glass, and then there was silence, silence not just from Margaret but from everyone in the room.

Enough with your cutting, insidious remarks, Schneiderman said to his daughter. I didn't know you were capable of such mean-spiritedness, Margaret, such vicious cruelty. Shame on you. Shame on you. Shame on you. Rose is a great and magnificent artist, and if you manage to accomplish one-tenth of what she's done in your life, you'll surpass my wildest expectations for you. But one needs a soul to accomplish even the smallest thing in this world, my dear, and from the way you've been acting tonight, I'm beginning to wonder if you have one.

It was the first time Ferguson had witnessed his stepfather's anger, which was a bellowing, apoplectic sort of anger, a wrath of such enormity and destructive force that he could only hope it would never be turned in his direction, but how satisfying it was to see it turned on Margaret that night, she who so fully deserved that brutal dressing-down from her father, and how glad he was to know that Schneiderman was willing to defend his new wife against the attacks of his own daughter, *a great and magnificent artist*, which augured well for the future of the marriage, he felt, and when Margaret inevitably collapsed into tears and a tearful Ella protested that he had no right to talk to her sister like that, Ferguson heard his mother pronounce a phrase, pronounce for the first time a phrase she would go on using whenever Schneiderman lost control of his temper in the months and years ahead, *Easy does it, Gil*, which somehow managed to carry the double weight of both a warning and a caress, and just after he heard his mother say those words for the first time, she stood up from her chair and went over to her husband, a man she had been married to for sixteen days, stood behind him as he went on sitting in his chair at the head of the table, put a hand on each of his shoulders, and then leaned over and kissed him on the back of the neck. Ferguson was impressed by her bravery and composure, which made him think of someone stepping into a cage with a lion, but apparently his mother knew what she was doing, for rather than push her away, Schneiderman reached up and wrapped his right hand around hers, and once he had it firmly in his grasp, he brought her hand down to his mouth and kissed it. They hadn't even looked at each other, but the tantrum had been quelled, or almost quelled, since there was still the matter of an apology to be negotiated, which the stern-voiced Schneiderman eventually pried out of the reluctant, weeping Margaret, who could barely bring herself to look up at her stepmother, but she said the words, she said, *I'm sorry*, and because the blowup had occurred over dessert (strawberries and cream!), the meal was essentially done, which allowed the sisters to make a prompt, face-saving exit with the excuse that they had a nine o'clock date to see some old high school friends, which Ferguson knew to be false, since the girls were supposed to spend the night at the apartment, sleeping in his bedroom while he sacked out on the sofa in the living room, a special foldout sofa bed his mother had bought specifically for that purpose, but that never happened, not that night or any other night, for on all future visits to New York the sisters stayed with their mother's brother and his wife in Riverdale, and if Schneiderman wanted to see them, he had to go to that other apartment or meet with them in public places, but not once did they return to the apartment on Central Park West, and years went by before they set foot in the new apartment overlooking the river.

Ferguson didn't care. He wanted nothing to do with either one of those girls, just as he wanted nothing to do with Schneiderman's father, who unfortunately came round to dinner about once a month, spouting all kinds of inanities about American politics, the Cold War, New York sanitation workers, quantum physics, and even Ferguson himself, *Watch out for that boy of yours, liebchen—he has sex on the brain and doesn't even know it yet*, but Ferguson did what he could to avoid him, always making sure to wolf down his main course in record time and then claim to be too full for dessert, at which point he would withdraw to his room to study for tomorrow's history test, which in fact had already been given that afternoon. His new not-grandfather was a bit less horrible than Margaret and Ella, perhaps, but not by much, not enough to make Ferguson want to sit around and listen to his crackpot harangues about J. Edgar Hoover's secret concentration camps in Arizona or the alliance between the John Birch Society and the Communist Party to poison the reservoirs of the New York City water system, which might have been funny in an odd sort of way if the old man hadn't shouted so much, but twenty or thirty minutes in his company was about all Ferguson could stomach. That made three new relatives he couldn't abide, three Schneidermans he gladly would have done without, but then there were the other Schneidermans, the ones who lived just thirteen and a half blocks away on West Seventy-fifth Street, and though he found it difficult to warm up to his stepaunt Liz, who struck him as a crabby, nervous sort of person, too fretful about the minutiae of daily life to understand that life could run out on you before you'd begun to live, he immediately took to Schneiderman's brother, Daniel, and the two Schneiderman offspring, stepcousins Jim and Amy, who made Ferguson feel welcome from the start and thought their Uncle Gil was *one lucky son of a bitch* (Jim's words) to have married a woman like Ferguson's mother, who (in Amy's words) was *just about perfect*.

Daniel worked as a commercial artist and sometime illustrator of children's books, a self-employed odd-jobber who spent eight to ten hours a day in a small room at the back of the family apartment that had been converted into a studio, a cluttered, dimly lit micro-atelier where he churned out drawings and paintings for greeting cards, advertisements, calendars, corporate brochures, and Tommy the Bear watercolors for his collaborations with writer Phil Costanza, bringing in enough money to feed, clothe, and house a family of four but with nothing left over for extravagances like long summer vacations or private schools for the kids. His work was skilled and professional, bearing the

marks of a deft hand and a capricious imagination, and although there
was nothing terribly original about what he did, it was never less than
charming, a word that was often used to describe Daniel Schneiderman
himself, who turned out to be one of the most unpretentious and jovial
people Ferguson had ever met, a person who liked to laugh and consequently laughed a lot, an altogether different kind of being from his
older brother, the little one who never had to struggle with a German
accent, the handsome one, the unserious one, *the one who liked sports*, as
did stepcousin Jim, long, lean, basketball-playing Jim, who had just
started his junior year at the Bronx High School of Science when Gil and
Ferguson's mother were married, and once the male contingent of the
other Schneidermans learned that their new nephew/cousin was as big
on basketball as they were, the duo became a trio, and every time Dan
and Jim went to see a game at the Garden, Ferguson was invited to go
along with them. That was the old Garden, the now demolished Madison Square Garden that had once stood on Eighth Avenue between
Forty-ninth and Fiftieth Streets, and so it was that Ferguson was taken
to see his first live basketball games during that 1959–60 season, Saturday afternoon college triple-headers, Harlem Globetrotter exhibitions,
and the shoddy, mediocre Knicks of Richie Guerin, Willie Naulls, and
Jumping Johnny Green, but there were only eight teams in the NBA back
then, which meant that the Boston Celtics played at the Garden at least
half a dozen times per season, and those were the games the trio made
a point of attending, since no one played the game better than that team
of Cousy, Heinsohn, Russell, and the Jones boys, they were a single, five-
part brain in constant motion, a single consciousness, utterly selfless
players who thought only of the team and not of themselves, *basketball
as it was meant to be played*, as Uncle Dan kept repeating as he watched
them, and yes, it was astonishing to observe how much better they were
than the Knicks, who seemed sluggish and awkward beside them, but
much as Ferguson admired the team as a whole, there was one player
who stood out for him and captured the bulk of his attention, sinewy,
wire-thin Bill Russell, who always seemed to be at the heart of what the
Celtics did, the one whose brain seemed to hold the four other brains
inside his head, or a man who had somehow dispersed his brain into
the heads of his teammates, for Russell moved strangely and didn't
look like an athlete, he was a limited player who rarely took shots or
scored, who rarely even dribbled the ball, and yet there he was snagging

another crucial rebound, making another impossible bounce pass, blocking another shot, and because of him the Celtics kept winning game after game season after season, champions or competing for the championship every year, and when Ferguson asked Jim what made Russell so great when in many ways he wasn't even good, Jim paused for a moment to think, shook his head, and replied, I don't know, Archie. Maybe he's just smarter than everyone else, or maybe it's because he sees more than other people do and always knows what's going to happen next.

Beanpole Jim was the answer to Ferguson's age-old prayers, the wish for an older brother, or at least an older cousin-friend he could look up to and draw strength from, and Ferguson exulted in their connection, in the way the sixteen-year-old Jim seemed to have no qualms about embracing his younger stepcousin as a comrade, little understanding that Jim, with a sister and two girl cousins, had no doubt been longing for a brother just as much as he had. In the two years before Jim graduated from high school and went off to study at MIT, he turned out to be an essential figure for the often confused and rebellious Ferguson, who was doing well in his classes at the Riverside Academy but continued to have an *attitude problem* (talking back to his teachers, quick to flare up when provoked by thugs like Billy Nathanson), and there was Jim, all curiosity and high spirits, a bighearted math-and-science boy who loved to talk about irrational numbers, black holes, artificial intelligence, and Pythagorean dilemmas, with no anger in him, never a rude word or a pugnacious gesture toward anyone, and surely his example helped tamp down the excessiveness of Ferguson's behavior somewhat, and there too was Jim giving Ferguson the lowdown on female anatomy and what to do about the ever more persistent problem of *sex on the brain* (cold showers, ice cubes on your dick, three-mile runs around the track), and best of all there was Jim on the basketball court with him, the five-foot-eleven-inch high school junior, the six-foot-one-inch senior who would meet Ferguson on Saturday mornings at the midway point between their two apartments and walk down to Riverside Park with him, where they would find an empty court and practice together for three hours, seven sharp every Saturday as long as the weather gods were with them, drizzles being acceptable but not downpours, flurries but not sleet or heavy snow, and nothing doing if the temperature dropped below twenty-five degrees (frozen fingers) or

rose above ninety-five (heat prostration), which meant they were out
there on most Saturdays until Jim packed his bags and left for college.
No more trotting along beside his mother on weekend photo outings
for young Mr. Ferguson, those days were finished forever, and from
now on it was basketball, which he had discovered at twelve when the
ball stopped being too large and heavy for him to control, and by the
time he was twelve and a half it had become the new passion of his
life, the next best thing to movies and kissing girls, and how fortunate
it was that Jim had arrived on the scene just then and was willing to
give up three hours every week instructing him on how to play, what
a miraculous turn that was, the right person at the right time—how
often did that happen?—and because Jim was a good and conscientious player, more than good enough to have made his high school team
if he had chosen to go out for it, he was a good teacher of fundamentals,
and one by one he led Ferguson through the basic drills of how to execute a proper layup, how to move his feet on defense, how to box out for
rebounds, how to throw a bounce pass, how to shoot free throws, how
to bank the ball off the backboard, how to release the ball at maximum
altitude when taking a jump shot, so many things to learn, dribbling
with his left hand, setting picks, keeping his arms up on defense, and
then the games of O-U-T and H-O-R-S-E at the end of each session, which
turned into games of one-on-one in the second year, as Ferguson
sprouted up to five-four, five-six, and five-seven, always losing to the
taller, more experienced Jim but beginning to hold his own after his
fourteenth birthday, at times respectable enough to pour in five or
six straight jumpers through the netless rims of Riverside Park, the
same denuded rims to be found in every public park across the city,
and because they played by the New York rule of winners-out, whenever Ferguson went on one of his shooting sprees, he would come dangerously close to not losing. As Jim put it after one of the last games
they played together: Give it another year, Archie, grow another two
or three inches, and you'll be wiping my ass off the court. He spoke
those words with the proud satisfaction of a teacher who had taught
his pupil well. And then it was Boston and good-bye, and a new hole
was dug in Ferguson's heart.

Within a year and a half of his mother's marriage to Gil, Ferguson
had gathered enough information about the Schneidermans to have

reached some definitive conclusions about his new family. In the left-hand column of his mental ledger he placed the names of three duds and one semi-dud: the unmentionable uglies (2), the demented patriarch (1), and the well-meaning but inconstant and overwrought Aunt Liz (½). In the right-hand column were the names of the four others: admirable Gil, amiable Dan, ardent Jim, and increasingly attractive Amy. In sum, he counted three and a half negatives as opposed to four positives, which mathematically proved that there was more to be thankful for than to grumble about, and with the Adlers all but gone from the land of the living and the Fergusons entirely absent now (Uncle Lew in prison, Aunt Millie somewhere in Florida, Uncle Arnold and Aunt Joan in Los Angeles, cousin Francie in Santa Barbara—married, the mother of two kids—and his other cousins scattered across the country and no longer in touch), the four good Schneidermans were essentially all Ferguson had left, and because one of those Schneidermans was married to his mother and the other three lived just minutes away on the same Riverside Drive where he lived, Ferguson grew ever more attached to them, for the positives in his family ledger were far more positive than the negatives were negative, and even though his life had been diminished in some ways, it had been greatly enhanced in others.

Amy was the Schneiderman bonus, the birthday present hidden under a pile of bunched-up wrapping paper that doesn't get found until after the party is over and all the guests have gone home. It was Ferguson's fault for not paying more attention to her, but there had been so many things to adjust to in the beginning, and he hadn't known what to make of the gawky, grinning creature who waggled and flung out her arms when she talked and couldn't seem to sit still, such an odd-looking girl with those braces on her teeth and that head of tangled, dirty-blond hair, but then the braces came off, her hair was cut into a short bob, and by the time Ferguson turned thirteen he noticed that breasts were beginning to grow inside Amy's formerly useless training bra and that his already thirteen-year-old stepcousin no longer resembled the girl she had been at twelve. A week after the move from Central Park West to Riverside Drive, she called him up after school one day and boldly announced that she was coming over for a visit. When he asked her why she wanted to see him, she said: Because we've known each other for six months, and in all that time you haven't said more than three words to me. We're supposed to be cousins now, Archie, and I want to find out if it's worth the trouble to be friends with you or not.

His mother and stepfather were both out that afternoon, and with no snack material in the cupboard beyond a half-eaten box of stale Fig Newtons, Ferguson felt at a loss, uncertain how he should handle this abrupt intrusion. After Amy hung up the phone in her apartment, it took just eighteen minutes before she was pushing the downstairs buzzer of his apartment, but in that interval Ferguson toyed with and discarded at least half a dozen ideas about what he could do to entertain her (watch television? look at family photo albums? show her the complete thirty-seven-volume set of Shakespeare plays and poems Gil had given to him for his birthday?), then decided to haul out the movie projector and portable screen from the utility closet and set them up for a viewing of one of his Laurel and Hardy films, which was probably a terrible mistake, he realized, since girls didn't like Laurel and Hardy, at least none of the girls he had ever known, starting with the beautiful Isabel Kraft two or three years earlier, who had made a face when he asked her what she thought of them, a sentiment that had been echoed just recently by his current number one, Rachel Minetta, who had called them *juvenile and idiotic,* but then in walked Amy on that cool afternoon in March 1960, dressed in a white sweater, a gray pleated skirt, saddle shoes, and white cotton socks—the ubiquitous bobby socks of the moment—and when Ferguson announced his intention to show her *Blotto,* a Laurel and Hardy two-reeler from 1930, she smiled and said: Great. I love Laurel and Hardy. After the Marx Brothers, they're the best team ever. Forget the Three Stooges, forget Abbott and Costello—Stan and Ollie are the cheese.

No, Amy wasn't like any of the other girls he knew, and as Ferguson watched her laughing at the film, heard her laughing at the film for a good fourteen of the twenty-six minutes it lasted, he concluded that it would indeed be worth the trouble to try to become friends with her, for her laugh wasn't the squealing, out-of-control noise of a child, he noted, but a succession of gut-deep, resonant guffaws—merry yaps, to be sure, but at the same time thoughtful, as if she understood why she was laughing, which made her laugh an intelligent laugh, a laugh that laughed at itself even as it laughed at what it was laughing at. Too bad that she went to public school and not the Riverside Academy, which

eliminated the possibility of daily contact, but in spite of their involvement with their separate friends, and in spite of their various after-school
activities (piano and dance lessons for Amy, sports for Ferguson), they
managed to get together once every ten days or so following Amy's
impromptu visit in March, which worked out to three or four times a
month, not counting the additional times when they saw each other for
joint family outings, holiday dinners, trips to Carnegie Hall with Gil,
and special events (Jim's high school graduation party, the old buzzard's
eightieth birthday bash), but for the most part they saw each other alone,
walking through Riverside Park when the weather was good, sitting in
one of their two apartments when it was bad, occasionally going to the
movies together or working on school assignments at the same table
together or hanging around together in one of their apartments on Friday night to watch the new television program they were both so keen
on (*The Twilight Zone*), but mostly when they were together they talked,
or Amy talked and Ferguson listened, for no one he knew had more to
say about the world than Amy Schneiderman, who seemed to have an
opinion on every subject and knew so much more than he did about
nearly everything. Brilliant, obstreperous Amy, who teased her father
and joked with her brother and warded off her mother's perpetual fuss-
ing with acerbic, know-it-all put-downs that she somehow managed to
get away with without being scolded or punished, most likely because
she was a girl who spoke her mind and had trained the people in her
family to respect her for that, and not even Ferguson, who had rapidly
become her new *ace copain,* was altogether immune from her insults and
criticisms. No matter how vociferously she claimed to like him and
admire him, she often found him lazy in the head and was continually
appalled by his lack of interest in politics, by how little thought he was
giving to Kennedy's presidential campaign and the civil rights movement, but Ferguson couldn't be bothered, he said, he hoped Kennedy
would win, but even if he did become president, things wouldn't get
any better than they were now, they just wouldn't get a whole lot worse,
and as for the civil rights movement, of course he was in favor of it, how
could anyone be against justice and equality for all, but he was only
thirteen years old, for heaven's sake, no more than an insignificant speck
of dust, and what the hell could a speck do about changing the world?

No excuses, Amy said. You're not going to be thirteen forever—and
then what happens to you? You can't spend your life thinking only about

yourself, Archie. You have to let something in, or else you'll turn into one of those hollowed-out people you hate so much—you know, one of the walking dead from Zombieville, U.S.A.

We shall overcome, Ferguson said.

No, my funny little speck-man. You shall overcome.

It was odd being so close to a girl, Ferguson discovered, especially a girl he had no desire to kiss, which was an unprecedented form of friendship in his experience, as intense as any friendship he had ever had with a boy and yet, in that Amy was a girl, there was a different tonality to their interactions, a girl-boy buzz just below the surface that was nevertheless unlike the buzz he felt with Rachel Minetta, or Alice Abrams, or any of the other girls he had crushes on and kissed when he was thirteen, a loud buzz as opposed to the soft buzz he felt with Amy, since she was supposed to be his cousin, a member of his own family, which meant he had no right to kiss her or even think about kissing her, and so great was the interdiction that it never once crossed Ferguson's mind to go against it, knowing that such an act would have been *highly improper*, if not *deeply shocking*, and even though Amy was becoming more and more attractive to him as he watched her body unfurl into the high bloom of her early adolescent womanhood, not pretty in the way Isabel Kraft was pretty, perhaps, but arresting, alive in her eyes as no girl had ever been for him, Ferguson continued to resist the urge to break the code of family honor. Then they turned fourteen, first Amy in December, followed by Ferguson in March, and suddenly he found himself inhabiting a new body that was no longer under his control, a body that produced unbidden erections and much shortness of breath, the early masturbation phase in which no thought that wasn't an erotic thought could fit inside his skull, the delirium of becoming a man without the privileges of being a man, turmoil, consternation, relentless chaos within, and whenever he looked at Amy now his first and only thought was how much he wanted to kiss her, which he sensed was beginning to be true for her whenever she looked at him. One Friday evening in April, with Gil and his mother off at some dinner party downtown, he and Amy sat alone in the seventh-floor apartment discussing the term *kissing cousins*, which Ferguson admitted he didn't fully understand, since it seemed to conjure up an image of cousins politely kissing each other on the cheek, which didn't seem right, somehow, since that kind of kissing didn't qualify as genuine kissing, and therefore why *kissing cousins* when the people in his head were just normal cousins, at which point Amy laughed and said, No, silly, this is what *kissing cousins* means, and without saying another word she leaned toward Ferguson on the sofa, put her arms around him, and planted a kiss on his mouth, which soon became a kiss that was traveling into his mouth, and from that moment on Ferguson decided they weren't really cousins, after all.

2.4

AMY SCHNEIDERMAN HAD BEEN SLEEPING IN HIS OLD BEDROOM for the past four years, Noah Marx had vanished for a time and then resurfaced, and the thirteen-year-old Ferguson, who had just entered the eighth grade, wanted out. Since he wasn't in a position to run away from home (where would he have gone, and how could he have lived without money?), he asked his parents for the next best thing: Would they please ship him off to a boarding school the following September and allow him to spend his four years of high school in a place far from the town of Maplewood, New Jersey.

He wouldn't have asked unless he had known they could afford the expense, but life on a grander scale had continued to flourish at ever more exalted heights since the family moved into the new house in 1956. Two more stores had been added to his father's growing empire (one in Short Hills, the other in Parsippany), and with local consumers now splurging on two and three television sets per household, with dishwashers, washing machines, and clothes dryers now considered standard equipment in every middle-class home, with half the population sinking money into voluminous deep-freeze receptacles to store the frozen foods they now preferred to eat, Ferguson's father had become a wealthy man—not yet a Rockefeller, perhaps, but a king of suburban retail, the renowned *prophet of profits* whose low prices had killed off the competition in seven counties.

The spoils from this expanding income now included a pistachio-green four-door Eldorado for Ferguson's father, a snappy red Pontiac convertible for his mother, membership at the Blue Valley Country Club, and the demise of Roseland Photo, which marked the end of his mother's brief career as independent breadwinner and artist (the fad for painted-over photographs had run its course, the studio was just barely break-ing even, so why bother to go on when sales at the five stores were stronger than they had ever been?), and with all this getting and spend-ing, all this jitterbugging opulence, Ferguson failed to see how board-ing school could possibly be a burden to them. And if they happened to object to his plan (meaning if his father happened to object, since he had the last word on all matters concerning money), Ferguson would counter by offering to give up Camp Paradise and work summer jobs instead, which would help reduce their share of the costs.

He had been researching the matter for several months, he told them, and the best schools seemed to be in New England, mostly in Massachusetts and New Hampshire, but also in Vermont and Connect-icut, with some good ones in upstate New York and Pennsylvania, and even a couple in New Jersey. It was only September, he realized, twelve whole months before the start of the next school year, but applications had to be sent in by mid-January, and unless they began narrowing the list of potential schools now, there wouldn't be enough time to make an informed decision.

Ferguson could hear his voice trembling as he spoke to them, he and his smug, unknowable parents sitting around the dining room table on a Tuesday night during the fall of the Kennedy-Nixon campaign, a family dinner for once, something that happened less and less often now because of the late closings of the stores and his mother's newfound pas-sion for bridge, which kept her out of the house two and three nights a week, and there they were in the dining room as Angie Bly shuttled back and forth between the kitchen and the table, bringing in the dishes for each new course and removing the ones from the old, vegetable soup to begin with, followed by thick slices of roast beef with mashed pota-toes and a mound of buttery string beans, such excellent food cooked by the brusque and capable Angie Bly, who had been cleaning house and cooking meals for them five days a week for the past four years, and now that Ferguson had swallowed his last morsel of roast beef, he finally spoke up, finally found the courage to talk about the thing that had been burning inside him for months.

He watched his parents carefully as the words left his mouth, studying their faces for signs that would tell him what they thought of his plan, but mostly they looked blank, he thought, as if they couldn't quite absorb what he was saying, for why would he want to leave the perfect world he lived in, he who was doing so well at school, who took such pleasure in playing on his baseball and basketball teams, who had so many friends and was invited to all the weekend parties, what more could a thirteen-year-old boy possibly want, and because Ferguson was loath to insult his parents by confessing that they were the reason why he wanted to go away, that living under the same roof with them had become almost intolerable to him, he lied and said he was hungry for a change, that he was feeling restless, smothered by the smallness of their small town and longing to take on new challenges, to test himself in a place that wasn't home.

He understood how ridiculous he must have sounded to them, trying to put his points across and make compelling, sophisticated arguments with his out-of-control, unpredictable voice, his post-boy-pre-man pipes still oscillating from high to low and back again as they sought their ultimate register, a vocal instrument that lacked all authority and command, and how ridiculous he must have looked to them as well, with his chewed-down fingernails and the newborn pus blob sprouting just to the left of his left nostril, a little no one who had been blessed with every material advantage in life, food and shelter and a thousand comforts, and Ferguson was old enough to know how lucky he was to dwell in the upper echelons of good fortune, old enough to know that nine-tenths of humanity was cold and hungry and menaced by want and perpetual fear, and who was he to complain about his lot, how dare he express the smallest note of dissatisfaction, and because he knew where he stood in the big picture of human struggle, he felt ashamed of his unhappiness, revolted by his inability to accept the bounties he had been given, but feelings were feelings, and he couldn't stop himself from feeling angry and disappointed, for no act of will could change what a person felt.

The problems were the same problems he had identified years earlier, but now they were worse, so much worse that Ferguson had concluded they were beyond fixing. The absurd pistachio-green Cadillac, the lifeless, immaculately tended precincts of the Blue Valley Country Club, the talk about voting for Nixon in November—they were all symptoms of an illness that had long infected his father, but his father had been a lost cause from the start, and Ferguson had watched his rise into the ranks of nouveau riche vulgarians with a sort of numb resignation. Then came the death of Roseland Photo, which had thrown him into a funk that had lasted for months, since he knew there had been more to it than a simple matter of dollars and cents. Closing down the studio had been a defeat, a declaration that his mother had given up on herself, and now that she had surrendered and gone over to the other side, how grim it was to see her turn into one of *those women*, yet one more country club wife who golfed and played cards and knocked back too many drinks at cocktail hour. He sensed that she was just as unhappy as he was, but he couldn't talk to her about it, he was too young to meddle in her private affairs, and yet it was clear to him that his parents' marriage, which had always made him think of a bathful of lukewarm water, had now gone cold, degenerating into a bored and loveless cohabitation of two people who went about their own business and intersected only when they had to or wanted to, which was almost never.

No more Sunday morning tennis at the public courts, no more Sunday lunches at Gruning's, no more Sunday afternoons at the movies. The day of national rest was now spent at the country club, a Valhalla of silent putting greens, whooshing water sprinklers, and squealing children romping in the all-weather pool, but Ferguson rarely accompanied his parents on those forty-minute drives to Blue Valley, since Sunday was the day when he practiced with his baseball, football, and basketball teams—even on the Sundays when there was no practice. Seen from a distance, there was nothing inherently wrong with golf, he supposed, and no doubt a case could be made for the benefits of lunching on shrimp cocktails and triple-decker sandwiches, but Ferguson missed his hamburgers and bowls of mint-chip ice cream, and the closer he came to the world that golf represented, the more he learned to despise golf—not so much the sport itself, perhaps, but certainly the people who played it.

Priggish, sanctimonious Ferguson. Ferguson the enemy of upper-middle-class customs and manners, the know-it-all scourge who looked down upon the new American breed of status seekers and conspicuous consumers—the boy who wanted out.

His one hope was that his father would think sending him to a well-known boarding school would enhance his prestige at the club. *Yes, our*

boy is at Andover now. So much better than public school, don't you agree? And
damn the expense. There's no greater gift a parent can give his child than a good
education.

A long shot, to be sure, a vain hope hatched from the self-deluding
optimism of a thirteen-year-old mind, for in point of fact there was no
reason to hope. Sitting across the table from him on that warm September evening, his father put down his fork and said: You're talking like a
greenhorn, Archie. What you're asking me to do is pay twice for the
same thing, and no person in his right mind would fall for a con like
that. Think about it. We pay taxes on this house, don't we? Very high
taxes, some of the highest property taxes in the state. I don't like it, but
I'm willing to fork over the money because I get something back for it.
Good schools, some of the best public schools in the country. That's why
we moved to this town in the first place. Because your mother knew
you'd get a good education here, as good as any education they can offer
at one of your fancy private schools. So no dice, kid. I'm not going to
pay double for something I already have. *Farshtaist?*

Apparently, boarding schools were not on his father's list of show-
off expenditures, and because his mother then piped in and said it would
break her heart if he left home at such a young age, Ferguson didn't even
bother to mention his idea about working summer jobs in order to help
with the tuition. He was stuck now. Not only for the rest of that year,
but for the four additional years it would take until he graduated from
high school—five years in all, which was more time than many people
served for armed robbery or manslaughter.

Angie came into the dining room with dessert, and as Ferguson
looked down at his bowl of chocolate pudding, he wondered why there
wasn't a law that allowed children to divorce their parents.

BECAUSE NOTHING HAD changed or ever would change, because the
old system of family governance was still intact after Ferguson's efforts
to amend the constitution had been voted down, the unfallen ancien
régime continued to rule by reflex and ingrained whimsy, and so it was
decreed that the vanquished malcontent should be rewarded with yet
another summer at his beloved Camp Paradise, his sixth consecutive
year in that parentless haven of ball fields, canoe expeditions, and the
rowdy companionship of his New York friends. Not only was Ferguson

about to leave his mother and father for two long months of respite and freedom, but standing beside him on the platform at Grand Central on the morning of his departure was Noah Marx, who was on his way up north for yet another summer as well, for Noah was back, and after missing the second half of the 1956 season and all eight weeks of 1957, he had resumed his connection with Camp Paradise and was about to embark on his fourth straight session there in the company of his step-mother's nephew, also known as his stepcousin and friend, the now fourteen-year-old Ferguson, who at five feet, seven inches stood half a head taller than Noah, who still went by the name of Harpo at camp.

It was a curious story. Ferguson's Aunt Mildred had remained Noah's stepmother because she and Uncle Don had never bothered to divorce, and when Noah's father returned from his eighteen-month sojourn in Paris, where he had begun writing a biography of Montaigne, he moved back to his old address on Perry Street. Not into the third-floor apartment he had previously shared with Mildred, however, but into a smaller, second-floor studio that had been vacated during his absence and which Mildred had rented for him prior to his return. That was the new arrangement. After a year and a half of turmoil and inde-cision, punctuated by three trips to Paris when Mildred was on break from teaching at Brooklyn College, they had concluded that they couldn't live apart. On the other hand, they also understood that they were incapable of living together—at least not all the time, at least not as a conventionally married couple, and unless they allowed for sporadic interruptions of the domestic routine, they would end up devouring each other in a bloodbath of cannibalistic rage. Hence the compro-mise of the two apartments, the so-called Escape-Hatch Conciliation, for theirs was one of those impossible loves, a fraught mixture of pas-sion and incompatibility, an electric storm-field of equally charged neg-ative and positive ions, and because Don and Mildred were both selfish and volatile and utterly devoted to each other, the wars they fought were never-ending—except at those moments when Don moved downstairs into his second-floor apartment and a new era of peace began.

It was quite a muddle in Ferguson's opinion, but not one he dwelled on at any length, since all marriages in his experience were flawed in one way or another, the savage conflicts of Don and Mildred as opposed to the weary indifference of his parents, but both marriages flawed just the same, not to mention his grandparents, who had barely spoken fifty words to each other in the past ten years, and as far as he could tell, the only grown-up man or woman who seemed to take pleasure in the mere fact of being alive was his Great-aunt Pearl, who no longer had a husband and would never have one again. Still and all, Ferguson was glad that Don and Mildred had been reunited, if not for their sakes then at least for his own, since Don's return had brought Noah back into his life, and after an eighteen-month interval, during which they had been barred from each other's company by Noah's quasi-insane mother, Ferguson was astonished by how quickly they became friends again, as if the long separation had lasted no more than a matter of days.

Noah was still all flap and fury, the fast-talking needler of yore, but far less combustible at eleven than he had been at nine, and as the boys staggered through late childhood into early adolescence, each one found support in what he perceived to be the other's strengths. For Noah, Ferguson was the handsome prince who excelled at everything he touched, the top dog who hit for the highest batting average and earned splendid marks at school, the one the girls liked, the one most looked up to by the other boys, and to be the cousin, friend, and confidant of such a person was an ennobling force in his life, which otherwise was a tormented life, the transitional life of a fourteen-year-old who fretted daily about his frizz-headed, gawky looks, about the disfiguring metal wires that had been bolted onto his teeth for the past year, about his appalling lack of physical grace. Ferguson knew how much Noah admired him, but he also knew that this admiration was misjudged and unwarranted, that Noah had turned him into a heroic, idealized being who in fact did not exist, whereas he, Ferguson, in the dark inner space where he actually lived, understood that Noah possessed a first-class mind, and that when it came to the things that truly mattered, the young Mr. Marx was more advanced than he was, at least one step ahead of him at every moment, often two steps, and occasionally four steps and even ten steps. Noah was his pathfinder, the quick-moving scout who explored the woods for Ferguson and told him where the best hunting was—books to read, music to listen to, jokes to laugh at, films to watch, ideas to think about—and now that Ferguson had ingested *Candide* and *Bartleby*, J. S. Bach and Muddy Waters, *Modern Times* and *Grand Illusion*, Jean Shepherd's late-night monologues and Mel Brooks's two-thousand-year-old man, *Notes of a Native Son* and *The Communist Manifesto* (no, Karl

Marx wasn't a relative—and neither, alas, was Groucho), he couldn't help imagining how impoverished his life would have been without Noah. Anger and disappointment could take you just so far, he realized, but without curiosity you were lost.

So there they were in July 1961, about to set off for Camp Paradise at the start of that eventful summer when all the news from the outside world seemed to be bad news: the wall going up in Berlin, Ernest Hemingway blasting a bullet through his skull in the mountains of Idaho, mobs of white racists attacking the Freedom Riders as they traveled on their buses through the South. Menace, despondency, and hatred, abundant proof that rational men were not in charge of running the universe, and as Ferguson settled into the pleasant and familiar bustle of camp life, dribbling basketballs and stealing bases in the mornings and afternoons, listening to the barbs and blather of the boys in his cabin, exulting in the chance to be with Noah again, which above all meant being able to participate in a nonstop, two-month-long conversation with him, dancing in the evenings with the New York City girls he liked so much, the spirited and busty Carol Thalberg, the slender and thoughtful Ann Brodsky, and eventually the acne-ridden but exceptionally beautiful Denise Levinson, who was of one mind with him about slipping away from the post-dinner "socials" for intense mouth-and-tongue exercises in the back meadow, so many good things to be thankful for, and yet now that he was fourteen and his head was filled with thoughts that wouldn't even have occurred to him just six months earlier, Ferguson was forever looking at himself in relation to distant, unknown others, wondering, for example, if he hadn't been kissing Denise at the precise moment when Hemingway was blowing his brains out in Idaho or if, just as he was hitting a double in the game between Camp Paradise and Camp Greylock last Thursday, a Mississippi Klansman hadn't been driving his fist into the jaw of a skinny, short-haired Freedom Rider from Boston. One person kissed, another person punched, or else one person attending his mother's funeral at eleven o'clock in the morning on June 10, 1857, and at the same moment on the same block in the same city, another person holding her newborn child in her arms for the first time, the sorrow of the one occurring simultaneously with the joy of the other, and unless you were God, who was presumably everywhere and could see everything that was happening at any given moment, no one could possibly know that those two events were taking place at the same time, least of all the grieving son and the laughing mother. Was that why man had invented God? Ferguson asked himself. In order to overcome the limits of human perception by asserting the existence of an all-encompassing, all-powerful divine intelligence?

Think of it this way, he said to Noah one afternoon as they were walking to the dining hall. You have to go somewhere in your car. It's an important errand, and you can't be late. There are two ways to get there—by the main road or the back road. It happens to be rush hour, and normally things are pretty clogged up on the main road at that time of day, but unless there's an accident or a breakdown, the traffic tends to move slowly and steadily, and chances are the trip will take you about twenty minutes, which would get you to your appointment just in time—on the dot, without a second to spare. The back road is a bit longer in terms of distance, but there are fewer cars to worry about, and if all goes well, you can count on a travel time of about fifteen minutes. In principle, the back road is better than the main road, but there's also a hitch: it has only one lane going in each direction, and if you happen to run into a breakdown or an accident, you're liable to get stuck for a long time, which would make you late for your appointment.

Hold on, Noah said. I need to know more about this appointment. Where am I going, and why is it so important to me?

It doesn't matter, Ferguson replied. The car trip is just an example, a proposition, a way of talking about the thing I want to discuss with you—which has nothing to do with roads or appointments.

But it does matter, Archie. Everything matters.

Ferguson let out a long sigh and said: All right. You're going to a job interview. It's the job you've been dreaming about all your life—Paris correspondent for the *Daily Planet*. If you get the job, you'll be the happiest person in the world. If you don't, you'll go home and hang yourself.

If it means that much to me, why would I leave at the last minute? Why not start the trip an hour earlier and make sure I won't be late?

Because . . . because you can't. Your grandmother has died, and you had to go to her funeral.

Fair enough. It's what we call a momentous day. I've just spent six hours weeping for my grandmother, and now I'm in my car, heading for the job interview. Which road do you want me to take?

Again, it doesn't matter. There are only two choices, the main road and the back road, and each one has its good points and bad points. Say you choose the main road and get to your appointment on time. You won't think about your choice, will you? And if you go by the back road and get there in time, again, no sweat, and you'll never give it another thought for the rest of your life. But here's where it gets interesting. You take the main road, there's a three-car pileup, traffic is stalled for more than an hour, and as you sit there in your car, the only thing on your mind will be the back road and why you didn't go that way instead. You'll curse yourself for making the wrong choice, and yet how do you really know it was the wrong choice? Can you see the back road? Do you know what's happening on the back road? Has anyone told you that an enormous redwood tree has fallen across the back road and crushed a passing car, killing the driver of that car and holding up traffic for three and a half hours? Has anyone looked at his watch and told you that if you had taken the back road it would have been your car that was crushed and you who were killed? Or else: No tree fell, and taking the main road was the wrong choice. Or else: You took the back road, and the tree fell on the driver just in front of you, and as you sit in your car wishing you had taken the main road, you know nothing about the three-car pileup that would have made you miss your appointment anyway. Or else: There was no three-car pileup, and taking the back road was the wrong choice.

What's the point of all this, Archie?

I'm saying you'll never know if you made the wrong choice or not. You would need to have all the facts before you knew, and the only way to get all the facts is to be in two places at the same time—which is impossible.

And?

And that's why people believe in God.

Surely you jest, Monsieur Voltaire.

Only God can see the main road and the back road at the same time—which means that only God can know if you made the right choice or the wrong choice.

How do you know he knows?

I don't. But that's the assumption people make. Unfortunately, God never tells us what he thinks.

You could always write him a letter.

True. But there wouldn't be any point.

What's the problem? Can't afford the airmail postage?

I don't have his address.

THERE WAS A new boy in the cabin that year, the one first-timer among Ferguson's old comrades from summers past, a non–city boy who lived in the Westchester town of New Rochelle, which made him the only other suburban dweller in Ferguson's circle of acquaintances, less boisterous and verbally aggressive than the boys from New York, quiet in the way that Ferguson was quiet, but even more so, a boy who said almost nothing, and yet, when he did speak, the people within hearing distance found themselves paying close attention to his words. His name was Federman, Art Federman, universally know as Artie, and because *Artie Federman* was so close in sound to *Archie Ferguson*, the boys in the cabin often joked that they were long-lost brothers, identical twins who had been separated at birth. What made the joke funny was that it wasn't a real joke but an anti-joke, a joke that made sense only if it was understood as a joke about the joke itself, for while Ferguson and Federman shared certain physical characteristics—similar in size and build, both with big hands and the lean, muscled bodies of young ballplayers— they bore little resemblance to each other beyond their common initials. Ferguson was dark and Federman was fair, Ferguson's eyes were gray-green and Federman's were brown, their noses, ears, and mouths were all shaped differently, and no one seeing them together for the first time ever would have mistaken them for brothers—or even, for that matter, distant cousins. On the other hand, the boys in the cabin were no longer seeing them together for the first time, and as the days passed and they continued to observe the two A.F.s in action, perhaps they understood that the joke that was not a joke was something more than a joke, for even if it wasn't a question of two flesh-and-blood brothers, it was a question of friends, of two flesh-and-blood friends who were rapidly becoming as close as brothers.

One of the odd things about being himself, Ferguson had discovered, was that there seemed to be several of him, that he wasn't just one person but a collection of contradictory selves, and each time he was with a different person, he himself was different as well. With an outspoken extrovert like Noah, he felt quiet and closed in on himself. With a shy and guarded person like Ann Brodsky, he felt loud and crude, always talking too much in order to overcome the awkwardness of her long silences. Humorless people tended to transform him into a jokester. Quick-witted clowns made him feel dull and slow. Still other people seemed to possess the power to draw him into their orbit and make him act in the same way they did. Pugnacious Mark Dubinsky, with his endless opinions about politics and sports, would bring out the verbal battler in Ferguson. Dreamy Bob Kramer would make him feel fragile and unsure of himself. Artie Federman, on the other hand, made him feel calm, calm in a way no other person had ever made him feel, for being with the new boy brought the same sense of selfhood he felt when he was alone.

If either one of the two A.F.s had been a slightly different person, they easily could have wound up as enemies. Ferguson in particular had every justification to resent the newcomer's arrival on the scene, for it turned out that Federman was better at sports than he was, and for the past five years Ferguson had been the best, especially at baseball, which meant he had always played shortstop and batted fourth for the traveling team, but when Federman showed up for practice on the first day, it quickly became apparent that he had more range and a stronger arm than Ferguson, that his bat was faster and more powerful, and by the next day, when he hit two home runs and a double in an intrasquad game, eliminating any doubt that his first day's performance had been a fluke, Bill Rappaport, the twenty-four-year-old coach of the team, pulled Ferguson aside and announced his decision: Federman was the new shortstop and cleanup hitter, and Ferguson was being switched over to third base and would bat one notch up in the order. You understand why I have to do this, don't you? Bill said. Ferguson nodded. Given the strength of the evidence, what else could he do but nod? Nothing against you, Archie, Bill continued, but this new kid is phenomenal.

No matter how you looked at it, Bill's new lineup was a demotion, a small drop in the ranks, and it stung Ferguson to have lost his position as supreme commander of the Camp Paradise baseball army, but just as feelings were always feelings, subjectively true one hundred percent of the time, facts were also facts, and in this case the objective, unarguable fact was that Bill had made the right decision. Ferguson was the number two man now. The old boyhood dream of one day making it to the major leagues slowly dissolved into a gunky residue at the bottom of his stomach. It left a bitter taste for a while, but then he got over it. Federman was simply too good to want to compete with him. In the face of such a talent, the only proper response was to be thankful he was on your side.

What made that talent so unusual, Ferguson felt, was that Federman was all but oblivious to it. No matter how earnestly he played, no matter how many games he won with last-inning hits or diving stops in the field, he never seemed to understand how much better he was than everyone else. Excelling at baseball was merely something he could do, and he accepted it in the same way he accepted the color of the sky or the roundness of the earth. A passion to do well, yes, but at the same time indifference, even a touch of boredom, and whenever someone on the team remarked that he should think about turning pro after he finished high school, Federman would shake his head and laugh. Baseball was a fun thing to do, he'd say, but it was essentially meaningless, no more than *kid's stuff*, and when he graduated from high school his plan was to go on to college and study to become a scientist—either a physicist or a mathematician, he wasn't sure which one yet.

There was something both lunkheaded and disarming about that response, Ferguson thought, which struck him as a typical example of what defined his almost-namesake and set him apart from the others, since it was a foregone conclusion that all the boys would eventually go on to college, that was the world they lived in, the third-generation Jewish-American world in which all but the most feebleminded were now expected to earn an undergraduate degree, if not a professional or advanced degree, but Federman didn't understand the nuances of what the others were saying to him, he failed to realize they weren't telling him he *shouldn't* go to college but that he didn't *have to go* if he didn't want to, which meant they thought he was in a stronger position than they were, more in control of his own destiny, and because he was indeed an excellent student in math and science and had every intention of going to college (he was teaching himself calculus that summer, for God's sake, and how many fourteen-year-olds could grasp the principles of calculus?), he had ignored the compliment and given them a blunt, straight-from-the-heart answer that was so obvious and beside the point (everyone knew he was studying calculus and was inevitably bound for college) that he needn't have said it at all.

But that was one of the things Ferguson liked best about the other A.F.—his innocence, his unworldly remove from the ironies and contradictions of the society he belonged to. Everyone else seemed to be trapped in the throes of a perpetual agitation, a chaos of clashing impulses and turbulent inconsistencies, but Federman was still, pensive, and apparently at peace with himself, so locked into his own thoughts and his own way of doing things that he paid little attention to the noise around him. An uncontaminated being, Ferguson sometimes thought, so pure and rigorously himself that it was often difficult to make sense of him, which was no doubt why he and Noah had formed such different impressions of their new cabinmate. Noah was willing to grant that Federman was both highly intelligent and a superb ball-player, but he was too sincere for his taste, too lacking in the humor department to qualify as good company, and the stillness that ema-nated from him, which had such a calming effect on Ferguson, was altogether unnerving to Noah, who felt that Federman was something less than fully human, *a weird ghosty-boy*, as he once put it, a specter who had been born with parts of his brain missing. Ferguson understood what Noah was trying to express with those comments, but he didn't agree with him. Federman was different, that was all, a person who lived on a separate plane from the others, and what Noah saw as weak-nesses of character—Federman's shyness with girls, his inability to tell a joke, his reluctance to argue with anyone—Ferguson tended to read as strengths, for he spent more time with Federman than Noah did, and he understood that what Noah perceived as shallowness or even emptiness was in fact depth, a largeness of soul that was not present in anyone else he knew. The problem was that Federman didn't do well in groups, whereas alone with a single counterpart he was a different person, and now that three weeks had gone by and the two A.F.s had walked back and forth to the baseball field together dozens of times, Ferguson had come to know that other person, or at least was begin-ning to know him, and the thing that impressed him most about Federman was how observant he was, how remarkably attuned his senses were to the world around him, and whenever he pointed to a cloud passing overhead, or to a bee alighting on the stamen of a flower, or identified the call of an invisible bird crying out from the woods, Ferguson felt he was seeing and hearing those things for the first time, that without his friend to alert him to the presence of those things, he never would have known they were there, for walking with Federman was above all an exercise in the art of paying attention, and paying attention, Ferguson discovered, was the first step in learning how to be alive.

Then came the exceptionally warm Thursday afternoon toward the end of the month, more or less the midpoint of the summer, just two days before the start of parents' weekend, with a basketball-baseball doubleheader scheduled for Saturday morning and afternoon against much-feared and much-hated rival Camp Scatico, whose teams would be visiting Camp Paradise for the day, games that would be watched by the mothers and fathers of the Paradise boys, the roly-poly women in their sleeveless cotton dresses, the chunky men in their Bermuda shorts, the sleek and formerly sleek women in their pedal-pusher slacks and stiletto heels, the men with thinning hair in their white business shirts with the sleeves rolled up to the elbow, it was the biggest sports day of the summer, which would be followed in the evening by a performance of the old Marx Brothers play *The Cocoanuts*, which had been turned into their first film in 1929, and bizarrely and yet most fittingly, Noah, who was widely known throughout the camp as Harpo, had been cast in the role of Groucho, a part for which his talents were far better suited, and not only was Ferguson looking forward to the games he would be involved in two days hence, he couldn't wait to see his cousin walk the Groucho walk as he pranced about the stage with a cigar wedged between the second and third fingers of his right hand and a greasepaint mustache smeared across the skin between his nose and upper lip. So much anticipation leading up to the events of that day, and because Camp Paradise was almost certain to lose the basketball game (they had been trounced on their visit to Camp Scatico ten days earlier), Bill Rappaport was determined to repeat their victory in baseball, and to that end he had put the boys through several grueling practices over the past days, with endless precision drills in fundamentals (bunting, hitting the cutoff man, holding runners on base) and strenuous calisthenic exercises *to keep them in shape* (push-ups, sit-ups, wind sprints, laps around the field), and on that particular Thursday in late July, which was the warmest, muggiest day that had fallen upon the camp all summer, Ferguson's body had been awash in sweat throughout the entire practice, and now that the two-hour session was over and he and Federman were walking back to the cabin, where they would be changing into their bathing suits for the obligatory pre-dinner swim, he felt exhausted from his exertions on the field, *sapped of energy*, as he put it to Federman, as if each one of his legs weighed two hundred pounds, and even the normally indefatigable New Rochelle calculus boy admitted that he, too, was feeling *rather pooped*. About halfway to the cabin, Ferguson began talking about the book he had finished reading during the post-lunch rest hour, *Miss Lonely-hearts*, a tiny novel by Nathanael West that had been included by his Aunt Mildred in her annual package of summer books for him, and just as he was starting to explain that Miss Lonelyhearts was in fact a man, a journalist writing in the voice of a woman for an advice col-umn to the lovelorn, he heard Federman emit a small, muffled noise, something that sounded like the word *oh*, and when he swiveled his head to the right and looked at his friend, he saw that Federman was staggering, as if he had been overcome by a fit of dizziness, and before Ferguson could ask him what was wrong, Federman's knees buckled and he slowly fell to the ground.

Ferguson assumed it was a joke, that after all the talk about how tired they were Federman had gotten it into his head to do a comic demonstration of what happens to a body after too much exercise on hot and humid summer days, but the laugh Ferguson was expecting to hear didn't come, for the truth was that Artie wasn't a person who traf-ficked in jokes, and as Ferguson bent down to examine his friend's face, he was startled to see that his eyes were neither open nor closed but half-open, half-closed, with only the whites visible, as if his eyes had rolled up into his head, which seemed to suggest that he had passed out, so Ferguson began to tap Federman's cheeks with his fingers, first tapping and then pinching the cheeks as he told him to wake up, as if a few taps and a few pinches would be enough to rouse him to con-sciousness, but when Federman didn't respond, when his head lolled back and forth as Ferguson began to shake his shoulders and his inert eyelids refused to open or shut or even flutter with the smallest sign of life, Ferguson started to grow afraid, and so he pressed his ear against Federman's chest in order to listen to the beating of his heart, in order to feel his rib cage rising and falling as the air went in and out of his lungs, but there was no heartbeat, there was no breath, and an instant later Ferguson stood up and began to howl: Help me! Help me, someone! Please—someone—help me!

BRAIN ANEURYSM. THAT was the official cause of death, someone said, and since the Columbia County medical examiner performed the autopsy himself, those were the words he inscribed on Federman's death certificate: *brain aneurysm.*

Ferguson knew what a brain was, but it was the first time he had come across the word *aneurysm,* so he walked over to the head counselor's office and looked it up in the *Webster's Collegiate Dictionary* that sat on the top shelf of the bookcase: *a permanent abnormal blood-filled dilation of an artery, resulting from disease of the vessel wall.*

THE GAMES WITH Camp Scatico were canceled until further notice. The Marx Brothers comedy would be held back until sometime the following month. The family songfest scheduled for Sunday morning was erased from the calendar.

AT THE ALL-CAMP gathering that convened in the Big Barn after dinner on Thursday, half the children wept, many of whom had never even known Federman. Jack Feldman, the head counselor, told the boys and girls that the ways of God were incomprehensible, beyond the grasp of human understanding.

BILL RAPPAPORT BLAMED himself for Federman's collapse. He had pushed the team too hard, he told Ferguson, he had put everyone in danger with those punishing workouts in that intolerable heat and humidity. What the fuck had he been thinking? Ferguson remembered the words from the dictionary: *permanent, abnormal, blood-filled . . . disease.* No, Bill, he said, it was bound to happen sooner or later. Artie was walking around with a time bomb in his head. It's just that no one knew about it—not him, not his parents, not one doctor who ever examined him. He had to die before anyone found out that the time bomb had been there his whole life.

□ □ □

DURING REST HOUR on Friday afternoon, his name was announced over the loudspeaker. *Archie Ferguson,* the voice of the camp secretary said. *Archie Ferguson, please come to the main office. You have a telephone call.*

It was his mother. Such a terrible thing, Archie, she said. I feel so sorry for that boy, for you . . . for everyone.

It wasn't just a terrible thing, Ferguson replied. It was the worst thing, the worst thing that's ever happened.

A long pause followed on the other end of the line, and then his mother said that she had just received a call from Artie's mother. An unexpected call, of course, an excruciating call, of course, but purely for the purpose of inviting Ferguson to attend the funeral in New Rochelle on Sunday—assuming he could get permission to leave the camp, and assuming he felt up to going.

I don't understand, Ferguson said. No one else is invited. Why me?

His mother explained that Mrs. Federman had been reading and rereading the letters her son had sent home from camp, and in nearly all of them Ferguson had been mentioned, often several times in the space of three or four paragraphs. *Archie is my best friend,* his mother said, quoting from a passage that had been read to her over the phone, *the best friend I've ever had.* And again: *Archie is such a good person, it makes me happy just to be near him.* And again: *Archie is the closest thing I've ever had to a brother.*

Another long pause, and then Ferguson said, in a voice so quiet he could barely hear his own words, That's how I felt about Artie.

IT WAS SETTLED, then. There would be no weekend visit from his parents. Instead, Ferguson would take the train down to New York in the morning, his mother would meet him at Grand Central Station, they would spend the night in the city at her parents' apartment, and the next morning the two of them would drive up to New Rochelle together. Not one to ignore the exigencies of public occasions, his mother promised to carry along clothes for him to wear at the funeral—his white shirt, jacket, and tie, his black shoes, black socks, and charcoal-gray pants.

She said: Have you grown much since you've been up there, Archie?

I'm not sure, Ferguson answered. Maybe a little.

I'm wondering if those things will still fit you.

Does it matter?

Maybe yes, maybe no. If the buttons pop off your shirt, we can always buy some new clothes tomorrow.

THE BUTTONS DIDN'T pop off, but the shirt was too small for him now, as was everything else except the tie. What a nuisance to go out shopping in ninety-four-degree weather, he thought, trudging through the streets of the broiling city because he'd grown two and a half inches since the spring, but he couldn't go to New Rochelle in his camp jeans and tennis shoes, and so off he went with his mother to Macy's, prowling the men's department for more than an hour in search of something decent to wear, without question the most boring activity on earth even in the best of times, which these times most definitely were not, and so little was his heart in what they were doing that he allowed his mother to make all the decisions, selecting this shirt, this jacket, and this pair of pants for him, and yet, as he would soon learn, how preferable was the boredom of shopping to the wretched hopelessness of sitting in the synagogue the next day, the hot sanctuary crowded with more than two hundred people, Artie's mother and father, his twelve-year-old sister, his four grandparents, his aunts and uncles, his boy and girl cousins, his friends from school, his various teachers going all the way back to kindergarten, his friends and coaches from the sports teams he had played on, friends of the family, friends of friends of the family, a mob of people baking in that airless room as tears spurted from clenched eyes and men and women sobbed, as boys and girls sobbed, and there was the rabbi at the pulpit reciting prayers in both Hebrew and English, none of that Christian claptrap about going to a better place, no fairy-tale afterlife for Ferguson and his people, these were the Jews, the demented, defiant Jews, and for them there was only one life and one place, this life and this earth, and the only way to look at death was to praise God, to praise the power of God even when the death belonged to a fourteen-year-old boy, to praise their fucking God until their eyes fell out of their heads and their balls fell off their bodies and their hearts shriveled inside them.

□ □ □

AT THE CEMETERY, as the casket was being lowered into the ground, Artie's father tried to jump into his son's grave. It took four men to pull him back, and when he tried to break free of them and do it again, the biggest of the four, who turned out to be his younger brother, put him in a headlock and wrestled him to the ground.

AT THE HOUSE after the burial, Artie's mother, a tall woman with thick legs and broad hips, threw her arms around Ferguson and told him he would always be part of the family.

FOR THE NEXT two hours, he sat on the sofa in the living room talking to Artie's little sister, whose name was Celia. He wanted to tell her that he was her brother now, that he would go on being her brother for as long as he lived, but he couldn't find the courage to push the words out of his mouth.

SUMMER CAME TO a close, another school year began, and in mid-September Ferguson started writing a short story, which slowly grew into a rather long story by the time he finished it in the days before Thanksgiving. He suspected it had been inspired by the joke that was not a joke about the two A.F.s, but he wasn't quite sure, since the story had come to him out of nowhere as a fully formed idea, and yet some-how or other Federman must have been in there, too, given that Feder-man was always with him now, would always be with him from now on. Not Archie and Artie, as he had been tempted to use at first, but Hank and Frank, those were the names of the principal characters, a rhyming pair rather than an assonant pair, but a lifelong pair for all that, in this case a pair of shoes, which was how the story got its title: *Sole Mates.*

Hank and Frank, the left shoe and the right shoe, meet for the first time in the factory where they were made, arbitrarily thrown together when the last person on the assembly line puts them into the same shoe box. They are a sturdy, well-crafted pair of brown leather lace-ups commonly known as brogans, and while their personalities are slightly different (Hank tends to be anxious and introspective while Frank is blunt and fearless), they are not different in the way that Laurel and Hardy are different, for example, or Heckle and Jeckle, or Abbott and Costello, but different, perhaps, in the way that Ferguson and Federman had been different—two peas from the same pod, yet by no means identical.

Neither one of them is happy in the box. They are still strangers at this point, and not only is it dark and stuffy in there, they have been jammed up against each other in a most intimate and compromising way, which leads to some unfriendly bickering at first, but then Frank tells Hank to get a grip on himself and settle down, they're stuck with each other whether they like it or not, and Hank, understanding that he has no choice but to make the best of a bad situation, apologizes for having gotten them off on *the wrong foot*, to which Frank says, *Is that supposed to be funny?*, meaning he didn't find the remark funny at all, and so Hank comes back at him by dropping his voice and speaking in a broad southern accent: *Ah shoe hope so, brothuh brogan. Can't live this life without no funnies, can we?*

The box containing Hank and Frank is put on a truck and driven to New York City, where it ends up in the back room of the Florsheim shoe store on Madison Avenue, one more box added to the hundreds of boxes stacked on shelves waiting to be sold. That is their destiny—to be sold, to be de-boxed by a man with size eleven feet and led away from the back room of that store forever—and Hank and Frank are impatient to begin their lives, to be out in the open air walking with their master. Frank is confident about their chances for a quick sale. They're an everyday sort of pair, he tells Hank, not some novelty item like patent leather dress shoes or Santa Claus slippers or fleece-lined snow boots, and since everyday shoes are the ones most in demand, it shouldn't be long before they can say good-bye to this dreary, stinking box of theirs. Maybe so, Hank says, but if Frank wants to talk about odds and statistics, he should think about the number eleven. Size eleven worries him. It's much bigger than average, and who knows how long they'll have to wait before Mr. Bigfoot walks in and asks to try them on? He'd be much happier with an eight or a nine, he says. That's what most men wear, and most means faster. The bigger the shoe, the longer it's going to take, and size eleven is one hell of a big shoe.

Just be glad we're not a twelve or thirteen, Frank says.

I am, Hank replies. I'm also glad we're not a six. But I'm not glad
we're an eleven.

After three days and three nights on the shelf, a bleak span that only
prolongs their doubts and febrile calculations about when and how they
will be rescued, if indeed they will be rescued at all, a clerk finally comes
in the next morning, pulls out their box from the tower of boxes they
were consigned to, and carries them into the showroom at the front of
the store. A customer is interested! The clerk removes the lid from the
box, and in that first moment when the light of the world shines upon
them, Hank and Frank start to tingle with joy, a joy so vast and intoxicating that it spreads all the way to the tips of their laces. They can see
again, see for the first time since the factory worker put them in their
box, and now that the clerk is taking them out of the box and putting
them on the floor in front of the seated customer, Frank says to Hank,
I think we're in business, pal, to which Hank responds, *I certainly hope so.*

(Note: At no point in the story does Ferguson address the question
of how shoes can talk, in spite of the fact that all lace-up shoes are
equipped with tongues. If it is a problem, he solves the problem by refusing to consider it. Nevertheless, the language spoken by Hank and
Frank is apparently inaudible to human beings, since the two of them
carry on conversations wherever and whenever they like, with no fear
of being overheard—at least not by living people. In the presence of other
shoes, however, they must be more circumspect, for all shoes in the story
speak Shoe. As it happened, none of Ferguson's early readers objected
to his use of that absurd, make-believe language. They all seemed to
go along with it as a legitimate case of *poetic license,* but several people
thought he had gone too far by giving Hank and Frank the ability to
see. Shoes are blind, one person said, everybody knows that. How on
earth can shoes possibly see? The fourteen-year-old author paused for
a moment, shrugged his shoulders, and said: *With their eyelets of course.
How else?*)

The customer is a big man, a great hulking fellow of broad girth
with a pair of swollen ankles and the moist, pallid skin of someone who
might or might not be suffering from diabetes or heart trouble. Not an
ideal master, perhaps, but as Hank and Frank have told each other countless times over the past three days, *shoes can't choose.* They must submit
to the will of the person who buys them, no matter who that person hap-

pens to be, for their job is to protect feet, any and all feet under any and all circumstances, and whether those feet belong to a madman or a saint, shoes must perform that job in perfect compliance with the wishes of their master. Still, it is an important moment for the newly manufactured brogans, so young and gleaming in the stiffness of their cowhide uppers and untrammeled soles, for this is the moment when they will at last begin their lives as fully functioning shoes, and as the clerk slips Hank onto the customer's left foot and then slips Frank onto the right, they both groan with pleasure, astonished by how good it feels to have a foot inside them, and then, miraculously, the pleasure only increases as the laces are tightened and the two ends are knotted into a crisp, firm bow.

It seems to be a good fit, the clerk says to the customer. Would you like to have a look in the mirror?

And so it is that Hank and Frank are able to see themselves together for the first time—by looking into the mirror as the fat man looks into the mirror as well. What a handsome pair we are, Frank says, and for once Hank is in accord with him. The finest brogans ever made, he says. Or, as the bard might have put it: *the very kings of Cobbledom.*

While Hank and Frank are admiring themselves in the mirror, however, the fat man is beginning to shake his head. I'm not sure, he says to the clerk, they look a bit clunky to me.

A man of your bulk needs a hardy shoe, the clerk replies, delivering his words in a matter-of-fact tone so as not to offend the customer.

Of course, the fat man mutters, that goes without saying, doesn't it? But that doesn't mean I have to walk around in these clodhoppers.

They're classics, sir, the clerk says drily.

Cop shoes. That's what they look like to me, the fat man says. Shoes for a plainclothes cop.

After a considerable pause, the clerk clears his throat and says: May I suggest we look at something else? A pair of wingtips, perhaps?

Yeah, wingtips, the customer says, nodding in agreement. That's the word I was looking for. Not brogans—wingtips.

Hank and Frank are put back in their box, and a few moments later they are lifted off the floor by a pair of invisible hands and carried back to the back room, where they once again join the ranks of the unsold. Hank is burning with indignation. The fat man's comments have incensed him, and as he spits out the words *clunky* and *clodhopper* for the forty-third time in the past hour, Frank finally speaks up and implores him to stop. Don't you realize how lucky we are? he says. Not only was that man a numskull, he was an obese numskull, and the last thing we want is to be saddled with too much heft. If old Mr. Chunko-witz didn't weigh three hundred pounds, he must have been a good two-sixty or two-seventy, and just imagine the day-to-day wear and tear of walking around with a mountain like that on top of us. Little by little, we would have been crushed, used up before our time, junked before we'd even had a chance to live. There might not be a lot of feath-erweights who wear size eleven, but at least we can hope for someone who's lean and fit, a man with a light and even step. No waddlers or plodders for us, Hank. We deserve the best because we're *classics*.

Two more misses follow over the next three days, one of them a near miss (a man who falls in love with them but discovers he needs a size ten and a half) and the other one a dud from the word go (a scowling teenage giant who mocks his mother for making him try on such *ugly gunboats*), and the wait goes on, so dispiriting in its languorous monot-ony that Hank and Frank begin to wonder if they aren't doomed to remain on the shelf forever—unwanted, out of style, forgotten. Then, three full days after the gunboat insult, when all hope has disappeared from their hearts, a customer walks into the store, a thirty-year-old man named Abner Quine, six feet tall and a trim one hundred and seventy pounds, a size eleven who not only is looking for a pair of brogans but will not settle for anything but a pair of brogans, and so Hank and Frank are taken off the shelf for the fourth time, which turns out to be the last time, the end of their fretful week in black shoe-box limbo, for when Abner Quine sticks his feet into them and walks around the store to test them out, he says to the clerk, *Excellent, they're just what I wanted*, and the two sole mates have finally found their master.

Does it make any difference that Quine turns out to be a cop? Not really, not in the long run it doesn't, but after Hank and Frank were rejected by the fat customer for looking like a pair of *cop shoes*, it is some-thing of a sore point with them, and rather than laugh at the coinci-dence they feel hurt and bewildered, for if brogans are the quintessential cop shoe, then it would seem they were fated all along to be worn by a flatfoot, a figure of immense ridicule in popular lore, and to be the shoe of preference for the flatfeet of this world, that is, the very embodiment of flat-footedness, means there must be something ridiculous about them as well.

Let's face it, Hank says. We weren't built for tuxedos and wild nights out on the town.

Maybe not, Frank replies, but we're solid and dependable.

Like two tanks.

Well, who wants to be a sports car, anyway?

Cop shoes, Frank. That's what we are. The lowest of the low.

But look at our cop, Hank. What a fine figure of a man he is. And he wants us. Low or not, he wants us, and that's good enough for me.

The tough, fast-walking Abner Quine has recently been promoted to the rank of detective. He has traded in his nightstick and patrolman's gear for a couple of business suits, a woolen one for the winter, a light-weight drip-dry for the summer, and has splurged on an expensive pair of shoes at Florsheim's (Hank and Frank!), which he intends to wear for his detective work every day the year round, regardless of the weather. Quine lives alone in a small, one-bedroom apartment in Hell's Kitchen, not the best of neighborhoods in 1961, but the rent is low and his precinct house is just four blocks away, and even though the apartment is often less than clean (the detective has little appetite for housework), Hank and Frank are impressed by how well he takes care of them. Though young in age, their master is a man of the old school, and he treats his shoes with respect, methodically undoing the laces at night and leaving them on the floor beside his bed rather than kicking them off and/or shutting them up in the closet, since shoes like to be near their master at all times, even when they are not on duty, and kicking off shoes without untying the laces can cause severe struc-tural damage over the long haul. Quine tends to be busy and distracted while at work on his cases (robberies, mostly), but let anything fall on either one of his shoes, whether a white splat of pigeon shit or a red blob of ketchup, and he is quick to remove the offending substance with one of the Kleenex tissues he carries in his right front pocket. Best of all, there are his frequent jaunts to Penn Station to consult with his prime snitch, an old black man named Moss, who happens to run the shoe-shine stand in the main hall, and as Quine plunks himself down in the chair to get the latest dope from Moss, more often than not he will ask for a shine to cover up the true purpose of his visit, thus killing two

birds with one stone, as it were, doing his job and caring for his brogans, and Hank and Frank are the happy beneficiaries of this ruse,
for Moss is an expert, with the fastest, most agile hands in the business, and to be rubbed by his cloths and massaged by his brushes is
an unsurpassed pleasure for everyday shoes like Hank and Frank, a
swooning plunge into the depths of footwear sensuality, and once they
have been buffed and boffed by Moss's sure hands, they end up spank-
ing clean and waterproofed as well, winners on all fronts.

It is a good life, then, about the best life they could have hoped for,
but *good* must not be mistaken for *easy*, since it is the lot of shoes to work
hard, even under the most positive circumstances, particularly in a place
like New York, where a sole can go for months without stepping on a
single tuft of grass or the tiniest patch of soft ground, where the extremes
of hot and cold can cause havoc to the long-term health of leathery
things, not to mention the damage wrought by downpours and snow-
falls, of inadvertent missteps into puddles and drifts, of repeated dousings and drenchings, all the indignities that are visited upon them when
the weather turns wet and foul, many of which could be avoided if their
conscientious master were even more conscientious, but Quine is not a
man who believes in rubbers or galoshes, and even in the heaviest blizzards he has no truck with snow boots, preferring at all times the company of his beleaguered brogans, who are both honored by his trust in
them and vexed by his thoughtlessness.

Pounding the pavement: day in and day out, that is what Quine does,
and therefore that is what Hank and Frank do as well. If there is any
consolation in having their heels and soles worn down by the steady,
abrasive interactions of leather and asphalt, it is that the two of them are
in it together, brothers sharing their fate as one. Like most brothers, however, they have their moments of discord and petulance, their feuds
and hot-tempered outbursts, for even if they are attached to one man's
body, they themselves are two, and each one's relationship to that body
is slightly different, since Quine's left foot and right foot are not always
doing the same thing at the same time. Sitting in chairs, for example.
As a left-handed person, he tends to cross his left leg over his right leg
far more often than his right leg over his left, and few sensations are
more enjoyable than feeling yourself being lifted into the air, of quitting the ground for a while and having your sole bared to the world,
and because Hank is the left shoe and consequently is able to enjoy this

experience more often than Frank, Frank harbors a certain resentment toward Hank, which he mostly struggles to suppress, but sometimes the liftoff puts Hank in such buoyant spirits that he can't stop himself from rubbing it in, laughing from his high perch as he dangles to the right of the master's right knee and calling out to Frank, *How's the weather down there, Frankie boy?*, at which point Frank will inevitably lose his composure, telling Hank to butt out and mind his own business. At the same time, Frank often pities Hank for being the left shoe of a left-handed man, since Quine generally takes his first step with his left foot, and whenever they pause for a red light on rainy or snowy days, the first step across the street is always the most perilous one, the often catastrophic fording of the gutter, and how many times has Hank been dunked in puddles and immersed in soaking mounds of slush when he himself has remained dry? Too many times to count. Frank rarely laughs in the face of his brother's humiliations and near drownings, but sometimes, when he is in a particularly sour mood, he just can't help himself.

Still and all, in spite of their occasional spats and misunderstandings, they have become the best of friends, and whenever they look at the brogans worn by their master's partner, a pair of grizzle-guts named Ed and Fred (all shoe couples in Ferguson's story have rhyming names), Hank and Frank know how blessed they are to have fallen in with an upstanding sort like Abner Quine rather than the slovenly thug he works with, Walter Benton, who seems happiest with his job when he's punching out suspects in the interrogation room or kicking them in the back with his shoes. Ed and Fred have done this dirty work for him often enough over the years to have been brutalized by it, and they have turned into an ornery pair of low-life cruds, so cynical and disgusted with the world that they haven't talked to each other for close to a year— not because they don't get along anymore but simply because they can't be bothered. On top of that, Ed and Fred are beginning to fall apart, for Benton is a neglectful master as well as a stupid one, and he has allowed the heels of his shoes to wear down without replacing them, has done nothing about the hole developing in Ed's underbottom or the cracked leather skin in the toe crease of Fred's upper, and not once in all the time that Hank and Frank have known those *ratty buggers* (Hank's phrase for them) have they ever been polished. By contrast, Hank and Frank are polished twice a week, and in the two years they have been serving their master they have each been given four new heels and two new soles. They still feel young, whereas Ed and Fred, who went on the job only six months before they did, are old, so old now they're just about finished and ready to be junked.

Because they are work shoes, they rarely get to accompany their master when he steps out with the ladies. The pursuit of love requires something less homely and down to earth than brogans, so Hank and Frank are cast aside in favor of Abner Q.'s triple-eyeletted dress shoes or his black alligator slip-ons, which always fills them with disappointment, not only because they dread being left alone in the dark but because they have been with Quine on several of his amorous excursions (when he was too pressed to go home after work and change), and they know how much fun those outings can be, especially when the master spends the night in a woman's bed, which means that Hank and Frank get to spend the night on the floor beside the bed, and because it is the woman's apartment, the woman's shoes are there as well, most often right next to them, and how raucous and jolly it was the first time, when they chatted and laughed and sang songs with Flora and Nora, an adorable pair of red satin high heels, and all the other times since then in a different woman's apartment, a big blonde the master calls either Alice or Darling, cavorting in her place on Greenwich Street with a pair of black pumps named Leah and Mia and a pair of penny loafers named Molly and Dolly, and how those girls carried on and giggled when they saw the master take off his clothes and strip down to the altogether, and how they gawked when they saw the ample breasts of their mistress bouncing up and down in the throes of love. Such splendid times they were, so scintillating when compared to the drab world of sweaty criminals and judges in black robes, and all the more precious to Hank and Frank for having been so few.

Months go by, and it becomes more and more apparent to them that Alice is the One. Not only has the master stopped seeing other women, but most of his spare time is now spent with her, his beloved Darling, who has rapidly acquired several other names as well, among them Angel, Sweetheart, Gorgeous, and Monkey Face, signs of an ever-increasing intimacy that leads to the inevitable moment in late May when, sitting on a bench in Central Park with Alice, Quine at last pops the big question. Because it is a workday, Hank and Frank are there to witness the proposal, and they are more than encouraged by Alice's tender response, *I'll do everything to make you happy, my love,* which seems to suggest they will be happy, too, as happy with the new arrangement as they have been with the old.

What Hank and Frank have failed to understand, however, is that marriage changes everything. It isn't just a question of two people deciding to live together, it's the beginning of a long struggle that pits one partner's will against the will of the other partner, and although the husband often appears to have the upper hand, it is the wife who is ultimately in control. The newlyweds abandon their respective apartments in Hell's Kitchen and Greenwich Village and take up residence in a larger, more comfortable place on West Twenty-fifth Street. Since Alice has left her secretarial job in the D.A.'s office, she is in charge of all household affairs, and while she routinely asks her husband for his opinion about the new curtains she wants to buy, the new rug she is planning to put in the living room, the new chairs she is dreaming about for the dining room table, Quine's response is always the same—*Whatever you want, Babe, it's your call*—which means, in effect, that Alice makes all the decisions. But no matter, think Hank and Frank. Alice might be the ruler of the roost now, but they still get to spend their days with the master, pounding the pavement in search of crooks, grilling suspects in the interrogation room, appearing in court to testify at trials, following up leads on the telephone, typing reports, running down alleys whenever a bad guy is foolish enough to bolt, going to Penn Station for their twice-weekly buffings from Moss, and now that Benton has given Ed and Fred the old heave-ho, they have a new pair of associates to work with, Ned and Ted, surly customers to be sure, but not half as bad as the recently departed ratty buggers, which would suggest that while many things are different now, the essential things are the same, perhaps even slightly better than they were before. Or so Hank and Frank tell themselves, but what they don't know, and what their complacency prevents them from grasping, is that sweet-voiced Alice is on a mission, and her efforts to improve the master's life will not stop at curtains and rugs. Within three months of the wedding ceremony, she is forging on into the realm of her husband's clothes, in particular the clothes he wears at work, which she contends are too dull and shabby for a man who is destined to become a captain one day, and though Quine responds somewhat defensively at first, saying that his suits are good enough, more than adequate for the kind of job he does, Alice wears down his resistance by telling him how handsome he is and what a dashing figure he'd cut in a top-of-the-line outfit. Both flattered and annoyed by her compliments, the master makes a witless crack about how money doesn't grow on trees, but he knows he has lost the battle, and on his next day off he reluctantly follows his wife to a men's store on Madison Avenue, where his wardrobe is refurbished with a couple of new suits, four white shirts, and six of the skinny ties that are now in fashion. Three mornings later, as the master dons one of those new suits before heading off to work, Alice breaks into a broad smile and tells him how impressive he looks, but then, before he can get a word out of his mouth, she glances down at his feet and says: I'm afraid we'll have to do something about those shoes.

What's wrong with them? Quine asks, beginning to show some irritation.

Nothing really, she says. They're just old, that's all—and they don't go with the suit.

That's ridiculous. They're the best pair of shoes I've ever owned. I bought them at Florsheim's the day after my promotion, and I've been wearing them ever since. They're my lucky shoes, Angel. Three years on the job, and in all that time not one shot fired at me, not one punch thrown at my face, not a single bruise anywhere on my body.

That's just it, Abner. Three years is a long time.

Not for a pair of brogans like these. They're not even fully broken in yet.

Alice purses her lips, cocks her head, and playfully strokes her chin, as if trying to assess the shoes with the solemn detachment of a philosopher. At last she says:

Too clunky. The suit makes you look like an important man, but the shoes make you look like a cop.

But that's what I am. A cop. A goddamned flatfoot.

Just because you're a cop, that doesn't mean you have to look like a cop. The shoes give you away, Abner. You walk into a room, and everyone thinks: There's a cop. With the right pair of shoes, they'd never even guess.

Hank and Frank wait for the master to speak up for them, to say a few more words in their defense, but Quine says nothing, answering Alice's last remark with an inscrutable grunt, and a moment later they are traveling with him as he walks to the front door of the apartment and leaves for work. The day is no different from any other day, nor is the next day any different from the day that preceded it, and Hank and Frank begin to hope the conversation with Alice was no more than a false alarm, that her harsh judgments about their value to the master are not shared by Quine himself, that the whole nasty business will blow away like a thin, passing cloud. Then it is Saturday, another day off from police work, and out goes Quine with their new enemy, the obtrusive, opinionated Alice, out in his weekend loafers as they stand beside the bed and wait for the couple to return, never once suspecting that they are about to be betrayed by the man they have served so loyally for the past three years, and when the master comes back later that afternoon and tries on his new pair of oxfords, Hank and Frank suddenly understand that they have been booted out and dismissed, purged by the upstart regime that has taken over the household, and because they have no recourse, no tribunal in which to lodge a complaint or present their side of the story, their lives are over and done with, stomped out by the palace coup that otherwise goes by the name of *marriage*.

What do you think? Quine asks Alice, as he finishes lacing the oxfords and stands up from the bed.

Beautiful, she says. The best of the best, Abner.

As Quine walks around the room, acquainting his feet with the spring and texture of his new workday companions, Alice points to Hank and Frank and says, What should I do with these old fogeys?

I don't know. Put them in the closet.

You don't want me to throw them out?

No, put them in the closet. You never know when I might need them again.

So Alice puts Hank and Frank in the closet, and while the master's parting words seem to offer some hope that they will be recalled to duty one day, months pass without any changes, and little by little they resign themselves to the fact that the master will never slip his feet into them again. The two brogans are bitter about their enforced retirement, and all through their early weeks in the closet they talk about how cruelly they have been treated, wailing forth their grievances in long, foul-mouthed diatribes against the master and his wife. Not that this moaning and groaning does them any good, of course, and as dust begins to settle upon them, and as they begin to understand that the closet is their world now, that they will never leave it until the day they are junked,

they give up their complaining and start to talk about the past, preferring to relive the old days instead of dwelling on the miseries of the present, and how good it is to remember their adventures with the master
when they were young and vigorous and had their place in the world,
how pleasant it is to recall the weathers they walked in, the myriad sensations of being outdoors in the fluctuating airs of planet Earth, the
sense of purpose that had been given to them by belonging to the bigness of human life. More months go by, and their reminiscing slowly
comes to an end, for it is becoming difficult to talk now, difficult even
to remember, not because Hank and Frank are sinking into old age but
because they have been cast aside, and shoes that are no longer taken
care of go downhill rapidly, their exteriors dry up and crack when they
cease to be shined and polished, their interiors stiffen when human feet
no longer enter them to provide the oils and perspiration necessary to
keep them soft and pliable, and slowly but surely cast-aside shoes begin
to resemble blocks of wood, and wood is a substance incapable of thinking or speaking or remembering, and now that Hank and Frank have
come to resemble two blocks of wood, they are nearly comatose, living
in a shadow world of black voids and barely flickering candle flames,
and so insensitive have their bodies become during their long incarcera-
tion that they feel nothing when the Quines' three-year-old son Timothy
slips his feet into them one afternoon and clomps around the apartment
laughing, and when his mother sees his little feet inside those enormous, comatose shoes, she starts laughing as well. What are you doing,
Timmy? she asks. I'm pretending to be Daddy, he says, and then his
mother shakes her head and frowns, telling the boy she'll give him a
nicer pair of big shoes to play with, those brogans are so filthy and used
up that it's time to get rid of them. How fortunate it is that Hank and
Frank can no longer hear anything or feel anything, for once Alice has
given her son his father's current pair of dress shoes, she picks up Hank
and Frank with her left hand, puts her right hand on top of Timmy's
head, and then leads him out into the hall toward the incinerator chute,
which is located in a minuscule box of a room behind an unlocked door.
I'd forgotten all about these ratty old buggers, she says, pushing down
on the handle of the incinerator chute door and allowing her son to *do
the honors*, meaning he can perform the task of disposing of the shoes,
and so little Timothy Quine takes hold of Hank, and as he casts him
seven floors down into the basement furnace, he says, *Good-bye, shoe,*

and then he takes hold of Frank and repeats the operation, saying *Good-bye, shoe*, as Frank follows his brother into the fire below, and before another day has dawned over the island of Manhattan, the two sole mates have been transformed into an indistinguishable mass of red, glowing cinders.

FERGUSON WAS IN the ninth grade now, technically the first year of high school but in his case the last year of junior high, and among the subjects he studied during the first semester was typing, an elective course that proved to be more valuable to him than anything else he took that year. Because he was so keen on mastering this new skill, he went to his father and asked for the money to buy a typewriter of his own, managing to persuade the prophet of profits to cough up the cash with the argument that he was going to need one eventually and prices would never be lower than they were now, and thus Ferguson secured himself a new toy to play with, a solid, elegantly designed Smith-Corona portable, which instantly acquired the status of *most treasured possession*. How he came to love that writing machine, and how good it felt to press his fingers against the rounded, concave keys and watch the letters fly up on their steel prongs and strike the paper, the letters moving right as the carriage moved left, and then the ding of the bell and the sound of the cogs engaging to drop him down to the next line as black word followed black word to the bottom of the page. It was such a grown-up instrument, such a serious instrument, and Ferguson welcomed the responsibilities it demanded of him, for life was serious now, and with Artie Federman never more than half an inch away from him, he knew it was time to start growing up.

When Ferguson completed the handwritten first draft of *Sole Mates* in early November, he had made enough progress in his typing course to do the second draft on the Smith-Corona. After he corrected that version and typed up the story again, the finished manuscript came to fifty-two double-spaced pages. It seemed incomprehensible to him that he had written so much, that somehow or other he had managed to crank out more than fifteen thousand words about *a dumb pair of shoes*, but after the idea came to him, one thing kept leading to another, his head kept filling up with new situations to write about, new aspects of the characters to explore and develop, and by the time he was finished

more than two months of his life had been given over to the project. He
felt a certain satisfaction in having done it, of course, the mere fact of
having composed such a long work was something any fourteen-year-
old would have felt proud of, but when he read it over for the fifth time
and made the last of his final revisions, he still didn't know if it was any
good or not. Since neither one of his parents was capable of judging the
story, let alone any story ever written in the history of mankind, and
since Aunt Mildred and Uncle Don were in London for the fall semester (Mildred had been given a half-year sabbatical)—which meant that
Noah was living full-time with his mother and was therefore inaccessible until January—and since he was too frightened to share it with the
one classmate whose opinion he would have trusted, he reluctantly gave
it to his English teacher, Mrs. Baldwin, who had been standing in front
of ninth-grade classrooms since the 1920s and was just a year or two
from retirement. Ferguson knew he was taking a risk. Mrs. Baldwin
excelled at giving vocabulary quizzes and spelling tests, she was mas-
terful at explaining how to diagram a sentence and terrifically good
at clarifying the tough points of grammar and diction, but her taste in
literature belonged to the fuddy-duddy school of superannuated trea-
sures, as evinced by her enthusiasm for Bryant, Whittier, and Longfel-
low, those turgid, insipid has-beens who dominated the curriculum
when she led the class through *the wonders of nineteenth-century American verse,* and while Ferguson's dark-browed E. A. Poe was there with
his obligatory black bird, there was no Walt Whitman—*too profane!*—and
no Emily Dickinson—*too obscure!* To her credit, however, Mrs. Baldwin
had also assigned them *A Tale of Two Cities,* which was his first exposure to Dickens on the page (he had once watched a movie version of *A
Christmas Carol* on TV), and though Ferguson had gladly joined his
friends in the age-old tradition of referring to the novel as *A Sale of Two
Titties,* he had fallen hard for the book, had found the sentences ferociously energetic and surprising, an inexhaustible inventiveness that
mixed horror and humor in ways he had never encountered in any other
book, and he was grateful to Mrs. Baldwin for having introduced
him to what he now considered to be *the best novel he had ever read.* That
was why he decided to give her his story—because of Dickens. Too bad
he couldn't write as well as old Charles, but he was just a beginner, an
amateur author with only one work to his name so far, and he hoped
she would take that into account.

It wasn't as bad as he thought it might be, but in other ways it was much worse. Mrs. Baldwin corrected his typos, spelling errors, and grammatical blunders, which not only was a help to him but proved that she had read the story with some care, and when they sat down for their after-school conference six days after he had given her the manuscript, she praised him for his perseverance and the richness of his imagination, and to be perfectly frank, she added, she was stunned that an apparently normal, well-adjusted boy should have such dark, disturbing thoughts about the world. As for the story itself, well, it was ludicrous, of course, a blatant example of the pathetic fallacy gone wrong, but even granted that a pair of shoes could think and feel and carry on conversations, what had Ferguson been trying to accomplish by inventing this comic-book world of his? There were unquestionably some touching and amusing moments, some flashes of genuine literary talent, but much of the story had offended her, and she wondered why Ferguson had chosen her to be his first reader, since he must have known she would be put off by his use of four-letter words (pigeon *shit* on page 17, holy *shit* on page 30—which she pointed out to him by tapping her finger on the lines in which those words appeared), not to mention his mockery of the police throughout, beginning with the derisory terms *flatfoot* and *cop shoes*, then deepening the insult with his portrayal of Captain Benton as a drunken, abusive sadist—didn't Ferguson know that her father had been Maplewood chief of police when she was a girl, hadn't she told the class enough stories about him to make that clear?— but worst of all, she said, worse than anything else was the smutty tone of the story, not just that Quine hops in and out of bed with various unsavory women before he proposes to Alice but that Alice herself is willing to sleep with him before their marriage—an institution, by the way, that Ferguson seemed to hold in absolute contempt—and then, even worse than worst of all, the fact that the sexual innuendos don't stop with the human characters but go all the way down to the shoes themselves, what a preposterous notion that was, the erotic lives of shoes, for pity's sake, and how could Ferguson look at himself in the mirror after writing about the pleasure a shoe feels when a foot steps into it, or the ecstasy that comes from being shined and polished, and how on earth did he ever think up the *shoe orgy* with Flora and Nora, that truly was the limit, and didn't Ferguson feel the least bit ashamed of himself for dwelling on such filth?

He didn't know how to answer her. Until Mrs. Baldwin started hammering him with her criticisms, he had assumed they would be talking about the mechanics of fiction writing, technical matters such as structure, pace, and dialogue, the importance of using one word instead of three or four words, how to avoid needless digressions and drive the story forward, the small but essential things he was still trying to figure out for himself, but it had never occurred to him that Mrs. Baldwin would attack him on what seemed to be moral grounds, calling into question the very substance of what he had written and condemning it as *indecent*. Whether she approved of the story or not, it was his work, and he was free to write whatever he wanted, to use the word *shit* if he felt it was necessary, for example, since people in the real world said that word a hundred times a day, and even if he was still a virgin, he had learned enough about sex to know that you didn't have to be married in order to do it, that human lust paid little or no heed to the laws of matrimony, and as for the sexual life of shoes, how could she not see how funny it was, funny in such an absurd, innocent way that anyone reading those passages would have to be half-dead not to crack a smile, and fuck her, Ferguson said to himself, she had no right to be reproaching him like this, and yet in spite of his resistance her words were doing the job she had intended them to do, they were scalding his insides and peeling off his skin, and so dazed was he by the assault that he didn't have the strength to defend himself, and when he was finally able to speak, he could get no more than two words out of his mouth, two mumbled words that surely ranked as the most pathetic words he had ever spoken:

I'm sorry.

I'm sorry, too, Mrs. Baldwin said. I know you think I'm being hard on you, but it's for your own good, Archie. I'm not saying your story is obscene, not when you compare it to some of the books they've been publishing these past few years, but it's vulgar and distasteful, and I just want to know what you were thinking when you wrote it. Did you have anything in mind, or were you simply trying to shock people with a bunch of off-color jokes?

Ferguson didn't want to be there anymore. He wanted to stand up and leave the room and never have to look at Mrs. Baldwin's wrinkled face and watery blue eyes again. He wanted to quit school and run away from home and ride the rails like a Depression hobo, begging for meals at kitchen doors and writing dirty books in his spare time, a man beholden to no one, laughing as he spat in the face of the world.

I'm waiting, Archie, Mrs. Baldwin said. Don't you have anything to say for yourself?

You want to know what was in my mind, is that it?

Yes, what you were thinking.

I was thinking about slavery, Ferguson said. About how some people were actually owned by other people and had to do what they were told from the minute they were born until the minute they died. Hank and Frank are slaves, Mrs. Baldwin. They come from Africa—the shoe factory—then they're put in chains and shipped to America on a boat— the shoe box, the truck ride to Madison Avenue—and then they're sold off to their master at a slave auction.

But the shoes in your story like being shoes. You're not going to tell me that slaves liked being slaves, are you?

No, of course not. But slavery lasted for hundreds of years, and how many times did the slaves rise up and revolt, how many times did slaves kill their masters? Almost never. Slaves did the best they could under bad conditions. They even told jokes and sang songs when they were able to. That's the story of Hank and Frank. They have to serve the will of their master, but that doesn't mean they don't try to make the most of what they have.

None of this comes through in the writing, Archie.

I didn't want to make it too obvious. Maybe that's a problem, or maybe you just missed it, I don't know. In any case, that's what I had in mind.

I'm glad you told me this. It doesn't change my opinion of the story, but at least I know you were trying to do something serious. I dislike it with all my heart, you understand, dislike it all the more because some of it is so good, and because I'm such an old woman now, I suppose I'll always dislike what you do—but keep writing, Archie, and don't listen to me. You don't need advice, you just need to keep at it. As your dear friend Edgar Allan Poe once wrote to an aspiring author: *Be bold—read much— write much—publish little—keep aloof from the little wits—and fear nothing.*

HE DIDN'T TELL her about the final pages of the story or what he had been thinking when Alice puts Hank and Frank in the closet. If Mrs. Baldwin had missed the secret references to slavery, how could she have understood that the closet is a concentration camp and that Hank and Frank are no longer black Americans at that point but European Jews in the Second World War, wasting away in captivity until they are finally burned to death in the incinerator-crematorium? It wouldn't have done any good to tell her that, nor was there any reason to talk about friendship, which was the true subject of the story as far as he was concerned, because that would have meant having to talk about Artie Federman, and he had no desire to share his grief with Mrs. Baldwin. She could have been right about not making those things visible enough for a reader to detect them, but then again she could have been blind, so rather than put the story away and stop thinking about it, he corrected the errors Mrs. Baldwin had circled on the manuscript and typed up yet another version, this time using carbon paper in order to make a second copy, which he airmailed to Aunt Mildred and Uncle Don the following afternoon. Twelve days after that, he received a letter from London, which in fact was two letters in a single envelope, a separate response from each of them, both favorable and enthusiastic, neither one of them blind to the things his teacher had failed to notice. What a puzzle, he said to himself, as a great surge of happiness swept through him, for even if his aunt and uncle had pronounced *Sole Mates* to be a good story, their verdict did nothing to change the fact that Mrs. Baldwin still thought it was a bad story. The same manuscript perceived differently by different pairs of eyes, different hearts, different brains. It was no longer a question of one person being punched while another person was being kissed, it was the same person being punched and kissed at the same time, for that was how the game worked, Ferguson realized, and if he meant to go on showing his story to other people in the future, he would have to prepare himself to be punched as often as he was kissed, or punched ten times for every kiss, or a hundred times with no kiss at all.

Rather than mail the story directly back to Ferguson, Uncle Don had sent it to Noah with instructions to return the manuscript to his cousin when he had finished reading it. Early one Saturday morning, about a week after the letters had arrived from London, the telephone rang in the kitchen as Ferguson was polishing off his breakfast of scrambled eggs and toast, and there was Noah on the other end of the line, spitting out words like tommy-gun bullets, saying he had to talk fast because

4 3 2 1

his mother had stepped out to do some shopping and would probably kill him if she walked in and caught him on a long-distance call, especially a call to Ferguson, who was not to be contacted under any circumstances *from the sanctuary of her apartment*, not only because he wasn't Noah's real cousin but because he was tied by blood to the *bitch-devil* (yes, Noah said, she was out of her mind, everyone knew that, but he was the one who had to live with her), and yet once he finished that breathless prologue of his, Noah immediately began to slow the pace of his delivery, and before long he was talking at normal speed, which was fast but not outrageously fast, and sounding like someone with all the time in the world to settle in for a nice lengthy chat.

Well, pisshead, he began. You've really done it this time, haven't you?

Done what? Ferguson replied, feigning ignorance, since he was more or less certain that Noah was referring to the story.

An odd little thing called *Sole Mates*.

You've read it?

Every word. Three times.

And?

Fantastic, Archie. Just fucking, flat-out fantastic. To tell the truth, I didn't know you had it in you.

To tell the truth, I didn't either.

I'm thinking we should turn it into a movie.

Very funny. And how do we do that without a camera?

An insignificant detail. We'll remedy that problem in due course. Anyway, we don't have time to work on it now. Because of school, for one thing, and the distance between New York and New Jersey, and assorted maternal impediments I won't go into today. But there's always the summer. I mean, we're finished with camp now, aren't we? We're too old for it, and after what happened to Artie, well, I don't think I could ever go back there.

I agree. No more camp.

So we'll spend the summer making the movie. Now that you've turned yourself into a writer, I suppose you'll be giving up all that sports nonsense.

Only baseball. But I'm still doing basketball. I'm on a team, you know, a ninth-grade team sponsored by the West Orange Y. We play other Y teams around Essex County twice a week, once on Wednesday night and once on Saturday morning.

I don't get it. If you want to go on being a jock, why quit baseball? It's your best sport.

Because of Artie.

What does Artie have to do with it?

He was the best player we've ever seen, wasn't he? And he was also my friend. Not so much your friend, but my friend, my good friend. Now Artie's dead, and I want to go on thinking about him, it's important to me to have him in my thoughts as much as possible, and the best way to do that, I realized, was to give up something in his honor, something I care about, something important to me, so I chose baseball, baseball because that was Artie's best sport, too, and from now on, whenever I see other people playing baseball, or whenever I think about why I'm not playing baseball myself, I'll think about Artie.

You're a strange person, do you know that?

I guess. But even if I am, what can I do about it?

Nothing.

That's right. Nothing.

So play basketball. Join a summer league if you want to, but as long as you're down to just one sport, you'll have lots of time to work on the movie.

Agreed. Assuming we manage to get hold of a camera.

We'll get it, don't worry. The important thing is that you've written your first masterpiece. The door has opened, Archie, and there'll be many more to come—a whole lifetime of masterpieces.

Let's not get carried away. I've written one thing, that's all, and who knows if I'll ever come up with another idea. Besides, I still have my plan.

Not *that*. I thought you'd dropped it ages ago.

Not really.

Listen to me, pisshead. You're never going to be a doctor—and I'm never going to be a strong man in the circus. You don't have a math and science brain, and I don't have a single muscle in my body. Ergo, no Doctor Ferguson—and no Noah the Magnificent.

How can you be so sure?

Because the idea came to you from a book, that's why. A stupid novel you read when you were twelve years old and which I had the misfortune to read myself because you insisted it was so good, which it isn't, and if you looked at it again I'm sure you'd finally see that it isn't what you thought it was, that it isn't any damned good at all. Idealistic young doctor blows up contaminated sewer system in order to rid town of disease, idealistic young doctor loses his ideals for money and a posh address, formerly idealistic not-so-young doctor regains his ideals and thus saves his soul. Hogwash, Archie. Just the kind of crap to move an idealistic young boy like yourself, but you're not a young boy anymore, you're a strapping fellow with a man's dick yowling between your legs and a head that can produce literary masterpieces and God knows what else, and you're telling me you're still in thrall to that abomination of a book whose title escapes me now because I've done everything in my power to forget it?

The Citadel.

That's it. And now that you've reminded me, never say it again in my presence. No, Archie, a person doesn't become a doctor because he's read a book. He becomes a doctor because he needs to become a doctor, and you don't need to become a doctor, you need to become a writer.

I thought this was going to be a short call. You haven't forgotten about your mother, have you?

Damnit. Of course I have. Gotta go, Arch.

Your father's coming back in a couple of weeks. We'll get together then, okay?

You bet. We'll talk Shoe to each other with thick brogan brogues— and figure out how to steal a camera.

ON DECEMBER NINETEENTH, three days after Ferguson's conversation with Noah, the *New York Times* reported that American G.I.s had entered the war zone in South Vietnam and were now taking part in tactical operations with instructions to *shoot if fired upon.* Along with a shipment of forty helicopters, four hundred American combat troops had arrived in South Vietnam one week earlier. Additional aircraft, ground vehicles, and amphibious ships were on the way. In all, there were now two thousand Americans in uniform in South Vietnam, *instead of the officially reported 685 members of the military advisory group.*

Four days after that, on December twenty-third, Ferguson's father left on a two-week trip to southern California to visit his brothers and their families. It was the first pause he had taken from work in years, the last one dating all the way back to December 1954, when he and Ferguson's mother had gone to Miami Beach for a ten-day winter vacation. This time, Ferguson's mother didn't go with him. Nor did she accompany Ferguson's father to the airport to say good-bye to him on the day he left. Ferguson had heard his mother bad-mouth her brothers-in-law often enough to understand that she had no interest in seeing them, but still, there must have been more to it than that, for once his father was gone, she looked more agitated than usual, preoccupied, morose, unable, for the first time in memory, to follow what he was saying when he talked to her, and so deep was her distraction that Ferguson wondered if she wasn't brooding about the state of her marriage, which seemed to have taken some definitive turn with his father's solo departure to Los Angeles. Perhaps the bathtub wasn't merely cold anymore. Perhaps it was frigid now, on the point of freezing over into a block of ice.

The carbon copy of his story had been sent back by Noah as promised, and since it showed up in Maplewood before his father left for California, Ferguson had given it to him on the off chance that he might read it on the trip. His mother had read it weeks earlier, of course, on the Saturday after Thanksgiving, curled up on the couch in the living room with her shoes off and smoking half a pack of Chesterfields as she worked her way through the fifty-two typed pages, telling him afterward that she thought it was *just wonderful, one of the best things I've ever read*, which was to be expected, he supposed, since she would have delivered the same verdict if he had copied out last month's shopping list and passed it off as an *experimental poem*, but far better to have your mother on your side than not, especially with a father who seemed to be on no side at all. Now that *Sole Mates* had passed through the hands of Aunt Mildred, Uncle Don, and Noah, he figured it was time to *screw up his courage* (a phrase he loved for its double, contradictory meanings) and show it to Amy Schneiderman, the one person in Maplewood whose opinion he could trust—and therefore the person he had been most terrified to approach, since Amy was too honest to pull any punches, and a punch from her would have flattened him.

In some ways, if not in many ways, Ferguson thought of Amy Schneiderman as a female version of Noah Marx. A more attractive version, to be sure, in that she was a girl and not a bug-eyed, muscle-less boy, but she was smart in the way Noah was smart, the same kind of lit-up person he was, all ablaze and crackling with spirit, and over the years Ferguson had come to realize how much he depended on them both, as if the two of them were a pair of butterfly wings he wore on his back to keep himself aloft, he who could be so heavy at times, so earthbound, and yet, in the case of the more attractive Amy, the physical attraction was not so great as to plant any amorous thoughts in Ferguson's head, and therefore she was still *just a friend*, albeit an essential friend, his most important comrade in the ever-expanding war against suburban dullness and mediocrity, and how fortunate it was that she, of all the people in the world, should be the one to occupy his old room, a narrative caprice in the story of their lives, perhaps, but it had formed a bond between them, a peculiar kind of closeness that they both took for granted now, for not only did Amy breathe the same air he had breathed in that house, she spent her nights in the same bed he had slept in when he lived there, a bed his mother had deemed too small for his room in the new house and had consequently given to Amy's less than wealthy parents before they moved in. That was more than five years ago now, late summer 1956, and although Amy was supposed to have started the fifth grade in September, two days before the school year began she fell off a horse on a riding trail in the South Mountain Reservation and broke her hip, and by the time the injury healed, it was already the middle of October, and so her parents decided to have her repeat the fourth grade instead of plunging her into a new school six weeks behind the other children in her class. That was how she and Ferguson wound up in the same grade together, the two of them born just three months apart but destined to have slightly different trajectories in school, but then the broken hip intervened, and their trajectories became identical, beginning with that first year when they were fellow members of Miss Mancini's fourth-grade class and continuing on through their last two years at Jefferson Elementary School and then all three years at Maplewood Junior High—always in the same classes together, always competing against each other, and because there had never been any romantic entanglements to divide them with the inevitable misunderstandings and hurt feelings that come with romance, always friends.

The morning after Ferguson's father left for California, Sunday, December twenty-fourth, the day before the holiday neither one of their families celebrated, Ferguson called Amy at ten-thirty and asked if he could come over to her house. He had something to give her, he said, and if she wasn't too busy, he would like to give it to her right away. No, she said, she wasn't busy, just lounging around in her pajamas reading the paper, trying not to think about the essay they were supposed to be writing over winter vacation. It was a fifteen-minute walk from his house to her house, a trip he had made on foot many times in the past, but the weather was ugly that morning, a fine drizzle falling with the temperature at thirty-one or thirty-two degrees, snow weather without any snow, but foggy, windy, and wet, so Ferguson said he would ask his mother to drive him there. In that case, Amy said, why didn't they both come for brunch? Jim had bagged out on them about ten minutes earlier and was still in New York with friends, but the food had been bought, there was enough to feed ten starving people, and it would be a pity to waste it. Just a minute, she said, as she put down the phone and yelled out to her parents, asking if Archie and Mrs. Ferguson could come over and *share our grub with us* (Amy had a weakness for quaint idioms), and twenty seconds later she picked up the phone again and said: It's fine. Come between twelve-thirty and one.

Thus, the manuscript of *Sole Mates* was finally put in Amy's hands, and as Ferguson sat in his old room with the girl who spent her nights sleeping in his old bed, the two of them talked while the adults prepared the meal in the kitchen directly below them, first of all about their current love dramas (Ferguson pining for a girl named Linda Flagg, who had turned him down when he'd asked her out to the movies on Friday, and Amy pinning her hopes on a boy named Roger Saslow, who had yet to call her but had hinted he would, assuming she had read the hint correctly), then about big brother Jim, an MIT freshman who had been one of the stalwarts of the Columbia High School basketball team in his junior and senior years, and how upset he was, Amy said, about Jack Molinas and the college point-shaving scandal, dozens of games fixed over the past few seasons by bribing players with a few hundred bucks while Molinas and his gambler pals cashed in big with tens of thousands a week. Everything in this country was fixed, Amy said. TV quiz shows, college basketball games, the stock market, political elections, but Jim was too pure to understand that. Maybe so, Ferguson said, but Jim was pure only because he saw the best in people, which was a good quality, he felt, one of the things he most admired about Amy's brother, and no sooner did Ferguson say the word *admire* than the conversation shifted to another subject—the essays they had to write for the school-wide competition in January. The topic was *The Person I Most Admire*, and everyone had to participate, every seventh, eighth, and ninth grader, with prizes going to the best three essays in each of the three grades. Ferguson asked Amy if she had chosen anyone yet.

Of course I have. It's getting late, you know. We have to hand them in on January third.

Don't make me guess. I'm bound to get it wrong.

Emma Goldman.

The name rings a bell, but I don't know much about her. Just about nothing, in fact.

I didn't either, but then my Uncle Gil gave me her autobiography as a present, and now I'm in love with her. She's one of the greatest women who ever lived. (*A brief pause.*) And what about you, Mr. Ferguson? Any ideas yet?

Jackie Robinson.

Ah, Amy said, the baseball player. But not just any baseball player, right?

The man who changed America.

Not a bad choice, Archie. Go for it.

Do I need your permission?

Of course you do, silly.

They both laughed, and then Amy jumped to her feet and said: Come on, let's go downstairs. I'm famished.

ON TUESDAY, FERGUSON went outside to retrieve the mail and found a hand-delivered letter sitting in the box—no stamp, no address, just his name written across the front. The message was succinct:

Dear Archie,

I hate you.

Love, Amy

P.S. I'll return the ms. tomorrow. I need one more ride with Hank and Frank before I let go.

His father returned to Maplewood on January fifth. Ferguson was expecting him to say something about the story, if only to apologize for not having read it, but he said nothing, and when he continued to say nothing over the days that followed, Ferguson assumed he had lost it. Since Amy had returned the original typescript by then, the loss of the copy was of little importance. What counted was how little his father seemed to care about that matter of little importance, and because Ferguson resolved never to speak to him about it unless his father spoke to him about it first, it grew into a matter of great importance, of greater and greater importance as time went on.

3.1

THERE WAS PAIN. THERE WAS FEAR. THERE WAS CONFUSION. TWO VIRgins deflowering each other with no more than the dimmest understanding of what they were up to, prepared only in the sense that Ferguson had managed to procure a box of condoms and that Amy, anticipating the blood that would inevitably flow out of her, had put a dark brown bath towel over the bottom sheet of her bed—a precaution inspired by the enduring power of old legends and which in fact proved unnecessary. Joy to begin with, the ecstatic sensation of being entirely naked with each other for the first time since their long-forgotten mattress romp as small children, the chance to touch every square centimeter of the other's body, the delirium of bare skin pressing against bare skin, but once they were fully aroused, the difficulty of advancing to the next step, the anxiety of entering another person for the first time, of being entered by another person for the first time, Amy tensing up in those first instants because it hurt so much, Ferguson feeling wretched for causing that hurt and therefore slowing down and ultimately withdrawing altogether, after which there was a three-minute time-out, and then Amy grabbed hold of Ferguson and instructed him to begin again, saying, Just do it, Archie, don't worry about me, just do it, and so Ferguson did it, knowing he couldn't not worry about her but also knowing that the line had to be crossed, that this was the moment they had been given, and in spite of the inner bruising that must have made her feel as if she were being torn apart, Amy laughed when it was over, laughed her big laugh and said, *I'm so happy, I think I could die.*

What a strange weekend it was, never once leaving the apartment as they sat on the sofa and watched Johnson being sworn in as the new president, watched Oswald being carted off to jail in his bloodied T-shirt, protesting to the cameras that he was nothing but a *patsy*, a word that Ferguson would forever associate with the frail young man who either killed or didn't kill Kennedy on his own, watched a brief respite from the news when an orchestra played the dirge from Beethoven's *Eroica* Symphony, watched the funeral procession through the streets of Washington on Sunday as Amy choked up at the sight of the riderless horse, and watched Jack Ruby slip into the Dallas police station and shoot Oswald in the stomach. *Unreal city.* The line from Eliot kept exploding in Ferguson's head throughout those three days as he and Amy gradually ate up the food in the kitchen, the eggs, the lamb chops, the sliced turkey, the packages of cheese, the cans of tuna fish, the boxes of breakfast cereal and cookies, Amy smoking more than he had ever seen her smoke and Ferguson smoking with her for the first time since they had met, the two of them sitting on the sofa together and stubbing out their Luckys in unison, then throwing their arms around each other and kissing, unable to stop themselves from committing the sacrilege of kissing at such a solemn moment, from leaving the sofa every three or four hours for another visit to the bedroom, shedding their clothes and climbing onto the bed again, both of them sore now, not just Amy but Ferguson as well, but they couldn't stop themselves, the pleasure was always stronger than the pain, and grim as it was to be there on such a miserable weekend, it was the biggest, most important weekend of their young lives.

The pity was that no more chances came their way for the next two months. Ferguson kept going to New York every Saturday, but Amy's apartment was never empty long enough for them to return to the bedroom. One of her parents was always around, often both of her parents, and with nowhere else for them to go, the only solution was for the Schneidermans to leave town again—which they didn't. That was why Ferguson accepted his cousin's invitation to go on the skiing trip to Vermont in late January. Not that he had any interest in skiing, which he had tried once and felt no need to try again, but when Francie told him that the only house they had been able to rent for the weekend was a sprawling old place with five bedrooms, Ferguson thought there might be some hope. Plenty of room, Francie said, which explained why she had thought of calling him, and if he wanted to bring along a friend, there would be room for that person as well. Do girlfriends count as friends? Ferguson asked. Of course they do! Francie said, and from the way she replied to his question, from the spontaneous enthusiasm of that ringing *Of course,* Ferguson naturally supposed she understood he was telling her that he and Amy were a couple now and wanted to sleep in the same bedroom, for Francie had been married at eighteen, after all, just one year older than Amy was now, and if anyone knew about thwarted teenage lust, it had to be his twenty-seven-year-old cousin, who had been his favorite cousin ever since he was in diapers. Amy was dubious about Ferguson's optimistic reading of Francie's *Of course,* knowing how far the two of them had strayed from the accepted rules of sexual conduct, which not only didn't allow for intercourse between unmarried teenagers but considered it to be a positive scandal, but still, she said, she had never been to Vermont, had never been on skis, and what could be better than *a weekend in the snow with Archie?* As for the other business, they would just have to see who was right and who was wrong, and if it turned out she was right, that didn't mean there couldn't be some late-night room-hopping for a silent crawl into someone else's bed. They left on a cold Friday afternoon, as Amy and Ferguson wedged themselves into a cramped blue station wagon with Francie, her husband, Gary, and the two Hollander children, six-year-old Rosa and four-year-old David, and it was a lucky thing for the big ones that the little ones slept for most of the five hours it took them to reach Stowe.

Francie had named her daughter after Ferguson's mother, even though the names were not identical. The injunction against giving children the names of living parents, grandparents, and relatives was a law that even nonpracticing Jews still followed, which accounted for the one-letter difference between Rose and Rosa, a subtle point that Gary the lawyer had come up with in order to outflank the traditionalists in his family, but nevertheless the name was there for everyone to see, Rosa in honor of Rose, and with that gesture Francie and Gary were telling the world they had turned their backs on Arnold Ferguson, who had broken apart the family with the crime he had committed against his brother, and henceforth their loyalties would be shifted over to that brother, victim Stanley and his wife, Rose, whom Francie had loved from the moment she first set eyes on her as a young girl. It wasn't easy for Francie to take that step, to denounce her father when she still felt so close to her mother, brother, and sister, but Gary's contempt for his father-in-law was so strong, his disgust at the man's moral weakness and dishonesty was so absolute, that Francie had little choice but to go along with her husband. They had already been married for two years when the robbery took place, living in northwestern Massachusetts as Gary finished his undergraduate work at Williams, one of the three "baby couples" in his class, and the twenty-year-old Francie was already pregnant with her own first baby, who was born several months after her father's involvement in the warehouse cleanout came to light. The rest of the family had all moved to California by then, not just her parents but the docile young Ruth as well, who had just finished high school and was enrolled in a secretarial course in L.A., and even Jack, who dropped out of Rutgers in his last year to join them, a decision Francie and Gary urged him not to make, which led to Jack telling them both to *fuck off*, and by the time Rosa was born, only Francie's mother and sister made the trip back east to hold the child in their arms. Jack said he was too busy to come, and the disgraced Arnold Ferguson couldn't come, because he could never come back east again.

Francie had suffered, then, no more or no less than anyone else in the family, perhaps, but each one had suffered in his or her own way, and as far as Ferguson could tell, Francie's suffering had turned her into a quieter, less ebullient person than she had once been, a duller version of her former self. On the other hand, she was getting older now, already past the point of what Ferguson liked to call *a fully grown grown-up*, and even if her marriage seemed to be a good one, there was no question that Gary could be pompous and overbearing at times, more and more given to long, blowhard monologues about the decline and fall of Western civilization, especially now that he had been with his father's firm for the past couple of years and was starting to earn big-man lawyer money, which must have worn her down to some degree, not to mention motherhood, which wore down everyone, even a caring and affectionate mother like Francie, who lived for her children in the same way Aunt Joan had once lived for hers. No, Ferguson said to himself, as the station wagon headed north through the gathering darkness, he mustn't exaggerate. Even if life had kicked her around a little bit, Francie was still the same old Francie, the same *magic cousin* of his early boyhood, somewhat hobbled now, he supposed, burdened as she was by the memory of her father's betrayal, but how happy she had sounded when he accepted her invitation for the weekend, and how generous of her to have included Amy with that surprising *Of course!*, and now that they were all sitting in the car together, Ferguson in the back with the two sleeping children and Francie up front between Gary and Amy, he could see his cousin's still beautiful face in the rearview mirror every time the headlights of a passing car shone into it, and one of those times, about halfway through the trip, when she glanced up and saw that he was looking at her, she turned around, stretched out her left arm, and took hold of his hand, which she then gave a long, hard squeeze. Everything okay? she asked. You're awfully quiet back there.

It was true that he hadn't said much in the past hour, but that was only because he hadn't wanted to wake the children, and therefore his mind had been wandering, floating around among ancient family matters as he stopped listening to what Amy and Gary were talking about up front, his body lulled by the rumbling of the tires below him, the old blur-in-the-head car sensation as they moved along at sixty miles an hour, but now that Francie had squeezed his hand and he was starting to pay closer attention, he gathered that the issue was politics, above all the assassination, which had happened just two months earlier and was still the subject no one could stop talking about, the obsessive conversations about who and why and how, since it scarcely seemed credible that Oswald had done it alone, and numerous alternative theories had already begun to circulate, Castro, the mob, the C.I.A., and even Johnson himself, the big-nosed Texan who had succeeded the man of the future, still an X factor as far as Amy was concerned, but Gary, who had been quick to make up his mind, called him a *slippery character*, an old-style backroom politician who wasn't up to the job, and Amy, though she acknowledged he could have been right, nevertheless countered by bringing up Johnson's speech from earlier that month, the announcement of the war against poverty, which was the best presidential speech of her lifetime, she said, and he had to admit that no one had ever stood up and said something like that since Roosevelt, not even Kennedy. Ferguson smiled as he heard Gary concede the point, and then his mind drifted away again as he started thinking about Amy, remarkable Amy who was making such a big hit with the Hollanders, who had won them over with the first handshake, the first hello, just as she had won him over at the Labor Day barbecue, and now that they were approaching the Vermont border, he could only pray that everything would work out as planned, that it wouldn't be long before the two of them were naked under the covers again in a strange room in a strange house in the middle of a New England nowhere.

The house was as big as advertised, and nowhere was the top of a hill that stood about ten miles from the ski resort. Three stories instead of the customary two, their weekend digs had been built sometime in the early nineteenth century, and every floorboard in that drafty wooden structure creaked. The creaking was a potential problem, since it turned out that Amy's interpretation of Francie's *Of course* had been the correct one, something Ferguson was obliged to admit when the six-person party made its first tour of the house, understanding that their hosts had never considered allowing them to sleep together in the same room, and therefore they would have to go with their backup plan, which Ferguson referred to as the *French farce solution*, the midnight frolics of doors opening and shutting on rusty hinges, of lovers creeping down darkened, unfamiliar hallways, of bodies crawling into beds they weren't supposed to be in, and groaning floorboards were not going to aid them in their deceptions. Fortunately, Gary and Francie suggested that the *big kids* sleep in the two attic bedrooms so the *little kids* could spend the night on the same floor as their parents, who would be nearby in case of a bad dream (Rosa) or a bed-wetting incident (David). That would help, Ferguson thought. The creaking floorboards would be right on top of the others, of course, resonating throughout the ceilings below, but then again, people sometimes left their beds in the thick of night to stumble off to the bathroom, and in an old house like this one who could prevent the floors from making their horror-movie sound effects? With any luck, they would be able to pull it off. And if they had no luck, what was the worst that could happen to them? Nothing much, Ferguson said to himself, perhaps nothing at all.

For the first little while, everything went smoothly. They had arranged the tryst for half past eleven, a full ninety minutes after the children had been tucked in and their weary parents had said good night, and at the appointed hour all was still in the house except for an occasional gust of wind pouring through the fissured walls and rattling the weathervane overhead. Planting his bare feet on the floor, Ferguson stood up from the iron cot and began the slow journey toward Amy's room, tiptoeing cautiously over the loose planks, halting after any and all squeaks emitted by the wood, then counting to five before hazarding the next step. He had left the door ajar to avoid having to turn the knob, which eliminated the risk of creating a sudden, too-loud noise from the latch, and while the hinges were indeed a bit rusty, they proved to be quieter than the wind. Next the hallway, with the fourteen additional steps that phase of the journey required, and then the gentle push against Amy's door, which had been left ajar as well, and at last he was in.

The bed was exceedingly narrow, but Amy was naked in that bed, and once he stripped off his jockey shorts and slipped in beside her, Ferguson was naked in that bed, too, and everything felt so good to him, so perfectly in accord with how he imagined it would feel, that for once in his life the real and the imagined were identical, absolutely and as never before one and the same thing, which had to make it the happiest moment of his life so far, he believed, since Ferguson was not someone who subscribed to the notion that desire fulfilled was desire disappointed, at least not in this case, where wanting Amy was no good now without having Amy, no good without having Amy want him, and the miracle was that she did want him, and therefore desire fulfilled was in fact desire fulfilled, the chance to spend a few moments in the ephemeral kingdom of earthly grace.

They had learned so much during that tumultuous weekend two months earlier, fumbling at first because they had known next to nothing about almost everything, but gradually achieving a certain knowledge about what they were trying to do, not an advanced knowledge, perhaps, but at least the rudiments of how the other's body worked, for without that knowledge there could be no true pleasure, especially for Amy, who had to teach the ignorant Ferguson about the various ways in which women differed from men, and now that Ferguson was beginning to get the hang of it, he felt calmer and more confident than he had in New York, which made everything better this time, so much better that after a few minutes in the pitch-black dark of that room in Vermont they had stopped thinking about where they were.

The bed was an old iron bed with a thin mattress poised on top of two dozen coiled springs, and like the wooden floor that supported the bed, it creaked. It creaked under the weight of one body, but when two bodies began to move around on that mattress together, it thundered. The noise made Ferguson think of a steam locomotive traveling at seventy miles an hour, whereas Amy found the noise similar to the one

made by a printing press churning out half a million copies for the
morning edition of a tabloid newspaper. Either way, the noise was too
loud for the delicate French farce they had written in their heads, and
now that they had begun to hear the noise, there was no longer anything in their heads but the noise, the infernal screech of their frantic
coupling, and yet how to stop themselves when they were on the brink,
tottering on the very precipice of desire fulfilled? They couldn't, and
therefore the two of them went on until they had both fallen off the edge,
and when the locomotive stopped moving and they could hear something other than the noise, they heard another noise coming from
the floor below, the wail of a startled, frightened child, no doubt the
little one, David, who had been jolted from sleep by the ruckus they
had made upstairs, and a moment after that they heard the sound of
footsteps, no doubt Francie's, mother Francie going in to comfort her boy
as father Gary snored on, at which point the horrified and embarrassed
Ferguson leapt out of Amy's bed and scampered back to his room,
and thus the curtain came thudding down on their Grand Boulevard
entertainment.

At seven-thirty the next morning, Ferguson walked into the kitchen
and found Rosa and David sitting at the table, banging the surface with
knives and forks as they cried out in unison: *We want pancakes! We want
pancakes!* Gary was sitting across from them, quietly drinking a cup of
coffee and smoking his first Parliament of the day. Francie, on her feet
by the stove, flashed an irritated look at her cousin and then returned
to the job of cooking scrambled eggs. Amy was nowhere in sight, which
probably meant she was still asleep in her little bed upstairs.

Gary put down his coffee and said: We promised them pancakes
yesterday, but then we forgot to pack the stuff to make them with. As
you can see, they're not too happy with the idea of scrambled eggs.

Red-headed Rosa and blond-haired David continued to attack the
table with their knives and forks, timing the blows to the drumbeat of
their favorite chant: *Wé wánt páncákes!*

There must be a store somewhere around here, Ferguson said.

Down the hill, then left for three or four miles, Gary answered,
blowing out a large puff of smoke that seemed to suggest he had no
intention of driving there himself. I'll go, Francie said, as she transferred
the now finished eggs from the frying pan into a large white bowl.
Archie and I will go together, won't we, Archie?

Anything you say, Ferguson replied, somewhat startled by the vehemence of Francie's question, which didn't sound like a question so much as a command. She was angry at him. First the hostile look when he walked into the kitchen and now the aggressive tone in her voice, which could only mean she was still thinking about last night's attic commotion, the damned locomotive bed that had blasted the little one awake on the second floor, an inexcusable offense he had hoped she would tactfully pretend to have forgotten, and although Ferguson knew he should apologize to her right then and there, he was too embarrassed to say a word. Going out to buy pancake mix and maple syrup had nothing to do with appeasing the children. That was her excuse, but the real motive was to get him alone with her for a little while in order to scold him, to have it out with him.

Meanwhile, the children were clapping and cheering, celebrating their victory by blowing kisses to their valiant mother, who was about to brave the cold and the snow on their behalf. Gary, who seemed oblivious to what was going on, or at least indifferent to it, put out his cigarette and dug into the scrambled eggs. After one bite, he filled up his fork again and held it out to David, who leaned forward and took it into his mouth. Then a forkful for Rosa, followed by another forkful for himself. Pretty good, he said, don't you think? Yummy, said Rosa. Yummy in the tummy! said David, who laughed at his own joke and then opened his mouth for another bite. Watching this scene as he laced up his boots and put on his winter jacket, Ferguson thought of two infant birds at feeding time. Worms or scrambled eggs, he said to himself, the hunger was the same hunger, and the open mouths were the same open mouths, stretched open as far as they could go. Pancakes, yes, but first a little something to get the morning off to a good start.

There were real birds outside, a speckled brown sparrow, an olive-green female cardinal with a dull scarlet crest, a red-winged blackbird—sudden splotches of color darting across the white-gray sky, a few bits of breathing life in the austere winter morning—and as Ferguson and his cousin crossed the snow-covered yard and climbed into the blue station wagon, he found it a pity that the weekend was about to be spoiled by a senseless argument. He and Francie had never argued in all the years they had known each other, not one unkind word had ever passed between them, their mutual devotion had been constant and unbending, the one deep friendship he had formed with any relative on that side of his family, the fractured clan of crazy, destructive Fergusons, only he and Francie among all the cousins and brothers and sisters and aunts and uncles had been able to avoid those stupid animosities, and it pained him to think she might turn on him now.

It was a cold morning, but not exceptionally cold for that time of year, four or five notches below freezing, and the engine kicked over with the first turn of the key. As they sat there waiting for the car to warm up, Ferguson asked if she would prefer that he do the driving instead. He wouldn't have his license until he turned seventeen in another six weeks or so, but he had his learner's permit, and given that she was a licensed driver who happened to be in the car with him, it was perfectly legal for them to switch places. Ferguson added that he was a good driver, and for many months now his parents had been letting him handle the chauffeuring duties whenever he had to go somewhere with them, either singly or together, and neither his mother nor his father had ever complained about the results. Francie smiled a tight little smile and said she was sure he was an excellent driver, probably a better driver than she was, but she was behind the wheel now, and they were about to get started, and going down the hill could be a bit tricky for someone who had never driven on a dirt road, and so she would do the driving, thank you, and once they got to the store and bought the things they needed to buy, maybe they could switch places for the ride back home.

As it happened, there was no ride back home. They couldn't return from Miller's General Store because they never managed to reach the store, and on that morning, which Ferguson would always think of as *the morning of mornings*, both cousins paid a price for that interrupted journey in the mountains of Vermont, especially Ferguson, who wound up paying for it long into the future, and while no one held him responsible for the accident (how could he be responsible if he wasn't driving the car?), he nevertheless blamed himself for causing Francie to turn her eyes from the road, for if she hadn't glanced over to look at him instead, she never would have skidded on that patch of ice and crashed into the tree.

The point was that he knew better than to allow himself to be drawn into the argument. Francie had every right to feel annoyed with him, and he decided the best course of action would be to say as little as possible to her, to nod his head and agree with whatever harsh judgment she pronounced on him, to resist the temptation to defend himself. Let her be angry, he thought, but as long as he could prevent that anger from inciting an anger of his own, perhaps the confrontation would be short and small and soon forgotten.

Or so Ferguson thought. His mistake was to assume that the central issue was the noise, the indiscretion of that noise and the selfishness he had shown by inflicting it on the others, but the noise was only part of it, the least part of it, and once he understood that the attack was far bigger than the one he had prepared himself for, he was caught with his guard down, and when Francie lashed out at him, he lashed back at her.

She managed to navigate the car down the mile-long hill without any trouble, but when she came to the bottom and paused, she turned right instead of left, and since Gary had said the store was to the left, Ferguson mentioned it to her, but Francie merely strummed her fingers on the steering wheel and said not to worry about it, Gary had no sense of direction, he was always mixing things up, and if he said they should go left, that must have meant they should go right. It was a funny thing to say, Ferguson thought, but the words didn't sound funny when they came out of Francie's mouth, they sounded bitter and slightly contemptuous, as if Francie were peeved at Gary about something, or peeved at someone else about some other thing, her brother Jack, for instance, who was rarely in touch with her anymore, or her pain-in-the-neck father, who had just lost another job and was on unemployment again, or perhaps all three men at the same time, which would have made Ferguson the fourth man she was on the outs with that morning, and the fact that she had indeed taken the wrong turn and was driving farther and farther away from the store didn't help to soften her mood when she discovered her mistake, which meant that the second half of the interrupted journey was spent on a series of twisting back roads in search of a route back to the county highway where they had started, and in the frazzle of bad temper and frustration that descended upon his normally uncombative first cousin, Francie finally got down to the business that had prompted them to leave the house in the first place and let him have it.

How sad, she said, how sad and disappointing it was to discover that her darling boy had turned into a lying cheat, that he was just another crumb in a long line of crumbs, and how dare he *use her* in the way he had, dragging his girlfriend up to Vermont in order to *fuck her* behind everyone's back, it was disgusting, two horny kids charming everyone on the ride up and then sneaking around in the attic at night, fucking on top of *two little children*, and how could he do this to her, she who had loved him since the day he was born, she who had bathed him and cared for him and watched him grow up, and what was she supposed to say to his mother, who had let him go to Vermont because she knew he would be safe with his cousin, there was trust involved in all this, she said, and how could he break that trust under her very roof, an out-of-control teenager who couldn't even keep it in his pants for one night, and the truth was she didn't want him there anymore, she would put him and his slut girlfriend on the bus this afternoon and send them back to New York, and good-bye and good riddance to them both . . .

That was the beginning. Five minutes later, she was still talking, and when Ferguson finally told her to shut up and stop the car, shouting that he'd had enough and would walk back to the house to fetch his things, Francie turned to him and said, with something like madness in her eyes, Don't be ridiculous, Archie, you'll freeze to death out here, which convinced him that something was wrong with her, that her mind was wobbling, on the verge of cracking up, and because she went on looking at him as if she no longer remembered what she had just been saying, he smiled at her, and when she smiled back at him, he realized that she had stopped looking at the road, and a moment later the car slammed into the tree.

No SEAT BELTS, not in 1964, and consequently they were both injured in the crash, even though the car had been traveling at a moderate speed, somewhere between thirty and thirty-five miles an hour. Francie: a concussion, a broken left clavicle caused by the impact when she was flung forward into the steering wheel, and once she was released from the Vermont hospital, transfer to a New Jersey hospital to recover from what the doctors told Gary was a nervous breakdown. Ferguson: unconscious and bleeding from his head, his arms, and his left hand, which had gone through the windshield first, and while no bones were broken (a long-odds fluke that confounded the staff and inspired some of the nurses to call it a *medical miracle*), two of the fingers on that left hand were severed by the windshield glass, both joints of the thumb and the top two joints of the index, and because the fingers were buried in the snow and not recovered until spring, Ferguson was fated to march through the rest of his life as an eight-fingered man.

He took it hard. He knew he should be glad he wasn't dead, but his survival was a fact, something that no longer had to be questioned, and the question before him now was not so much a question as a cry of despair: What was going to happen to him? He had been deformed, and when they removed the bandages and showed him what his hand looked like, what it would always look like from now on, he was revolted by what he saw. His hand was no longer his hand. It belonged to some-one else, and as he gazed down at the stitched-up, smoothed-over spots that had once been his thumb and index finger, he felt sick and turned his head away. So ugly, so hideous to look at—*the hand of a monster*. He had joined the brigade of the damned, he told himself, and from now on he would be looked upon as one of those crippled, distorted people who no longer counted as full-fledged members of the human race. And then, to compound the agony of those insidious humiliations, there would be the trial of having to relearn a hundred things he had mas-tered as a small boy, the myriad manipulations that a two-thumbed person performed unconsciously every day, how to tie his shoes, how to button his shirt, how to cut his food, how to use a typewriter, and until those tasks became automatic for him again, which could take months, perhaps even years, he would be constantly reminded of how far he had fallen. No, Ferguson wasn't dead, but other words beginning with the letter *d* clung to him like a flock of starving children in the days that followed the accident, and he found it impossible to free himself from the spell of those emotions: demoralized, depressed, dumb-founded, discouraged, dejected, down in the dumps, desperate, defen-sive, despondent, discombobulated, distressed, deranged, defeated.

His greatest fear was that Amy would stop loving him. Not that she would want to, and not that she would even understand her own feel-ings, but how could anyone enjoy being touched by that maimed and disfigured hand, it would turn a person's stomach, it would kill all desire, and little by little the revulsion would mount until she started to back away from him and eventually let him go, and if he lost Amy not only would his heart be broken but his life would be ruined for-ever, for what woman in her right mind could possibly be attracted to a man like him, a pitiable, mutilated creature who walked around with *a claw* jutting from his left arm instead of a hand? Endless sorrow,

endless loneliness, endless disappointment—that would be his lot—
and even as Amy sat with him in the hospital throughout the weekend
and then cut school to stay with him through Monday, Tuesday, and
Wednesday, stroking his face and telling him that everything would be
exactly as it had been before, that losing a couple of fingers was a rotten
blow but hardly the end of the world, that millions of people lived with
far worse and forged on bravely without giving it a second thought,
and even as Ferguson listened to her and watched her face as she talked
to him, he wondered if he wasn't looking at an apparition, a substitute Amy who was going through the motions of the real Amy, and if
he shut his eyes for a couple of seconds, he wondered if she wouldn't
disappear before he had a chance to open them again.

His parents had left Montclair to be with him as well, and they were
wonderfully kind to him, just as Amy was wonderfully kind to him, just
as the doctors and nurses were wonderfully kind to him, and yet how
could any of them know what he was feeling, how could they understand that contrary to what they all kept telling him, it was indeed *the
end of the world*, at least the little part of the world that had belonged
to him, and how could he open up to them about the devastation he felt
whenever he thought about baseball, *the dumbest game ever invented*,
according to the long-gone Anne-Marie Dumartin, but how deeply he
still loved it, and how much he had been looking forward to the first
indoor varsity practices, which were scheduled to begin in mid-February,
and now the baseball part of his world had ended as well, for he would
never be able to hold a bat again with those two fingers missing from
his left hand, not in the proper way, not in the way he needed to hold it
to swing with power, and how could he control a glove that had been
designed for five fingers with only three fingers, he would be cast down
into mediocrity if he tried to play with his handicap, and that would be
unacceptable to him, especially now, when he had been preparing himself for the season of his life, an all-conference, all-county, all-state kind
of season, causing such a stir that the pro scouts would start coming to
watch the *wizard* at third base with the .400 batting average, which would
lead to an eventual signing with a major league club, thus making him
the first baseball-playing poet in the annals of American sport, winner
of both the Pulitzer Prize and the Most Valuable Player Award, and
because he had never dared to confess this fantastical daydream to anyone, he couldn't begin now, not when he found himself on the brink of

tears every time he thought about returning to Montclair and telling his coach he could no longer play on the team, holding up his miserable left hand to demonstrate why his career was over, at which point the terse, undemonstrative Sal Martino would nod his head in commiseration, mumbling a few short words that would come out more or less as follows: *Tough break, kid. We're going to miss you.*

Amy and his father both left on Thursday morning, but his mother stayed with him until he was discharged from the hospital, sleeping in a nearby motel and traveling around in a small rented car. The extremity of her compassion was almost too much for him, the sympathetic maternal eyes that kept watching him and telling him how deeply his suffering had become her suffering, and yet, because she understood how much he disliked it when she fussed and doted, he was thankful to her for not dwelling on his injuries, for not offering any advice, for not encouraging him to *buck up*, for not shedding any tears. He knew what a frightful mess he was and how painful it must have been for her to look at him, not only the still healing sutures on his left hand, which were still red and raw and swollen, but also the bandages wrapped around his forearms, temporarily masking the sixty-four stitches that had closed up his gouged flesh, and the weird patches of shorn hair dotting his scalp, where more stitches had been applied to the worst cuts and gashes, but none of those future scars seemed to disturb her, the only thing that mattered was that he had come through the accident with his face intact, which again and again she called *a blessing*, the one lucky turn in this whole unlucky business, and while Ferguson was in no mood to count his blessings just then, he understood her point, since there was a hierarchy of destruction to be reckoned with, and living with a destroyed hand was far less terrible than living with a destroyed face.

It was hard to admit to himself how much he wanted his mother to be there with him. Every time she sat down in the chair next to his bed, things felt a little better than they were when he was alone, often vastly better, and yet he still held back from confiding in her, he couldn't quite bring himself to tell her how afraid he was when he thought about his stunted, abysmal future, the long years of loveless desolation that stood in front of him, all the childish, self-pitying fears that would have sounded so inane if he had spoken them out loud, and so he continued to say next to nothing about himself, and his mother didn't press him to say more. In the long run, it probably didn't make any difference if he talked or not, since it was all but certain that she already knew what he was thinking anyway, she had always known somehow, ever since he was a small boy she had known, and why should it be any different now that he was in high school? Nevertheless, there were other things to talk about besides himself, above all Francie and the mystery of her breakdown, which they continued to discuss all through their final days in Vermont, and now that Francie had left the hospital and was checked into another hospital in New Jersey, what was going to happen to her? His mother wasn't sure. All she knew was what Gary had told her, and she couldn't make sense of it, nothing was clear except that the problems had apparently been growing for some time. Distress about her father—perhaps. Trouble in the marriage—perhaps. Regret over having married too young—perhaps. All of the above—or none of them. The puzzling thing was that Francie had always seemed so healthy and stable. A diamond of joyful exuberance, the light of everyone's eye. And now this.

Poor Francie, his mother said. My beloved girl is ill. Her family is three thousand miles away, and there's no one to take care of her. It's up to me, Archie. We'll be home in a couple of days, and once we're there, that's my new job. To make sure Francie gets well.

Ferguson asked himself if anyone but his mother could have made such an outrageous declaration, willfully ignoring the possibility that psychiatrists might have any role in Francie's recovery, as if love and the persistence of love were the only reliable cure for a shattered heart. It was such a mad and ignorant thing to say that he couldn't help laughing, and once the laugh came out of his throat, he realized that it was the first time he had laughed since the accident. Good for him, he thought. And good for his mother, too, he thought, whose statement deserved to be laughed at, even though it had been wrong of him to laugh, for the beautiful thing about his mother's words was that she believed them, believed with every bone in her body that she was strong enough to carry the world on her back.

THE WORST PART about going home was having to return to school. The hospital had been torture enough, but at least he had felt protected there, walled off from others in the sanctuary of his room, but

now he had to walk back into his old world and let everyone see him—
and the last thing he wanted was to be seen.

It was February, and in preparation for his return to Montclair High,
his mother knitted him a pair of special gloves, one normal glove and
one with three and a third fingers, shaped to fit the contours of his newly
diminished left hand, and a most comfortable pair of gloves they were,
made of the softest imported cashmere in an innocuous pale brown, a
bland hue that didn't assault the eyes and call attention to itself as
a bright color would have, and therefore the gloves were almost unno-
ticeable. For the rest of the month and halfway into the next, Ferguson
wore the left glove indoors at school, claiming he had to do it because
of doctor's orders—to protect the hand as it continued to heal. That
helped a little bit, as did the stocking cap he wore to hide his patchwork
head, which he also had to keep on both outside and inside because of
doctor's orders. Once his hair grew back and the bald spots were gone,
he would abandon the cap, but it served him well during the early stages
of his reentry, as did the long-sleeved shirts and sweaters he wore to
school every day, typical clothing for February but also a way to cover
the crosshatched scars on his two forearms, which were still an awful
shade of red, and because he had been excused from gym class until
his doctor declared him fully mended, he didn't have to undress and
shower in front of his eleventh-grade cronies, which meant that no one
saw the scars until they had turned white and were nearly invisible.

Those were some of the ploys Ferguson used to make the trial somewhat less difficult for himself, but it was difficult all the same, difficult
to return as a piece of *damaged goods* (as one of his former baseball teammates put it when Ferguson overheard him talking behind his back),
and while his friends and teachers all felt sorry for him and tried not to
stare at the gloved left hand, not everyone in that school was his friend,
and those who actively disliked him were not the least bit dismayed to
see the haughty, standoffish Ferguson get his comeuppance. It was his
fault that so many people had turned against him in the past few months,
since he had more or less abandoned them when he started seeing
Amy, declining all Saturday invitations and making himself scarce on
Sundays, and the popular little boy whose double portrait still stood in
the window of Roseland Photo had transformed himself into an outsider. About the only thing that had still kept him connected to the
school was the baseball team, and now that baseball was gone, he was

beginning to feel gone as well. He continued to show up every day, but every day a little less of him was there.

In spite of his estrangement, there were still some friends, still some people he cared about, but apart from dumb Bobby George, his base-ball pal and ex–*National Geographic* sidekick, there was no one he cared about deeply, and why he still should have cared about Bobby was inexplicable to him—until the night he returned from Vermont and Bobby came over to his house to welcome him back, and when the young George saw the gloveless, hatless, sweaterless young Fergu-son, he started to say something and then burst out crying, and as Ferguson watched his friend give way in that spontaneous gush of infantile tears, he understood that Bobby loved him more than anyone else in the town of Montclair. All his other friends felt sorry for him, but Bobby was the only one who cried.

For Bobby's sake, he went to one of the after-school indoor practices to watch the pitcher-catcher drills. It was hard for him to stand in that echoing gym as balls popped back and forth into gloves and bounced across the hardwood floor, but Bobby would be starting behind the plate that season, and he had asked Ferguson to come and see if his throw-ing had improved over last year, and if it hadn't, to tell him what he was doing wrong. Only players were allowed to be in the gym during those two-hour practice sessions, but even though Ferguson was no longer a member of the team, he still retained certain privileges, which had been granted to him by Coach Martino, whose response to his injuries had been much less restrained than Ferguson had imagined it would be, not holding back as he usually did but cursing loudly at the *goddamned, fucked-up thing that had happened*, telling Ferguson that he was one of the best players he had ever coached and that he had been expecting great things from him in his junior and senior years. Then, almost immedi-ately, he started talking about converting him into a pitcher. With an arm like his, he could probably pull it off, Mr. Martino said, and then no one would give a *flying fuck* about his batting average or how many home runs he hit. If it was too soon to begin now, why not think about it for next year? Meanwhile, for this year, he could stay with the team as a sort of unofficial assistant coach, hitting fungoes at practice, leading the players through their drills and calisthenics, discussing strategy with him on the bench during games. But only if he wanted to, of course, and though Ferguson was tempted to take him up on his offer, he knew he couldn't, he knew it would kill him to be part of the team and not part of the team, a wounded mascot cheering the others on, and so he thanked Mr. Martino and politely said no, explaining that he *just wasn't ready*, and the old World War II first sergeant, who had fought in the Battle of the Bulge and had belonged to the unit that liberated Dachau, patted Ferguson on the shoulder and wished him luck. Then, by way of conclusion, as he reached out to shake Ferguson's hand for the last time, Coach Martino said: The only constant in this world is shit, my boy. We're all in it up to our ankles every day, but sometimes, when it gets up to our knees or waists, we just have to pull ourselves out of it and move on. You're moving on, Archie, and I respect you for it, but if you ever happen to change your mind, remember that the door is always open.

Bobby George's tears and Sal Martino's *always open*. Two good things in a world of otherwise all bad things, and yes, Ferguson was moving on now, he had already moved on since he and the coach parted that day, and whether he was headed in the right direction or the wrong direction, the best thing about that second good thing was that no matter where he happened to find himself in the future, he would never forget Mr. Martino's eloquent words about the pervasive, all-enduring power of shit.

He mostly kept to himself until the end of winter, going straight home after school every day, sometimes hitching rides with seniors who had cars, sometimes making the twenty-minute journey on foot. The house was always empty then, which meant it was quiet, and quiet was what he craved most after spending six and a half hours at school, a large, enveloping quiet that allowed him to recover from the ordeal of dragging his gloved and hatted body in front of the two thousand other bodies that filled the hallways and classrooms for those six and a half hours, and nothing was better than to withdraw into himself again and vanish. His parents generally came home a little past six, which gave him about two and a half hours to loll around in his empty fortress, for the most part upstairs in his room with the door closed, where he could crack open the window and smoke one or two of his mother's forbidden cigarettes, relishing the irony of how the new report from the surgeon general about the perils of smoking had coincided with his own growing interest in the pleasures of tobacco, and as he smoked his mother's life-threatening Chesterfields, Ferguson would pace around the room listening to records, alternating between big choral works (Verdi's *Requiem*, Beethoven's *Missa Solemnis*) and solo compositions by Bach (Pablo Casals, Glenn Gould), or else lie on the bed and read books, working his way through the recent bundle of paperbacks sent to him by Aunt Mildred, the unstinting tour guide of his literary education, who had just mapped out his second visit to France in the past nine months, and so Ferguson spent those late-afternoon hours reading Genet (*The Thief's Journal*), Gide (*The Counterfeiters*), Sarraute (*Tropisms*), Breton (*Nadja*), and Beckett (*Molloy*), and when he wasn't listening to music or reading books, Ferguson felt lost, so deeply at odds with himself that he sometimes felt he was bursting apart. He wanted to begin writing poems again, but he couldn't concentrate, and every idea that entered his head seemed worthless. The first baseball-playing poet in history could no longer play baseball, and suddenly the poet in him was dying as well. *Help me*, he wrote one day. *Why should I help you?* the message to himself continued. *Because I need your help*, the first voice answered. *Sorry*, the second voice said. *What you need is to stop saying you need help. Start thinking about what I need for a change.*

And who are you?

I'm you, of course. Who else do you think I am?

The one constant in his world that wasn't shit were his nightly talks on the phone with Amy. Her first question to him always was *How are you doing, Archie?*, and every night he would give her the same answer: *Better. A little better than yesterday*—which was in fact true, not only because his physical condition was slowly getting better as time went on but because talking to Amy always seemed to give his old self back to him, as if her voice were the snapping fingers of a hypnotist ordering him to come out of his trance and wake up. No one else had that power over him, and as the weeks passed and Ferguson continued to recover, he began to suspect it had something to do with Amy's reading of the accident, which was unlike anyone else's, for she refused to regard it as a tragedy, and therefore, among the people who loved Ferguson, she was the one who felt least sorry for him. In her view of the world, tragedies were reserved for death and ravaging disabilities— paralysis, brain damage, brutal disfigurement—but the loss of two fingers was no more than a trivial matter, and given that a car smashing into a tree should have led to death or brutal disfigurement, one could only rejoice that Ferguson had survived the accident without any tragic consequences. Too bad about baseball, of course, but that was a small debt to pay for the privilege of being alive with only two missing fingers, and if he was having trouble writing poems just now, then give poetry a rest for a while and stop worrying about it, and if it turned out that he never managed to write another poem, that would only mean he hadn't been cut out to write poetry in the first place.

You're beginning to sound like Dr. Pangloss, Ferguson said to her one night. Everything always happens for the best—in this, the best of all possible worlds.

No, not at all, Amy said. Pangloss is an idiot optimist, and I'm an intelligent pessimist, meaning a pessimist who has occasional flashes of optimism. Nearly everything happens for the worst, but not always, you see, nothing is ever *always*, but I'm *always* expecting the worst, and when the worst doesn't happen, I get so excited I begin to sound like an optimist. I could have lost you, Archie, and then I didn't. That's all I can think about anymore—how happy I am that I didn't.

For the first weeks after he came home from Vermont, he wasn't strong enough to travel into New York on Saturdays. Going back and forth to school from Monday to Friday was just barely feasible, but Manhattan would have been too hard on his aching, stitched-together body, the jostling bus to begin with, but also the long climb up subway stairways, the crowds of people bumping into him in the pedestrian tunnels, and then the impossibility of walking for any length of time through the cold winter streets with Amy, so they reversed the process for all of February and halfway into March, and for five Saturdays in a row Amy visited him in Montclair instead. The new arrangement was short on outward stimulation, but it also had several advantages over the old routine of wandering in and out of bookstores and museums, of sitting in coffee shops, of going to films and plays and parties, the first one being that Ferguson's parents worked on Saturday, and because they worked the house was empty, and because the house was empty he and Amy could go upstairs into his room, shut the door, and lie down on the bed with no fear that anyone would discover what they were doing. But still there was fear, at least for Ferguson, who had convinced himself that Amy would want no part of him anymore, and the first time they went into his room in the Montclair house, his fear was no less great than it had been the first time they went into Amy's room in the New York apartment, but once they were on the bed and their clothes began to come off, Amy surprised him by taking hold of his wounded hand and kissing it, slowly kissing it twenty or thirty times, and then she put her mouth against his bandaged left forearm and kissed it a dozen times, followed by another twelve kisses on his bandaged right forearm, and then she pulled him down against her chest and began kissing the small bandages on his head, one by one by one, each one six times, seven times, eight times. When Ferguson asked her why she was doing that, she said it was because those were the parts of him she loved best now. How could she say that? he replied, they were disgusting, and how could anyone love what was disgusting? Because, Amy said, those wounds were a memory of what had happened to him, and because he was alive, because he was with her now, what happened to him was also what hadn't happened to him, which meant that the marks on his body were signs of life, and because of that they weren't disgusting to her, they were beautiful. Ferguson laughed. He wanted to say, *Pangloss to the rescue again!*, but he didn't say anything, and as he looked into Amy's eyes, he wondered if she was telling the truth. Could she possibly believe what she had just said to him, or was she only pretending to believe it for his sake? And if she didn't believe it, how could he believe her? Because he had to believe her, he decided, because believing her was the only choice he had, and the truth, the so-called almighty truth, meant nothing when he considered what not believing her would have done to them.

Sex for five straight Saturdays, sex in the early afternoon as the thin February light wrapped itself around the edges of the curtains and seeped into the air around their bodies, and then the pleasure of watching Amy climb back into her clothes, knowing that her naked body was inside those clothes, which somehow prolonged the intimacy of sex even when they weren't having sex, the body he carried around in his mind as they went downstairs to fix themselves some lunch or listened to records or watched an old movie on television or took a short walk around the neighborhood or he read out loud to her from *Pictures from Brueghel* by William Carlos Williams, his newly anointed favorite, who had pushed Eliot off the throne following a bloody skirmish with Wallace Stevens.

Sex for five straight Saturdays, but also the chance to talk face to face again after the long-distance phone conversations during the school week, and on three of those Saturdays Amy hung around long enough to be there when his parents came home from work, which led to three dinners with just the four of them sitting together in the kitchen, his mother so much happier now that he was with Amy and not that *drunken Belgian girl* and his father amused by her volubility and offbeat remarks, as when, to cite one example from late February, which had been the month of the Beatles' conquest of America and Cassius Clay's triumph over Sonny Liston, the two big subjects everyone was talking about, Amy made the nutty but insightful comment that John Lennon and the new heavyweight champion were one and the same person divided up into two different bodies, young men in their early twenties who had captured the attention of the world in precisely the same way, by not taking themselves seriously, by having a gift for saying the most obnoxious things with a boldness and theatricality that made people laugh, *I am the greatest, We're more popular than Jesus Christ,* and when Amy repeated those ridiculous but unforgettable statements, Ferguson's father suddenly started to laugh, not only because Amy had done spot-on imitations of Lennon's Liverpudlian burr and Clay's Kentucky drawl, but because she had imitated their facial expressions as well, and once Ferguson's father had stopped laughing, he said: You've got a good point there, Amy. *Wise guys with fast tongues and even faster minds.* I like that.

Ferguson had no idea if his parents were aware of how he and Amy spent those Saturday mornings and afternoons alone in the house. He suspected his mother might have been onto them (she had come home unannounced on the second Saturday to retrieve a sweater and had caught them smoothing out the covers on the bed), which could have meant she had discussed it with his father, but even if they did know, neither one of them said a word about it, since it was manifestly clear by then that Amy Schneiderman was a positive force in their boy's life, a one-girl emergency team who was single-handedly nursing him through the agonizing adjustment to his post-accident world, and therefore they encouraged them to be together as often as possible, and even though money was particularly tight just then, they never objected to the high cost of the long-distance calls, which had more than quadrupled their monthly telephone bill. *That girl is good stuff, Archie,* his mother said to him one day, and as she watched her ex-boss's granddaughter minister to her son, she herself was ministering to her niece Francie by going to the hospital every afternoon at four o'clock for a one-hour visit, where she steadfastly carried on with her all-love-and-nothing-but-love treatments. Ferguson paid close attention to her nightly reports about Francie's progress, but he kept worrying that his cousin would say something to his mother about *the squeaking bed* and how angry she had been at him on the morning of the crash, which could have led to some unpleasant questions from his mother that he would have been compelled to lie about in order to cover up his embarrassment, but when he finally found the courage to raise the subject himself, asking his mother what Francie had told her about the accident, his mother claimed that Francie had never mentioned it. Was that true? he asked himself. Could Francie have blanked out the crash, or was his mother merely playing dumb about the argument because she didn't want to upset him?

And what about my hand? Ferguson asked. Does she know about that?

Yes, his mother said. Gary told her.

Why would he do that? It seems rather heartless, don't you think?

Because she has to know. She'll be getting out of the hospital soon, and no one wants her to be shocked when she sees you again.

She was discharged after three weeks of rest and therapy, and although there would be further breakdowns and hospitalizations in the years to come, she was back on her feet for now, still wearing a sling around her left arm because the clavicle had been slow in mending, but *altogether radiant* as Ferguson's mother said after her final visit to the hospital, and when the sling came off a week later and Francie invited Ferguson and his parents for Sunday brunch at her house in West Orange, he found her looking radiant as well, fully restored, no longer the harried, spooked-out woman she had been during that catastrophic weekend in Vermont. It was a fraught moment for both of them, facing each other for the first time since the accident, and when Francie looked at his hand and saw what the accident had done to it, she teared up and threw her arms around him, blubbering out an apology that made Ferguson understand, for the first time since the accident, how much he secretly blamed Francie for what had happened to him, that even if it wasn't her fault, even if her final glance at him in the car had been the glance of a mad person, someone no longer in control of her thoughts, she was the one who had smashed the car into the tree, and while he wanted to forgive her for everything, he couldn't quite do it, not all the way down in the deepest part of himself, and even as his mouth was saying all the right words, assuring her that he didn't hold it against her and all was forgiven, he knew that he was lying and would always hold it against her, that the accident would stand between them for the rest of their lives.

He turned seventeen on March third. Several days after that, he went to the local branch of the DMV and took the road test for his New Jersey driver's license, demonstrating his skill at the wheel with his smoothly negotiated turns, the steady pressure he applied to the gas pedal (*as if you were putting your foot on an uncooked egg*, his father had told him), his mastery at braking and driving in reverse, and last of all his understanding of the maneuvers involved in parallel parking, the tight-squeeze operation that was the downfall of so many would-be motorists. Ferguson had taken hundreds of tests over the years, but passing this one was far more important to him than anything he had accomplished at school. This one was for real, and once he had the license in his pocket, it would have the power to unlock doors and let him out of his cage.

He knew his parents were struggling, that business was down for both of them and the family's resources were pinched—not yet hard times, perhaps, but getting close, getting closer by the month. Blue Cross/Blue Shield had covered the bulk of the costs for his stay in the Vermont hospital, but there had been some cash expenditures as well, out-of-pocket deductibles and sundry long-distance telephone charges, along with the money spent on the motel room and his mother's rented car, which couldn't have been easy on them, walking out into their rainy day with torn umbrellas and no shoes on, and so when March third came around and the only birthday present he received from his parents was a toy car—a miniature replica of a white 1958 Chevy Impala—he interpreted it as a kind of joke present, at once a good-luck charm for the driving exam he was about to take and an admission from his parents that they couldn't afford anything better. Oh well, he thought, it actually was rather funny, and since both of his parents were smiling, he smiled back at them and said thank you, too distracted to pay attention to what his mother said next: Fear not, Archie. Out of little acorns do mighty oaks grow.

Six days later, an oak appeared in the driveway in the form of a full-sized car, a mammoth replica of the acorn that now sat on Ferguson's desk as an all-purpose paperweight, or almost a replica, since the white Chevy Impala parked in the driveway had been built in 1960, not 1958, with two doors instead of the four doors in the model, and both of Ferguson's parents were sitting in the car and honking the horn together, honking and honking until their son came down from his room to see what the commotion was about.

His mother explained that they had been planning to give it to him on the third, but the car had needed some work, and the repairs had taken a little longer than expected. She hoped he liked it, she said. They had thought about letting him choose one on his own, but then it wouldn't have been a surprise, and the fun of giving a present like this was the surprise.

Ferguson said nothing.

His father frowned at him and asked: Well, Archie, what do you think? Do you like it or not?

Yes, he liked it. Of course he liked it. How could he not like it? He liked the car so much he wanted to get down on his knees and kiss it.

But how did you come up with the money? he finally asked. It must have cost a lot.

Less than you'd think, his father said. Only six-fifty.

Before or after the repairs?

Before. An even eight hundred after.

That's a lot, Ferguson said. Way too much. You shouldn't have done it.

Don't be ridiculous, his mother said. I've taken a hundred portraits in the past six months, and now that the book is finished, what do you think is hanging on the walls of my famous men and women?

Ah, I see, Ferguson said. Not just the grant, but bonus money, too. How much did you charge them for the pleasure of looking at themselves?

A hundred and fifty a pop, his mother said.

Ferguson made a little whistling sound, nodding his head in appreciation.

A cool fifteen grand, his father added, just in case Ferguson was having trouble with the arithmetic.

You see? his mother said. We're not going to the poorhouse, Archie, at least not today, and probably not tomorrow either. So shut up, get into your car, and take us somewhere, all right?

Thus began the Season of the Car. For the first time in his life, Ferguson was the master of his own comings and goings, the sovereign ruler of the spaces that surrounded him, with no god before him now but a six-cylinder internal combustion engine, which asked nothing more of him than a full tank of gas and an oil change every three thousand miles. Throughout the spring and into the early days of summer, he drove the car to school every morning, most often with Bobby George next to him up front and sometimes with a third person in back, and when school let out at a quarter past three, he no longer went straight home to sequester himself in his small bedroom but climbed back into the car and drove, drove for an hour or two without purpose or destination, drove for the pure satisfaction of driving, and after not knowing where he wanted to go for the first minutes or quarter hours of those drives, he often found himself meandering up to the South Mountain Reservation, the only patch of wilderness in all of Essex County, acres and acres of forests and hiking trails, a sanctuary that harbored owls and hummingbirds and hawks, a place of a million butterflies, and when he reached the top of the mountain he would get out of the car and look down at the immense valley below, town after town filled with houses and factories and schools and churches and parks, a view that encompassed more than twenty million people, one-tenth of the population of the United States, for it went all the way to the Hudson River and across into the city, and at the farthest limit of what Ferguson could see from the top ledge of the mountain, there were the tall buildings of New York, the Manhattan skyscrapers jutting out from the horizon like tiny stalks of grass, and once, as he looked at Amy's city, he got it into his head that he should go see Amy herself, and suddenly he was in the car again, impulsively driving to New York through the mounting rush-hour traffic, and when he arrived at the Schneidermans' apartment an hour and twenty minutes later, Amy, who was in the middle of doing her homework, was so surprised to see him when she opened the door that she let out a shriek.

Archie! she said. What are you doing here?

I'm here to kiss you, Ferguson said. Just one kiss, and then I have to be off.

Just one? she said.

Just one.

So Amy opened her arms and let him kiss her, and just as they were in the middle of their one kiss, Amy's mother walked into the entrance-way and said: Good God, Amy, what are you doing?

What does it look like, Ma? Amy said, as she jerked away her lips from Ferguson's mouth and looked at her mother. I'm kissing the coolest guy on two legs.

It was Ferguson's finest moment, the very pinnacle of his adolescent aspirations, the grand and foolish gesture he had dreamed of so often but had never found the courage to try, and because he didn't want to spoil it by going back on his word, he bowed to Amy and her mother and then headed for the stairs. Out on the street, he said to himself: Without the car, it never would have happened. A car had nearly killed him in January, and now, just two months later, a car was giving his life back to him.

On Monday, March twenty-third, he decided not to wear the hat to school, and since his hair had grown back by then and his head looked more or less as it had always looked before the Vermont scalping, no one mentioned the absence of the hat except for three or four girls in his French class, among them Margaret O'Mara, who had once sent him a secret love note when they were in the sixth grade. On Thursday morning, the weather was so warm for that time of year that he decided to dispense with the glove as well. Again, no one said much of anything, and of all the people in his dwindling circle of friends, only Bobby George asked to take a close look at it, which Ferguson reluctantly allowed him to do—sticking out his left arm and letting Bobby take hold of the hand, which he then brought up to within six inches of his face and examined with the rapt scrutiny of a veteran surgeon, or perhaps a young, brainless child—it was hard to tell with Bobby—turning the hand back and forth and gently rubbing his fingers against the injured areas, and when he finally let go of it and Ferguson dropped his arm back down to his side, Bobby said: It's looking real good, Archie. All healed up now and back to its old color.

Ever since the accident, people had been telling him stories about famous men who had also lost fingers and then had gone on to flour-ish in life, among them the baseball pitcher Mordecai Brown, better known as Three Finger Brown, who had won 239 games in a fourteen-year career and was elected to the Hall of Fame, and the silent film come-dian Harold Lloyd, who had lost the thumb and forefinger of his right hand in a property bomb explosion, and still he managed to hang from the hands of that gigantic clock and perform a thousand other impossible stunts. Ferguson tried to take heart from those inspirational narratives, to see himself as a proud member of the fraternity of eight-fingered men, but rah-rah stuff of that ilk tended to leave him cold, or embarrass him, or repulse him with its treacly optimism, and yet still and all, with or without the examples of those other men to guide him, he was slowly coming to terms with the altered shape of his hand, *beginning to get used to it*, and when he finally took off the glove on March twenty-sixth, he figured the worst was behind him. What he failed to consider, however, was how comforting the glove had been to him, how much he had depended on it as a shield against the squirming horrors of self-consciousness, and now that the hand was naked again, now that he was trying to act as if *everything had returned to normal*, he fell into the habit of sticking his left hand into his pocket whenever he was with other people, which at school meant nearly all the time, and the demoralizing thing about this new habit was that he wasn't aware of what he was doing, the gesture was made out of pure reflex, entirely independent of his will, and it was only when he had to take the hand out of the pocket for one reason or another that he understood the hand had been in the pocket in the first place. No one outside the school was aware of this tic, not Amy, not his mother and father, not his grandparents, since it wasn't difficult to be brave around the people who cared about him, but Ferguson had turned into a coward at school and was beginning to despise himself for it. And yet how could he stop himself from doing something he didn't even know he was doing? There seemed to be no answer to the problem, which was yet another instance of the old and intractable mind-body problem, in this case a mindless body part acting as if it had a mind of its own, but then, after a month of fruitless searching, an answer finally came to him, an altogether practical answer, and one by one he gathered up the four pairs of pants he wore to school, gave them to his mother, and asked her to sew up the front and back left pockets on each pair.

On April eleventh, Amy received her acceptance letter from Barnard. No one who knew her was surprised, but for several months she had been anguishing over the 81 she had been given in Algebra II–Trigonometry last year, which had pulled down her overall average from 95 to 93, and wondering if her SAT scores weren't just a trifle too low, 1375 instead of the 1450 she had been gunning for, and whenever

Ferguson had tried to reassure her during those anxious months of waiting, she would tell him that nothing was certain in this life, that the
world doled out disappointments as quickly and eagerly as a politician
could shake hands, and because she didn't want to be disappointed, she
was preparing herself to be disappointed, and therefore, when the happy
news arrived at last, she wasn't happy so much as relieved. But Ferguson was happy, not just for Amy but for himself, above all for himself,
since there had been a number of backup choices in case Barnard had
turned her down, each one in a city not named New York, and Ferguson had been living in dread that she would land in one of those far-off
places like Boston or Chicago or Madison, Wisconsin, which would have
made everything so complicated and lonely for him, seeing her only a
few times a year, the rushed holiday returns to West Seventy-fifth Street
and then gone again, nine long months with little or no contact, writing letters to her that she would be too busy to answer, and slowly and
inevitably they would have drifted apart, nothing could have stopped
her from meeting someone else, the college boys would have been circling around her and sooner or later she would have fallen for one of
them, a twenty- or twenty-one-year-old history major/civil rights activist who would have made her forget all about poor Ferguson, who still
hadn't graduated from high school, and then the letter from Barnard
arrived, and he no longer had to contemplate the grim details of what
might have been. Ferguson was still young, but he was old enough to
have learned that worst nightmares sometimes became real—brothers
robbing brothers, presidents shot down by assassins' bullets, cars crashing into trees—and that sometimes they didn't, as with the crisis two
years earlier, when the world was supposed to have ended but didn't, or
as with Amy's going off to college, which could have taken her away from
New York but didn't, and now that she would be spending the next four
years in New York, Ferguson understood that when the time came for
him to go to college, he would have to head to New York as well.

The baseball season had started by then, but Ferguson did everything he could not to think about it. He avoided going to the games, and
whatever he knew about the team came from his conversations with
Bobby George on their morning rides to school. Andy Malone, who had
taken over Ferguson's spot at third base, was apparently having trouble adjusting to his new position and had cost the team a couple of wins
with late-inning errors. Ferguson felt sorry for him and everyone else

on the team, but not too sorry, not sorry enough to prevent him from feeling somewhat glad as well, for much as it pained him to admit it, there was a perverse satisfaction in knowing that the team was less good without him. As for Bobby—nothing to worry about, as usual. He had always been good, but now he was the best player on the squad, a power-hitting catcher who could field as well as he hit, and when he finally talked Ferguson into going to a home game against Columbia High School in the second week of May, Ferguson was astonished by how enormously Bobby had improved. A single, a double, and a three-run homer—along with two runners thrown out trying to steal second base. The snot-clogged little boy who had breathed through his mouth and sucked his thumb was now a six-foot-two-inch adolescent, a muscular, quick-footed hulk of more than two hundred pounds who looked like a full-grown man on the field and played with an intelligence that was nothing less than bewildering to Ferguson, for Bobby George was a blockhead at all pursuits that were not baseball or football or laughing at dirty jokes, and the only reason why he wasn't flunking half his classes was because his parents had hired a tutor from Montclair State to help keep his average from dropping below a C, which was the academic minimum required to participate in interscholastic sports. Put him on a ball field, however, and he played smart, and now that Ferguson had seen how good Bobby had become, there was no need to torture himself by going to another game that spring. Maybe next year, he told himself, but for now it still hurt too much.

Summer was approaching, and with the business of college finally off the table for her, Amy was talking politics again, pouring out her ideas to Ferguson in long conversations about SNCC, CORE, and the direction of the movement, bitterly frustrated that she was too young to go down south to take part in the Mississippi Summer Project that was being organized during the last months of the school year, the three-pronged initiative launched by SNCC that involved the recruitment of a small army of college students from the North, a thousand extra pairs of hands to help with (1) a voter registration drive for the disenfranchised Negroes of the state, (2) the running of the Freedom Schools that would be set up for Negro children in dozens of towns and small cities, and (3) the founding of the Mississippi Freedom Democratic Party, which would elect a slate of alternative delegates to go to the convention in Atlantic City at the end of August in order to unseat the all-white, racist delegation of the regular Democrats. Amy would have given anything to go down into that danger zone of violence and bigotry, to put herself on the line for the cause, but nineteen was the cutoff age and she wasn't eligible to apply, which was all to the good from Ferguson's perspective, for much as he believed in the cause himself, a summer without Amy would have been intolerable to him.

Many intolerable things occurred in the months that followed, but not to them, not directly to them, and in spite of their summer jobs as clerk at the Eighth Street Bookshop (Amy) and staff member at Stanley's TV & Radio (Ferguson), they managed to see each other often, not just on the weekends but on many weeknights as well, with Ferguson driving into the city the moment he got off from work, picking up Amy at the bookstore and then on to hamburgers at Joe Junior's and a movie at the Bleecker Street Cinema or a walk through Washington Square or a naked tumble in the apartment of one of Amy's absent friends, free to go wherever they wanted now because of Ferguson's car, the Freedom Car of that Freedom Summer, the Saturdays and Sundays when they would drive out to Jones Beach or drive up north to the country or drive down to the Jersey shore, a summer of big thoughts and ferocious love and immense pain, which began so encouragingly when the Civil Rights Bill was passed by the Senate on June nineteenth, and then, immediately afterward, just seventy-two hours later, the intolerable things began to happen. On June twenty-second, three of the young men who had joined the Mississippi Summer Project were reported missing. Andrew Goodman, Mickey Schwerner, and James Chaney had left the project's Ohio training center ahead of the other students in order to investigate the bombing of a church and had not been heard from since the day of their departure. There was no question that they had been murdered, beaten and tortured and killed by white segregationists out to terrorize the invading horde of Yankee radicals who were plotting to destroy their way of life, but no one knew where the bodies were and not one white person in the state of Mississippi seemed to care. Amy wept when she heard the news. On July sixteenth, the day Barry Goldwater won the Republican nomination for president in San Francisco, a white cop shot and killed a black teenager in Harlem, and Amy wept again when James Powell's death was answered by six straight nights of rioting and looting in Harlem and Bedford-Stuyvesant, with the New York police shooting live bullets over the heads of people standing on rooftops and throwing stones and garbage down on them in the streets, not the fire hoses and dogs used to disperse black mobs in the South but real bullets, and Amy wept not only because she finally understood that racism was just as strong in the North as it was in the South, just as strong in *her own city,* but because she also understood that her innocent idealism was dead, that her dream of a color-blind America in which blacks and whites stood together was no more than stupid wishful thinking, and not even Bayard Rustin, the man who had organized the March on Washington just eleven months earlier, had the least bit of influence anymore, and when he stood in front of the crowd in Harlem and begged them to stop the violence so no one would be hurt or killed, the crowd shouted him down and called him an Uncle Tom. Peaceful resistance had lost its meaning, Martin Luther King was yesterday's news, and Black Power had become the supreme gospel, and so great was that power that within a matter of months the word *Negro* had been erased from the American lexicon. On August fourth, the bodies of Goodman, Schwerner, and Chaney were discovered in an earth dam near Philadelphia, Mississippi, and the photographs of their half-buried corpses, lying in the mud at the bottom of the dam, were so horrible and disturbing to look at that Ferguson turned away his head and groaned. The next day, word was released that two U.S. destroyers patrolling the Gulf of Tonkin had been attacked by North Vietnamese P.T. boats, or so it was stated in the official government report, and on August seventh Congress passed the Gulf of Tonkin Resolution, giving Johnson the power "to take all necessary measures to repel any armed attack against the forces of the United States and to prevent further aggression." The war was on, and Amy was no longer weeping. She had made up her mind about Johnson now, and she was furious, so exalted in her anger that Ferguson was almost tempted to crack a joke to see if she would ever smile again.

It's going to be big, Archie, she said, bigger than Korea, bigger than anything since World War Two, and just be glad you won't be part of it.

And why is that, Dr. Pangloss? Ferguson asked.

Because one-thumbed men don't get drafted. Thank God.

3.2

A MY DIDN'T LIKE HIM ANYMORE, AT LEAST NOT IN THE WAY FER-
guson wanted her to like him, and after the splendid days of last
spring and summer when the kissing cousins had left behind their
cousinhood for a stab at true love, they were back to being just plain
cousins. Amy was the one who had called off the romance, and there
was nothing Ferguson could do to change her mind, for once a Schneiderman mind was made up, it was unbudgeable. Her chief complaints
about Ferguson were that he was too self-involved, too pushy with
his embraces (the persistent assaults on her breasts, which she wasn't
ready to bare to him at age fourteen), too passive in all other matters
not related to her breasts, too immature, too lacking in a social conscience for them to have anything *meaningful* to talk about. It wasn't
that she didn't feel a great and enduring fondness for him, she said,
or that she didn't enjoy having the movie-crazed, basketball-playing,
lazy-boned Ferguson as a member of her newly expanded family, but
as a boyfriend he was hopeless.

The fling ended a couple of weeks before the end of the summer
(1961), and when school started again after Labor Day, Ferguson felt
bereft. Not only would there be no more kissing rampages with Amy,
but their pre-fling camaraderie had been smashed as well. No more visits to each other's apartments to do homework together, no more *Twilight Zone* episodes on TV, no more games of gin rummy, no more
listening to records, no more outings to the movies, no more walks in
Riverside Park. He still saw her at family gatherings, which tended to

occur two or three times a month, the dinners and Sunday brunches at
the two Schneiderman apartments, the excursions to the Szechuan Palace on Broadway and the Stage Deli on Seventh Avenue, but he found it
painful to look at her now, painful to be near her after being cast aside,
rejected because he didn't measure up to her standards of what constituted a worthy, dependable human being, and instead of sitting next to
her at those meals as he always had in the past, he now positioned himself at the other end of the table and tried to act as if she wasn't there. In
the last week of September, midway through a dinner at Uncle Dan and
Aunt Liz's place, with the old goat blathering on about the poisonous
radium the East Germans had planted in the Berlin Wall, Ferguson
stood up in disgust, mumbled an excuse about having to visit the bathroom, and left the table. He did go into the bathroom, but only to hide
from the others, since it was all getting to be too much for him, the obligation to maintain a mask of politeness in front of Amy at these family
events, the still fresh wound reopening each time he saw her again, not
knowing what to do or say in her presence anymore, and so he ran the
water in the sink and flushed the toilet a couple of times to make the
others believe he had gone in there to empty his bowels rather than to
indulge in the miserable pleasure of feeling sorry for himself. When he
opened the door three or four minutes later, Amy was standing in the
hall with her hands on her hips, a defiant, combative posture that
seemed to demonstrate that she too had had enough.

What the hell is going on? she asked. You don't look at me anymore.
You don't talk to me anymore. All you do is sulk, and it's getting on my
nerves.

Ferguson looked down at his feet and said: My heart is broken.

Come off it, Archie. You're disappointed, that's all. And I'm disappointed, too. But at least we can try to be friends. We've always been
friends, haven't we?

Ferguson still couldn't bring himself to look her in the eyes. There's
no going back, he said. What's done is done.

You're joking, right? I mean, tough titties and all that, but nothing
is done. Nothing has even started yet. We're fourteen years old, schmuck-
face.

Old enough to have our hearts broken.

Toughen up, Archie. You're talking like a pathetic little child, and

I hate that. I just hate that. We're going to be cousins for a long, long time, and I need you to be my friend, so please don't make me hate you.

Ferguson tried to toughen up. Hard as it was to listen to Amy tear into him with those scolding remarks, he understood that he had allowed his soft-minded, self-pitying impulses to get the better of him, and unless he put a stop to it, he would turn into Gregor Samsa and *awake one morning from uneasy dreams to find himself transformed into a gigantic bug.* He was in the ninth grade now, the first year of high school, and although his academic performance at the Riverside Academy had always been respectable, his marks had slipped a little in the seventh and eighth grades, perhaps from boredom, perhaps from an over-reliance on his natural abilities to carry him through with less than an all-out effort, but the work was more demanding now, and it wouldn't be possible to answer test questions about how to conjugate irregular French verbs in the *passé simple* or put dates on things such as the Defenestration of Prague and the Diet of Worms (the Diet of Worms!) if he didn't put in the study time to master those abstruse particulars. Ferguson resolved to lift his grades to the highest level he could imagine for himself—nothing less than A's in English, French, and history, and nothing less than B+'s in biology and math—a stringent but realistic plan of action, since striving for A's in the last two subjects would have taken so much extra work that basketball would have been pushed out of the picture, and when tryouts began after the Thanksgiving break, he was determined to make the freshman team. He did make it (as a starting forward), and his course work met expectations as well, although not precisely in the way he had predicted, for the A in French wound up as a disappointing B+, and the B+ in biology evolved into a miraculous A−. But no matter. Ferguson made the honor roll for the first semester, and if Amy had been a student at the Riverside Academy, she would have known how well he had done. But she wasn't, and therefore she didn't, and because her angry, heartsick cousin was too proud to tell her that he had *toughened up,* she never knew how deeply she had shamed him into trying to prove her wrong about who he was.

All that said, it went without saying that he still wanted her, that he would have done anything to win Amy back, but even if he eventually managed to make her want him again, it was going to take time, perhaps a long time, and in the interval between not having her anymore and perhaps having her again, he figured the best strategy for turning things around would be to find himself a new girlfriend. Not only would that show he had lost interest in her and had put their breakup behind him (which was essential), it would distract him from thinking about her all the time, and the less he thought about her, the less he would mope, and the less he moped, the more attractive he would appear to her. A new girlfriend would make him a happier person, and emboldened by his newfound happiness, he would surely be nicer to Amy at family gatherings, more charming, more in control of his feelings, and whenever the occasion presented itself, he would talk to her about *current events*. That was one of her principal gripes against him—his indifference to politics, his lack of concern about what was happening in the big world of national and international affairs—and to remedy that deficit Ferguson resolved to follow the news more closely from now on. Two papers were delivered to the apartment every morning, the *Times* and the *Herald Tribune*, although Gil and his mother read the *Times* and largely ignored the *Herald Tribune*, even if it was Gil's employer, for the joke in the family was that the *Herald Tribune* was too pro-Republican to be taken seriously by anyone who lived on the Upper West Side. Nevertheless, Gil's reviews and articles appeared roughly every other day in that Park Avenue organ of Wall Street money and American power, and Ferguson's morning job was to cut out the pieces with Gil's byline on them and stow the clippings in a box for his mother, who was planning to put together a scrapbook of Gil's writings one day, and Gil was forever telling him not to bother with that *rubbish*, but Ferguson, who understood that Gil was both embarrassed by the attention and secretly pleased by it, would shrug and say, Sorry, orders from the Boss, the Boss being yet another name for the already double-named Rose Adler/Rose Schneiderman, and Gil would nod with feigned resignation and reply, *Natürlich, mein Hauptmann*, you mustn't get in trouble for not following orders. So the *Times* and the *Herald Tribune* were there for him to read in the morning, and when the afternoon rolled around and he came home from school, a copy of the *New York Post* had generally found its way into the apartment as well, and on top of the dailies there were *Newsweek*, *Life*, and *Look* (in which his mother sometimes published photographs), *I. F. Stone's Weekly*, the *New Republic*, the *Nation*, and assorted other magazines, and Ferguson diligently plowed through them now instead of turning straight to the film and book reviews in the back, reading the political articles in order to figure out what was going on *out there* and thus figure out how to hold his own in a conversation with Amy. Such were the sacrifices he was willing to make in the cause of love, for even as he turned himself into a more informed citizen, a more vigilant observer of the battles between Democrats and Republicans, of America's interactions with friendly and unfriendly foreign governments, he still found politics to be the dullest, deadliest, dreariest subject he could think of. The Cold War, the Taft-Hartley Act, underground nuclear testing, Kennedy and Khrushchev, Dean Rusk and Robert McNamara—none of it meant much to him, and in his opinion all politicians were either stupid or tainted or both, and even handsome John Kennedy, the much-admired new president, was just another stupid or tainted politician to Ferguson, who found it much more nourishing to admire men like Bill Russell and Pablo Casals than to waste his feelings on pompous windbags scrambling for votes. The only three things from *out there* that truly engaged his attention in the last months of 1961 and the first months of 1962 were the Eichmann trial in Jerusalem, the crisis in Berlin—because Gil and Uncle Dan were so wrapped up in it—and the civil rights movement at home—because the people were so brave and the injustices they had exposed him to were so obscene that they made America look like one of the most backward countries on earth.

The quest for a substitute Amy was not without its problems, however. It wasn't that Ferguson was expecting to discover anyone who resembled her, since Amy was not the sort of girl who had been designed for mass production, but he was reluctant to settle for anything less than a top-quality alternative—nothing to compare to Amy, perhaps, but a scintillating person who would bowl him over and quicken the pace of his heart. Unfortunately, the most promising candidates had already given their hearts to others, among them the ever more beautiful Isabel Kraft, the Hedy Lamarr of the freshman class, who was dating a boy from the sophomore class, as was her attractive cousin, Alice Abrams, as was Ferguson's former flame, the honey-voiced Rachel Minetta. That was one of the central facts of ninth-grade life: most of the girls were more advanced than most of the boys, which meant that the most impressive girls shunned the boys from their year for the more advanced boys from the next year, if not the next year plus one. Hoping for a quick result, success by mid-October at the latest, that is, three weeks after

Amy had told him to *toughen up,* Ferguson was still searching well into November, not from any lack of effort on his part (four movie dates with four different girls on four successive Saturdays) but simply because none of the girls he went out with was the right one. By the time school recessed for the Thanksgiving break, he was beginning to wonder if any girl at the Riverside Academy would ever be the right one.

Basketball helped to distract him from the disappointments of love, at least for five days of the week, with loveless weekends to be endured by seeking further distraction from such things as pickup games with his friends, occasional Saturday night parties, movies with whatever person he could find to go with him (often his mother), and concerts with Gil or Gil and his mother both, but there was no question that playing basketball for the eleven weeks the season lasted helped to keep him from falling into too many mope-holes, beginning with the one-week tryout period and the grand satisfaction of making the last cut, followed by an exhausting week of after-school practices as the team knit together under the direction of Coach Nimm, often referred to as Coach Numb because of his placid disposition, and then nine weeks of games, eighteen games in all, one on Tuesday afternoon and the other on Friday evening, half the games on their home court and the other half on the courts of other private schools scattered around the city, the newsreel-cartoon freshman game before the curtain rose on the main-feature varsity game, and there was Ferguson, the oddball who had asked to wear number 13, running onto the court with the other members of the starting five and taking his position for the center jump.

All those Saturday mornings in Riverside Park with cousin Jim had helped transform the raw, twelve-year-old beginner into a solid if unspectacular player by the time he scored seven points in his first game for the Riverside Rebels at the age of fourteen years and nine months. Ferguson knew that his talents were limited, that he lacked the exceptional speed required for basketball greatness, and because he was less nimble with his left hand than his right, he would never be more than an iffy ball handler when pressured by quick and aggressive opponents. No flash, no razzle-dazzle, no fake-them-out-of-their-pants one-on-one moves, but there were enough strong points about Ferguson's game to keep him off the bench and make him an indispensable part of the team, most of all the spring in his legs, which allowed him to jump higher than anyone else, and when you combined that ability with the reckless enthusiasm of his play—an insane form of hustle that earned him the nickname of Commando-in-Chief—the result was an unusual knack for muscling deft, clean rebounds when he crashed the boards against taller players. He rarely missed layups, and his outside shot was good, with the potential to become very good, but the accuracy he showed at practice was seldom matched by his performance in games, since he tended to rush his shots in the heat of competition, which made him an erratic offensive player that first year, someone capable of scoring ten or twelve points when his shot was on or two points or no points when it was off. Thus the seven points he scored in the first game, which turned out to be his average for the season, but with the games only thirty-two minutes long and the point totals somewhere in the thirty-five-to-forty-five range for each team, seven a game wasn't bad. Not terribly exciting, perhaps, but not bad.

Rah-rah-sis-koom-bah! Rebels! Rebels! Yah-yah-yah!

The numbers meant little to him, however, and as long as the team won he didn't care how many points he scored, but even more important than winning or losing was the mere fact that he was on the team in the first place. He loved wearing the red-and-yellow Rebels' uniform with the number 13 on it, he loved the nine other boys he played with, he loved Coach Nimm's pepless but insightful pep talks in the locker room at halftime, he loved riding on the bus to the away games with his teammates and the ten varsity boys and the six varsity cheerleaders and the four freshman cheerleaders, he loved the chaos of merriment and loud jokes on the bus and especially when junior-class cutup Yiggy Goldberg got suspended for two games for pulling down his pants and sticking his bare ass against the window to moon the people in the passing cars, he loved playing so hard that he was no longer aware of being inside his own body, no longer conscious of who he was, he loved working himself into a sweat at practice and then feeling the hot water from the shower blast the sweat from his skin, he loved that the team had started off slowly and gotten better as the season went along, losing most of the games in the first half and then winning most of them in the second half to wind up with an almost even 8 and 10 record, and he loved it that one of the wins came against Hilliard at home when he scored just three points but led the team in rebounds.

Ho-ho-tic-tac-toe! Rebels! Rebels! Go-go-go!

The best part of it was that people came to watch, that there was always a crowd in the small gym at Riverside for the two games, not thousands or even hundreds but enough to make it feel like a spectacle, with Chuckie Showalter pounding on the bass drum to urge the team on, and nearly everyone in Ferguson's family showed up at one time or another to root for the Commando-in-Chief, Uncle Dan most of all, who didn't miss a single home game, and his mother next, who failed to come only when she was out of town for her work, and several times an appearance from Mr. No-Sport Gil, and once cousin Jim, down from Boston on his midwinter break from college, and once, for the game against Hilliard, Miss Amy Schneiderman herself, who saw Ferguson take a hard tumble trying to save a ball from going out of bounds, who saw him thrust his shoulder into a Hilliard player and knock him to the floor as they battled for an errant pass, who saw him block a layup from going into the basket in the fourth quarter to keep Riverside ahead by three points, and after the game was over she said to him: Good show, Archie. A little scary at times, but fun to watch.

Scary? he asked. What does that mean?

I don't know. Intense, maybe. Super intense. I hadn't realized basketball was supposed to be a contact sport.

Not always. But under the boards, you have to be tough.

Is that what you are now, Archie—tough?

Don't you remember?

What are you talking about?

Toughen up. You don't remember?

Amy smiled and shook her head. Ferguson found her so unbearably beautiful at that moment, he wanted to throw his arms around her and attack her mouth with kisses, but before he could do anything that foolish and disgraceful, Uncle Dan walked up to him and said: Terrific job, Archie. The jump shot might have been a little off, but I think it was your best all-around game so far.

THEN THE BASKETBALL season was over, and it was back to the no-girlfriend void of no Amy and no one else. The only girl he saw with any regularity was last year's Miss April in the copy of *Playboy* Jim had passed on to him before heading off to college, but Wanda Powers of Spokane, Washington, a grinning twenty-two-year-old with gravity-defying cantaloupe breasts and a body that seemed to have been manufactured from a rubber model of the real Wanda Powers, had begun to lose her hold over Ferguson's imagination.

Antsy and demoralized, ever more frustrated by the stuckness of his position in the world, dragged down by his dulled hopes and the feverish daydreams that had supplanted those hopes, the useless and incessant mental journeys into realms of voluptuous happiness where everything he wished for came true, Ferguson decided to make a last attempt to patch things up with Amy and start their romance again, but when he called her five days after the end of the season, asking her to accompany him to the team party that would be held at Alex Nordstrom's place on Saturday night, she said she was busy. Well, he asked, what about the day after that? No, she said, she was busy on Sunday as well, and then he learned that she would continue to be busy for as long as *it* lasted, *it* being the mutual love she had formed with a person she refused to name, and that was that, Ferguson said to himself, Amy had a boyfriend, Amy was gone, and the green fields of hope had turned to mud.

A number of unpleasant incidents occurred in the wake of that dispiriting phone call. *One*: Getting drunk for the first time in his life on the evening of the party when he and fellow team member Brian Mischevski broke into the Nordstroms' liquor cabinet and stole an unopened bottle of Cutty Sark, which they hid in the inside pocket of Ferguson's winter coat and then carried back to Brian's apartment when the fête at the Nordstroms' was over. Fortunately, Brian's parents were out of town for the weekend (which explained why they picked his apartment as their watering hole), and fortunately Brian remembered to tell Ferguson to call his own parents and ask permission to spend the night before they cracked open the bottle and downed two-thirds of its contents, two-thirds of that two-thirds scalding its way down Ferguson's throat and landing in his stomach, where, unfortunately, it didn't remain for long, for Ferguson had drunk just one can of beer and two glasses of wine before that night and had no experience with the intoxicating powers of eighty-six-proof distilled scotch, and not long before he passed out on the living room sofa, he puked up the entire swizzle on the Mischevskis' Oriental rug. *Two*: Just ten days after that binge of weepy, semi-suicidal drunkenness, he tangled with Bill Nathanson, formerly known as Billy, the large toad who had been tormenting him since his first year at the Riverside Academy, at long last letting loose with a barrage of punches to Nathanson's fat belly and pimple-studded face when the cretin called him a *stupid prick* in the lunchroom, and even though Ferguson was punished with three days of after-school detention, along with a sharp warning from Gil and his mother to *shape up*, he had no regrets about having lost his temper, and as far as he was concerned, the satisfaction of pummeling Nathanson was well worth the price he had to pay for it. *Three*:

On a Tuesday afternoon in late March, less than a month after his fifteenth birthday, he skipped out of school immediately following lunch, walked from West End Avenue to Broadway, and went to the movies. It was going to be a one-time-only exception, he told himself, but the rules had to be broken that day because the film he wanted to see would not be showing the next day, or on any other day in the foreseeable future, and cousin Jim, who had seen *Children of Paradise* at the Brattle Theatre in Cambridge, had told Ferguson that he must see it the next time it came to New York or else lose the right to call himself a human being. The picture was scheduled to start at one, and Ferguson covered the ten blocks to West Ninety-fifth Street and the Thalia Theater as quickly as he could, telling himself that if he had been a little bit older, he wouldn't have had to resort to truancy, since there was another showing of the film at eight o'clock, but Gil and his mother never would have given him permission to go on a school night, especially not to a movie that was over three hours long. There would be the matter of inventing an excuse for them, he supposed, but nothing had come to mind so far, and the best and simplest one—that he had felt sick after lunch and had gone home to lie down—was not going to work in this case because Gil and his mother were almost certainly in the apartment, Gil in his study working on his book about Beethoven and his mother in her darkroom developing pictures, and even if his mother happened to be out, there was a ninety-nine percent chance that Gil would be in. Not having an excuse was a problem, but as with most of the problems Ferguson created for himself, he tended to jump first and worry about the consequences later, for he was a young man who wanted what he wanted precisely when he wanted it, and woe to the person who stood in his way. On the other hand, Ferguson reasoned, as he half-walked and half-trotted up the crowded sidewalk in the frigid March air, he wasn't missing much of anything by cutting his Tuesday afternoon classes, which consisted of gym and study hall, and since Mr. McNulty and Mrs. Wohlers rarely bothered to take attendance, he might even get away with it. And if he didn't, and if he still hadn't managed to come up with a false explanation by the time he saw Gil and his mother again, he would simply tell the truth. He wasn't committing a crime or an immoral act, after all. He was going to the movies, and few things in this world were better than going to the movies.

The Thalia was a small, oddly shaped theater of roughly two hundred seats with thick, sight-obstructing columns and a sloping floor that stuck to the bottoms of your shoes because of all the sodas that had been spilled on it over the years. Cramped and dingy, almost laughable in the range of its discomforts, with the ancient springs in the seat cushions digging into your ass and the smell of burnt popcorn wafting into your nose, it was also the best place on the Upper West Side for watching old films, which the Thalia presented at the rate of two per day, every day a different double feature, two French films today, two Russian films tomorrow, two Japanese films the day after that, which explained why *Children of Paradise* was on the Thalia program that afternoon and not showing anywhere else in the city, perhaps anywhere else in the country. Ferguson had been there a couple of dozen times by then, with Gil and his mother, with Amy, with Jim, with Jim and Amy together, with friends from school, but as he showed his student ID and paid the forty cents for his discount ticket, he realized that he had never been there alone, and then, as he found a seat in the middle of the fifth row, he further realized that he had never been to any movie alone, not just at the Thalia but anywhere, not once in his life had he sat in a movie theater alone, for movies had always been about companionship as much as the movies themselves, and while he had often watched his Laurel and Hardy movies alone when he was a small boy, that was because he had been alone in the room where he was watching them, but now there were other people in the theater with him, at least twenty-five or thirty other people, and he was still alone. He couldn't tell if that was a good feeling or a bad feeling—or simply a new feeling.

Then the film started, and it no longer mattered if he was alone or not. Jim had been right about this one, Ferguson said to himself, and all through the three hours and ten minutes that *Children of Paradise* played before him on the screen, he kept thinking about how much it had been worth it to risk punishment in order to see this film, which was just the sort of film that would appeal to a fifteen-year-old of Ferguson's temperament, a florid, high Romantic love saga punctuated by bursts of humor, violence, and cunning depravity, an ensemble piece in which every one of the characters is essential to the story, the beautiful, enigmatic Garance (Arletty) and the four men who love her, the mime played by Jean-Louis Barrault, a soulful, passive dreamer destined to limp through a life of longing and regret, the exuberant, bombastic, supremely entertaining actor played by Pierre Brasseur, the coldhearted, ultra-dignified count played by Louis Salou, and the devious monster played by Marcel Herrand in the role of Lacenaire, the poet-murderer who stabs the count to death, and when the film ended with Garance disappearing into a vast Parisian crowd as the heartbroken mime chases after her, Jim's words came rushing back to Ferguson (*The best French film ever made, Archie. The* Gone with the Wind *of France—only ten times better*), and although Ferguson had seen only a handful of French films at that point in his life, he agreed that *Les Enfants du Paradis* was much better than *Gone with the Wind*, so much better that it was useless even to compare them.

The lights came on, and as Ferguson stood up and stretched his arms, he noticed someone three seats to his left, a tall boy with dark hair who must have been a couple of years older than he was, in all probability another hooky-playing cinephile, and when he glanced over at his fellow renegade, the boy smiled at him.

Some film, the stranger said.

Some film, Ferguson repeated. I loved it.

The boy introduced himself as Andy Cohen, and as he and Ferguson walked out of the theater together, Andy said that this was the third time he had seen *Children of Paradise,* and did Ferguson know that the criminal Lacenaire, the mime Duburau, and the actor Lemaître had all been real people from France in the 1820s? No, Ferguson confessed, he hadn't known that. Nor had he known that the film had been shot in Paris during the German occupation, nor that Arletty had gotten herself into a heap of trouble at the end of the war for having an affair with a German officer, nor that the writer Jacques Prévert and the director Marcel Carné had collaborated on several films in the thirties and forties and were the inventors of what critics called *poetic realism*. This Andy Cohen was certainly a well-informed young man, Ferguson said to himself, and while he might have been showing off a little, trying to impress the backward young neophyte with his superior knowledge of film history, he was doing it in a friendly way, somehow, more from an excess of enthusiasm than from any kind of arrogance or condescension.

They were out on the street by then, walking south down Broadway, and within four blocks Ferguson had learned that Andy Cohen was eighteen, not seventeen, and that he hadn't cut any classes to go to the movie because he was a freshman at City College and had no classes that afternoon. His father was dead (a heart attack six years ago), and Andy and his mother lived in an apartment on Amsterdam Avenue and 107th Street, and because he didn't have any plans for the rest of the day, maybe he and Ferguson could go to a coffee shop somewhere and have a bite to eat? No, Ferguson said, he had to be home by four-thirty or else, but maybe they could get together another time, Saturday afternoon, for instance, when he knew he would be free, and the moment Ferguson said the word *Saturday*, Andy reached into his coat pocket and pulled out the Thalia program for March. *The Battleship Potemkin*, he said. It's playing at one o'clock.

The Thalia at one on Saturday, Ferguson replied. I'll see you there.

He extended his right arm, shook Andy Cohen's hand, and the two parted company, the one continuing south toward Riverside Drive between Eighty-eighth and Eighty-ninth Streets and the other turning around and heading north toward what might or might not have been home.

As expected, Gil and his mother were in the apartment when Ferguson walked in, but, as not expected, the school had already called to report his unauthorized departure. Gil and his mother had those worried looks on their faces that always saddened Ferguson and made him realize how unpleasant it must have been for them to be the grown-ups responsible for taking care of someone like him, for the call from the school meant that his whereabouts had been unknown from twelve-thirty to four-thirty, which was more than enough time for conscientious parents to start fretting about their missing teenager. That was why his mother had established the four-thirty rule: Be home by then or else call home to explain where he was. The limit had been extended to six o'clock for the basketball season because of after-school practices, but the basketball season was over now and the four-thirty deadline was back in effect. Ferguson had walked into the apartment at four twenty-seven, which on any other day would have kept him in the clear, but he hadn't counted on the school to call so promptly, and for that stupid oversight he was sorry, not just because of the scare he had put into Gil and his mother but because it made him feel like an idiot.

Half of his allowance was docked for the following week, and for the three school days that remained from the current week he was held after dismissal to work in the lunchroom mopping floors, scrubbing pots, and scouring the large eight-burner stove. The Riverside Academy was an enlightened, forward-looking institution, but it still believed in the punitive virtues of K.P. duty.

On Saturday, a day of relaxed curfews and relative freedom, Ferguson announced at breakfast that he was going to the movies with a friend that afternoon, and since Gil and his mother were generally good about not asking too many unimportant questions (no matter how much they might have wished to know the answers), Ferguson didn't name the movie or the friend, and he left the apartment in time to reach the Thalia by ten to one. He wasn't expecting Andy Cohen to be there, not when it seemed so unlikely that he would have remembered their hastily plotted rendezvous at the theater door, but now that Ferguson had discovered the pleasures of watching films alone, the prospect of being alone again didn't bother him. Nevertheless, Andy Cohen had remembered, and as the two of them shook hands and bought their forty-cent tickets, the college boy was already launching into a brief lecture on Eisenstein and the principles of *montage*, the technique that had supposedly revolutionized the art of filmmaking. Ferguson was told to pay special attention to the scene on the Odessa Steps, which was one of the most famous sequences in movie history, and Ferguson said he would, although the word *Odessa* had a somewhat troubling effect on him, given that his grandmother had been born in Odessa and had died in New York just seven months earlier, and Ferguson regretted that he had paid so little attention to her when she was alive, no doubt assuming she was immortal and that there would be plenty of time to get to know her better in the future, which of course never happened, and thinking about his grandmother made him think about his grandfather, whom he still missed terribly, and by the time Ferguson and Andy Cohen took their seats in the fifth row—which they agreed was the best row in the house—the expression on Ferguson's face had changed so radically that Andy asked him if anything was wrong.

I'm thinking about my grandparents, he said. And my father, and all the dead people I've known. (*Pointing to his left temple.*) It gets pretty dark in there sometimes.

I know, Andy said. I can't stop thinking about my father—and he's been dead for six years.

It helped that Andy's father was dead, too, Ferguson thought, that they were both the sons of nonexistent men and spent their days in the company of ghosts, at least on the bad days, the worst days, and because the glare of the world was always brightest on the bad days, perhaps that explained why they sought out the darkness of movie theaters, why they felt happiest when sitting in the dark.

Andy said something about the hundreds of cuts that had gone into editing the big scene, but before he could tell Ferguson exactly how many there were (a number he surely knew by heart), the lights dimmed, the projector went on, and Ferguson turned his attention to the screen, curious to discover what all the fuss was about.

The townspeople of Odessa waving to the striking sailors from the top of the steps. A wealthy woman opens her white umbrella, a legless boy doffs his cap, and then the word SUDDENLY, and the face of a terrified woman fills the screen. A crowd of people charging down the stairs, the legless boy among them, as the white umbrella rushes into the foreground. Fast music, hectic music, music racing faster than the fastest pounding heart. The legless boy in the center as the crowd streams down on either side of him. A reverse shot of the soldiers in their white uniforms chasing the people down the steps. A close-up of a woman getting up from the ground. A man's knees buckle. Another man falls. Still another man falls. A wide shot of the running crowd as the soldiers run down the stairs in pursuit. Close shots of people hiding in the shadows. The soldiers take aim with their rifles. More cowering people. Lateral shots of the crowd, frontal shots of the crowd, and then the camera begins to move, sprinting along beside the crowd of sprinting people. Rifles blasting from above. A mother running with her little boy until the boy in the white shirt falls down face-first. The mother keeps running, the crowd keeps running. The boy in the white shirt is crying, blood is dripping from his head, the white shirt is speckled with blood. The crowd keeps running, but now the mother realizes that her son is no longer with her and stops. The mother turns around, looking for her boy. A close-up of her anguished face. The crying boy in the bloodied shirt passes out. The mother opens her mouth in horror and grabs hold of her hair. A tight shot of the unconscious boy as legs and more legs rush past him. The music continues to pound. A close-up of the mother's horrified face. The endless crowd continues to pour down the steps. A boot comes down on the boy's outstretched hand. A closer shot of the crowd pouring down the steps. Another boot comes down on the boy. The bleeding boy rolls over onto his back. An extreme close-up of the mother's horrified eyes. She begins to move forward, mouth open, hands in hair. The crowd pours down. The mother approaches her fallen son. She bends down to pick him up. A wide shot of the frenzied, charging crowd. A reverse shot of the mother carrying the boy back up the stairs in the direction of the soldiers. Her mouth is moving, angry words are coming out of her. A broad shot of the dense crowd. A closer shot of some people crouching behind a stone wall, among them the Woman with the Pince-Nez . . .

So it began, and as Ferguson watched the sequence unfold, he found the slaughter so gruesome that his eyes eventually filled up with tears. It was unbearable to watch the mother being gunned down by the czar's soldiers, unbearable to watch the killing of the second mother and the awful journey of the baby carriage down the steps, unbearable to watch the Woman with the Pince-Nez howling with her mouth wide open and one lens of her pince-nez shattered and blood gushing from her right eye, unbearable to watch the Cossacks pull out their swords to slice the baby in the carriage to bits—unforgettable images, and therefore images to go on producing nightmares for fifty years—and yet, even as Ferguson recoiled from what he was watching, he was thrilled by it, astonished that anything as vast and complex as that sequence could possibly have been put on film, the pure magnitude of the energy unleashed by those minutes of footage nearly split him in two, and by the time the film was over, he was so shattered, so exhilarated, so mixed up in a confusion of sorrow and elation that he wondered if any film would ever affect him in that way again.

There was a second Eisenstein feature on the program—*October*, known in English as *Ten Days That Shook the World*—but when Andy asked Ferguson if he wanted to see it, Ferguson shook his head, saying he was too exhausted and needed to get some air. So they went out into the air, not quite certain what to do next. Andy suggested they go back to his apartment so he could lend Ferguson his copy of Eisenstein's *Film Form and The Film Sense* and maybe scrounge up some food as well, and

Ferguson, who had no plans for the rest of the day, thought *Why not?* During the walk to West 107th Street and Amsterdam Avenue, the mysterious Andy Cohen divulged some more facts about his life, first of all the fact that his mother was a registered nurse at St. Luke's Hospital and was working the twelve-to-eight shift that day and wouldn't (thank God) be at home when they got there, and the fact that he had been accepted by Columbia but had decided to go to City College because the tuition was free there and his mother couldn't afford to send him to Columbia (and yet what a nice kick in the pants to know he had the stuff to make the Ivy League), and the fact that much as he loved movies he loved books even more, and if everything went according to plan he would get a Ph.D. and wind up as a professor of literature somewhere, maybe even—hah!—at Columbia. As Andy talked and Ferguson listened, Ferguson was struck by the enormous gap that separated them intellectually, as if the three-year difference in their ages represented a journey of several thousand miles that Ferguson had yet to begin, and because he felt so ignorant when he compared himself to the big-brained college student walking beside him, Ferguson asked himself why Andy Cohen seemed to be working so hard at trying to become his friend. Was he one of those lonely people who had no one to talk to, Ferguson wondered, a person so hungry for companionship that he would settle for anything that dropped in front of him, even when it came in the form of a know-nothing high school boy? If so, it didn't make much sense. Some people had flaws, character flaws or physical flaws or mental flaws that tended to isolate them from others, but Andy didn't seem to be one of them. He was amiable and relatively good-looking, he was not without a sense of humor, and he was generous (e.g., the offer to lend Ferguson the book)—in short, someone who fell into the same category of person as cousin Jim, who was just one year older than Andy and had many friends, more friends than he could count on the fingers of twelve hands. In fact, now that Ferguson thought about it, the effect of being with Andy was not dissimilar to what it felt like to be with Jim—the comfortable sense of not being looked down upon by someone older than he was, of older and younger walking down the street together at the same pace. But Jim was his cousin, and it was normal to be treated like that by someone in your family, whereas Andy Cohen, at least for now, was little more than a stranger to him.

The future professor lived in a small two-bedroom apartment on the third floor of a run-down, eleven-story building, one of the many Upper West Side residential towers that had sunk into decrepitude since the end of the war, once a modest dwelling place for members of the middle middle class and now occupied by an assortment of struggling people who spoke several different languages behind the locked doors of their apartments. As Andy showed Ferguson around the sparsely furnished, well-ordered rooms, he explained that he and his mother had been living there since his father's third and final heart attack, and Ferguson understood that this was just the kind of place he and his mother might have rented if there had been no life insurance money to carry them through the rough years after his own father's death. Now that his mother had married again and was earning decent money as a photographer, just as Gil was earning decent money from writing about music, they were so much better off than Andy and his poor nurse mother that Ferguson felt ashamed of his good fortune, which he had done nothing to contribute to, just as Andy had done nothing to contribute to his less than good fortune. Not that the Cohens were poor, exactly (the refrigerator was well-stocked with food, Andy's bedroom was crammed with paperback books), but when Ferguson sat down in the small kitchen to eat one of the salami sandwiches Andy had prepared for them, he noticed that this was a household that collected Green Stamps and cut out discount coupons from the *Journal-American* and the *Daily News*. Gil and his mother counted dollars and tried not to overspend, but Andy's mother counted pennies and spent whatever she had.

After the snack in the kitchen, they went into the living room and talked for a while about *Madame Bovary* (which Ferguson hadn't read), *The Seven Samurai* (which Ferguson hadn't seen), and other films on the Thalia program for next month. Then something strange happened, or something interesting, or something strangely interesting, which in any case was unexpected, or at least it seemed so at first, but then, as Ferguson began to think about it a little, not as unexpected as all that, for once Andy asked the question, Ferguson finally understood why he was there.

He was sitting on the sofa across from Andy, who was sitting in an armchair by the window, and after a short lull in the conversation, Andy leaned forward in his chair, looked at Ferguson for a long moment, and then asked, apropos of nothing: Do you ever jerk off, Archie?

Ferguson, who had been a dedicated onanist for close to a year and a half, answered the question promptly. Of course, he said. Doesn't everyone?

Maybe not everyone, Andy replied, but almost everyone. It's perfectly natural, *n'est-ce pas?*

If you're too young for real sex, what else can you do?

And what do you think about, Archie? I mean, what goes through your head while you're jerking off?

I think about naked women and how nice it would be to be naked with a naked woman instead of jerking off into the toilet.

Sad.

Yes, a little sad. But it's better than nothing.

And has anyone ever jerked you off? One of your high school girlfriends, maybe?

No, I can't say I've had the pleasure.

I have—a few times.

Well, you're older than I am. It makes sense that you've had more experiences.

Not many experiences. Just three, in fact. But I can tell you it's a lot better when someone else does it to you than when you do it yourself.

I can believe that. Especially if the girl knows what she's doing.

It doesn't have to be a girl, Archie.

What's that supposed to mean? Are you saying you don't like girls?

I like girls very much, but they don't seem to like me. I don't know why, but I've never had any luck with them.

So you've been jerked off by boys?

Just one boy. George, my friend from Stuyvesant, who never had any luck with girls either. So last year we decided to experiment—just to see what it felt like.

And?

It was great. We jerked each other off those three times, and we both decided that it doesn't matter who does it to you. A girl or a boy—the feeling is the same, and who cares if it's a girl's hand or a boy's hand wrapped around your dick?

I never thought about it that way.

No, I hadn't either. It's what I would call *a major discovery.*

Why just three times, then? If you and George liked it so much, why did you stop?

Because George is at the University of Chicago now, and he's finally found himself a girlfriend.

Too bad for you.

I suppose, but George isn't the only person in the world. There's you, Archie, and if you'd like me to do it to you, I'd be happy to jerk you off. Just so you'll know what I've been talking about.

But what if I don't want to jerk you off? Maybe George liked doing that, but I don't think I'd be interested. Nothing against you, Andy, but I really do like girls.

I would never ask you to do something you don't want to do. That would be wrong, and I don't believe in pressuring people. It's just that you're such a nice boy, Archie. I like being with you, I like looking at you, and I would love to be able to touch you.

Ferguson told him to go ahead. He was curious, he explained, and Andy could jerk him off if he wanted to, but just this once, he added, and only if they turned out the lights and pulled down the shades, for a thing like that had to be done in the dark, so Andy stood up from his chair and one by one turned out the lights and pulled down the shades, and once he had completed those tasks, he sat down on the sofa next to the anxious, slightly panicked Ferguson, unzipped the younger boy's pants, and dug in.

It felt so good that Ferguson started to moan, within seconds his soft and nervous penis began to stiffen and grow progressively longer with each stroke of the older boy's hand, which was a skilled and deeply knowledgeable hand, Ferguson thought, a hand that seemed to know precisely what a dick needed and wanted on its journey from slumber to arousal and beyond, the exquisite back-and-forth between rough and gentle manipulations, so good, he said, when Andy asked him how it felt, and then Ferguson unbuckled his belt and slipped his pants and jockey shorts down to his knees, giving the wondrous hand more room to operate, and suddenly the other hand was on him as well, playing with his balls as the first hand worked on what was now a full-scale erection, Ferguson's fifteen-year-old cock at the very limit of where it could go, and once again Andy asked him how it felt, but this time Ferguson could only grunt forth a wordless response as the pleasure spread through his thighs and up into his groin and the journey to beyond was done.

Now you know, Andy said.

Yes, now Ferguson knew.

Just two and a half minutes, Andy said.

The best two and a half minutes of his life, Ferguson thought, and then he glanced down at his shirt, which was visible now that his eyes had adjusted to the dark, and saw that it was splattered with the stains of his ejaculation.

Damnit, he said. Look at my shirt.

Andy smiled, patted Ferguson on the head, and then leaned over and whispered into his ear: D. H. Lawrence comes in torrents when his Balzac with desire.

Ferguson, who had never heard that old college ditty, let out a long squeal of surprised laughter. Then Andy recited the dirty limerick about the young man from Kent, another classic that was not yet familiar to Ferguson, and the young innocent, who was rapidly losing his innocence, burst out laughing again.

When calm was restored, Ferguson pulled up his pants and rose from the couch. Well, he said, I guess I should rinse out this shirt, and as he started walking from the living room to the kitchen, undoing the buttons as Andy stood up and followed him, he explained that the shirt was new, a birthday present from his mother and stepfather, and he had to get the spots out or else find himself in the unpleasant position of being asked questions he would prefer not to answer. Strike fast, he said, remove the stains before they settled into the fabric, and *destroy the evidence*.

As the two of them stood at the sink together, Andy asked Ferguson if he was a one-and-done sort of guy or someone with the staying power to go an extra round or two. Ferguson, who had forgotten all about *just this once*, asked him what he had in mind. Something good, Andy said, unwilling to reveal the secret, but he assured Ferguson that it would surpass the pleasures of the living room sofa and make him feel even better than he did now.

The stains were concentrated on the bottom part of the shirt, from the midpoint of the shirt tails to an area between the second and third buttons, and Andy washed them out for Ferguson, quite quickly as it happened, with little scrubbing required, and when the job was done, Andy carried the wet shirt into his bedroom and put it on a hanger, which he looped over the knob on the closet door. There you go, he said. Good as new.

Ferguson was touched by the sweetness of that small gesture, which showed how thoughtful and considerate Andy was, and Ferguson enjoyed being doted on in that way, cared for by someone kind enough to wash out his shirt and put it on a hanger for him, not to mention the kindness to jerk him off without asking to be jerked off in return. Whatever qualms or hesitations Ferguson might have felt in the beginning were gone now, and when Andy suggested he take off his clothes and lie down on the bed, Ferguson happily took off his clothes and lay down on the bed, anticipating the next good thing that was about to be done to him. He understood that most people would have frowned on what he was doing, that he had entered the dangerous territory of forbidden, deviant impulses, Faggot-Land in all its corrupting, lascivious glory, and that if anyone found out he had traveled to that wicked country he would be mocked and hated and possibly even beaten up for it, but no one was ever going to find out because no one would ever be told, and even if it had to remain a secret, it would never be a dirty secret, for what he was doing with Andy didn't feel dirty to him, and what he felt was all that mattered.

His cock grew hard again as Andy ran his palms over Ferguson's naked skin, and when Andy put that hardened cock into his mouth and gave Ferguson the first blow job of his life, Ferguson was long past caring whether it was a girl or a boy who was giving it to him.

HE WASN'T QUITE sure what to think. Undeniably, the two orgasms that had swept through him and out of him in Andy's apartment that day were the strongest, most gratifying physical pleasures he had ever experienced, but at the same time the means to the end had been purely mechanical, a one-sided operation in which Andy did to him what he had no desire to do to Andy. What they had done, then, was not quite sex in the strictest sense of the word, at least not sex as Ferguson understood it, since for him sex had always been about two rather than one, the physical expression of an extreme emotional state, the longing for another person, and in this instance there had been no longing, no emotion, no anything but the desires of his dick, meaning that what had happened with Andy wasn't sex so much as a higher, more enjoyable form of masturbation.

Was he attracted to boys? Until then, he had never even asked himself the question, but now that he had allowed Andy to jerk him off and suck him off and run his hands over his naked body, he began paying more attention to the boys in his school, especially the boys he knew best and liked best, which included everyone on the freshman basketball team, all of whom he had seen naked in the shower and locker room scores of times without giving the matter a second thought, but now that he was starting to think about it, he tried to imagine what it would feel like to kiss elegant Alex Nordstrom on the lips, a true kiss with tongues digging into each other's mouths, or to jerk off muscular Brian Mischevski until he came all over his bare stomach, but neither one of those pretend scenes produced much of a reaction from Ferguson, not that he was repulsed by them or scared by the thought of engaging in real boy-on-boy sex, for if it turned out that he was a faggot boy without having known it until now, then he wanted to know for sure, beyond any doubt or possibility for error, but the fact was that the idea of embracing other boys didn't excite him, didn't make his dick grow hard, didn't fill him with the lustful thoughts that sprang from the wells of deepest yearning. But Amy excited him, and even now the thought of his never-again-to-be-touched-or-kissed lost first love continued to fill him with deepest yearning, and Isabel Kraft excited him, especially after he saw her walking around in her red bikini last June twenty-eighth on the ten-person group outing to Far Rockaway, and when he thought about the naked bodies of his friends and compared them to the almost naked body of Isabel Kraft, he understood that girls aroused him and boys didn't.

But maybe he was deluding himself, he thought, maybe he was wrong to think that emotions were an essential part of sex, maybe he should consider the various forms of loveless sex that brought physical release but no emotions of any kind, masturbation, for example, or men screwing whores, and what that must have been like in relation to what being with Andy had been like, sex without kisses or feelings, sex for the sole purpose of attaining physical pleasure, and maybe love had nothing to do with it, maybe *love* was just a high-flown word to cover up the dark, uncontrollable demands of animal lust, and if you were in the dark and couldn't see the person who was touching you, what difference did it make how you managed to get your juices flowing?

An unanswerable question. Unanswerable because Ferguson was still just fifteen years old, and whether time would transform him into a man who sought the company of women, or a man who sought the company of men, or a man who sought the company of both women and men, it was far too early for him to know who he was or what he wanted when it came to matters of sex, for at that point in his life, which was also that point in history, that particular moment in that particular place, America in the first half of 1962, he was barred from having sex with members of what he believed to be the right sex, for even if he managed to win back the affections of Amy Schneiderman or make a surprise conquest of Isabel Kraft, neither one of those girls would allow herself to do to him what Andy Cohen had already done, and now that his body had evolved into the body of a man, he still found himself trapped in his boy's world of enforced virginity, even as he reached the moment when he had begun to crave sex with a passion that would not be equaled at any other moment in his life, and because the only sex available to him at that moment of thwarted desire was sex with a member of the wrong sex, he showed up at the Thalia Theater the next Saturday afternoon to see *Rashomon* with Andy Cohen, not because he had formed any special attachment to the City College boy who lived with his mother on Amsterdam Avenue and West 107th Street but because the things that boy did to him felt so good, so excessively and extraordinarily good, that the feeling was all but irresistible.

They got down to it more quickly the second time, dispensing with the preliminaries on the living room sofa and heading straight for Andy's bedroom, where they both wound up with their clothes off, and while Ferguson couldn't bring himself to touch Andy where he wanted to be touched, to jerk him off in the same way Andy was jerking him off, he watched as Andy did it to himself and didn't mind when the cum landed on his chest, which felt rather nice, actually, the warmth of it, the suddenness of it, and then the languor of Andy's slowly moving hand as he rubbed the ejaculation into Ferguson's skin. It was becoming more about two now, less about one and more about leaving behind the good of glorified wanking for the better of something more like real sex, and for three Saturdays in a row following that second time together, the Saturdays of *The Blue Angel*, *Modern Times*, and *La Notte*, Ferguson gradually eased his way into abandoning himself to Andy's bolder and bolder seductions, no longer holding back as he submitted to the promptings of Andy's tongue as it moved up and down the length of his body, no longer frightened to be kissed or to kiss in return, no longer hesitant to take hold of Andy's stiffened cock and put it in his mouth, for reciprocity was fundamental, Ferguson realized, two was infinitely more satisfying than one, and only by seducing the seducer could he thank him for the pleasure of being seduced.

Andy was softer and flabbier than Ferguson, skinny and tall but with the no-muscle body of someone who never played sports or did any exercise, and he was fascinated by the hardness of Ferguson's muscles, the basketball body Ferguson had built for himself by lifting weights and doing a hundred push-ups and a hundred sit-ups every night, and again and again Andy would tell Ferguson how beautiful he was, running his hand over Ferguson's taut stomach and marveling at its flatness, telling him that his face was beautiful, that his ass was beautiful, that his cock was beautiful, that his legs were beautiful, so many *beautifuls* that by the second of the last three Saturdays they spent together Ferguson was beginning to feel oppressed by them, as if Andy were talking about him in the way that he (Ferguson) would talk about a girl, which was another subject Ferguson was beginning to have some doubts about, the question of girls, since every time he mentioned Isabel Kraft's remarkable looks or said something about how much he still loved Amy Schneiderman, Andy would make a face and then come out with some insulting crack about girls in general, saying that their brains were genetically inferior to the brains of men, for example, or that their cunts were cesspools of infection and disease, ugly, ridiculous statements that seemed to suggest that Andy had not been telling the truth in March when he said he liked girls, for not even his mother was exempt from his bitter condemnations, and when Ferguson heard him call her a *sad, dumb cow* and another time call her a *revolting tub of shit*, he countered by saying he loved his own mother more than anyone else in the world, to which Andy replied: *Not possible, kid, just not possible.*

Later on, Ferguson understood how badly he had misread the situation from the start. He had assumed that Andy was just another sexed-up boy like himself, unlucky with girls and therefore willing to have a go at it with a boy, two boys rolling around with each other for the fun of it, fuck-fun for adolescent virgins, but it had never once crossed his mind that anything serious could come of it. Then, on the last Saturday they spent together, just minutes before Ferguson had to leave the apartment, as the two of them lay side by side on the bed, still naked, still sweaty and out of breath, each one drained by the exertions of the past quarter hour, Andy took Ferguson into his arms and said that he loved him, that Ferguson was the love of his life and he would never stop loving him, not even after he was dead.

Ferguson said nothing. Any word would have been the wrong word at that moment, so he held his tongue and said nothing. Sad, he thought, so sad and demoralizing to have created such a mess, but he didn't want to hurt Andy's feelings by telling him about his own feelings, which were that he didn't love him back and would never love him back for as long as he lived, and this was good-bye, and too bad it had to end this way because the fun had been so much fun, but damn it all, he shouldn't have said that, and how could he be so stupid?

He kissed Andy on the cheek and smiled. Gotta go, he said.

Ferguson sprang off the mattress and began collecting his clothes from the floor.

Andy said: Same time next week?

What's playing? Ferguson asked, as he climbed into his jeans and buckled his belt.

Two Bergmans. *Wild Strawberries* and *The Seventh Seal*.

Whoops.

Whoops? What's whoops?

I just remembered. I have to go up to Rhinebeck with my parents next Saturday.

But you still haven't seen any Bergmans. That's more important than a day with Moms and Pops, no?

Probably. But I have to go with them.

The week after next, then?

Ferguson, who was slipping into his shoes at that point, mumbled a barely audible *Uh-huh*.

You're not going to come, are you?

Andy sat up in bed and repeated the words at the top of his voice: *You're not going to come, are you?*

What are you talking about?

You bitch! Andy yelled. I pour my heart out to you, and you don't say a fucking word!

What do you want me to say?

Ferguson zipped up his spring jacket and headed for the door.

Fuck off, Archie. I hope you fall down the stairs and die.

Ferguson left the apartment and walked down the stairs.

He didn't die.

Instead, he walked home, went into his room, and lay down on the bed, where he spent the next two hours looking up at the ceiling.

3.4

ON THE FIRST SATURDAY OF 1962, THREE DAYS AFTER FERGUSON handed in his nine-hundred-word essay about Jackie Robinson, he and the six other players on his YMHA basketball team traveled from their home base in West Orange to a gym in Newark for a morning game against a YMCA team from the Central Ward. Two more games were scheduled to be played on that court immediately afterward, and the bleachers were filled with members of those four other teams along with friends and relatives of the players from those teams, not to mention the team that Ferguson and his friends were about to square off against in the first part of the triple-header, which made for a crowd of about eighty or ninety people. Except for the seven white boys from the Jewish Y and their coach, a high school math teacher named Lenny Millstein, everyone in the gym that morning was black. There was nothing unusual about that, since the West Orange boys often played against all-black teams in their Essex County Y League, but what was unusual about that morning in Newark was the size of the crowd, close to a hundred instead of the customary ten or twelve. At first, no one seemed to be paying much attention to what was happening on the court, but when the game ended in a tie and had to go into overtime, the people who had come for the two other games began to grow restless. As far as Ferguson could tell, the crowd didn't care which team won or lost—they just wanted the game to be done with so the other games could start—but then the five-minute overtime ended in another tie score, and the mood of the crowd swelled from restlessness to agitation. Get the jokers off the court, yes, but if one of those two teams eventually had to win, then the onlookers were going to pull for the Newark boys over the suburban boys, the Christian boys over the Jewish boys, the black boys over the white boys. Fair enough, Ferguson said to himself as the second overtime began, it was only natural for people to root for the home team, only natural for people to shout from the stands during a close game, only natural for people to insult the visiting players, but then the second overtime ended in yet another tie score, and everything suddenly seemed to catch fire: the small, dilapidated gym in central Newark was ablaze with sound, and a no-account basketball game between fourteen-year-old boys had been turned into a symbolic blood match between *us and them*.

Both teams were playing poorly, both teams were missing nine-tenths of their shots and throwing away a third of their passes, both teams were tired and distracted by the noise from the crowd, both teams were doing their best to win and yet performing as if they wanted to lose. The crowd was unanimous in its support of one team over the other team, stomping and roaring its approval every time a Newark player wrestled away a rebound or intercepted a pass, hooting with derision whenever a West Orange player clanked a jump shot or bounced the ball off his foot, yowling in raucous ecstasy every time Newark scored a basket, booing in prolonged bursts of outrage and disgust whenever West Orange answered with a score of its own. With ten seconds left on the clock, Newark led by one point. Lenny Millstein called a time-out, and as the West Orange players gathered around their coach, the clamor from the stands was so loud that he had to shout to make himself heard, the sage Lenny Millstein, who not only was an excellent basketball man but an excellent person as well, who knew how to handle fourteen-year-old boys because he understood that fourteen was the worst possible age on the calendar of human life, and therefore all fourteen-year-olds were confused and fractured beings, not one of them a child anymore and not one of them an adult, none quite right in the head or at home in his unfinished body, and in the furnace of that claustrophobic arena of belligerent, bellowing partisans, the astute man with the curly blond hair and the jocular, no-discipline approach to running a team was shouting at his charges and reminding them how to break a full-court press, and before the boys put their right hands on top of Lenny's right hand for a last *Let's go!*, the thirty-four-year-old husband and father of two pointed to an exit door in the side wall of the gym and told the boys that no matter what happened in the next ten seconds, whether they won the game or lost the game, at the instant the final buzzer sounded they should all run for that door and jump into his station wagon parked at the curb because, as he put it, *things are getting a little nuts in here*, and he didn't want anyone to be injured or killed in the mayhem that was sure to follow. Then the five hands and the one hand came together, Lenny barked the last *Let's go!*, and Ferguson and the other starters trotted back onto the court.

They were the longest ten seconds of Ferguson's life, an absurd, high-speed ballet that seemed to be unfurling in slow motion because he was the only player on the court who wasn't moving, fixed in his position at the top of the far circle to receive a long desperation pass if all else failed, the last option out of several desperate options, and for that reason he could see it all from where he stood, the whole dance sharply etched in space, vivid and indelible, called up again and again over the ensuing months and years, never not remembered at any point in his life, Mike Nadler's inbounds pass to Mitch Goodman after faking out a leaping, arm-waving Newark defender, Goodman's no-dribble wheel-around pass to Alan Schaeffer at midcourt, and then Schaeffer's blind shot-put heave as the clock ticked down to three seconds, two seconds, one second, followed by the astonishment on Schaeffer's pudgy face as the ball made its improbable journey through the air and went straight through the hoop without touching the rim, the longest buzzer beater in the history of the Essex County Y League, an ending to trump all other endings for the rest of time.

He saw Lenny bounding off in the direction of the side door. As the West Orange player standing farthest from that door, Ferguson started running before anyone else, started running the second he saw the ball go through the basket, not even pausing to congratulate Schaeffer or celebrate the win, for Lenny had been right to suspect trouble, and now that Newark had been robbed of its victory, the people in the gym were incensed. A howl of collective shock to begin with, eighty or ninety brains clobbered by the sight of that cheap, lucky basket, and an instant later half the crowd was surging onto the court, crying out in anger and disbelief, an army of thirteen-, fourteen-, and fifteen-year-old boys, four dozen black boys bent on tearing apart half a dozen white boys for the injustice that had been committed against them, and for a few moments as he sprinted across the court Ferguson felt in real danger, afraid that the mob would catch up to him and knock him to the floor, but he managed to rush through the swarming labyrinth of bodies with just one random punch delivered to his right arm, a punch that hurt and continued to hurt for the next two hours, and then he was out the door and running toward Lenny's station wagon in the cold air of that bleak January morning.

Thus ended the miniature race riot that almost happened but didn't. All during the trip home, the other boys in the car whooped it up in a high-octane surge of manic good cheer, again and again reliving the last ten seconds of the game, congratulating themselves for having escaped the wrath of the avenging crowd, conducting pretend interviews with the still incredulous and ceaselessly smiling Schaeffer, laughing, laughing, so much laughter that the very air was thick with jubilation, but Ferguson took no part in it, couldn't take part in it because he had no desire to laugh, even though Schaeffer's last-second shot had been one of the funniest, most unlikely things he had ever seen, but the game had been ruined for him by what had happened after the game, and the punch still hurt, and the reason why the punch had been thrown hurt even more than the pain still throbbing in his arm.

Lenny was the only other person in the car who wasn't laughing, the only other one who seemed to understand the dark implications of what had happened in the gym, and for the first time all season he reprimanded the boys for their sloppy, incompetent play, dismissing Schaeffer's fifty-footer as an accident and asking them why they hadn't trounced that mediocre team by twenty points. The others took those words as a sign of anger, but Ferguson realized that he wasn't angry but upset, or scared, or disheartened, or all three at once, and that the game meant nothing in light of the ugly scene that had followed the game.

It was the first time Ferguson had witnessed a crowd turn into a deranged mob, and hard as it was to take, the irrefutable lesson he had learned that morning was that a crowd could sometimes express a hidden truth that no one person in the crowd would have dared to express on his own, in this case the truth about the resentment and even hatred many black people felt toward white people, which was no less strong than the resentment and even hatred many white people felt toward black people, and Ferguson, who had just spent the last days of the Christmas holiday writing an essay about the courage of Jackie Robinson and the need for total integration in every aspect of American life, couldn't help feeling upset, scared, and disheartened by what had happened in Newark that morning, fifteen years after Jackie Robinson had played his first game for the Brooklyn Dodgers.

Two Mondays after the Saturday in Newark, Mrs. Baldwin stood in front of Ferguson's ninth-grade English class and announced that he had won first prize in the essay contest. The second prize had been awarded to Amy Schneiderman for her *impressive encomium on the life of Emma Goldman,* and how proud she was of them both, Mrs. Baldwin said, the top two submissions coming from the same class, *her class,* which was one of thirteen ninth-grade English classes in the school, and not once in all her years of teaching at Maplewood Junior High had she been *granted the privilege of having two winners in the annual writing contest.*

Good for Mrs. Baldwin, Ferguson thought, as he watched his literary nemesis gloating over the dual triumph at the blackboard, as if she were the one who had written the essays herself, and happy as Ferguson was to be the winner from among the three hundred and fifty students in his grade, he understood that the victory was of no importance, not only because whatever Mrs. Baldwin judged to be good necessarily had to be bad but because he himself had turned against his own essay since the debacle in the Newark gym, knowing that what he had written was too optimistic and naïve to make any sense in the real world, that while Jackie Robinson deserved all the praise Ferguson had given him, desegregating baseball was just a midget step in a much larger struggle that would have to go on for many more years, no doubt for more years than Ferguson himself would ever get to live, perhaps for another century or two, and that next to his hollow, idealistic portrait of a transformed America, Amy's piece on Emma Goldman had been much better, not just better written and better thought-out but at once more subtle and more passionate, and the only reason why she hadn't been given the first prize was because the school couldn't award the blue ribbon to an essay about a *revolutionary anarchist,* who by definition was to be regarded as a thoroughly un-American American, a person so radical and dangerous to the American way of life that she had been deported from her own country.

Mrs. Baldwin was still droning on in front of the class, explaining that the three winners from each grade would be reading their essays out loud at an all-school assembly scheduled for Friday afternoon, and as Ferguson glanced over at Amy—who sat one row in front of him and two desks to the right—he was amused that when his eyes landed on her back, dead center between her two shoulder blades, she instantly turned around to look at him, as if she had felt his eyes touching her, and, even more amusing, once their eyes met, she scrunched up her face and stuck out her tongue at him, as if to say, Pooh on you, Archie Ferguson, I should have won and you know it, and when Ferguson smiled at her and shrugged, as if to say, You're right, but what can I do about it?, Amy's scrunch turned into a smile, and a moment later, unable to suppress the laugh gathering in her throat, she let out one of her weird snorts, an unexpectedly loud noise that prompted Mrs. Baldwin to interrupt what she was saying and ask, Is everything all right, Amy?

Just fine, Mrs. Baldwin, Amy said. I burped. I know it's an unladylike thing to do, but I couldn't help it. Sorry.

EVERYONE HAD ALWAYS told Ferguson that life resembled a book, a story that began on page 1 and pushed forward until the hero died on page 204 or 926, but now that the future he had imagined for himself was changing, his understanding of time was changing as well. Time moved both forward and backward, he realized, and because the stories in books could only move forward, the book metaphor made no sense. If anything, life was more akin to the structure of a tabloid newspaper, with big events such as the outbreak of a war or a gangland killing on the front page and less important news on the pages that followed, but the back page bore a headline as well, the day's top story from the trivial but compelling world of sports, and the sports articles were nearly always read backward as you turned the pages from left to right instead of from right to left as you did with the articles in the front, going in reverse as if plowing through a text in Hebrew or Japanese, steadily working your way toward the middle of the paper, and once you hit the no-man's-land of the classifieds, which were not worth reading unless you were in the market for trombone lessons or a used bicycle, you would jump over those pages until you wound up in the central territory of movie ads, theater reviews, Ann Landers's advice column, and the editorials, from which point, if you had started reading from the back (as Ferguson, the sports enthusiast, usually did) you could keep going all the way to the front. Time moved in two directions because every step into the future carried a memory of the past, and even though Ferguson had not yet turned fifteen, he had accumulated enough memories to know that the world around him was continually being shaped by the world within him, just as everyone else's experience of the world was shaped by his own memories, and while all people were bound together by the common space they shared, their journeys through time were all different, which meant that each person lived in a slightly different world from everyone else. The question was: What world did Ferguson inhabit now, and how had that world changed for him?

For one thing, he wasn't going to be a doctor anymore. He had spent the past two years dwelling in a far-off future of noble self-sacrifice and unstinting good works, a man utterly unlike his own father, working not for money and the acquisition of lime-green Cadillacs but for the benefit of humanity, a doctor who would treat the poor and the downtrodden by setting up free clinics in the worst urban slums, who would travel to Africa to work in tent hospitals during cholera epidemics and murderous civil wars, a heroic figure to the many who depended on him, a man of honor, a saint of compassion and courage, but then clear-eyed Noah Marx came along to tear down the scenery of those outlandish hallucinations, which in fact were the stuff of cornball Hollywood doctor movies and weak-minded, sentimental doctor novels, an appropriated vision of a future calling that Ferguson had not found within himself but had always seen from the outside, as if watching an actor in a black-and-white film from the 1930s, with a comely nurse-companion-wife hovering at the edge of the frame and soulful music playing in the background, never the real Ferguson with his complex and tormented inner life but a mechanical toy hero born out of a desire to forge a heroic destiny for himself, which would prove that he, the one and only, was better than any other man on this earth, and now that Noah had shown him how badly deluded he was, Ferguson felt ashamed of himself for having squandered so much energy on those childish dreams.

At the same time, Noah was wrong to think he had any interest in becoming a writer. It was true that reading novels was one of the fundamental pleasures life had to offer, and it was also true that someone had to write those novels in order to give people the chance to experience

that pleasure, but as far as Ferguson was concerned, neither reading
nor writing could be construed as a heroic activity, and at that point in
his journey toward adulthood Ferguson's sole ambition for the future
was, as his number one author had put it, to become *the hero of his own life*.
Ferguson had read his second Dickens novel by then, all 814 pages of that
long, circuitous slog through the fictional life of the author's favorite
child, consumed in its entirety during the two-week Christmas break,
and now that his marathon reading jag had come to an end, Ferguson
found himself at odds with his phantom companion from the previous year, Holden Caulfield, who had bad-mouthed Dickens with his
comment about *all that David Copperfield kind of crap* on the first page of
The Catcher in the Rye, for books were beginning to talk to books in Ferguson's head now, and good as J. D. Salinger might have been, he wasn't
fit to shine Charles Dickens's shoes, least of all if the old master were
decked out in a pair of brogans named Hank and Frank. No, there
would never be any question about it: reading fiction was great fun, and
writing fiction was great fun as well (fun mixed with anguish, struggle, and frustration, but fun for all that, since the pleasure of writing a
good sentence—especially when it started out as a bad one and slowly
improved after being rewritten four times—was unsurpassed in the
annals of human fulfillment), and anything that was so much fun and
caused so much pleasure could not, by definition, be looked upon as
heroic. Forget the saintly doctor routine, but there were countless heroic
alternatives Ferguson could imagine for himself, among them a career
in the law, for instance, and given that daydreaming was the talent he
continued to excel at above all others, in particular daydreaming about
the future, he spent the next several weeks projecting himself into courtrooms where his eloquence would save wrongly accused men from
going to the electric chair and cause every member of the jury to break
down and weep after each one of his closing arguments.

Then he turned fifteen, and at the birthday dinner held in his honor
at the Waverly Inn in Manhattan, a celebration that included his parents, his grandparents, Aunt Mildred, Uncle Don, and Noah, Ferguson
was given a present or presents by each of the families in his family, a
check for a hundred dollars from his mother and father, another check
for a hundred dollars from his grandmother and grandfather, and three
separate packages from the Marx contingent, a boxed set of Beethoven's
late string quartets from Aunt Mildred, a hardcover book from Noah

entitled *The Funniest Jokes in the World*, and four paperback books
by nineteenth-century Russian authors from Uncle Don, works that
Ferguson knew by reputation but had not yet taken the trouble to read:
Fathers and Sons by Turgenev, *Dead Souls* by Gogol, *Three Novellas* by Tolstoy (*Master and Man*, *The Kreutzer Sonata*, *The Death of Ivan Ilyich*), and
Crime and Punishment by Dostoyevsky. It was the last of those titles that
put a stop to Ferguson's crude fantasies about becoming the next Clar-
ence Darrow, for reading *Crime and Punishment* changed him, *Crime and
Punishment* was the thunderbolt that crashed down from heaven and
cracked him into a hundred pieces, and by the time he put himself
together again, Ferguson was no longer in doubt about the future, for
if *this* was what a book could be, if *this* was what a novel could do to a
person's heart and mind and innermost feelings about the world, then
writing novels was surely the best thing a person could do in life, for
Dostoyevsky had taught him that made-up stories could go far beyond
mere fun and diversion, they could turn you inside out and take off the
top of your head, they could scald you and freeze you and strip you
naked and thrust you out into the blasting winds of the universe, and
from that day forward, after flailing about for his entire boyhood, lost
in an ever-thickening miasma of bewilderment, Ferguson finally knew
where he was going, or at least knew where he wanted to go, and not
once in all the years that followed did he ever go back on his decision,
not even in the hardest years, when it looked as though he might fall
off the edge of the earth. He was just fifteen years old, but already he
had married himself to an idea, and for better or worse, for richer or
poorer, in sickness and in health, young Ferguson meant to pledge his
troth to that idea until the end of his born days.

THE SUMMER MOVIE project was off. Noah's maternal grandmother
had died back in November, and now that his mother had come into a
bit of extra money, she decided to spend a portion of it on furthering
her son's education. Without consulting Noah, she enrolled him in
a summer-long program for foreign high school students in Montpel-
lier, France—eight weeks of *total immersion* in the French language, at the
end of which, if the booklet about the program was to be believed, he
would return to New York speaking with the fluency of a home-grown,
snail-eating Frog. Three days after Ferguson finished reading *Crime*

and Punishment, Noah called to announce the change in plans, cursing his mother for having *pulled a fast one* on him, but what could he do about it, he said, he was too young to be the master of his own life, and for now the mad queen still called the shots. Ferguson covered his disappointment by telling Noah how lucky he was, that if he were in his shoes he'd jump at the chance to go, and as for their own pair of shoes, well, too bad, but the fact was they still had no camera and hadn't even begun to outline the script, so no harm done, and just think of what was waiting for him in France—Dutch girls, Danish girls, Italian girls, a harem of high school beauties all to himself, since not many boys went to those programs, and with little competition standing in his way, he was sure to have the time of his life.

Ferguson would miss Noah, of course, miss him badly, for summer had always been the season when they could be together every day, all day every day for eight full weeks, and a summer without his grouchy harpist cousin-friend would scarcely feel like summer anymore—just a long stretch of time marked by hot weather and a new kind of loneliness.

Fortunately, the one-hundred-dollar check was not the only present his parents had given him for his fifteenth birthday. He had also gained the right to travel to New York on his own, a new liberty he intended to exercise as often as possible, for the beautiful but dreary town of Maplewood had been built for the sole purpose of making people want to get out of it, and with another, larger world suddenly available to him, Ferguson was out of it nearly every Saturday that spring. There were two ways to travel to Manhattan from where he lived: by the 107 bus, which set off every hour from the depot in Irvington and took you to the Port Authority building at Eighth Avenue and Fortieth Street, or by the four-car train run by the Erie Lackawanna Railroad, which left from the station in Maplewood and stopped at the terminus in Hoboken, where there were two further options for finishing off the trip to the city: underground on the Hudson tube or above ground over the water on the Hudson ferry. Ferguson preferred the train-ferry solution, not only because he could walk to the station in about ten minutes (whereas going to the depot in Irvington required someone to give him a lift) but because he loved the train, which was one of the oldest trains still in use anywhere in America, with cars that had been built in 1908, dark green metal hulks that evoked the early days of the industrial revolution, and inside the car the antiquated wicker seats and the seat backs that could be flipped in either direction, the low-speed anti-express that rattled and lurched and sang forth a ruckus of screams as the wheels churned over the rusty tracks, such happiness to be sitting in one of those cars alone, looking out the window at the gruesome, deteriorating landscape of northern New Jersey, the swamps and rivers and iron drawbridges against a background of crumbling brick buildings, remnants of the old capitalism, some of it still functioning, some of it in ruins, so ugly that Ferguson found it inspiring in the same way nineteenth-century poets had found inspiration from the ruins on Greek and Roman hills, and when he wasn't looking out the window at the collapsed world around him he was reading his book of the moment instead, the Russian novels that were not written by Dostoyevsky, Kafka for the first time, Joyce for the first time, Fitzgerald for the first time, and then standing on the deck of the ferry if the weather was anywhere close to decent, the wind in his face, the engine vibrating in the soles of his feet, the seagulls circling above him, such an ordinary trip when all was said and done, a trip made by thousands of commuters every morning from Monday to Friday, but this was Saturday, and to the fifteen-year-old Ferguson it was pure romance to be traveling toward lower Manhattan in this way, the best of all good things he could possibly be doing—not just leaving home behind, but going to this, *to all this*.

Seeing Noah. Talking to Noah. Arguing with Noah. Laughing with Noah. Going to movies with Noah. On Perry Street Saturdays, lunch in the apartment with Aunt Mildred and Uncle Don, then out with Noah and off to wherever they had decided to go, which was often nowhere, the two of them ambling through the streets of the West Village as they gawked at pretty girls and discussed the fate of the universe. Everything had been decided now. Ferguson was going to write books, Noah was going to direct films, and therefore they mostly talked about books and films and the numerous projects they would work on together over the years. Noah was a different Noah from the one Ferguson had met as a small boy, but he still had that aggravating side to him, what Ferguson thought of as his wise-ass, Marx Brothers side, his rambunctious displays of exuberant anarchism, which would burst forth in nonsensical exchanges with greengrocers (*Hey, buddy, what's with this eggplant stuff— I don't see no egg there*) or waitresses in coffee shops (*Sweetheart, before you give us our check, kindly rip it up so we won't have to pay*) or movie-house cashiers standing in their glass boxes (*Tell me one good thing about the film that's playing or I'll cut you out of my will*), provocative gibberish that only proved what a pest he could be, but that was the price you paid for being Noah's friend, feeling amused and embarrassed by him at the same time, as if you were walking around with an obstreperous toddler, and then, without warning, he would do an abrupt about-face and start talking about Albert Camus's *Reflections on the Guillotine*, and after you told him you still hadn't read a word of Camus, he would rush into a bookstore and steal one of his novels for you, which of course you couldn't accept, and consequently you would be put in the awkward position of having to tell him to reenter the store and put the book back on the shelf, which of course made you feel like a sanctimonious prig, but still he was your friend, the best friend you had ever had, and you loved him.

Not every Saturday was a Perry Street Saturday, however. On the weekends Noah spent with his mother on the Upper West Side, it wasn't always possible for Ferguson to see him, so he made other arrangements for those blackout Saturdays, twice traveling into New York with a Maplewood friend named Bob Smith (yes, there was such a person as Bob Smith), once by himself to visit his grandparents, and several times with Amy, as in Amy Ruth Schneiderman, who was especially keen on looking at art, and because Ferguson had recently discovered how much he enjoyed looking at art himself, they spent those Saturdays walking through museums and galleries, not just the big ones everyone went to, the Met, the Modern, the Guggenheim, but smaller ones such as the Frick (Ferguson's favorite) and the midtown photography center, all of which kept them talking for hours afterward, Giotto, Michelangelo, Rembrandt, Vermeer, Chardin, Manet, Kandinsky, Duchamp, so much to take in and think about, seeing nearly everything for *the first time*, again and again the destabilizing jolt of *the first time*, but the most memorable experience they shared together didn't happen in a museum but in the more confined space of a gallery, the Pierre Matisse Gallery in the Fuller Building on East Fifty-seventh Street, where they saw an exhibition of recent sculptures, paintings, and drawings by Alberto Giacometti, and so pulled in were they by those mysterious, tactile, lonely works that they stayed for two hours, and when the rooms began to empty out, Pierre Matisse himself (Henri Matisse's son!) noticed the two young people in his gallery and walked over to them, all smiles and good humor, happy to see that two new converts had been made that afternoon, and much to Ferguson's surprise, he stood there and talked to them for the next fifteen minutes, telling them stories about Giacometti and his studio in Paris, about his own *transplantation* to America in 1924 and the founding of his gallery in 1931, about the tough years of the war when so many European artists were destitute, great artists like Miró and so many others, and how they wouldn't have survived without help from their friends in America, and then, on an impulse, Pierre Matisse led them to a back room of the gallery, an office with desks and typewriters and bookcases, and one by one he took down from the shelves of those bookcases a dozen or so catalogues from past exhibitions by Giacometti, Miró, Chagall, Balthus, and Dubuffet and handed them to the two astonished teenagers, saying, You two children are the future, and maybe these will help with your education.

They walked out of there wordless and agape, carrying their gifts from Henri Matisse's son as they propelled themselves along Fifty-seventh Street, walking quickly because *they were the future*, because their bodies were demanding that they walk quickly after such an encounter, after being blessed by an act of such unexpected kindness, and so they walked down the crowded, sunlit street as fast as two walkers could walk without breaking into a run, and after a couple of hundred yards Amy finally interrupted the silence and declared that she was hungry, *famished* was the word she used, as she often did, since Amy could never be merely hungry as other people were, she was starved or ravenous, she could eat an elephant or a flock of penguins, and now that she was talking about filling up her belly with *some tasty chow*, Ferguson realized that he could go for some food himself, and given that they were walking down Fifty-seventh Street, he proposed that they head for the Horn & Hardart automat between Sixth and Seventh Avenues, not just because it was close but because on an earlier trip to the city he and Amy had both decided that the Horn & Hardart automat was the most splendid eating spot in all of New York.

Not that the bland, inexpensive food served there could be categorized as *splendid*, the bowls of Yankee bean soup, the Salisbury steaks with mashed potatoes doused in gravy, the thick slabs of blueberry pie, no, it was the place itself that lured them in, the amusement park atmosphere of that vast emporium of chrome and glass, the novelty of eating *automated food*, twentieth-century American efficiency in its craziest, most delightful incarnation, wholesome, hygienic cuisine for the hungry masses, and how enjoyable it was to go to the cashier and load up with a pile of nickels and then walk around looking at the dozens of offerings in their glassed-in receptacles, windows barricading tiny rooms of food, each one an individual portion *made especially for you*, and once you had chosen your ham-and-cheese sandwich or slice of pound cake, you would insert the appropriate number of nickels into the slot and the window would open, and just like that the sandwich was yours, a solid, dependable, freshly made sandwich, but before you left to start searching for a table there was the further enjoyment of seeing how quickly the empty receptacle filled up with another sandwich, a sand-wich identical to the one you had just bought for yourself, for there were people back there, men and women in white uniforms who took care of the nickels and replenished the empty containers with more food, what a job that must have been, Ferguson thought, and then the quest for an unoccupied table, carrying your meal or snack around and among the motley crowd of New Yorkers eating and drinking their automated food and beverages, many of them old men who sat there for hours every day consuming cup after cup of slowly drunk coffee, the old men from the vanished left still arguing after forty years about where the revolution had gone wrong, the stillborn revolution that had once seemed immi-nent and now was no more than a memory of what had never been.

So Ferguson and Amy went into the Horn & Hardart automat toward the close of that resplendent afternoon to have a bite to eat, to browse through the thin, densely illustrated catalogues of past exhibi-tions at the Pierre Matisse Gallery, and to discuss what they both felt had been a good day, all in all a very good day. He needed more days like this one, Ferguson said to himself, more good days to counteract the effect of so many rough days in the past few months, which had been the days of no baseball for one thing, a decision that had so con-fused his friends that he had stopped trying to explain himself to them, for the experiment in self-denial was turning out to be much harder to stick to than he had thought, giving up something he had loved so thor-oughly for so many years, a thing so thoroughly a part of him that his body sometimes ached to hold a bat in his hands again, to put on his glove and have a catch with someone, to feel his spikes digging into the dirt as he ran to first base, but he couldn't back down now, he would have to keep the promise he had made or else admit to himself that Artie's death had meant nothing, had taught him nothing, which would have turned him into someone so weak and unheroic that he might as well have asked to be turned into a dog, an abject, groveling mutt who begged for scraps and licked up his own vomit from the floor, and if not for his weekly escapes into the city, which kept him far from the ball fields where his friends played every Saturday, who knows if he wouldn't have given in and allowed himself to become that dog?

Worse still, the spring of no baseball was also the spring of no love. Ferguson had thought he was smitten with Linda Flagg, but after pursuing her throughout the fall and winter, determined to win the affections of Maplewood's most enticing and enigmatic heartthrob, who by turns had encouraged him and rebuffed him, had let him kiss her and not let him kiss her, had given him hope and wrenched that hope away from him, Ferguson had come to the conclusion that not only did Linda Flagg not love him but that he didn't love her. The moment of revelation occurred on a Saturday in early April. After weeks of effort, Ferguson had finally persuaded her to accompany him on one of his trips to Manhattan. The plan was simple: lunch at the automat, a crosstown walk to Third Avenue, and then a couple of hours in the dark watching *The Loneliness of the Long Distance Runner*, a film that Jim Schneiderman had been urging him to see, and if, during the course of the film, Ferguson was able to hold Linda's hand, or kiss Linda on the mouth, or run his hand up and down Linda's leg, so much the better. It turned out to be a gloomy day, dank with drizzles and intermittent downpours, colder than they would have wished, darker than seemed normal for that time of year, but nothing about early spring was ever normal, Ferguson said, as they walked to the station under opened umbrellas and dodged the puddles forming on the sidewalk, and he was sorry about the rain, he continued, but it wasn't really his fault, since he had written a letter to Zeus last week asking for sunny weather, and how could he have known they were in the middle of a month-long postal strike on Mount Olympus? Linda laughed at the inane remark, or else laughed because she was feeling no less jittery and hopeful than he was, which seemed to suggest they were off to a promising start, but then they boarded the Erie Lackawanna for Hoboken, and Ferguson understood that nothing was going to go right that day. The train was dirty and uncomfortable, Linda said, the view was depressing, it was too wet to take the ferry (even though the sky was beginning to clear), the Hudson tube was even dirtier and more uncomfortable than the train, the automat was interesting but scary, what with all the derelicts shuffling in and out, the three-hundred-pound black woman sitting alone at that table over there talking to herself about baby Jesus and the end of the world, the half-blind, whiskery old man reading a rumpled, three-day-old newspaper with a magnifying glass, the ancient couple just next to them dipping old, used-up tea bags into cups of hot water, everyone who came in here was either poor or crazy, and what kind of city was this that allowed crazy people to wander around the streets, she said, and you, Archie, what makes you think New York is so much better than everywhere else when in fact it's so disgusting?

It wasn't her fault, Ferguson told himself. She was a bright, fetching girl who had been raised in a hermetically sealed dome of upper-middle-class comforts and civilities, a colorless, rational world of tidy front lawns and air-conditioned rooms, and to find herself rubbing up against the squalor and tumult of big-city life filled her with an instinctive revulsion, a physical response she was powerless to control, as if she were breathing in a bad smell and suddenly felt sick to her stomach. She couldn't help it, Ferguson repeated to himself, and therefore she couldn't be blamed, but what a disappointment to discover how unadventurous she was, how squeamish, how thrown by what was unfamiliar to her. *Difficult.* That was the word he often used to describe her to himself, and surely the hot-and-cold Linda Flagg had made life difficult for him over the past six months, but she was by no means a stupid or empty person— just afraid, that was all, afraid of the irrationality of vast, repellent cities, and no doubt afraid of boys as well, even though that pretty face of hers was a lure few boys could resist. But not vapid, not without wit and thoughtfulness, for she had a good mind and always spoke intelligently about the books they read in English class, and now that Ferguson had wrapped his hand around her elbow and was guiding her eastward along Fifty-seventh Street, he wondered if her spirits wouldn't begin to improve once they entered the theater and settled in to watch the film. The theater was on the other side of Park Avenue, in one of the richest, *least dirty* neighborhoods of Manhattan, and the movie was supposed to be good, and since Linda had a taste for good books and a nose for good art, perhaps a good movie would put her in a good mood and something good could be salvaged from the rotten day they were having so far.

The movie was certainly good, so good and so absorbing that

Ferguson soon forgot about rubbing Linda's leg or trying to kiss her on the mouth, but *The Loneliness of the Long Distance Runner* was a young man's story and not a young woman's story, which meant that it appealed to Ferguson more than it did to Linda, and even though she granted that it was *an excellent film*, she wasn't carried away by it as Ferguson was, who felt it was one of the best films ever made, *a masterpiece*. After the lights came on, they walked to a Bickford's on Lexington Avenue and ordered coffee and doughnuts at the counter (coffee was a new pleasure in Ferguson's life, and he drank it as often as he could, not only because he liked the taste but because drinking it made him feel more grown-up—as if each sip he took of that hot brown liquid were carrying him farther and farther from the prison house of childhood), and as they sat there among the less fat, less poor, less crazy people than the ones who frequented Horn & Hardart's, they continued to discuss the film, in particular the final sequence, the long-distance championship race at the reform school where the hero (played by a new British actor named Tom Courtenay) is supposed to win the trophy for his pompous headmaster (played by Michael Redgrave) but changes his mind at the last minute and stops, allowing the pretty-boy rich kid from the fancy school (played by James Fox) to win instead. For Ferguson, the decision to lose *on purpose* was a magnificent act of defiance, a thrilling gesture of revolt against authority, and it had warmed his cold and angry heart to see that brazen *Fuck you* depicted on screen, for by insulting the headmaster in that way, the hero had said no to the corrupt and used-up world the headmaster represented, the crumbling British system of empty rewards and arbitrary punishments and unjust class barriers, and in so doing the hero had found his honor, his strength, *his manhood*. Linda rolled her eyes. Nonsense, she said. In her opinion, throwing the race was a dumb move, the worst thing the hero could have done, since long-distance running was his ticket out of that hellhole of a reform school, and now he would be pushed all the way to the bottom again and have to start over from scratch, and what was the point, she asked, he had won his moral victory, but at the same time he had ruined his life, and how could anyone call that *magnificent*?

It wasn't that Linda was wrong, Ferguson said to himself, but she was arguing for expediency over valor, and he hated arguments of that sort, *the practical approach to life*, using the system to beat the system, playing by a set of broken rules because no other rules were in place, whereas those rules needed to be smashed and reinvented, and because Linda believed in the rules of their world, their little suburban world of getting ahead and moving up and settling into a good job and marrying someone who thought the way you did and mowing the lawn and driving a new car and paying your taxes and having 2.4 children and believing in nothing but the power of money, he understood how useless it would have been to prolong the discussion. She was right, of course. But he was right, too, and suddenly he didn't want her anymore.

Linda was henceforth expunged from the list of possibles, and with no other possibles in sight, Ferguson dug in for what promised to be a sad and lonely end to a sad and lonely year. Many years after that year, when he was well into his adulthood, he would look back on that period of his adolescence and think: *Exile in the rooms of home.*

His MOTHER WAS worried about him. Not just because of Ferguson's increasing hostility toward his father (to whom he rarely spoke anymore, refusing to initiate conversations with him and replying to Stanley's questions with sullen, one- and two-word answers), not just because her son persisted in trekking out to New Rochelle for bimonthly dinners with the Federmans (about which he said nothing after he returned home, claiming it was simply too grim to talk about *those destroyed, grieving people*), not just because he had abruptly and inexplicably given up baseball (arguing that basketball was enough for him now and that baseball had become *boring*, which couldn't have been true, Rose felt, not after the season started in April and she saw how carefully Ferguson read the box scores in the morning paper, studying the numbers with the same avidity he had always shown in the past), and not just because her once popular boy seemed to have no girlfriend at the moment and was attending fewer and fewer weekend parties, but because of all those things, and especially because there was something new in Ferguson's eyes, a look of inwardness and detachment that had never been there in all the years she had known him, and on top of those concerns about the state of her son's emotional health, there was a piece of news she had to share with him, a piece of bad news, and therefore it became necessary for the two of them to sit down together and have a talk.

She organized it for a Thursday, which happened to be Angie Bly's day off, and with Ferguson's father not expected to return home until ten or ten-thirty, there would be ample time for both a one-on-one dinner and a long conversation afterward. Wary of starting off the post-dinner tête-à-tête by confronting Ferguson with intrusive questions about himself, which likely would have caused him to clam up and leave the table, Rose held him there by breaking the bad news first, the sad bad news about Amy's mother, Liz, who had just been diagnosed with cancer, a particularly wretched form of cancer that was going to end her life within a matter of months, perhaps even weeks, pancreatic cancer, no hope, no cure, nothing but pain and certain death ahead of her, and at first it was difficult for Ferguson to absorb what his mother was saying, since Amy hadn't so much as breathed a syllable to him about her mother's condition, which was altogether bizarre, given that Amy was his close friend and confided in him about all manner of frets and fears and anxious uncertainties, so before Ferguson could begin to delve into the words *pancreatic cancer*, he had to find out how his mother had been made privy to this information, which Mrs. Schneiderman's own daughter seemed to know nothing about. *Dan told me*, his mother said, which only deepened her son's confusion, for why would a man share such news with a friend before talking to his own child, but then Ferguson's mother explained that Dan wanted to tell both his children at the same time, feeling that Jim and Amy together would be able to handle the news better than Jim and Amy alone, and therefore he was waiting for Jim to come down from Boston tomorrow afternoon before he spoke to either one of them. Liz had been in the hospital for several days, she added, but both children had been told she was in Chicago visiting her mother.

Poor Amy, Ferguson thought. She had been in conflict with her mother for years, and now that her mother was going to die, the unfinished business between them would never be resolved. How hard it would be on her, so much harder than having to cope with the early death of someone you had always been on good terms with, someone you had adored without reservation, for at least then you could carry the memory of that person inside you with an ongoing tenderness, even happiness, an awful, aching sort of happiness, whereas Amy would never be able to think about her mother without feeling regret. Such a perplexing woman, Mrs. Schneiderman, such an odd presence to Ferguson from the day he met her as a young boy, a muddle of contradictory strengths and weaknesses that encompassed the virtues of a good brain, skillful management of the household, insightful opinions on political matters (she had majored in history at Pembroke), and relentless devotion to her husband and two children, but at the same time there was something nervous and frustrated about Mrs. Schneiderman, a feeling that she had missed out on doing what she was supposed to have done in life (a career of some sort, perhaps, a job that would have been important enough to turn her into *an influential person*), and because she had settled for the less exalted job of housewife, she seemed determined to prove to the world that she was smarter than everyone else, knew more than everyone else, not just about some things but about all things, and the fact was that she did know an astonishing amount across an enormous range of subjects, she was without question the most deeply informed human being Ferguson had ever encountered, but the problem with being a know-it-all of the nervous, frustrated variety was that you found it impossible not to correct people when they said something you knew to be wrong, which happened again and again with Mrs. Schneiderman, for she was the only person in the room who knew how many milligrams of Vitamin A were in an average-sized raw carrot, she was the only person who knew how many electoral votes Roosevelt had won in the 1936 presidential election, she was the only person who knew the horsepower differential between a 1960 Chevy Impala and a 1961 Buick Skylark, and even though she was always right, it could be maddening to be around her for any length of time, for one of Mrs. Schneiderman's deficits was that she talked too much, and Ferguson often wondered how her husband and two children could stand to live under the bombardment of all those words, that ceaseless yammering which failed to make any distinction between important things and unimportant things, talk that could impress you with its intelligence and perspicacity or else bore you half to death with its utter meaninglessness, as when Ferguson and Amy were sitting in the backseat of the Schneidermans' car one night on the way to the movies and Mrs. Schneiderman went on for half an hour describing to her husband how she had rearranged the clothes in his bedroom bureau drawers, patiently marching him through the entire series of decisions she had made to arrive at her new system, why long-sleeved shirts belonged in one place, for example, and short-sleeved shirts belonged in another, why black socks had to be separated from blue socks, which in turn had to be separated from the white socks he wore when playing tennis, why his more numerous sleeveless undershirts had to sit on top of and not below his V-neck undershirts, why boxer shorts had to sit to the right of jockey shorts and not to the left, and on and on, one inconsequential detail piled upon another inconsequential detail, and by the time they reached the movie theater, after living inside those bureau drawers for *half an hour,* one half of one of the precious twenty-four hours that comprise a day, Amy was digging her fingers into Ferguson's arm—unable to scream, and therefore screaming in code with her clenched, dug-in fingers. It wasn't that her mother was an inadequate or uncaring mother, Ferguson said to himself. If anything, she cared too much, loved too much, had too much faith in her daughter's golden future, and the curious effect of that *too much,* Ferguson realized, was that it could generate the same resentments as *not enough,* especially when the *too much* was so strong that it blurred the boundaries between parent and child and became a pretext for meddlesome interference, and because the one thing Amy wanted above all else was *breathing room,* she pushed back hard whenever she began to feel suffocated by her mother's persistent involvement in the smallest aspects of her life— from questions about her homework assignments to lectures on the proper method of brushing her teeth, from probing interrogations about the dalliances of her school friends to criticisms of the way she did her hair, from warnings about the perils of alcohol to quiet, monotonous harangues about not tempting boys by wearing too much lipstick. *She's driving me straight to the funny farm,* Amy would tell Ferguson, or: *She thinks she's the captain of the mind police and has a right to be in my head,* or: *Maybe I should get myself pregnant so she can worry about something real,* and Amy fought back by accusing her mother of bad faith, of having it in for her while pretending to be on her side, and why couldn't she just let her alone in the same way she let Jim alone, and again and again they clashed, and if not for her even-tempered, amiable father—*her fun-loving father*—who was continually trying to make peace between them, the intense flare-ups between Amy and her mother would have escalated into an all-out permanent war. Poor Mrs. Schneiderman. She had lost her daughter's love because she had loved her unwisely. Then, taking that thought one step further, Ferguson said to himself: Pity the fate of unloved parents after they're buried in the ground—and pity their children as well.

Still, it was difficult for Ferguson to understand why his mother was telling him about Mrs. Schneiderman's illness, the fatal illness that not even Jim and Amy knew anything about at that point, and once he had said all the things one says at such a moment, *how terrible, how unfair, how cruel to be cut down in the middle of your life*, he asked his mother why she was giving him this advance warning. There was something presumptuous and furtive about it, he said, it made him feel as if they were whispering behind the Schneidermans' backs, but no, his mother replied, not at all, she was telling him now so he wouldn't be shocked when Amy broke the news to him, he would be prepared for the blow and be able to take it calmly, which would help him be a better friend to Amy, who was going to need his friendship now more than ever, and not just now but almost certainly for a long time to come. That made some sense, Ferguson supposed, but not a lot of sense, by no means enough sense, and because his mother was usually sensible when she talked about complicated situations like this one, he wondered if she wasn't hiding something from him, holding back part of the story even as she divulged other parts of it, above all a plausible account that would explain the words *Dan told me*, for why had Dan Schneiderman chosen to confide in her about his wife's cancer in the first place? They were old friends, yes, acquaintances of more than twenty years, but not close friends, as far as Ferguson could tell, not close in the way he and Amy had become close, and yet Amy's father had gone to Ferguson's mother in his hour of greatest trouble and unburdened himself to her, which was an act that first of all required a deep level of mutual trust, but also the kind of intimacy that could exist only between the closest of close friends.

They went on talking about Mrs. Schneiderman for a few more minutes, not wanting to say anything unkind about her but both agreeing that she had never figured out the right approach to take with her daughter and that her biggest problem was not knowing when to *back off* (Rose's words) or *butt out* (Ferguson's words), and then, almost imperceptibly, the troubled relations between Amy and her mother turned into a discussion about the difficulties between Ferguson and his father, and once they arrived at that subject, which was where Rose had been subtly pushing the conversation since the beginning, she startled her son by asking him an unexpectedly blunt question—*Tell me, Archie, why have you turned against your father?*—which so discombobulated him that he couldn't think fast enough to invent a false answer. Exposed and defenseless, with no will to evade the truth anymore, he blurted out the whole petty business about the missing copy of *Sole Mates* and how burned up he was that nearly six months had gone by and his father still hadn't said a word to him about it.

He's too embarrassed, his mother said.

Embarrassed? What kind of an excuse is that? He's a man, isn't he? All he has to do is speak up and tell me what happened.

Why don't you ask him?

It's not my job to ask him. It's his job to tell me.

You're being awfully hard, aren't you?

He's the hard one, not me. He's so hard and so wrapped up in himself that he's turned this family into a nightmare.

Archie . . .

All right, maybe not a nightmare. A disaster area. And this house— it's like living inside one of his goddamn deep freezers.

Is that how it feels to you?

Cold, Ma, so cold, especially between you and him, and I wish to hell you hadn't let him talk you into shutting down your studio. You should be taking photographs, not wasting your time on bridge.

Whatever problems your father and I might be having are entirely separate from what's been happening between *you* and your father. You need to give him another chance, Archie.

I don't think so.

Well, I know so, and if you come upstairs with me, I'll show you why.

With that mysterious request, Ferguson and his mother stood up from the table and left the dining room, and since Ferguson had no idea where his mother was intending to go, he followed her up the stairs to the second floor, where they turned left and entered his parents' bedroom, a room he rarely went into anymore, and then he watched his mother open the door of the closet where his father kept his clothes, disappear inside, and reemerge a few moments later holding a large cardboard box in her arms, which she carried to the middle of the room and put down on top of the bed.

Open it, she commanded him.

Ferguson lifted up the flaps, and once he could see what was in the box, he felt so confused that he didn't know if he should burst out laughing or crawl under the bed in shame.

There were three neatly stacked piles of pamphlets inside, sixty or seventy in all, stapled pamphlets of forty-eight pages each with plain white covers and the following words printed across the front in bold black letters:

SOUL MATES
BY ARCHIE FERGUSON

As Ferguson picked up one of the pamphlets and began leafing through the pages, stunned to see the words of his story looking back at him in eleven-point type, his mother said: He wanted to surprise you, but then the printer screwed up the job by misspelling the title, and your father felt so bad about it, so stupid for not having checked to make sure everything had been done right, he couldn't bring himself to tell you about it.

He should have told me, Ferguson said, speaking in a voice so low that his mother could barely hear him. Who cares about the title?

He's so proud of you, Archie, his mother said. He just doesn't know what to say or how to say it. He's a man who never learned how to talk.

WHAT FERGUSON DIDN'T know at the time, and what continued to be unknown to him until his mother spoke about it seven years later, was that she and Dan Schneiderman had been carrying on a clandestine affair for the past eighteen months. The two or three nights of bridge every week were in fact just one night, and Dan's poker nights and bowling nights were no longer used for poker or bowling, and Ferguson's parents' marriage wasn't merely the icy, passionless charade it appeared to be, it was defunct, deader than the deadest body in the county morgue, and if they continued to stay together in their nonsensical union, it was only because divorce was considered to be so scandalous in that part of the world that they needed to protect their boy from the stigma of coming from *a broken home*, which in many ways was worse than being the son of an embezzler or a door-to-door vacuum cleaner salesman. Divorce was for movie stars and rich people who lived in New York townhouses and summered in the south of France, but in the New Jersey suburbs of the fifties and early sixties unhappy couples were supposed to stick it out, which was what Ferguson's parents were intending to do until their offspring graduated from high school and left Maplewood for good, at which point they would call it quits and go their separate ways, preferably to two different towns, each one as far from Maplewood as possible. Meanwhile, his father had started spending his nights in the guest bedroom, supposedly because his snoring had become so loud that Ferguson's mother was having trouble falling asleep, and not once did Ferguson suspect his parents might not have been telling the truth.

Ferguson's father was the only person who knew about Rose's affair with Dan Schneiderman, and Ferguson's mother was the only person who knew that Stanley had recently taken up with a widow from Livingston named Ethel Blumenthal. The grown-ups were cavorting just as rashly and impetuously as the fifteen-year-olds, but they went about it with such stealth and discretion that no one in Maplewood or anywhere else had the smallest inkling of what they were up to. Not Liz Schneiderman, not Jim or Amy, not Ferguson's grandparents, not Aunt Mildred or Uncle Don, and not Ferguson himself—although the words his mother had spoken that night after dinner, *Dan told me*, had pushed open the door an inch or two, but not enough for him to see anything in the room behind it, since it was still too dim in there and he didn't know where to look for the light switch.

His parents weren't bitter, and they didn't detest each other, and neither one wished the other ill. They simply didn't want to be married anymore, and for the time being they were trying to make the best of it by keeping up appearances. Eighteen years had been ground into a thimbleful of dust, a powdery residue no heavier than the ashes from a single extinguished cigarette, and yet one thing nevertheless remained, an unbroken solidarity about the welfare of their son, and for that reason Rose was doing what she could to mend the rift that had developed between Stanley and Archie, for even though Stanley was a less than adequate father, he wasn't the villain Archie had made him out to be, and long after their little family had been blown apart, Stanley would go on being Archie's father, and it wouldn't do Archie any good to travel through the rest of his life bearing a grudge against him. Luckily, there had been those botched pamphlets. Such a pathetic attempt to ingratiate himself with his son, of course, about whom he understood almost nothing, and how passive Stanley had been when the pamphlets came out wrong (why not go back to the printer and have them done again?), but at least they were something, at least they proved something, and Archie would have to take them into account whenever he thought about his father in the months and years ahead.

It seemed that Daniel Schneiderman had fallen for Rose as far back as 1941, in the days after she started working at his father's studio on West Twenty-seventh Street, but Rose had been engaged to David Raskin at the time, and when Raskin was killed at Fort Benning the following August, Schneiderman was already engaged to Elizabeth Michaels and about to go into the army himself. As he confessed to Rose years later, he would have broken off that engagement if he'd thought he had even the slightest chance with her, but Rose was in mourning then, walled off from the world in a dark closet of deadness and despair, not sure if she wanted to go on living or die, and the farthest thing from her thoughts was putting herself back in circulation, since she had no interest in seeing other men or falling for another man, least of all a man who was about to marry someone else, and therefore nothing happened, which is to say, Dan married Liz, Rose married Stanley, and Rose never knew that Dan secretly wished she had married him.

Ferguson was told about the affair but never anything specific about it—how it began, where they met on the evenings they spent together, what they were planning or not planning for the future—only that it started two days after Kennedy's inauguration and that his mother went into it with a clear conscience because her marriage to his father was already over, a mutual decision arrived at six months earlier that had freed both of them from the vows they had made in 1944, with nothing left to discuss but the formalities of an eventual divorce and what to tell Archie about Stanley's removal to another bed. Dan was in a much trickier spot, however, since he and Liz hadn't had that sort of throw-in-the-towel conversation and were still married, would always be married, he feared, because he didn't have the heart to walk out on her after two decades of rugged, contentious, but not entirely miserable wedlock, and unlike Ferguson's mother, Jim and Amy's father suffered from the guilt of his adulterous infidelities. Then came more guilt, guilt for both of them now, the corrosive, gut-consuming guilt of Liz's cancer, for how many times had each one of them thought about the happier life they would have had together if Dan were no longer married to Liz, and now the gods were about to remove Liz from the story, and the good thing they had both daydreamed about but had never dared to express out loud had turned into something exceedingly bad, the worst thing either one of them could have imagined, for how not to feel that their thoughts were pushing that luckless, dying woman into her grave?

That was all the fifteen-year-old Ferguson knew back then—that Mrs. Schneiderman was going to die—and when Amy called him late Sunday night, three days after his mother had warned him of the disaster that was about to fall on the Schneiderman children, he was prepared for Amy's tears and capable of uttering more or less cogent sentences in response to the grotesque things she was telling him on the phone, the Saturday and Sunday visits to the hospital where her mother was lying in a morphine-induced blur of panicked dissociation, pain and then less pain, then more pain and a slow, stuporous withdrawal into sleep, her face so gaunt and gray now, *as if she were no longer herself,* lying alone in the bed as her rotting, burned-up insides went about the job of killing her, and why had her father lied about it, she moaned, why had he kept it back from her and Jim with that dumb story about going to Chicago to be with Grandma Lil, how awful of him to have done that and how awful that she had been thinking about buying *black lipstick* in order to shock her mother at the very moment when her mother was being taken to the hospital, she felt so bad about that now, so bad about so many things, and Ferguson did what he could to calm her down, saying that her father had done the right thing in waiting for Jim to come home from college so he could break the news to them together, and remember that he, Ferguson, would always be there for her, and whenever she needed a shoulder to cry on, he wanted her to think about using his shoulder first.

Mrs. Schneiderman held on for another four weeks, and in late June, just as the school year was coming to a close, Ferguson attended his second funeral in the past eleven months, a smaller and quieter affair than the massive obsequies for Artie Federman, no uncontrollable outbursts of howling and sobbing this time but rather stillness and shock, a subdued farewell to a woman who had died on the morning of her forty-second birthday, and as Ferguson listened to Rabbi Prinz recite the customary prayers and say the customary words, he looked around and saw that only a few people who were not close relatives of the Schneidermans had tears in their eyes, his mother among them, who wept throughout the entire service, but not even Jim was crying, he just sat there holding Amy's hand and looking down at the floor, and afterward, in the pause between the service and the drive to the cemetery, he was moved to see his weeping mother throw her arms around the weeping Dan Schneiderman and hang on for a long, hard hug, little understanding the full import of that hug or why they held on to each other for so long, and then he was throwing his own arms around the weeping, swollen-eyed Amy, who had cried on his shoulder countless times in the past month, and because he felt so sorry for her, and because it felt so good to be holding her body in his arms, Ferguson decided that he must and should and with all due haste would fall in love with her. Her situation was so precarious now that it demanded something more than friendship from him, something more than the old Archie-and-Amy routine they had perfected over the years, but Ferguson never had a chance to tell her about his sudden change of heart, since that was the last he saw of Amy for the next two months. After the day of her mother's funeral, her father let her skip the last four days of the semester, and the fifth day, which was the day their class graduated from Maplewood Junior High, the three Schneidermans took off on a summer-long journey through England, France, and Italy, which Ferguson's mother thought was a brilliant idea, the best possible medicine for a family that had suffered as much as they had.

His father had to work on the morning of Ferguson's graduation, so his mother came to the ceremony alone. Afterward, they drove to South Orange Village and stopped in for lunch at Gruning's, the site of so many delectable hamburgers in the years before the Blue Valley Country Club had destroyed the old Sunday ritual, and for the first several minutes after they found a table in the back, they discussed Ferguson's plans for the summer, which included a job at his father's outlet in Livingston (a multipurpose, minimum-wage position that would have him working at such tasks as mopping floors, squirting Windex onto the screens of the show-room televisions, washing down the refrigerators and other appliances on display, and installing air conditioners with the delivery man, Joe Bentley), two outdoor basketball games a week in the Maplewood–South Orange Twilight League, and as many hours at his desk as possible: he had come up with ideas for a couple of new stories and was hoping to finish them before school started again. Not to speak of books, of course, all the dozens of books he wanted to read, and then, with whatever time he had left, he would write Amy as many letters as he could and hope she would be at the addresses he mailed them to.

His mother listened, his mother nodded, his mother smiled a distant, thoughtful sort of smile, and before Ferguson could think of what to say next, she interrupted him and said: Your father and I are splitting up, Archie.

Ferguson wanted to make sure he had heard her correctly, so he repeated the words back to her: Splitting up. As in *divorce*?

That's right. As in *So long, it's been good to know ya.*

And when did you decide this?

Ages ago. We were planning to wait until you went off to college, or wherever you go after you finish high school, but three years is a long time, and what's the point of waiting? As long as you approve, of course.

Me? What do I have to do with it?

People will talk. People will point fingers. I don't want you to feel uncomfortable.

I don't care what people think. It's none of their business.

So?

By all means. By any means. As far as I'm concerned, it's the best news I've heard in a long time.

You mean it?

Of course I mean it. No more lies, no more pretending. The age of truth begins!

TIME PASSED, AND again and again during the months that followed, Ferguson would stop, take a good look at the things around him, and tell himself that life was getting better. Not only was he finished with junior high school now, which meant that nothing he wrote would ever be judged by Mrs. Baldwin again, but the breakup of his parents' marriage seemed to be breaking up many other things as well, and with the old, predictable routines no longer in place, it was becoming more and more difficult to know what would happen from one day to the next. Ferguson enjoyed that new feeling of instability. Things might have been in flux, at times verging on out-and-out confusion, but at least they weren't dull.

For the time being, he and his mother were to go on living in the big house in Maplewood. His father had rented a smaller house in Livingston, not far from the house of his lady friend Ethel Blumenthal, who was still a secret at that point and therefore not known to Ferguson, but

the long-range plan was to sell the big house within a certain number
of months after the divorce was finalized and for both of his parents to
move elsewhere. It went without saying that Ferguson would go on living with his mother. He would be free to see his father whenever he
wished, but if it turned out he didn't want to see his father, then his
father would have the right to see him for two dinners every month.
That was the minimum. There was no maximum. It seemed to be a fair
arrangement, and they all shook hands on it.

His father was writing a monthly check to his mother for what was
termed *sundry and essential living expenses*, each of them had a lawyer,
and the amicable parting that was supposed to have been *wrapped up
in a matter of weeks* dragged on for months in less than amicable disputes
about alimony payments, the division of common property, and the
deadline for putting the house on the market. From Ferguson's point of
view, it seemed that his father was the one who was gumming up the
works, that something in him was unconsciously but actively resisting
the divorce, and although he felt frustrated on his mother's behalf (who
wanted it over and done with as quickly as possible), in the early days
of his parents' wrangling Ferguson felt oddly reassured by his father's
obstructionism, since it seemed to suggest that the prophet of profits was
capable of normal human feelings after all, which had not been apparent to his son for many years, and whether it was because Stanley
Ferguson still harbored an abiding love for the woman he had married almost two decades earlier (the sentimental reason) or because the
ignominy of divorce represented failure and humiliation in the eyes of
others (the social reason) or simply because he was reluctant to see Ferguson's mother walk off with half the money from the sale of the big
house (the financial reason) was less important than the fact that he felt
something, and even though he ultimately gave in and signed the divorce
agreement in December after Ferguson's mother said she would be willing to relinquish her share of the house, that didn't mean money alone
had had the last word, for Ferguson sensed that the sentimental and
social reasons were the true cause of the conflict and that holding
out for the money was merely an attempt to save face.

At the same time, using that money as a wedge in the negotiations
struck Ferguson as an unforgivable act. The largest asset his parents
owned in common was the house, the big house Ferguson had always
detested, the show-off Tudor-style manor he had never wanted to move

to in the first place, and by depriving his soon-to-be ex-wife of her share of the proceeds from that most valuable asset, Ferguson's father was in effect pauperizing Ferguson's mother, making it all but impossible for her to buy a new house of her own, thus condemning her *and his own son* to a diminished life in a cheap, cramped apartment somewhere near the railroad tracks. He was punishing her for not loving him anymore, and the fact that Ferguson's mother had agreed to such a harsh stipulation only proved how desperately she wanted to be liberated from the marriage, even if it wrecked her financially, and so Ferguson's father forged on with his cruel demand and wouldn't back down. If there was any hope in the wording of the final agreement, it was that the house wouldn't have to be put on the market until two years after the divorce became final, which would more or less cover the three years Ferguson would be in high school, but still, after trying to give his father the benefit of the doubt ever since the Sole-Soul contretemps, after doing his best to treat his father amicably and politely all during the long, tedious summer of working at the Livingston store, Ferguson now turned against him with something close to hatred, and he resolved never to accept another penny from his father for the rest of his life, not for spending money, not for clothes or a secondhand car, not for college tuition, not for anything ever again, and even after Ferguson was a grown man and had failed to publish any of his books and was living as a wino on the lowest block of the Bowery, he would refuse to unclench his fist when his father tried to press a fifty-cent piece into his hand, and when the old man finally left this world and Ferguson inherited eighty million dollars and the ownership of four hundred and seventy-three appliance stores, he would close the stores and distribute the money equally among the bums he had known from his days of living as a forgotten man on the sidewalks of skid row.

Still and all, life was getting better, and once his father moved out of the house on July second, Ferguson was impressed by how quickly his mother adjusted to their new circumstances. Everything was suddenly different, and the limitations of the monthly allowance forced her to abandon most of the comforts and all of the luxuries that had come from being married to a man with money: the services of Angie Bly for one thing (which had relieved her of tiresome domestic chores such as cooking and cleaning the house), the Blue Valley Country Club for another (no longer possible under the circumstances, which abruptly put an end to the pleasures of golf), but most of all the free-and-easy spending on clothes and shoes, the twice-weekly hairdresser appointments, the pedicures and massages, the bracelets and necklaces bought on impulse and then seldom worn afterward, all the trappings of the so-called good life she had been leading for the past ten years and which she gave up—or so it appeared to Ferguson—without a moment's regret. She spent that first summer of pre-divorce separation working in the backyard garden, taking care of the house, and cooking in the kitchen, cooking up a storm in the kitchen, which led to such abundant and delicious dinners for her son after he came home from work that he spent the better part of his days at his father's store thinking about what his mother would be feeding him at home that night. She rarely went out and rarely talked to anyone on the phone besides her mother in New York, but there were many visits that summer from her friend Nancy Solomon, the loyal comrade of her earliest childhood, who began to remind Ferguson of one of those next-door neighbors in a TV sitcom, the funny-looking fellow housewife who was always available to drop in for a cup of coffee and a long chat, and after Ferguson had gone upstairs to read or work on his new story or write another letter to Amy, nothing made him happier than to hear the women laughing in the kitchen below. His mother was laughing again. The dark circles under her eyes were slowly erasing themselves, and bit by bit she was beginning to look like her old self—or perhaps her new self, since the old one had vanished so long ago that Ferguson could barely even remember it.

Dan Schneiderman and his children returned from Europe at the end of August. In the sixty-two days since their departure, Ferguson had written Amy fourteen letters, half of which had managed to find her in the right place at the right time, while the other half continued to languish unclaimed in various American Express offices across Italy and France. He hadn't dared to talk about love in any of those letters, since it would have been presumptuous and unfair of him to put her on the spot, to ask a question she wouldn't have been able to answer to his face, but the letters had been full of affectionate and sometimes highly emotional declarations of undying friendship, and again and again he had told her that he missed her, that he longed to see her again, and that the little world he lived in was an exceedingly empty place when she wasn't in it. From her end, Amy had sent off five letters and eleven picture postcards, all of which arrived safely in New Jersey, and though the cards from London, Paris, Florence, and Rome were necessarily short (and riddled with exclamation marks!!), the letters were long and mostly talked about how she was adjusting to her mother's death, which seemed to change from day to day and sometimes even from hour to hour, with some tolerable moments, some painful moments, and weirdly enough some altogether good moments when she didn't think about it at all, but when she did think about her mother it was hard not to feel guilty, she wrote, that was the most difficult thing to accept, the unending guilt, because a part of her knew she would be better off without her mother in her life, and to admit to that feeling was *a terrible admission of her own rottenness*. Ferguson responded to that grim, self-hating letter with further news about his parents' separation and impending divorce, telling her that not only was he glad it was happening but that he was thrilled to know he would never have to spend another night under the same roof with his father and that he didn't feel the least bit guilty about it. *We feel what we feel*, he wrote, *and we're not responsible for our feelings. For our actions, yes, but not for what we feel. You never did anything wrong to your mother. You argued with her sometimes, but you were a good daughter, and you mustn't torture yourself for what you're feeling now. You're innocent, Amy, and you have no right to feel guilty about things you haven't done.*

Half of what he wrote to her that summer was lost, but those sentences happened to be in one of the letters that wound up reaching her— in London, just one day before she flew back to New York with her father and brother.

The day after they returned, the three Schneidermans came to the house for dinner. It was the first of many dinners Ferguson's mother would cook for them throughout that first year of high school, the two and three and sometimes even four dinners a week that were mostly just with Dan and Amy after Jim went off to college again, and because Ferguson still had no idea that his mother and Amy's father were anything more to each other than the good friends of the *Dan told me* era back in the spring, he interpreted those invitations as gestures of kindness and goodwill, a sympathetic reaching out to a family in mourning, father and daughter still too distracted by their grief to handle the business of shopping and cooking for themselves, their household a chaos of unmade beds and unwashed dishes now that Liz was no longer around to maintain domestic order, but on top of the generosity there were personal motives as well, Ferguson realized, for his mother was alone now and had been alone since the beginning of the summer, her life suspended between a dead past and a blank, unknowable future, and why wouldn't she welcome the company of pleasant Dan Schneiderman and his daughter, Amy, who brought words and feelings and affection into the house, and surely those dinners were good for all of them during that transitional period of post-burial melancholy and imminent divorce, not least for Ferguson himself, who found those sit-downs at the kitchen table to be one of the strongest arguments yet advanced to support his theory that life was indeed getting better.

Better, of course, did not mean good, possibly not even close to good. It simply meant that things were less bad than they had been before, that the overall condition of his life had improved, but given what happened at the first dinner with the Schneidermans in late August, things still hadn't improved as much as Ferguson would have hoped. He had not been with Amy for more than two months, and therefore the contours of her face had grown less and less familiar to him, and as he studied her across the table as the five of them tucked into his mother's pot roast, he understood that the beauty of Amy's eyes had something to do with her eyelids, that the folds in her eyelids were different from the folds in most other people's eyelids, and because of that her eyes seemed both poignant and innocent, a rare combination he had never seen in anyone else, young eyes that would go on being young even after she herself had become old, and that was why he had fallen for her, he suspected, the moment of revelation had occurred when he saw those eyes gush forth tears at her mother's funeral, he had been so moved by those weeping eyes that he could no longer think of her as *just a friend,* suddenly it was love, the *in-love* sort of love that surpassed all other forms of love, and he wanted her to love him back in the same way he now loved her. After dessert, he took her out into the backyard for a one-on-one conversation while the three others continued to sit around the table talking. It was one of those warm and muggy late-summer New Jersey nights, the thick air dotted with the blinks and pulsing flashes of a hundred fireflies, the same creatures he and Amy had captured on summer nights when they were children, putting them in clear glass jars and walking around with those glowing shrines of light in their hands, and now they were walking around in the same backyard talking about Amy's trip to Europe and the end of Ferguson's parents' marriage and the letters they had written to each other in July and August. Ferguson asked if she had received the last one, the one he had sent to London ten days earlier, and when she said yes, he asked if she understood what he had been trying to tell her. I think so, Amy said. I'm not sure it helps, but maybe it will start to help at some point, the not-being-responsible-for-our-feelings stuff, I'm really going to have to chew on that for a while, Archie, since I still can't help feeling responsible for what I feel.

That was when Ferguson put his right arm around her shoulder and said: I love you, Amy. You know that, don't you?

Yes, Archie, I know that. And I love you, too.

Ferguson stopped walking, turned to face her, and then put his left arm around her as well. As he pulled her body up against his, he said: I'm talking about real love, Schneiderman, all-out, forever-and-ever love, the biggest love of all time.

Amy smiled. A moment later, she put her arms around him, and as her long bare arms came into contact with his bare arms, Ferguson's legs started to buckle.

I've been thinking about this for months, she said. Whether we should try it or not. Whether we're meant to be in love with each other or not. I'm so tempted, Archie, but I'm scared. If we try and it doesn't work out, we probably won't be friends anymore, at least not the way we are now, which is the best friends in the world, close in the way brothers and sisters can be close, that's how I've always thought of us, as brother and sister, and every time I try to imagine kissing you, it feels like incest to me, something wrong, something I know I would regret, and I don't want to lose what we have, it would kill me not to be your sister anymore, and would it be worth losing all the good things we have together for a few kisses in the dark?

Ferguson was so crushed by what she said that he disentangled his arms from hers and took two steps back. Brother and sister, he said, with anger mounting in his voice, what nonsense!

But it wasn't nonsense, and when Amy's father and Ferguson's mother were married eleven months and four days after the night of that first dinner, the two friends officially became brother and sister, and even though the word *step* was factored into the designation, they were henceforth members of the same family, and the two bedrooms they slept in until the end of high school stood side by side in the same second-floor hallway of their new family house.

4.1

THE HOUSING POLICY SET FORTH IN THE BARNARD COLLEGE
Student Handbook stated that all out-of-town freshmen were
required to live in one of the on-campus dormitories, whereas freshmen
from New York could choose between living in a dormitory and living
at home with their parents. Independent Amy, who had no desire to
stay with her parents and no desire to share a room with someone in
an over-regulated dormitory, outfoxed the system by claiming her
parents had moved from West Seventy-fifth Street to a bigger apartment on West 111th Street, a much bigger apartment that was in fact
occupied by four students who were not freshmen, a sophomore and a
junior from Barnard and a junior and a senior from Columbia, and when
Amy moved into that immense place with the long corridors and ancient
plumbing fixtures and beveled glass doorknobs, she became the sole
occupant of the fifth bedroom. Her parents went along with the decep-
tion because Amy had shown them the numbers, which proved that it
was cheaper to pay one-fifth of the two-hundred-and-seventy-dollar
apartment rent than to live in a dormitory, and also because, and especially because, they knew it was time for their willful daughter to leave
home. A little more than a year had passed since the cookout in the
Fergusons' backyard, and now the Schneidermans' daughter and
the Fergusons' son had been granted their most ardent wish: a room
with a lock on the door and a chance to fall asleep together in the same
bed whenever they wanted to.

The problem was that *whenever* turned out to be a sticky concept,

more an idealized possibility than a workable proposition, and with one
of them still stuck in Montclair and the other caught in the whirl of confusions and adjustments that come with the start of college life, they
wound up sharing that bed less often than they had expected. There
were the weekends, of course, and they took advantage of them whenever they could, which was most weekends in September, October, and
early November, but the freedoms of the summer had been curtailed,
and only once in all that time was Ferguson able to make one of his
weeknight dashes into the city. They continued to talk about the things
they had always talked about, which that fall included such matters
as the Warren Commission Report (true or false?), the Free Speech
Movement at Berkeley (long live Mario Savio!), and the victory of the
bad Johnson over the infinitely worse Goldwater (not three cheers but
two, perhaps one), but then Amy was invited on a weekend outing to
Connecticut and they had to cancel their plans, which was followed
by another cancellation the next week (a touch of the flu, she said,
although she wasn't in the apartment when he called her on Saturday
night and again on Sunday afternoon), and bit by bit Ferguson sensed
that she was slipping away from him. His old fears returned, the black
ruminations of last winter when he thought she might have to leave
New York, conjuring up the other people she would come to know in
those imagined other places, the other boys, the other loves, and why
should it be any different in her home city? She was living in a new
world now, and he belonged to the old world she had left behind. Just
thirty-six blocks to the north, and yet the customs were entirely different up there, and the people spoke another language.

It wasn't that she seemed bored with him or loved him any less, it
wasn't that her body stiffened up when he touched her or that she wasn't
happy with him in the new bed in the new apartment, it was simply
that she seemed distracted now, unable to focus her attention on him
as she had in the past. After those two missed weekends, he managed
to arrange a visit to the empty apartment on the Saturday after Thanksgiving (her roommates had all gone home for the holiday), and as they
sat in the kitchen together drinking wine and smoking cigarettes, he
noticed that Amy was looking out the window instead of looking at
him, and rather than ignore it and go on with what he was saying, he
stopped in midsentence and asked her if something was wrong, and
that was when it happened, that was when Amy turned her head

back in his direction, looked him in the eyes, and pronounced the seven small words that had been forming in her mind for close to a month: *I think I need a break, Archie.*

They were only seventeen years old, she said, and it was beginning to feel as if they were married, as if they had no future anymore except to go on being together, and even if they did wind up together in the long run, it was too soon to lock themselves into that commitment now, they would feel smothered, trapped by promises they might not be able to keep, and before long they would start to resent each other, and why not take a deep breath and just *relax* for a little while?

Ferguson knew he was being dumb, but there was only one question his dumb heart could think of asking: Are you saying you don't love me anymore?

You haven't been listening to me, Archie, Amy said. All I'm saying is that we need more air in the room. I want us to keep the doors and windows open.

Which means that you've fallen for someone else.

Which means that someone has his eye on me and I've flirted with him a couple of times. It's nothing serious, believe me. In fact, I'm not even sure I like him. But the point is that I don't want to feel guilty about it, and I have been feeling guilty because I don't want to hurt you, and then I ask myself: What's wrong with you, Amy? You're not married to Archie. You're not even halfway through your first year of college, and why shouldn't you have a chance to explore a little, to kiss another boy if you want to, maybe even to go to bed with another boy if you feel like it, to do the kinds of things people are supposed to do when they're young?

Because it would kill me, that's why.

It isn't forever, Archie. All I'm asking for is a time-out.

THEY WENT ON talking for more than an hour, and then Ferguson left the apartment and drove back to Montclair. Four and a half months would go by before he saw Amy again, four and a half dreary months of no kissing, no touching, and no talking to the one person he most wanted to kiss and touch and talk to, but Ferguson managed to weather that time without going to pieces because he was convinced that he and Amy had not come to the end, that the long and complicated journey they had embarked on together had merely run into its first detour, a rockslide that had fallen onto their path and had forced them to head off into the woods, where they had momentarily lost sight of each other, but sooner or later they would find the road again and continue on their way. He was convinced of this because he had taken Amy at her word, for Amy was the one person he had ever known who didn't lie, who couldn't lie, who always told the truth no matter what the circumstances, and when she'd said that she wasn't dumping him or sending him into permanent exile, that all she was asking for was a break, a pause to open the windows and air out the room, Ferguson had believed her.

The strength of that belief kept him going through those empty, Amy-less months, and he hunkered down and tried to make the best of them, refusing to succumb to the temptations of self-pity, which had been so attractive to him at earlier stages of his adolescence (the loss of Anne-Marie Dumartin, the injury to his hand), striving for a tougher, more resolute approach to the conundrums of pain (the pain of disappointment, the pain of living in Mr. Martino's *world of shit*), girding himself to absorb blows now rather than crumbling under their force, standing his ground rather than running away, digging in for what he now understood would be a long siege of trench warfare. Late November 1964 to mid-April 1965: a time of no sex and no love, a time of inwardness and disembodied solitude, a time of forcing himself, at long last, to grow up, to have done with everything that still connected him to his childhood.

It was his last year of high school, the last year he would spend in the town of Montclair, New Jersey, the last year he would live under the same roof with his parents, the last year of the first part of his life, and now that he was alone again, Ferguson looked out at his old, familiar world with renewed concentration and intensity, for even as he kept his gaze fixed on the people and places he had known for the past fourteen years, he felt they were already beginning to vanish before his eyes, slowly dissolving like a Polaroid image moving in reverse, undeveloping itself as the outlines of buildings blurred and the features of his friends' faces grew less distinct and the bright colors faded into white rectangles of nothingness. He was among his classmates again as he hadn't been in over a year, no longer slinking off to New York on the weekends, no longer a person with a secret life, a one-thumbed shadow reinserted into the midst of the seventeen- and eighteen-year-olds he had known since the age of three and four and five, and now that they were beginning to disappear, he found himself looking at them with something close to tenderness, the same *boring suburban crowd* he had turned his back on so abruptly after Amy went upstairs with him on the afternoon of the Labor Day cookout were his sole companions again, and he did what he could to treat them with tolerance and respect, even the most ridiculous and empty-headed among them, for he was no longer in the judgment business, he had given up his compulsion to hunt out the flaws and weaknesses in others because he had learned by now that he was just as weak and flawed as they were, and if he meant to grow up into the kind of person he was expecting himself to be, he would have to keep his mouth shut and his eyes open and never look down on anyone again.

No Amy for now, no Amy for what threatened to be a long and unbearable stretch of time, but Ferguson's irrational conviction that the two of them were destined to be together again at some point in the future pushed him into making plans for that future when the moment came for him to send off his applications to college. That was one of the curious things about being in the last year of high school, the fact that you spent most of your time thinking about next year, knowing that a part of you was already gone even as you remained where you were, as if you were living in two places at once, the drab present and the uncertain future, boiling down your existence into a set of numbers that included your grade point average and SAT scores, approaching the teachers you liked best and asking them to write letters of recommendation for you, composing the absurd, impossible essay about yourself in which you hoped to impress a panel of anonymous strangers of your worthiness to attend their institution, then putting on a jacket and tie and traveling to that institution to be interviewed by someone whose report would weigh heavily on whether they accepted you or not, and suddenly Ferguson started worrying about his hand again, for the first time in months he felt anxious about his missing fingers when he sat down across from the man who would help to decide his future, asking himself whether the man saw him as a handicapped person or merely as someone who had been in an accident, and then, even as he was replying to the man's questions, he remembered the last time he and Amy had talked about his hand, back in the summer when for some reason he had looked down at it and said how much it revolted him, which had annoyed her so greatly that she'd shouted at him, saying that if he ever mentioned his hand again she would take out a cleaver and chop off her own left thumb and give it to him as a present, and the ferocity of her anger was so magnificent that he promised never to bring up the subject again, and as he went on talking to the man who was interviewing him, he realized that not only must he not talk about it again but he must not think about it either, and bit by bit he forced himself to push it out of his mind and settled into his conversation with the man, who was a music professor at Columbia, which needless to say was his first choice, the only college he had any interest in attending, and when the genial, humorous, thoroughly sympathetic composer of twelve-tone comic operas found out that Ferguson was interested in poetry and hoped to become a writer one day, he walked over to the bookshelf in his office and pulled out four recent issues of the *Columbia Review*, the undergraduate literary magazine, and handed them to the nervous, self-conscious applicant from the other side of the Hudson. You might want to have a look at these, the professor said, and then they were shaking hands and saying good-bye to each other, and as Ferguson left the building and walked out onto the campus, which was already familiar to him because of his half dozen weekend trysts with Lady Schneiderman back in the fall, he wondered if he might not run into her that afternoon (he didn't) or if he shouldn't go down to her apartment on West 111th Street and ring the bell (he didn't, he wouldn't, he couldn't), and so rather than torment himself with thoughts about his absent, inaccessible love, he opened one of the issues of the *Columbia Review* and stumbled across a poem with a most amusing and vulgar refrain, a line so shocking in its directness that Ferguson laughed out loud when he read it: *A steady fuck is good for you.* It might not have been much of a poem, but Ferguson couldn't help agreeing with the sentiment, which contained a truth that no other poem had ever expressed so bluntly, or at least no other poem he had read, and on top of that he found it encouraging to know that Columbia was a place that allowed its students to publish such thoughts without fear of being censored, which meant that one could be free as a student there, for if any student had written that line for the Montclair High School literary magazine, he would have been expelled at once and likely thrown in jail.

His parents were indifferent. Neither one of them had gone to college, neither one of them knew anything about the distinctions between one college and another, and therefore they would be happy for their boy wherever he went, whether to the state university in New Brunswick (Rutgers) or to Harvard University in Cambridge, Massachusetts, since they were too ignorant to have developed into snobs about the prestige of one school over another and were simply proud of Ferguson for having been such a good student all his life. Aunt Mildred, however, who had recently been promoted to full professor at Berkeley, had other ideas about the academic destination of her one and only, and in a long coast-to-coast phone call in early December she tried to steer her nephew around to her way of thinking. Columbia was an excellent first choice, she said, no problem with that, the undergraduate program was one of the strongest in the country, but she also wanted him to consider other options, Amherst and Oberlin, for example, small, isolated schools where the atmosphere would be calmer and less distracting than in New York, more conducive to the rigors of focused study, but if he had his heart set on a big university, why not give some thought to Stanford and Berkeley, how dearly she would love to have him out in California with her for the next four years, and either one of those places was every bit as good as Columbia if not better, but Ferguson told her that his mind was made up, it was New York or nothing, and if Columbia turned him down, he would go to NYU, which accepted nearly everyone who applied, and if something went wrong there, his high school diploma would allow him to enroll in courses at the New School, which turned down no one, and that was the plan, he said, just three possibilities, all of them in New York, and when his aunt asked him why it had to be New York when there were so many more attractive places to choose from, Ferguson reached back into his memory and pulled out the words Amy had spoken to him on the first day they met—because, he said, New York is *it*.

A STATE OF limbo, perhaps, but in the narrow slit between the not-here and not-there of the drab present, something happened to Ferguson that altered his thinking about what would happen next. In early December, he landed a job at the *Montclair Times*, which more accurately could be said to have been a job that landed on him, since it came his way unexpectedly, with no serious effort on his part, a gift of blind happenstance, but once he started doing it, he discovered that he wanted to keep on doing it, for not only did he enjoy the work but the effect of that enjoyment was to narrow the infinite spaces of a future anywhere into a precise somewhere, and with that narrowing a multitude of anythings was suddenly turned into a single something. In other words, three months short of his eighteenth birthday, Ferguson accidentally stumbled upon a calling in life, something to do over the long haul, and the perplexing thing was that it never would have occurred to him to do it if he hadn't been thrust into doing it in the first place.

The *Montclair Times* was a weekly newspaper that had been covering local events since 1877, and since Montclair was larger than most of the towns in the area (population: 44,000), the paper was more substantial, more thorough, and carried more advertising than other Essex County weeklies, even if most of the stories it published were more or less the same as those found in the smaller rags: Board of Education meetings, gatherings of the Ladies Garden Club, Boy Scout banquets, automobile accidents, engagements and marriages, break-ins, muggings, and acts of teenage vandalism as reported in the Police Blotter, reviews of exhibitions at the Montclair Art Museum, lectures at Montclair State Teachers College, and sports in all of their indigenous manifestations: Little League baseball, Pop Warner football, and extensive coverage of the games played by the high school varsity teams, the redoubtable Montclair Mounties, whose football squad had just finished the most successful season in its history—a perfect 9–0 record, a state championship, and a number three ranking in the country, which meant that of all of the thousands of high school football teams spread across the United States, only two were considered to be better than Montclair. Ferguson had missed every one of those Saturday games, but now, just ten days after his glum, post-Thanksgiving conversation with Amy, his mother told him about a possible opening at the *Times*—assuming he was interested. It seemed that Rick Vogel, the young man who reported on high school sports for the paper, had done such an impressive job chronicling the football team's glorious season that he had been hired away by the *Newark Evening News*, a daily paper with twenty times the circulation of the Montclair weekly and a large enough budget to pay twenty times the salary, and the editor in chief of the *Times* found himself in what Ferguson's mother called *a hell of a fix*: the varsity basketball season was scheduled to begin next Tuesday, and he had no one to write about the games.

Until then, the thought of working for a newspaper had never crossed Ferguson's mind. He saw himself as a literary man, a man whose future would be dedicated to the writing of books, and whether he wound up becoming a novelist or a playwright or the heir to New Jersey's Walt Whitman and William Carlos Williams, he was headed in the direction of art, and whatever the importance of newspapers, it was certain that writing for them had nothing to do with art. On the other hand, an opportunity had presented itself to him, he was at loose ends, restless and dissatisfied with just about everything, and perhaps a stint at the *Times* would inject some color into the drab present and lure him away from dwelling on his own miserable circumstances. More than that, there was some money involved—a nominal ten-dollar fee per article—but even more than the money there was the fact that the *Times* was a legitimate newspaper, not a joke publication like the *Mountaineer* at Montclair High, and if Ferguson managed to wrangle himself a job there, he would be entering the ranks of the grown-up world—no longer an almost-eighteen-year-old high school boy but a young adult, or, just as good if not more satisfying to his ears, *a boy wonder*, meaning a boy who was doing the work of a man.

Not to be forgotten was that Whitman had started out as a journalist for the *Brooklyn Eagle* and that Hemingway had written for the *Kansas City Star* and that Newark-born Stephen Crane had been a reporter for the *New York Herald*, and so when Ferguson's mother asked him if he had any interest in taking over for the precipitously departed Vogel, Ferguson needed no more than half a minute to say yes. It wasn't going to be easy, his mother added, but Edward Imhoff, the fat sourpuss who edited the *Times*, might be desperate enough to chance going with an untested kid, at least for one game, which would buy him a little time if Ferguson didn't pan out, but as they both knew, his mother said, he *was* going to pan out, and because she had been publishing photographs in Imhoff's paper for more than a dozen years and had included his portrait in her book of Garden State notables (an act of uncalled-for generosity if there ever was one), the windbag owed her, she said, and without wasting another second she picked up the phone and called him. Such was the way Ferguson's mother handled herself when something needed to be done—she seized the moment and did it, unafraid and unstoppable, and how Ferguson relished her gutsy bravura as he listened to her half of the conversation with Imhoff. Not once in the seven minutes they talked did she sound like a mother begging a favor for her son. She was a clever talent scout who had just solved a problem for an old friend, and Imhoff should get down on his knees and thank her for saving his ass.

On the strength of that call, Ferguson was granted an audience with the moody, dyspeptic editor in chief, and although he came armed with two samples of his writing in order to prove that he was not an illiterate numskull (an English paper on *King Lear* and a short, jocular poem that ended with the lines *If life is a dream, / What happens when I wake up?*), the bulbous, balding Imhoff barely glanced at them. I assume you know something about basketball, he said, and I assume you can write a coherent sentence, but what about newspapers—do you even bother to read them? Of course he read them, Ferguson replied, three papers every day. The *Star-Ledger* for local news, the *New York Times* for world and national news, and the *Herald Tribune* because it had the best writers.

The best? Imhoff said. And who in your opinion are the best?

Jimmy Breslin on politics for one. Red Smith on sports for another. And the music critic Gilbert Schneiderman, who happens to be the uncle of a close friend of mine.

Bully for you. And how many newspaper articles have you written, Mr. Hotshot?

I think you already know the answer to that question.

Ferguson didn't care. Not about what Imhoff thought of him, and not even if Imhoff turned him down for the job. His mother's boldness had emboldened him into a position of absolute indifference, and indifference had power, Ferguson realized, and no matter what the outcome of the interview, he wasn't going to let himself be pushed around by that bilious sack of haughtiness and bad manners.

Give me one good reason why I should hire you, Imhoff said.

Because you need someone to cover the game on Tuesday night, and I'm willing to do it. If you didn't want me to do it, why would you be wasting your precious time talking to me now?

Six hundred words, Imhoff said, as he slapped his palms against the desk. You fuck up, and you're out. You cut the mustard, and you get to live another day.

Writing a newspaper article was going to be different from any other kind of writing Ferguson had done in the past. Not just the writing of poems and short stories, which were so different from journalism they didn't even belong in the discussion, but also the other forms of nonfiction writing he had been engaged in for most of his life: personal letters (which sometimes reported on real events but were predominantly filled with opinions about himself and others: I love you, I hate you, I'm sad, I'm happy, our old friend turns out to be a despicable liar) and papers for school, such as his recent essay on *King Lear*, which was essentially a group of words responding to another group of words, as was the case with nearly all scholarly endeavors: words responding to words. By contrast, a newspaper article was a group of words responding to the world, an attempt to put the unwritten world into words, and in order to tell the story of an event that had occurred in the real world you paradoxically had to begin with the last thing that had happened rather than the first, the effect rather than the cause, not *George Bliffle woke up yesterday morning with a stomach ache* but *George Bliffle died last night at age seventy-seven*, with something about the stomach ache two or three paragraphs down. The facts above all else, and the most important fact before all other facts, but just because you had to stick to the facts didn't mean you were supposed to stop thinking or weren't allowed to use your imagination, as Red Smith had done earlier that year when reporting on the defeat of Sonny Liston for the heavyweight title: "Cassius Marcellus Clay fought his way out of the horde that swarmed and leaped and shouted in the ring, climbed like a squirrel onto the red velvet ropes and brandished his still-gloved hand aloft. 'Eat your words,' he howled to the working press rows. 'Eat your words.' " Just because you were confined to the real world didn't make you any less of a writer if you had it in you to write well.

Ferguson knew that sports were of no consequence in the long run, but they lent themselves to the written word more readily than most other subjects because each game had a built-in narrative structure, the agon of competition necessarily resulted in a victory for one team and a defeat for the other, and Ferguson's job was to tell the story of how the winner won and the loser lost, whether by one point or by twenty points, and when he showed up for the first game of the season on that Tuesday night in mid-December, he had already figured out how he was going to shape his story, since the central drama of the Montclair basketball team that year was the youth and inexperience of its players, not one member of the starting five had been a starter last season, eight seniors had graduated in June and with one exception the current squad was composed entirely of sophomores and juniors. That would be the thread that ran through his coverage of the team from game to game, Ferguson decided, charting whether a collection of raw beginners would evolve into a solid unit as the season unfolded or simply stagger along from one defeat to the next, and even though Imhoff had promised to boot him out if the first article failed to *deliver the goods*, Ferguson wasn't planning to fail, he most emphatically was not going to fail, and therefore he looked upon that first article as the opening chapter of a saga he would go on writing until the season ended after the eighteenth game in mid-February.

What he hadn't expected was how inordinately alive he would feel when he walked into the school gym and took his seat beside the official scorer at the table that straddled the midcourt line. Everything was suddenly different. No matter how many games he had seen in that gym over the years, no matter how many physical education classes he had attended there since entering high school, no matter how many indoor practice sessions he had taken part in there as a varsity baseball player, the gym was no longer the same gym that evening. It had been transformed into a site of potential words, the words he would write about the game that had just begun, and because it was his job to write those words, he had to look at what was happening more closely than he had ever looked at anything, and the sheer attentiveness and singularity of purpose that sort of looking required seemed to lift him up and fill his veins with massive jolts of electric current. The hair on his head was sizzling, his eyes were wide open, and he felt more alive than he had in weeks, alive and alert, all lit up and awake in the moment. He had a pocket-sized notebook with him, and all through the game he jotted down what he was seeing on the hardwood court, for long stretches he found himself seeing and writing simultaneously, the pressure to translate the unwritten world into written words was pulling out the words with surprising quickness, it was utterly unlike the slow, brooding agonies that went into writing a poem, all was speed now, all was haste, and almost without thinking about it he was writing down words such as *a short, redheaded ball handler with the quickness of a hamster* and *a skinny rebounding machine with elbows as deadly as sharpened pencils* and *a foul shot that fluttered in and out of the rim like an indecisive hummingbird*, and then, after Montclair fell to Bloomfield in *a closely fought 54–51 defeat*, Ferguson concluded the story with: *The Mountie faithful, unaccustomed to losing after an autumn of football perfection, shuffled out of the gym in silence.*

The article was due the following morning, so Ferguson rushed back home in the white Impala and went up to his room, where he spent the next three hours writing and rewriting the piece, whittling down the eight-hundred-word first draft to six hundred and fifty words and then down to five hundred ninety-seven, just under Imhoff's limit, which he typed up in a final typo-free version on his Olympia portable, the indomitable, German-made machine his parents had given him on his fifteenth birthday. Assuming Imhoff accepted the article, it would be the first bit of writing Ferguson had ever published outside of school magazines, and as he faced the imminent loss of his authorial virginity, he dithered back and forth about what name he should use to sign his work. *Archie* and *Archibald* had always posed a problem for him, *Archie* because of that damnable idiot in the comic books, Archie Andrews, the friend of Jughead and Moose, the birdbrained teenager who could never decide whether he loved the blond-haired Betty more than the dark-haired Veronica or vice versa, and *Archibald* because it was a fusty, oldfangled embarrassment that was all but defunct now, and the only literary man known as Archibald anywhere in the world was Ferguson's least favorite American poet, Archibald MacLeish, who won every prize and was considered to be *a national treasure* but was in fact a boring, no-talent dud. Except for his long-dead great-uncle, whom Ferguson had never met, the sole Archie-Archibald he felt any kinship with was Cary Grant, who had been born in England as Archibald Leach, but no sooner had the showman-acrobat come to America than he'd changed his name and turned himself into a Hollywood film star, which never would have happened if he had stuck with the name of *Archibald*. Ferguson liked being *Archie* to his friends and family, there was nothing wrong with *Archie* when he heard it in the intimate discourses of affection and love, but there was something juvenile and even laughable about *Archie* in a public context, especially for a writer, and because Archibald Ferguson was not to be considered under any circumstances, the almost eighteen-year-old budding newspaperman decided to suppress his name altogether and go with his initials, in the same way T. S. Eliot and H. L. Mencken had gone with theirs, and thus the career of A. I. Ferguson began. A.I.—known to some as a field of study called Artificial Intelligence—but there were other references buried in those letters as well, among them *Anonymous Insider*, which was the one Ferguson chose to think about whenever he saw his new name in print.

Because he had to go to school the next morning, his mother agreed to stop in at Imhoff's office and give him the article herself, since her studio was only two blocks from the *Times* building in downtown Montclair. A day of anxious breathing followed—would Ferguson be let in the door or shut out, would he be asked to cover Friday night's game or was his job as a basketball reporter finished after one game?—for now that he had taken the plunge, he was no longer indifferent, and pretending that he didn't care would have been a lie. Six and a half hours of school, and then the drive to Roseland Photo for the verdict, which his mother delivered with a certain dose of bemused irony:

It's all okay, Archie, she said, getting down to the most important fact first, he's running your story in tomorrow's paper, and you're hired for the rest of the basketball season, and the baseball season, too, if that's what you want, but good God, what a piece of work that man is, humphing and grumphing as I stood there watching him read your article, pouncing on your new pen name first of all—which I like a lot, by the way—but he couldn't get over what he called the *pretentiousness* of it, A.I., A.I., A.I., he kept saying it over and over, and then he would add, Asshole Intellectual, Arrogant Imbecile, Absolute Ignoramus, he couldn't stop himself from insulting you because he realized what you'd written was good, Archie, unexpectedly good, and a man like that doesn't want to encourage young people, he wants to crush them, so he picked on a couple of things just to show how superior he is to everyone else, the remark about the *indecisive hummingbird*, he just hated that one and crossed it out with his blue pencil, and a couple of other things made him snort or curse under his breath, but the upshot is that you're a working member of the local press now, or, in Ed Imhoff's words, when I asked him whether he wanted you or not, *The boy will do.* The boy will do! I burst out laughing when I heard that, and then I asked him, Is that all you have to say, Ed?, to which he answered, Isn't that enough? Well, maybe you'd like to thank me for finding you a new reporter, I said. Thank *you*? he said. No, my dear Rose, it's you who should be thanking *me*.

One way or another, Ferguson was in the door, and the good thing about the arrangement was that he rarely had to see or talk to Imhoff, since he was required to be at school on Wednesday and Monday mornings, the respective deadlines for the articles about the Tuesday and Friday night games, which were published together when the paper came out on Thursday afternoon. Ferguson's mother therefore continued to hand in the pieces to Imhoff, and although Ferguson went in twice for Saturday meetings with the Big Fish (in a small pond) to be dressed down for the sin of *overwriting* (if phrases such as *existential despair* and *a balletic move that challenged the principles of Newtonian physics* could be considered overwriting), most of his conversations with Imhoff took place on the telephone, as when the boss asked him to do a feature-length profile of the basketball coach, Jack McNulty, after the team won six in a row to lift its record to 9 and 7, or when he instructed Ferguson to start wearing a jacket and tie to the games because he was *a representative of the* Montclair Times *and needed to comport himself as a gentleman while carrying out his duties,* as if wearing a jacket and tie had anything to do with writing about basketball games, but those were the days when questions of clothing and hair had begun to divide the old and the young, and like many of the boys in his school Ferguson had let his hair grow longer that year, the old 1950s crew cuts were passé now, and changes were happening among the girls as well, more and more of them had stopped teasing their hair into the cotton-candy bouffants and beehives of yore and were simply brushing it out and letting it hang loosely around their shoulders, which Ferguson found far more attractive and sexy, and as he studied the human landscape in those early weeks of 1965, he felt that everyone was starting to look better, and there was something in the air that pleased him.

ON FEBRUARY SEVENTH, eight American soldiers were killed and 126 wounded in a Vietcong attack against a military base in Pleiku—and the bombing of North Vietnam began. Two weeks later, on February twenty-first, just days after the end of the high school basketball season, Malcolm X was gunned down by Nation of Islam assassins while delivering a speech at the Audubon Ballroom in Washington Heights. Those were the only two subjects that seemed to exist anymore, Ferguson wrote in a letter to his aunt and uncle in California, the expanding bloodshed in Vietnam and the civil rights movement at home, white America at war with the yellow people of Southeast Asia, white America in conflict with its own black citizens, who were more and more in conflict with themselves, for the movement that had already split into factions was splitting further into factions of factions and perhaps even factions of factions of factions, everyone in conflict with everyone else, the lines drawn so sharply that few dared step over them anymore, and so divided had the world become that when Ferguson innocently asked Rhonda Williams out on a date sometime in January, he discovered that those lines were now sheathed in barbed wire. This was the same Rhonda Williams he had known for the past ten years, the slender, talkative girl who was in most of his academic classes and who happened not to be a white person but a black person, as were many other students at Montclair High, which was the most racially integrated school in the area, a segment of northern New Jersey in which every one of the surrounding schools was nearly all white or nearly all black, and Rhonda Williams, whose family was wealthier than Ferguson's and who happened to have black skin, which in truth was pale brown skin, just one or two shades darker than Ferguson's skin, vivacious Rhonda Williams, who was the daughter of the chief of internal medicine at the V.A. hospital in nearby Orange and whose younger brother was a substitute guard on the Montclair basketball team, bright, college-bound Rhonda Williams, who had always been Ferguson's friend and shared his love of music, was consequently the first person who sprang to mind when he read that Sviatoslav Richter would be performing an all-Schubert program at the Mosque Theatre in Newark the Saturday after next, and so he asked Rhonda if she would like to go with him, not just because he thought she would enjoy the concert but because it had been two months since he had last seen Amy and he was aching for female companionship, longing to be with someone who was not a basketball player or Bobby George or odious Edward Imhoff, and of all the girls in his school, Rhonda was the one he liked best. The prospect of an early Saturday night meal at the Claremont Diner and then Schubert played by one of the world's finest pianists struck Ferguson as something no music lover would want to turn down, but incredibly enough she did turn him down, and when Ferguson asked her why, Rhonda said:

I just can't, Archie.

Does that mean you have a boyfriend I don't know about?

No, there's no boyfriend. I just can't.

But why? If you're not busy that night, what's the problem?

I'd rather not say.

Come on, Rhonda, that's not fair. This is me, remember? Your old friend Archie.

You're smart enough to figure it out for yourself.

No, I'm not. I can't even begin to guess what you're talking about.

Because you're white, that's why. Because you're white, and I'm black.

Is that a reason?

I think it is.

I'm not asking you to marry me. I just want to go to a concert with you.

I know, and I appreciate your asking me, but I can't.

Please tell me it's because you don't like me. That I can accept.

But I do like you, Archie. You know that. I've always liked you.

Do you realize what you're saying?

Of course I do.

It's the end of the world, Rhonda.

No, it's not. It's the beginning—the beginning of a new world—and you just have to accept it.

Whether it was the end of the world or the beginning of the world, Ferguson would never bring himself to accept it, and he walked away from that conversation feeling both sucker-punched and angry, appalled that such a conversation could still have been possible one hundred years after the end of the Civil War. He wanted to talk to someone about it, to pour out the thousand reasons why he was so upset by what had happened, but the only person he had ever been able to open up to about such things was Amy, and Amy was the one person he couldn't talk to now, and as for his friends at school, there was no one he trusted deeply enough to confide in anymore, and even Bobby, who still rode to school with him every morning and continued to regard himself as Ferguson's staunchest pal, wouldn't have had much to contribute to a discussion of that sort, and besides, Bobby was having problems of his own just then, love problems of the most devastating adolescent variety, an unrequited crush on Margaret O'Mara, who herself had had a crush on Ferguson for the past six years, which was now causing no end of trouble and consternation for Ferguson, since immediately after his post-Thanksgiving talk with Amy he had toyed with the idea of asking Margaret out on a date, not that he had any burning desire to become entangled with Margaret, who was a dull, friendly girl with an uncommonly attractive face, but after Amy had declared her interest in kissing other boys Ferguson had wondered, not without some bitterness, whether he shouldn't respond by going out to look for other girls to kiss, and Margaret O'Mara was a prime candidate because he felt almost certain she would want to be kissed by him, but then, just as he was preparing himself to call her, Bobby had confessed how enamored he was of the same Margaret O'Mara, who was the first monumental love of his life, but she seemed to have no interest in him, she barely even listened when he talked to her, and would Ferguson kindly intercede on his behalf and explain to Margaret what a good and worthy fellow he was (shades of *Cyrano de Bergerac,* a film that Ferguson and Margaret had seen together in their tenth-grade French class), and so when Ferguson went to Margaret and tried to put in a word for Bobby (instead of asking her out himself), she laughed at him and called him *Cyrano.* The laugh was the end of it—resulting in a double washout, failure on both fronts. Bobby was still pining for her, and even though Margaret would have leapt at the chance to go out with Ferguson, Ferguson had resolved not to ask her out because he couldn't do that to his friend. Which led to no dates with anyone for the next two months, and then, when he did ask someone out, it was Rhonda Williams, who politely kicked him in the face and taught him that the America he wanted to live in didn't exist—and probably never would.

Under different circumstances, he might have gone to his mother and talked out his frustrations with her, but he was feeling too old for that now, and he didn't want to depress her with a long emotional rant about the bleak future he envisioned for the Republic. His parents' future was already bleak enough, and with income dwindling from both Roseland Photo and Stanley's TV & Radio, and with the supplemental fifteen thousand all but exhausted now, drastic changes were imminent, it was only a matter of time before the family would have to rethink how it lived and worked and perhaps even where it lived and where it worked. Ferguson felt especially sorry for his father, whose small retail business could no longer compete with the large discount stores that were popping up in towns such as Livingston, West Orange, and Short Hills, and why would anyone want to buy a television from Ferguson's father when the same set could be found for forty percent less at E. J. Korvette's just a few miles away? When Mike Antonelli was let go in the second week of January, Ferguson understood that the store was on its last legs, but still his father persisted in maintaining the old routine, arriving at nine sharp every morning to install himself at his workbench in the back room, where he continued to repair broken toasters and badly functioning vacuum cleaners, more and more reminding Ferguson of old Dr. Manette from *A Tale of Two Cities*, the half-deranged prisoner of the Bastille who sat at the bench in his cell cobbling shoes, year after year cobbling shoes, year after year fixing damaged household appliances, and more and more Ferguson came to acknowledge the incontestable fact that his father had never fully recovered from Arnold's betrayal, that his faith in the family had been destroyed, and then, in the ruins of his crumbled certainties, the one person in the family he still loved had crashed her car into a tree and maimed his son for life, and even though he never talked about the accident, both Ferguson and his mother knew that he rarely stopped thinking about it.

The fortunes of Roseland Photo were also sinking, not as quickly as those of Stanley's TV & Radio, perhaps, but Ferguson's mother knew the days of studio photography were nearly done, and for some time she had been reducing the number of hours she kept the studio open, from five ten-hour days in 1953 to five eight-hour days in 1956 to four eight-hour days in 1959 to four six-hour days in 1961 to three six-hour days in 1962 to three four-hour days in 1963, devoting more and more of her energies to photo work for Imhoff at the *Montclair Times*, where she had been put on salary as the paper's chief photographer, but then her book of Garden State notables was published in February 1965, and within two months the book had landed in the waiting rooms of most doctors' offices, dentists' offices, lawyers' offices, and municipal offices around the state, and Rose Ferguson was no longer an invisible no one but a recognizable someone, and on the strength of her success with the book, she decided to go to the editor of the *Newark Star-Ledger* (whose picture was in the book) and ask for a job as a staff photographer, for even though Ferguson's mother was forty-three by then (too old, perhaps?), to most people she looked six or eight years younger than that, and as the editor scanned the contents of her voluminous portfolio and remembered the flattering portrait she had taken of him, which was hanging on a wall in his den at home, he suddenly reached out and shook her hand, for the fact was that they did have an opening, and Rose Ferguson was just as qualified to fill that slot as anyone else. The salary wasn't much, more or less the same amount she had managed to cobble together with studio portraits and her work with Imhoff in an average year, which would neither hurt nor help the family's overall financial situation, but then Ferguson's father came up with the bright idea of shutting down Stanley's TV & Radio, which had been running in the red for the past three years, and a negative was turned into a positive, which became slightly more positive when Sam Brownstein talked him into accepting a job at his sporting goods store in Newark (or, as Ferguson's father put it, in one of his rare moments of levity, *trading in air conditioners for catcher's gloves*), and thus, in the spring of 1965, both Roseland Photo and Stanley's TV & Radio closed their doors for good, and with Ferguson about to go off to college in the fall, his parents said it was time to start thinking about selling the house and renting a smaller place closer to their new jobs, which would free up more than enough money to cover Ferguson's college expenses, since for some reason Ferguson's father was opposed to the idea of asking for a scholarship (stupid pride or proud stupidity?) or reducing the burden by taking part in a work-study program, because, as his father explained, he didn't want his boy *to work while he studied but to work at his studies*, and when Ferguson protested that his father was being absurd, his mother walked over to his father, kissed him on the cheek, and said: No, Archie, you're the one who's absurd.

FERGUSON'S BIRTHDAY FELL on a Wednesday that year. He was eighteen now, which gave him the right to drink alcohol in any bar or restaurant in New York City, to marry without his parents' consent, to die for his country, to be judged as a man in a court of law, but not to vote in municipal, state, or federal elections. The next afternoon, March fourth, he came home from school to find a letter from Amy sitting in the mailbox. *Dear Archie,* it said, *A big kiss to you on your birthday. Soon, my sweetheart, sooner and sooner and sooner—as long as you're still interested. I've done my best not to think about you, but it hasn't worked. Such a chilly winter it's been, living in this room with the windows open. I'm freezing! Love, Amy.*

Not knowing what *soon* meant, much less *sooner and sooner and sooner,*

Ferguson couldn't quite make sense of what Amy had written, although the tone of the letter seemed encouraging. He was tempted to respond with a gushing letter of his own, but then he decided to wait until the question of college had been settled, which wouldn't happen until the middle of next month. On the other hand, if Amy sent another letter before then, he would write back at once—but she didn't, and the standoff continued. Ferguson imagined he was being strong, but later on, when he looked back on his actions from the perspective of his future self, he understood that he was merely being stubborn. Stubbornly proud, which was finally just another term for *stupid*.

On March seventh, two hundred Alabama state troopers attacked 525 civil rights demonstrators in Selma as they were preparing to cross the Edmund Pettus Bridge and begin a march toward Montgomery to protest voting rights discrimination. Forever after, that date would be remembered as *Bloody Sunday*.

The next morning, U.S. Marines landed in Vietnam. The two battalions, which had been sent to protect the air base in Da Nang, were the first combat forces to be posted in the country. U.S. personnel in Vietnam was now up to 23,000. By late July, the number would be increased to 125,000 and draft quotas would be doubled.

On March eleventh, the Reverend James J. Reeb of Boston, Massachusetts, was beaten to death in Selma. Two other white Unitarian ministers were injured in the attack.

Six days later, a local judge ruled that the march from Selma to Montgomery could proceed. President Johnson federalized the state National Guard, and after he sent in another 2,200 troops to protect the demonstrators, the walk began on March twenty-first. That same evening, Viola Liuzzo, a mother of five from Detroit, who had driven down to Alabama to take part in the action, was shot to death in her car by members of the Ku Klux Klan because a black man was sitting next to her in the front seat.

On Monday (March twenty-second), a distraught, bewildered Ferguson began working for the *Montclair Times* again. A month had gone by since the end of the basketball season, and now it was time for baseball, dreaded, beautiful baseball, which would be an entirely different proposition from covering basketball, so much so that Ferguson had initially thought he wouldn't be up to doing it, but not writing for the paper had been hard on him, he had missed reporting on the games in the way a smoker misses cigarettes when the pack runs out, and the extra time he had been given to work on his poems had not produced any poems worth mentioning, nothing but a string of failed poems that had so discouraged him that he was beginning to question whether he had any gift for poetry at all, and now that he was fourteen months removed from the accident and a full season removed from any involvement with baseball, perhaps the moment had come to test himself and see whether he could walk back onto a ball field without tumbling into a funk of useless sorrows and regrets. There would be the excitement of high-speed electric writing, he told himself, there would be the fun of watching Bobby George swat balls over the fence and of talking to the big-league scouts who would surely be coming around to look at Bobby, and as long as he could endure not being part of it anymore, there would be the old sensations of smelling the cut grass and looking up at white balls darting across blue skies and hearing the sounds of balls colliding with bats and leather gloves, and those things he would welcome, he thought, would welcome because he had missed them so much, and therefore, without once sharing his qualms with Imhoff, he kept to the bargain they had struck in December and went into Sal Martino's office on March twenty-second to interview the coach about the upcoming season, which turned into the first of twenty-one articles he wrote that spring about the Montclair High School varsity baseball team.

It wasn't as difficult as he had thought it would be, in fact it wasn't difficult at all, and when the season opened with an away game at Columbia High School in early April, Ferguson drove there thinking less about the game that would be played that afternoon than the words he would use to write about it. He felt infinitely older than he had felt a year ago, so much older than anyone else his age, especially the boys on the team, which would have been his team as well if not for the accident, and just to prove how thoroughly things had changed for him, when he dropped off his Impala at Krolik's Garage for a tune-up the following week and rode on the team bus to another away game in East Orange, he sat up front with Sal Martino rather than with his classmates in the back, for the boisterous wisecracking and loud laughter of the boys had lost its appeal to him, and suddenly one more childish thing had been put behind him, and it was strange to feel so old, he said to himself, strange because it made him feel both sad and glad at the same time, which was a new emotion for him, something unprecedented in the history of his emotional life, sadness and gladness merging into a single mountain of feeling, and once that image occurred to him, he found himself thinking about the White Rock girl on the seltzer bottle and his conversation with Aunt Mildred about Psyche six years ago when they had discussed the transformation of caterpillars into butterflies, for the puzzling thing about turning from the one into the other was that caterpillars were probably quite content to be caterpillars, creeping over the earth without once thinking about becoming something else, and sad as it must have been for them to stop being caterpillars, surely it was better and altogether astonishing to start over again as butterflies, even if the life of a butterfly was more precarious and sometimes lasted just a single day.

In the first five games of the season, the lovesick Bobby George hit four doubles, three home runs, and had a .632 average with five walks and eight runs batted in. Whatever Margaret O'Mara had done to the poor boy's heart, she hadn't affected his ability to play baseball. *And just think*, a scout for the Minnesota Twins said to Ferguson as he watched Bobby throw out a runner at second base, *the kid won't be eighteen until the summer.*

On April sixteenth, Ferguson finally sat down and wrote a short letter to Amy. *I'm in*, he began. *Columbia has accepted me as a member of the class of '69—a deliciously evocative number that seems to suggest all sorts of exciting activities in the future. Unlike you, I haven't made any effort not to think about you but have kept you in mind steadily and lovingly (and sometimes despondently) for the past four and a half months. So yes, in reply to your rhetorical question, I am still interested and will always be interested and will never not be interested because I love you madly and cannot bear to think of living my life without you. Please tell me when it will be possible to see you again. Your Archie.*

She didn't bother to write this time but called, called him at home just hours after she had received the letter, and the first thing that struck him was how good it was to hear her voice again, her New York voice with the softened r's that turned his name into something that sounded like *Ahchie*, and an instant later she was repeating the last sentence of his note, saying *When will it be possible to see me?*, to which he said, *That's right, when?*, and out came the answer he had been hoping she would give him: *Anytime you like. Anytime starting now.*

And so the banished Ferguson once again found himself in the good graces of his temperamental queen, and because she judged him to have behaved nobly during his exile, with no begging letters or phone calls, no whining exhortations to be reinstated to his former position at court, the first words she said to him when he drove into New York to see her the following night were *You're my one and only, Archie, my one in a million one and only*, and because she started to cry the moment he put his arms around her, Ferguson suspected that life had been somewhat rocky for her in the past four and a half months, that there were things she felt ashamed of having done, no doubt things concerning sex, and for that reason he decided not to ask her any questions, not then and not ever, for he didn't want to hear about the other people she had slept with and have to imagine her naked body in bed with another naked body sporting a long, fat erection that was traveling into the space between her parted legs, no names or descriptions, please, not one detail of any kind, and since he didn't ask her any of the questions she must have been expecting him to ask, she clung to him all the more tightly because of that.

It was the most beautiful spring of his life, the spring of being with Amy again, of having Amy to talk to again, of holding the naked Amy in his arms again, of listening to Amy blast forth against Johnson and the CIA for shipping twenty thousand soldiers down to the Dominican Republic to stop the freely elected writer-historian Juan Bosch from reclaiming the presidency because he was supposedly under the influence of the Communists, which was untrue, and why meddle in that little country's business when America was already doing so much damage in other parts of the world? How Ferguson admired her for the purity of her indignation, and how satisfying it was to be spending the weekends with her in New York again, which in a few short months would be where he lived as well, and beyond Amy the spring was beautiful because his worries about next year were at last behind him, which meant he could slack off for the first time in all the years he had been in school, just as everyone else in the senior class was slacking off during those two months of *dolce far poco*, which had somehow reduced ancient conflicts and animosities and seemed to be drawing everyone closer together as the end of their lives together approached, and then, as the weather warmed up, there was the new ritual he established with his father, the two of them waking at six o'clock every weekday morning and leaving the house by six-thirty for an hour or an hour and a half of tennis on the empty public courts in town, his fifty-one-year-old father still able to beat him in every set by scores of 6–2 and 6–3, but the exercise was putting Ferguson back in shape, and after a long stretch of no sports since the day of the crack-up the tennis was fulfilling an old and still powerful need in him, and he was glad to see his father win, glad to see how painless it was for the old man to be dismantling his store, selling off the remaining stock of TVs, radios, and air conditioners for one-third off, one-half off, two-thirds off, the struggle was over now, his father no longer cared about anything, all his former ambitions had vanished into thin air, and with his mother in the process of dismantling her own business as well, each of them scheduled to vacate by May thirtieth and start their new jobs in mid-June, there was something giddy about them that spring, giddy in the way small, exuberant children could be when someone grabbed hold of their ankles and turned them upside down, as he and Amy must have been when they bounced naked on the bed together during those blacked-out moments of the distant past, and how lucky it was that even after his mother had given the *Montclair Times* notice of her impending departure, Imhoff hadn't sacked him out of revenge, so Ferguson was continuing to cover the twice-weekly baseball games of the Montclair varsity, and with Bobby George on his way to a first-team all-state season and most likely a contract with a major league club, Ferguson was impressed by how well Bobby was handling his newfound stardom, which had made him the talk of the school, and even though he was still battling with his studies and couldn't resist laughing at unfunny jokes about farmers' daughters and traveling salesmen, there was a new aura of greatness around him, which was slowly beginning to seep into Bobby and change how he thought about himself, and now that Margaret O'Mara had started talking to him, one seldom saw Bobby walking around without a smile on his face, the same sweet smile Ferguson remembered from their days together as four- and five-year-old boys.

One of the best things about that beautiful spring was anticipating the summer, making plans with Amy for the trip they were going to take to France, a month-long journey from the middle of July to the

middle of August, one month because that was all they could afford
after stitching together money saved from past summer jobs, the fees
from Ferguson's *Montclair Times* articles that had not been spent on
gas for his car and hamburgers for his stomach, a sizable graduation
present from Ferguson's grandparents (five hundred dollars), a smaller
contribution from Amy's paternal grandfather, and additional sums
chipped in by both sets of parents, which would cover four and a half
weeks of bare-bones living once the fares for the charter flight had been
dispensed with, so rather than try to cram a grand European tour into
that limited amount of time, they chose to stick to one country and
immerse themselves in it as fully as they could. France was the inevitable choice because they were both studying French and wanted to
become more fluent in the language, but also because France was the
center of all things that were not American, with the best poets, the best
novelists, the best filmmakers, the best philosophers, the best museums,
and the best food, and with no luggage but the knapsacks on their backs
they left American soil from Kennedy Airport at eight o'clock in the evening on July fifteenth, one day after the annual celebration of Bastille
Day in France. It was their first trip abroad. For Ferguson, it was also
the first time he had flown in an airplane, which meant it was the first
time he had ever lost contact with the earth.

Paris for the most part, Paris for twenty-two of the thirty-one days
they spent in France, with one excursion by train to the north (Normandy and Brittany, with visits to Omaha Beach, Mont Saint-Michel,
and Chateaubriand's family castle in Saint-Malo) and one excursion to
the south (Marseille, Arles, Avignon, and Nîmes). A vow to converse in
French with each other as often as possible, to shun American tourists,
to strike up conversations with local residents in order to practice their
French, to read only French books and newspapers, to see only French
films, to send home postcards written in French. The Paris hotel they
lived in was so obscure that it didn't even have a name. The sign above
the front door simply read HOTEL, and the simple room they shared on
the rue Clément in the sixth arrondissement, directly facing the Marché
Saint-Germain, the small but large enough *chambre dix-huit*, which had
no telephone or television or radio in it, which was equipped with a cold-
water sink but no toilet, cost ten francs a night, the equivalent of two
dollars, which came to one dollar apiece, and what difference did it make
that the toilet down the hall wasn't always free when you wanted to use

it, or that the shower was a cramped metal box jammed into the wall at the top of the stairs and wasn't always free when you wanted to use it, the essential thing was that the room was clean and light and that the bed was big enough for two people to sleep in it comfortably, and even more essential was the fact that the owner of the hotel, a stout man with a mustache named Antoine, could not have cared less that Ferguson and Amy were sharing that bed, even though they were clearly not married and were young enough to have been Antoine's children.

That was the first thing that endeared them to France (the blessed indifference to the private lives of others), but more things soon followed, such as the hard-to-understand fact that everything seemed to smell better in Paris than in New York, not just the bakeries and restaurants and cafés but even the nethermost bowels of the metro, where the disinfectant used to wash down the floors was scented with something akin to perfume, whereas the New York subways were rank and often unbreathable, and the constant motion of the sky, with clouds continually massing overhead and then breaking apart, which created a shimmering, mutating sort of light that was both soft and full of surprises, and the northern latitude that kept the midsummer sky aglow for many more hours than at home, still not dark until ten-thirty or a quarter to eleven at night, and the pleasure of simply wandering through the streets, of being lost and yet never fully lost, as in the streets of the Village in New York, but now an entire city was like the Village, with no grid and few right angles in the neighborhoods they went to as one sinuous, cobbled path wound around and flowed into another, and of course there was the food, *la cuisine française*, rapturously ingested at the one restaurant meal they had every night after a breakfast of buttered bread and coffee (*tartine beurré* and *café crème*) and a lunch of homemade ham sandwiches (*jambon de Paris*) or homemade cheese sandwiches (*gruyère, camembert, emmental*), nightly dinners at the good but inexpensive restaurants noted in *Europe on Five Dollars a Day*, and at places such as Le Restaurant des Beaux Arts and Wadja in Montparnasse and La Crémerie Polidor (supposedly one of James Joyce's eating spots), they dug into foods and dishes they had never encountered in New York or anywhere else, *poireaux vinaigrette, rillettes, escargots, céleri rémoulade, coq au vin, pot au feu, quenelles, bavette, cassoulet, fraises au crème chantilly*, and the beguiling sugar bomb known as *baba au rhum*. Within a week of setting foot in Paris, they had both turned into rabid Francophiles, with

Amy suddenly announcing her decision to major in French as she worked her way through novels by Flaubert and Stendhal and Ferguson made his first halting attempts to translate French poetry as he sat in *chambre dix-huit* or the back room at La Palette and read Apollinaire, Éluard, Desnos, and other pre-war French poets for the first time.

Needless to say, there were moments when they quarreled and got on each other's nerves, for they were together nearly every second for thirty-one days and nights, and Amy was a person prone to the occasional storm and foul-mouthed snit, and Ferguson had a tendency to lapse into fugues of morose introspection and/or inexplicable silences, but none of their disagreements lasted more than an hour or two, and most if not all of them occurred while they were on the road, under the duress of travel and sleepless nights on trains. Needless to say as well, America was constantly on their minds throughout the trip, even if they were glad to be away from it for the time being, and they talked at length about the two encouraging things that happened while they were gone—Johnson signing the Medicare Bill on July thirtieth and then the Voting Rights Act on August sixth—and also about the calamitous thing that happened on August eleventh, just five days before they flew home: the race riots in Los Angeles, the rage riots of the black population in a neighborhood called Watts. After which Amy said: Forget about studying French. My first impulse was the right one all along. History and political science. To which Ferguson raised an imaginary glass and said: Ask not what your country can do for you. Ask Amy Schneiderman to run your country.

The day before they were scheduled to return to New York, they made two embarrassing discoveries: 1) they had bought too many books to carry on the plane; 2) their money was precariously low—no doubt because buying books had not been factored into their budget. They had both lost weight during their month abroad (Ferguson seven pounds, Amy five pounds), but that was to be expected of people determined to subsist on only one full meal a day, and yet in spite of those economies they had overspent on their frequent visits to bookstores, mostly to the Librairie Gallimard across from l'Église Saint-Germain and to the shop run by left-wing publisher François Maspero across from l'Église Saint-Séverin, and in addition to the twenty-one volumes of poetry Ferguson had bought and the eleven thick novels Amy had bought, they had been unable to resist purchasing a number of political books by Frantz Fanon (*Les Damnés de la terre*), Paul Nizan (*Aden Arabie*), and Jean-Paul Sartre (*Situations I, II, III*), which increased the total to thirty-seven books. Several hours of their last day in Paris were therefore squandered on packing up those books in cartons, lugging them to the post office, and shipping them to Amy's apartment on West 111th Street (all of them to Amy's apartment, even the ones that belonged to Ferguson, because his parents had accepted a down payment on their house in early June and it was unclear whether they were still living in Montclair or had moved somewhere else by now), and the cost of the stamps required to send those cartons across the ocean by slow boat—with delivery expected sometime around Christmas—so depleted their remaining cash that they were left with just fourteen dollars, eight of which would be needed for the bus ride to the airport in the morning. Their plans for a large farewell meal at the Restaurant des Beaux Arts that evening were consequently destroyed, and they were reduced to dining on flat, dessicated hamburgers at the Wimpy's on Boulevard Saint-Michel. Fortunately, they both found it funny, for bad planning on that scale proved that they were indeed the Most Ridiculous People on Earth.

So the skinny, bedraggled eighteen-year-olds returned from their Gallic adventures, hobbling into the New York air terminal with their overloaded backpacks and bushy heads of hair, and once they had gone through passport control and customs, their parents opened their arms and welcomed them back, greeting them with an enthusiasm and intensity normally reserved for returning war heroes and discoverers of new continents. Amy and Ferguson, who had already arranged to meet up again in a couple of days, kissed each other good-bye, and then they marched off with their respective families to be driven home for baths, haircuts, and brief visits with their parents, grandparents, and aunts and uncles.

As Ferguson quickly learned while walking to the car, home was no longer the house in Montclair but an apartment in the Weequahic section of Newark. Neither one of his parents seemed upset by this backward move out of the suburbs, this apparent fall in social status, or economic status, or worldly status, or any other measure of what constituted success or failure in American life, which relieved him of the obligation to feel upset on their behalf, for the truth was that he didn't care one way or the other.

His mother was laughing. Not only are we back in Newark, she said, but we're in the same building we used to live in when we were first married—25 Van Velsor Place. Not the same apartment, but one on the same floor, the third floor, right across the hall from where you spent the first three years of your life. Pretty extraordinary, don't you think? I wonder if you'll remember anything about it. An identical apartment, Archie. Not the same one, but one just like it.

An hour later, when Ferguson stepped into the two-bedroom flat on the third floor of 25 Van Velsor Place, he was impressed by how cozy and lived-in it felt after such a short time. In just three weeks his parents had already managed to settle in, and compared to the narrow confines of *chambre dix-huit*, its proportions struck him as immense. Nothing like the house in Montclair, of course, but big enough.

Well, Archie? his mother said, as he wandered in and out of the rooms, does anything come back to you?

Ferguson wished he could have thought of some clever remark to echo the hopefulness in his mother's voice, but all he could do was shake his head and smile.

He remembered nothing.

4.2

43

THE SUMMER OF 1962 BEGAN WITH A TRIP TO A FAR-OFF PLACE and ended with a second trip to an even farther far-off place, four back-and-forth journeys by air that took Ferguson to California (by himself) and to Paris (with his mother and Gil), where he spent a total of two and a half weeks not having to worry about running into Andy Cohen. In between his travels, he stayed at home on Riverside Drive, avoiding the Thalia but going to as many old and new movies as he could, participating in two outdoor basketball leagues, and, at Gil's suggestion, reading twentieth-century American literature for the first time (*Babbitt, Manhattan Transfer, Light in August, In Our Time, The Great Gatsby*), but for the fifteen-year-old Ferguson, who never once laid eyes on Andy Cohen during the months between his freshman and sophomore years, the most memorable part of the summer was traveling in airplanes for the first time and seeing what he saw and doing what he did in California and Paris. *Memorable*, of course, did not mean that all his memories were good ones, but even the worst one, the memory that continued to cause him the most pain, had come from an experience that proved to be instructive to him, and now that he had learned his lesson, he hoped he would never make the same mistake again.

The California trip was a present from his Aunt Mildred, the once elusive and mysterious relative who had boycotted her sister's wedding in 1959 and had appeared to want nothing more to do with the family, but she had returned to New York twice since that nasty, inexplicable snub, once for her father's funeral in 1960 and again for her mother's funeral in 1961, and now she was back in the fold, on reasonably good terms with her sister again and on excellent terms with her new brother-in-law, and so changed was her attitude that on the second visit she willingly showed up for a dinner at the apartment on Riverside Drive, where one of the guests was her ex-husband, Paul Sandler, Ferguson's former uncle, who had remained a fast friend of the Adler-Schneiderman household, Paul Sandler in the company of his second wife no less, a forthright, outspoken painter by the name of Judith Bogat, and Ferguson was impressed by how relaxed and comfortable his aunt seemed at that dinner, trading pleasantries with her ex as if there were no history between them, discussing the progress of the not-yet-completed Lincoln Center with Gil, actually deigning to compliment her sister on some of her recent photographs, and asking Ferguson all sorts of friendly, challenging questions about films and basketball and the agonies of adolescence, which led to a sudden, spontaneous invitation to visit her in Palo Alto—*on her dime*—and thus it was arranged that her nephew would fly out to spend a week with her after the end of the school year. Two hours later, as the last of the dinner guests dispersed into the night, Ferguson asked his mother why Aunt Mildred seemed so different now, so *happy*.

I think she's in love, his mother said. I don't know any of the details, but she mentioned a person named Sidney a couple of times, and I have a feeling they might be living together now. You can never tell with Mildred, but there's no question she's in a good mood these days.

He was expecting his aunt to meet him at the airport, but someone else was waiting for him in the terminal the day he landed in San Francisco, a younger woman of perhaps twenty-five or twenty-six who stood by the exit door holding up a copy of Mildred's book on George Eliot, a diminutive, lively-looking, almost pretty girl with short brown hair dressed in blue jeans rolled up at the bottoms, a red-and-black checkered shirt, two-toned alligator boots with pointy tips, and a yellow bandanna cinched around her neck—Ferguson's first Westerner, a genuine cowgirl!

The *Sidney* Ferguson's mother had told him about was in fact *Sydney*, a Sydney with the last name of Millbanks, and as the young woman accompanied the weary traveler out of the terminal and led him toward

her car in the parking lot, she explained that Mildred was teaching summer classes that quarter and had been held up at a department meeting
on campus, but she would be joining them for dinner at the house in a
couple of hours.

Ferguson inhaled his first whiff of California air and said: Are you
the cook?

Cook, housekeeper, back rubber, and bedmate, Sydney replied. I
hope you aren't shocked.

The truth was that Ferguson did feel a little shocked, or at least surprised, or perhaps confused, since this was the first time he had heard
of two people of the same sex living together, and no one had ever told
him or dropped the smallest hint that his aunt secretly preferred the
bodies of women to the bodies of men. The divorce from Uncle Paul had
an explanation now, or seemed to have an explanation, but even more
interesting was that Sydney the cowgirl saw no point in hiding the truth
from him, and there was something admirable about her candor, he
thought, it was good not to feel ashamed of being *different*, and so rather
than admit to being a little shocked or confused by this unexpected
revelation, Ferguson smiled and said: No, not at all. I'm just happy that
Aunt Mildred isn't alone anymore.

It took about forty minutes to drive from the San Francisco airport
to the house in Palo Alto, and as Sydney tooled down the freeway in
her pale green Saab, she told Ferguson about how she had met Mildred
some years back when she was looking for a new place to live and had
rented the garage apartment attached to her house. In other words, it
had been an accidental meeting, something that never would have happened if she hadn't stumbled across four lines of minuscule type in a
newspaper, but not long after she settled in they had become friends,
and a couple of months after that they had fallen in love. Neither one of
them had been with a woman before, but there they were, Sydney said,
a university professor and a third-grade schoolteacher, a woman in her
early forties and a woman in her mid-twenties, a Jew from New York
and a Methodist from Sandusky, Ohio, swept up in the greatest romance
of their lives. The most confounding thing about it, Sydney continued,
was that she had never thought about women in the past, she had always
been a girl who was crazy for boys, and even now, after being *shacked
up* with a woman for close to three years, she still didn't think of herself

as a lesbian, she was simply a person in love with another person, and because that other person was beautiful and entrancing and unlike anyone else in the world, what difference did it make if she was in love with a man or a woman?

She probably shouldn't have been talking to him in that way. No doubt there was something inappropriate and perhaps indecent for a grown woman to be sharing such confidences with a fifteen-year-old boy, but the fifteen-year-old Ferguson was thrilled by her openness, at no point in his adolescence had any adult ever been so honest with him about the chaos and ambiguities of erotic life, and even though he had only just met Sydney Millbanks, Ferguson decided that he liked her, that he liked her enormously, and because he himself had been wrestling with these same matters for the past several months, struggling to figure out where he stood on the boy-girl spectrum of desire and whether he belonged in the zone of boys and girls or boys and boys or girls and boys interchangeably, he felt that this California cowgirl, this lover of both men and women, this person who had just entered his life and was taking him to his aunt's house in Palo Alto, might be someone he could talk to without fear of being laughed at or insulted or misunderstood.

I agree, Ferguson said. It doesn't matter if it's a man or a woman.

Not many people think that way, Archie. You know that, don't you?

Yes, I know, but I'm not many people, I'm just me, and the weird thing about me so far is that the only sex I've ever had was with another boy.

That's very common for people your age. So common that you shouldn't worry about it—just in case you *have* been worrying. What's a boy to do, right?

Ferguson laughed.

I hope you enjoyed it, at least, Sydney said.

I enjoyed *it*, but after a while I didn't enjoy *him*, so I put a stop to it.

And now you're wondering: What's next?

Until I get a chance to do it with a girl, I won't really know what's next.

It's not much fun being fifteen, is it?

It has its good points, I suppose.

Really? Name one.

Ferguson closed his eyes, paused for a long moment, and then turned to her and said: The best thing about being fifteen is that you don't have to be fifteen for more than a year.

THERE WERE NO flies or mosquitoes in California, and the Palo Alto air smelled like a box of cough drops, spicy-sweet throat lozenges with a eucalyptus flavor because eucalyptus trees turned out to be everywhere, giving off an all-pervasive scent that seemed to cleanse your nasal passages every time you inhaled. Vicks VapoRub dispensed free of charge into the northern California atmosphere for the health and happiness of the human population!

The town, on the other hand, felt bizarre to Ferguson, less a real place than the idea of a place, a quasi-urban-quasi-suburban outpost designed by a master planner with no tolerance for dirt or imperfection, which made the town seem dull and artificial, a quaint little Spookville inhabited by people with trim haircuts and straight white teeth, all of them dressed in good-looking, up-to-the-minute casual clothes. Luckily, Ferguson didn't spend much time there, going once to shop for groceries with Sydney in the largest, cleanest, most beautiful supermarket he had ever seen, once to a filling station to put gas in her primitive, lawn-mower-engine Saab (seven parts gasoline to one part oil, both poured directly into the tank), and twice to the local art house theater to watch films in that week's Carole Lombard Festival (*My Man Godfrey*, *To Be or Not to Be*), primarily because Sydney believed Mildred bore a strong resemblance to Carole Lombard, which, upon reflection, Ferguson granted was more or less true, but what splendid comedies those films were, and now that he had seen them, not only did Ferguson have a new actress to admire but a new insight into Aunt Mildred, who had laughed harder at those films than anyone else, and since Ferguson's mother had often told him how her big sister had mocked her in the old days for liking movies so much, he wondered if love hadn't softened his aunt's attitude toward what she had once called *trashy, low-life entertainment* or if she had always been a hypocrite, lording it over her sister by asserting her superior taste and intelligence in all things while privately reveling in the same trash everyone else did.

Twice, the three of them left Palo Alto and went on all-day excursions in Mildred's black Peugeot, first to Mount Tamalpais on Wednesday, with a return trip down the coast that included a two-hour pause at Bodega Bay, where they had dinner in a restaurant overlooking the water, and a Saturday outing to San Francisco that triggered dozens of tourist yelps from the startled Ferguson as they drove up and down the steep hills and then stopped for lunch at a Chinese restaurant where he ate dim sum for the first time (food that tasted so good his eyes filled with tears as he gorged himself on three different varieties of dumplings— tears of thanks, tears of joy, tears of hot sauce surging through his nostrils), but for the most part Mildred was busy with her classes and student conferences that week, which meant that until she came home for dinner at six or six-thirty Ferguson was either alone or with Sydney, although far less alone than with Sydney, who was on a ten-week vacation from her school, just as he was from his, and because Sydney professed to being *the laziest person in the world*, a title Ferguson had always thought belonged exclusively to him, they spent the bulk of their time together sprawled out on blankets in the yard behind the house, which was a one-story stucco cottage with a terra-cotta roof, or inside the house, which was pleasantly cluttered with books and rec- ords and was the first house Ferguson had ever set foot in that had no television, and as the days passed and he got to know Sydney better, he was intrigued that the almost pretty cowgirl was turning into the pretty cowgirl, and then the very pretty cowgirl, for the longish nose he had first seen as a defect now struck him as alluring and distinctive, and the blue-gray eyes that had once seemed so ordinary now looked alive and full of feeling. He had known her for just a few days, but he already felt they were friends—in much the same way, he imagined, that he and cousin Francie had once been friends in the long-ago world before the Newark fire.

So it went for the first five days of his visit, that is, the three days that weren't spent traveling around in Mildred's car, the quiet, unevent- ful days when Ferguson and Sydney would lie around in the backyard and talk about anything that came into their heads, not just about the question of who fucked whom and why but also about Sydney's girl- hood in Ohio and Ferguson's double boyhood in New Jersey and New York, about the different ways in which stories were told in books and movies and the pleasures and frustrations of teaching young children, about how Mildred felt both excited and nervous to have her nephew staying in the house, excited for all the obvious reasons but nervous because she was hesitant to expose her sister's son to the way she was living now, which explained why she had asked Sydney to sleep in the garage apartment while Ferguson was with them, *to spare the boy any embarrassment,* as she had put it, meaning her own embarrassment, and when Ferguson asked Sydney why she had gone ahead and told him the real story just minutes after picking him up at the airport, the pretty cowgirl said: I hate dissembling, that's why. It means you don't believe in your own life, or that you're scared of your own life, and I believe in my life, Archie, and I don't want to be scared of it.

Around four o'clock, they would pull themselves together and shuffle into the kitchen to start making dinner, continuing to talk as they chopped onions and peeled potatoes, the two of them twelve years apart in age, which paradoxically was much larger than the fifteen years that stood between Sydney and Mildred, but for all that he and Sydney were closer in spirit than Sydney was to Mildred, Ferguson felt, two mutts as opposed to the thoroughbred from Stanford University, a question of temperament more than of age, he supposed, but when Mildred finally returned to the house at six or six-thirty, Ferguson would pay close attention to how the two women acted around him, aware that Mildred was pretending not to be involved with Sydney in the way he knew she was while Sydney stubbornly ignored the injunction to pretend, showering endearments on his aunt that seemed to make Mildred more and more uncomfortable as the days went on, the *darlings* and *angels* and *sugar-pies* that no doubt would have pleased her if he hadn't been sitting at the table with them, and after five days Ferguson sensed they were locked in a silent quarrel that had been provoked by his presence, and on the evening of the sixth day, which was the next to last day of his visit, the increasingly anxious and out-of-sorts Mildred drank too much wine at dinner and eventually lost her composure—lost it because she wanted to lose it and needed the wine to push her over the edge—and the surprising thing about her outburst was that she didn't lash out at Sydney but at her nephew, as if he were the cause of her troubles, and the moment the assault began, Ferguson understood that Sydney had been talking behind his back, that the cowgirl had betrayed him.

Since when have you been a Bulgarian, Archie? Mildred said.

A Bulgarian? Ferguson replied. What are you talking about?

You've read *Candide*, haven't you? Don't you remember the Bulgarians?

I'm not following you.

The buggering Bulgarians. That's where the word comes from, you know. Bul-gar, bug-gar. *Bugger*.

And what's that supposed to mean?

Men fucking other men up the ass.

I still don't know what you're talking about.

A little birdie told me you've been buggering other boys. Or maybe other boys have been buggering you.

A little birdie?

At that point Sydney jumped into the conversation and said: Leave him alone, Mildred. You're drunk.

No, I'm not, Mildred said. I'm mildly intoxicated, and that gives me the right to tell the truth, and the truth of the matter is, my beloved Archie, the truth is that you're too young to be going down that road now, and if you don't get a grip on yourself, you'll turn into a queer before you know it, and then there'll be no turning back. There are enough queers in this family already, I'm afraid, and the last thing we need is another one.

Without uttering a word, Ferguson stood up from the table and started walking out of the room.

Where are you going? Mildred asked.

Away from you, Ferguson said. You have no idea what you're talking about, and I don't have to sit here listening to your crap.

Oh, Archie, Mildred said, come on back. We need to talk.

No we don't. I'm done talking with you.

Ferguson stomped off, struggling to push back the tears that were gathering in his eyes, and when he came to the corridor at the front of the house, he turned left and walked down the tiled hallway until he reached the guest bedroom at the far end. In the distance, he could hear Mildred and Sydney arguing behind him, but he didn't listen to what they were saying, and by the time he entered the room and shut the door, their voices were too muffled for him to make out the words.

He sat down on the bed, put his hands over his face, and started to sob.

No more sharing of secrets, he said to himself, no more unguarded confessions, no more trusting in people who didn't deserve to be trusted. If he couldn't say what he wanted to say in front of everyone in the world, he would keep his mouth shut and say it to no one.

He understood now why his mother had always looked up to her older sister—and why she had always been disappointed by her. So much intelligence there, he said to himself, so much humor when she had a mind to be humorous, so much generosity when she had a mind to be generous, but Mildred could be mean, meaner than any other person on earth, and now that Ferguson had been scalded by that meanness, he wanted nothing more to do with her and would henceforth cross her off his list. No more Aunt Mildred, and no more Sydney Millbanks, who had shown such promise as a friend—but how could you be friends with someone who seemed to be your friend but wasn't?

A moment later, Sydney was knocking on the door. He knew it was Sydney because she was calling out his name, asking if he was all right, asking if she could come in and talk to him, but Ferguson said no, he didn't want to see her or talk to her, he wanted her to leave him alone, but unfortunately the door had no lock, and Sydney came in anyway, cracking open the door until he could see her face and the tears that were rushing down her cheeks, and then she was all the way in, apologizing for what she had done, saying I'm sorry, I'm sorry, I'm sorry.

Fuck off, *little birdie*, Ferguson said. I don't care if you're sorry or not. Just leave me alone.

I'm a stupid blabbermouth, Sydney said. Once I start talking, I don't know when to stop. I didn't mean it, Archie, I swear I didn't.

Of course you meant it. Breaking a secret is bad enough, but lying is even worse. So don't start lying too, okay?

What can I do to help, Archie?

Nothing. Just go.

Please, Archie, let me do something for you.

Besides getting you out of this room, there's only one thing I want.

Tell me what it is, and it's yours.

A bottle of scotch.

You're not serious.

A bottle of scotch, preferably unopened, and if it is open, as close to full as possible.

It'll make you sick.

Listen, Sydney, either you bring it in to me or I go out and get it myself. But I'd rather not go out there right now because my aunt is in the other room, and I don't want to see her.

All right, Archie. Give me a few minutes.

So Ferguson got his scotch, a half-empty bottle of Johnnie Walker Red hand-delivered to him by Sydney Millbanks, a half-empty bottle that Ferguson chose to think of as half full, and once Sydney left the room again, he began drinking the scotch and went on drinking it in small, slow swallows until the first slivers of dawn cut through the slats of the venetian blinds and the bottle was empty, and for the second time that year Ferguson puked up his binge on the floor of another person's house and passed out.

PARIS WAS DIFFERENT. Paris was all about the sensation of being in Paris and roaming around the streets with his mother and Gil, about attending the opening of his mother's first solo exhibition at the Galerie Vinteuil on the rue Bonaparte, about the two evenings spent with an old friend of Gil's named Vivian Schreiber, about discovering that in spite of his B's and B+'s at the Riverside Academy he had learned enough French to be able to hold his own in the language, about deciding that Paris was the city where he eventually wanted to live. After a summer of watching old and new French films, it was impossible to walk through the streets of Montmartre without thinking he might run into the young Antoine Doinel from *The 400 Blows*, to walk down the Champs-Élysées without hoping to brush past the gorgeous Jean Seberg as she strolled back and forth in her white T-shirt hawking copies of the *Herald Tribune*— the same paper his stepfather worked for!—or to glide along the banks of the Seine and glance over at the *bouquinistes'* stalls without remembering the roly-poly bookstore owner who dives into the water to rescue the vagabond Michel Simon in *Boudu Saved from Drowning*. Paris was the movie of Paris, an agglomeration of all the Paris movies Ferguson had seen, and how inspiriting it was to find himself in the real place now, real in all of its sumptuous and stimulating reality, and yet to walk around feeling that it was an imaginary place as well, a place both in his head and out in the air that encircled his body, a simultaneous *here* and *there*, a black-and-white past and a full-color present, and Ferguson took pleasure in shuttling between the two of them, his thoughts moving so fast at times that the two blurred into one.

It was unusual for an exhibition to open at the end of August, when half the population of Paris was gone from the city, but that was the only available slot in the gallery's schedule—August twentieth to September twentieth—and Ferguson's mother had gladly accepted it, knowing that the director had done everything he could to *fit her in*. Forty-eight pictures in all, about half from previously published work and half from a new book that would be coming out next year, *Silent City*. Ferguson had already been told that he was the subject of one of the photographs, but still, he found it somewhat destabilizing to see himself hanging on the far wall when he entered the gallery, the familiar old picture his mother had taken of him seven years ago in the pre-Gil days when they were living together in the apartment on Central Park West, a long shot of him from behind as he sat on the living room floor watching Laurel and Hardy on television, his eight-year-old torso enveloped in a striped, short-sleeved T-shirt, and the moving thing about the photo, which bore the one-word title *Archie*, was the curve of his skinny back, each vertebra of his spine protruding into the shirt to create the bumpy-bony effect of childhood vulnerability, the portrait of an exposed being, a little boy locked in total concentration before the bowler-hatted buffoons on screen and therefore oblivious to everything else around him, and how proud Ferguson was of his mother for having produced such a good picture, which could have been nothing more than a banal snapshot but wasn't, as was the case with the forty-seven other pictures on view that evening, and as Ferguson looked at his young faceless self sitting on the floor of an apartment they no longer occupied, he couldn't help going back to the months of the curious interregnum and the Hilliard School disaster and remembering how his mother had ultimately replaced God in his mind as the supreme being, the human incarnation of the divine spirit, a flawed and mortal deity prone to the sulks and restless confusions that afflict all human beings, but he had worshipped his mother because she was the one person who *never let him down*, and no matter how many times he had disappointed her or proved himself to be less than he should have been, she had never not loved him and would never not love him to the end of her life.

Pretty and jittery, Ferguson said to himself, as he watched his mother smile and nod and shake hands with the guests at the *vernissage*, which had attracted about a hundred people in spite of the August holiday, a large noisy crowd crammed into the smallish exhibition space of the gallery, noisy because the eight or nine dozen people who had come there were apparently more interested in talking to one another than in looking at the pictures on the walls, but this was the first opening of any

kind that Ferguson had attended, and he was unfamiliar with the protocols of such gatherings, the sophisticated hypocrisies of supposed art
lovers coming to an art show in order to ignore the artworks on display,
and if the young barman serving drinks at a table in a corner of the
room hadn't been kind enough to pour Ferguson a glass of *vin blanc*, followed by a second glass twenty minutes later, Ferguson might have
walked out in protest, since this was his mother's big moment, and he
wanted everyone there to be fixed on Rose Adler's work, to be trans-
fixed by it to such a degree that all of them would be hammered into a
state of speechless awe, and when that failed to happen Ferguson stood
in the corner feeling ticked off and let down, too inexperienced to understand that the small red dots posted next to the frames on the walls
meant those pictures had already been sold and that his mother was in
excellent spirits that evening, not the least put off by the chatter and
noise of those rude, ignorant people.

Midway through his second *vin blanc*, Ferguson saw Gil slicing
through the crowd with his arm around a woman's shoulder. The two
of them were moving in his direction, steadily advancing toward the
drinks table in spite of the intervening bodies, and when they drew close
enough for Ferguson to see that they were both smiling, it occurred to
him that the woman must have been Gil's old friend Vivian Schreiber.
Gil had already told him something about her, but Ferguson hadn't been
paying much attention and had retained little of the story, which was a
rather complicated one, he remembered, having to do with the war and
Vivian's older brother, Douglas Gant or Grant, who had served in Gil's
intelligence unit and was his closest friend, and somehow or other Gil
had *pulled the strings* that allowed Vivian, the much younger sister of his
much younger army comrade, to enter France in September 1944, just
one month after the liberation of Paris and three months after she graduated from college in the United States. Why Vivian had needed to go
to France was unclear to Ferguson, but not long after she got there she
married Jean-Pierre Schreiber, a French citizen born of German-Jewish
parents in 1903 (which made him twenty years older than Vivian) who
had managed to avoid arrest by the Germans and/or the Vichy police
by traveling to neutral Switzerland just days before the fall of France,
and according to what Gil had told Ferguson, Schreiber was rich, or had
been rich, or soon became rich again because of his family's resurrected
wine-export business, or wine-growing business, or wine-bottle-

manufacturing business, or some other commercial enterprise that had nothing to do with the harvesting or selling of grapes. No children, Gil had said, but a successful marriage that lasted until the end of 1958, when the trim and youthful Schreiber unexpectedly dropped dead while running to catch a plane at Orly Airport, which had turned Vivian into a young widow, and now that she had sold off her husband's share of the business to his two nephews, she was a wealthy young widow, and, he added, *the most charming and intelligent woman in all of Paris, a great friend.*

All these facts or partial facts or possible anti-facts were rolling around in Ferguson's head as Gil and Vivian Schreiber came nearer to where he was standing. His first impression of the great friend was that she ranked among the three or four most beautiful women he had ever seen. Then, as she came closer and he could make out her features with more precision, he realized that she wasn't beautiful so much as impressive, a thirty-eight-year-old woman who projected a radiant aura of assurance and ease, whose clothes and makeup and hair were so elegantly and unpretentiously arranged that they seemed to have required no effort on her part to achieve the effect they achieved, who didn't simply occupy space in the room where everyone was standing but seemed to dominate the room, to own the room, as she no doubt owned every room she happened to enter anywhere in the world. A moment later, Ferguson was shaking her hand and looking into her large brown eyes and smelling the good smells of the perfume that hovered around her body as he listened to her unusually deep voice say how honored she was to meet him (honored!), and all of a sudden everything began to glow more brightly in Ferguson, for surely Vivian Schreiber was an exceptional person, a full-fledged movie-star sort of person, and knowing her was bound to make a difference in his sadly unexceptional fifteen-year-old's life.

Vivian was present at the dinner that followed the opening, but there were twelve people sitting at the table in the restaurant, and Ferguson was too far away from her for them to have a chance to talk, so he contented himself with watching her throughout the meal, noting how carefully the others around her listened to what she said whenever she contributed something to the conversation, and once or twice she looked over at him and saw that he was looking at her and smiled, but other than that, and other than the word spreading at his end of the table that Vivian had bought six of his mother's photographs (including *Archie*), there was no contact between them that night. Three nights later, when Ferguson, his mother, and Gil met Vivian for dinner at La Coupole, there were no impediments to the give-and-take of talking and listening, but for some reason Ferguson felt shy and overwhelmed in Vivian's presence and said little, preferring to listen to the conversation of the three adults, who had much to say on any number of subjects, including his mother's photographs, which Vivian praised as *sublimely human and uncannily direct*, and Vivian's older brother, Douglas Gant or Grant, who worked as a marine biologist in La Jolla, California, and the progress Gil had made on his book about Beethoven's string quartets, and Vivian's own work on a book she had been writing about an eighteenth-century painter named Chardin (who was still unknown to Ferguson at that point, but by the time he left Paris four days later he had made it his business to see every Chardin at the Louvre and had absorbed the mysterious fact that looking at a glass of water or an earthen jug on a painted canvas could be more involving and significant to the soul than looking at the crucified son of God on a similar painted rectangle), but even though Ferguson was mostly silent at the dinner, he was alert and happy, fully engaged in what the others were saying, and how much he enjoyed sitting in La Coupole, that huge, cavernous restaurant with the white tablecloths and the brisk waiters in their black-and-white uniforms, and all the people around him talking at once, so many people talking and looking at one another at the same time, the heavily rouged women with their little dogs and the somber men chain-smoking their Gitanes and the outlandishly decked-out couples who seemed to be auditioning for a play in which they were the central characters, *the Montparnasse scene*, as Vivian called it, the never-ending *jeu du regard*, and there was Giacometti, she said, and there was the actor who performed in all of Beckett's plays, and there was another artist whose name meant nothing to Ferguson but who must have been a famous figure known to everyone in Paris, and because they were in Paris his mother and Gil let him drink wine at dinner, such a luxury to be in a place where no one cared about how old you were, and several times during the two hours they spent at their corner table in the restaurant Ferguson sat back and looked at his mother and Gil and the luminous Vivian Schreiber and found himself wishing the four of them could go on sitting there forever.

Afterward, as Gil and his mother were about to put Vivian in a taxi, the young widow took hold of Ferguson's face, kissed him once on each cheek, and said: Come back and see me when you're a little older, Archie. I think we're going to be great friends.

BETWEEN THE TRIPS to California and Paris there was the hot summer in New York, the outdoor basketball games in Riverside Park, the four or five nights a week spent in air-conditioned movie theaters, the big and small American novels Gil continued to leave on his bedside table, and the poor planning that had kept him stuck in the city when every one of his school friends had gone somewhere else for July and August, not to mention the nineteen-year-old Jim, who was working as a counselor at a sleepaway camp in Massachusetts, and the confounding, ever-elusive Amy, who had managed to get herself shipped off to Vermont to take part in a two-month-long immersion program in French, which was precisely what he should have done and no doubt would have done if he hadn't lacked the wit to propose it to his mother and Gil, who almost certainly would have been able to afford the tuition, which Uncle Dan and Aunt Liz could not, but fast-talking Amy had pried loose the necessary cash from her grandmother in Chicago and the old goat in the Bronx, and there she was sending him jocular, teasing postcards from the New England woods (*Cher Cousin, The word "con" in French doesn't mean what I thought it meant. The English equivalent would be "jerk" or "asshole"—not you-know-what. Whereas "queue," which means "tail," also means you-know-what in French. Which reminds me: How is my favorite con man doing in N.Y. these days? Hot enough for you, Archie, or is that pretend sweat I see dripping from your forehead? Baisers à mon bien-aimé, Amy*), while Ferguson languished in the torrid drool of dog-day Manhattan, trapped in yet another loveless stretch of masturbation reveries and grimly persistent wet dreams.

The biggest topic in the household that summer was Lincoln Center and Gil's long-term dispute with his colleagues over the new Philharmonic Hall, which would finally be opening on September twenty-third. *The pus-ridden eyesore* (as Ferguson's grandfather used to call it) had been part of the West Sixties landscape for as long as Ferguson and his mother had been living in New York—a gigantic, thirty-acre slum-clearance project financed by Rockefeller money that had razed hundreds of buildings and kicked out thousands of people from their apartments to make way for what was being called a *new cultural hub*. All those mountains of dirt and bricks, all those steam shovels and pile drivers and holes in the ground, all that noise blasting through the neighborhood for all those years, and now that the first building of the sixteen-acre Lincoln Center complex was nearly done, the controversy was about to erupt into one of the angriest public shouting matches in the city's history. Size versus acoustical balance, arrogance and presumption versus mathematics and reason, and Gil was in the thick of it because the feud had been provoked by the *Herald Tribune*, in particular by two of the people he worked with most closely at the paper, arts editor Victor Lowry and fellow music critic Barton Crosetti, who had led an aggressive campaign to expand the number of seats in the original blueprints for the new hall because, they insisted, a great metropolis like New York deserved something bigger and better. Bigger, yes, Gil had argued, but not better, since the acoustical design had been calibrated for an auditorium of twenty-four hundred seats, not twenty-six hundred, and even though the architects and engineers responsible for the plan had said the quality of the sound would be *different*, which was another way of saying *worse* or *unacceptable*, the city gave in to the *Herald Tribune*'s demands and increased the size of the hall. Gil saw that capitulation as a defeat for the future of orchestral music in New York, but now that the larger version of the building was almost finished, what could he do but hope the results would be somewhat less disastrous than he feared? And if they weren't less, that is, if the results were fully as bad as he expected them to be, then he would launch a public campaign of his own, he said, and throw himself into an effort to help save Carnegie Hall, which the city was already intending to demolish.

The joke in the family that summer was: How do you spell the word *hub*? Answer: f-l-u-b.

Gil could joke about it because the only other option was to feel angry, and walking around with anger inside you was a bad way to live, he told Ferguson, it was pointless and self-destructive and cruel to the people who depended on you *not* to be angry, especially when the cause of your anger was something you couldn't control.

Do you understand what I'm trying to say, Archie? Gil asked.

I'm not sure, Ferguson said. I think so.

(*I'm not sure*: a subtle reference to Gil's volcanic outburst against

Margaret at the old apartment on Central Park West. *I think so*: an acknowledgment that he had not seen his stepfather lose his temper again on such a grand scale since that night. There could be only two reasons to account for the change in Gil: (1) His character had improved over time or (2) His marriage to Ferguson's mother had turned him into a better, calmer, happier man. Ferguson chose to believe the second possibility—not just because he wanted to believe it but because he knew it was the correct answer.)

It's not that the issue isn't important to me, Gil went on. My whole life is music. My whole life is writing about the music performed in this town, and if those performances are going to be less good now because of stupid decisions made by wrongheaded but well-meaning people—some of them my friends, I'm sad to say—then of course I'm going to feel angry, so angry that I've even thought about quitting the paper, just to let them know how seriously I take this business. But what good would that do me—or you, or your mother, or anyone else? I suppose we could get along without my salary if we had to, but the fact is I love my job, and I don't want to quit.

You shouldn't quit. There might be some problems over there, but you shouldn't quit.

It's not going to last much longer anyway. The *Herald Tribune* is sinking financially, and I doubt it will hold on for more than another two or three years. So I might as well go down with the ship. A loyal crew member to the last, standing by the mad captain who steered us into such dangerous waters.

You're joking, right?

Since when have you known me to joke, Archie?

The end of the *Herald Tribune*. I remember the first time you took me there—and how much I liked it, how much I still like it every time we go to the building together. It's hard to believe it won't exist anymore. I even thought . . . well, never mind . . .

Thought what?

I don't know . . . that one day . . . it sounds so idiotic now . . . that one day I might end up working there, too.

What a beautiful idea. I'm touched, Archie—deeply touched—but why would a boy with your talents want to be a newspaperman?

Not a newspaperman, a movie critic. In the same way you write about concerts, maybe I could write about films.

I've always imagined you'd end up making your own films.

I don't think so.

But you love movies so much . . .

I love watching them, but I'm not sure I'd enjoy making them. It takes too much time to make a movie, and during that time you don't have any time left over to watch other movies. Do you see what I'm talking about? If the thing I enjoy most is watching movies, then the best job for me would be to watch as many movies as I can.

SCHOOL HAD BEEN in session for close to a month when the new hall opened with a gala concert performed by the New York Philharmonic under the direction of Leonard Bernstein, an event considered so important that it was televised by CBS—a live national broadcast beamed into every home in America. In the days that followed, more concerts were performed by some of the most admired symphony orchestras in the country (Boston, Philadelphia, Cleveland), and by the end of the week both the press and the public had pronounced their verdict on the acoustical qualities of Lincoln Center's flagship venue. PHILHAR-MONIC FLOP read one headline. PHILHARMONIC FOLLY read another. PHILHARMONIC FIASCO read a third. The double-*f*-sound was apparently irresistible to newspaper editors, given how neatly it flew off the tongues of indignant music lovers, professional naysayers, and barroom wags alike. Some people differed, however, claiming the results weren't as bad as all that, and so began the screaming contest between fors and againsts, the uncivil debate that would go on filling the New York air for months and years to come.

Ferguson followed these events out of loyalty to Gil, pleased that his stepfather had been on the winning side of the argument, no matter what harm the defective hall would do to the eardrums of the city's classical music patrons, and one Sunday afternoon he even stood in front of Carnegie Hall with Gil and his mother holding a sign that read PLEASE SAVE ME, but mostly Ferguson didn't care, and mostly his thoughts were zeroed in on the demands of school and the never-ending quest for love, even when all the newspapers in New York shut down during the printers' strike that lasted from early December to the final day of March—which he generously chose to interpret as a long-deserved rest for Gil.

Amy had broken up with last year's boyfriend, the one Ferguson had never met and whose name he had never known, but she had found a new *ami intime* during her Francophone summer in Vermont, someone who lived in New York and therefore was *disponible pour les rencontres chaque weekend*, which pushed Ferguson out of the running once again, disqualifying him from even considering a new assault on the fortress of Amy's heart. The same held true of the attractive girls at the Riverside Academy—all locked up and out of bounds, just as they had been the year before, which meant that Isabel Kraft was still no more than a phantom sylph running through the forests of his imagination, a figment other writhing in the light of the nocturnal bone— more real than Miss September, perhaps, but not by much.

If only Andy Cohen hadn't said those words last spring, Ferguson sometimes thought, if only their simple arrangement hadn't become so messy and impossible. Not that he even liked Andy Cohen anymore, but the way things were shaping up for his sophomore year, those Saturday afternoon romps on West 107th Street were beginning to make sense again, at least when you considered how much better it was to be with someone than with no one. On the other hand, Onan's muse had never come to him in the form of a male body. It was always a female person who crawled under the blankets with him, for when it wasn't Isabel Kraft slipping out of her red bikini and pressing her skin against his skin, it was Amy, or else—and this he found bizarre—it was Sydney Millbanks, the two-faced cowgirl who had stabbed him in the back, or Vivian Schreiber, who had spoken approximately forty-seven words to him and was old enough to be his mother, but there they were, the two women from his travels across continents and oceans in July and August, and there was nothing he could do to stop either one of them from entering his thoughts at night.

The contrast seemed clear enough, a rigid divide between what he wanted and what his circumstances allowed him to have, the soft flesh of women that would necessarily have to be deferred for another year or two and the stiff cocks of boys that could be savored now if the opportunity ever arose again, the impossible as opposed to the possible, nighttime fantasies as opposed to daytime realities, love on the one hand and adolescent lust on the other, all so neat and unambiguous, but then he discovered that the line was less sharply drawn than he had supposed, that love could exist on either side of that mental boundary

and could do to him what the cowgirl said it had done to her, and to
understand that about himself after pushing away the unwanted love of
Andy Cohen came as a shock to Ferguson—and it frightened him,
frightened him so much that he scarcely seemed to know who he was
anymore.

   In late September, he left New York again for yet another far-off
place, traveling to Cambridge, Massachusetts, to spend the weekend
with his cousin Jim. Not by air this time but five and a half hours by
land on two buses to Boston with a change in Springfield, his first long-
distance bus ride anywhere, and then two nights sleeping in Jim's dormitory room at MIT, camped out on the bed normally occupied by Jim's
roommate, who had left campus on Friday morning and wouldn't be
back until Sunday night. The plan was nebulous. Take in the sights,
play some one-on-one basketball in the gym on Saturday morning, visit
a few labs at MIT, have a look at the Harvard campus, wander around
Back Bay and Copley Square in Boston, have lunch and/or dinner at
Harvard Square, go to a movie at the Brattle Theatre—an unstructured,
spur-of-the-moment kind of weekend, Jim said, since the purpose of the
visit was *to hang out and spend some time together* and what they wound
up doing was of little importance. Ferguson was thrilled. No, more than
thrilled—out of his skin with anticipation, and the mere thought of
spending the weekend with Jim instantly parted the clouds that had
been gathering overhead and turned the sky a bright, bright blue. No
one was better than Jim, no one was kinder or more generous than Jim,
no one was more admirable than Jim, and all during the bus ride to
Boston Ferguson reflected on how lucky he was to have been thrown into
the same family as his remarkable stepcousin. He loved him, he said to
himself, *he loved him to pieces,* and he knew that Jim loved him back
because of all those Saturday mornings in Riverside Park, teaching the
runty twelve-year-old how to play roundball when there were a hundred other things he could have been doing, he loved him because he
had called to invite him to go up to Cambridge for no other reason than
to hang out and spend some time together, and now that Ferguson had tasted
the pleasures of boy-boy intimacy, there was nothing he wouldn't have
done to find himself naked in Jim's arms, to be kissed by Jim, to be fon-
dled by Jim, yes, to be *buggered* by Jim, which was something that had
never happened with the boy from City College last spring, for whatever Jim wanted him to do he would do, since this was love, a big, burn-

ing love that would go on burning for the rest of his life, and if Jim turned out to be the kind of ambidextrous boy he himself seemed to be turning into, which was altogether unlikely, of course, then a kiss from Jim would carry him to the gates of heaven, and yes, those were the words Ferguson said to himself when he thought that thought in the middle of his journey to Boston: *the gates of heaven.*

It was the happiest weekend of his life—and also the saddest. Happy because being with Jim made him feel so protected, so secure in the comforting nimbus of the older boy's calm, and at every moment he could count on being listened to as carefully as he listened to Jim, who never made him feel lesser or lower or left out. The big breakfasts at the little diner across the Charles, the talk about the space program and mathematical puzzles and the enormous computers that one day would be small enough to fit in your palm, the Bogart double bill of *Casablanca* and *To Have and Have Not* at the Brattle Theatre on Saturday night, so many things to be thankful for during the long hours they spent with each other between Friday night and Sunday afternoon, but through it all the constant pain of knowing that the kiss he wanted would never be given to him, that having Jim was also not having Jim, that to have and have not meant never exposing his true feelings without running the risk of perishing in a fire of eternal humiliation. Worst of all: looking at his cousin's naked body in the locker room after one-on-one basketball, standing naked together with no possibility of extending his arm and putting his fingers on the lean, muscular body of his forbidden love, and then, on Sunday morning, Ferguson's brazen ploy to test the waters by walking around the dorm room with no clothes on for more than an hour, tempted to ask Jim if he wanted a rubdown but not daring to, tempted to sit down on his bed and start jerking off in front of Jim but not daring to, hoping his nakedness would elicit some response from his thoroughly heterosexual cousin, which needless to say it didn't, for Jim was already in love with someone else, a girl from Mount Holyoke named Nancy Hammerstein, who drove in on Sunday to have lunch with them, a perfectly decent and intelligent girl who saw in Jim precisely what Ferguson saw, and so even in his happiness Ferguson suffered through much sorrow that weekend, aching for the kiss that would never be given to him and knowing how deluded he was even to want it, and as he sat on the bus that carried him back to New York on Sunday, he cried a little bit, then cried a lot as the sun went down and darkness engulfed the bus. He was crying more and more often these days, he realized . . . and who was he? he kept asking himself . . . and what was he? . . . and why on earth did he persist in making life so hard for himself?

HE WOULD HAVE to get over it or die, and because Ferguson didn't feel ready to die at age fifteen and a half, he did what he could to get over it, throwing himself with scattershot fervor into a maelstrom of contradictory pursuits. By the time the Cuban missile crisis started and ended two weeks later, with no bombs dropped and no wars declared, leaving no war in sight other than the ever-present Cold War of long duration, Ferguson had published his first film review, had smoked his first cigarette, and had lost his virginity to a twenty-year-old prostitute in a small brothel on West Eighty-second Street. The following month, he made the Riverside Academy's varsity basketball team, but as one of only three sophomores on the ten-man squad, he sat on the bench and rarely saw more than one or two minutes of action per game.

Published. The piece wasn't a review but an overview, a discussion of the equal but contrasting merits of two films Ferguson had been pondering for the past several months. It appeared in the dismal, sloppily printed biweekly school paper called the *Riverside Rebel,* an eight-page broadsheet that published out-of-date news items about interscholastic athletic events, articles about meaningless school controversies (the declining quality of the cafeteria food, the headmaster's decision to ban the playing of transistor radios in the halls between classes), and poems, short stories, and occasional drawings by the students who fancied themselves poets, short-story writers, and artists. Mr. Dunbar, Ferguson's English teacher that year, was the *Rebel's* faculty adviser, and he encouraged the fledgling cinephile to contribute as many articles as he cared to write, claiming that the paper was in desperate need of *new blood,* and regular columns on films, books, art, music, and theater would be *a step in the right direction.* Intrigued and flattered by Mr. Dunbar's request, Ferguson set to work on a piece about *The 400 Blows* and *Breathless,* his two favorite French films of the past summer, and now that he had been to France himself, it seemed only natural that he should begin his career as a film critic by writing about the French New Wave.

Other than the fact that both films were shot in black and white and set in contemporary Paris, Ferguson argued, they had nothing in common. The two works were radically different in tone, sensibility, and narrative technique, so different that it would be useless to compare them and even more useless to waste a single moment questioning which one was the better film. About Truffaut he wrote: *heartbreaking realism, tender but tough-minded, deeply human, rigorously honest, lyrical.* About Godard he wrote: *jagged and disruptive, sexy, disturbingly violent, funny and cruel, constant in-joke references to American films, revolutionary.* No, Ferguson wrote in the final paragraph, he would not come down on the side of one film or the other because he loved them both, in the same way he loved both Jimmy Stewart Westerns and Busby Berkeley musicals, loved both Marx Brothers comedies and James Cagney gangster films. Why choose? he asked. Sometimes we want to sink our teeth into a nice fat hamburger, and at other times nothing tastes better than a hard-boiled egg or a dry saltine. *Art is a banquet,* he concluded, *and every dish on the table is calling out to us—asking to be eaten and enjoyed.*

Smoked. On Sunday morning, one week after Ferguson's trip to Cambridge, the two Schneiderman households jammed their six bodies into a rented station wagon and drove north to Dutchess County, where they stopped for lunch at the Beekman Arms in Rhinebeck and then scattered in several directions throughout the town. As usual, Ferguson's mother disappeared with her camera and was not seen again until it was time to return to New York. Aunt Liz headed off for the main drag to browse in the antique shops, and Gil and Uncle Dan climbed back into the car, saying they wanted to have a look at the autumn foliage when in fact they were planning to discuss what to do with their declining father, who was in his mid-eighties now and suddenly in need of twenty-four-hour palliative care. Neither Ferguson nor Amy had any interest in poking around old furniture stores or looking at the mutating colors of dying leaves, so they turned right when they saw Amy's mother turn left and kept on walking until they reached the edge of town, where they chanced upon a small hillock that was still covered with green grass, a pleasant little clump of soft ground that seemed to be begging them to sit on it, which they both promptly did, and a few seconds later Amy reached into her pocket, pulled out a pack of unfiltered Camels, and offered Ferguson a cigarette. He didn't hesitate.

It was high time he gave one of those cancer sticks a shot, he said to himself, Mr. He-Man-Athlete-Who-Would-Never-Smoke-Because-It-Was-Bad-For-His-Wind, and of course he coughed after each of the first three puffs, and of course he felt dizzy for a while, and of course Amy laughed because it was funny to see him doing the things all novice smokers inevitably did, but then he settled down and began to get the hang of it, and before long he and Amy were talking, talking in a way that hadn't been possible for them in over a year, with no wise-cracks or insults or accusations, with all the rancor and built-up resent-ments gone like the smoke that was gusting from their mouths and vanishing into the autumn air, and then they stopped talking and just sat on the grass smiling at each other, happy to be friends again and no longer at odds, never again at odds, at which point Ferguson wrapped his arm around her in a pretend headlock and croaked softly into her ear: Another cigarette, please.

Lost. There was a wicked and exciting boy in the senior class named Terry Mills, a brilliant good-for-nothing who knew more about what teenage boys were not supposed to know than anyone else at the school. He was the supplier of scotch for weekend parties, the purveyor of amphetamine pills for those who wanted to fly fast and stay up all night, the dispenser of marijuana for those who preferred a more subdued approach to intoxication, and the panderer who could help you lose your virginity by taking you to the whorehouse on West Eighty-second Street. One of the richest boys at the Riverside Academy, the plump and sar-castic Terry Mills lived with his divorced and frequently absent mother in a townhouse between Columbus Avenue and Central Park West, and although there was much about his behavior that Ferguson found repugnant, he also found it difficult not to like him. According to Terry, legions of Riverside Academy boys both past and present had left their boyhoods behind them in the rooms of the Eighty-second Street bor-dello, it was a long-established tradition, he said, one that he himself had embraced two years ago as a sophomore, and now that Ferguson had ascended to the rank of sophomore as well, might he be interested in paying a visit to that enchanted realm of sensual delights? Yes, Fer-guson said, of course he would, most certainly he would, when could they go?

That conversation took place on a Monday afternoon over lunch, the Monday following the Sunday that Ferguson had spent in Rhinebeck smoking cigarettes with Amy, and the following morning Terry reported that everything had been arranged for Friday afternoon at around four, which wouldn't pose a problem for Ferguson because his curfew had been extended that year to six o'clock, and fortunately he had the twenty-five dollars that would be needed to *turn him into a man*, although Terry was still hoping that Mrs. M., the director of the establishment, could be talked into giving Ferguson a student discount. Not knowing what to expect, since he had no experience of brothels outside of what he had seen in gaudy, Technicolor Hollywood Westerns, Ferguson walked into the apartment on West Eighty-second Street with no images in his head—nothing but a blank of uncertainty, zip plus zero minus null. He found himself in one of those large Upper West Side apartments with crumbled plaster and yellowing walls, a once elegant place that had no doubt housed a prominent New York burgher and his voluminous family, but who would stop to examine plaster and walls when the first room you entered was a broad living room with six young women in it, half a dozen professional love-makers sitting around on chairs and divans in various stages of undress, two of them in fact entirely undressed, which made them the first naked women Ferguson had seen in his life.

He had to choose. That was a problem because he had no idea which one of the six would be the best love-maker for an unpracticed boy-girl virgin whose sexual history so far had been confined to one male partner, and he had to choose quickly because it made him feel uncomfortable to be sizing up those women as if they were packages of fuck-meat without brains or souls, and therefore Ferguson eliminated the four partially dressed ones and narrowed it down to a choice between the two all-naked ones, figuring there would be no surprises that way when the action began, and suddenly it wasn't difficult at all, since one of the two was a chubby, large-breasted Puerto Rican woman well past thirty and the other was a good-looking black girl who couldn't have been more than a few years older than Ferguson—a slender, small-breasted sprite with short hair and a long neck and what looked to be remarkably smooth skin, skin that promised to feel better than any skin his hands had ever touched.

Her name was Julie.

He had already paid his twenty-five dollars to the rotund, chain-smoking Mrs. M. (no discounts for youthful beginners), and because

Terry had loudly and crudely announced that *Ferguson's dick had never seen the inside of a pussy*, there was no point in pretending he had been down this road before, the road in this case being a narrow hallway that led to a cramped, windowless room with a bed, a sink, and a chair in it, and as Ferguson walked down that corridor behind the young Julie's sweet, swaying behind, the bulge in his pants was steadily growing, so much so that when they entered the room and Julie instructed him to take off his clothes, she looked down at his cock and said, You sure get hard fast, don't you, kid?, which pleased Ferguson immensely, knowing that he was virile enough to produce more rapid hard-ons than most of her adult customers, and suddenly he felt happy, not at all nervous or afraid, even if he didn't fully understand the ground rules of the encounter, as when he tried to kiss her on the lips and she jerked her head away, saying, We don't do that, honey—gotta save that stuff for your girlfriend, but she didn't mind it when he put his hands on her little breasts or kissed her on the shoulder, and how good it felt when she washed his dick with soap and warm water at the sink, and how much better it felt when he agreed to something called *half-and-half* without knowing what it was (fellatio+copulation) and they lay down on the bed together and the first half of half-and-half proved to be so pleasurable that he was afraid he wouldn't make it to the second half, but somehow he did, and that was the best part of the whole adventure, the long-hoped-for, long-dreamed-of, long-delayed entrance into another person's body, *the act of coupling,* and so powerful were the sensations of being inside her that Ferguson couldn't hold back anymore and came almost immediately—so fast that he regretted his lack of control, regretted that he hadn't been able to put off the climax by even a few seconds.

Can we do it again? he asked.

Julie burst out laughing—a great gut yawp of hilarity that bounced around the walls of the tiny room. Then she said: You come, you're done, funny man—unless you have another twenty-five dollars.

I barely have twenty-five cents, Ferguson said.

Julie laughed again. I like you, Archie, she said. You're a good-looking boy with a pretty pecker.

And I think you're the most beautiful girl in New York.

The skinniest, you mean.

No, the most beautiful.

Julie sat up and kissed Ferguson on the forehead. Come back and see me sometime, she said. You know the address, and that loudmouthed friend of yours has the telephone number. Call first to make an appointment. You wouldn't want to show up when I'm not here, would you?

No, ma'am. Not on your life.

Sat. Making the varsity team as a sophomore was a reflection of how much Ferguson's game had improved over the summer. The outdoor leagues had been highly competitive, the rosters crammed with poor black kids from Harlem who took their basketball seriously, who knew that being good at basketball meant starting for a high school team, which could mean playing for a college team and a chance to get out of Harlem for good, and Ferguson had worked hard to improve his outside shooting and ball handling, had put in long hours of extra practice with one of the eager kids from Lenox Avenue named Delbert Straughan, a fellow forward on the tougher of the two teams he had played for, and now that he had grown another two inches and stood at a sturdy five-nine and a half, he had advanced from mere proficiency to something close to excellence, with such potent spring in his legs that even at his height he could dunk the ball once in every two or three tries. The problem with making the varsity as a sophomore, however, was that you were automatically relegated to the second team, which doomed you to spend the season picking up splinters as a lowly benchwarmer. Ferguson understood the importance of hierarchies and would have been content with his subordinate role if he hadn't felt that he was a better player than the first-string small forward, a senior by the name of Duncan Nyles, sometimes referred to as No-Dunk Nyles—for, as it happened, he wasn't only just a little better than Nyles, he was a lot better. If Ferguson had been the only one who felt that way, it wouldn't have rankled so much, but nearly all the players shared his opinion, none more vociferously than the other proletarian scrubs, among them his old friends from last year's freshman team, Alex Nordstrom and Brian Mischevski, who were positively disgusted by the coach's decision to put Ferguson on the bench and kept reminding him of how unfairly he was being treated, since the evidence was there for everyone to see: Whenever the first team and the second team squared off in practice scrimmages, Ferguson consistently outshot, outhustled, and outrebounded No-Dunk Nyles.

The coach was a perplexing person—half genius and half idiot—and

Ferguson never quite managed to figure out where he stood with him. A former backcourt star for St. Francis College in Brooklyn, one of the smallest schools on the metro region's Catholic circuit, Horace "Happy" Finnegan knew the game thoroughly and taught it well, but in all other respects his brain seemed to have atrophied into a gummy mass of melted thought wires and burned out language tubes. *Pair up in threes*, he would say to the boys at practice, or *Make a circle, men, three hundred and sixty-five degrees*, and beyond the incessant malapropisms there were the questions the boys would ask just for the pleasure of seeing him scratch his head, such as, *Hey, Coach, do you walk to school or carry your lunch?* or *Is it hotter in the city or the summer?*, nonsensical beauties that never failed to elicit the desired scratch, the desired shrug, the desired *You got me, kid*. On the other hand, Happy Finnegan was a perfectionist when it came to the finer points of basketball, and Ferguson marveled at how he seethed with indignation whenever a player missed a free throw (*the one gimme in the whole damn game*) or saw a player drop a neatly fired pass (*Keep your eyes open, fucker, or I'll yank you off the court*). He demanded efficient and intelligent play, and even though everyone laughed at him behind his back, the team won most of its games, consistently performing above and beyond its meager talents. Still, Nordstrom and Mischevski kept urging their friend to go in for a private meeting with the coach, not that it would necessarily change anything, they said, but they wanted to know why he insisted on starting the wrong man at small forward. Yes, the team was winning most of its games, but didn't Finnegan want to win *every* game?

A good question, the coach said, when Ferguson finally knocked on his door in early January. A very good question, and I'm glad you asked it. Yes, any idiot can see you're better than Nyles. You go up against each other one-on-one, and there'd be nothing left of him but an empty jockstrap and a puddle of sweat on the gym floor. Nyles is a lump. You're a Mexican, Ferguson, a goddamn human jumping bean, and you play as hard as anyone I've got, but I need the lump out there on the court. Chemistry, that's what it is. Five-on-five, not one-on-one—you follow? With those four other guys sprinting around like jazzed-up dots and dashes, the fifth has to be a sack of potatoes, a lump of flesh with sneakers on his feet, a big nobody to fill up space and think about digesting his food. You see what I mean, Ferguson? You're too good. Everything would change if I put you in there. The pace would get too fast, too revvy-revvy. You'd all have heart attacks and epileptic fits, and we'd start to lose. We'd be a better team, but we'd be worse. Your day will come, kid. I've got plans for you—but not until next year. The chemistry will be different after the dots and dashes fly the coop, and then I'll need you. Be patient, Ferguson. Bust your ass at practice, say your prayers at night, keep your hands off your willy, and everything will work out just so.

He was tempted to quit the team right then and there, for what Finnegan seemed to be offering him was no chance to play no matter what happened for the rest of the season—unless the so-called chemistry began to go wrong and the team stopped winning, but how in good conscience could he root for the team to lose and go on calling himself a loyal member of the team? Still, Finnegan had all but promised him a starting spot for next year, and on the strength of that promise Ferguson reluctantly swallowed his medicine and held on, working hard to impress Finnegan by *busting his ass* every day at practice, although he didn't say his prayers at night and couldn't keep his hands off his willy.

When the next season began, however, he found himself on the bench again, and the awful thing about it was that there was no one to blame—not even Finnegan, especially not Finnegan. The new boy had turned up out of nowhere, a six-foot-two-inch sophomore whose family had moved to Manhattan from Terre Haute, Indiana, and Hoosier phenom Marty Wilkinson was so damned good, so much better than Ferguson and everyone else on the team, that the coach had no choice but to start him at forward, and with the other starting forward back from last year, the solid and dependable Tom Lerner, who had been voted captain of the team, there was no room for Ferguson to crack the first-string lineup. Finnegan made some efforts to increase his playing time, but five or six minutes a game wasn't enough, and Ferguson felt himself withering on the bench. He had been turned into an afterthought, a combination hatchetman-noncombatant whose skills quietly seemed to be eroding, and the mounting frustration, as he confessed to his mother and stepfather at dinner one night, was *killing his spirit*, and so it was that four games into the season, which happened to fall four weeks after Kennedy's assassination, one month minus two days after that grotesque Friday when even the skeptical, unduped Ferguson had shed tears along with everyone else, allowing himself to succumb to the general mood of the country without understanding that the murder of the president had been a reenactment of his own father's murder nine years ago, the full horror of his private grief now played out on a grand public scale, and on December 20, 1963, a few minutes after the end of Riverside's fourth game, Ferguson went into the coach's office and announced that he was quitting the team. No hard feelings, he said, but he just couldn't take it anymore. Finnegan said he understood, which was probably true, and then the two of them shook hands, and that was that.

He wound up playing in a league sponsored by the West Side Y instead. It was still basketball, and he still enjoyed it, but even though he was recognized as the strongest player on his team, it wasn't the same, it couldn't be the same, and it would never be the same again. No more red-and-yellow uniforms. No more bus rides. No more Rebel fanatics cheering from the stands. And no more Chuckie Showalter pounding on his bass drum.

By the beginning of 1964, the almost-seventeen-year-old Ferguson had published a dozen more film articles under the stewardship of Mr. Dunbar, often with help from Gil on matters of prose style, diction, and the always daunting problem of figuring out exactly what he meant to say and then saying it as clearly as possible. His pieces tended to alternate between American and foreign subjects, an examination of the language in W. C. Fields comedies, for instance, followed by something on *The Seven Samurai* or *Pather Panchali*, *A Walk in the Sun* followed by *L'Atalante*, *I Am a Fugitive from a Chain Gang* followed by *La Dolce Vita*— an elemental sort of criticism that was less interested in making judgments about the films than in trying to capture the experience of watching them. Bit by bit, his work was improving, bit by bit his friendship with his stepfather had deepened, and the more he went to the movies, the more he wanted to go to the movies, for moviegoing wasn't a hunger so much as an addiction, and the more movies he consumed, the more his appetite for them increased. Among the theaters he went to most often were the New Yorker on Broadway (just two blocks from his apartment), the Symphony, the Olympia, and the Beacon on the Upper West Side, the Elgin in Chelsea, the Bleecker Street and Cinema Village downtown, the Paris next door to the Plaza Hotel, the Carnegie next door to Carnegie Hall, the Baronet, the Coronet, and Cinemas I and

II in the East Sixties, and, following a pause of several months, the Thalia again, where he had yet to run into Andy Cohen after twelve visits. In addition to the commercial theaters, there was the Museum of Modern Art, an indispensable resource for classic films, and now that Ferguson was a member (a present from Gil and his mother when he turned sixteen), he could go to any and all of those films merely by flashing his card at the door. How many films had he seen in that span between October 1962 and January 1964? An average of two every Saturday and Sunday and one other on Friday, which came to a total of more than three hundred—a good six hundred hours of sitting in the dark, or the number of clock ticks repeated in the course of twenty-five consecutive days and nights, and when you subtracted the minutes lost to sleep and various drunken swoons, over a month of his waking life during the fifteen months that had ticked by.

He had also smoked a thousand more cigarettes (both with and without Amy) and had pursued his love affair with strong spirits by drinking three hundred glasses of Scotland's finest product at weekend parties thrown by Terry Mills and his equally dissolute successors the following year, no longer upchucking on rugs when he overindulged but passing out quietly and contentedly in a corner of the room, single-mindedly pursuing these alcoholic oblivions in order to purge the dead and the damned from his thoughts, having come to the conclusion that unmediated life was too horrible to bear and that swallowing liquids designed to dull the senses could bring comfort to the troubled heart, but it was important to exercise caution and not go too far, which was why binges were reserved for the weekends, not every weekend but roughly every other one, and he found it curious that he never craved the stuff unless it happened to be right in front of him, and even then he found it altogether resistible, but once he took the first drink, he couldn't stop until he had drunk too much.

Pot was becoming more and more available at those weekend bashes, but Ferguson had decided it wasn't for him. After three or four puffs, the unfunniest things would start to seem funny to him, and he would dissolve in a fit of giggles. Then he would begin to feel weightless, all silly and stupid inside, which had the unpleasant effect of thrusting him back into some childish incarnation of himself, for even though Ferguson was struggling to grow up just then, falling down as often as he managed to stay on his feet, he didn't want to think of himself as a child anymore, so he shunned grass and stuck to booze, preferring to be plastered rather than stoned, and in that way he could feel he was acting as an adult.

Last but not least, that is, first and foremost, he had gone back to Mrs. M.'s place six times in those fifteen months. He would have gone more often, but the twenty-five dollars presented a problem, since his allowance was only fifteen dollars a week and he had no job and no chance of getting one (his parents wanted him to concentrate on his schoolwork), and once he had spent the first twenty-five in October (1962) his bank account was all but empty until his sixteenth birthday in March (1963), when his mother wrote him a check for one hundred dollars to supplement the gift of his museum membership card, which covered four sessions with Julie at the apartment on West Eighty-second Street, but the other two visits were paid for by appropriating things that didn't belong to him and converting them into cash, criminal acts that tormented Ferguson and ate away at his crumbling conscience, but the sex was so important to him, so fundamental to his well-being, so indisputably the only thing that could keep him from cracking apart, that he couldn't stop himself from bartering his soul for a few moments in Julie's arms. God had been dead for years, but the devil had returned to Manhattan and was making a strong comeback in the northern sector of the borough.

It was always Julie because she was much the prettiest and most desirable girl who worked at Mrs. M.'s, and now that she understood how young Ferguson was (she had thought he was seventeen the first time he showed up, not fifteen), her attitude toward him had softened into a kind of droll camaraderie as she watched his limbs continue to grow from one encounter to the next, not that she treated him with anything that could be called tenderness or affection, but she was friendly enough to bend the rules now and let him kiss her on the lips when he wanted to, sometimes even to drive his tongue into her mouth, and the good thing about being with Julie was that she never talked about herself and never asked him any questions (beyond how old he was), and other than the fact that she worked at Mrs. M.'s every Tuesday and Friday, Ferguson knew nothing about Julie's life, whether she was employed as a prostitute in other houses around the city, for example, or whether the two days with Mrs. M. were helping to fund her college education, perhaps even at City College for all he knew, where she sat next to Andy

Cohen in their Russian literature seminar, or whether she had a boy-friend or a husband or a little child or twenty-three brothers and sisters, or whether she was planning to rob a bank or move to California or eat chicken pot pie for dinner. It was better not to know, he felt, better that it should be about nothing but the sex, which he found to be such deeply rewarding sex that twice during those fifteen months Ferguson was willing to break the law by entering bookstores on the Upper West Side with a woolen coat over his multipocketed winter jacket and fill the pockets of both coat and jacket with paperback books, which he then marked up with numerous dog-ears and underlinings and sold to a used bookstore across the street from Columbia at one-fourth the cover price, stealing and selling dozens of classic novels in order to earn the extra money he needed to have more sex with Julie.

He wished it could have been sixty times instead of six times, but just knowing that Julie would be there whenever the urge overpowered him was enough to kill his interest in chasing after the girls at his school, the fifteen- and sixteen-year-olds who would have swatted away his curious hands as he struggled to remove their sweaters and bras and panties, not one of them would have marched around naked in front of him as Julie did, not one of them would have allowed him to penetrate the inner sanctum of her holy womanhood, and even assuming that such a miracle could have come to pass, what work would have been required to achieve what he had already achieved with Julie, and with Julie there could never be any of the heartbreak that would inevitably come from falling for one of those *nice girls*, none of whom he loved in any case, only his adored Amy, who didn't go to the Riverside Acad-emy but attended Hunter High School in another part of town, his lost and rediscovered best beloved kissing cousin of the unfiltered cigarettes and the mighty laugh, she was the only one worth the effort and the risk, the only girl with whom sex would also mean love, for everything had changed in the past fifteen months, the world of his desires had been turned upside down, and one by one Isabel Kraft and Sydney Mill-banks and Vivian Schreiber had all vanished from his thoughts at night, the only two who came to him anymore were the Schneiderman boy and the Schneiderman girl, the ferociously desired Jim and Amy, every night it was either one or the other who crawled into bed with him, on some nights first one and then the other, and that made sense, he supposed, sense to a person who was cut down the middle and

couldn't make sense of who he was, the soon-to-be seventeen-year-old
Archibald Isaac Ferguson, variously known as a whoremongering sex
maniac and petty criminal, an ex–high school basketball player and
sometime film critic, a twice-rejected lover of his male and female stepcousins, and a devoted son and stepson of Rose and Gil—who both
would have dropped dead if they had found out what he was up to.

WHEN OLD MAN Schneiderman gave up the ghost at the end of February, there was an after-funeral gathering at the apartment on Riverside
Drive, a small gathering because Gil's widowed father had made no new
friends in the past twenty years and most of the old ones had already
found permanent accommodations elsewhere, a collection of perhaps
two dozen people that included Gil's daughters, Margaret and Ella, making their first family appearance since the fall of 1959, accompanied by
their newly acquired fat, balding husbands, one of whom had made
Margaret pregnant, and in spite of his prejudice against them, Ferguson had to admit that his stepsisters showed no signs of hostility toward
his mother, which was a lucky thing for them, since nothing would have
made Ferguson happier than to stir up a scene and boot them out of the
house, a violent impulse that was entirely uncalled for under the circumstances, but after standing out in the cold February weather for close
to an hour as the family laid the old goat to rest, Ferguson was feeling
agitated, *revvy-revvy*, as Happy Finnegan would have put it, perhaps
because he had been thinking about his not-grandpa's hot temper and
outspoken contentiousness, or perhaps because every death made him
think of his father's death, so by the time the assembled mourners
returned to the apartment, Ferguson was feeling wretched enough to
down two quick whiskeys on an empty stomach, which might have contributed to the events that followed, for once the post-funeral gathering
began, he wound up misbehaving in a manner so bold and outlandishly
inappropriate that it wasn't clear to him if he had lost his mind or accidentally solved the mystery of the universe.

This was what happened. *First*: Everyone present was either standing or sitting in the living room, food was being eaten, drinks were
being drunk, conversations were going back and forth between and
among pairs and groups of people. Ferguson saw Jim standing in a
corner by the front window talking to his father, maneuvered his way

into that corner himself, and asked Jim if he could have a word with him in private. Jim said yes, and the two of them walked down the hall and went into Ferguson's bedroom, where, with no word or preamble of any kind, Ferguson threw his arms around Jim and told him he loved him, loved him more than anyone in the world, loved him so much he would be willing to die for him, and before Jim could respond, the now six-foot Ferguson covered the face of the six-foot-one-inch Jim with numerous kisses. The good Jim was neither angry nor shocked. He assumed that Ferguson was either drunk or gravely upset about something, so he wrapped his arms around his younger cousin, held him in a long, fervent hug, and said: I love you, too, Archie. We're friends for life. *Second*: Half an hour later, everyone present was still either standing or sitting in the living room, food was still being eaten, drinks were still being drunk, conversations were still going back and forth between and among pairs and groups of people. Ferguson saw Amy standing in a corner by the front window talking to her cousin Ella, maneuvered his way into that corner himself, and asked Amy if he could have a word with her in private. Amy said yes, and the two of them walked down the hall and went into Ferguson's bedroom, where, with no word or preamble of any kind, Ferguson threw his arms around Amy and told her he loved her, loved her more than anyone in the world, loved her so much he would be willing to die for her, and before Amy could respond, Ferguson kissed her on the mouth, and Amy, who was familiar with Ferguson's mouth because of the many kisses he had given her in the bygone days of their pubescent fling, opened her own mouth and let Ferguson dive in with his tongue, and before long she had wrapped her arms around her cousin and the two of them had fallen onto the bed, where Ferguson reached under Amy's skirt and began running his hand up her stockinged leg and Amy reached into Ferguson's pants and took hold of his stiffened penis, and after each one had finished off the other, Amy smiled at Ferguson and said: This is good, Archie. We've been needing to do this for a long time.

Everything improved after that. Egregious, unacceptable social offenses were apparently not always egregious and unacceptable, for not only had Ferguson managed to open his heart and declare his love to the two Schneidermans but his friendship with Jim had grown stronger because of it, and he and Amy had become a couple again. The week after the funeral, his mother and Gil gave him two hundred dollars for his birthday, but he didn't need the money for Julie anymore, he could spend it on Amy and buy her beautiful lace underwear for the nights when Gil and his mother went out and they had the apartment to themselves, or the nights when Amy's parents went out, or the nights when someone else's parents went out and one of their friends gave them a room to hole up in for a few hours, and how much better things were between them now that he was writing his film articles and Amy could see that he wasn't the dolt she used to think he was, suddenly she respected him, suddenly it didn't matter if he was wrapped up in politics or not, he was a film boy, an art boy, a *sensitive boy*, and that was good enough for her, and what a pleasant jolt it was to discover that neither one of them was a virgin, that neither one of them was afraid, that they had both learned enough by then to know how to satisfy each other, surely that made all the difference, to be happy in bed with a person you loved and who loved you back, and for a short time Ferguson walked around feeling that yes, it was true—by throwing his arms around Jim and Amy he had *unlocked the secret of the universe*.

It couldn't last, of course, the big love would have to be put aside and perhaps even forgotten because Amy was a year ahead of him in school and would be going to the University of Wisconsin in the fall, not to nearby Barnard as originally planned but to the far-off American tundra because Amy had decided, *after long weeks of tormented soul-searching*, that she had to get as far away from her mother as possible. Ferguson begged her not to go there, actually got down on his knees and begged, but the sobbing Amy said she had no choice because she would be *strangled and suffocated* in New York by her relentlessly interfering mother, and much as she loved her darling Archie, she felt she was *fighting for her life* and had to go, simply had to go and couldn't let herself be talked out of it. That conversation was the beginning of the end, the first step in the slow dismantling of the perfect world they had created for themselves, and because the next day was the start of the weekend when Amy was supposed to make her long-planned trip to Cambridge to visit her brother, Ferguson found himself alone in New York on that Friday night in April, and he who had not drunk a drop of alcohol since the afternoon of the old man's funeral and had not attended a single one of his friends' disreputable parties went to one of those disreputable parties and drank himself into such a stupor that he overslept the next morning and missed going to school to take the SATs, which had been scheduled to begin at nine sharp.

There would be another chance to take the test in the fall, but his mother and Gil were annoyed with him for being so *irresponsible,* and though he couldn't fault them for being miffed by his failure to show up for the exam, their anger nevertheless stung, stung far more than it should have, and for the first time in his life Ferguson was beginning to understand how fragile he was, how difficult it was for him to steer his way through even the smallest conflicts, especially conflicts brought on by his own flaws and stupidities, for the point was that he needed to be loved, loved more than most people needed to be loved, entirely loved without respite through every waking minute of his life, loved even when he did things that made him unlovable, especially when reason demanded that he not be loved, and unlike Amy, who was pushing her mother away from her, Ferguson could never let go of his mother, his unsmothering mother whose love was the source of all life for him, and merely to see her frown at him with that sad look in her eyes was a devastation, a bullet in the heart.

The end came at the beginning of summer. Not the fall, when Amy would be going to Wisconsin, but early July, when she left on a two-month backpacking trip through Europe with one of her friends, another whiz-kid Hunter girl named Molly Devine. Later that same week, Ferguson left for Vermont. His mother and stepfather had granted him his wish to follow Amy's example and take part in the French immersion program at Hampton College. It was a fine program, and Ferguson's French improved enormously in the weeks he was there, but it was a sexless summer filled with dread about what was waiting for him when he returned to New York: a last kiss with Amy—and then good-bye, no doubt a definitive good-bye.

So there was Ferguson after Amy flew off to Madison, Wisconsin, a senior in high school *with his whole life in front of him,* as he was informed by his teachers, his relatives, and every adult he crossed paths with, but he had just lost the love of his life, and the word *future* had been erased from every dictionary in the world. Almost inevitably, his thoughts turned to Julie again. It wasn't love, of course, but at least it was sex, and sex without love was better than no sex at all, particularly when no books would have to be stolen in order to pay for it. Most of his

birthday money was gone by then. He had spent it on lingerie and perfume and linguine dinners with Amy in the spring, but he still had
thirty-eight dollars left over, which was more than enough for another
tumble in the apartment on West Eighty-second Street. Such were the
contradictions of manhood, Ferguson discovered. Your heart could be
broken, but your gonads kept telling you to forget about your heart.

He called Mrs. M., hoping to schedule a Friday afternoon appointment with Julie, and though Mrs. M. had some trouble remembering
who he was (it had been months since his last visit), he reminded her
that he was the kid who had been sitting around in the living room talking to the girls when that cop walked in to collect his weekly envelope
and shooed him out of the place. Yeah, yeah, Mrs. M. said. I remember
you now. Charlie Schoolboy. That's what we used to call you.

And what about Julie? Ferguson asked. Can I see her on Friday?

Julie ain't here, Mrs. M. said.

Where is she?

Don't know. Word is she's on smack, honey. I doubt we'll be seeing
her again.

That's terrible.

Yeah, it's terrible, but what can we do about it? There's another black
girl here now. Much prettier than Julie. More flesh on her bones, more
personality. Cynthia, that's her name. Want me to pencil you in?

Black girl—what's that got to do with it?

I thought you went for black girls.

I go for all girls. I just happened to like Julie.

Well, if you go for all girls, there's no problem, is there? The stable's
full these days.

Let me think about it, Ferguson said. I'll call you back.

He hung up the phone, and for the next thirty or forty seconds he
repeated the word *terrible* to himself thirty or forty times, struggling not
to imagine Julie's limp body as she nodded out somewhere in a drugged-
up haze, hoping Mrs. M.'s information was wrong and that Julie wasn't
working there anymore because she had graduated from City College
with honors in philosophy and was studying for her doctorate at
Harvard, and then his eyes teared up for a moment as an image formed
in his mind: Julie lying dead on a bare mattress, naked and stiff in a
dingy room at the Auberge Saint Hell.

A week later, he was ready to give it a shot with Cynthia or anyone else at Mrs. M.'s establishment who had two arms, two legs, and something that resembled a woman's body. Unfortunately, he had spent the last of his birthday money on a record-buying spree at Sam Goody's and had to resort to less than savory means of acquiring the money, so on a warm Friday afternoon in early October, one day before his rescheduled appointment to take the SATs, he donned his thief's gear of woolen overcoat and multipocketed winter jacket and entered a bookstore across from the Columbia campus called Book World, which sounded so much like the burned-down business that had once been Home World that at first he hesitated to go in, but in he went despite his qualms, and as he stood by the paperback fiction section along the southern wall of the store, slipping novels by Dickens and Dostoyevsky into his pockets, he felt a hand come crashing down on his shoulder from behind, and then a voice was roaring in his ear, *I've got you, fucker—don't move!*, and just like that Ferguson's book-stealing operation came to a sorry, idiotic end, for what person in his right mind would wear a woolen overcoat on a day when the temperature was sixty-two degrees outside?

They slammed down hard on him and gave him the works. The book-stealing epidemic that had spread across the city was driving many booksellers to the verge of ruin, and the law needed to make an example of someone, and since the owner of Book World was fed up and enraged by what had been happening to his business, he called the cops and told them he wanted to press charges. Never mind that there were only two slender books in Ferguson's pockets—*Oliver Twist* and *Notes from Underground*—the boy was a thief and had to be punished. The stunned and mortified Ferguson was therefore handcuffed, arrested, and driven in a squad car to the local precinct house, where he was booked, fingerprinted, and photographed from three angles as he held up a little board with his name on it. Then they put him in a holding cell with a pimp, a drug dealer, and a man who had stabbed his wife, and for the next three hours Ferguson sat there waiting for one of the cops to come back and fetch him so he could be arraigned before a judge. That judge, Samuel J. Wasserman, had the authority to dismiss the charges and send Ferguson home, but he didn't do that because he too felt that someone needed to be made an example of, and what better candidate than Ferguson, a snot-nosed rich boy from a so-called progressive private school who had broken the law for no reason other than the pure sport of it? The gavel came down. The trial was scheduled for the second week in November, and Ferguson was released without bail—on condition that he remain in the custody of his parents.

His parents. They had been called, and they were both standing in the courtroom when Wasserman set the date for the trial. His mother cried, emitting no sounds as she slowly shook her head back and forth, as if not yet able to absorb what he had done. Gil didn't cry, but he too was shaking his head back and forth, and from the expression in his eyes, Ferguson gathered that he wanted to smack him.

Books, Gil said, as the three of them stood at the curb waiting for a taxi, what in the world were you thinking? I give you books, don't I? I give you all the books you could possibly want. Why the hell did you have to steal them?

Ferguson couldn't tell him about Mrs. M. and the apartment on West Eighty-second Street, couldn't tell him about the money he was hoping to raise because he wanted to fuck a whore, couldn't tell him about the seven times he had fucked a vanished junkie whore named Julie or about the other books he had stolen in the past, so he lied and said: It's about this thing that's going on with some of my friends—stealing books as a test of courage. It's a kind of competition.

Some friends, Gil said. Some competition.

They all climbed into the backseat of the cab, and suddenly Ferguson felt everything go limp inside him, as if there were no bones left under his skin. He leaned his head against his mother's shoulder and started to cry.

I need you to love me, Ma, he said. I don't know what I'd do if you didn't love me.

I love you, Archie, his mother said. I'll always love you. I just don't understand you anymore.

IN ALL THE confusion, he had forgotten about the SATs he was supposed to take in the morning—and so had his mother and Gil. Not that it mattered much, he said to himself as the days wore on, for the truth was that the idea of college had lost its attraction to him, and given how much he had always disliked school, the prospect of not going to school beyond this year was something to be taken into careful consideration.

□ □ □

THE FOLLOWING WEEK, when word got out about Ferguson's run-in with the authorities, the Riverside Academy took it upon itself to suspend him for a month, an action permitted under the by-laws of the code governing student conduct. He would have to keep up with his homework during that time or else risk being expelled when he returned, the headmaster said, and he would also have to find a job. What job? Ferguson asked. Bagging groceries at the Gristedes on Columbus Avenue, the headmaster said. Why there? Ferguson asked. Because one of our parents owns it, the headmaster said, and he's willing to let you work there during your suspension. Will they pay me? Ferguson asked. Yes, they'll pay you, the headmaster said, but you can't keep the money. It all has to go to charity. We were thinking the American Booksellers Association might be a worthy recipient. How does that strike you?

I'm all for it, Mr. Briggs. I think it's an excellent idea.

THE PRESIDING JUDGE at the November trial, Rufus P. Nolan, found Ferguson guilty as charged and sentenced him to six months in a juvenile detention facility. The harshness of the verdict hung in the air for three or four seconds (seconds as long as hours, as years) and then the judge added: *Sentence suspended.*

Ferguson's legal representative, a young criminal lawyer named Desmond Katz, asked that the stain of the verdict be expunged from his client's record, but Nolan refused. He had shown remarkable leniency in suspending the sentence, he said, and the good counselor should refrain from pushing his luck. The crime revolted him. As a son of privilege, Ferguson seemed to think he was above the law and that stealing books was nothing more than *a lark*, whereas his wanton disrespect of private property and cruel indifference to the rights of others showed a callousness of spirit that needed to be dealt with harshly in order to ensure that his criminal tendencies would be *nipped in the bud*. As a first offender, he deserved another chance. But he also deserved to have this mark on his record—to make him think twice before he ever considered pulling another stunt like this one again.

□ □ □

Two WEEKS LATER, Amy wrote to tell him she had fallen for someone else, a certain senior classman named Rick, and that she wouldn't be coming home to New York for the Christmas holidays because Rick had invited her to spend that time with him at his family's place in Milwaukee. She said she was sorry to have to break such bad news to him, but something like this was bound to happen sooner or later, and how good it had been during those beautiful weeks in the spring, and how much she still loved him, and how glad she was that they would always be *the best cousin-friends on earth.*

She added in a postscript that she was relieved to know he wouldn't be going to jail. Such a stupid business, she said. *Everybody steals books, but you had to be the one who got caught.*

FERGUSON WAS DISINTEGRATING.

He knew he had to pull himself together—or else his arms and legs would start to fall off and he would spend the rest of the year writhing on the ground like a worm.

On the Saturday after he tore up Amy's letter and burned it in the kitchen sink, he sat through four movies in three different theaters between the hours of noon and ten—a double bill at the Thalia and one movie each at the New Yorker and the Elgin. On Sunday, he sat through four others. The eight films were so scrambled in his head that he couldn't remember which was which anymore by the time he fell asleep on Sunday night. He decided that from then on he would jot down a one-page description of every film he saw and keep those pages in a special three-ring binder on his desk. That would be one way of holding on to his life instead of losing it. Plunging into the dark, yes, but always with a candle in his hand and a box of matches in his pocket.

In December, he published two more articles for Mr. Dunbar's newspaper, a long one on three non-Westerns by John Ford (*Young Mr. Lincoln, How Green Was My Valley, The Grapes of Wrath*) and a short one on *Some Like It Hot*, which mostly ignored the story and concentrated on the men disguised in drag and Marilyn Monroe's half-naked body spilling out of her diaphanous dress.

The irony was that his suspension from school had not turned him into an outcast. Quite the contrary, it seemed to have elevated his standing among his male friends, who now looked upon him as a daring rebel, *a tough hombre*, and even the girls seemed to find him more attractive now that he had been officially transformed into a dangerous person. His interest in those girls had ended when he was fifteen, but he asked a few of them out just to see if they could stop him from thinking about Amy. They couldn't. Not even when he took Isabel Kraft in his arms and kissed her—which suggested that it was going to take time, a long time before he was ready to start breathing again.

No COLLEGE. THAT was his final decision, and when he told his mother and Gil that he wouldn't be registering to take the SATs in early January, that he wouldn't be sending out applications to Amherst or Cornell or Princeton or any of the other colleges they had been discussing for the past year, his parents looked at him as if he had just announced that he was planning to commit suicide.

You don't know what you're talking about, Gil said. You can't stop your education now.

I won't be stopping it, Ferguson said. I'll just be educating myself in a different way.

But where, Archie? his mother asked. You're not planning to sit around this apartment for the rest of your life, are you?

Ferguson laughed. What a thought, he said. No, I wouldn't stay here. Of course I wouldn't stay here. I'd like to go to Paris—assuming I manage to graduate from high school, and assuming you'd be willing to give me a graduation present that would cover the price of a cheap, one-way charter ticket.

You're forgetting the war, Gil said. The moment you're out of high school, they'll draft you into the army and ship you off to Vietnam.

No, they won't, Ferguson said. They wouldn't dare.

FOR ONCE, FERGUSON was right. Six weeks after he stumbled his way to the end of high school, having made his peace with Amy, having blessed Jim on his engagement to Nancy Hammerstein, having lived through an unexpectedly warm and comforting springtime affair with his good friend Brian Mischevski, which had convinced the now eighteen-year-old Ferguson that he was indeed someone who had been built to love both men and women and that his life would be more complicated than most other lives because of that doubleness but also perhaps richer and more invigorating as well, having written a new article for Mr. Dunbar's paper every other week until the end of the final semester, having added close to a hundred pages to his loose-leaf three-ring binder, having worked with Gil to prepare a comprehensive reading list for his first year as a student attached to no college or university, having gone back to the Gristedes on Columbus Avenue to shake hands with his former co-workers, having gone back to Book World to apologize to the owner, George Tyler, for having stolen the books, having understood how lucky he was to have been caught and not severely punished, having vowed never to steal anything from anyone ever again, Ferguson received his *Greetings* letter from the United States government and was told to report to the draft board on Whitehall Street for his army physical, which needless to say he passed because he was a fit young man with no physical problems or abnormalities, but because he had a criminal record, and because he openly confessed to the staff psychiatrist that he was attracted to men as well as to women, a new draft card was issued to him later that summer with his new classification typed onto the front: 4-F.

Feckless—frazzled—fucked-up—and free.

$\boxed{4.4}$

IN HIS THREE YEARS AS A HIGH SCHOOL STUDENT IN THE NEW JERSEY suburbs, the sixteen-, seventeen-, and eighteen-year-old Ferguson started twenty-seven short stories, finished nineteen of them, and spent no less than one hour every day with what he called his *work notebooks*, which he filled with various writing exercises he invented for himself in order to *stay sharp, dig down, and try to get better* (as he once put it to Amy): descriptions of physical objects, landscapes, morning skies, human faces, animals, the effect of light on snow, the sound of rain on glass, the smell of burning wood, the sensation of walking through fog or listening to wind blow through the branches of trees; monologues in the voices of other people in order to become those other people or at least try to understand them better (his father, his mother, his stepfather, Amy, Noah, his teachers, his friends at school, Mr. and Mrs. Federman), but also unknown and more distant others such as J. S. Bach, Franz Kafka, the checkout girl at the local supermarket, the ticket collector on the Erie Lackawanna Railroad, and the bearded panhandler who cadged a dollar from him in Grand Central Station; imitations of admired, demanding, inimitable writers from the past (take a paragraph from Hawthorne, for example, and compose something based on his syntactical model, using a verb wherever he used a verb, a noun wherever he used a noun, an adjective wherever he used an adjective—in order to feel the rhythms in your bones, to feel how the music was made); a curious sequence of vignettes generated by puns, homonyms, and one-letter displacements of words: ail/ale, lust/lost, soul/soil, birth/berth; and impetuous jags of automatic writing to *clear his brain* whenever he was feeling stuck, as with a four-page scribble-gush inspired by the word *nomad* that began: *No, I am not mad. Nor am I even angry, but give me a chance to discombobulate you, and I'll pick your pockets clean.* He also wrote one one-act play, which he burned in disgust one week after finishing it, and twenty-three of the foulest stinker poems ever hatched by a citizen of the New World, which he tore up after promising himself never to write another poem again. He mostly hated what he did. He mostly thought he was stupid and talent-less and would never amount to anything, but still he persisted, driv-ing himself to keep at it every day in spite of the often disappointing results, understanding there would be no hope for him unless he kept at it, that becoming the writer he wanted to be would necessarily take years, more years than it would take for his body to finish growing, and every time he wrote something that seemed slightly less bad than the piece that had come before it, he sensed he was making progress, even if the next piece turned out to be an abomination, for the truth was that he didn't have a choice, he was destined to do this or die, because not-withstanding his struggles and dissatisfaction with the dead things that often came out of him, the act of doing it made him feel more alive than anything else he had ever done, and when the words began to sing in his ears and he sat down at his desk and picked up his pen or put his fingers on the keys of his typewriter, he felt naked, naked and exposed to the big world rushing in on him, and nothing felt better than that, nothing could equal the sensation of disappearing from himself and entering the big world humming inside the words that were humming inside his head.

Stubborn. That was the word that best described him during those years—and every year more stubborn than the year before, more locked into himself, more unwilling to budge when someone or something pushed up against him. Ferguson had grown hard—hard in his con-tempt for his father, hard in the abnegations he continued to impose on himself years after Artie Federman's death, hard in his opposition to the suburban society that had held him prisoner since the beginning of his conscious life. If Ferguson hadn't yet turned into an insufferable scold who made people flee from him the moment he walked into a room, it was because he didn't look for fights and generally kept his thoughts to himself. Most of his fellow high school students saw him as an okay sort

of guy—a bit morose at times, a bit *lost in his own head*, but not someone
with a chip on his shoulder, and definitely not a bore, since Ferguson
wasn't against all people, only some people, and the people he wasn't
against he tended to like, and the people he liked he treated with a
reserved but thoughtful affection, and the people he loved he loved in
the way a dog loves, with every part of himself, never judging, never
condemning, never thinking an ill thought, simply worshipping them
and exulting in their presence, for he knew he was utterly dependent
on the small band of people who loved him and whom he loved back
and that without them he would have been lost, another Hank or Frank
tumbling down the shaft of the all-devouring incinerator, a flake of ash
floating across the night sky.

He was no longer the boy who had written *Sole Mates* as a fourteen-
year-old nitwit nobody, but he still carried that boy inside him, and he
sensed that the two of them would go on walking together for a long
time to come. To combine the strange with the familiar: that was what
Ferguson aspired to, to observe the world as closely as the most dedicated realist and yet to create a way of seeing the world through a different, slightly distorting lens, for reading books that dwelled only on
the familiar inevitably taught you things you already knew, and reading books that dwelled only on the strange taught you things you didn't
need to know, and what Ferguson wanted above all else was to write
stories that would make room not only for the visible world of sentient
beings and inanimate things but also for the vast and mysterious unseen
forces that were hidden within the seen. He wanted to disturb and dis-
orient, to make people roar with laughter and tremble in their boots, to
break hearts and damage minds and dance the loony dance of the dizzy-
boys as they swung into their doppelgänger duet. Yes, Tolstoy was ever
so moving, and yes, Flaubert wrote the best sentences in creation, but
much as Ferguson enjoyed following the dramatic, increasingly drastic
turns in the lives of Anna K. and Emma B., at that moment in his life
the characters who spoke most forcefully to him were Kafka's K., Swift's
Gulliver, Poe's Pym, Shakespeare's Prospero, Melville's Bartleby, Gogol's
Kovalyov, and M. Shelley's monster.

Early efforts from his sophomore year: a story about a man who
wakes up one morning to discover he has a different face; a story about
a man who loses his wallet and passport in a foreign city and sells his
blood in order to eat; a story about a little girl who changes her name

on the first day of every month; a story about two friends who stop being friends because of a dispute in which both of their arguments are wrong; a story about a man who accidentally kills his wife and then decides to paint every house in his neighborhood a bright shade of red; a story about a woman who loses the power of speech and finds herself growing progressively happier as the years go on; a story about a teenage boy who runs away from home and then, when he decides to return, discovers that his parents have vanished; a story about a young man writing a story about a young man writing a story about a young man writing a story about a young man . . .

Hemingway taught him to look at his sentences more carefully, how to measure the weight of each word and syllable that went into the building of a paragraph, but admirable as Hemingway's writing could be when he was writing at his best, his work didn't say much to Ferguson, all that manly bluster and tight-lipped stoicism seemed slightly ridiculous to him, so he left Hemingway behind for the deeper, more demanding Joyce, and then, when he turned sixteen, another bundle of paperbacks was given to him by Uncle Don, among them books by the heretofore unknown Isaac Babel, who quickly became Ferguson's number one short-story writer in the world, and Heinrich von Kleist (the subject of Don's first biography), who quickly became Ferguson's number two short-story writer, but even more valuable to him, not to say *precious* and *everlastingly fundamental*, was the forty-five-cent Signet edition of *Walden and Civil Disobedience* that was wedged in among the books of fiction and poetry, for even if Thoreau wasn't a writer of novels or short stories, he was a writer of sublime clarity and precision, a creator of such beautifully constructed sentences that Ferguson felt their beauty as one feels a blow to the chin or a fever in the brain. Perfect. Every word seemed to fall perfectly in place, and every sentence seemed to be a small work unto itself, an independent unit of breath and thought, and the thrill of reading such prose was never knowing how far Thoreau would leap from one sentence to the next—sometimes it was only a matter of inches, sometimes of several feet or yards, sometimes of whole country miles—and the destabilizing effect of those irregular distances taught Ferguson how to think about his own efforts in a new way, for what Thoreau did was to combine two opposing and mutually exclusive impulses in every paragraph he wrote, what Ferguson began to call the impulse to *control* and the impulse to *take risks*. That was the secret, he felt. All control would lead to an airless, suffocating result. All risk would lead to chaos and incomprehensibility. But put the two together, and then maybe you'd be onto something, then maybe the words singing in your head would start to sing on the page and bombs would go off and buildings would collapse and the world would begin to look like a different world.

But there was more to Thoreau than just style. There was the savage need to be himself and no one but himself even at the cost of offending his neighbors, the stubbornness of soul that so appealed to the ever more stubborn Ferguson, the *adolescent* Ferguson, who saw in Thoreau a man who had managed to remain an adolescent for his entire life, which is to say, a man who had never abandoned his principles, who had never turned into a corrupt, sellout grown-up—a brave boy to the bitter end, which was precisely how Ferguson wanted to imagine his own future. But beyond the spiritual imperative to transform himself into a bold, self-reliant being, there was Thoreau's critical examination of the American premise that money rules all, the rejection of the American government and his willingness to go to jail in order to protest that government's actions, and then, of course, there was the idea that had changed the world, the idea that had helped make India an independent country five months after Ferguson was born, which was the same idea now spreading across the American South and perhaps would help change America as well, *civil disobedience*, nonviolent resistance to the violence of unjust laws, and how little had changed in the one hundred and twelve years since *Walden*, Ferguson told himself, the Mexican-American War now turned into the Vietnam War, black slavery now turned into Jim Crow oppression and Klan-run state governments, and just as Thoreau had written his book in the years leading up to the Civil War, Ferguson felt that he too was writing at a moment when the world was about to blow apart again, and three times in the weeks both before and after his mother married Jim and Amy's father, as he watched the televised images and studied the newspaper photographs of Buddhist monks in South Vietnam *burning themselves to death* to protest the policies of the American-backed Diem regime, Ferguson understood that the quiet days of his boyhood were over, that the horror of those immolations proved that if men were willing to die for peace, then the steadily expanding war in their country would eventually become so big that it would obscure everything and end up making everyone go blind.

□ □ □

THE NEW HOUSE was in South Orange, not Maplewood, but since the two towns were governed by a single board of education, Ferguson and Amy stayed on as students at Columbia High School, which was the only public high school in the district. They had already finished their sophomore year when their parents were married on August 2, 1963, and the dispiriting conversation that had taken place in the backyard of Ferguson's old house eleven months earlier was all but forgotten. Amy had found herself a boyfriend, Ferguson had found himself a girlfriend, and their brother-sister friendship had forged on just as Amy had hoped it would, although now that they were actually brother and sister, perhaps the old metaphor had become a trifle redundant.

Ferguson's father was taking all the money from the sale of the old house, but Dan Schneiderman still owned the old-old house, the first Maplewood house, which young Ferguson had never wanted to leave, and by selling that house for twenty-nine thousand dollars, he had been able to buy the somewhat larger house in South Orange for thirty-six thousand dollars, for even though Ferguson's mother was nearly penniless because the monthly checks from his father had stopped coming after she married Dan, Dan himself was no longer broke, since he and Liz had both taken out one-hundred-and-fifty-thousand-dollar life insurance policies early in their marriage, and now that he had collected that sum in the wake of Liz's hideous, premature death, the newly formed family of Adlers, Fergusons, and Schneidermans was comfortably solvent for the time being. It was hard not to think about where the money had come from, the gruesome translation of terminal cancer into dollars, but Liz was dead, and life was moving on, and what choice did any of them have but to move along with it?

They all loved the new house. Even Ferguson, who was strongly opposed to living in a small town, who would have given almost anything to move to New York or any other large city anywhere in the world, admitted that it was a fine choice and that the two-story white clapboard house built in 1903 and situated on an out-of-the-way cul-de-sac known as Woodhall Crescent was a far better place to park your bones than the chilly Castle of Silence he had been forced to live in for the past seven years. They probably could have used one more bedroom on top of the four they had, since the room that would have been Jim's was converted into a studio for Dan, but no one saw it as a hardship, least of all the phlegmatic Jim, who visited only rarely and seemed content to sleep on the living room sofa, and if he didn't mind, why should anyone else mind? The important thing was that they were all in it together, and because Ferguson approved of Dan, and Amy and Jim approved of Ferguson's mother, and Dan approved of Ferguson, and Ferguson's mother approved of Amy and Jim, they all settled in peacefully together and paid no attention to the gossips in the two towns who felt that with all the twists and commotions of the past year—death, divorce, remarriage, a new house, and two sexed-up teenagers living side by side on the same floor in that house—something *strange* or *unnatural* or *not quite right* must have been going on over there at 7 Woodhall Crescent. The man was nothing more than a *struggling artist*, for pity's sake, meaning a slovenly, wisecracking *luftmensch* (according to the Jews) or a long-haired nonconformist with doubtful political leanings (according to the non-Jews), and how could Stanley Ferguson's wife have walked out on her marriage and all the money that came with it to join forces with a character like that?

The biggest change for Ferguson had nothing to do with his mother's marriage to Dan Schneiderman. She had been married before, after all, and in that Dan was a better, more compatible husband for her than his father had been, Ferguson endorsed the union and didn't think about it much because he didn't have to. What he did think about, however, and what represented a far more significant upheaval in the basic conditions of his life, was that he was no longer an only child. As a young boy, he had prayed for a brother or a sister, again and again he had begged his mother to produce a baby for him so he wouldn't be alone anymore, but then she had told him it wouldn't be possible, that she had no more babies in her, which meant that he would be her one and only Archie until the end of time, and little by little Ferguson had come to terms with his solitary fate, evolving into the pensive, dreamy fellow who now wanted to spend his adulthood sequestered in a room writing books, missing out on the rough-and-tumble joys and high-spirited camaraderie that most children live through with their siblings, but also avoiding the conflicts and hatreds that can turn childhood into a hellish, unrelenting brawl that ends in lifelong bitterness and/or permanent psychosis, and now, at the age of sixteen, having eluded both the good and the bad of not being the only one for his entire life, Ferguson's childhood wish had been granted in the form of a sixteen-year-old sister and a twenty-year-old brother—but too late, too long deferred to be of much use to him anymore, and even though Jim was mostly absent and Amy was his close friend again (after a long spell of resenting her for having turned him down the previous summer), there were days when he couldn't help longing for his old life as an only child, even if that life had been much worse than this one.

It would have been different if Amy had loved him in the way he had come to love her, if they had taken advantage of their new circumstances to indulge in various sorts of carnal mischief, impromptu hanky-panky sessions when their parents' backs were turned, secret lust frolics and midnight assignations in either one of their adjacent bedrooms, culminating in the mutual sacrifice of their two virginities to the cause of love and greater mental health, but Amy wasn't interested, she really and truly just wanted to be his sister, and the sex-mad Ferguson, whose primary goal in life was to stick his penis into a naked girl's body and put his virginhood behind him forever, had to go along with it or else explode from the continual agitation of wanting what he couldn't have, for thwarted desire was a poison that seeped into every part of you, and once your veins and inner organs were fully saturated with the stuff, it traveled upward toward your brain and burst right through the top of your skull.

The early weeks in the new house were the most difficult for him. Not only did he have to suppress the urge to grab hold of Amy and smear her face with kisses every time they were alone together, and not only did he have to tamp down the nighttime erection reveries of slipping into bed with her in the room next door, but there were numerous practical adjustments that had to be made as well, which largely revolved around the question of how not to infringe on each other's privacy, and until they established a set of hard-and-fast rules about how to coexist in the spaces they shared (knock first, tidy up the bathroom before leaving it, wash your own dishes, don't crib the other's homework unless the answer is freely given to you, and no snooping in the other's room, which meant that Ferguson couldn't peek at Amy's diary and Amy couldn't peek at Ferguson's work notebooks and stories), there were several awkward moments and a couple of downright embarrassments, as when Amy opened the bathroom door and saw the freshly showered Ferguson sitting naked on the toilet jerking off—*I didn't see that!* she yelped, as she slammed the door shut—or when Ferguson popped out of his room at the precise instant Amy was walking down the hall trying to adjust the towel that was wrapped around her body, and when the towel suddenly fell off, unveiling the whiteness of her bare skin to the startled Ferguson, who was looking at the small-nippled breasts and curly brown pubes of his stepsister for the first time, Amy let out a loud *Fuck!*, which Ferguson answered with an almost witty retort—*I always suspected you had a body*, he said. *Now I'm sure of it*—and Amy laughed, then raised her arms in a mock-cheesecake pose, and said, *Now we're even, <u>Mr. Dick</u>*, which referred not only to the funny character in their beloved *David Copperfield* but to what she had seen in the bathroom several days earlier.

It was true that Ferguson had a girlfriend, but it was also true that he would have dropped her in an instant if Amy's *Barkis* had been willing, but it wasn't, and now that Ferguson had seen the body that would never be given to him, he no longer had to torture himself with trying to imagine what it looked like, and that was a small step forward, he felt, a way to begin curing himself of an unhealthy obsession that would never take him anywhere except into the Bottomless Well of Eternal Sadness, and by way of recompense he tried to fix his thoughts on his girlfriend's body, which he had seen naked only from the waist up so far, but their explorations were becoming bolder and more reckless now that they had been reunited at the start of their junior year, which meant there was cause for hope, and after a rough summer of not knowing where he stood with Amy or how he should act with her, Ferguson decided to capitulate, to burn his arsenal of weapons and sign a mental treaty of absolute surrender, and from that moment on he began to settle into his new job of acting as a brother to Amy's sister, knowing that was the only way he could go on loving her and still be loved in return.

Sometimes they fought, sometimes Amy shouted and slammed doors and called him names, sometimes Ferguson hid in his room and refused to talk to her for entire evenings, entire blocks of ten or twelve uninterrupted hours, but mostly they made an effort to get along, and mostly they did get along. In effect, their friendship returned to what it had been before Ferguson got it into his head that they should be more than *just friends*, but there was an added intensity to the friendship now that they were living with their newly married parents in the house on Woodhall Crescent, with longer, more intimate conversations that

sometimes lasted three or four hours and at some point always managed to come around to Amy's mother's death and Artie Federman's
death, with more hours of studying and preparing for tests together
(which pushed Ferguson's grades up from B+'s and occasional A–'s to
Amy's level of all A's and A–'s), more cigarettes smoked together, more
alcohol drunk together (almost all of it beer, cheap Rolling Rock in long
green bottles or even cheaper Old Milwaukee in the stumpy brown
ones), more old movies watched on TV together, more records listened to
together, more games of gin rummy played together, more trips to New
York together, more joking, more teasing, more arguing about politics,
more laughing, and no more inhibitions about picking noses and farting in each other's company.

THE SCHOOL HAD more than twenty-one hundred students, just over
seven hundred per grade, and in that factory of secondary public education that served the towns of Maplewood and South Orange, there
was a mix of Protestants, Catholics, and Jews, a largely middle-class
population with a chunk from the blue-collar laboring class and another
chunk from the upper strata of white-collar wealth, boys and girls whose
families had come to America from England, Scotland, Italy, Ireland,
Poland, Russia, Germany, Czechoslovakia, Greece, and Hungary, but not
a single Asian family and only twenty-four students of color in the entire
school, making it one of the many one-color high schools in Essex
County, and even at that late date, nineteen and twenty years after the
liberation of the death camps at the end of the Second World War, traces
of anti-Semitism lingered on in the two towns, mostly in the form of
whispers, silences, and unwritten exclusions at places such as the Orange
Lawn Tennis Club, but sometimes it was worse than that, and neither
Ferguson nor Amy ever forgot the cross that was burned on the front
lawn of one of their Jewish friends from Maplewood the year they
turned ten.

More than two-thirds of the seven hundred–plus students in their
class would go on to attend college, some at the best private colleges in
the country, some at mediocre private colleges along the eastern sea-
board, some at state-run colleges in New Jersey, and for the boys who
didn't attend college there was the army and Vietnam, and after that, if
there was an after that, work as mechanics and gas pumpers at garages

and filling stations, careers as bakers and long-distance truck drivers, fitful or steady employment as plumbers, electricians, and carpenters, twenty-year stints in the police department, the fire department, and the sanitation department, or else shooting for the jackpot in high-risk trades such as gambling, extortion, and armed robbery. For the girls who didn't attend college, there was marriage and motherhood, secretarial school, nursing school, beautician school, dental technician school, work in offices, restaurants, and travel agencies, and the chance to spend the rest of their lives within ten miles of the town where they were born.

There were some exceptions, however, some girls who would not be going on to college and would not be staying put either, some girls with altogether different pasts and futures from the home-grown New Jersey girls Ferguson had been studying all his life, and one such figure happened to turn up in his English class on the first day of his first year as a high school student, a dark-haired, dark-skinned girl who was neither pretty nor not pretty but singularly arresting to Ferguson's eyes, all coiled into herself like an unafraid animal trapped in a zoo, calmly observing the observers through the bars, wondering which one would be brave enough to feed her, and when Mrs. Monroe began the session by pointing her finger at each of the twenty students and asking them to give their names and introduce themselves to the other members of the class, he heard the dark-haired girl speak with what he took to be a British accent, and without pausing to reflect on the matter Ferguson made up his mind to pursue her, not only because a girl from somewhere else was automatically more desirable than a local girl from the Jersey suburbs but because it had been exactly seven days since Amy had rebuffed him in the backyard and he was free, disgustingly free to pursue any girl who crossed his path. Fortunately, Amy was not in his English class that year, which meant her eyes would not be looking at him as he looked at the dark-haired girl and plotted how to approach her, woo her, and win her over, and with no Amy around to spy on his intentions, he could make those intentions as transparent as he wished.

Dana Rosenbloom. Not British but South African. The second of four daughters born to Maurice and Gladys Rosenbloom in Johannesburg, currently residing in the United States because Dana's prosperous, factory-owning father was not only a capitalist entrepreneur but a socialist, a man so opposed to the apartheid government that had been ruling the country since 1948 that he had actively worked against it,

and by engaging in those subversive activities he had offended the
South African legal authorities to such an extent that they had wanted
to put him in prison, a place that would not have been good for Maurice
Rosenbloom's health or the morale of his family, so off the six of them
went, hightailing it out of South Africa to London, leaving behind their
factory, their house in Johannesburg, their cars, their cats, their horse,
their country house, their boat, and the better part of their money.
From everything to nearly nothing, and with Dana's sixty-two-year-old
father too frail to work anymore, her much younger mother, whom
Ferguson guessed to be somewhere in her mid-forties, had taken it
upon herself to support the family in London, a task she had accomplished by rising to a position of great prominence at Harrods department store within three years, and having risen as far as she could go
at Harrods, she had accepted a more important position for double the
salary at Saks Fifth Avenue in New York. Thus the Rosenblooms landed
on American soil in the spring of 1962, and thus they found their way to
a large, creaking house on Mayhew Drive in South Orange, New Jersey,
and thus Dana Rosenbloom wound up sitting two desks over from
Ferguson in Mrs. Monroe's tenth-grade English class at Columbia High
School.

A white South African with the swart complexion of a North African, Eastern European origins layered upon older, deeper origins in
Middle Eastern deserts, the exotic Jewess of Germanic and Nordic literature, the gypsy girl of nineteenth-century operas and Technicolor films,
Esmeralda, Bathsheba, and Desdemona rolled into one, the black fire of
crinkled, unruly hair burning like a crown on her head, slender limbs
and narrow hips, a slight slouch to the shoulders and upper neck as she
scratched out her notes in class, languid movements, never rushed or
frazzled, calm, mild and calm, not the Levantine temptress she appeared
to be but a solid girl with warm, affectionate impulses, in many ways
the most ordinary girl Ferguson had ever been attracted to, not beautiful in the way Linda Flagg was beautiful, not brilliant in the way Amy
was brilliant, but older and more poised than either one of them because
of what she and her family had been through, older than Ferguson himself, an untormented sensualist with enough experience and daring to
make her receptive to his early advances, and before long he understood
that she was crazy about him and would never hack him to pieces as
Amy sometimes did, the disputatious Schneiderman who burst out

laughing when Ferguson pulled out a pipe and lit it after dinner one evening during the Year of Many Dinners before their parents were married, the pipe he had bought to smoke while writing because he thought all writers were meant to smoke pipes when they sat at their desks and wrote, and how thoroughly she had mocked him for that, calling him a *pretentious oaf* and the *silliest boy who had ever lived*, words that Dana Rosenbloom never would have spoken to him or anyone else, and so he courted the dark-eyed newcomer from Johannesburg and London and won her over, not because he knew what he was doing when it came to the art of seduction but because she had fallen for him and wanted to be seduced.

He wasn't in love with her, he would never be in love with her, right from the start he understood that Dana would never be the grand passion he was looking for, but his body needed to be touched, he craved intimacy with someone, and Dana touched him and kissed him well, so well and so often that the physical pleasures obtained by her caresses all but obliterated the need for a grand passion at that point in his life. A little passion with a lot of touching and kissing was enough for now, and when they broke through to bare-skin, all-out sex in the winter of their junior year, it was more than enough to satisfy him.

Wordless animal sex with the gypsy girl who loved him, communication by looks and gestures and touch, few verbal exchanges about anything but the most trivial matters, not a meeting of minds as with Amy or the future girl of his dreams but a meeting of bodies, an understanding between bodies, a lack of inhibition that was so new to Ferguson that he sometimes trembled when he thought about what they did to each other in the empty rooms where they managed to be alone together, skin burning with happiness, sweat flowing from their pores as they slathered each other with kisses, and how kind she was to him, how accepting of his funks and self-indulgent despairs, how unconcerned that he loved her less than she loved him, but they both knew their connection was no more than a temporary business, that America was his place and not hers and for now she was just biding her time until graduation and her eighteenth birthday, when she would be heading off to Israel to live on a kibbutz between the Sea of Galilee and the Golan Heights, that was all she wanted, no college, no books, no big ideas, just planting her body in a place with other bodies and doing whatever she had to do in order to belong to a country that would never kick her out.

Inevitably, there were times when he felt bored with her, disengaged because she cared so little about the things that were most important to him, and all through the years they were in school together he wobbled and drifted, set his sights on other girls, took up with other girls during the summers when Dana visited her relatives in Tel Aviv, but he couldn't ever break with her entirely, her sweetness kept luring him back, the sweetness of her good heart was irresistible, and the sex was necessary, the one thing that blotted out all other things for the minutes or hours it lasted and seemed to make him understand why he had been born and what it meant to belong to the world, the beginning of erotic life, the beginning of real life, and none of that would have been possible with any other girl in the school, the Linda Flaggs and Nora McGintys and Debbie Kleinmans were all militant virgins, professional maidens locked up in iron chastity belts, and therefore, even if his affections wavered from time to time, he knew how lucky he was to have found Dana Rosenbloom and would never let go of her until he had to, for beyond giving herself to him Dana had also given him her family, and Ferguson had come to love that family, love the very idea that such a family could exist, and every time he stepped into their house and was engulfed by the Rosenbloomian aura, he felt so happy to be there he didn't want to leave.

What that aura was seemed to elude any precise definition, although Ferguson made numerous attempts over the years to understand what made it so distinctive, so unlike any other household he had entered before. A mixture of the posh and the humdrum, he sometimes thought, but one in which the poshness was never tainted by the humdrumness and the humdrum was never influenced by the posh. The elegant, beautifully controlled British manners of the parents flourishing side by side with the anarchic tendencies of the children, yet neither camp seemed to resent the other, and an air of peacefulness seemed to hover around the house at all times, even when the two youngest daughters were shouting at each other in the living room. One snapshot: the tall, slim, aristocratic Mrs. Rosenbloom in one of the Chanel and Dior suits she wore to her office at Saks Fifth Avenue patiently talking about birth control to her eldest daughter, Bella, who had gone beatnik since her arrival in America and was listening patiently to her mother as she adjusted her black turtleneck sweater and brushed on black eyeliner, which slowly transformed her into a raccoon. A second snapshot: the smallish, somewhat emaciated Mr. Rosenbloom with his silk ascot and gray goatee discoursing on the virtues of good penmanship to his youngest daughter, Leslie, a scrawny nine-year-old with scabs on her knees and a pet hamster named Rodolfo sleeping in a pocket of her dress. Such was the Rosenbloomian aura, or one or two of its transient emanations, and when Ferguson considered the turmoil those people had gone through together, when he thought about what it must have been like to lose everything and have to start all over again in another part of the world, and then have to start over again for a second time in yet another part of the world, he wondered if he had ever met a braver, more resilient family than this one. That was the aura, too: We're alive, and from now on it's live and let live, and may the gods turn their backs on us and butt out of our affairs for good.

There was much to learn from Mr. Rosenbloom, Ferguson decided, and because Dana's sixty-six-year-old father no longer worked and spent most of his days at home reading books and smoking cigarettes, Ferguson began stopping in to see him from time to time, most often immediately after school when the late-afternoon light would flow into the living room and cast complex, crisscrossing shadows on the floor and furniture, and there they would sit, the young man and the old man in that half-dark, half-bright room, talking about nothing in particular, rambling around among politics and the peculiarities of American life, occasionally discussing a book or a film or a painting, but the bulk of it was Mr. Rosenbloom telling stories about the past, frivolous, charming anecdotes about storm-tossed voyages on steamship liners to Europe, the bons mots he had uttered as a young man, the shock of delight that coursed through him when he took the first sip of his first martini, references to *gramophone records, the wireless,* and rolled-up silk stockings sliding off women's legs, nothing of any consequence, nothing of any depth, but fascinating to listen to, and how rarely he talked about his troubles in South Africa, Ferguson noticed, and when he did say something there was never any rancor in his voice, none of the anger or indignation that might have been expected from a man in exile, and that was why Ferguson was so drawn to Mr. Rosenbloom and took such pleasure in his company—not because he was a man who had suffered but because he was a man who had suffered and could still crack jokes.

Mr. Rosenbloom never read any of Ferguson's stories, never even glanced at a single word Ferguson had written, but of all people he was the one who came up with the solution to a problem that had vexed Ferguson for many months and no doubt would have gone on plaguing him for years.

Archie, the old man said one afternoon. A nice name for everyday use, but not a very good name for a novelist, is it?

No, Ferguson said. It's tragically inappropriate.

And *Archibald* isn't much better, is it?

No, not any better at all. Worse.

So what are you going to do when you start publishing your work?

If I ever do start publishing, you mean.

Well, let's assume that you will. Do you have any alternatives in mind?

Not really.

Not really, or not at all?

Not at all.

Hmmm, Mr. Rosenbloom said, as he lit up a cigarette and looked off into the shadows. After a long pause he asked: What about your middle name? Do you have one?

Isaac.

Mr. Rosenbloom exhaled a large plume of smoke and repeated the two syllables he had just heard: *Isaac*.

It was my grandfather's name.

Isaac Ferguson.

Isaac Ferguson. As in Isaac Babel and Isaac Bashevis Singer.

A fine Jewish name, don't you think?

Not so much the *Ferguson* part, but definitely the *Isaac* part.

Isaac Ferguson, novelist.

Archie Ferguson the man, Isaac Ferguson the writer.

Not bad, I'd say. What do you say?

Not bad at all.

Two people in one.

Or one person in two. Either way, it's good. Either way, that's the name I'll use to sign my work: Isaac Ferguson. If I ever manage to get published, of course.

Don't be so modest. *When* you manage to get published.

Six months after that conversation, as the two of them sat in the house discussing the differences between the light of South African afternoons and the light of New Jersey afternoons, Mr. Rosenbloom stood up from his chair, walked to the far end of the room, and came back with a book in his hand.

Maybe you should read this, he said, as he gently let the book fall from his hand into Ferguson's hand.

It was Alan Paton's *Cry, the Beloved Country: A Story of Comfort in Desolation*. Published by Jonathan Cape, Thirty Bedford Square, London.

Ferguson thanked Mr. Rosenbloom and promised to return the book within the next three or four days.

You don't have to give it back, Mr. Rosenbloom said, as he sat down in his chair again. It's for you, Archie. I don't need it anymore.

Ferguson opened the book and saw that there was an inscription on the first page that read: *23 September 1948. Many Happy Birthdays, Maurice—Tillie and Ben.* Under the two signatures, written out in thick block letters, there were two more words: HOLD FAST.

IF HE WASN'T going to take money from his father, then it was out of the question to spend another summer working in one of his stores. At the same time, if Ferguson wouldn't take money from his father, then he would have to start earning money of his own, but two-month summer jobs were hard to come by in that part of the world, and he didn't know where to look for one. Now that he was sixteen, he supposed he could go back to Camp Paradise and work as a waiter there, but he would earn nothing except for the tips the parents handed out on the last day of the summer, which would amount to a paltry two hundred dollars or so, and besides, Ferguson was finished with camp and never wanted to go back, the mere thought of setting foot on the ground where he had seen Artie Federman die was enough to make him see the death again, see it again and again until it was Ferguson himself who was emitting the faint little *Oh* that came from Artie's mouth, Ferguson himself who was falling down on the grass, Ferguson himself who was dead, and it simply wouldn't be possible to go there, not even if the salary for camp waiters was four hundred dollars a meal.

In the spring of his sophomore year, with his mother's wedding already announced for early August and no solution in sight, Jim put Ferguson in touch with one of his old high school friends, a two-hundred-and-thirty-pound ex–football tackle named Arnie Frazier, who had flunked out of Rutgers in his freshman year and was running a

moving business in Maplewood and South Orange. The fleet consisted
of one white Chevy van, and the operation was an under-the-table affair
transacted on a strict cash-only basis, with no insurance, no bonded
employees, no formal business structure, and no taxes paid because no
income was declared. Even though Ferguson wouldn't be old enough
to drive until next March, Frazier took him on as a shotgun man to
replace his current sidekick, who had been drafted into the army and
would be heading off to Fort Dix at the end of June. Jim's friend would
have preferred a full-time, year-round worker, but Jim was Frazier's
friend because he had once rescued Frazier's twin sister from a touchy
situation at a high school party (decking a drunken lacrosse player who
was pawing her in a corner of the room), and Frazier felt he owed Jim
and couldn't say no. That was how Ferguson got his foot in the door and
began his career as a moving man, which lasted for all three of his high
school summers from 1963 to 1965, since his services were required
again the next year when the new shotgun man was forced to quit
because of a herniated disk in his lower back and again the third year
when the fleet expanded to two vans and Frazier was in urgent need of
a second driver. It was strenuous work at times, and every year when
Ferguson started up again half the muscles in his body would be excru-
ciatingly sore for the first six or seven days, but he found manual work
to be a good counterbalance to the mental work of writing, for not only
did it keep him in good physical shape and serve a legitimate purpose
(moving people's belongings from one place to another), it allowed
him to think his own thoughts rather than have to give his thoughts to
someone else, which was the case with most nonmanual work, helping
someone else make money with your brains while getting as little as
possible for it in return, and even if Ferguson's salary was low, every
job ended with five- and ten- and sometimes twenty-dollar bills being
shoved into his hand, and because work was abundant during those
years before the millions burned on Vietnam wrecked the national economy, he wound up earning close to two hundred tax-free dollars every
week. So Ferguson spent those three summers lugging beds and sofas
up and down narrow staircases, delivering antique mirrors and Louis
XV escritoires to interior decorators in New York, moving college
students in and out of their dorm rooms on campuses in Pennsylvania,
Connecticut, and Massachusetts, hauling old refrigerators and broken-
down air conditioners to the town dump, and in the process he met

many people who never would have brushed up against his life if he had been sitting in an office or making ice cream cones for noisy children at Gruning's. More than that, Arnie treated him well and seemed to respect him, and while it was true that Ferguson's twenty-one-year-old boss voted for Goldwater in the '64 election and wanted to drop nuclear bombs on Hanoi, it was also true that the same Arnie Frazier hired two black men when the second van was bought and the crew expanded to four, and the last summer Ferguson worked for him brought the inestimable bonus of riding around every day with one of those black men, Richard Brinkerstaff, a broad, big-bellied giant who would look through the windshield of the van as Ferguson drove them to their next destination, carefully absorbing the passing landscapes of empty suburban roads and potholed city streets and crowded industrial highways, and again and again in the same tone of voice, whether he was talking about something that delighted him or saddened him or repelled him, he would point his finger at the little girl playing with her collie on the front lawn of her house or the disheveled wino staggering through the intersection at Bowery and Canal and say: *How sweet it is, Archie. How sweet it is.*

Ferguson knew that his father had no idea what to make of him. Not just because he found it impossible to understand why anyone would want to go into such an iffy field as writing books, which struck him as a delusional folly, an all but certain descent into impoverishment, failure, and mind-shattering disappointment, but also because his properly raised son, who had been exposed to the benefits of traditional, up-from-the-bootstraps American enterprise from the day of his birth, now shunned the opportunities that had been given to him for advancement and success in life to fritter away his summers working as a common laborer, toiling under an idiot college dropout who cheated the IRS. There was nothing wrong with the money he was earning, but the problem was that it would never become more money, for bottom-rung work of that sort would always keep him at the bottom, and when his son started talking about supporting himself in the future as a factory worker or a sailor in the merchant marine, the father cringed at the thought of what would become of him. What had happened to the little boy who had wanted to be a doctor? Why had everything gone so wrong?

That was how Ferguson imagined his father must have thought

about him, if in fact he did think about him, and in the two- and three-page monologues he wrote in his father's voice, he struggled to understand his father's way of thinking, digging down and trying to excavate the few things he knew about Stanley Ferguson's early life, the difficult, no-money years when his grandfather was murdered and his screaming, quasi-hysterical grandmother took charge of the clan, and then the mysterious departure of his father's two older brothers to California, never fully explained, never fully understood, and after that the push to become the richest man on earth, the great prophet of profits who believed in money as other people believed in God or sex or good works, money as salvation and fulfillment, money as the ultimate measure of all things, and anyone who resisted that belief was either a fool or a coward, as his ex-wife and son were surely fools and cowards, their brains stuffed with the romantic claptrap dished out by novels and cheap Hollywood films, and his ex-wife was mostly to blame for what had happened, his once beloved Rose, who had turned the boy's head away from his father and coddled him with all that soft-minded nonsense about discovering his *true self* and forging his own *unique destiny*, and now it was too late to undo the damage and the boy was lost.

Still, none of that explained why his father continued to nod off in front of movie and TV screens, or why, as his wealth had grown, he had become cheaper and more tightfisted and took his son only to lousy, inexpensive restaurants for their twice-monthly dinners, or why he had changed his mind about selling the house in Maplewood and had moved back in after Ferguson and his mother had left, or why, after going to the trouble of having *Sole Mates* printed, he never asked to see any of Ferguson's new stories, never inquired about how he was getting on with his stepfather and stepsiblings in the house on Woodhall Crescent, never asked what college he wanted to go to, never said a word about the Kennedy assassination or seemed to care that the president had been shot, and the more Ferguson tried to tunnel his way into his father's soul, searching for something that wasn't dead or cut off from other people, the less he was able to find. Even the complex Mr. Rosenbloom, who no doubt hid much if not most of his inner life from the world, made more sense to Ferguson than his father did. Nor could the differences between them be boiled down to the fact that his father worked and Mr. Rosenbloom didn't. Dan Schneiderman worked. Not the twelve- and fourteen-hour days his father put in, but a steady seven to eight hours five or six

days a week, and even if he wasn't the most dazzling artist in the world,
he knew the limitations of his modest talent and took pleasure in his
work, which he did well enough to cobble together a living as *a self-
employed artisan of the brush*, as he sometimes put it, not the big-money
income Stanley Ferguson raked in, of course, but a more generous heart
in spite of that, as shown by the new car he bought for his new wife,
which turned Ferguson and Amy into joint owners of her old Pontiac
when they passed the test for their licenses, by the clever mobiles and
whirling little mechanical sculptures he made as presents for everyone's
birthday, by the surprise outings to restaurants, concerts, and films,
by the allowance he insisted on giving Ferguson along with the one he
gave his daughter—shelling out weekly to both of them because he
wanted their summer earnings to be deposited in the bank and not
touched while they were still in high school—but most of all by the
generosity of his person, his high spirits and loving solicitudes, his boy-
ishness, his whimsy, his passion for poker and all games of chance,
his somewhat reckless disregard of tomorrow in favor of today, which
added up to a man so different from Ferguson's father that the son/
stepson had trouble reconciling them as members of the same species.
Then there was Dan's older brother, Gilbert Schneiderman, Ferguson's
new, impressively intelligent uncle, who worked as hard as anyone else,
teaching music history full-time at Juilliard and writing entry after entry
on classical composers for a soon-to-be-published music encyclopedia,
and Uncle Don worked as well, the intense, sometimes crabby father
of best-friend Noah never stopped working as he plugged away at his
Montaigne biography and spilled forth two and sometimes three book
reviews a month, and even Arnie Frazier worked, the flunk-out, 4-F, IRS-
chiseling ex–football player worked his ass off, as Ferguson well knew,
but that didn't prevent him from drinking a six-pack of Löwenbräu
every night and keeping up amorous relations with three different
girls from three different towns at the same time.

Ferguson tried not to feel angry when he was with his father, even
though he was appalled by how willing the appliance king had been to
let Dan Schneiderman give him the money for his allowance, which
legally and morally should have been given to him by his father, but
Ferguson suspected his father was angry as well, not so much at him
but at his mother, who not only had pressed for the divorce but had
remarried so soon afterward, and by abdicating his responsibility

toward his son, Ferguson's father had his miser's reward of not having
to part with his money when he didn't want to (which was almost always
now) along with the additional satisfaction of sticking it to his ex-wife's
new husband. Fun and games in the flea circus of petty animosities and
tortures, Ferguson said to himself, as his heart contracted ever more
tightly within him, but perhaps it was just as well that his father had
reneged on his allowance obligation, since Ferguson would have refused
the money if it had been offered to him, and he didn't want to confront
his father with the decision he had made not to accept his money, which
would have been seen as an act of hostility, something close to a declaration of war, and Ferguson wasn't looking to pick a fight with his father,
he just wanted to endure their meetings as quietly as possible and have
nothing happen that would cause either one of them pain.

No MONEY FROM his father—and no baseball because Artie Federman's ghost was still walking beside him and Ferguson wouldn't back
down from his promise. Other sports were permitted, but none of them
had ever counted as much as baseball, and after starting at forward for
the J.V. basketball team in his first year of high school, Ferguson decided not to go out for the varsity the following year, which brought an
abrupt and definitive end to his participation in organized sports. It
had once meant everything to him, but that was before he had read
Crime and Punishment, before he had discovered sex with Dana Rosenbloom, before he had smoked his first cigarette and downed his first
drink, before he had become the future writer who spent his evenings
alone in his room filling up his precious notebooks with words, and
while he still loved sports and would never think of abandoning them,
they had been relegated to the category of idle amusements—touch
football, pickup basketball games, ping-pong in the basement of the new
house, and occasional Sunday morning tennis with Dan, his mother, and
Amy, for the most part doubles matches, either children versus parents or father-daughter versus mother-son. Recreational diversions,
as opposed to the do-or-die battles of his boyhood. Play hard, work up
a sweat, win the game or lose the game, and then go back home for a
shower and a smoke. But it was still beautiful to him, especially the
sport he cared about most, forbidden baseball, which he would never
play again, and he kept on pulling for his newly invented team from

Flushing, even if the fate of the Western world no longer hung in the balance when Choo Choo Coleman stepped into the batter's box with two outs and two men on in the bottom of the ninth. His stepfather and stepbrother would groan when the inevitable third strike was called, but Ferguson would merely nod or shake his head and then stand up and calmly turn off the TV. The Choo Choo Colemans of this world had been born to strike out, and the Mets wouldn't have been the Mets if he hadn't.

Two dinners every month with his father, and one dinner every other month with the Federmans in New Rochelle, a ritual Ferguson held fast to in spite of his misgivings, since it was never clear to him why Artie's parents kept asking him back and even less clear why he found himself willing to make the long trek out there to see them when in fact he wasn't willing, when in fact each one of those dinners filled him with dread. *Murky.* Their motives escaped him, for neither he nor the Federmans understood what they were doing or why they persisted in doing it, and yet the impulse had been there from the start: Mrs. Federman throwing her arms around him after the funeral and telling him he would always be part of the family; Ferguson sitting beside twelve-year-old Celia in the living room for two hours, struggling to find the words to say he was her brother now and would always take care of her. Why had they said those things and thought those things—and what did any of it mean?

He and Artie had been friends for only one month. Long enough to have turned into the A.F. twins, long enough to have felt they were at the beginning of what would be a long and close friendship, but not long enough for either one of them to have become *a part of the other's family.* At the time of his friend's death, Ferguson had never even set eyes on Ralph and Shirley Federman. He hadn't even known their names, but they had known about him because of the letters their son had written from Camp Paradise. Those letters were crucial. The shy, untalkative Artie had opened up to them about his new and wonderful friend, and therefore his parents were already convinced that Ferguson was wonderful before they ever met him. Then Artie died, and three days later the wonderful friend showed up at the funeral, not the spitting image of their son but a boy much like him, tall and strong, with the same young athlete's body, the same Jewish background, the same good marks at school, and for such a boy to enter their lives at the precise moment they had lost their son, the very boy their son had referred to as a *brother*, must have had a powerful effect on them, Ferguson reasoned, an uncanny effect, as if their vanished boy had outmaneuvered the gods and sent them another boy to stand in for him, a changeling son from the world of the living swapped for the one who had died, and by keeping up contact with Ferguson, they could see what would have happened to their own boy as he slowly grew up and turned into a man, the gradual shifts that made a fifteen-year-old different from a fourteen-year-old, a sixteen-year-old different from a fifteen-year-old, a seventeen-year-old different from a sixteen-year-old, and an eighteen-year-old different from a seventeen-year-old. It was a kind of performance, Ferguson realized, and every time he traveled to New Rochelle for another Sunday dinner, he had to take on the job of pretending to be himself by being himself, by enacting himself as fully and truthfully as he could, for they all knew they were playing a game, even if they weren't aware they knew, and Archie would never be Artie, not just because he didn't want to be but because the living could never replace the dead.

They were good people, kind people, unexceptional people, and they lived in a little white house on a tree-lined street with other little white houses owned by other hard-working middle-class families with two or three children and a car or two cars in the white wooden garage. Ralph Federman was a tall, thin man in his late forties who had trained as a pharmacist and owned the smallest of the three drugstores on the main street of the New Rochelle shopping district. Shirley Federman, also tall but not thin, was a few years younger than her husband. A graduate of Hunter College, she worked part-time at the local library, canvassed for Democratic candidates during state and national elections, and had a thing for Broadway musicals. They both treated Ferguson with a quiet sort of deference, a bit shocked perhaps and also grateful that he went on accepting their invitations out of loyalty to their son, and because they didn't want to lose him, they tended to sit back at the dinners and let Ferguson do most of the talking. As for Celia, she rarely said a word, but she listened to him, listened more closely than either of her parents did, and as Ferguson watched her evolve from a timid, grieving child into a self-possessed girl of sixteen, it occurred to him that she was the reason why he kept going back there, for it had always been apparent to him how bright she was, but now she was

becoming pretty, too, a slender, swanlike, long-limbed kind of prettiness, and even though she was still too young for him, in another year
or two she wouldn't be, and lodged somewhere in a deep, inaccessible
part of Ferguson's brain was the unformed idea that he was destined to
marry Celia Federman, that the narrative of his life demanded he marry
her in order to negate the injustice of her brother's early death.

It was essential that he talk, that he not just sit there making polite
conversation but really talk, telling them everything he could about
himself so they would begin to understand who he was, and more and
more after the first few visits that was what he did, talk to them about
himself and the things that were happening to him, because by then
there was less and less to say about Artie, it was too gruesome to keep
going over the same ground again and again, and Ferguson could see
with his own eyes how in the course of nine months Mr. Federman's
hair had gone from dark brown to a mix of brown and gray to mostly
gray and then to all white, how Artie's father grew much thinner for a
time and his mother kept putting on weight, ten more pounds by October 1961, fifteen more pounds by March 1962, twenty more pounds by
September, their bodies were telling Ferguson what was happening to
their souls as they went on living with Artie's death, and there was no
need to discuss their son's exploits as a ten-year-old Little Leaguer anymore, no need to mention his A+'s in science and math ever again, and
so Ferguson came up with a new strategy for getting through those
dinners, which was to push Artie out of the room and force them to
think about something else.

Never a word about giving up baseball because of their son, never
a word about his lustful thoughts toward Amy Schneiderman, never a
word about having sex with Dana Rosenbloom, never a word about the
night he drank too much with Amy's boyfriend, Mike Loeb, and wound
up puking all over his pants and shoes, but other than hiding those
secrets and indiscretions, Ferguson made a point of not censoring himself, a difficult task for someone as reticent as he was, but he trained
himself to be honest with them, *to perform for them,* and at the two dozen
New Rochelle dinners he attended over the four years between Artie's
death and his graduation from high school, he talked about many things,
including the various upheavals that had occurred in his family (his
parents' divorce, his mother's second marriage, his frigid relations with
his father) and the curious experience of having acquired a new set of

relatives, not just his stepfather and two stepsiblings but Dan's brother, Gil, an erudite and sympathetic man who took an interest in his stepnephew's writerly aspirations (*You have to learn everything you can, Archie*, he once said to him, *and then you have to forget it, and what you can't forget will create the foundation of your work*) and Gil's dour wife, Anna, and his plump, smirking daughters, Margaret and Ella, along with Dan's crotchety old father, who lived in a room on the third floor of a nursing home in Washington Heights and was either cracked or in the early stages of dementia, but still, he did come out with some unforgettable remarks from time to time in that Sig Ruman accent of his: *I vant ve all shut up now so I can piss!* One of the best results of his mother's marriage, he told them, was that by some mysterious sleight of hand, which had strung together so many different families and overlapping lineages, his dearest friend and cousin by marriage, Noah Marx, was now related to his new stepsister and stepbrother as well, cousins by marriage once or twice removed (no one was quite sure which), a fact that made him dizzy every time he thought about it—Noah and Amy bound together with him in the same mixed-up tribe!—and what an improvement it was to see how well Dan Schneiderman hit it off with Donald Marx, which had not been the case with his father, who had disliked Uncle Don and had once called him a *pompous schmuck*, and this was better, Ferguson said, even if his mother's relations with her sister had not improved and never would, but at least now it was possible to sit down and have dinner with the Marxes without wanting to scream or pull out a gun and shoot someone.

He could tell them things he never told anyone else, which made him a different person when he was with them, a more forthright and entertaining person than he was at home or at school, *a person who could make people laugh*, and perhaps that was another reason why he kept on going back there, because he knew they would want to listen to the stories he told, the amusing anecdotes about Noah, for example, someone he never tired of bringing into the conversation, his staunch fellow traveler through the thickets of life who had been given a full scholarship to the Fieldston School in Riverdale, one of the best private schools in the city, the taller, post-wire-toothed Noah who had managed to find himself a girlfriend and was directing plays at Fieldston, contemporary stuff like *The Chairs* and *The Bald Soprano* by Ionesco, older stuff like *The White Devil* by John Webster (what a bloodbath!), and making little movies with his Bell & Howell eight-millimeter camera. Still one of the world's most cunning saboteurs, he accompanied Ferguson on the second of his semi-monthly meetings with his father in May 1964, not to a cheap restaurant this time but to the dreaded Blue Valley Country Club, an invitation Ferguson rashly accepted by insisting Noah be included in the party, a proposal he assumed his father would reject, but his father surprised him by agreeing to his demand, and so the appliance king and the two boys set out one Sunday afternoon for lunch at the club, and because Noah knew all about Ferguson's struggles with his father and how much he detested that club, he mocked the place and the things it stood for by wearing a plaid tam-o'-shanter with a white pom-pom on top for the occasion, such a ludicrous, oversized headpiece that Ferguson and his father both laughed when they saw it, perhaps the only time they had laughed in unison for more than a decade, but Noah deadpanned it and didn't crack a smile, which made a funny thing even funnier, of course, telling them this was his first visit to a golf club and he wanted to *look right*, since golf was a Scottish game and therefore all golfers must needs (he actually said *must needs*) adorn themselves with Scottish hats as they worked their way around the links. It was true that Noah got a little carried away once they arrived at the club, perhaps because he felt uncomfortable to be rubbing shoulders with what he called the *filthy rich*, or perhaps because he wanted to show his solidarity with Ferguson by saying out loud what Ferguson himself would never have dared to say, as when an obese man waddled by, pointed to the tam-o'-shanter, and called out, *Nice hat!*—to which Noah replied (with an enormous grin plastered across his face), *Thanks, fatso*—but Ferguson's father was walking ten or twelve feet in front of them and missed the insult, thus sparing the boys the dressing-down that would have been given to them if he had heard it, and for once Ferguson managed to get through a day at the Blue Valley Country Club without wishing he were somewhere else.

That was one side of Noah, he told the Federmans, the zany *agent provocateur* and impish clown, but at bottom he was a thoughtful, serious person, and nothing proved that more than how he had behaved on the weekend Kennedy was shot. By pure happenstance, Noah had been invited to come out to New Jersey to spend a couple of days and nights with Ferguson and Amy in the new house on Woodhall Crescent. The plan was to make a movie together with his eight-millimeter camera, a silent adaptation of Ferguson's short story *What Happened?*, the one about the boy who runs away from home and returns to find his parents missing, with Noah cast as the boy and Ferguson and Amy as the parents. Then, on Friday, November twenty-second, just hours before Noah was supposed to leave New York from the Port Authority bus terminal, Kennedy was shot and killed in Dallas. It would have made sense for him to cancel the visit, but Noah didn't want to, and he called to tell them to pick him up at the Irvington bus station as scheduled. They all watched television for the entire weekend, Ferguson and his stepfather sitting together at one end of the long sofa in the living room and Amy and her stepmother curled up together at the other end, Rose with her arms around Amy and Amy with her head resting on Rose's shoulder, and Noah had the wit to take out his camera and film them, all four of them for the better part of two days, moving back and forth between their faces and the black-and-white images on the television screen, the face of Walter Cronkite, Johnson and Jackie Kennedy on the plane as the vice president was sworn in as the new president, Jack Ruby shooting Oswald in a corridor of the Dallas police station, the riderless horse and John-John's salute on the day of the burial procession, all those public events alternating with the four people on the sofa, grim-faced Dan Schneiderman, his blank, burned-out stepson, and the two wet-eyed women watching those events on the screen, all in silence, of course, since the camera couldn't record sound, a mass of footage that must have come to ten or twelve hours, an intolerable length that no one could have sat through from start to finish, but then Noah took the rolls of film back to New York, found a professional editor to help him, and cut those hours down to twenty-seven minutes, and the result was stupendous, Ferguson said, a national catastrophe written across the faces of those four people and the television set in front of them, a real film by a sixteen-year-old boy that was more than just a historical document but a work of art as well, or, as Ferguson expressed it, using the word he always used when describing something he loved, *a masterpiece.*

There were many stories about Noah, but also about Amy and Jim, about his mother and grandparents, about Arnie Frazier and their near crack-up on the New Jersey Turnpike, about Dana Rosenbloom and her family, about his talks with Mr. Rosenbloom, and about his friendship with Mike Loeb, Amy's boyfriend, then ex-boyfriend, then boyfriend redux, who not only knew who Emma Goldman was and had read her autobiography, *Living My Life*, but was the only person in the school who had also read Alexander Berkman's *Prison Memoirs of an Anarchist*. Beefy Mike Loeb, budding anti-Soviet Marxist radical, who believed in the movement, in organizing, in mass action, and consequently took a dim view of Ferguson's interest in Thoreau, who was all about the individual, the solitary man of conscience acting out of moral principle but with no theoretical foundation for attacking the system, for rebuilding society both from the bottom up and the top down, an excellent writer, yes, but what a pinched and prudish fellow he was, and so frightened of women he probably went to his grave a virgin (Celia, fourteen at the time, snickered when Ferguson repeated those words), and even if his idea of civil disobedience had been picked up by Gandhi, King, and others in the civil rights movement, passive resistance wasn't enough, sooner or later it would come down to armed struggle, and that was why Mike preferred Malcolm X to M. L. King and had taped a poster of Mao to his bedroom wall.

No, Ferguson replied, when Artie's parents asked if he agreed with this boy, but that was what made their conversations so instructive, he said, because every time Mike challenged him he would have to think harder about what he believed in himself, and how could you ever learn anything if you only talked to people who thought exactly as you did?

Then there was Mrs. Monroe, his favorite subject of all, the one person who made life as a high school student bearable, and the great good luck to have had her as his English teacher for both his sophomore and junior years, the young and spirited Evelyn Monroe, just twenty-eight when Ferguson entered her class for the first time, the vibrant antidote to the dowdy, reactionary, anti-modernist Mrs. Baldwin, Monroe née Ferrante, a tough Italian girl from the Bronx who rode off to Vassar on a full scholarship, formerly married to jazz saxophonist Bobby Monroe, frequenter of Village hangouts, friend of musicians, artists, actors, and poets, the hippest teacher ever to grace the halls of Columbia High School, and what separated her from all the other teachers Ferguson had ever had was that she looked upon her students as fully formed, independent human beings, young grown-ups rather than large children, which had the effect of making them all feel good about themselves when they sat in her class and listened to her talk about the books she had assigned, Mr. Joyce, Mr. Shakespeare, Mr. Melville, Miss Dickinson, Mr. Eliot, Miss Eliot, Miss Wharton, Mr. Fitzgerald, Miss

Cather, and all the rest, and there wasn't a single student in either one of the two classes Ferguson took with her who didn't adore Mrs. Monroe, but no one more than Ferguson himself, who showed her every one of the stories he wrote throughout high school, even in the last year when she wasn't his teacher anymore, not that she was a better judge than Uncle Don or Aunt Mildred were, he supposed, but he felt she was more honest with him than they were, more detailed in her criticisms and at the same time more encouraging, as if it were a foregone conclusion that he had been born to do this and no other choice was possible.

She kept a sign posted above the blackboard, a sentence from the American poet Kenneth Rexroth that she had copied out in letters large enough to be read by someone in the back row, and because Ferguson often found himself looking at the sign during class, he later calculated that he must have read it several thousand times during the years he studied with her: AGAINST THE RUIN OF THE WORLD, THERE IS ONLY ONE DEFENSE: THE CREATIVE ACT.

Mrs. Federman said: Every young person needs a Mrs. Monroe, Archie, but not every young person gets one.

What a frightening thought, Ferguson said. I don't know what I'd do without her.

NEW YORK KEPT pulling at him, and Ferguson continued to go there as often as he could on his free Saturdays, sometimes alone, sometimes with Dana Rosenbloom, sometimes with Amy, sometimes with Amy and Mike Loeb, sometimes just with Mike Loeb, and sometimes with all three of them together, where he (and they) would link up with Noah on the weekends when young Groucho was camping out in the Village with his father and Mildred, or just with his father if Uncle Don and Aunt Mildred happened to be living apart again. *Density, immensity, complexity,* as Ferguson once put it when asked why he preferred the city to the suburbs, a sentiment shared by all five members of his little gang, and except for Dana, who had already made up her mind about where she wanted to go after high school, the other four decided they should all stay in New York for college. That meant Columbia for the three boys and Barnard for Amy, assuming they were accepted there, which seemed likely or more than just a long shot because of their strong records, but even though three of them managed to get in, only one of them wound up moving to Morningside Heights the following September. Noah, the rejected applicant, had brought the defeat upon himself by cultivating a new habit in the summer after his junior year, and so fond did he become of smoking pot that he temporarily lost interest in school, which caused his grades and test scores to crash in the first semester of his senior year, and Columbia, which was his father's alma mater, the place where everyone in his family hoped he would be spending the next four years, turned him down. Noah laughed it off. He would be going to NYU instead, which would allow him to stay in New York as planned, and even though it was universally recognized as a worse college than Columbia, with a mediocre undergraduate program for listless, unmotivated students, NYU would give him the chance to study filmmaking, a subject not offered to Columbia undergraduates, and besides, he said, he would be living downtown in the coolest part of the city rather than in that shithole slum wedged between Harlem and the Hudson River.

Noah to Washington Square, Mike to the uptown grid at West 116th Street between Broadway and Amsterdam Avenue, and Ferguson and his stepsister to colleges beyond the borders of the city. Amy's decision had everything to do with Mike. They had already broken up once before, when he cheated on her with a girl named Moira Oppenheim in the middle of their junior year, but after a protracted separation that had ended with groveling gestures of contrition from Mike, Amy had given him another chance, and now, just four months later, he had gone off and done it again, betraying her with the same Moira Oppenheim no less, *the mousey little tramp who wouldn't take no for an answer,* and Amy was fed up, furious, and finished with Mike for good. The letters from the colleges she had applied to landed in the mailbox on Woodhall Crescent the following week. Yes from Barnard and yes from Brandeis, her first and second choices, and because she wanted to be nowhere near Mike Loeb or ever have to look at his fat face and bloated body again, she said no to New York and yes to Waltham, Massachusetts, convinced that the one would be just as good as the other and relieved that she had no second thoughts about her decision. The pig had humiliated her and broken her heart, and Ferguson agreed that she would be better off going somewhere else, and just to prove how much he was on her side, he offered to give her the Pontiac they owned together when she left for Massachusetts in the fall and to cut off his friendship with Mike Loeb right now, *starting this minute.*

Ferguson's situation was more complicated than hers. He had been accepted by Columbia and wanted to go to Columbia, and even if he had been forced to share a dormitory room with Mike Loeb, he still would have wanted to go to Columbia, but there was the question of money to think about, the unanswerable question of who was going to pay for it. He could have backed down and gone to his father, who no doubt would have come through for him, however reluctant he might have been about it, knowing in the end that it was his responsibility to cough up for his son's education, but Ferguson refused even to consider that as an option. His mother and Dan knew where he stood on that point, had always known from the beginning, and even though they thought his position was *bullheaded and self-defeating*, they respected him for it and didn't try to change his mind, for his mother had withdrawn from the battle, the days of fighting to patch things up between Ferguson and his father were done, and after the shabby trick his father had pulled on her about the sale of the old house, Rose understood that her boy's decision not to accept any money from Stanley was a way of defending her—a highly emotional and unreasonable one, perhaps, but also an act of love.

Ferguson sat down with his mother and stepfather to discuss these matters in November of his senior year. The time was approaching to send off his college applications, and while Dan told him not to worry, that the money would be there for him no matter what the cost, Ferguson had his doubts. He figured a year of college would come to about five or six thousand dollars (tuition, room and board, books, clothes, supplies, travel money, and a small monthly allotment of pocket cash), which would come to a total of twenty to twenty-five thousand dollars by the time he made it through the full four years. The same held true for Amy—twenty to twenty-five thousand over the next four years. Jim would be graduating from MIT just as Amy and Ferguson were graduating from high school, which would eliminate the need to pay for a third tuition, but Jim was applying to graduate school in physics, and even though he was bound to get in somewhere that would give him a fellowship along with a stipend for living expenses, the stipend wouldn't be enough to cover everything, and therefore Dan would have to go on forking out another thousand or fifteen hundred dollars a year for Jim, which would bring the overall disbursement of cash for sustaining two Schneidermans and one Ferguson in institutions of higher learning to roughly eleven, twelve, or thirteen thousand dollars per annum. On average, Dan earned thirty-two thousand dollars a year—which explained why Ferguson had his doubts.

There was the extra money from Liz's life insurance policy, but the one hundred and fifty thousand dollars paid out to Dan in the summer of 1962 was down to seventy-eight thousand by the end of November 1964. Twenty thousand of the seventy-two thousand already spent had gone into paying off the double mortgage on the old-old house, then selling that house and buying the new one with cash, which had put his mother and stepfather in the good position of owning 7 Woodhall Crescent outright, with no bank breathing down their necks, with nothing more to pay but the property taxes and the water bill. Another ten thousand of the seventy-two thousand already spent had gone into the house as well, for painting, repairs, and improvements, which would only make the house more valuable if they ever chose to sell it. Still, another forty-eight thousand dollars had vanished since the marriage on cars, restaurant dinners, vacations, and drawings by Giacometti, Miró, and Philip Guston. Much as Ferguson hated his father's tightness with money, he was also somewhat alarmed by how freely his stepfather scattered it around him, for if Dan's income was too small to cover the tuitions, then the seventy-eight thousand left from the insurance money would be their only recourse, and according to Ferguson's calculations that sum would be reduced to just over or under thirty thousand by the time he and Amy finished college, and far less than that if Dan and his mother kept on spending as they had over the past two years. For that reason, Ferguson wanted to take as little as possible from them—nothing if he could. It wasn't that he felt anyone was about to starve to death, but it frightened him to think that one day in the not-too-distant future, when his mother was less than young, and perhaps in less than good health after a lifetime of smoking her daily packs of Chesterfields, she and Dan might find themselves in a rough spot.

He had saved twenty-six hundred dollars from his two summers of work for Arnie Frazier. If he cut back on buying books and records, he could probably add another fourteen hundred to his bank account by the end of the summer, which would lift the total to four thousand dollars even. His grandfather had already confided to his mother that he was planning to give him two thousand dollars as a graduation present, and if his money and his grandfather's money were both used to pay for college, then Dan's share would be reduced to nothing. So much for the first year, but what about the three years after that? He would continue to work during the summers, of course, but doing what and earning what were no more than question marks at that point, and even though his grandfather would probably be willing to chip in something, it would be wrong to count on it, especially now that his grandmother had come down with heart trouble and their medical bills were mounting. One year of New York if he was lucky enough to get into Columbia—and after that, what else could a sane man do but fly to Las Vegas and put everything he owned on number thirteen?

There was one far-fetched solution available to him, a roll of the dice that would solve all their money problems if the winning combination came up, but if Ferguson won the bet, he would also lose the thing he wanted most, for New York and Columbia would be off the table for good. Even worse, it would mean having to spend four more years in New Jersey, the last place in the world where he wanted to be, and not just New Jersey, but a small town in New Jersey that was no bigger than the one he lived in now, which would put him in the same situation he had been trying to run away from for most of his life. Still, if the solution presented itself to him (and there was every reason to believe it wouldn't), he would gladly accept it and kiss the dice he had rolled.

Princeton was starting something new that year, the Walt Whitman Scholars Program, which had been funded by a 1936 alumnus named Gordon DeWitt, who had grown up in East Rutherford and had attended the public schools there, and DeWitt's money would be paying for full scholarships to four graduates from New Jersey public high schools every year. Financial need was one of the requirements, along with academic excellence and soundness of character, and as the son of a well-heeled businessman, one would have assumed Ferguson had no right to apply, but that was not the case, for in addition to reneging on his allowance obligation to his son, Stanley Ferguson had broken the divorce agreement he had signed with his ex-wife, which stipulated that he contribute half the money needed for the boy's upkeep, that is, to reimburse Ferguson's mother for half of what she and her new husband spent on the food Ferguson ate and the clothes he wore as well as half his medical and dental bills, but six months into her second marriage, when no money from her ex-husband had arrived, Ferguson's mother consulted a lawyer, who wrote a letter threatening to haul Ferguson's father into court to make him pay what he owed, and when Ferguson's father countered by offering a compromise—no money for his half of the boy's upkeep, but from now on he would stop claiming his son as a dependent on his income tax returns and hand that honor over to Dan Schneiderman—the matter was settled. Ferguson himself had known nothing about this dispute, but when he told his mother and stepfather about the Walt Whitman scholarships at Princeton, explaining that he wanted to send in an application but didn't think he fit all the requirements, they assured him he did, for even though Dan made a respectable income, the burden of sending three children to universities at the same time practically qualified Ferguson as a hardship case. As far as the law was concerned, the link between father and son had been severed. Ferguson was a minor, and because his sole financial support now came from his mother and stepfather, in the eyes of Princeton and everyone else, it was as if his father had ceased to exist. That was the good news. The bad news was that Ferguson had finally learned the truth about his father, and he was so upset by what the man had done, so angry at him for his cheapness and meanness toward the woman he had once been married to, that nothing would have satisfied Ferguson more than to slug his father in the face. The son of a bitch had disowned him, and now he wanted to disown him back.

I know I promised to have dinner with him twice a month, Ferguson said, but I don't think I want to see him anymore. He broke his promise to you. Why can't I break my promise to him?

You're almost eighteen now, his mother said, and you can do anything you want. Your life belongs to you.

Fuck him.

Easy does it, Archie.

No, I mean it. *Fuck him.*

He figured there would be thousands of applicants, the top boys from around the state, all-county athletes in football and basketball, class presidents and debating club champions, science prodigies with double 800s on their SATs, such sterling candidates that he himself wouldn't have the smallest chance of making the first cut, but he sent in his application anyway, along with two of his stories and a list of people who had offered to write letters of recommendation for him: Mrs. Monroe; his French teacher, Mr. Boldieu; and his current English teacher, Mr. MacDonald. He wanted to be a lion, but if it turned out that fate had chosen him to become a tiger, he would make every effort to wear his stripes proudly. Black and orange instead of powder blue and white. F. Scott Fitzgerald instead of John Berryman and Jack Kerouac. Did any of it really matter? Princeton might not have been New York, but it was only an hour away by train, and the one advantage Princeton had over Columbia was that Jim had applied there for graduate work in physics. He was sure to be accepted, which Ferguson was not, but one could nevertheless dream, and how pleasant it was to imagine the two of them spending the next four years together in that woodsy world of books and fellowship as the ghost of Albert Einstein flitted among the trees.

After his conversation with his mother and Dan in late November, Ferguson wrote a long letter to his father in which he explained why he wanted to suspend their twice-a-month dinners. He didn't quite come out and say he never wanted to see him again, for it still wasn't clear to Ferguson if that was his position or not, though he suspected it was, but he was only seventeen, and he lacked the courage and confidence to issue life-altering ultimatums about the future, which he hoped would be a long one, and who knew what turns his relationship with his father would take in the years ahead? What he did bring up, however, and what constituted the heart of the letter, was how distressed he was to have learned that his father had removed him as a dependent on his income tax returns. It felt as if he had been erased, he wrote, as if his father were trying to forget the past twenty years of his life and pretend they had never happened, not only his marriage to Ferguson's mother but the fact that he had a son, whom he had now given over entirely to the care of Dan Schneiderman. But putting all that aside, Ferguson continued, after devoting two full pages to the subject, the dinners they had together had become infinitely depressing to him, and why go on with the dreary charade of making lifeless small talk with each other when the truth was that neither of them had anything to say anymore, and how sad it was to sit together in those grimy places looking at the clock and counting the minutes until the torture was over, and wouldn't it be better to take a pause for a while and reflect on whether they wanted to start up again at some future point or not?

His father wrote back three days later. It wasn't the answer Ferguson wanted, but at least it was something. *Okay, Archie, we'll give it a rest for now. I hope you're doing well. Dad.*

Ferguson wasn't going to reach out to him again. He had decided that much, and if his father wasn't willing to court him and try to win him back, then that would be the end of it.

He mailed off his applications to Columbia, Princeton, and Rutgers in early January. In mid-February, he took a day off from school and went to New York for his interview at Columbia. He was already familiar with the campus, which had always reminded him of a fake Roman city, with the two massive libraries confronting each other in the middle of the small campus, Butler and Low, each one a hulking granite structure in the classical style, elephants lording it over the less voluminous brick buildings around them, and once he found his way to Hamilton Hall, he went upstairs to the fourth floor and knocked. The interviewer was an economics professor named Jack Shelton, and what a jolly man he was, cracking jokes throughout the conversation and even making fun of *stuffy, sclerotic Columbia*, and when he learned of Ferguson's ambition to become a writer, he ended their talk by handing the Columbia High School senior several issues of the Columbia College literary magazine. Flipping through them half an hour later as he rode downtown on the IRT express, Ferguson chanced upon a line of poetry that amused him greatly: *A steady fuck is good for you.* He laughed out loud when he read it, happy to realize that Columbia couldn't have been as stuffy as all that, for not only was the line funny, it was true.

The following week, he made his first visit to Princeton, where he doubted many students published poems with the word *fuck* in them, but the campus was much larger and more attractive than Columbia's, bucolic splendor to compensate for the fact that it wasn't in New York but in a small New Jersey town, Gothic architecture as opposed to classical architecture, impressively subtle, near-perfect landscaping filled with carefully tended shrubs and tall, thriving trees, but somewhat antiseptic, as if the vast plot of land on which Princeton stood had been converted into a giant terrarium, smelling of money in the same way the Blue Valley Country Club did, a Hollywood version of the ideal American university, *the northernmost southern school*, as someone had once said to him, but who was he to complain about anything, and why should he ever want to complain if he happened to win a free pass to walk on those grounds as a Walt Whitman Scholar?

They must have known that Whitman was a man who had no interest in women, he said to himself, as he completed his tour of the campus, a man who believed in love between men and men, but old Walt had spent the last nineteen years of his life just down the road in Camden, which made him New Jersey's own national monument, and even if his work was both astonishingly good and astonishingly bad, the best of it was the best poetry ever written in this part of the world, and bravo to Gordon DeWitt for having put Walt's name on his scholarships for New Jersey boys rather than the name of some dead politician or Wall Street pooh-bah, which was precisely what DeWitt had been for the past twenty years.

There were three interviewers this time, not one, and even though Ferguson was properly dressed for the occasion (white shirt, jacket, and tie) and had reluctantly given in when his mother and Amy had begged him to get a haircut before going down there, he felt nervous and out of place in front of those men, who were no less friendly to him than the Columbia professor had been and asked all the questions he was expecting to be asked, but when the hour-long interrogation finally ended, he walked out of the room feeling he had made a botch of it, cursing himself for having mixed up the titles of books by William James and his brother Henry for one thing, and, even worse, having garbled Sancho Panza into Poncho Sanza for another, and in spite of having corrected those errors the instant the words had flown out of his mouth, they were the blunders of a true and thorough idiot, he felt, and not only was he convinced he would come in dead last among all the candidates for the scholarship, he was disgusted with himself for having performed so badly under pressure. For some reason, or reasons, or no reason that anyone but the three men who had talked to him could understand, the committee did not share his opinion, and when he was asked to return for a second interview on March third, Ferguson was perplexed—but also, for the first time, beginning to wonder if there wasn't some cause for hope.

It was a curious way to spend his eighteenth birthday, decking himself out in a jacket and tie again and traveling down to Princeton for a one-on-one conversation with Robert Nagle, a classics professor who had published translations of plays by Sophocles and Euripides and a book-length study of the pre-Socratics, a man in his early forties with a long, sad face and a watchful, no-nonsense look in his eyes, the best literary mind in all of Princeton according to Ferguson's high school English teacher, Mr. MacDonald, who had gone to Princeton himself and was rooting hard for Ferguson to win the scholarship. Nagle was not a man to waste his breath chatting about irrelevant things. The first interview had been filled with questions about Ferguson's academic achievements (good but not spectacular), his work as a moving man during the summers, why he had stopped playing competitive sports, his feelings about his parents' divorce and his mother's remarriage, and what he hoped to accomplish by studying at Princeton and not somewhere else, but Nagle ignored those matters and seemed to be interested only in the two stories Ferguson had included with his application and in finding out which writers he had read and hadn't read and which ones he cared about most.

The first story, *Eleven Moments from the Life of Gregor Flamm*, was the longest piece Ferguson had written in the past three years, twenty-four typed pages that had been composed between early September and mid-November, two and a half months of steady work during which he had put aside his notebooks and ancillary projects to concentrate on the task he had set for himself, which was to tell the story of someone's life without telling it as a continuous story, simply jumping in at various disjointed moments to investigate an action, a thought, or an impulse, and then hopping on to the next one, and in spite of the gaps and silences left between the isolate parts, Ferguson imagined the reader would stitch them together in his mind so that the accumulated scenes would add up to something that resembled a story, or something more than just a story—a long novel in miniature. A six-year-old in the first episode, Gregor looks into a mirror to examine his own face and comes to the conclusion that he wouldn't be able to recognize himself if he saw himself walking down the street, then the seven-year-old Gregor is at Yankee Stadium with his grandfather, standing up with the crowd to applaud a double hit by Hank Bauer and feeling a wet, slithery something land on his bare right forearm, a gob of human spit, a thick lozenge of phlegm that makes him think of a raw oyster creeping along his skin, no doubt an expectoration launched by someone sitting in the upper deck, and beyond the disgust Gregor feels as he wipes it off with his handkerchief and then throws the handkerchief away, there is the conundrum of trying to figure out whether the person who spat on him did it on purpose or not, whether he was aiming for Gregor's arm and hit his target or whether it was chance that propelled the spit to land where it did, an important distinction in Gregor's mind, since an

intentional hit would postulate a world in which nastiness and evil are
the governing forces, a world in which invisible men attack unknown
boys for no reason but to indulge in the pleasure of harming others,
whereas an accidental hit would postulate a world in which unfortunate things happen but no one is to blame, and further on there is the
twelve-year-old Gregor discovering the first pubic hair that has sprouted
on his body, the fourteen-year-old Gregor watching his best friend drop
dead before his eyes, killed by something called a brain aneurysm, the
sixteen-year-old Gregor lying naked in bed with the girl who has helped
him lose his virginity, and then, in the final episode, the seventeen-
year-old Gregor sitting alone on top of a hill, studying the clouds as
they pass overhead, asking himself whether the world is real or nothing
more than a projection of his mind, and if it is real, how will his mind
ever be able to encompass it? The story concludes: *And then he walks
down the hill, thinking about the pain in his stomach and whether eating lunch
will make him feel better or worse. It is one o'clock in the afternoon. The wind
is blowing from the north, and the sparrow that was sitting on the telephone
wire is gone.*

The other story, *Right, Left, or Straight Ahead?*, was written in December and consisted of three separate episodes, each one about seven
pages long. A man named Lazlo Flute is out taking a walk in the country. He comes to a crossroads and must choose between the three possibilities of going left, right, or straight ahead. In the first chapter, he goes
straight ahead and runs into trouble when he is attacked by a pair of
thugs. Beaten and robbed, left for dead by the side of the road, he
eventually regains consciousness, climbs back to his feet, and staggers
on for another mile or so until he comes to a house, knocks on the
door, and is let in by an old man, who inexplicably apologizes to Flute
and begs his forgiveness. The man leads Flute to the kitchen sink and
helps wash the blood off his face, still rattling on about how sorry he is
and what a terrible thing he has done, but sometimes, he says, *my imagination runs away from me and I just can't help myself.* He takes Flute into
another room, a small study at the far end of the house, and points to a
pile of handwritten pages on the desk. Take a look if you want, he says,
and when the battered hero picks up the manuscript, he sees that it
is an account of the things that have just happened to him. *Such vicious
characters,* the old man says, *I don't know where they came from.*

In the second part, Flute turns right instead of going straight ahead.

He has no memory of what happened to him in the first chapter, and because the new episode starts with a blank slate, the fresh beginning seems to offer the hope that something less awful will happen to him this time, and indeed, after walking a mile and a half down the road to the right, he comes upon a woman standing beside a broken-down car, or what appears to be a broken-down car, for why would she be standing there in the middle of the countryside if the car worked, but as Flute approaches her, he sees that none of the tires is flat, the hood is not up, and the radiator is not spewing forth clouds of steam into the air. Still, there must be a problem of one sort or another, and as the unmarried Flute draws closer to the woman, he sees that she is exceptionally attractive, or at least to his eyes she is, and therefore he jumps at the chance to help her, not just because he wants to help her but because an opportunity has presented itself to him and he wants to make the most of it. When he asks her what the trouble is, she says she thinks the battery is dead. Flute opens the hood and sees that one of the cables has come loose, so he reconnects the cable and tells her to get back into the car and give it a try, which she does, and when the car starts up with the first turn of the key, the beautiful woman gives Flute a big smile, blows him a kiss, and promptly drives off, departing so quickly that he doesn't even have time to jot down her license plate number. No name, no address, no number, and no way ever to reconnect with the enchanting specter who bolted in and out of his life in a matter of minutes. Flute walks on, sickened by his own stupidity, wondering why his chances in life always seem to slip through his fingers, tempting him with the promise of better things and yet always disappointing him in the end. Two miles later, the thugs from the first chapter reappear. They jump out from behind a hedge and try to wrestle Flute to the ground, but this time he fights back, kneeing one of them in the groin and poking the other one in the eye, and he manages to get away, running down the road as the sun sets and night begins to fall, and just when it is becoming difficult to make out much of anything, he comes to a bend in the road and sees the woman's car again, parked next to a tree this time, but the woman is gone, and when he calls out to her and asks where she is, no one answers. Flute runs off into the night.

In the third part, he turns left. It is a gorgeous afternoon in late spring, and the fields on either side of him are crammed with wildflowers, two hundred birds are singing in the crystalline air, and as

Flute contemplates the various ways in which life has been both kind and cruel to him, he comes to the realization that most of his problems have been caused by himself, that he is responsible for having made his life such a dull and unadventurous one, and if he means to live life to the fullest, he should spend more time with other people and stop taking so many solitary walks.

WHY DO YOU give your characters such odd names? Nagle asked.

I don't know, Ferguson said. Probably because the names tell the reader those characters are in a story, not the real world. I like stories that admit they're stories and don't pretend to be the truth, the whole truth, and nothing but the truth, so help me God.

Gregor. A reference to Kafka, I suppose.

Or Gregor Mendel.

A brief smile flitted across the long, sad countenance. Nagle said: But you've read Kafka, haven't you?

The Trial, The Metamorphosis, and about ten or twelve other stories. I'm trying to take it slowly because I like him so much. If I sat down and barreled through all the Kafka I still haven't read, then there'd be no new Kafka to look forward to, and that would be sad.

Hoarding your pleasures.

That's it. You're given just one bottle, and if you drink it down all at once, you won't have a chance to drink from the bottle again.

In your application, you say you want to be a writer. What do you think about the work you've done so far?

Most of it is bad, revoltingly bad. A few things are a little better, but that doesn't mean they're good.

And what's your opinion of the two stories you sent us?

So-so.

Then why send them?

Because they're the most recent ones, and also because they're the longest ones I've written.

Off the top of your head, give me the names of five writers not named Kafka who've had the greatest impact on you.

Dostoyevsky. Thoreau. Swift. Kleist. Babel.

Kleist. Not many high school boys are reading him these days.

My mother's sister is married to a man who wrote a biography of Kleist. He's the person who gave me the stories.

Donald Marx.

You know him?

I know of him.

Five is too small a number. I feel I've left out some of the most important names.

I'm sure of that. Dickens for one, right? And Poe, definitely Poe, and perhaps Gogol, not to speak of the moderns. Joyce, Faulkner, Proust. You've probably read them all.

Not Proust. The others, yes, but I still haven't gotten around to *Ulysses*. I'm planning to read it this summer.

And Beckett?

Waiting for Godot, but nothing else so far.

And Borges?

Not a word.

What fun awaits you, Ferguson.

At this point, I've barely even made it to the beginning. Other than a few plays by Shakespeare, I still haven't read anything written before the eighteenth century.

You mentioned Swift. What about Fielding, Sterne, and Austen?

No, not yet.

And what is it about Kleist that attracts you so much?

The speed of his sentences, the propulsion. He tells and tells but doesn't show much, which everyone says is the wrong way to go about it, but I like the way his stories charge forward. It's all very intricate, but at the same time it feels as if you're reading a fairy tale.

You know how he died, don't you?

He shot himself in the mouth when he was thirty-four. After he'd killed a woman friend in a double-suicide pact.

Tell me, Ferguson, what would happen if you were accepted by Princeton but turned down for the scholarship? Would you come here anyway?

It all depends on what Columbia says.

That's your first choice.

Yes.

May I ask why?

Because it's in New York.

Ah, of course. But you'd come here if we gave you the scholarship.

Absolutely. It's all about the money, you see, and even if I do get into Columbia, I'm not sure my family could afford to send me there.

Well, I don't know what the committee will decide, but I just want to tell you that I enjoyed reading your stories and think they're much better than *so-so*. Mr. Flute is still searching for another second road, I believe, but *Gregor Flamm* is a lovely surprise, an excellent piece of work for someone your age, and with a few small revisions in the third and fifth parts, I'm sure you could publish it somewhere. But don't. That's what I wanted to say to you, my one word of advice. Hold off for a while, don't rush to get yourself into print, keep working, keep growing, and before long you'll be ready.

Thank you. No, not thank you—but yes, as in *yes, you're right*, even if you could be wrong, about not being so-so, I mean, but it means so much to . . . Christ, I don't know what I'm saying anymore.

Don't say anything, Ferguson. Just stand up from that chair, shake my hand, and go home. It's been a privilege to meet you.

SIX WEEKS OF uncertainty followed. All through March and halfway into April, Robert Nagle's words blazed in Ferguson's mind, the *excellent piece of work* and the *privilege to meet you* kept him warm through the chilly days of late winter and early spring, for he realized that Nagle was the first stranger, the first neutral person, the first utterly indifferent outsider who had ever read his work, and now that the *best literary mind in all of Princeton* had judged his stories to be worthy, the young author wished he could stop going to school and spend ten hours a day sitting in his room with the new work that was taking shape in his head, a multipart epic called *Mulligan's Travels*, which was sure to be the best thing he had ever done, the great leap forward at last.

One morning in the midst of the long waiting period, as Ferguson sat in the kitchen brooding about lions and tigers and the odds of ending up as an ant in the big ant factory known as Rutgers, situated in the world-renowned metropolis of New Brunswick, New Jersey, his mother walked into the room with that day's *Star-Ledger*, plopped it down on the breakfast table in front of him, and said, *Get a load of this, Archie*. Ferguson looked, and what he saw was so unexpected, so outside the realm of what seemed possible, so egregiously wrong and ridiculous, that he had to look at it three more times before he could begin to assimilate the news. His father had married again. The prophet of profits had hitched himself to forty-one-year-old Ethel Blumenthal, widow of the late Edgar Blumenthal and mother of two children, sixteen-year-old Allen and twelve-year-old Stephanie, and as Ferguson looked down at the photograph of his grinning father and the not unpresentable second Mrs. Ferguson, he saw that she bore a certain resemblance to his mother, especially in her height and shape and the darkness of her hair, as if his father had gone out looking for a new version of the original model, but the replacement was only half as pretty and had a guarded look in her eyes, something sad and shut off and perhaps a little cold, whereas Ferguson's mother's eyes were a port of refuge for everyone who came near her.

He supposed he should have been outraged that his father had never introduced him to this woman, who was technically his stepmother now, and deeply offended that he had not been invited to the wedding, but Ferguson was neither one of those things. He was relieved. The story was over, and Stanley Ferguson's son, who no longer had to pretend he felt any filial attachment to the man who had sired him, looked at his mother and shouted, *Adios, papa—vaya con Dios!*

Three weeks after that, on the same day in three different parts of the country—New York City, Cambridge, Massachusetts, and a small town in New Jersey—the youngest members of the mingled, mixed-up tribe opened their mailboxes and found the letters they had been waiting for. Except for the one no to Noah, it was a clean sweep of yeses for all of them, an unprecedented triumph that put the Schneiderman-Ferguson-Marx quartet in the enviable position of being able to choose where they wanted to go for the next four years of their lives. In addition to NYU, Noah could attend City College or the American Academy of Dramatic Arts. Jim could go west to Caltech, south to Princeton, or stay where he was at MIT. In addition to Barnard and Brandeis, Amy's options included Smith, Pembroke, and Rutgers. As for Ferguson, the ants had come through for him as expected, but so had the two jungle beasts, as not expected, and when he looked over at the exultant Amy, who was throwing her letters around the kitchen and laughing her head off, he stood up and said to her, in his best imitation of her grandfather's accent: Ve valtz together now, ja liebchen? Then he walked over to where she was standing, wrapped his arms around her, and kissed her smack on the lips.

Walt Whitman Scholar.

In spite of the heartening letter from Columbia, New York would have to wait. The money made it imperative for him to go to Princeton, but beyond the money there was the distinction of having won the scholarship, which was unquestionably the biggest thing that had ever happened to him, *a gigantic feather in his cap,* as Dan had put it, and even for the hardened, undemonstrative Ferguson, who was normally so shy about his accomplishments that he would rather have left the room than open his mouth and brag about himself, the Princeton scholarship was different, a thing so big that it felt good to carry it around with him and let others see it, and when word got out at school that he was one of the four anointed ones, he soaked up the compliments without feeling embarrassed or making any of his usual self-deprecatory remarks, he was greedy for the adulation, he enjoyed being at the center of a world that was suddenly revolving around him, admired and envied and talked about by everyone, and even though he had wanted to move to New York in September, the thought of becoming a Walt Whitman Scholar at Princeton was more than enough to live on for now.

Two months went by, and the day after he graduated from high school, Ferguson received a letter from his father. In addition to a short note congratulating him on the scholarship (which had been announced in the *Star-Ledger*), the envelope contained a check for one thousand dollars. Ferguson's first impulse was to tear it up and mail the pieces back to his father, but then he thought better of it and decided to deposit the check in his account. Once it cleared, he would write out two checks for five hundred dollars each, one of them to SANE (National Committee for a Sane Nuclear Policy) and the other one to SNCC (Student Nonviolent Coordinating Committee). There was no sense in tearing up money when it could be put to good use, and why not give it away to the ones who were fighting against the imbecilities and injustices of the messed-up world he lived in?

That same evening, Ferguson locked himself in his room and cried for the first time since he had moved out of the old-old house. Dana Rosenbloom had left for Israel earlier that day, and because her parents were moving back to London for yet another fresh start, it was more than likely he would never see her again. He had pleaded with her not to go, explaining that he had been wrong about many things and wanted another chance to prove himself to her, and after she told him her mind was made up and nothing could stop her, he had impulsively asked her to marry him, and because Dana understood that it wasn't a joke, that Ferguson meant every word he was saying, she told him he was the love of her life, the one man she would ever care about with her whole heart, and then she kissed him for the last time and walked away.

The next morning, he started working for Arnie Frazier again. Mr. College was back in the moving business, and as he sat in the van listening to Richard Brinkerstaff talk about his childhood in Texas and the whorehouse in his little town where the madam was so cheap she recycled used condoms by dousing them in warm water and then unrolling them onto the ends of broomsticks to dry out in the sun, Ferguson understood that the world was made of stories, so many different stories that if they were all gathered together and put into a book, the book would be nine hundred million pages long. The summer of Watts and the American invasion of Vietnam had begun, and neither Ferguson's grandmother nor Amy's grandfather would live to see it to the end.

5.1

H E HAD BEEN ASSIGNED A ROOM ON THE TENTH FLOOR OF Carman Hall, the newest dormitory on campus, but once Ferguson unpacked his bags and put away his things, he walked over to an adjacent dormitory a few yards to the north, Furnald Hall, and rode the elevator to the sixth floor, where he stood in front of Room 617 for a few moments, and then he went downstairs, walked east along the brick pathway that ran alongside Butler Library and headed for a third dormitory building, John Jay Hall, where he rode the elevator up to the twelfth floor and stood in front of Room 1231 for a few moments. Federico García Lorca had lived in those two rooms during the months he spent at Columbia in 1929 and 1930. Six-seventeen Furnald and 1231 John Jay were the work sites where he had written "Poems of Solitude at Columbia University," "Return to the City," "Ode to Walt Whitman" (*New York of filth / New York of wires and death*), and most of the other poems collected in *Poet in New York*, a book that was ultimately published in 1940, four years after Lorca was beaten, murdered, and thrown into a mass grave by Franco's men. Holy ground.

Two hours later, Ferguson walked over to Broadway and West 116th Street and met up with Amy at Chock Full o'Nuts, home of the *heavenly coffee* that was reputed to be so good that not even Rockefeller's money could buy a better brand (according to the TV commercial). Chock Full o'Nuts was the same company that employed Governor Rockefeller's friend Jackie Robinson as vice president and director of personnel, and after Amy and Ferguson had mused on those weird, entangled facts for a couple of minutes—ubiquitous Nelson Rockefeller, whose family owned coffee plantations in South America, and post-baseball Jackie Robinson, whose hair had turned white even though he was still relatively young, and a chain of eighty New York coffee shops with mostly black people working in them—Amy put her arm around Ferguson's shoulder, drew him toward her, and asked him how it felt to be in college now, a free man at last. *Jolly good, my love, positively ripping*, he said, as he kissed Amy on her neck, ear, and eyebrow—except for one small detail, which had nearly caused him to be punched in the face one hour after he arrived on campus. He was referring to the Columbia tradition of forcing incoming freshmen to wear powder-blue beanies during Orientation Week (with the class year stitched onto the front, in this case the laughable '69), which in Ferguson's opinion was a revolting custom that should have been abolished decades ago, a throwback to the humiliating initiations of rich-boy undergraduate life in the nineteenth century, and there he was, Ferguson said, minding his own business as he trundled through the quad on his way from here to there, with the name tag identifying him as a freshman pinned to his chest, when he was confronted by two upperclassmen, so-called monitors whose job was to help first-year underlings find their way around campus, but those short-haired hulks in the tweed jackets and ties, who must have been linemen on the varsity football team, were not interested in helping Ferguson find his way but in stopping him to ask why he wasn't wearing his beanie, sounding more like unfriendly cops than friendly students, and Ferguson bluntly told them it was upstairs in his room and he had no intention of wearing it anytime that day or any other day that week, at which point one of the cops called him a *puke* and ordered him to go back to his room and fetch it. Sorry, Ferguson said, if you want it so much, you'll have to fetch it yourself, a response that so irked the monitor that for a moment Ferguson thought he was about to haul off and flatten him, but the other cop told his friend to calm down, and rather than prolong the confrontation, Ferguson simply walked away.

Your first lesson in the anthropology of male-college kinship groups, Amy said. The world you belong to now is split into three tribes. The frat boys and the jocks, who make up about a third of the population, the grinds, who make up another third, and the pukes, who make up the last third. You, dear Archie, I'm glad to say, are a puke. Even though you used to be a jock.

Maybe so, Ferguson said. But a jock with the heart of a puke. And also, perhaps—I'm just guessing here—*the mind of a grind.*

The heavenly coffee was set down before them on the counter, and just as Ferguson was about to take his first sip, a young man walked in and smiled at Amy, a medium-sized young man with long rumpled hair who was unquestionably one of the pukes, a fellow member of the tribe Ferguson now seemed to belong to, since length of hair (according to Amy) was one of the factors that distinguished pukes from jocks and grinds, the least important factor in a list that included leftward political inclinations (anti-war, pro–civil rights), belief in art and literature, and suspicion of all forms of institutional authority.

Good, Amy said. There's Les. I knew he would come.

Les was a junior named Les Gottesman, a casual friend of Amy's, no more than a dim acquaintance, in fact, but everyone on both sides of Broadway knew who Amy Schneiderman was, and Les had agreed to show up at Chock Full o'Nuts that afternoon as Amy's *welcoming gift* to Ferguson on his first day of college because he, Les Gottesman, was the author of the line that had so amused and exhilarated Ferguson on his visit to the campus six months earlier: *A steady fuck is good for you.*

Oh *that*, Les said, as Ferguson hopped off his stool and shook the poet's hand. I guess it seemed funny at the time.

It's still funny, Ferguson said. And vulgar and offensive, too, at least to some people, probably to most people, but also an undeniable statement of fact.

Les smiled modestly, looked back and forth between Amy and Ferguson a couple of times and then said: Amy tells me you write poems. You might want to show some of them to the *Columbia Review.* Come around and knock one day. Ferris Booth Hall, third floor. It's the office with all the people shouting in it.

On October sixteenth, Ferguson and Amy took part in their first anti-war demonstration, a march organized by the Fifth Avenue Vietnam Peace Parade Committee that attracted tens of thousands of people ranging from Maoist student activists to Orthodox Jewish rabbis, the largest crowd either one of them had ever been in outside of a baseball or football stadium, and on that bright Saturday afternoon in early fall, under the perfect blue skies of a perfect New York day, as the marchers headed down Fifth Avenue and then turned east toward U.N. Plaza, some of them singing, some of them chanting, most of them walking in silence, which was how Ferguson and Amy chose to go about it, holding hands and walking side by side in silence, throngs of non-marchers sat on the low perimeter wall of Central Park applauding or shouting out encouragement, while another faction, the pro-war faction, the ones Ferguson eventually came to think of as the anti-anti-war people, shouted insults and abuse, and in several instances threw eggs at the marchers, or ran into the crowd and punched them, or doused them with red paint.

Two weeks later, the pro and anti-anti forces staged their own march in New York City on what they called Support America's Vietnam Effort Day as twenty-five thousand people walked past a contingent of elected officials who cheered them on from elevated viewing stands. Few Americans were willing to concede the errors of their government's war at that point, but with one hundred and eighty thousand U.S. combat troops now posted in Vietnam and the bombing campaign known as Operation Rolling Thunder in its eighth month, with American units on the offensive and G.I. death counts coming in from battles at Chu Lai and Ia Drang, the swift and inevitable victory that Johnson, McNamara, and Westmoreland had all promised the American public seemed less and less certain. In late August, Congress had passed a law fixing a penalty of five years in prison and up to ten thousand dollars in fines for anyone convicted of destroying Selective Service documents. Nevertheless, young men continued to burn their draft cards in public protests as the Resist the Draft movement expanded across the country. One day before Ferguson and Amy marched down Fifth Avenue, three hundred people had gathered in front of the Armed Forces Induction Center on Whitehall Street to watch twenty-two-year-old David Miller put a match to his draft card in the first open defiance of the new federal law. Four other young men attempted to do the same thing at Foley Square on October twenty-eighth and were engulfed by a mob of hecklers and police. The following week, when five others were about to burn their draft cards during a demonstration at Union Square, a young anti-anti jumped out from the crowd and sprayed them with a fire extinguisher, and once the five drenched boys managed to ignite their sodden cards, hundreds of people standing behind the police barricades shouted, "Give us joy, bomb Hanoi!"

They also shouted, "Burn yourselves, not your cards!," an ugly reference to the anti-war Quaker pacifist who had burned himself to death four days earlier on the grounds of the Pentagon. After reading an account by a French Catholic priest who had seen his Vietnamese parishioners *burned up in napalm*, thirty-one-year-old Norman Morrison, the father of three young children, drove from his house in Baltimore to Washington, D.C., sat down not fifty yards from the window of Robert McNamara's office, poured kerosene over his body, and immolated himself as a silent protest against the war. Witnesses said the flames rose ten feet into the air, an eruption of fire equal in force to that caused by napalm when dropped from a plane.

Burn yourselves, not your cards.

Amy had been right. The small, almost invisible disturbance called "Vietnam" had grown into a conflict *bigger than Korea, bigger than anything since World War Two*, and day by day it was continuing to grow, every hour more troops were being sent to that remote, impoverished country on the other side of the world to fight the menace of communism by preventing the North from conquering the South, two hundred thousand, four hundred thousand, five hundred thousand young men from Ferguson's generation shipped off to jungles and villages no one had ever heard of or could locate on a map, and unlike Korea and World War II, which had been fought in places thousands of miles from American ground, this war was being fought both in Vietnam and at home. The arguments against military intervention were so clear to Ferguson, so persuasive in their logic, so self-evident after a thorough scrutiny of the facts that it was difficult for him to understand how anyone could support the war, but millions did, many more millions at that point than the millions who opposed it, and in the eyes of the pro and anti-anti forces, anyone who objected to the policies of his government was an agent of the enemy, an American who had given up the right to call himself an American. Every time they saw another dissenter risk five years in prison by burning his draft card, they yelled out *traitor* and *commie scum*, whereas Ferguson looked up to those boys and considered them to be among the bravest, most principled Americans in the country. He was all in behind them and would march against the war until the last soldier came home, but he could never be one of them, never stand next to them because of the missing thumb on his left hand, which had already spared him from the threat his fellow students would be facing once they finished college and were called up for their physicals. Defying the draft was not a job for the maimed or the handicapped but for the fit, the ones who would qualify as good soldier material, and why risk going to prison on the strength of a meaningless gesture? It was a lonely spot to be in, he often felt, as if he were an exile who had been exiled even from the exiles, and consequently there was a sense of shame attached to being who he was, but like it or not the car crash had exempted him from the future battle of whether to resist or abscond, he alone among his acquaintances did not have to live in fear of the next step, and surely that helped him stay on his feet during a time when so many others lost their balance and fell, for the country had already split in two by September and October 1965, and from that point on it was impossible to say the word *America* without also thinking of the word *madness*.

We had to destroy the village in order to save it.

Then, on November ninth, one week after Norman Morrison's suicide on the grounds of the Pentagon, roughly six weeks into Ferguson's first semester at Columbia, when he was still feeling his way forward and not yet sure whether college was all it had been cracked up to be, the lights went out in New York. It was 5:27 P.M., and within thirteen minutes an area covering eighty thousand square miles of the northeastern United States had lost electrical power, leaving more than thirty million people in the dark, among them eight hundred thousand New York City subway riders on their way home from work. Unlucky Ferguson, who seemed to have perfected the art of being in the wrong place at the wrong time by then, was alone inside an elevator traveling upward toward the tenth floor of Carman Hall. He had gone back to his dormitory to drop off some books and change into a heavier jacket, but he hadn't been planning to spend more than one minute in his room, since he and Amy were supposed to begin cooking their spaghetti dinner in her apartment at six o'clock, after which he would be reading a history paper she had finished that afternoon, fifteen pages on the 1866 Haymarket Square riot in Chicago, an editorial service he provided each time she wrote a paper because it always made her *feel better*, she said, if he looked over her work before she handed it in. Then they were going to sit on the sofa in the living room together for a couple of hours catching up on their assignments for tomorrow's classes (Thucydides for Ferguson, John Stuart Mill for Amy), and after that, if they were in the mood, they would walk up Broadway to the West End Bar for a beer or two, perhaps talk to some of their friends if any of them happened to be there, and once they had had enough of sitting in the bar, they would go back to the apartment for another night in Amy's small but deliciously comfortable bed.

He was never quite sure which happened first, the sudden halt of the elevator or the extinguishing of the lights, or whether the two events occurred at the same time, the brief sputtering of the fluorescent bulbs overhead and the violent lurch of the elevator car all around him, a hiss followed by a bang, a bang followed by a hiss, or a hiss and a bang together, but however it happened it happened fast, and within two seconds the lights had gone out and the elevator had stopped moving. Ferguson was stuck somewhere between the sixth and seventh floors, and there he would remain for the next thirteen and a half hours, alone in the dark with nothing to do but examine the thoughts in his head and hope the lights would come back on before his bladder failed him.

Right from the start, he understood that it wasn't just his problem but everyone's problem. People were shouting throughout the building—*Blackout! Blackout!*—and as far as Ferguson could tell, there was no panic in their voices, if anything the tone was exuberant and celebratory, an outrush of wild laughter was rising up through the elevator shaft and resounding against the walls of the car, the boring old routines had lost their purpose, something new and unexpected had fallen from the sky, a black comet was streaking across the city, and let's have a party and whoop it up! That was good, Ferguson thought, and the longer the merriment went on, the more it would help him from panicking himself, for if no one else was afraid, why should he be afraid?— even though he was trapped inside a metal box and could see no more than the blindest blind man on a starless winter night at the North Pole, even though he felt as if he had been locked up in a coffin and might starve to death before he managed to crawl out.

Within two or three minutes, some of the more conscientious students started banging on the elevator doors and asking if anyone was inside. *Yes!* several voices answered, and Ferguson discovered he wasn't the only unfortunate who had been stranded in midair, that both elevators were in fact occupied, but the other box had half a dozen people in it whereas Ferguson was alone, not only imprisoned as the others were but cast into solitary confinement, and when he yelled out his name and room number (1014B), a voice called back: Archie! You poor sucker! To which Ferguson replied: Tim! How long is it going to last? Tim's answer was less than encouraging: Who the hell knows?

There was nothing to be done. He would have to sit there and wait it out, the bumbling Mr. Mishap who had been on his way to his girl-friend's apartment when he was accidentally turned into Experiment Number 001, now confined to a sensory-deprivation tank suspended six and a half floors above ground, the Harry Houdini of the Ivy League, the Robinson Crusoe of New York City and the greater metropolitan area, and if it hadn't felt so awful to be sealed up in that pitch-black cell, he would have laughed at himself and taken a bow for being the world's number one comic dunce, the number one *cosmic* dunce.

He would have to pee in his pants, he decided. If and when it became necessary to empty his bladder, he would have to revert to the self-sopping practices of early toddlerhood rather than inundate the floor and find himself—for the next however many hours—sitting in a pud-dle of cold, sloshing urine.

No cigarettes, and no matches either. Smoking would have helped pass the time, and the matches would have allowed him to see some-thing every now and then, not to speak of the glowing tips of the ciga-rettes each time he inhaled, but he had run out of both cigarettes and matches earlier that afternoon and had been intending to buy a new pack on his way down to dinner at Schneiderman's Spaghetti House on West 111th Street. *Dream on, funny man.*

It was impossible to know if the telephones were still working, but on the off chance they were, he called out to Tim again, wanting to ask his roommate to contact Amy and tell her what had happened to him so she wouldn't worry when he failed to show up at six, but Tim wasn't there anymore, and when Ferguson called out this time, no one answered. The whoops and laughter had quieted down in the past few minutes, the crowds in the hallways had largely dispersed, and no doubt Tim had gone upstairs to smoke pot with his pothead friends on the tenth floor.

So dark in there, so disconnected from everything, so outside the world or what Ferguson had always imagined to be the world that it was slowly becoming possible to ask himself if he was still inside his own body.

He thought about the wristwatch his parents had given him for his sixth birthday, a small child's watch with a flexible metallic band and numbers on the face that glowed in the dark. How comforting those green illuminated numbers had been to him as he lay in bed before sleep closed his eyes and pulled him under, little phosphorescent companions who disappeared in the morning when the sun came up, friends by night but mere painted numerals by day, and now that he no longer wore a watch, he wondered what had happened to that long-ago birthday present and where it could have gone to. Nothing to see anymore, and no sense of time anymore either, no way of knowing if he had been in the elevator for twenty or thirty minutes, or forty minutes, or an hour.

Gauloises. Those were the cigarettes he had been planning to buy on his walk down Broadway, the brand that he and Amy had started smoking during their trip to France in the summer, the overstrong, brown-tobacco fat boys in the pale blue packages with no cellophane around them, the cheapest of all French cigarettes, and merely to light up a Gauloise in America now was to return to the days and nights they had spent in that other world, the smells of the rough, cigar-like smoke were so different from the blond-tobacco smells of Camels and Luckys and Chesterfields that one puff, one exhale could send them back to *chambre dix-huit* in their little hotel across from the market, and suddenly their minds would be traveling through the Paris streets again as they relived the happiness they had felt there together, cigarettes as a sign of that happiness, of the new and bigger love that had taken hold of them during their month abroad and could express itself now by such acts as conjuring up surprise meetings with bawdy undergraduate poets as a gift to the newest member of the Morningside Heights Puke Battalion, blessed Amy and her talent for the unpredictable gesture, her lightning-fast improvisations, her resourceful, generous heart.

Ferguson had been tempted to take Les up on his offer and submit some of his work to the *Columbia Review*, but a month and a half had gone by since then, and he still hadn't come around and knocked. Not that he would have given Les any of his recent poems, which had all been disappointments to him and didn't deserve to be published, but the translations he had started doing in Paris had become a more serious enterprise by now, and after investing in several dictionaries that had helped improve his less than perfect French (*Le Petit Robert, Le Petit Larousse Illustré*, and the indispensable French-to-English *Harrap's*), he was no longer misreading lines and making idiotic blunders, and bit by bit his versions of Apollinaire and Desnos were beginning to sound like English poems rather than French poems that had been shoved through a linguistic meat grinder and rendered into Fringlish, but they weren't quite ready yet, there was still work to be done in order to make them right, and he didn't want to knock on the door until he felt good about every word in every line of those lyric glories, which he admired too deeply not to give them everything he had, again and again everything he had. It wasn't clear that the magazine would want to publish translations, but it would be worth making the effort to find out, since the *Review* had attracted some of the most interesting freshmen he had met so far, and by becoming part of it himself Ferguson would be able to join forces with poets and prose writers such as David Zimmer, Daniel Quinn, Jim Freeman, Adam Walker, and Peter Aaron, all of whom were in various classes with him, and he had seen enough of them in the past six weeks to know how intelligent and well-read they were, beginning writers who seemed to have the stuff to go on and become real poets and novelists one day, and not only were they smart, ferociously gifted first-year pukes, but each one of them had made it through Freshman Orientation Week without ever putting on his beanie.

No more poems for Ferguson, not for now in any case, and even if the adventure started up again sometime in the future, for the moment he had no choice but to think of himself as a *poet in remission*. The illness he had contracted in his mid-teens had led to a two-year-long fever that had produced close to a hundred poems, but then Francie had cracked up the car in Vermont, and suddenly the poems had stopped coming, for reasons he still couldn't understand he had felt cautious and afraid since then, and the few poems he had managed to write had not been good, or not good enough, by no means ever good enough. The prose of journalism had rescued him from the impasse, but a part of him missed the slowness of poetic labor, the feeling of shoveling down into the earth and tasting the earth in his mouth, and therefore he had followed Pound's advice to young poets and taken a stab at translation. At first, he had thought of it as nothing more than an exercise to keep his hand in, an activity that would bring him the pleasures of writing poetry with none of the frustrations, but now that he had been at it for a while, he understood there was much more to it than that. If you loved the poem you were translating, then taking apart that poem and putting it back together in your language was an act of devotion, a way of serving the master who had given you the beautiful thing you held in your hands, and the great master Apollinaire and the little master Desnos had written poems that Ferguson found beautiful and daring and astonishingly inventive, each one of them imbued with a spirit of melancholy and buoyancy at the same time, a rare combination that somehow joined the contradictory impulses at war in Ferguson's eighteen-year-old heart, and so he kept at it in whatever spare time he could create for himself, reworking, rethinking, and refining his translations until they would be solid enough for him to come knocking on the door.

The door was the door of 303 Ferris Booth Hall, the student activities center located flush against his dormitory building at the southwestern edge of the campus, the building he was trapped in now, and assuming he didn't lose his mind in the blackness first, he would have to write about this experience if he ever managed to get out of it, write some witty and provocative first-person article that the *Columbia Daily Spectator* would run because he was a member of the staff now, one of the forty undergraduates who worked on the student paper with no interference from the university administration or faculty censors, for even though he still hadn't found the courage to knock on the door of Room 303, he had walked into the larger office at the other end of the hall on the second day of Freshman Orientation Week, Room 318, and had told the person in charge that he wanted to join up. That was all there was to it. No trial period, no test articles, no need to show them the stories he had written for the *Montclair Times*—just go out and do it, and if you met your deadlines and proved you were a competent reporter, you were in. *Auf wiedersehen, Herr Imhoff!*

The possible beats for freshmen were Academic Affairs, Student Activities, Sports, and coverage of the surrounding community, and when Ferguson had said, *No sports, please, anything but sports,* they had given him Student Activities, which entailed filing two stories per week on average, most of them short, barely half the length of the pieces he had written on high school basketball and baseball games last year. His contributions so far had touched on a number of political issues involving both left-wing and right-wing causes, the May 2 Committee's plan to organize an anti-draft union on campus to fight against what they called "an unjust war of repression," but also an article about a band of

Republican students who had decided to back William F. Buckley's candidacy for mayor because the current mayor, John Lindsay, had "drifted away from the principles of the Republican Party." Other articles, which Ferguson called *lightweight stuff and trivial fluff*, had involved him in some parochial university matters, such as the thirteen freshmen who were still without dormitory rooms three weeks after the start of the semester, or the contest to name the new "café" in John Jay Hall, which was now offering "vending machine delicacies in a Horn & Hardart–style cafeteria," a competition sponsored by the University Food Services that would reward the winner with a free meal for two at any restaurant in New York City. Now, in the days just before the blackout, Ferguson had been working on a story about a Barnard freshman who was facing suspension for having a male guest in her room at an unlawful hour, since the current policy allowed visits from men only on Sunday afternoons between two and five o'clock, and the accused's guest had been with her at one in the morning. The girl, whose name was protected and could not be mentioned in the article, felt the punishment was unfair "because others do it and I was just the one who got caught." No wonder Amy had lied and cheated to scam her way out of living in one of those dormitory-prisons when she was a freshman. Reporter A. I. Ferguson wrote the story as a straight news article, as he was obliged to do, but fellow first-year student Archie Ferguson wished he could have defended the girl by quoting the refrain from Les Gottesman's poem in the first sentence of his article.

Let the facts speak for themselves.

Newspaper work was both an engagement with the world and a retreat from the world. If Ferguson meant to do his job well, then he would have to accept both elements of the paradox and learn to live in a state of doubleness: the demand to plunge into the thick of things and yet remain on the sidelines as a neutral observer. The plunge never failed to excite him—whether it was the high-speed plunge of writing about a basketball game or the slower, deeper excavations required to investigate outmoded parietal rules at a women's college—but the holding back was a potential problem, he felt, or at least something he would have to adjust to over the months and years ahead, for taking the journalist's vow of impartiality and objectivity was not unlike joining an order of monks and spending the rest of your life in a glass monastery—removed from the world of human affairs even as it continued to whirl around you on all sides. To be a journalist meant you could never be the person who tossed the brick through the window that started the revolution. You could watch the man toss the brick, you could try to understand why he had tossed the brick, you could explain to others what significance the brick had in starting the revolution, but you yourself could never toss the brick or even stand in the mob that was urging the man to throw it. Temperamentally, Ferguson was not someone inclined to throw bricks. He was, he hoped, a more or less reasonable person, but the agitations of the times were such that the reasons for not throwing bricks were beginning to look less and less reasonable, and when the moment finally came to throw the first one, Ferguson's sympathies would be with the brick and not the window.

His mind drifted off for a while, bogged down in the netherness of the infinite dark around him, and once he emerged from the mental fugue, he found himself thinking about the last lines of his translation of a short poem by Desnos:

> Somewhere in the world
> At the foot of a mountain
> A deserter is talking to sentinels
> Who do not understand his language.

Then, after four hours of captivity in the black box, his bladder finally gave out on him and he wet his pants in the same way he had done as a guiltless, smiling little chap in diapers. What a disgusting thing to do, he said to himself, as the warm liquid coursed through his underpants and corduroy trousers—but also, at the same time, how much better to be empty rather than full.

He remembered peeing with Bobby George one afternoon in the Georges' backyard when they were five years old and Bobby turning to him and asking: Archie, where does it all go? Millions of people and millions of animals peeing for millions of years, why aren't the oceans and rivers made of pee instead of water?

It was a question Ferguson had never been able to answer.

His old childhood friend had signed a contract with the Baltimore Orioles the day after he graduated from high school, and in the last article Ferguson ever wrote for the *Montclair Times* he had reported on the forty-thousand-dollar bonus that came with the contract along with Bobby's imminent departure for Aberdeen, Maryland, where he would be starting at catcher for the Orioles' short-season A-level team in the New York–Penn League. The kid had managed to put twenty-seven games under his belt that summer (and bat .291) before the draft board called him up for his physical, and with no student deferment to prevent him from serving his country now instead of four years from now, he had been inducted into the United States Army in mid-September and was currently nearing the end of his basic training at Fort Dix. Ferguson prayed that Bobby would be shipped off to a comfortable post in West Germany, where they would put him in a baseball uniform and allow him to play ball for the next two years as a way to discharge his patriotic duty, for the thought of little Bobby George tramping through the jungles of Vietnam with a rifle on his back was so repellent to Ferguson, he found the thought almost unthinkable.

How long was the war going to last?

Lorca, murdered by a fascist death squad at thirty-eight. Apollinaire, killed at the same age by the Spanish flu forty-six hours before the end of World War I. Desnos, killed at forty-four by typhus at Theresienstadt just days after the camp had been liberated.

Ferguson fell asleep and dreamed he was dreaming he was dead.

When power was restored at seven o'clock the next morning, he staggered back to his room on the tenth floor, stripped off his damp clothes, and stood under the shower for fifteen minutes.

The previous day, twenty-two-year-old Roger Allen LaPorte had sprinkled his clothes with gasoline and set himself on fire in front of the Dag Hammarskjöld Library at the U.N. With second- and third-degree burns over ninety-five percent of his body, he had been taken by ambulance to Bellevue Hospital, still conscious and able to speak. His last words were: I'm a Catholic Worker. I'm against war, all wars. I did this as a religious action.

He died not long after the blackout ended.

FRESHMAN HUMANITIES (REQUIRED). Fall Semester: Homer, Aeschylus, Sophocles, Euripides, Aristophanes, Herodotus, Thucydides, Plato (*Symposium*), Aristotle (*Aesthetics*), Virgil, Ovid. Spring Semester: Assorted books from the Old and New Testaments, Augustine (*Con-*

fessions), Dante, Rabelais, Montaigne, Cervantes, Shakespeare, Milton, Spinoza (*Ethics*), Molière, Swift, Dostoyevsky.

Freshman CC (Contemporary Civilization—required). Fall Semester: Plato (*Republic*), Aristotle (*Nicomachean Ethics, Politics*), Augustine (*City of God*), Machiavelli, Descartes, Hobbes, Locke. Spring Semester: Hume, Rousseau, Adam Smith, Kant, Hegel, Mill, Marx, Darwin, Fourier, Nietzsche, Freud.

Studies in Literature. Fall Semester (in lieu of required Freshman Composition course because of F.'s good score on A.P. exam): A seminar focused on the study of one book—*Tristram Shandy*.

The Modern Novel. Spring Semester: A bilingual seminar with books read alternately in English and French—Dickens, Stendhal, George Eliot, Flaubert, Henry James, Proust, Joyce.

French Poetry. Fall Semester—Nineteenth Century: Lamartine, Vigny, Hugo, Nerval, Musset, Gautier, Baudelaire, Mallarmé, Verlaine, Corbière, Lautréamont, Rimbaud, Laforgue. Spring Semester—Twentieth Century: Péguy, Claudel, Valéry, Apollinaire, Jacob, Fargue, Larbaud, Cendrars, Perse, Reverdy, Breton, Aragon, Desnos, Ponge, Michaux.

It didn't take long for him to decide that the best things about Columbia were the courses, the professors, and his fellow students. The reading lists were superb, the classes were small and led by tenured faculty members who took a special interest and pleasure in teaching undergraduates, and the other students were sharp, well prepared, and not afraid to speak up in class. Ferguson said little, but he absorbed everything that was discussed in those one- and two-hour sessions, feeling he had landed in a kind of intellectual paradise, and because he quickly understood that in spite of the many books he had read in the past ten or twelve years he still knew close to nothing, he diligently read all the texts that were assigned, hundreds of pages a week, sometimes more than a thousand, stumbling now and then but at least skimming the books and poems that resisted him (*Middlemarch, City of God*, and the dreary pomposities of Péguy, Claudel, and Perse) and at times doing more than was asked of him (plowing through all of *Don Quixote* when selections totaling only half the book had been assigned—but how could one not want to read *all* of that best and mightiest of all great books?). Two weeks into the fall semester, his parents drove in from Newark and took him out to dinner with Amy at the Green Tree, the inexpensive Hungarian restaurant on Amsterdam Avenue Ferguson had grown so fond of that he'd renamed it Yum City, and when he started talking about how much he enjoyed his courses and how astounding it was that his main job in life now was to read and write about books(!), his mother told him the story of her own *grand adventure* during the months before he was born, confined to bed with nothing to do but read, all the excellent books that Mildred had recommended, dozens of works that Stanley had checked out of the library for her and which she still thought about today, so many of them so well remembered after so many years, and since Ferguson could not recall ever having seen her read anything except for a handful of thrillers and some books about art and photography, he was moved by the image of his young, expectant mother lying alone all day in the first Newark apartment with novels propped up against her ever-growing belly, the bulge under her skin that was none other than his own unborn self, and yes, his mother said, smiling warmly at the thought of those long-ago days, How could you not love books after all the books I read while I was pregnant with you?

Ferguson laughed.

Don't laugh, Archie, his father said. It's what biologists call *osmosis*.

Or metempsychosis, Amy said.

Ferguson's mother looked confused. Psychosis? she said. What are we talking about?

The transmigration of souls, Ferguson explained.

But of course, his mother said. That's what I've been trying to tell you. My soul is in your soul, Archie. And it always will be, even after my body is gone.

Don't even think about that, Ferguson said. I've made special arrangements with the boys upstairs, and they've promised me you're going to live forever.

Good classes, good teachers, good classmates, but not all aspects of the Columbia experience were joyful ones, and among the things Ferguson liked least about the place were its stodgy, Ivy League pretensions, its backward-looking rules and rigid protocols, its lack of interest in the welfare of its students. All power was in the hands of the administration, and with no due process or impartial investigative board to oversee matters of discipline, they could kick you out at any moment without having to explain themselves. It wasn't that Ferguson was planning to get into trouble, but time would prove that others were, and when large numbers of them decided to make trouble in the spring of 1968, the entire institution went berserk.

More about that later.

Ferguson was pleased to be in New York, pleased to be with Amy in Amy's New York, at last a full-time resident of the capital of the twentieth century, but even though he was already familiar with the Columbia neighborhood, or somewhat familiar with it, now that he was living there he finally began to see Morningside Heights for what it was: a wounded, disintegrating zone of poverty and desperation, block after block of worn-out buildings with most of the apartments in those buildings housing mice, rats, and cockroaches along with the people who lived in them. The dirty streets were often strewn with uncollected garbage, and half of the pedestrians walking down the streets were out of their minds, or about to lose their minds, or recovering from mental breakdowns. The neighborhood was kilometer zero for the lost souls of New York, and every day Ferguson passed a dozen men and women locked in deep, incomprehensible dialogues with invisible others, people who did not exist. The one-armed vagrant with the overstuffed shopping bag, his hunched body doubled over itself as he stared down at the sidewalk and muttered his paternosters in a small, rasping voice. The bearded midget ensconced in various doorways on the side streets off Amsterdam Avenue, reading month-old copies of the *Daily Forward* with the jagged shard of a broken magnifying glass. The fat woman who floated around in her pajamas. On the traffic islands in the middle of Broadway, the drunk, the elderly, and the mad crowded together on benches above the subway gratings, sitting shoulder to shoulder as each one stared off silently into the distance. *New York of filth. New York of wires and death.* Then there was the person everyone referred to as the Yumkee Man, the aging crackpot who stood on the corner in front of Chock Full o'Nuts every day intoning the words *yawveh yumpkee,* a haranguer of the old school variously known as Dr. Yumkee and Emsh, self-proclaimed son of Napoleon, self-proclaimed messiah, and true-blue American patriot who never went anywhere without carrying his American flag, which on cold days he would wrap around his shoulders and use as a shawl. And the bald, bullet-headed boy-man Bobby, who spent his days carrying out errands for the owners of Ralph's Typewriter Shop on Broadway and 113th Street, sprinting down the sidewalk with outstretched arms pretending to be an airplane, weaving in and out of the human traffic as he made the engine noises of a B-52 in full-throttle flight. And hairless Sam Steinberg, the ever-present Sam S., who rode three different subway trains from the Bronx every morning to sell candy bars on Broadway or in front of Hamilton Hall, but also to sell his crude, Magic Marker pictures of imaginary animals for one dollar, little works done on the laundry cardboards that came with pressed shirts, calling out to anyone who would listen to him, *Hey, mistah, new paintings here, beauteeful new paintings here, the most beauteeful paintings in the woild*. And the great enigma of the Hotel Harmony, the crumbling hotel for down-and-out men that stood on the corner of Broadway and 110th Street, the tallest building for blocks around, and written on the brick wall in letters large enough to be read from a quarter of a mile away was the hotel's motto, which surely qualified as the most dumbfounding oxymoron on earth: THE HOTEL HARMONY—WHERE LIVING IS A PLEASURE.

It was a cracked-up world up there on the upper Upper West Side, and it took some getting used to before he could harden himself to the squalor and misery of his new stomping grounds, but not all was bleakness on the Heights, young people were wandering around the streets as well, pretty girls from Barnard and Juilliard often figured in the landscape, fluttering past him like optical illusions or spirits from dreams, there were bookstores to browse in on Broadway between 114th and 116th Streets, even a basement store for foreign books around the corner and down the stairs on 115th Street, where Ferguson could spend the odd half hour rummaging through the French poetry section, the Thalia and the New Yorker showed the best old and new movies just twenty and twenty-five blocks to the south, Edith Piaf was on the jukebox of a greasy-spoon diner called the College Inn, where he could stuff himself with cheap breakfasts and talk to the blowsy, bleached-blond waitress who called him *honey*, Chock Full o'Nuts for ten-minute coffee breaks, life-sustaining hamburgers at Prexy's (*The Hamburger with a College Education*), *ropa vieja* and espresso at the Ideal (Ee-day-al), the Cuban-Chinese place on Broadway between 108th and 109th Streets, and goulash and dumplings at Yum City, the restaurant he and Amy went to so often for dinner that the plump husband-and-wife owners began offering them free desserts, but the central point of refuge in that cracked-up neighborhood was the West End Bar and Grill, situated on Broadway between 113th and 114th Streets, with its immense oval bar of smoothly polished oak, the booths for four or six along the northern and eastern walls, and the large, movable chairs and tables in the back room. Amy had already introduced him to the West End the previous year, but now that Ferguson was a year-round resident himself, that ancient, dimly lit watering hole soon became his principal hangout, his study hall by day and meeting place by night, his second home.

It wasn't the beer or the bourbon that interested him, it was the talk, the chance to talk to his friends from the *Spectator* and the *Columbia Review*, to talk to Amy's political friends and various West End regulars, drinks were merely liquid props to be nursed along in order to go on sitting in the booth, for this was the first time in Ferguson's life that he had been surrounded by people he wanted to talk to, not just Amy anymore, who for the past two years had been his sole interlocutor, the one person in his life worth talking to, now there were several, now there were many, and the conversations he took part in at the West End were just as valuable to him as anything that was said in his classes at Hamilton Hall.

The *Spectator* boys were a serious, hard-working lot, more grinds than pukes when it came to how they dressed and cut their hair, but grinds with the hearts of pukes, and Ferguson's fellow beginners from the class of '69 were already dedicated newspapermen, just out of high school but dug in and committed to their jobs as if they had been working at them for years. The older members of the *Spectator* staff tended to frequent another bar a couple of blocks down Broadway, the Gold Rail, which was the saloon of preference for the frat boys and jocks, but Ferguson's cronies preferred the dingier, less raucous atmosphere of the West End, and of the three who sometimes joined him for drinks and talk in one of the side booths, there was the calm and thoughtful Robert Friedman, a kid from Long Island who covered Academic Affairs and at the absurd age of eighteen could write as skillfully and professionally as any reporter from the *Times* or the *Herald Tribune*, the fast-talking Greg Mullhouse from Chicago (Sports), and the dogged, probing, wryly sarcastic Allen Branch from San Francisco (Community Affairs), and they all agreed that the managing board of the paper was too conservative, too timid in its treatment of the university's bad policies concerning the war (allowing military recruiters on campus, failing to cut ties with the ROTC—pronounced *Rotsy*—the Naval Reserve Officers' Training Corps program) as well as its slumlord tactics in evicting poor tenants from university-owned apartment buildings to further Columbia's expansion through the surrounding neighborhood, and when their turn came to take control of the *Spectator* in the spring of their junior year, they would elect Friedman editor in chief and quickly get to work at *changing everything*. The plans for this eventual coup only confirmed what Ferguson had already figured out about the freshman class that year. They were different from the classes above them—more aggressive, more impatient, more willing to stand up and fight against stupidity, complacency, and unfairness. The postwar children born in 1947 had little in common with the wartime children born just two and three years earlier, a generational rift had opened up in that short span of time, and whereas most of the upperclassmen still bought into the lessons they had learned in the 1950s, Ferguson and his friends understood that they were living in an irrational world, a country that murdered its presidents and legislated against its citizens and sent its young men off to die in senseless wars, which meant that they were more fully attuned to the realities of the present than their elders were. A small example, a trivial example, but nevertheless a pertinent example: the beanie battles of Freshman Orientation Week. Ferguson had instinctively refused to wear his, but so had the *Columbia Review* and *Spectator* boys, so had scores of others, and in a class of six hundred and ninety-three students, more than a third of them stared down and bumped shoulders with the football monitors in the days before the start of classes. Nothing had been organized. Each anti-beanie boy had acted on his own, appalled by the idea of having to march around campus as a conscript in the Tweedledee and Tweedledum brigade, and the contagion of resistance had spread until it was turned into a de facto mass movement, a general boycott, a struggle between tradition and common sense. The result? The administration announced that beanies would henceforth be dispensed with for all incoming freshmen in the future. A microscopic victory, yes, but perhaps a sign of things to come. Beanies today—who knew what tomorrow?

By the end of Thanksgiving week, Ferguson had built up a pile of half a dozen translations that seemed more or less finished to him, and when they passed the all-important Amy Test, he finally gathered them together, put them in a manila envelope, and submitted them to the

Review. Contrary to what he had been expecting to be told, the editors were not averse to the principle of including translations in the magazine—*as long as they weren't too long,* as one of them said—and so it was that Ferguson's English rendering of the Desnos poem about the deserter and the sentinels, *At the Edge of the World,* was accepted for publication in the spring issue. Even if he was no longer a full-fledged poet, he could still participate in the act of writing poetry by translating poems that were far superior to anything he could have written himself, and the young poets connected to the *Review,* whose ambitions for themselves were much greater than his were for himself, who risked everything when they sat down to write while he risked almost nothing when he sat down to translate, recognized his value to the group as someone who could judge the merits of some works over other works, who brought a wider, more inclusive perspective to their conversations about poetry, but they never embraced him as a member of the inner circle, which was entirely fair and just, Ferguson thought, since in the end he wasn't truly one of them, and yet as far as hanging out at the West End was concerned, they were all good friends, and Ferguson loved talking to them, especially David Zimmer, who impressed him as the most brilliant and precocious of the bunch, along with Zimmer's non-writer pal from Chicago, Marco Fogg, an eccentric, wild-haired boy who walked around in an Irish tweed suit and was so deeply informed about literature that he could crack jokes in Latin and make you laugh, even if you didn't understand Latin.

The journalists and the poets were the ones Ferguson gravitated to because he found them to be the ones who were most alive, the ones who had already begun to figure out who and what they were in relation to the world, but there were others in the class of '69 who had no clue about themselves or anything else, the floundering teenage boys who had amassed good grades in school and could score knockout numbers on standardized tests but who still had the minds of children, the horde of inexperienced ephebes and virgin wankers who had grown up in small provincial cities and suburban tract houses and who clung to the campus and their dorm rooms because New York was too big, too rough, too fast, and the place threatened and confused them. One such innocent was Ferguson's roommate, a genial fellow from Dayton, Ohio, named Tim McCarthy, who had entered college thoroughly unprepared to take on the freedom of living away from home for the first time, but unlike many of the others in that position, he didn't withdraw into himself and hide from the city, he rushed straight into it, bent on losing himself in the twin pleasures of monumental beer consumption and a steady intake of marijuana, with a couple of acid trips thrown in for good measure. Ferguson didn't know what to do. He spent most nights with Amy at the apartment on 111th Street, and his room in Carman Hall served as little more than an office for him, the place where he kept his books, typewriter, and clothes, and whenever he was in that room he tended to be sitting at his desk with the typewriter in front of him, working on his news articles for the *Spectator*, composing the various short and long papers he was required to hand in for his courses, or else fiddling with yet another draft of one of his translations. He didn't see Tim often enough to have formed a connection with him, their relations were friendly but *deeply superficial*, as he had once heard a woman say to another woman on the 104 bus, and while Ferguson sensed that the boy was headed for what could have been serious trouble, he was reluctant to pry into Tim's personal business. He had already seen enough to know that he himself had no interest in experimenting with the silliness that was pot or the craziness that was LSD, but what right did he have to tell Tim McCarthy to refrain from ingesting those things? One afternoon in mid-December, however, when Tim stumbled into the room squealing and giggling after his latest pot session with the gang down the hall, Ferguson finally spoke up and said: It might seem funny to you, Tim, but it's not funny to anyone else.

The Dayton boy flopped down on his bed and smiled: Don't be such a grump, Archie. You're beginning to sound like my father.

I don't care how many drugs you take, but it wouldn't be so nice for you if you flunked out of here, would it?

You're talking through your nose, Mr. New Jersey. I'm all A's and B's this semester, with more A's than B's, and if I do what I should on the finals next month, I'll probably make the dean's list. Won't Daddy be proud.

Good for you. But if you go on getting stoned every day, how much longer can you keep it up?

Keep it up? It's always up, man, always up and raring to go, and the higher I am, the more up it is. You should try it sometime, Archie. The hardest hard-ons this side of the Rock of Gibraltar.

Ferguson emitted a brief snort of a laugh—not unlike one of Amy's snorts—but in this case it was an admission of defeat rather than a genuine laugh. He had started an argument he was bound to lose.

We'll never be younger than we are right now, Tim said, and after you're young, it all goes downhill pretty fast. Boring adulthood. The blahs of the big blah-blah-blah. A job, a wife, a couple of kids, and then you're shuffling around in your slippers, waiting for them to cart you off to the glue factory—sans teeth, sans everything. So why not live it up and have some fun while we can?

It depends on what you call fun.

Letting go, for one thing.

Agreed. But what's your idea of letting go?

Juicing up and jumping out of my skin.

That might work for you, but it's not for everyone.

Wouldn't you rather fly than crawl on the ground? There's nothing to it, Archie. You just open your arms and take off.

Some of us don't want that. And even if we thought we did, we wouldn't be able to do it.

Why not?

Because we can't, that's all. We just can't.

IT WASN'T THAT Ferguson was unable to fly or let go or jump out of his skin, but he needed Amy in order to do those things, and now that they had lived through their first breakup, their first reconciliation, and their first experience of sleeping-together-every-night in France, he could no longer separate the idea of being who he was from the necessity of being with her. New York was the next step forward, everyday life with the chance to see each other every day, to be together almost constantly if they wished, but Ferguson understood that he couldn't take any of those possibilities for granted, for the breakup had taught him that Amy was a person who needed more room than most people did, that her suffocating mother had made her allergic to any and all forms of emotional pressure, and if he demanded more from her than she was willing to give, she would eventually withdraw from him again. He sometimes wondered if he didn't love her too much, or if he hadn't yet learned how to love her in the correct way, because the truth was that Ferguson happily would have married her tomorrow, even as an eighteen-year-old student in his first months of college he felt prepared to march through the rest of his life with her and never look at another woman again. He knew how excessive those thoughts were, but he couldn't stop himself from thinking them. Amy was all tangled up inside him. He was who he was because she was in there with him now, and why pretend he could ever be anything even remotely human anymore without her?

He never said a word about any of this. The idea wasn't to scare her off but to love her, and Ferguson did his best to stay alert to Amy's moods and respond to the subtle, unvoiced indications that told him whether tonight would be a good night for sleeping in her bed, for example, or whether she would prefer to wait until tomorrow night, to make a point of asking whether she wanted to get together for dinner that evening or meet up later at the West End or stay in because they both had papers to write or else chuck everything and go to a movie at the Thalia. He let her make all those decisions because he knew she felt freer and happier when she was the one to decide, and above all the Amy he wanted was the fierce, tender, wisecracking girl who had saved his life after the accident, the intrepid co-conspirator who had traveled through France with him and not the sullen monarch who had expelled him from her court last fall for four months of lonely rustication in his New Jersey backwater.

Mostly, he wound up spending the night with her, on average four or five nights a week, often as many as six, with one or two or sometimes three nights alone in his single bed on the tenth floor of Carman Hall. It was a workable arrangement, he felt, even though he wished the numbers could have been a consistent seven and zero, but the important thing was that after two years their bodies still caught fire when they crawled under the sheets together, and it was the rare night that Ferguson slept in Amy's bed when they didn't make love before falling asleep. To reverse the Gottesman proposition, not only was the steady sex good for them, but the good sex steadied them and made them stronger: two twined into one rather than one and one standing apart. The physical intimacy that had developed between them was so intense now that Ferguson sometimes felt he knew Amy's body better than his own. But not always, and therefore it was essential that he listen to her and follow her lead in physical matters, that he *pay close attention to what she*

was telling him with her eyes, for every now and then he would miscon-
strue the signals and do the wrong thing, such as grabbing hold of her
and kissing her when she didn't want him to, and even though she never
pushed him away (which only added to his confusion), he could tell that
her heart wasn't fully in it, that sex wasn't on her mind just then as it
was on his, as it always was on his, but she would go ahead and let him
make love to her anyway because she didn't want to disappoint him,
submitting to his desires with a passive sort of involvement, *mechanical
sex,* which was worse than no sex at all, and the first time it happened
Ferguson felt so ashamed of himself he vowed never to let it happen
again, but it did happen again, twice more over the next few months,
which made him understand, finally, that men and women were not the
same, and if he meant to do right by his woman, he would have to pay
even closer attention and learn how to think and feel as she did, for there
was no doubt in his mind that Amy knew exactly what he was thinking and feeling, which explained why she tolerated his lustful blunders
and love-blind acts of stupidity.

Another error he sometimes committed was overestimating Amy's
confidence in herself. The great roar of being that emanated from the
Schneiderman soul seemed to preclude any lapses into doubt or
uncertainty, but she had her bad moments just as everyone else did, her
moments of sadness and weakness and grim introspection, and because
they occurred so rarely, they always seemed to catch Ferguson by surprise. Intellectual doubts above all, whether her political ideas were
sound or not, whether anything she ever did or said or thought would
be of value to anyone, whether it was worth fighting the *system* when
the system would never change, whether the fight to make things
better would only make them worse because of all the people who would
rise up against the people fighting to make them better, but also doubts
about herself, the small *girl things* that would suddenly torment her for
no apparent reason, her lips were too thin, her eyes were too small, her
teeth were too big, there were too many moles on her legs, the same
light-brown dots that Ferguson loved so much, but no, she would say,
they're ugly, and she would never wear shorts again, and now she was
getting too fat, and now she had lost too much weight, and why were
her breasts so small, and goddamn that big Jewish nose of hers, and
what the fuck to do with her crazy, kinky hair, it was impossible,
impossible to do anything with it, and how could she still want to go

on wearing lipstick when the cosmetic companies were brainwashing women into conforming to some skewed, artificial vision of woman-hood in order to feed the great capitalist profit machine that ran on making people want what they didn't need? All this from a vibrant, attractive girl in the flower of her young adulthood, and if such a person as Amy Schneiderman could succumb to questioning the body that belonged to her in that way, what about the fat girls and the homely girls and the deformed girls who didn't even have a chance? Not only were men and women not the same, Ferguson concluded, but it was more difficult to be a woman than a man, and if he should ever forget that, he told himself, then the gods should come down from their mountain and pluck out the eyes from his head.

In the spring of 1966, an SDS chapter was formed at Columbia. Students for a Democratic Society was a national organization by then, and one by one most of the left-wing student groups on campus voted to join up with SDS or disband their ranks and dissolve into it. Among them were the Committee for Social Mockery, which had marched around College Walk last year holding up blank signs in a general protest against everything (a spectacle Ferguson dearly wished he had seen), the May 2 Movement, which was backed by the Progressive Labor Party, members of the Progressive Labor Party itself (the hard-line, Maoist PL), and the group that Amy had belonged to since her freshman year, the ICV (Independent Committee on Vietnam), which had fought with the police last May when twenty-five of its members disrupted the NROTC awards ceremony on Low Library plaza. The SDS slogan was *Let the People Decide!*, and Ferguson supported the group's positions just as enthusiastically as Amy did (against the war, against racism, against imperialism, against poverty—and for a democratic world in which all citizens could live with one another as equals), but Amy joined the organization and Ferguson didn't. The reasons were obvious to both of them, and they didn't spend much time discussing the matter, nor any time at all in trying to talk the other into making a different decision, since he in fact encouraged her to join up, and she understood why he would never join anything, for Amy was someone who could imagine herself throwing bricks, who no doubt had been born to throw bricks, whereas Ferguson was someone who couldn't and wasn't, and even if he had burned his press badge and resigned from the *Spectator*, he still wouldn't have joined under any circumstances. He walked down Fifth Avenue with her again on March twenty-sixth in another anti-war demonstration, but that was as far as he would go in doing his bit for the cause. There were just so many hours in a day, after all, and once he had finished his school-work and newspaper work, the prospect of spending some time with his French poets was far more attractive to him than attending loud, contentious political meetings to plan out the next action the group would be taking against the next issue on the agenda.

WHEN THE SECOND semester ended in early June, Ferguson shook hands with Tim McCarthy, said good-bye to Carman Hall, and moved to more spacious digs off-campus. Only freshmen were required to live in dormitories, and now that his freshman year was behind him, he was free to go wherever he wished. All along, his wish had been to move in with Amy, but as a point of pride (and perhaps a test of love), Ferguson had held back from asking her if he could rent one of the two bedrooms that would likely be opening up in her apartment (both occupied by seniors), waiting for her to ask the question herself, which she did at the end of April, just hours after she learned that her two graduating apart-ment mates would be leaving New York on the same day they were given their diplomas, and how much sweeter it was to be living there at her invitation than to have invited himself, to know that she wanted him just as much as he wanted her.

They promptly took over the two vacated rooms, both of which were larger and brighter than Amy's cramped little hole at the back of the apartment, two rooms standing side by side along the main hallway, both equipped with double beds, desks, bureaus, and bookcases, which they bought from the departing tenants for a grand total of forty-five dollars each, and Ferguson's shuttle existence of the past year came to an end, no more daily treks up and down Broadway between his dorm room and Amy's apartment, they lived together now, they slept together in the same bed seven nights out of every seven now, and all through that summer of 1966, the nineteen-year-old Ferguson walked around with the uncanny sensation that he had entered a world in which it was no longer necessary to ask the world for anything more than it had already given him.

An unprecedented moment of equipoise and inner fulfillment. Having his cake and eating it too. No one, but no one, was ever supposed to be that happy. Ferguson sometimes wondered if he hadn't pulled a fast one on the author of *The Book of Terrestrial Life*, who was turning the pages too quickly that year and had somehow left the page for those months blank.

Summer in hot, unbreathable New York, one ninety-degree day after another as the broiling asphalt melted in the sun and the concrete pavement slabs burned into the soles of their shoes, the air so dense with humidity that even the bricks on the façades of buildings seemed to be oozing sweat, and everywhere the stink of garbage rotting on the sidewalks. American bombs were falling on Hanoi and Haiphong, the heavyweight champion was talking to the press about Vietnam (No Vietcong ever called me nigger, he said, thus conflating the two American wars into a single war), the poet Frank O'Hara was run over by a dune buggy on a Fire Island beach and killed at the age of forty, and Ferguson and Amy were both trapped in boring summer jobs, bookstore clerk for him, typing and filing for her, low-paid work that forced them to ration their Gauloises, but Bobby George was playing baseball in Germany, the West End Bar had air-conditioning, and once they returned to their hot, airless apartment, Ferguson could run cool washcloths over Amy's naked body and dream they were back in France. It was the summer of politics and movies, of dinners at the Schneidermans' apartment on West Seventy-fifth Street and the Adlers' apartment on West Fifty-eighth Street, of celebrating Gil Schneiderman's move to the *New York Times* after the *Herald Tribune* shut down its presses and vanished from the scene, of going to concerts at Carnegie Hall with Gil and Amy's brother, Jim, of riding the 104 bus down Broadway to the Thalia and the New Yorker to escape the heat by watching movies, which they jointly decided should always be comedies, since the grimness of the moment demanded that they laugh whenever it was possible, and who better to get them going than the Marx Brothers and W. C. Fields, or the screwball inanities starring Grant and Powell, Hepburn, Dunne, and Lombard, they couldn't get enough of them, they jumped onto the bus the minute they found out another comedy double feature was playing, and what a relief it was to forget the war and the stinking garbage for a few hours as they sat in the air-conditioned dark, but when no comedies were to be seen in the neighborhood or anywhere else they returned to their summer project of grinding through what they called the *literature of dissent*, reading Marx and Lenin because

one had to read them, and Trotsky and Rosa Luxemburg, Emma Goldman and Alexander Berkman, Sartre and Camus, Malcolm X and
Frantz Fanon, Sorel and Bakunin, Marcuse and Adorno, looking for
answers to help explain what had happened to their country, which
seemed to be collapsing under the weight of its own contradictions, but
while Amy found herself moving closer to a Marxist reading of events
(the inevitable overthrow of capitalism), Ferguson had his doubts, not
just because the Hegelian dialectic turned on its head struck him as a
mechanical and simplistic view of the world but because there was no
class consciousness among American workers, no sympathy for socialist
thought anywhere in the culture, and therefore no chance for the great
upheaval Amy was predicting. In other words, they disagreed, even if
they were essentially on the same side, but none of those differences
seemed to matter, since neither one of them felt wholly certain about
anything at that point, and each understood that the other could have
been right, or that both of them could have been wrong, and better to
air their doubts freely and openly than to march together in blind lock-
step until they fell off the edge of a cliff.

Most of all, it was the summer of looking at Amy, of watching her
put on lipstick and brush her impossible hair, of studying her hands
as she rubbed body lotion into her palms and then ran those palms
over her legs and arms and breasts, of washing her hair for her as
she closed her eyes and sank into the lukewarm water in the tub, the
ancient tub with the claw feet and the rust stains running through
the cracked porcelain, of lying in bed in the morning and seeing her
dress herself in a corner of the room as light came through the window
and surrounded her, smiling at him as she slipped into her panties and
bra and cotton skirt, the small domestic details of living within her
feminine orbit, tampons, birth-control pills, the pills for when her
stomach cramped up during hard periods, the household chores they
did together, shopping for food, washing dishes, and the way she
would sometimes bite her lower lip as they stood in the kitchen slicing and chopping onions and tomatoes for the pot of chili that would
feed them for a weekend's worth of dinners, the concentration in her
eyes whenever she painted her fingernails or toenails *to make a good
impression at work*, watching her shave her legs and underarms as she
sat quietly in the bath, then climbing into the tub with her and soaping
down her slithery white skin, the unearthly smoothness of her skin

against his hands, and sex and sex and sex, sweaty summer sex with no cover or sheet on top of them as they rolled around on the bed in her room and the creaking old fan stirred the air a bit and cooled off nothing, the shudders and sighs, the yowls and groans, in her, on top of her, under her, beside her, the deep laughs trapped in her throat, the surprise tickling attacks, the sudden snatches of old pop songs from their childhood, lullabies, dirty limericks, Mother Goose poems, and grumpy Amy narrowing her eyes in another one of her snits, happy Amy gulping down ice water and cold beers, eating fast, shoveling it in *like a ravenous stevedore*, the snorts of laughter watching Fields and the M. Brothers—*There ain't no sanity clause, Archie!*—and the magnificent *Ah* she exhaled one evening when he handed her his translation of an early poem by René Char, a poem so short that it consisted of only six words, a brief blink entitled *Lacenaire's Hand*, which was a reference to the nineteenth-century criminal-poet who later surfaced as a character in *Children of Paradise*:

   Worlds of eloquence have been lost.

   It could never end. The sun was stuck in the sky, a page had gone missing from the book, and it would always be summer as long as they didn't breathe too hard or ask for too much, always the summer when they were nineteen and were finally, finally almost, finally perhaps almost on the brink of saying good-bye to the moment when everything was still in front of them.

5.2

5.3

O N NOVEMBER 7, 1965, FERGUSON CAME TO THE SIXTEENTH BOOK
of Homer's *Odyssey*. He was sitting at a desk in a small maid's
room on the sixth floor of an apartment building in the seventh
arrondissement of Paris, which had been his home for the past three
weeks, and now that Odysseus has finally made it back to Ithaka after
his endless journey from Troy, gray-eyed Athena has disguised him
in the garb and body of a wizened old vagabond, and as the man of
many wiles sits with the swineherd Eumaeus in a mountain hut on
the outskirts of town, in walks Telemachus, Odysseus's son, who was
no more than an infant when his father set off for Troy twenty years
ago and still knows nothing about his father's return, having himself
just returned from a long and dangerous voyage, and as Eumaeus
leaves the hut and heads for the palace in order to tell Penelope, the
young man's mother, that Telemachus has returned to Ithaka unharmed,
father and son are alone together for the first time, and while the father
is fully aware that he is looking at his son, the son still knows nothing.

Athena then shows up masquerading as a tall and handsome
Ithakan woman, seen only by Odysseus and therefore invisible to the
son, and when she beckons the father to step outside for a moment,
she tells him that the time for dissembling is over and that he must
reveal himself to Telemachus now. "Saying no more" (as rendered in the
newly published Fitzgerald translation that was sitting on Ferguson's
desk) "she tipped her golden wand upon the man, / making his cloak
pure white, and the knit tunic / fresh around him. Lithe and young she

made him, / ruddy with sun, his jawline clean, the beard / no longer grey upon his chin."

There was no God, Ferguson kept telling himself. There never had been and never would be a single God, but there were gods, many gods from many and all parts of the world, among them the Greek gods who lived on Mount Olympus, Athena, Zeus, Apollo, and the various others who had gamboled their way through the first two hundred and ninety-five pages of *The Odyssey*, and what the gods enjoyed more than anything else was meddling in the affairs of men. They simply couldn't help themselves, it was what they had been born to do. In the same way that beavers couldn't help themselves from building dams, Ferguson supposed—or cats couldn't help themselves from torturing mice. Immortal beings, yes, but beings with too much time on their hands, which meant that nothing could stop them from cooking up their juicy, often ghastly entertainments.

When Odysseus reenters the hut, Telemachus is thunderstruck by the transformation of the old man into what he now concludes must be a god. But Odysseus, on the verge of crumbling into tears, barely able to get the words out of his mouth, quietly says: "No god. Why take me for a god? No, no. / I am that father whom your boyhood lacked / and suffered pain for lack of. I am he."

That was the first stab, the tip of the blade puncturing Ferguson's skin somewhere in the boneless, unprotected area between his rib cage and groin, for reading the words of Odysseus's short reply produced the same effect in him that would have been produced if the lines had read: *It's going to be a cold day, Archie. Remember to wear your scarf to school.*

Then the blade went all the way in: "throwing / his arms around this marvel of a father / Telémakhos began to weep. Salt tears / rose from the wells of longing in both men, / and cries burst from both as keen and fluttering / as those of the great taloned hawk, / whose nestlings farmers take before they fly. / So helplessly they cried, pouring out tears, / and might have gone on weeping so until sundown."

It was the first time Ferguson had wept over a book. He had shed numerous tears in the darkness of both empty and crowded movie theaters, sometimes at the most soft-headed, sentimental rubbish, had choked up more than once while listening to the *Saint Matthew Passion* with Gil, especially at that spot on the first side of the third disk when the tenor's voice suddenly catches with emotion, but books had never done that to him, not even the saddest, most moving books, and yet now in the dim November light of Paris tears were falling on page 296 of his one-dollar-and-forty-five-cent paperback edition of *The Odyssey*, and when he turned away from the poem and tried to look through the window of his little room, everything in the room was blurred.

THE ODYSSEY WAS the second book on Gil's reading list. *The Iliad* had come first, and after plowing his way through the two epic poems by the anonymous bard or bards who had been given the name Hómēros, Ferguson had promised to read ninety-eight more books over the next two years, including Greek tragedies and comedies, Virgil and Ovid, portions of the Old Testament (King James version), Augustine's *Confessions*, Dante's *Inferno*, roughly half the contents of Montaigne's *Essays*, no fewer than four tragedies and three comedies by Shakespeare, Milton's *Paradise Lost*, selections from Plato, Aristotle, Descartes, Hume, and Kant, *The Oxford Book of English Verse*, *The Norton Anthology of American Poetry*, as well as British, American, French, and Russian novels by such writers as Fielding-Sterne-Austen, Hawthorne-Melville-Twain, Balzac-Stendhal-Flaubert, and Gogol-Tolstoy-Dostoyevsky. Gil and Ferguson's mother both hoped their 4-F, ex-book-thief son would change his mind about going to college in a year or two, but if Ferguson persisted in shunning the benefits of a formal education, at least those one hundred titles would give him some knowledge of some of the books every educated person was supposed to have read.

Ferguson meant to stick to his promise because he wanted to read those books and had every intention of reading every one of them. He didn't want to go through life as an untrained, undisciplined know-nothing, he merely didn't want to go to college, and even though he was willing to sit through five two-hour classes a week at the Alliance Française because one of his ambitions in life was to become wholly proficient in French, he had no desire to sit through classes anywhere else, least of all in a college, which would have been no better than any of the other maximum-security institutions he had been confined to since the age of five—and undoubtedly even worse. The only reason to surrender your ideals and go in for one of those four-year stretches was to be given a student deferment from the army, which would put off the dilemma of marching off to Vietnam or saying no to Vietnam, which in turn would put off the second dilemma of federal prison or permanent removal from the United States, all postponed for the length of your four-year sentence, but Ferguson had already solved the problem by other means, and now that the army had rejected him, he could reject college without ever having to face any of those dilemmas again.

He knew how lucky he was. Not only had he been spared from the war and each one of the odious choices that followed from the war, the terrible ayes and nays that every post–high school and post-college American male would have to confront for as long as the evil war went on, but his parents had not turned against him, that was crucial, nothing was more important to the prospects of his long-range survival than the fact that Gil and his mother had forgiven him for the transgressions of his senior year, and even though they continued to *worry about him* and question his mental and emotional stability, they had not forced him to start seeing a doctor for the psychotherapy Gil had suggested might do him an *enormous amount of good*, for Ferguson had argued that it wasn't necessary, that he had made his fair share of *dumb adolescent mistakes* but was essentially fine and that throwing away their money on such a nebulous proposition would only make him feel guilty. They gave in. They always gave in when he talked to them in a mature and sensible tone of voice, because whenever Ferguson was on top of himself and not under himself, which was about half the time, there were few people in the world as sweet as he was, as loving as he was, such sweetness and transparent love emanating from his eyes that few could resist him, least of all his mother and stepfather, who were perfectly aware that Ferguson could be other things besides sweet as well, but still they found themselves powerless to resist.

Two lucky things, and then a third lucky thing that came through for him at the last minute, the chance to live in Paris for a time, perhaps for a long time, which had not seemed possible at first, not with his mother fretting about the enormous distance that would stand between them and Gil stewing about the logistics of the venture and the dozens of practical difficulties it would present, but then, a couple of weeks after Ferguson's 4-F classification landed in the family mailbox, Gil wrote to Vivian Schreiber in Paris to ask for her advice, and the surprising answer she gave him in her return letter put an end to Gil's stewing and greatly diminished Ferguson's mother's alarm. "Send Archie to me," Vivian wrote. "The sixth-floor *chambre de bonne* that belongs to my apartment is empty now, since my brother's son Edward has gone back to America for his senior year at Berkeley and I haven't bothered to look for a new occupant, which means that Archie can have it if he doesn't mind living in minimal quarters. Rent-free, of course. And now that my Chardin book has been published in London and New York, I've been spending my time translating it into French for my Paris publisher, a tedious job that thankfully is nearly done, and with no new projects burning on the immediate horizon, I would be happy to take on the task of tutoring Archie as he works his way through the extraordinary books on your list, which will of course make it necessary for me to read them as well, and I must admit that the thought of plunging into all that good stuff again is exceedingly pleasant to me. The high school film articles you included in your letter show that Archie is a capable and intelligent young man. If he doesn't approve of my teaching methods, we can look for someone else. But I'm willing to give it a try."

Ferguson was euphoric. Not just Paris, but Paris under the same roof as Vivian Schreiber, Paris under the benevolent care of womankind's most glorious incarnation, Paris on the rue de l'Université in the seventh arrondissement, Left Bank Paris with all the comforts of a rich and tranquil neighborhood, just a short walk to the cafés of Saint-Germain, just a short walk across the river to the Cinémathèque at the Palais de Chaillot, and, most important of all, for the first time ever in his life, *life on his own*.

It was painful having to say good-bye to his mother and Gil, especially his mother, who cried a bit at the end of their last home-cooked dinner together on a wet night in mid-October, which almost made him want to tear up as well, but he averted that potential embarrassment by telling them about the book he had started writing in the days just after his army physical, at a moment when he still wasn't sure what would happen to him and was feeling entirely lost, a little book which already had a title that was forever fixed in stone, *How Laurel and Hardy Saved My Life*, which was essentially a book about his mother, he said, and the rough years they had gone through together between the night of the Newark fire and the day she married Gil, a book that would be broken down into three parts, "Glorious Oblivions" being the first one, an account of all the movies they had watched together during the Curious Interregnum and the months beyond, the importance of those movies to them, the life-saving power of those ridiculous studio films, watched together in the balconies of West Side theaters as his mother puffed away on her Chesterfields and Ferguson dreamed he was inside the movies playing on the two-dimensional screens in front of him, and then the second part would be called "Stan and Ollie," a history of his infatuation with those two morons and how he loved them still, and then a final section, not yet fully worked out, something with a title such as "Art and Trash" or "This Versus That," which would explore the differences between Hollywood garbage films and masterpieces from other countries and argue strongly for the value of garbage even as it defended those masterpieces, and maybe it was good for him to be going so far away, he said, away from his mother as she was now in order to write about her as she had been then, to be able to live for a while in the large, densely crowded spaces of memory with no interference from the present, nothing to distract him from living in the past for as long as he needed to be there.

His mother smiled at him through her tears. Stubbing out a half-smoked cigarette with her left hand, she reached out to Ferguson with her right, drew her son toward her, and kissed him on the forehead. Gil stood up from the table, walked over to where Ferguson was sitting, and kissed him as well. Ferguson kissed both of them, and then Gil kissed his mother, and they all said good night. By the evening of the next day, good night had turned into good-bye, and a minute later Ferguson was boarding the plane and was gone.

SHE HAD AGED somewhat since he had last seen her, or looked somewhat older than the person he had been carrying around in his head for the past three years, but she was forty-one now, almost forty-two, which was only two years younger than his mother, his still beautiful mother who had aged somewhat in the past three years as well, and undoubtedly Vivian Schreiber was still beautiful herself, just a little older, that was all, and even if she was objectively less beautiful than his mother, she still had that glow about her, that seductive glamour-glow of power and certainty that his mother didn't have, his hard-working artist mother who only bothered about looking her best when she went out into the world, whereas Vivian Schreiber wrote books about artists and was always out in the world, a well-heeled widow with no offspring and *a multitude of friends*, according to Gil, someone who hobbed and nobbed with artists, writers, journalists, publishers, gallery owners, and museum directors, while Ferguson's more subdued mother was hunkered down inside her work with no intimate others beyond her husband and her son.

Sitting in the backseat of the taxi on their way into town from the airport, Vivian (not Mrs. or Madame Schreiber, as she had instructed him in the terminal, but Vivian or Viv) asked Ferguson a hundred questions about himself and his plans and what he was hoping to accomplish by living in Paris, which he answered by talking about the book he had started writing back in the summer, about his determination to improve his French to such a degree that he would be able to speak it as well as he spoke English, about his eagerness to plunge into Gil's reading list and soak up every word of those one hundred books, about seeing as many films as he could and recording his observations in his three-ring loose-leaf binder, about his ambition to write articles on films and publish them in British or American or French-based English-language magazines if any editor would accept them, about wanting to play basketball somewhere and joining a league if there were such things as amateur basketball leagues in Paris, about the possibility of tutoring French kids in English to pad the allowance his parents would be sending him every month, an under-the-table cash arrangement since by law he wouldn't be allowed to work in France, and on and on the jet-lagged Ferguson talked in response to Vivian Schreiber's questions, no longer intimidated by her as his fifteen-year-old self had been, able to think boldly enough now to look upon her not as an auxiliary parent but as an adult acquaintance and possible friend, for there was no reason to suppose she had offered him a room in her building out of some dormant maternal impulse (childless woman seeks to take care of the child she might have had in her early twenties), no, proxy mothering was not at issue here, there was another reason, an as yet unknowable reason that continued to perplex him, and therefore, once he had answered her many questions, he had only one question to ask her, which was the same question he had been asking himself ever since Gil had received her letter: Why was she doing this? Not that he wasn't grateful, Ferguson said, not that he wasn't thrilled to be back in Paris, but they hardly knew each other, and why would she put herself out like this for someone she hardly knew?

A good question, she said. I wish I could answer it.

You don't know?

Not really.

Does it have something to do with Gil? To thank him for what he did for you during the war, maybe?

Maybe. But it's not just that. More about being at loose ends, I think. It took me fifteen years to write the Chardin book, and now that it's done, the thing in my life that used to be the book has turned into an empty space.

Fifteen years. I can't believe *fifteen years*.

Vivian smiled, a frowning sort of smile, Ferguson remarked, but nevertheless a smile. She said: I'm slow, honey.

I still don't get it. What does the empty space have to do with me?

It could be the photograph.

What photograph?

The picture your mother took of you when you were a little boy. I bought it, remember? And for the past three years it's been hanging on a wall in the room where I finished writing *Chardin*. I've looked at that photo thousands of times. The little boy with his back to the camera, his bony spine protruding as the striped T-shirt presses against the vertebrae, his thin right arm extended, his hand splayed out on the carpet, and Laurel and Hardy on the screen in the distance, which is the same distance from the front of you as the camera is from the back of you. The proportions are just perfect—sublime. And there you are, all alone on the floor, stranded in the middle of those two distances. Boyhood incarnate. The loneliness of boyhood. The loneliness of *your* boyhood. And needless to say, whenever I look at the photograph, I think about you, the boy I met in Paris three years ago, the same boy who had once been the little boy in the picture, and after thinking about you so often, it's hard for me not to think of us as friends. So when Gil wrote to me and said you wanted to come here, I said to myself, Good, now we can become real friends. I know it sounds a bit daft, but there it is. I think we're going to have an interesting time together, Archie.

THE SECOND-FLOOR APARTMENT was vast, the sixth-floor *chambre de bonne* was not. Seven large rooms below, one little room above, and each of those seven rooms was filled with furniture, standing lamps, Persian rugs, paintings, drawings, photographs, and books, books everywhere in the master bedroom and the study and along one wall of the living room, a spacious, high-ceilinged apartment with a simple, uncluttered feel to it because the rooms were ample enough to absorb the objects they contained without impinging on one's movements, a pleasant feeling of *just enough* and never *too little* or *too much*, and how taken Ferguson was by the huge, all-white, old-fashioned kitchen with the black and white tiles underfoot, and the mirrored double doors that stood between the living room and the dining room, with their slim French door handles as opposed to the stumpy doorknobs used in America, and the massive double windows in the living room, sheathed in thin, almost translucent muslin drapes, which allowed the light to filter through at all hours of the morning and afternoon and often to the point of dusk. Bourgeois heaven in the apartment below, but upstairs in the sixth-floor maid's room, which was technically on the seventh floor of the building, since the French counted the ground floor not as the first floor but the *rez-de-chaussée*, there was nothing but four bare walls, a sloped ceiling, and just enough space for a bed, a narrow five-shelf bookcase, a tiny desk with a creaking wood-and-wicker chair, a built-in storage drawer under the bed, and a cold-water sink. Communal toilet down the hall; no shower or bath. A floor that was reached by taking the elevator to the fifth floor and walking up the stairs to the floor above, where a long wooden corridor stretched along the northern face of the building, with six identical brown doors standing side by side in a row, each one the property of the owners of the apartments on floors zero through five, Ferguson's door being the second of those doors, while the rooms behind the other doors were occupied by the Spanish and Portuguese maids who worked for the apartment owners below. It was a grim little monk's cell, Ferguson realized, when he set foot in it with Vivian on the morning of his first day in Paris, not at all what he had been expecting, the smallest space he would ever have to live in since the beginning of his life, a *chambre* that would no doubt take some getting used to before he could learn to inhabit it without feeling he was about to suffocate, but it did have windows, or one window in two parts, a tall double window in the northern wall, with a Lilliputian balcony surrounded by a metal railing on three sides and just enough room to accommodate his size eleven-and-a-half feet, and from that balcony or through that double window he could look north and take in a prospect of the Quai

d'Orsay, the Seine, the Grand Palais on the other side of the river, and
up through the right bank all the way to the far-off ivory dome of the
Sacré-Coeur in Montmartre, and if he turned his head to the left and
leaned over the balcony railing, there was the Champs de Mars and the
Eiffel Tower. Not bad. Not bad at all, finally, because there had never
been any question that he would have to spend all his time in that room,
it was to serve as his place for writing, studying, and sleeping, but the
place for eating, bathing, and talking was downstairs in Vivian's apartment, where the cook Celestine gave him food whenever he asked for
it, the delicious bowls of coffee and *tartines beurrées* for breakfast in the
morning, the hot lunches when he wasn't eating sandwiches in little
cafés on or around the Boulevard Saint-Germain, and the dinners with
or without Vivian at home or the dinners with Vivian in restaurants
or with Vivian and other people in restaurants or at dinner parties in
Vivian's apartment or the apartments of other people, and as Vivian
slowly introduced him to the complex Parisian world she belonged to,
Ferguson slowly began to settle in.

For the first five months, the rhythm of his daytime routine was
as follows: work on his book every morning from nine to twelve, lunch
from noon to one, reading the books on Gil's list from one to four, except
on Tuesdays and Thursdays, when he read from one to two-thirty and
spent the next hour and a half in Vivian's study talking with her about
the books, an hour-long walk through various Left Bank neighborhoods
(mostly Saint-Germain, the Latin Quarter, and Montparnasse), and then
on to the Boulevard Raspail for his Monday-through-Friday classes at
the Alliance Française. Until he finished his book (which happened a
few days after his nineteenth birthday in March), and until he felt his
French was solid enough to forgo the classes (also in March), he rigidly
adhered to those three fundamental activities of writing, reading, and
studying to the exclusion of all others, which meant that for the time
being there was no time for watching movies except on Saturdays and
Sundays and the occasional weekday night, no time for basketball, and
no time to begin tutoring French children in English. Never before
had Ferguson shown such dedication and singleness of purpose, such
a fervent commitment to the tasks he had set for himself, but never
before had he felt so calm and steady when the light came through his
window in the morning, so glad to be where he was, even on those
mornings when he was hungover or not feeling at his best.

The book was everything to him. The book was the difference between being alive and not being alive, and although Ferguson was still young, no doubt extremely young to have embarked on such a project, the advantage of starting the book at eighteen was that he was still close to the time of his boyhood and remembered it well, and because of Mr. Dunbar and the *Riverside Rebel* he had been writing for some years now and was no longer strictly a novice. He had published twenty-seven articles of varying lengths in Mr. Dunbar's paper (one as short as two and a half typed pages, another one as long as eleven typed pages), and after he started recording his impressions of films in the loose-leaf binder, he had acquired the habit of writing nearly every day, since there were more than a hundred and sixty sheets in the binder now, and the jump from *nearly every day* to *every day come hell or high water* was not so much a jump as the natural next step. On top of his own efforts during the past three years, there had been the long conversations with Gil, the lessons learned from Gil about how to achieve concision, grace, and clarity in each sentence he wrote, how to join one sentence to another sentence in order to build a paragraph that had some muscles in it, and how to begin the next paragraph with a sentence that would either prolong or contradict the statements in the preceding paragraph (depending on your argument or your purpose), and Ferguson had listened to his stepfather and absorbed those lessons well, which meant that even though he was barely out of high school when he started working on his book, he had already sworn his allegiance to the flag of the Written Word.

The idea had come to him after the humiliations of his army physical on August second. Not only had he been forced to reveal the black mark on his name denoted by the words *criminal record*, but the doctor had pressed him to talk about the particulars as well, not just being caught for pinching books on the day George Tyler's hand had crashed down on his shoulder but how many other times he had stolen books without being caught, and because Ferguson had felt tense and frightened to be sitting in that government building on Whitehall Street talking to a U.S. Army doctor, he had told the man the truth, had said *several times* in answer to the question, but beyond the humiliation of being forced to delve into the larcenous activities of his senior year, there had been the greater humiliation of having to confess to his *unnatural sexual desires*, his attraction to boys as well as to girls, and then the

man, whose name was Dr. Mark L. Worthington, had asked Ferguson
to provide the particulars concerning that matter as well, and while
Ferguson had understood that telling the truth would guarantee that he
would never have to serve in the army or spend two to five years in a
federal prison for refusing to serve in the army, it had been hard to tell
the truth because of the disgust he had seen in Dr. Worthington's eyes,
the revulsion expressed by the tightening of his lips and the clenching
of his jaw, but the man had wanted to know the details and Ferguson
had had no choice but to give them, so one by one he had marched
through the erotic acts he had performed during his love affair with
the beautiful Brian Mischevski from early spring to the day Brian left
New York in early summer, and Yes, sir, Ferguson had said, they had
been on the bed together many times with no clothes on, that is, both of
them entirely naked, and Yes, sir, Ferguson had said, they had kissed
each other with their mouths open and had pushed their tongues into
those open mouths, and Yes, sir, they had put their hardened penises
into each other's mouths, and Yes, sir, they had ejaculated into each
other's mouths, and Yes, sir, they had put their hardened penises into
each other's bottoms and had ejaculated into those bottoms or onto the
buttocks flanking those bottoms or onto each other's faces or stomachs,
and the more Ferguson had talked, the more disgusted the expression
on the doctor's face had become, and by the time the interview was over,
the never-to-be-inducted Ferguson was trembling throughout the length
of his four limbs and sickened by the words that had tumbled from his
mouth, not because he felt ashamed of what he had done but because the
doctor's eyes had condemned him, had looked on him as a moral degen-
erate and a menace to the stability of American life, which had felt to
Ferguson as if his own life were being spat on by the government of
the United States, which was his country, after all, whether he liked it
or not, and by way of revenge, he had said to himself as he walked out
of that building into the hot summer air of New York, he would write a
little book about the dark years after the Newark fire, a book so powerful and so brilliant and so drenched in the truths of what it meant to be
alive that no American would ever want to spit on him again.

*I was seven years old when my father burned to death in an arsonist's fire.
His scorched remains were put in a wooden box, and after my mother and I put
that box in the ground, the ground we walked on began to crumble beneath our
feet. I was an only child. My father had been my only father, and my mother*

had been his only wife. Now she was no one's wife, and I was a boy without a
father, the son of a woman but no longer of a man.

We lived in a small Jersey town just outside New York, but six weeks after
the night of the flames, my mother and I left that town and moved to the city,
where we temporarily holed up in my mother's parents' apartment on West
Fifty-eighth Street. My grandfather called it "a curious interregnum." By that
he meant a time of no fixed address and no school, and in the months that
followed, the cold winter months of late December 1954 and early 1955, as my
mother and I tramped through the streets of Manhattan in search of a new place
to live and a new school for me to attend, we often took shelter in the darkness
of movie theaters . . .

A first draft of the first part of the book was completed before Ferguson left New York in mid-October. Seventy-two typed pages written in the two and a half months between the army physical and the flight across the Atlantic, roughly one page per day, which was the goal Ferguson had set for himself, one decent page per day and anything beyond that to be considered a miracle. He hadn't had the nerve to show that unrevised portion of the book to Gil or his mother, wanting to present them with the finished product only when it was well and truly finished, but most of the films he had seen with his mother during the Curious Interregnum were discussed in those pages, along with the Curious Interregnum itself, and then the beginning of his career at Hilliard, his war with God and the self-destructive program of willed failure, the countless forays to movie theater balconies to watch more Hollywood films with his mother during the Glorious Oblivions period, followed by his mother's new start as a photographer and the transformation of his once bright playroom into the darkroom where she developed her pictures, eleven and a half months of his early life beginning on the morning of November 3, 1954, when his mother told him his father had burned to death in the Newark fire, and ending on the afternoon of October 17, 1955, when Ferguson turned on the television in their third-floor apartment and stumbled across the *Cuckoos* theme song and the credits announcing the first Laurel and Hardy film he ever saw.

It took a couple of weeks for him to adjust to his new surroundings and make his peace with the smallness of his room, but by November first he was back inside the book, having prepared for the "Stan and Ollie" section by making a complete list of their films while still in New York and then, with his stepfather's help, arranging with Clement

Knowles, the head of the film department at the Museum of Modern Art, to watch all the Laurel and Hardy films in their collection, often by himself on Moviolas, sometimes projected for him on larger screens, and because Ferguson wrote down a detailed account of each film he saw, the films were fresh in his mind again when he began writing about them in Paris. Remarkably enough, only one book had been written about Laurel and Hardy in English, a 240-page double biography by John McCabe that was published in 1961, but other than that nothing, not one other book in English that Ferguson was aware of. Ollie had died in 1957, and the not terribly old Stan (seventy-four) had died in February 1965, not six months before Ferguson conceived of his plan to write about how the two of them had saved his life ten years earlier, and once he began that section of the book, he couldn't help thinking about the opportunity he had missed, for nothing would have made him happier than to have sent Stan the manuscript of his book when the final draft was done. As with the articles he had written as a student in New York, Ferguson's approach was all about looking at the movies themselves, the movies as he had first seen them as an eight- and nine-year-old boy, with no biographical information about his bowler-hatted friends, no historical information about how the team had been formed in 1926 by director Leo McCarey at the Hal Roach studio, and nothing about Ollie's three marriages and Stan's six marriages (three of them to the same woman!). Beyond writing his book, and fully just as important as writing the book, the subject that dominated Ferguson's thoughts most persistently was sex, and yet even now, at the advanced age of eighteen, he found it nearly impossible to imagine Stan Laurel having sex with anyone, let alone with his six wives, three of whom had been the same person.

He pushed on through November, December, and halfway into January, concluding the second section of the book by recounting his grandparents' surprise visit to the apartment on Central Park West in December, laden with the bulky presents of roll-up movie screen, sixteen-millimeter movie projector, and the ten cans of Laurel and Hardy shorts, a section that for some unfathomable reason was precisely the same length as the first, seventy-two pages, the last paragraph of which read: *Little matter that the projector had been bought secondhand—it worked. Little matter that the prints were scratched and the sound sometimes seemed to be coming from the bottom of a bathtub—the films were watchable. And with the films came a whole new set of words for me to master—"sprocket," for example, which turned out to be a far better word to think about than "scorched."*

Then Ferguson lost his way. The third section of the book, which in the intervening months had been given a new title, "Junkyards and Geniuses," was meant to explore the differences between art films and commercial films, mostly the differences between Hollywood and the rest of the world, and Ferguson had given much thought to the film-makers he had chosen to write about, three Hollywood *junkmen* who had excelled at making good commercial products in a wide range of genres and styles (Mervyn LeRoy, John Ford, Howard Hawks) and three *geniuses* from abroad (Eisenstein, Jean Renoir, and Satyajit Ray), but after spending two and a half troubled weeks trying to get his thoughts down on paper, Ferguson understood that the subject he was writing about had nothing to do with the rest of the book, that he was writing another book or another essay and that there was no room in his book about dead fathers and struggling widows and crushed little boys for speculations of that sort. It came as a shock to realize how badly he had misconstrued his project, but now, on the strength of that wrong turn, he felt he knew how to fix the damage. He put aside the first twenty pages of "Junkyards and Geniuses" and went back to the first section, which he now divided into two sections, "A Curious Inter-regnum," which covered his post-fire, pre-Hilliard days in New York and ended with the words his mother had spoken to the woman selling tickets at the movie theater on the Upper West Side—*Butt out, lady. Just give me my change*—and "Glorious Oblivions," which began in a different spot now, with Ferguson walking into Hilliard on his first day of school there, but still ended with the television and his first Laurel and Hardy film. In the third part, he added some paragraphs about his mother's reaction to the two morons and explored the *daily duties* gag a bit more thoroughly, but the chapter still ended with the word *scorched.* Then he added a fourth section, "Dinner in the Balcony," which he now understood was the logical conclusion of the book, the emotional heart of the book, and how could he have been so blind and so dumb as to have ignored that scene with his mother in the living room, to have considered leaving it out of the book when in fact everything in the book had been building toward that moment, and so, over three mornings in mid-February, three mornings of devastation and utterly focused work, feeling more alive in the words he was writing than with any other passage of the book, Ferguson wrote the ten pages he needed to write about breaking down and confessing to his mother, about the deluge of tears that had poured out of them as they sat on the living room carpet, about the silent-God-no-God-anti-God rehash and the reason for his bad marks at school, and then, after they had dried their tears and pulled themselves together, of course!—off they went to the movies at Ninety-fifth Street and Broadway, where they ate hot dogs in the balcony and washed them down with *fizzless, watery Cokes* as his mother lit up another Chesterfield and they watched Doris Day sing one of the stupidest songs ever written, *Que Sera, Sera*, in Hitchcock's Technicolor version of *The Man Who Knew Too Much*.

Writing about himself over the six months it had taken him to finish his short, 157-page book had thrust Ferguson into a new relationship with himself. He felt more intimately connected to his own feelings and at the same time more remote from them, almost detached, indifferent, as if during the writing of the book he had paradoxically become both a warmer and a colder person, warmer by the fact that he had opened up his insides and exposed them to the world, colder by the fact that he could look at those insides as if they belonged to someone else, a stranger, an anonymous anyone, and whether this new interaction with his writing self was good for him or bad for him, better for him or worse for him, he could not say. All he knew was that writing the book had exhausted him, and he wasn't sure if he would ever have the courage to write about himself again. About movies, yes, perhaps about other things as well someday, but autobiography was too wrenching, the demand to be both warm and cold was too difficult, and now that he had rediscovered his mother as she had been *back then,* he suddenly found himself missing her as she was *now,* missing both her and Gil, and with the *Herald Tribune* on the verge of collapse, he hoped they would come to visit him in Paris before long, for even though Ferguson was almost a man, there was much about him that was still a child, and having dwelled inside his childhood for the past six months, it wasn't easy to get out of it.

That afternoon, he went downstairs for his Thursday study session with Vivian carrying the unbound pages of *How Laurel and Hardy Saved My Life* instead of his copy of *Hamlet. Hamlet* would have to wait, Ferguson decided. Hamlet, who did nothing but wait, would have to go on waiting a little longer, because now that the book was finished, Ferguson was desperate for someone to read it, since he himself was incapable of judging what he had written and had no idea whether it came across as a real book or a failed book, a garden filled with violets and roses or a truckload of manure. With Gil on the other side of the ocean, Vivian was the best choice, the inevitable choice, and Ferguson knew he could trust her to give his work a fair and impartial reading, for she had already proved herself to be an excellent preceptor, always assiduously prepared for their twice-a-week tutorials and incredibly sharp, with countless things to say about the works they pored over together (close readings, the *explication de texte* method for certain crucial passages, as demonstrated by the chapter about Odysseus's scar in Auerbach's *Mimesis*) but also around the works and behind the works, social and political conditions in ancient Rome, for example, Ovid's exile, Dante's banishment, or the revelation that Augustine was from North Africa and consequently a black man or a brown man, a constant in-flow of reference books, history books, and critical studies checked out from the nearby American Library and the farther-off British Council Library, and Ferguson was both impressed and amused that the supremely *mondaine* and often frivolous Madame Schreiber (how she could laugh at parties, how she roared at dirty jokes) was at the same time a dedicated scholar and intellectual, a summa cum laude graduate from Swarthmore, a Ph.D. in art history from what she mockingly referred to as the Sore Bone in Paris (dissertation on Chardin—her first stab at the material that would eventually become her book), and a clear and fluid writer (Ferguson had read parts of that book), and in addition to instructing him on how to read and think about the literary works on Gil's list, she was taking the trouble to instruct Ferguson on how to look at and think about works of art with Saturday visits to the Louvre, the Musée de l'Art Moderne, the Jeu de Paume, or the Galerie Maeght, and even though Ferguson still found it incomprehensible that she should want to devote so much of her time to his education, he understood that his mind was steadily growing because of her, but why, he would ask, why are you doing all this for me, and the enigmatic Viv would always smile and say: Because I'm having fun, Archie. Because I'm learning so much.

By the time Ferguson went downstairs with his manuscript that afternoon in mid-February, he had been living in Paris for four months, and he and Vivian Schreiber had become friends, good friends, and perhaps (Ferguson sometimes thought) even a little bit in love with each other, or at least he was in love with her, and she had never failed to show him anything but the warmest, most complicitous affection, and when he knocked on the door of her study for their two-thirty appointment, he didn't wait for her to ask him in because that wasn't how they went about it, all he had to do was knock on the door to let her know he had arrived and then walk in, and so he walked in and found her sitting in her usual spot in the black leather armchair with her reading glasses on and a burning Marlboro wedged between the second and third fingers of her left hand (she still smoked American cigarettes after twenty-one years in France) and a paperback copy of *Hamlet* in her right hand, the text open somewhere in the middle of the book, and, as always, the picture of himself on the wall just behind her head, *Archie*, the photograph his mother had taken more than ten years ago, which he suddenly realized should be on the cover of the book if anyone ever wanted to publish it (good luck!), and as Vivian glanced up from the book and smiled at Ferguson, Ferguson walked across the room without saying a word and deposited the manuscript at her feet.

All done? she asked.

All done, he said.

Good for you, Archie. Bravo. And many *merdes* to mark the day.

I'm wondering if we could skip *Hamlet* this afternoon so you could take a look at it instead. It's short. I doubt you'll need more than two or three hours to finish it.

No, Archie, I'll need more time than that. I assume you want a real response, yes?

Of course. And whenever something jumps out at you, feel free to mark it up. The book isn't final yet, just finished for now. So read it with a pencil. Suggest changes, improvements, cuts, anything that occurs to you. I'm so sick of it, I can't look at it anymore.

This is what we'll do, Vivian said. I'll stay here, and you'll go out for a walk, for dinner, for a movie, for any old thing you want, and when you come back to the house, you'll go straight upstairs to your room.

Pushing me out, huh?

I don't want you around while I'm reading your book. Too much mental interference. *Tu comprends?* (You understand?)

Oui, bien sûr. (Yes, of course.)

We'll meet in the kitchen tomorrow morning at eight-thirty. That will give me the rest of the afternoon, all evening, and into the night if necessary.

What about your dinner with Jacques and Christine? Aren't you supposed to see them at eight?

I'll cancel. Your book is more important.

Only if it's good. If it's bad, you'll curse me for missing the dinner.

I'm not expecting it to be bad, Archie. But even if it is, your book is still more important than the dinner.

How can you say that?

Because it's your book, *your first book,* and no matter how many books you write in the future, you'll never write your first book again.

In other words, I've lost my virginity.

That's it. You've lost your virginity. And whether you've done it with a good fuck or a bad fuck, you'll never be a virgin again.

The next morning, Ferguson walked into the kitchen a few minutes before eight o'clock, hoping to fortify himself with a bowl or two of Celestine's café au lait before Vivian showed up to pronounce her verdict on his miserable excuse of a book and cast it into the dustbin of history, one more discarded human thing to rot among the millions of others. In spite of his calculations, however, Vivian had beaten him to the punch, and there she was when Ferguson entered the room, sitting at the white enamel table in the white kitchen dressed in her white morning bathrobe with the white-and-black pages of his manuscript standing in a pile next to her own white bowl of Celestine's café au lait.

Bonjour, Monsieur Archie, Celestine said. *Vous vous levez tôt ce matin* (You're up early this morning), addressing Ferguson with the formal *vous* of servants rather than the *tu* of familiar equals, a quirk of the language that still grated on his American ears.

Celestine was a brisk little woman of around fifty, reserved, unobtrusive, but exceedingly kind, Ferguson had always felt, and even though she insisted on calling him *vous,* he liked the way she pronounced his name in French, softening the hard *ch* sound into a less abrasive *sh,* which turned him into Ar-shee, which in turn invariably made him think of the French word for *archive,* ar-sheeve. Young as he still was, he had already become an archive, which meant he was someone to be kept for the ages—even if his book belonged in the dustbin of history.

Parce que j'ai bien dormi, Ferguson said to her (Because I had a good sleep), which was manifestly untrue, since one glance at his tousled hair and hollowed-out eyes would have told anyone he had drunk a full bottle of red wine last night and had hardly slept at all.

Vivian stood up and kissed him once on each cheek, their standard morning salutation, but then, diverging from the daily ritual, she put her arms around him and kissed him on each cheek again, two smacking busses this time, loud smooches that resonated throughout the tiled kitchen, after which she abruptly pushed him back, held him at arm's length, and asked: What's wrong with you? You look terrible.

I'm nervous.

Don't be nervous, Archie.

I'm about to shit in my pants.

Don't do that either.

What if I can't help myself?

Sit down, stupid, and listen to me.

Ferguson sat down. A moment later, Vivian sat down as well. She leaned forward, looked Ferguson in the eyes, and said: No worries, bub. *Tu piges?* (You get it?) *Tu me suis bien?* (You follow?) It's a beautiful, heartbreaking book, and I'm awed that someone your age could have written anything this good. If you don't change a word, it's strong enough to be published as is. On the other hand, it's still not perfect, and because you told me to go ahead and mark it up if I wanted to, I've marked it up. About six or seven pages of suggested cuts, I'd say, along with fifty or sixty sentences that could use more work. *In my opinion.* You don't have to follow my opinion, of course, but here's the manuscript (*shoving it across the table in Ferguson's direction*), and until you decide what you want to do, I won't say another word. They're only suggestions, remember, but *in my opinion*, I think the changes will make the book a better book.

How can I thank you?

Don't thank me, Archie. Thank your extraordinary mother.

Later that morning, Ferguson climbed back into the pages of his manuscript and began working his way through Vivian's comments, most of which were spot on target, he felt, a good eighty to ninety percent of them, at any rate, which was a large percentage, so many small but acute excisions, a phrase here, an adjective there, subtle but ruthless parings-down to increase the energy of the prose, and then the awkward sentences, there were far too many of them, he was ashamed to admit, blind spots he had failed to catch after dozens of readings, and over the next ten days Ferguson attacked each one of those stylistic flubs and aggravating repetitions, at times changing bits that Vivian had left unmarked, at times reversing those changes and going back to the original, but the essential thing was that Vivian had left the structure of the book intact, her pencil hadn't switched around paragraphs or sections, there were no serious overhauls or blotted out passages, and once Ferguson had incorporated the revisions into his now scratched-over, barely readable typescript, he typed up the book again, this time in triplicate (two carbons), which proved to be a hellish job because of his propensity for hitting the wrong keys, but when his nineteenth birthday rolled around on March third, he was nearly done, and six days later he was completely done.

Meanwhile, Vivian had been calling around, making inquiries among her British friends about potential publishers for Ferguson's book, choosing London over New York because she had better contacts there, and Ferguson, who was wholly ignorant about all matters concerning publishing, whether in England or the United States, left everything to Vivian and forged on with his typing, already starting to think about his partially written essay, "Junkyards and Geniuses," which might or might not have been the germ of a second book, and about reading over some of his longer high school pieces with the notion of reworking them (if he found they were worth the trouble) and trying to place them in magazines, but even after Vivian had narrowed down the British possibilities to two small literary houses, minute but aggressive concerns dedicated to publishing what she called *new talent*, Ferguson had no hope that either one of them would accept his book.

You decide where you want to send it first, Vivian said to him, as they sat in the kitchen on the morning of his nineteenth birthday, and when she told him that the names of the two presses were Io Books and Thunder Road, Ltd., Ferguson instinctively said Io, not because he had a clear sense of who Io was but because the word *thunder* seemed inimical to a book with the names *Laurel* and *Hardy* in the title.

They've been in business for about four years now, Vivian said, a kind of hobbyhorse for a well-to-do, thirtyish young man named Aubrey Hull, mostly a publisher of poets, they tell me, with some fiction and nonfiction, nicely designed and printed, good paper, but they put out only twelve to fifteen books a year, whereas Thunder Road publishes about twenty-five. Still want to go for Io?

Why not? They're going to reject it anyway. And when we send it to the Thunder people, they're going to reject it, too.

All right, Mr. Negative, one last question. The title page. The book will be going out sometime next week, and what name do you want to use for yourself?

What name? My name, of course.

I'm talking about Archibald or Archie, or A., or A. plus your middle initial.

My birth certificate and passport both say I'm Archibald, but no one has ever called me that. Archibald Isaac. I've never been Archibald, and I've never been Isaac. I'm Archie. I've always been Archie, and I'll always be Archie to the end. That's my name, Archie Ferguson, and that's the name I'll use to sign my work. Not that it matters now, of course, since no publisher in his right mind would ever want to publish such a weird little book, but it's good to think about it for the future.

So IT WENT during the daytime hours of Ferguson's early months in Paris, the satisfactions of intense study and hard work on his book, the steady improvement of his French after the summer-long program in Vermont, the classes at the Alliance Française, the dinners conducted entirely in French with Vivian's Paris friends, the daily conversations with Celestine, not to mention numerous encounters with strangers while standing at the bar and eating ham sandwiches in his lunch-hour cafés, which had turned him into an almost fifty-fifty bilingual American in France, and so immersed had he become in his second language that if not for his studies in English, his writing in English, and his all-English interactions with Vivian, his own English might have started to atrophy. He often dreamed in French now (once, comically, with English subtitles running below the action), and his head was continually churning with bizarre, often obscene bilingual puns, such as transforming the common French expression *au contraire* (on the contrary) into an English homonym of stupefying vulgarity: O cunt rare.

Cunts were on his mind, however, as were cocks, along with the imagined and remembered bodies of naked women and men from both the present and the past, for once the sun went down in the evening

and the city turned dark, the invigorating solitude of his daytime regi-
men often collapsed into a breathless sort of loneliness at night. The first
months were the hardest on him, the beginning period when he was
introduced to many people but no one he particularly liked, no one even
a millionth as much as he liked Vivian, and he would gut out those
empty, late-night hours in his small suffocation room by doing one of
several things to distract himself from the loneliness: reading (almost
impossible), listening to classical music on his pocket-sized transistor
radio (a bit more possible, but never for more than twenty or thirty minutes at a stretch), doing a second stint of work on his book (difficult but
sometimes productive, sometimes useless), stepping out for ten o'clock
showings of films in theaters behind and around the Boulevard Saint-
Michel (mostly enjoyable, even when the film was less than good, but
then he would return to his room at twelve-thirty and the loneliness
would still be waiting for him), prowling the streets of Les Halles in
search of a prostitute when the cunt-cock problem raged out of control
(the buzz in the groin from walking past all those sidewalk hookers,
temporary release, but the sex was brusque and dismal, impersonal
fucks of no account, which inevitably filled him with aching memories
of Julie on his long walks home in the dark, and with an allowance of
just eighty dollars a week from his mother and Gil, those ten- and twenty-
dollar tumbles had to be kept to a minimum). The last solution was
alcohol, which could be part of the other solutions as well, drinking and
reading, drinking and listening to music, drinking after coming back
from a film or another sad-eyed whore—the one solution that solved
everything whenever the loneliness became too big for him. Having
sworn off scotch after one too many blackout stupors in New York,
Ferguson had shifted over to red wine as his medicine of choice, and
with a liter of *vin ordinaire* selling for a paltry one franc at some of the
neighborhood *épiceries* close to his lunchtime haunts (twenty cents for
a bare, unlabeled bottle at grocery stores scattered through the sixth
arrondissement), Ferguson always had one or two of those bottles
stashed in his room, and whether he went out or stayed in on a given
night, the one-franc red wine was an effective balm for inducing
drowsiness and an eventual plunge into sleep, although those foul,
nameless vintages could be hard on his system, and he often found
himself battling the runs or a woozy, cracking head when he woke in
the morning.

On average, he dined alone with Vivian in the apartment once or twice a week, traditional cold-weather food such as *pot au feu, cassoulet,* and *boeuf bourguignon* prepared and served by Celestine, who had no husband or family in Paris and was always on call for extra duty when asked, such good-tasting meals that the ever-hungry Ferguson could seldom resist a second or even third helping of the main course, and it was during those quiet, one-on-one dinners that he and Vivian became friends, or solidified the friendship that had been there from the start, both of them sharing stories about their lives, with much of what he learned about her entirely unexpected: born and raised in the Flatbush section of Brooklyn, for example, the same part of town where the original Archie had lived, Jewish in spite of coming from a family named Grant (which prompted Ferguson to tell the story of how, in one day, his grandfather had gone from being Reznikoff to Rockefeller to Ferguson), daughter of a doctor and a fifth-grade schoolteacher, four years younger than her brilliant scientist brother, Douglas, Gil's good friend during the war, and then, even before she graduated from high school, a trip to France in 1939 at age fifteen to visit distant relatives in Lyon, where she met Jean-Pierre Schreiber, an even more distant relative, perhaps a fourth or fifth cousin, and even though he had just celebrated his thirty-fifth birthday, which made him a vast twenty years older than she was, *something happened,* Vivian said, *a spark was lit between them* and *she gave herself to Jean-Pierre,* he a widower in charge of a significant French export company and she just a second-year student at Erasmus High School in Brooklyn, a liaison that no doubt would have struck most outsiders as *a little perverse,* but it had never seemed that way to Vivian, who looked upon herself as a grown-up in spite of her young age, and then, when the Germans crossed into Poland in September, there was no chance for them to see each other again until the war was over, but Jean-Pierre was safe in Lausanne, and over the five years it took for Vivian to complete high school and graduate from college, she and Jean-Pierre exchanged *two hundred and forty-four letters* and were already committed to marrying each other by the time Gil managed to pull the strings that allowed her to slip into France just after Paris was liberated in August 1944.

It was pleasant to listen to Vivian's stories because she seemed to take such pleasure in telling them, even if it probably *was* a little perverse for a thirty-five-year-old man to have fallen for a fifteen-year-old girl, but Ferguson couldn't help noting that he too had been fifteen when he made his first trip to France, where he had met Vivian Schreiber through similar kinds of family connections, a woman who was not just twenty years older than he was but twenty-three years, yet why bother to count when it had already been established that one person was less than half the age of the other, and all through those lonely first months in Paris Ferguson actively lusted after Vivian and hoped they would wind up in bed together, for inasmuch as her love life and marriage had not been constricted by questions of age, it was possible to wonder if she might not be willing to experiment in the opposite direction with him, to be the older one this time while he took over her previous spot as the younger for what was bound to be an intoxicating adventure in erotic perversity. He found her beautiful, after all, old in comparison to him but not old in the big scheme of things, a woman who still shimmered with sensuality and allure, and there was no doubt in his mind that she found him attractive, since she had often remarked on how handsome he was, how smashing he looked when they left the apartment to go out for dinner, and what if that was the true and secret reason why she had invited him to live with her—because she had dreamed of his body and wanted to nuzzle against his young flesh? That would account for her inexplicable generosity toward him, the free rent and the free food, the free study sessions, the clothes she had bought for him on their first shopping blitz at Le Bon Marché in November, all the expensive shirts and shoes and sweaters she had sprung for that day, the three pairs of pleated corduroy trousers, the sports jacket with the double vents in back, the winter coat and the red woolen scarf, top-of-the-line French clothes, the fashionable clothes he took such pleasure in wearing, and why would she be doing all those things if she wasn't lusting after him just as feverishly as he was lusting after her? Sex toy. That was the term for it, and yes, he gladly would have become her sex toy if that was what she had in mind, but even though she often looked at him as if that was precisely what she had in mind (the thoughtful stares directed at his face, her eyes closely scrutinizing his smallest gestures), he was in no position to act, as the younger one he had no right to make the first move, it was up to Vivian to reach out to him, but much as he longed for her to take him in her arms and kiss him on the mouth, or even to extend her hand and touch his face with the tips of her fingers, she never did.

He saw her nearly every day, but the details of her private life were
a mystery to him. Did she have a lover, Ferguson asked himself, or several lovers, or a series of lovers, or no lover at all? Were her sudden ten
o'clock exits from their one-on-one dinners proof that she was on her
way to an appointment in some man's bed elsewhere in the city, or was
she merely going out for a late-night drink with friends? And what about
her occasional weekend departures, on average once or twice a month,
most of them to Amsterdam, she said, where it seemed plausible to think
a man might have been waiting for her, but then again, now that her
book on Chardin had been published, perhaps she was looking for a
new subject to write about and had chosen Rembrandt or Vermeer or
some other Dutch painter whose work could be found only in Holland.
Unanswerable questions, and because Vivian talked freely about the
past but not about the present, at least not about her personal affairs in
the present, the one soul Ferguson felt any connection to in all of Paris,
the one human being he loved, was also a stranger to him.

One or two one-on-one dinners per week in the apartment, two or
three dinners per week in restaurants, almost always with other people,
Vivian's friends, her horde of longtime Paris friends from the divergent
but often overlapping worlds of art and literature, painters and sculp-
tors, professors of art history, poets who wrote about art, gallery men
and their wives, all of them well advanced in their careers, which meant
that Ferguson was always the youngest person sitting at the table, suspected by many to be Vivian's sex toy, he realized, even if their suspicions were wrong, and while Vivian always introduced him as the
stepson of one of her dearest American friends, a fair number of the people
at those four- and six- and eight-person restaurant dinners simply ignored
him (no one could be colder or ruder than the French, Ferguson discovered), whereas others leaned in close and wanted to know everything
about him (no one could be warmer or more democratic than the French,
he also discovered), but even on the nights when he was ignored, there
was the pleasure of being in the restaurants, of taking part in the good
life those places seemed to represent, not just the grand spectacle of La
Coupole, which he had witnessed three years earlier and still stood
for him as the embodiment of all that was different between Paris and
New York, but other brasseries such as Bofinger, Fouquet's, and Bal-
zar, nineteenth-century palaces and mini-palaces of wood-paneled

walls and mirrored columns humming with the clink of flatware and the murmured roar of fifty or two hundred and fifty human voices, but also the grungier spots in the fifth arrondissement where he ate couscous and merguez for the first time in underground Tunisian and Moroccan restaurants and was initiated into the coriander savors of Vietnamese cuisine, the food of America's mortal enemy, and two or three times that fall, when the dinners turned out to be especially animated and the hour was pushing past midnight, the whole group of four or five or six or seven would tramp off to Les Halles for onion soup at the Pied de Cochon, a restaurant crowded with customers at one and two and three o'clock in the morning, the arty sophisticates and late-night revelers sitting at the tables while the neighborhood whores stood at the bar drinking *ballons de rouge* alongside the hefty butchers in their blood-spattered smocks and aprons, an intermix of such radical disjunction and unlikely harmony that Ferguson asked himself if such a scene could exist anywhere else in the world.

Many dinners but no sex, no sex that he didn't pay for and ultimately regret, and beyond those regrets no physical contact with anyone except for his morning cheek kisses with Vivian. De Gaulle was reelected president of the republic on December nineteenth, Giacometti was dying in Switzerland of a heart disease called pericarditis (it killed him on January eleventh), and every time Ferguson walked home at night after one of his post-dinner prowls, he was stopped by the police and asked to show his papers. On January twelfth, he launched into the ill-conceived third section of his book, which caused him much difficulty and many wasted hours of work until he finally scrapped it and figured out a new, more appropriate ending. On January twentieth, while still in the midst of those turmoils with his book, he received a letter from Brian Mischevski, who was in his first year at Cornell, and by the time Ferguson had finished studying the four short paragraphs of his friend's letter, he felt as if a building had fallen on top of him. Not only had Brian's parents reneged on their promise to pay for their son to visit Paris in the spring, a trip that Ferguson had been looking forward to with frantic anticipation, but Brian himself thought it was probably all for the best anyway, since he had a girlfriend now, and fun as it had been to *pal around* with Ferguson last year, what they had been up to was nothing more than *kids' stuff*, really, and Brian had outgrown that after landing in *college,* had put all that behind him for good, and even though Ferguson was still his *number one friend of all time,* their friendship would just be *a normal friendship from now on.*

Normal. What did *normal* mean, Ferguson asked himself, and why wasn't it *normal* for him to feel the way he did about wanting to kiss and make love to other boys, the sex of one-sex sex was just as normal and natural as the sex of two-sex sex, maybe even more normal and more natural because a cock was something boys understood better than girls, and therefore it was easier to know what the other person wanted without having to guess, without having to play the courtship and seduction games that could make the sex of two-sex sex so confounding, and why did a person have to choose between one or the other, why block out one-half of humanity in the name of *normal* or *natural* when the truth was that everyone was Both, and people and society and the laws and religions of people in different societies were just too afraid to admit it. As the California cowgirl had said to him three and a half years ago: *I believe in my life, Archie, and I don't want to be scared of it.* Brian was scared. Most people were scared, but scared was a stupid way to live, Ferguson felt, a dishonest and demoralizing way to live, a dead-end life, a dead life.

For the next several days, he walked around feeling ravaged by Brian's kiss-off letter—from Ithaca, New York, of all places (Ithaka!)—and the nights were almost unbearable in their loneliness. His intake of red wine doubled, and on two consecutive nights he vomited into the sink. Vivian, who had a good pair of eyes in her head to go along with a keen, observant brain, looked at him carefully during their first one-on-one dinner since the arrival of Brian's letter, hesitated for a couple of moments, and then asked him what was wrong. Ferguson, who felt confident she would never betray him as Sydney Millbanks had on his disastrous trip to Palo Alto, decided to tell her the truth, since he needed to talk to someone, and there was no one else but Vivian.

I've had a disappointment, he said.

I can see that, Vivian replied.

Yes, a ton of hurt landed on me the other day, and I'm still trying to get over it.

What kind of hurt?

Love hurt. In the form of a letter from a person I care about very much.

That's hard.

Extremely hard. Not only have I been dumped, but I've been told that I'm not normal.

What does normal mean?

In my case, an overall interest in all kinds of people.

I see.

Do you really see?

I assume you're talking about girl people and boy people, no?

Yes, I am.

I've always known that about you, Archie. From the first time we met at your mother's opening.

How could you tell?

From the way you were looking at the young man who was serving the drinks. And also from the way you were looking at me, from the way you still look at me.

Is it so obvious?

Not really. But I have a good sense of these things—from long experience.

You're saying you have a nose for two-way people?

I was married to one.

Oh. I had no idea.

You're so much like Jean-Pierre, Archie. Maybe that's why I wanted you to come here and stay with me. Because you remind me of him so much . . . so much.

You miss him.

Horribly.

It must have made for a complicated marriage, though. I mean, if I go on being the way I am, I don't think I'll ever marry anyone.

Unless it's to another two-way person.

Ah. I never though of that.

Yes, it can be a bit complicated at times, but it's worth the effort.

Are you telling me that you and I are the same?

That's right. But different, too, of course, in that I, through no doing of my own, am a woman, and you, dear boy, are a man.

Ferguson laughed.

Then Vivian laughed back at him, which induced Ferguson to laugh again, and once Ferguson laughed again, Vivian laughed back at him again, and before long the two of them were laughing together.

□ □ □

THE FOLLOWING SATURDAY, January twenty-ninth, two guests came to the apartment for dinner, both of them Americans, both of them old friends of Vivian's, a man of about fifty named Andrew Fleming, who had been Vivian's American history professor in college and now taught at Columbia, and a young woman of about thirty named Lisa Bergman, a transplant from La Jolla, California, who had recently moved to Paris to work for an American law firm and whose older cousin was married to Vivian's brother. After Ferguson's talk with Vivian earlier in the week, which had led to the startling double confession of their equal but opposite two-way proclivities, Ferguson wondered if Lisa Bergman might not be Vivian's current flame, and, if so, whether her presence at the table that evening was a sign that Vivian had cracked open the door a bit and was allowing him to have a glimpse of her private life. As for Fleming, who was in Paris on a one-semester sabbatical to complete the final draft of his book about what he called the American *old boys* in France (Franklin, Adams, Jefferson), he was so obviously not a man cut out for women, so obviously a man interested only in men, that after twenty or thirty minutes it flashed through Ferguson's head that he was taking part in his first all-queer dinner since that horrible night in Palo Alto. This time, however, he was having fun.

It felt good to be with Americans again, so comfortable and unforced, so pleasant to sit down with people who shared the same references and laughed at the same jokes, all four of them so different from one another and yet chatting away as if they had been friends for years, and the more Ferguson studied how Vivian was looking at Lisa, and the more he looked at how Lisa was looking at Viv, the more certain he became that his intuition had been correct, that the two of them were indeed *involved*, and that made Ferguson happy for Vivian, since he wanted her to have anything and everything her good heart desired, and this Lisa Bergman, as in Ingrid and Ingmar, a Swedish Bergman as opposed to a German or Jewish Bergman, was nothing if not a fascinating character, a vivacious and vivid match for the all-deserving Viv.

Big. That was the first thing you noticed about her, the bigness of her body, five foot ten and large-boned, a burly girl without a touch of fat on her, solid and broad-shouldered, thick, powerful arms, large breasts, and extremely blond hair, a southern California blonde, with a round, pretty face and pale, almost invisible eyelashes, the kind of woman Ferguson could have imagined winning medals as a shot-putter or discus thrower at the summer Olympics, a Swedish-American Amazon who looked as if she had stepped from the pages of a nudist magazine, clean-cut, health-conscious nudism, the champion female weight lifter of all nudist colonies throughout the civilized world, and funny, devilishly funny and unconstrained, laughing between every other sentence she spoke, delicious American sentences spiced with words that made Ferguson understand how much he had missed hearing them since he'd left New York, two-syllable standbys such as dinky, dorky, grotty, snazzy, goofy, snooty, crummy, cruddy, crappy, gunky, and wicked, as in *wonderful* or *marvelous*, and whatever kind of law Lisa was practicing in Paris, she said not a word about it.

By contrast, the middle-aged Fleming was small and chubby, five-six at the most, with a waddling sort of walk and a sizable paunch protruding against the V-neck sweater under his jacket, small, fleshy hands, a chinless, sagging face, and an unusual pair of horn-rimmed owl glasses perched on his nose. A young professor who suddenly and irrevocably was no longer young. A veteran academic with a slight stammer and a head of fewer and fewer thinning gray hairs, but also alive and alert to the three others sitting at the table, a man who had read much and knew much but didn't talk about himself or his work either, that was the game they were playing that night, Lisa the lawyer not talking about the law, Vivian the art writer not talking about art, Ferguson the memoirist not talking about his memories, Fleming the historian not talking about the old American boys in Paris, and in spite of occasional lapses into stuttering, Fleming expressed himself in clean, smoothly articulated sentences, actively participating in the general conversation about all things and no things, politics for one, *bien sûr*, the war in Vietnam and the anti-war movement at home (Ferguson was receiving twice-monthly reports about it from his cousin Amy in Madison), de Gaulle and the French elections, the recent suicide of a man named Georges Figon just before he was about to be arrested for the kidnapping of Mehdi Ben Barka, the Moroccan politician whose whereabouts were still unknown, but also trivial digressions into such matters as trying to remember the name of the actress in the movie with the title no one could remember or—Lisa excelled at this—reciting the lyrics of obscure pop songs from the 1950s.

The dinner lumbered on slowly and enjoyably, a languorous three hours of food and talk and large quantities of wine, and then they were on to the cognac, and as Ferguson and Fleming raised their glasses to toast each other, Vivian said something to Lisa about wanting to show her something somewhere else in the apartment (Ferguson had stopped listening by then, but he hoped they were going off to neck in the study or in Vivian's bedroom), and just like that the two women were gone, which left Ferguson alone at the table with Fleming, and after an awkward moment in which neither one of them said anything because neither one of them knew what to say, Fleming suggested they go upstairs to visit Ferguson's room, which earlier in the evening Ferguson had described as *the smallest room in the world*, and although Ferguson laughed and inanely commented that there wasn't much to see up there beyond a messy desk and an unmade bed, Fleming said it didn't matter, he was simply curious to see what the smallest room in the world looked like.

If it had been anyone else but Fleming, Ferguson probably would have said no, but he had come to like the professor over the course of the evening and felt drawn to him because of the kindness he saw in his eyes, something tender and compassionate and sad, an ache of suffering caused by what Ferguson imagined must have been a constant internal pressure to hide who he was from the world, a man from the generation of closet-men who had spent the past thirty years skulking around in shadowy corners and dodging the suspicious looks of his colleagues and students, all of whom had surely and always pegged him for the sissy he was, but as long as he behaved himself and kept his hands off the innocent or unsuspecting ones, they would grudgingly allow him to go on tending the grass at their Ivy League country club, and all through the dinner, as Ferguson had sat there contemplating the grimness of such a life, he had begun to feel sorry for Fleming, perhaps even to pity him, which was why he said yes to the journey upstairs instead of no, even if it was starting to give him the old Andy Cohen sensation of being with a person who said one thing and meant another, but what the hell, Ferguson thought, he was a big boy now and didn't have to accommodate anyone he didn't want to, least of all a sweet, aging man for whom he felt no physical attraction whatsoever.

□ □ □

OH MY, FLEMING said, when Ferguson opened the door and switched on the light in the room. It is indeed very, very small, Archie.

Ferguson hastily pulled the quilt over the bare bottom sheet on the bed and gestured for Fleming to sit down as he swung around the desk chair and sat down as well, face to face with Fleming, so close to him in the cramped room that their knees were almost touching. Ferguson offered Fleming a Gauloise, but the professor shook his head and declined, suddenly looking nervous and distracted, not at all sure of himself, as if he wanted to say something but didn't quite know how to say it. Ferguson lit up a cigarette for himself and asked: Is everything okay?

I was just wondering . . . wondering how much . . . you would want.

Want? I don't understand. Want what?

How much . . . money.

Money? What are you talking about?

Vivian tells me that you're . . . she tells me that you're strapped for cash, liv . . . living on a tight budget.

I still don't understand. Are you saying you want to give me money?

Yes. If it would please you . . . to . . . to be nice to me.

Nice?

I'm a lonely man, Archie. I need to be touched.

Ferguson understood now. Fleming hadn't come upstairs with any plan or expectation of seducing him, but he would be willing to pay for sex if Ferguson was willing to go along, pay for it because he knew that no young man would ever want to touch him without being paid, and for the pleasure of being touched by a desirable young man, Fleming would be willing to turn that young man into a whore, a male Julie to fuck him up the ass, although he probably wasn't thinking about it in such crude terms, since it wouldn't be the anonymous sex of whore and client but sex between two people who already knew each other, which would turn the transaction into a gesture of charity, an older man giving a younger man some much-needed money, for which the older man would be repaid by a different kind of charity, and as Ferguson's thoughts spun around in his head, arguing back and forth about how his small allowance couldn't be counted as a hardship because of the free rent and free food and free clothes that came from living under the protection of his wealthy benefactress, and yet, still and all, living on what amounted to ten dollars a day for all the rest wasn't easy, not when there were so many film books he wanted to buy and couldn't afford to buy, not when he longed for a record player and a collection of records to listen to at night instead of the broadcasts on boring France Musique, yes, more money would help him out, more money would make life better in dozens of different ways, but was he willing to do what Fleming wanted him to do in order to get that money, and what would it feel like to have sex with someone who was physically repellent to him, *how would that feel*, and once Ferguson asked himself that question, he suddenly imagined how rich he could become by indulging in such activities as a side occupation, sleeping with lonely, middle-aged American tourists for money, a studly young rentboy for the men, a charming young gigolo for the women, and even though there was something morally wrong about it, he supposed, something *wicked*, to use the word Lisa had used several times that evening, it was only a matter of sex, which was never wrong when both people wanted to do it, and beyond the money there would be the additional reward of experiencing many orgasms while working for that money, which was almost comical when you stopped and thought about it for a moment, since an orgasm was the one indisputably good thing in this world that money couldn't buy.

Ferguson leaned forward and said: Why did Vivian tell you I was hard up for cash?

I don't know, Fleming replied. She was just talking to me about you and . . . and . . . she mentioned that you lived . . . what were the words? . . . close . . . *close to the bone.*

And what made you think I'd be interested in being *nice* to you?

Nothing. Just a hope, that's all. A . . . a feeling.

What sort of money do you have in mind?

I don't know. Five hundred francs? A thousand francs? You tell me, Archie.

How about fifteen hundred?

I be . . . I believe I can do that. Let me have a look.

As Ferguson watched Fleming slide his hand into the inside breast pocket of his jacket and pull out his wallet, he understood that he was actually going ahead with this, that for the same amount of money he received from his parents for his monthly allowance he was going to take off his clothes in front of this fat, balding man and have sex with him, and as Fleming began counting the bills in his wallet, Ferguson realized that he was scared, *scared to death*, scared in the same way he had been scared when he had stolen the books from Book World in New York, a hotness under the skin caused by what he had once described to himself as *the sear of fear*, a burn that was spreading through his body so quickly now that the pounding in his head bordered on excitement, yes, that was it, the fear and excitement of going past the edge of what was allowed, and even though Ferguson had been found guilty and could have spent six months in jail, which theoretically should have taught him never to go near the edge again, he was still taunting the no-God impostor-God of his childhood to come down and smash him if He dared, and now that Fleming had extracted twelve one-hundred-franc bills and six fifty-franc bills from the wallet and had put the wallet back in his pocket, Ferguson was so angry at himself, so disgusted by his own weakness, that it shocked him to hear the cruelty in his voice when he spoke to Fleming:

Put the money on the desk, Andrew, and turn out the light.

Thank you, Archie. I . . . I don't know how to thank you.

He didn't want to look at Fleming. He didn't even want to see him, and by not looking and not seeing he was hoping to pretend that Fleming wasn't there, that it was someone else who had come up to the room with him and that Fleming himself had not been at the dinner that night and Ferguson had never met him, had never even known that such a man as Andrew Fleming existed anywhere on the face of the earth.

The operation would have to be carried out in darkness or not at all—hence the command to switch off the light—but now that Ferguson had risen from the chair and was beginning to take off his clothes, the light went on in the hall, the *minuterie* (one-minute light) that was turned on again and again by different people throughout the day, and because there were gaps between the door frame and the edges of the ill-fitting door, light was suddenly coming in, just enough light to make it not dark enough now that his eyes had adjusted to the darkness, enough light for him to make out the lumpy contours of Fleming's now naked body, and consequently Ferguson looked down at the floor as he lifted himself onto the high wooden platform bed with the deep built-in drawer under the mattress, and then, once he was on the bed, he turned his eyes upward and looked at the wall as Fleming began kissing his naked chest and sliding a hand onto his slowly stiffening cock, which, after some intense fondling, was eventually inserted into Fleming's mouth. Further on, when the unresisting Ferguson found himself on his back and was no longer able to look at the wall, he turned his eyes toward the window instead, thinking that a view of the outside might help him forget he was inside, trapped inside his too-small room, but just then the light in the hall went on again, turning the window into a mirror that reflected only what was inside, and there he was with Fleming on the bed, or rather there was Fleming on top of him on the bed, with the old man's flat, flabby ass thrust into the air, and the instant Ferguson saw that picture in the window that was a mirror, he shut his eyes.

He had always made love with his eyes open, always with his eyes wide open because he loved looking at the person he was with, and barring Andy Cohen and some of the streetwalkers in Les Halles, he had never been with anyone he had not felt powerfully attracted to, for the pleasure of touching and being touched by a person he cared about was enhanced by looking at that person as well, the eyes had as much to do with the enjoyment as any other part of the body, even the skin, but now for the first time since he could remember being with anyone Ferguson was going at it blind, which cut him off from the room and the present moment, and even as Fleming was asking Ferguson to take hold of his cock and spit on it, Ferguson wasn't fully there anymore, his mind was producing images that had nothing to do with what was happening on the bed in his top-floor room on the rue de l'Université, Odysseus and Telemachus were weeping in each other's arms, Ferguson was running his hand over the round, muscular half-moons of Brian Mischevski's lovely ass, which he would never see or touch again, and poor Julie, whose last name he had never even known, was lying dead on a bare mattress in her room at the Hôtel des Morts.

Now Fleming was asking Ferguson to go inside him, please, he said, yes, if you will, thank you, deep inside him, all the way in, and as the still blind Ferguson eased his hard-on into the invisible man's capacious hole, the professor grunted, then began to moan, then went on moaning as Ferguson's cock moved around inside him, a wave of agonizing sounds that couldn't be blocked out because Ferguson had not been prepared for them, unlike the visual things, which he had been prepared for and had managed to erase, but even if he covered his ears the sounds would still be heard, nothing could ever stop them, and then it was suddenly over, Ferguson's erection was softening and shrinking, it was no longer possible to keep it up, neither the erection nor what he was doing, it was all over now, he was slipping out, he was done without being done, but done for all that, done for good.

I'm sorry, he said. I can't go on with this.

Ferguson sat up in bed with his back turned toward Fleming, and all at once an enormous inrush of air filled his lungs, filled him to the point of choking, and then the air was rushing out of him in a single prolonged sob, a retched-up sound that was as loud as a loud cough, as loud as a dog's bark, a chopped-off howl that shot through his windpipe, burst into the space around him, and left him gasping for breath.

No feeling ever worse than this one. No shame ever more terrible.

As Ferguson wept quietly into his hands, Fleming touched his shoulder and said he was sorry, he never should have come up to the room and asked him to do this, it was wrong, he didn't know how it could have happened, but please, he said, you mustn't let it get you down, it's of no importance, they'd had too much to drink and weren't in their right minds, it was all a mistake, and here is another thousand francs, he said, here is another fifteen hundred francs, and please, Archie, go out and spend it on something nice for yourself, something that will make you happy.

Ferguson climbed off the bed and picked up the money from the desk. I don't want your stinking money, he said, as he crumpled up the notes in his fist. Not one bloody franc of it.

And then, still naked, he walked to the northern edge of the room, opened each half of the long double window, stepped onto the balcony, and tossed the wad of bills out into the cold January night.

5.4

He was eighteen, and she was sixteen. He was about to start college, and she was at the beginning of her junior year of high school, but before he lost any more time thinking about her, before he gave another second to imagining the possible future they might or might not have been destined to share one day, he decided the moment had come to give her the test. Linda Flagg had flunked that test three years ago, but Amy Schneiderman and Dana Rosenbloom had both passed it. Those two were the only girls he had ever loved, and while he still loved both of them in their different ways, Amy was his stepsister now and had never loved him in the way he loved her, and although Dana had loved him more than he had ever deserved to be loved by anyone, Dana was gone now and living in another country, gone from his life for good.

He knew there was something mad about the whole business, a wobbly four-in-the-morning logic to the idea that he could undo the curse of Artie's death by falling in love with his dead friend's sister, but there was more to it than that, he told himself, a genuine attraction to the ever more lovely Celia, who took after her lean father and bore no genetic resemblance to her stout, overweight mother, but beautiful as Celia was becoming, and sharp as her mind undoubtedly was, he had never been alone with her, not once since the day of the funeral had he ever talked to her without also talking to her parents at the same time, and it was still uncertain what she was made of, whether she was the demure and compliant middle-class girl who sat quietly at the dinner table during Ferguson's visits to New Rochelle or whether she was a person with spirit, someone with the stuff to make him want to pursue her when the time was right.

He called it the Horn & Hardart Initiation Exam.

If she was as entranced by her first visit to the automat as he had been, as each of his high school loves had been at approximately her age, then the door would remain open and he would continue to think about Celia and wait for her to grow up.

If not, the door would shut, and he would abandon his foolish fantasy about trying to rectify the wrongs of the world and never think about opening the door again.

He called the house in New Rochelle on the Thursday after Labor Day. He wouldn't be going down to Princeton for another two weeks, but the public schools were already in session, and he was hoping she might be free for an afternoon rendezvous this Saturday, or, if not this Saturday, the next one.

When Celia picked up the phone and heard his voice, she assumed he wanted to talk to her mother about arranging another dinner at the house. She nearly put the receiver down before he had a chance to tell her that, no, she was the one he wanted to talk to, and after asking her how it felt to be back in school (so-so) and whether she was taking biology, physics, or chemistry this year (physics), he asked whether she would be willing to meet up with him in Manhattan this Saturday or next Saturday for lunch and a movie or a visit to a museum or anything else she cared to do.

You're joking, of course, she said.

Why would I joke?

It's just that . . . well, never mind, it's not important.

Well?

Yes, I'm free. Both this Saturday afternoon and next Saturday afternoon.

Let's say this Saturday.

All right, Archie, this Saturday.

He met her at Grand Central Station, and after not having seen her in the past two and a half months, he was encouraged by how pretty she looked, her smooth maple-syrup skin a shade darker from a summer's worth of sun in New Rochelle, where she had worked as a junior counselor and swimming instructor at a day camp for small children, which made her teeth and the whites of her eyes shine with an enhanced clarity, and the simple white blouse and flowing azure skirt she had put on for the afternoon suited her well, he thought, as did the pinkish-red lipstick she was wearing, which added one more dab of color to the over-all picture of whites and blues and browns, and because it was a warm day, she had put up her dark, shoulder-length hair in a dancer's knot, which exposed the back of her long, graceful neck, and so impressed was Ferguson by that overall picture as she walked toward him and shook his hand, he had to remind himself that she was still too young for him, that this was nothing more than a friendly get-together, and that beyond their initial handshake and the one they would give each other at the end of the day, he must not, under any circumstances, even think of putting a hand on her.

Here I am, she said. Now tell me why I'm here.

As they walked uptown from East Forty-second Street toward the block between Sixth and Seventh Avenues on West Fifty-seventh, Ferguson tried to explain what had prompted him to call her *out of the blue*, but Celia was skeptical, unconvinced by the stories he told about why he had wanted to see her, shaking her head when he came out with non-sense such as, I'm going off to college soon, and there won't be many chances to see each other this fall, to which she replied, Since when has seeing me ever been important to you?, such as, We're friends, aren't we, isn't that enough?, to which she replied, Are we friends? You and my parents are friends, maybe, or sort of friends, but you've spoken a grand total of about one hundred words to me in the past four years, and why would you want to hang out with a person you barely even know is alive?

The girl had spirit, Ferguson said to himself, that much was clear, and that much was settled. She had evolved into a proud, smart girl who wasn't afraid to speak her mind, but with that newfound assertiveness she had also acquired a talent for asking questions that had no answers, at least none he could give her without sounding like a crazy person. No matter what, he would have to keep Artie out of the discussion, but now that she had challenged his motives, he understood that he would have to give her better answers than the lame ones he had given so far, truthful answers, the whole truth about all things and every thing except her brother, and so he started again by saying that he had called her the other night because he had honestly wanted to see her, which was in fact the case, and the reason why he had wanted to see her alone was because he felt it was time they established their own one-on-one friendship, independent of her parents and the house in New Rochelle. Still reluctant to accept any of his statements as even remotely or possibly true, Celia asked him why he would bother, why he would want to spend a moment of his time with her, a mere high school girl, when he was already on his way to Princeton, and again Ferguson gave her a simple, truthful answer: Because she was a big person now, he said, and everything was different and would go on being different from now on. She had fallen into the erroneous habit of looking up to him as a much older person, but the calendar said they were only two years apart, and before long those two years would cease to count for anything and they would be the same age. To give her an example, Ferguson started talking about his stepbrother Jim, who was a full four years older than he was and yet one of his closest friends, someone who regarded him as an absolute equal, and now that Jim had flunked his army physical because of a falsely diagnosed heart murmur and had chosen to do his graduate work at Princeton, which would put them on the same campus at the same time—what luck that was—they were planning to see each other as often as they could and were even mapping out a trip together for sometime in the spring or early summer—going from Princeton to Cape Cod on foot, all the way to the northernmost tip of the cape without once stepping into a car or a train or a bus or, perish the thought, mounting a bicycle.

Celia was beginning to relent, but still she said: Jim's your brother. That makes it different.

My stepbrother, Ferguson said. And only for the past two years.

All right, Archie, I believe you. But if you want to be my friend now, you'll have to stop acting like my big brother, my pretend big brother. Do you understand?

Of course I do.

No more fake-brother stuff, and no more Artie stuff, because I don't like it and never have. It's sick and stupid and doesn't do either one of us any good.

Agreed, Ferguson said. No more of that. Ever.

They had just turned west off Madison Avenue and were beginning to walk down Fifty-seventh Street. After fifteen blocks of doubt, perplexity, and contentious wrangling, a cease-fire had been declared, and

Celia was smiling now, Celia was listening to Ferguson's questions and telling him that of course she knew what an automat was, and of course she had heard of Horn & Hardart, but no, she admitted, as far as she could remember she had never set foot in the place, not even as a little girl. Then she asked: What is it like, and why are we going there?

You'll see, Ferguson said.

He was willing to give her every benefit of the doubt now because he wanted her to pass the test, even to the point of bending the rules and allowing indifference to count as much as all-out, passionate enthusiasm. Only antipathy or scorn would disqualify her, he said to himself, something equivalent to the disgust he had seen in Linda Flagg's eyes when she looked over and saw the three-hundred-pound black woman muttering to herself about the dead baby Jesus, but then, before he could take that thought any further, they had already come to the automat and were walking into that nutty glitter-box of chrome and glass, and the first words that came out of Celia's mouth put an end to his worries before they even had a chance to turn their dollars into nickels. Holy moly, she said. What a weird and nifty place.

They sat down with their sandwiches and talked, for the most part about the summer, which in Ferguson's case had been spent moving furniture with Richard Brinkerstaff, traveling to cemeteries to bury his grandmother and Jim and Amy's grandfather, and writing his little saga, *Mulligan's Travels*, which was going to have twenty-four parts in all, he said, each one about five or six pages long, each one an account of a voyage to another imaginary country, Mulligan's anthropological reports for the American Society of Displaced Souls, and with twelve of those pieces now written, he was hoping the work at college wouldn't be too crushing for him to go on with it after he moved to Princeton. As for Celia, not only had she been splashing around in pools with children during the day, she had been taking night classes at the College of New Rochelle in trigonometry and French, and now that she had earned those additional credits, she would be able to finish high school after her junior year by taking one extra course a semester, which would mean she could start college next fall, and when Ferguson asked her *Why the big rush?*, she told him she was fed up living in that *dinky suburban town* and wanted to get out and move to New York, either Barnard or NYU, she didn't care which one, and as Ferguson listened to her enumerate the motives behind her *early jailbreak*, he had the sudden, vertiginous feeling that he was listening to himself, for what she was saying and thinking about her life sounded almost identical to what he had been saying and thinking for years.

Rather than compliment her on being the world's most clever and ambitious student, which undoubtedly would have led to some talk about Artie's good grades and how those good grades seemed to run in the family, he asked her what she wanted to do after lunch. There were several films playing that afternoon, he said, among them the new thing with the Beatles (*Help!*) and the latest thing from Godard, *Alphaville*, which Jim had already seen and couldn't stop talking about, but Celia felt it would be more enjoyable to visit a museum or a gallery, where they could go on talking to each other rather than having to sit in the dark for two hours listening to other people talk. Ferguson nodded and said, Good point. They could walk over to Fifth Avenue, head uptown to the Frick, and spend the afternoon there looking at the Vermeers, Rembrandts, and Chardins. Okay? Yes, that was more than okay. But first, he added, one more cup of coffee before they left, and an instant later he bolted out of his chair and disappeared with their two cups.

He was gone for only a minute, but in that time Celia had noticed a man sitting at the table next to theirs, a small old man who had been blocked from her view by Ferguson's shoulder, and when Ferguson came back with their recharged coffees and two containers of cream, he saw that Celia was looking at the man, looking at him with such distress in her eyes that Ferguson asked her if anything was wrong.

I feel so sorry for him, she said. I'll bet he hasn't eaten anything all day. He just sits there staring into his coffee as if he's afraid to drink it, because once the coffee is gone, he won't have enough money to buy another cup, and he'll have to leave.

Ferguson, who had spotted the old man while walking back to the table, didn't feel it would be polite to turn around and look at him again, but yes, the man had struck him as a lonely down-and-outer, a grizzled, unkempt wino with dirty fingernails and a sad leprechaun's face, and Celia was probably right that he had just spent his last nickel.

I think we should give him something, she said.

We should, Ferguson replied, but we have to remember that he hasn't asked us for it, and if we just walk over there and hand him some money because we feel sorry for him, he might feel offended, and then all our good intentions would only make him feel worse than he already feels.

You could be right, Celia said, as she lifted her cup and brought it toward her mouth, but then again, you could be wrong.

They both finished and stood up from their chairs. Celia opened her purse, and as they walked toward the old man sitting at the next table, she reached into the purse, pulled out a dollar, and put it down in front of him.

Please, sir, she said, go and buy yourself something to eat, and the old man, taking hold of the dollar and putting it in his pocket, looked up at her and said, Thank you, miss. God bless you.

LATER WOULD BE later, no doubt a most fulfilling and instructive later, a later of more afternoons and possibly even nights with the admirable, still-too-young Celia, but now was now, and for now the world had moved to the cranberry bogs and marshy lowlands of central New Jersey, for now the world was all about being one of eight hundred incoming freshmen and trying to adjust to his new circumstances. He understood himself well enough to know that he probably wasn't going to fit in, that there would be things about the place he wasn't going to like, but at the same time he was determined to make the most of the things he was going to like, and to that end he had already laid down five personal commandments in advance of his departure for Princeton, five laws he meant to adhere to for the whole duration:

1) Weekends in New York whenever and as often as possible. After his grandmother's sudden and calamitous death in July (congestive heart failure), his now widowed grandfather had given him a key to the apartment on West Fifty-eighth Street along with unrestricted use of the spare bedroom, which meant there would always be a place to crash for the night. The promise of that room represented a singular instance of desire and opportunity joined, for on most Friday afternoons Ferguson would be able to leave campus and board the one-car shuttle train from Princeton to Princeton Junction (known as the Dinky, as in *dinky suburban town*) and then transfer to the longer, faster train that shot north to midtown Manhattan, the new and ugly Penn Station as opposed to the old and beautiful one, which had been demolished in 1963, but architectural blunders aside, it was still New York, and the

reasons for going to New York were multiple. The negative reason was that it would allow him to escape the stuffiness of Princeton for an occasional breath of fresh air (even if the air in New York wasn't fresh), which would make the stuffiness more tolerable to him and perhaps even pleasant (in its own stuffy way) during the time he spent on campus. The positive reason was the old reason of the past: *density, immensity, complexity.* Another positive reason was the chance he would be given to spend time with his grandfather and to keep up his friendship with Noah, which was vital to him. Ferguson hoped he would make friends at college, he wanted to make friends, he was expecting to make friends, but would any of those friends ever be as important to him as Noah?

2) No creative writing classes. A difficult decision, but Ferguson aimed to stick with it to the end. Difficult because the Princeton undergraduate program was one of the oldest in the country, which meant he could have earned academic credit for doing what he was already doing, that is, have been rewarded for the privilege of forging on with his book, which in turn meant his course load would have been effectively lightened by one course each semester, which would have given him more time not only to write but to read, to watch films, to listen to music, to drink, to pursue girls, and to go to New York, but Ferguson was opposed to the teaching of creative writing on principle, for he was convinced that fiction writing was not a subject that could be taught, that every future writer had to learn how to do it on his or her own, and furthermore, based on the information he had been given about how those so-called workshops were run (the word inevitably made him think of a roomful of young apprentices sawing through wooden planks and hammering nails into boards), the students were encouraged to comment on one another's work, which struck him as absurd (the blind leading the blind!), and why would he ever submit to having his work picked apart by a numskull undergraduate, his exceptionally bizarre and unclassifiable work, which would surely be frowned upon and dismissed as *experimental rubbish.* It wasn't that he was against showing his stories to older, more experienced people for one-on-one criticism and discussion, but the idea of a group horrified him, and whether that horror was caused by arrogance or fear (of the dreaded punch) was less important than the fact that he finally didn't give a rat's ass about anyone's work but his own, and why bother to pretend to care

when he didn't? He was still in touch with Mrs. Monroe (who had read the first twelve parts of *Mulligan's Travels*, which had led to twelve kisses and no punches along with some pertinent, mind-opening comments), and if and when she wasn't available, other trusted readers included Uncle Don, Aunt Mildred, Noah, and Amy, and if he ever found himself in a fix and couldn't track down any of those trusted ones, he would head for the office of Professor Robert Nagle, *the best literary mind in all of Princeton*, and humbly ask for his help.

3) No eating club. Three-quarters of his classmates would wind up joining one, but Ferguson wasn't interested. Similar to fraternities but not quite identical to fraternities, with the word *bicker* standing in for what other places called *rush*, they smacked of all the time-honored, backward-looking things about Princeton that left him cold, and by steering clear of the clubs and going "independent," he would be able to avoid one of the stuffiest aspects of that stuffy place and thus feel happier about being there.

4) The ban against baseball would continue, an injunction that would include all spinoff forms of the game as well: softball, wiffleball, stickball, and playing catch with anyone at any time, even with a tennis ball or a pink rubber *spaldeen* or a rolled-up pair of socks. Being out of high school would help put the struggle behind him, he felt, since he would no longer be in contact with his old baseball friends, who remembered what a good and promising player he had been, and because they had been mystified by his decision to stop playing and couldn't understand the false excuses he had given for abandoning the game, they had gone on questioning him about it all through high school. Mercifully, those questions would end now. On the other hand, now that he had escaped the halls and classrooms of Columbia High, he was about to go to one of the most sports-obsessed colleges in the country, the school that had taken on Rutgers in the first intercollegiate football game ever played in 1869, the school that just six months earlier had gone to the Final Four and come in third in the NCAA basketball tournament, the strongest finish ever for an Ivy League team, with the whole country swept up in Bill Bradley's headline battles with Cazzie Russell of Michigan, followed by Bradley's unprecedented fifty-eight points in the consolation-game victory for Princeton, and no doubt everyone on campus would still be rehashing those exploits when Ferguson arrived. Athletes would be everywhere, and Ferguson would

naturally want to jump in and take part in various games, but those games would have to be confined to such things as half-court basketball and touch football, and in order to guard against any future temptations to participate in the sport he had vowed to shun as a memorial to Celia's dead brother, he had given away his baseball gear at the end of August, casually handing over two bats, a pair of spikes, and the Luis Aparicio–model Rawlings glove that had been sitting on a shelf in his room for the past four years to Charlie Bassinger, the scrawny nine-year-old kid who lived next door to him on Woodhall Crescent. Take it, Ferguson had said to Charlie, I don't need this stuff anymore, and young Bassinger, who wasn't quite certain what his much admired almost-college-man neighbor was talking about, had looked up at Ferguson and asked, You mean for keeps, Archie? That's right, Ferguson answered. For keeps.

5) No overtures to his father. If his father made an overture to him, he would think carefully about how he should or shouldn't respond, but he wasn't expecting that to happen. Their last communication had been the short note Ferguson had written to thank his father for the high school graduation present in June, and because he had been feeling especially bitter and hopeless on the afternoon the check arrived (Dana had left for Israel earlier that day), he had told his father about his plan to contribute half the money to SNCC and the other half to SANE. It was unlikely his father had been pleased.

QUALMS AND FOREBODINGS, nerves and more nerves, and if not for the soothing presences of his mother and Jim, who were both in the van with Ferguson on the morning he made his way down to the bogs and marshes of COLLEGE LIFE, he probably would have lost his breakfast and staggered out onto the dewy swards of Princeton with half of that breakfast on his shirt.

It was an intense day for the whole family. Dan and Amy were in another car traveling north to Brandeis, Ferguson and company were traveling south in one of Arnie Frazier's white Chevy vans, which Arnie had been kind enough to let them borrow for free, and there they were cruising along the New Jersey Turnpike on that drizzly, mizzly morning, with Jim at the controls and Ferguson and his mother wedged in beside him on the front seat, the entire space in back filled

up to the ceiling with the worldly possessions of the two step-
brothers, the familiar hodgepodge of bedding and pillows and towels and clothes and books and records and record players and radios
and typewriters, and now that Ferguson had just finished reciting the
first three of his five commandments to them, Jim was shaking his
head and smiling his enigmatic Schneiderman smile, which was a
smile of thought and reflection rather than a smile that verged on or
even suggested laughter.

Loosen up, Archie, he said. You're taking this much too seriously.

Yes, Archie, his mother chimed in. What's with you this morning?
We haven't even gotten there, and already you're thinking about how
to get away.

I'm scared, that's all, Ferguson said. Scared that I'm about to get lost
in some reactionary, anti-Semitic dungeon and won't get out alive.

Now his stepbrother laughed.

Think of Einstein, Jim said. Think of Richard Feynman. They don't
kill Jews at Princeton, Archie, they just make them walk around with
yellow stars on their sleeves.

Now Ferguson laughed.

Jim, his mother said, you shouldn't joke like that, really you
shouldn't—but a moment later she was laughing, too.

About ten percent, Jim said. That's what I've been told. Which is a
lot higher than the national percentage of . . . of what? Two percent, three
percent?

Columbia is somewhere around twenty or twenty-five percent,
Ferguson said.

Maybe so, Jim replied, but Columbia didn't give you the scholarship.

BROWN HALL, AND a suite of two bedrooms on the third floor large
enough to house four freshmen with a common room and bathroom in
between. Brown Hall and a roommate named Small, Howard Small, a
solid, chunky fellow of around five-eleven with a clear gaze and an aura
of tranquil self-confidence about him, a person comfortably settled into
his own patch of ground, his own skin. A firm but not too firm or bone-
crunching grip when they shook hands for the first time, and a moment
later Howard was leaning forward and studying Ferguson's face,
which was an odd thing for someone to do, Ferguson thought, but

then Howard asked him a question that turned the odd thing into a thing that wasn't odd at all.

You didn't happen to go to Columbia High School, did you? Howard asked.

Yes, Ferguson said. As a matter of fact I did.

Ah. And while you were at Columbia, you didn't happen to play on the J.V. basketball team, did you?

I did. Just for my sophomore year, though.

I knew I'd seen you somewhere before. You played forward, right?

Left. Left forward. But you're right. Not that I know why you're right, but you are.

I was a benchwarmer on the West Orange J.V. that year.

Which means . . . how interesting . . . that we've already crossed paths twice.

Twice without even knowing it. Once for the home game and once for the away game. And just like you, I stopped playing after that one season. But I was a talentless oaf, truly awful and inept. Whereas you were pretty good, as I remember it, maybe even very good.

Not bad. But the point was: Did I want to go on thinking about jock-straps or turn my full attention to panties and bras?

They both smiled.

Not a difficult choice, then.

No, utterly painless.

Howard walked over to the window and gestured toward the campus. Look at this place, he said. It reminds me of the Duke of Earl's country retreat, or one of those mental hospitals for the insanely rich. P.U. the magnificent, thank you for letting me in here, and thank you for these sumptuous grounds. But please explain one thing to me. Why are there so many black squirrels prancing around out there? In my experience, squirrels have always been gray, but here at Princeton they're all black.

Because they're part of the decorating scheme, Ferguson said. You remember the Princeton colors, don't you?

Orange . . . and black.

That's right, orange and black. Once we start seeing some orange squirrels, we'll know why the black ones are there.

Howard laughed at Ferguson's mildly funny, mildly stupid joke, and because he laughed, the nerve-knot in Ferguson's stomach began to

unclench a little bit, for even if P.U. turned out to be a hostile or disappointing place, he was going to have a friend there, or so it seemed to
him when he heard his roommate laugh, and how fortunate he was to
have met that friend in the first minutes of the first hour on the first day.

As they went about the business of unpacking their bundles, boxes,
and bags, Ferguson was informed that Howard had started life on the
Upper West Side of Manhattan and had been turned into a bridge-and-
tunnel boy at age eleven when his father was appointed dean of students
at Montclair State, and how curious it was to learn that they had spent
the past seven years living within a few miles of each other and yet
had intersected only glancingly those two times on the hardwood
floors of their high school gyms. Testing each other out in the way
strangers tend to do when they have been arbitrarily thrown together
in the same cell, they quickly learned that they shared many likes
and dislikes but not all or even most, both preferring the Mets to the
Yankees, for one thing, but as of two years ago Howard had become
a staunch vegetarian (he was morally opposed to the slaughter of
animals) while Ferguson was an unthinking, bred-in-the-bone car-
nivore, and although Howard indulged in cigarette smoking from
time to time, Ferguson regularly consumed between ten and twenty
Camels a day. Books and writers were all over the map (Howard had
read little contemporary American poetry or European fiction; Ferguson
was more and more immersed in both of them), but their taste in films
was eerily congruent, and when they both judged their favorite comedy of the 1950s to be *Some Like It Hot* and their favorite thriller to be
The Third Man, Howard blurted out in a sudden rush of enthusiasm,
Jack Lemmon and Harry Lime!, and an instant later he was sitting down
at his desk, grabbing hold of a pen, and drawing a cartoon of a tennis
match between a lemon and a lime. Ferguson watched in wonder as
his prodigious roommate dashed off the sketch—the longer, bumpier
lemon with arms and legs and a tennis racket in its right hand playing
against the smaller, rounder, smoother lime with similar arms, legs,
and racket, each one with a face that resembled the Lemmon and Lime
originals (Jack L. and Orson W.), and then Howard added a net, a ball
flying through the air, and the cartoon was done. Ferguson looked
down at his watch. Three minutes from the first stroke to the last. No
more than three minutes, perhaps even two.

Good God, Ferguson said. You really can draw, can't you?

Lemmon versus Lime, Howard said, ignoring the compliment. It's pretty funny, don't you think?

Not just pretty funny. Very funny.

We might be onto something here.

Without a doubt, Ferguson said, as he tapped his finger against Howard's pen and said, *William Penn*, and then tapped his finger against the drawing and said, *versus Patti Page*.

Ah, but of course! There's no end to it, is there?

They kept it up for the next several hours, all through the unpacking and settling in, all through lunch in the dining hall, all through the afternoon as they wandered around the campus together and straight into dinner, by which time they had come up with forty or fifty more pairings. From beginning to end, they never stopped laughing, and so hard did they laugh at times and now and then for long intervals of time that Ferguson asked himself if he had ever laughed so hard at anything since the day he was born. Laughter to the point of tears. Laughter to the point of suffocation. And what a good sport it was for overcoming the fears and trembles of a young traveler who had just left home and found himself standing at the border crossing between the written past and the unwritten future.

Think of body parts, Howard said, and a moment or two later Ferguson answered: Legs Diamond versus Learned Hand. A few moments after that, Howard volleyed back with: Edith Head versus Michael Foot.

Think of sloshy bodies, Ferguson said, H-two-O in any one of its various states, and Howard answered: John Ford versus Larry Rivers, Claude Rains versus Muddy Waters. After several moments of concentrated thought, Ferguson matched those two with two of his own: Bennett Cerf versus Toots Shor, Veronica Lake versus Dick Diver.

Do fictional characters count? Howard asked.

Why not? As long as we know who they are, they're just as real as real people. Anyway, since when did Harry Lime stop being a fictional character?

Whoops, I forgot about old Harry. In that case, let me offer you C. P. Snow versus Uriah Heep.

Or two other English gentlemen: Christopher Wren versus Christopher Robin.

Smashing. Now think of kings and queens, Howard said, and after a long pause Ferguson answered: William of Orange versus Robert Peel. Almost at once, Howard came back with: Vlad the Impaler versus Charles the Fat.

Think of Americans, Ferguson said, and over the next hour and a half they produced:

Cotton Mather versus Boss Tweed.

Nathan Hale versus Oliver Hardy.

Stan Laurel versus Judy Garland.

W. C. Fields versus Audrey Meadows.

Loretta Young versus Victor Mature.

Wallace Beery versus Rex Stout.

Hal Roach versus Bugs Moran.

Charles Beard versus Sonny Tufts.

Myles Standish versus Sitting Bull.

On it went, and on they went with it, but when they finally returned to their room after dinner and sat down to make a list of the pairings, more than half of what they had come up with had already flown out of their heads.

We'll have to keep better records, Howard said. If nothing else, we've learned that brainstorms grow from highly flammable materials, and unless we walk around with a pen or a pencil at all times, we're bound to forget most of what we've done.

For every one we forget, Ferguson said, we'll always be able to invent another. Think crustacean, for example, cast out your net for a little while, and suddenly you have Buster Crabbe versus Jean Shrimpton.

Nice.

Or sounds. A sweet peep in the forest, a loud roar in the jungle, and there you are with Lionel Trilling versus Saul Bellow.

Or crime fighters with secretaries and girlfriends whose names go with addresses.

You've lost me.

Think Perry Mason and Superman, and what you get is Della Street versus Lois Lane.

Good. Awfully good. But then take a stroll on the beach, and before you know it you're looking at George Sand . . . versus Lorna Doone.

That's going to be a fun one to draw. An hourglass playing tennis with a cookie.

Yes, but what about Veronica Lake versus Dick Diver? Think of the possibilities.

Delicious. It's so sexy, it's almost obscene.

NAGLE WAS HIS faculty adviser. Nagle was the professor who taught him Classical Literature in Translation, the course that was doing more for the growth of Ferguson's mind than any other course he was taking. And almost surely Nagle was the person who had argued most strenuously on his behalf for the scholarship, and even though Nagle never would have talked about what he had done, Ferguson sensed that Nagle had hopes for him and was taking a special interest in his progress, and that was crucial to Ferguson's inner equilibrium in that time of transition and potential disarray, for Nagle's hopes were the difference between feeling estranged and feeling he might have belonged there, and when he handed in his first paper of the term, five pages on the reunion scene between Odysseus and Telemachus in the sixteenth book of *The Odyssey*, Nagle returned it to him with a cryptic note scrawled at the bottom of the last page, *Not bad, Ferguson—keep it up*, which Ferguson understood to be the laconic professor's way of telling him he had done a good job, a less than superlative job, perhaps, but a good job for all that.

Every other Wednesday throughout the first semester, Nagle and his wife, Susan, hosted an afternoon tea at their small house on Alexander Street for Nagle's six freshman advisees. Mrs. Nagle was a short, round brunette who taught ancient history at Rutgers and stood a full head shorter than her lean, long-faced husband. While she poured the tea, Nagle served the sandwiches, or while Nagle poured the tea, she served the sandwiches, and while Nagle sat in an armchair smoking cigarettes and talking or listening to some of his charges, Mrs. Nagle sat on the sofa talking and listening to his other charges, and so companionable and yet distantly polite were the two Nagles with each other that Ferguson sometimes wondered if they didn't communicate in ancient Greek when they didn't want their eight-year-old daughter, Barbara, to know what they were talking about. The idea of a formal tea had always struck Ferguson as the dullest sort of social business imaginable (he had never been to one until now), but in fact he enjoyed Nagle's ninety-minute parties and tried not to miss them, for they offered another chance to see the professor in action, and what they told him was that Nagle was more than he appeared to be in the classroom or his office, where he never talked about politics or the war or current issues, but here in his house every other Wednesday afternoon he welcomed in his six first-year charges, who happened to be two Jewish students, two foreign students, and two black students, and when you considered that there were only twelve black freshmen in the entire class of eight hundred (only twelve!) and no more than five or six dozen Jews and perhaps half or a third that many foreigners, it seemed clear to Ferguson that Nagle had quietly taken it upon himself to look after the outsiders and make sure they didn't drown in that forbidding, alien place, and whether he was motivated by political beliefs or a love of Princeton or simple human kindness, Robert Nagle was doing what he could to make the marginal ones feel at home.

Nagle and Howard and Jim—in the first month of Ferguson's new life as a discombobulated scholarship boy, a boy who had previously come to think of himself as a man and was now regressing into the anxious uncertainties of childhood, they were the ones who held him together. Howard was more than just a demon cartoonist and high-energy wit, he was a solid thinker and conscientious student with plans to major in philosophy, and because he was considerate and mostly self-contained and undemanding of Ferguson's attentions, it was possible for Ferguson to share the room with him and not feel that his privacy was being impinged upon. That had been one of Ferguson's greatest fears, having to live in a less than large room with someone else, which until now had happened to him only at Camp Paradise, where he had bunked in cabins with two counselors and seven other boys, but at home he had always been able to retreat into the four walls of his one-person sanctuary, even in the new house on Woodhall Crescent when Amy had been in the next room slamming doors and blasting out loud music, and the worry had been whether he would be able to read or write or even think with another person lying on a bed or sitting at a desk just six or seven feet from him. As it happened, Howard had been fretting about the same close-quarters problem, for he too had always had his own room while growing up, and in a frank conversation on the third day of Freshman Orientation Week, during which they both confessed to their fears of no solitude and too much air going from one set of lungs into the other, they worked out what they hoped would be an acceptable modus operandi. Their suitemates were a pre-med student from Vermont named Will Noyes and an 800 math wizard from Iowa named Dudley Krantzenberger, and Ferguson and Howard agreed that when the common room was empty, that is, when Noyes and Krantzenberger were in their bedroom or out of the building, one of them (Ferguson or Howard) would read-write-think-study-draw in the bedroom and the other in the common room, and when either Noyes or Krantzenberger or both was/were in the common room, Ferguson and Howard would take turns going to the library while the other remained in the bedroom. They shook hands on it, but then the semester began in earnest, and after a couple of weeks they had grown so comfortable with each other that the precautionary rules were no longer in force. They came and went as they pleased, and if they both decided to stay in at the same time, they discovered that they were able to sit in the room together for long stretches of silent work without breaking in on each other's thoughts or contaminating the air they both breathed. Potential problems sometimes turned into genuine problems, and sometimes they didn't. This one didn't. By the first of October, the two occupants of the third-floor room in Brown Hall had invented eighty-one more tennis matches.

As for Jim, he was adjusting to a new set of circumstances as well, feeling his way as a first-year graduate student in the roughly competitive Department of Physics, acclimating himself to life with a roommate in an off-campus apartment, no less frazzled than his stepbrother was during that early period in black squirrel heaven, but still they managed to have dinner together every Tuesday night, either spaghetti at the apartment with Jim's fellow MIT-graduate roommate, Lester Patel from New Delhi, or hamburgers at a crowded little place on Nassau Street called Bud's, along with an hour and a half of one-on-one basketball at Dillon Gym every ten days or so, where Ferguson always lost to the slightly taller, slightly more talented Schneiderman, but not by such embarrassing scores that it wasn't worth the effort. One evening about two weeks after the start of classes, Jim dropped by Brown Hall for an impromptu visit with Ferguson and Howard, and when Howard pulled out the list of tennis matches they had done so far and showed Jim some of the drawings that went with them (Claude Rains on one side of the net as a cluster of isolate droplets, Muddy Waters on the other side up to his waist in goo), Jim laughed as hard as Ferguson and Howard had

laughed on the morning they'd cooked up the game, and to see him doubled over and in stitches like that said something good about Jim's
character, Ferguson felt, just as passing the Horn & Hardart Initiation
Exam had said something good about Celia's character, for in each case
the reaction had proved that the person in question was a kindred spirit,
someone who appreciated the same screwball juxtapositions and unpredictable yokings of like and unlike that Ferguson did, for the unhappy
truth was that not everyone was enamored of Horn & Hardart's or
the poetic grandeur of automated, nickel-in-the-slot cuisine, and not
everyone laughed or even smiled at the tennis matches, as Ferguson and
Howard had observed with Noyes and Krantzenberger, who one by one
had looked at the pairings with blank faces, not understanding that they
were supposed to be funny, not capable of grasping the droll doubleness that occurred when a thing-word also posed as a name-word and
that putting two of those thing-names together could hoist you into a
realm of unexpected mirth, no, the whole venture had fallen flat for their
sober, literal-minded suitemates, whereas Jim was in a lather of extreme
jollification, clutching his sides and telling them he *hadn't laughed so
hard in years*, and once again Ferguson found himself looking at the old
punch-kiss problem, which appeared to be intractable, since the *what*
couldn't speak for itself except by being itself and therefore was forever
at the mercy of the *who*, and given that there was always just one *what*
and many *whos*, the *whos* inevitably had the last word, even when they
were wrong in their judgments, not just about big things such as books
and the design of eighty-story buildings but about small things such as
a random list of harmless, silly jokes.

THE COURSES NOT taught by Nagle were not as engaging as Classical
Literature in Translation, but they were good enough, and between the
work of settling into his new surroundings and the work for those
courses, which included a freshman requirement in prosody and composition along with Introduction to French Literature with Lafargue, the
European Novel from 1857 to 1922 with Baker, and American History I
with McDowell, there was little time left over in the first month for him
to think about poor Mulligan, and what time there was he squandered
on trips to New York.

His grandfather had gone down to Florida for the fall and winter, which gave Ferguson free access to the apartment whenever he wanted it, and with the apartment came the luxury of being entirely and bracingly alone. The rooms on West Fifty-eighth Street also provided him with the further indulgence of being able to make free telephone calls, since his grandfather had explicitly told him to use the phone *whenever his mouth felt the itch* and not to worry about the cost. The offer implied a certain degree of moderation, of course, an understanding that Ferguson would not lose control of himself and saddle his grandfather with excessive long-distance charges, which eliminated the possibility of calling Dana in Israel, for example (something he might have done anyway if he had known her number), but as it was he managed to stay in touch with various others on the domestic front, all of them women, the women he loved or had loved or might start to love later or soon or now.

Stepsister Amy had thrown herself into the anti-war movement at Brandeis, which had drawn *all the most interesting people on campus*, she said, among them a senior named Michael Morris, who had been one of the Freedom Summer volunteers in Mississippi last year, and Ferguson could only hope that this one would be better for her than the slob she had given her heart to in high school, duplicitous Loeb of the manifold deceptions and broken promises. Had that been an innocent mistake on Amy's part, he wondered, or, having rejected her future stepbrother on the night of the fireflies in the backyard of the old house, was she destined to fall for the wrong man again and again? Be careful, he said to her. This Morris seems to be a good fellow, but don't jump into it until you know who he really is. Ferguson in his self-appointed role as the new Miss Lonelyhearts, dispensing advice on matters he knew nothing about. A subtle form of unconscious revenge, perhaps, for much as he cared about Amy, the scald of her old rejection still stung from time to time, and he had never been able to tell her how badly she had hurt him.

His mother had found a job with the Hammond Map Company in Maplewood, a long-term assignment to take pictures for a series of New Jersey calendars and agendas they were planning to start publishing in 1967, that is, one year from now in the fall of 1966, New Jersey Notables, New Jersey Landscapes, New Jersey Historic Sites, and two editions of New Jersey Architecture (one for public buildings and one for private houses), which had been swung through the intervention of one of Dan's commercial clients, and Ferguson felt this was excellent news for several reasons, first of all because of the extra cash that would be coming into the household (a source of perpetual worry) but most of all because he wanted his mother to be busy with something again after his father had recklessly pulled the plug on her studio, and with no kids to look after at home anymore, why not do this, which was bound to be satisfying work for her and enliven her days, however far-fetched the notion of New Jersey calendars and weekly planners might have been.

The person he had once called Mrs. Monroe and now addressed as Evie, the short form of Evelyn she was known by to her friends, was back at C.H.S. doing her stuff in front of her several English classes and overseeing the new crop of editors in charge of the student literary magazine, but things had taken a rocky turn for her in early September when her boyfriend of the past three years, a political journalist at the *Star-Ledger* named Ed Southgate, had abruptly called off their affair and gone back to his wife, and Evie was down and feeling too much pain for her own good, spending the late weekend hours with a glass of scotch in her hand listening to scratchy blues records by Bessie Smith and Lightnin' Hopkins, and hell, Ferguson kept thinking to himself as the trees changed color and leaves started falling to the ground, how that woman's big soul could ache. Whenever he called her, he did what he could to pull her out of the doldrums and take her mind off the departed Ed because there was no point in looking back anymore, he felt, nothing for it but to jostle her out of her booze-hole by poking fun at Ed-ness, deadness, and despair, telling her not to worry because he, Ferguson, her former student, was coming to the rescue, and if she didn't want to be rescued she should lock the doors of her house or get out of town, because he was coming whether she liked it or not, and all at once the two of them would be laughing and the cloud would lift just long enough for her to start talking about other things besides sitting alone in the downstairs parlor with a bottle of scotch, the loveless nights in her half of the two-family house where she lived on a block of tall, undulating shade trees in East Orange, the half-house Ferguson had visited eight or ten times during the summer and knew well enough by now to have learned that it was one of the few places in the world where he felt utterly and only himself, and every time he called her he would think about those summer visits and the one night when they both drank too much and were on the verge of going to bed together when the doorbell rang and the little boy from across the street asked if his mother could borrow a cup of sugar.

Then there was Celia, a call every Friday evening or Saturday afternoon to his new friend, for no other purpose than to prove how seriously he was taking the job of being her friend, and he kept on calling because she always seemed happy when he did. Their early conversations had a tendency to meander over several or many unconnected subjects, but they seldom lagged, and Ferguson enjoyed listening to her earnest, intelligent voice as they zigzagged from the sociology of high school cliques to the war in Vietnam, from worried complaints about her *numb, debilitated parents* to wistful ruminations about the possibility of orange squirrels, but soon enough she was talking more and more about her preparations for the SATs, which would eliminate any more Saturday outings for the time being, and then, in late September, she announced that she had started seeing a boy named Bruce, who was apparently about to be turned into something that resembled a boyfriend, which jolted Ferguson when she told him about it and went on jolting him for a day or two after that, but once he calmed down he reasoned that it was probably for the best, since she had made too strong an impression on him during the day they had spent together in New York, and with no other girls anywhere in the picture just then, he might have made an impetuous lunge at her the next time they were together, something he would have regretted, something that could have ruined their chances down the road, and better that this Bruce person should be standing between them now, for high school romances rarely lasted beyond the end of high school, and next year she would be in college if things went as planned, as undoubtedly they would, and after that the whole situation would be different again.

Meanwhile, in the downtown blocks around Washington Square, Noah was sinking his teeth into the meaty pleasures of his newly independent life, his liberation from the claustrophobic confines of his mother's apartment on West End Avenue and the peace-and-quarrel cycles of his father's demented marriage to his neurasthenic stepmother. As he put it to Ferguson one day as he showed him around his dormitory, his small, two-by-four room was the next best thing to camping out in the Montana wilderness. *I'm no longer hemmed in, Arch,* he said, *I feel like an emancipated slave who's lit out for the territories,* and although Ferguson worried that he was smoking too much pot and too many cigarettes (close to two packs a day), his eyes were clear and he generally seemed to be in good form, even as he coped with the loss of his girlfriend, Carole, who had dumped him before going off to live under her own big skies in Yellow Springs, Ohio.

Two weeks into the first semester, Noah reported that NYU was much less demanding than Fieldston and that he could do his daily stint of work in about the same time it took *to consume a five-course dinner*. Ferguson wondered when Noah had last sat down to a five-course dinner, but he got the point, and he couldn't help admiring his cousin for being so relaxed about the business of college, which in his own case had nearly provoked a nervous breakdown. So there was young Mr. Marx, a new man in his old surroundings, stomping around the cobbled lanes of his West Village turf, going to jazz clubs and movies at the Bleecker Street Cinema, writing down story ideas for films as he sat in the Caffè Reggio and drank his sixth cup of espresso that day, and there he was making friends with young poets and painters from the Lower East Side, and when Noah began introducing Ferguson to some of those people, Ferguson's world expanded in ways that would ultimately reconfigure the landscape of his life, for those early encounters were the first steps toward discovering what kind of life would be possible for him in the future, and again, as always, Noah was the one to thank for steering him in the right direction. However opposed he might have been to the workshops at Princeton, Ferguson knew there was much to be gained by talking to other writers and artists, and because most of the downtown fledglings he met through Noah were three and four and five years older than he was, they were already publishing their work in little magazines and organizing group shows in tumbledown lofts and storefronts, which meant they were miles ahead of him at that point, and therefore Ferguson listened carefully to what they said. Most of them wound up teaching him something, even the ones he didn't take to personally, but the smartest one in his opinion turned out to be the one he liked best, a poet named Ron Pearson, who had come to New York from Tulsa, Oklahoma, four years earlier and had graduated from Columbia in June, and one evening at Ron's cramped little railroad flat on Rivington Street, as Ferguson and Noah and two or three others sat on the floor with Ron and his wife, Peg (he was already married!), the conversation spun around from Dada to anarchism, from twelve-tone music to Nancy and Sluggo porn cartoons, from traditional forms in poetry and painting to the role of chance in art, and suddenly John Cage was mentioned, a name that was only dimly recognizable to Ferguson, and when Ron learned that their new friend from the Jersey swamps had never read a word of Cage's writings, he jumped to his feet, walked over to the bookcase, and pulled out a hardcover copy of *Silence*. You have to read this, Archie, he said, or else you'll never learn how to think about anything except what other people want you to think.

Ferguson thanked him and promised to return the book as soon as possible, but Ron waved him off and said, Keep it. I have two other copies, so this one belongs to you now.

Ferguson opened the book, flipped through it for a couple of moments, and then fell upon this sentence on page 96: "The world is teeming: anything can happen."

It was Friday, October 15, 1965, and Ferguson had been a student at Princeton for one month, one of the most trying and exhausting months he could remember, but he was pulling out of it now, he felt, something was starting to shift in him again, and spending those hours with Noah and Ron and the others had helped push him away from the things that were weak and angry and arrested in him, and now he had the book, a hardcover copy of John Cage's *Silence*, and when the little party broke up and everyone left, he told Noah that he was feeling tired and wanted to head back to his grandfather's place uptown, which wasn't in fact true, since he wasn't the least bit tired and merely wanted to be alone.

Twice before, a book had turned him inside out and altered who he was, had blasted apart his assumptions about the world and thrust him onto a new ground where everything in the world suddenly looked different—and would remain different for the rest of time, for as long as he himself went on living in time and occupied space in the world. Dostoyevsky's book was about the passions and contradictions of the human soul, Thoreau's book was a manual on how to live, and now Ferguson had discovered a book that Ron had correctly called *a book about how to think*, and as he sat in his grandfather's apartment reading "2 Pages, 122 Words on Music and Dance," "Lecture on Nothing," "Lecture on Something," "45' for a Speaker," and "Indeterminancy," he felt as if a fierce, purifying wind were blowing through his brain and cleaning out the junk that had accumulated there, that he was in the presence of a man who was unafraid to ask first questions, to start all over from the beginning and walk down a path no one had ever traveled before him, and when Ferguson finally put down the book at three-thirty in the morning, he felt so stirred up and ignited by what he had read that he knew sleep was out of the question, that he wouldn't be able to close his eyes for the rest of the night.

The world is teeming: anything can happen.

He had made plans to get together with Noah at noon tomorrow and march down Fifth Avenue in what would be their first anti-war demonstration, New York's first large-scale protest against the buildup of American troops in Vietnam, an event that was sure to attract tens of thousands of people if not one hundred thousand or two hundred thousand, and nothing was going to stop Ferguson from taking part in it, not even if he was dead on his feet and had to shuffle down Fifth Avenue like a drunken somnambulist, but noon was many hours away, and for the first time since he had first set foot in Brown Hall last month, he was ready to start writing again, and nothing was going to stop him from doing that either.

Mulligan's first twelve voyages had taken him to countries that lived in a state of permanent war, countries of intense religious severity that punished their citizens for thinking impure thoughts, countries whose cultures were dedicated to the pursuit of sexual pleasure, countries whose people thought about little else but food, countries run by women in which the men served as low-paid lackeys, countries devoted to the making of art and music, countries governed by racist, Nazi-like laws and other countries in which the people could not distinguish between different colors of skin, countries in which merchants and businessmen cheated the public as a matter of civic duty, countries organized around perpetual sports competitions, countries besieged by earthquakes, erupting volcanoes, and continual bad weather, tropical countries in which the people wore no clothes, frigid countries in which the people were obsessed with fur, primitive countries and technologically advanced countries, countries that seemed to belong to the past and others that seemed to belong to the present or the distant future. Ferguson had made a rough map of the twenty-four journeys before starting the project, but he had found that the best way to enter a new chapter was by writing blindly, to put down whatever seemed to be bubbling in his head as he barreled along from sentence to sentence, and then, when the wild first draft was finished, he would go back and slowly begin to tame it, usually going through five or six more drafts before it reached its proper and definitive shape, the mysterious combination of lightness and heaviness he was searching for, the seriocomic tone that was necessary to pull off such outlandish narratives, the *plausible implausibility* of what he called *nonsense in motion*. He looked upon his little book as an experiment, an exercise that would allow him to flex some *new writerly muscles*, and when he had finished writing the last chapter, he was planning to burn the manuscript or, if not burn it, bury the book in a place where no one would ever find it.

That night in his grandfather's spare bedroom, which had once been the room his mother had shared with her sister Mildred, charged with the sense of freedom Cage's book had given him, hell-bent and exultant, reveling in the thought that his month-long silence had come to an end, he wrote the first and second drafts of what was undoubtedly his most crackpot effort so far.

THE DROONS

The Droons are happiest when complaining about the condition of their land. The mountain dwellers envy the people who live in the valleys, and the people in the valleys long to migrate to the mountains. The farmers are dissatisfied with the yield of their crops, the fishermen grumble about their daily catch, and yet no fisherman or farmer has ever stepped forward to accept responsibility for his failure. They prefer to blame the land and the sea rather than admit that they are less than good farmers and fishermen, that the old knowledge has gradually been lost and they are no more skilled at what they do than untrained beginners.

For the first time in my travels, I have come across what I would call a *lazy people*.

The women have lost hope in the future and are no longer interested in bearing children. The wealthiest ones spend their days stretched out naked on smooth slabs of rock, drowsing in the warmth of the sun. The men, who seem to prefer roaming among jagged outcrops and areas of extreme declivity, resent the indifference of their women toward them, but they do little about it and have no clear plan about how to change the situation. Every now and then, they will mount a feeble assault and throw stones at the recumbent women, but the stones usually fall short of their target.

For some time now, each newborn child has been drowned at birth.

On my arrival at the palace, I was greeted by the Princess of Bones and her retinue. She led me away from the latest skirmish into her garden, where she served me a bowl of apples and discussed the passions of her people. What new defiance were they preparing against the custodians of virtue? she asked. Although she spoke of grave matters, the princess did not seem perplexed or unduly alarmed. She laughed often, as though at some private joke, and went on fanning herself throughout our conversation with the bamboo fan that had been given to her as a girl, she said, by the ambassador of China. In the morning, she gave me provisions for my journey.

There are many villages, all of them ringing the tower in a series of eight concentric circles. From the shore, icebergs are always in sight.

The tower is said to be the oldest structure on the island, built in a time before memory. It is no longer inhabited, but legend tells that it was once a site of worship and that the oracles emitted there by the soothsayer Botana governed the Droons in their golden age.

I mounted my horse and decided to head for the hinterlands of the interior. After three days and three nights, I arrived at the village of Flom, where, I had been told, a new cult has infected the imaginations of the people and is threatening to destroy them. According to my source (a scribe at the palace), the contagion of self-loathing that is spreading among the citizens of Flom has reached such proportions that they have turned against their own bodies and seek to diminish them or disfigure them or render them useless in what the scribe called an *orgy of dismemberment*.

Orgy is not the word for it. *Orgy* suggests transport and ecstatic pleasure, but there is no pleasure among the people of Flom. They go about their business with the intense calm of religious zealots.

Once a day, a ceremony known as the Endurance is performed in the central square of the village. The participants wrap themselves tightly in gauze from head to toe, leaving only a small hole for the nostrils to prevent suffocation, and then four servants of those mummy-like figures are ordered to pull on the limbs of their master or mistress, to pull as energetically as possible for as long as possible. The test is to withstand the torture. In the event that a limb should be ripped off in the process, a great roar of exaltation rises up from the crowd. The Endurance has now been transformed into

what is known as the Transcending. The severed limbs are pre-
served in a glass case in the Town Hall and worshipped as sacred
objects. Amputees are accorded the privileges of royalty.

The new laws passed by the municipal government all reflect the
principles of the Transcending. Services to the community are
rewarded with painless amputations, whereas convicted criminals
are forced to submit to a lengthy operation, during which additional
body parts are sewn onto their flesh. For a first offense, it is usual
to attach a hand to the area around the stomach. For repeated
offenders, however, more humiliating punishments are prepared. I
once saw a man with the head of a young girl attached to his back.
Another had baby's feet sprouting from his palms. There are even
some who seem to be carrying around another entire body.

In their daily comings and goings, the people of Flom try to dis-
pel the fears one might associate with their precarious existence.
They are not inclined to forgetfulness—their anguish persists even
when no sign of it is visible to the naked eye. They have therefore
chosen to confront it and in that way overcome the obstacles that
have prevented them from knowing themselves. They make no
excuses for having transformed their solipsism into a fetish.

It is not merely their bodies that they wish to overcome but their
feeling of separateness from one another. One man put it to me
this way: "We can't seem to find a common ground. Each one of us
carries around his own world, which seldom overlaps with anyone
else's world. By reducing the size of our bodies, we hope to diminish
the spaces that lie between us. Remarkably enough, it is a proven
fact that amputees are more inclined to participate in the lives of
others than most four-limbed Flomians. Some have even been able to
marry. Perhaps when we shrink down to almost nothing, we will at
last find one another. Life is, after all, very difficult. Most of us die
here simply because we forget to breathe."

Including the time he spent pacing around the room between
paragraphs, along with the minutes lost in making a cup of instant coffee and retrieving a fresh pack of Camels from his overnight bag, it took
Ferguson a little under two hours to compose that preliminary draft.
When he had finished writing it, he put down his pencil and carefully
read over what he had done, sat back in the chair, paused for a while to

smoke and scratch and think, and then picked up his pencil and started writing the chapter again. Six versions and nine days later, only four sentences from the original draft remained.

ON THE WEDNESDAY before Thanksgiving, Ferguson went home for the first time in more than two months, traveling with Jim to the house on Woodhall Crescent as Amy made a similar journey from Boston, and there they were again, all five of them together for the long weekend, but beyond sitting down for the annual turkeyfest on Thursday afternoon, Ferguson spent little time at the house. Dan and his mother were so deeply married now, they were beginning to look like each other, he thought, but Amy had descended on them in a foul and contentious mood, and when Ferguson tried to buck up her spirits at the holiday dinner by reeling off a dozen of the newest tennis matches he had concocted with Howard (Arthur Dove versus Walter Pidgeon, John Locke versus Francis Scott Key, Charles Lamb versus Georges Poulet, Robert Byrd versus John Cage), all the others laughed, including Jim, who had already heard most of them twice, but Amy let out a prolonged groan and then tore into him for wasting his time on what she called *trivial, asinine, college-boy humor*. Didn't he know that America was fighting an illegal and immoral war? Didn't he know that black people were being gunned down and killed all across the country? And what gave him the right, Mr. Pampered Princeton Know-It-All, to ignore those injustices and fritter away his education by indulging in *dumb dormitory pranks*?

Ferguson gathered that Amy's romance with Freedom Summer hero Michael Morris was not going well or perhaps not going at all, but he held back from asking her about her love life and simply said: Yes, Amy, I agree with you. The world is a cesspool of shit and pain and horror, but if you're telling me you want to start a country where it's against the law to laugh, then I think I'd rather live somewhere else.

You're not listening to me, Amy said. Of course we need to laugh. If we didn't laugh, we'd probably all be dead within a year. It's just that your tennis matches aren't funny—and they don't make me laugh.

Dan told his daughter *to calm down and take it easy*. Jim told his sister to take an *anti-grumpus pill*, which he quickly amended to *an anti-pill pill*, and Ferguson's mother asked Amy if there was *something on her mind*, a question Amy answered by looking down at her napkin and chewing on her lower lip, and from that point on until the end of the meal Ferguson said almost nothing to anyone. After the pumpkin pie, they all went into the kitchen to wash dishes and scrub pots and pans together, and then Dan and Jim went into the living room to watch the news and the results of the Thanksgiving football games on TV while Amy and Ferguson's mother sat down at the kitchen table to have what Ferguson presumed would develop into *a serious heart-to-heart talk* about the thing that happened to be on Amy's mind (no doubt Michael Morris). It was a little past six o'clock. Ferguson went upstairs to use the telephone in the master bedroom, the only phone in the house that would give him the privacy to talk without being overheard. Evie had told him last weekend that she would be having Thanksgiving dinner with the Kaplans, the couple who lived next door to her and were her best friends in the neighborhood, but on the off chance that the party had broken up early, he called her house first. No answer. That would mean having to call the Kaplans, which in turn would oblige him to have a long talk with the Kaplan family member who happened to pick up the phone, either George or Nancy or one of their two college-age kids, Bob or Ellen, all of whom were Ferguson's friends, all of whom he normally would have been glad to talk to, but on that particular night he wanted to talk only to Evie.

Some of his best memories of growing up were connected to the Kaplans' house, which he had visited many times during his years in high school, the Friday and Saturday night gatherings in that two-story, sagging wooden structure crammed with thousands of overspill books from George's secondhand bookstore, often with Dana, often also with Mike Loeb and Amy, and on most of those evenings a small crowd of twelve or sixteen would be there, an unusual mix of adults and teenagers together, an even more unusual mix of white and black teenagers together, but that part of East Orange was more or less half white and half black by then, and because the Kaplans and Evie Monroe were ban-the-bomb-pro-integration leftists with no money and no intention of running away, and also because everyone who showed up there was nimble enough to joke about George's name and call him the Man Who Didn't Exist (a reference to the false name given to Cary Grant in *North by Northwest*—GEORGE KAPLAN), Ferguson sometimes thought of that house as the last outpost of sanity anywhere in America.

Bob was the one who picked up, which was a good thing for Ferguson, since Bob was the least talkative of the Kaplans and tended to have four things on his mind at once, so after a short conversation about the pluses and minuses of college and *the goddamn fucking mess in Vietnam* (Bob's words), the phone was passed to Evie.

What's up, Archie? she asked.

Nothing. I just want to see you.

Dessert begins in about ten minutes. Why not hop in your car and come over?

Just you. Alone.

Anything wrong?

Not really. A sudden need for air. Amy's in one of her grand snits, the guys are talking football, and I'm hankering to see you.

That's nice, *hankering*.

I don't think I've ever used that word before, not once in my whole life.

Nancy has a headache, and George seems to be coming down with the flu, so I doubt this thing will go on much longer. I should be home in about an hour.

You don't mind?

No, of course not. I'd love to see you.

Good. I'll be at your place in an hour.

It was no secret that they were fond of each other, that the eighteen-year-old Ferguson and the thirty-one-year-old Evie Monroe had long since moved beyond the teacher-student formalities of the classroom. They were friends now, good friends, possibly the best of friends, but along with their friendship there had been a growing physical attraction on both sides, which had remained a secret to everyone, even to themselves at first, the unbidden lustful thoughts that neither one of them was prepared to act on out of fear or inhibition, but then came the disinhibiting effect of one too many scotches on a Thursday night in mid-August, and from one moment to the next the tamped-down flames of their mutual attraction combusted into a savage necking binge on the sofa in the downstairs parlor, the love play that was interrupted in mid-squeeze by the ringing doorbell, a notable event not only because of its ferocity but because it had taken place during the time of Ed, albeit toward the end of the time of Ed, and now that Ed was gone and Dana Rosenbloom was gone and Celia Federman was no more than a figment on the far horizon and neither Ferguson nor Evie had touched anyone for longer than he or she cared to remember, it seemed almost inevitable that they should want to touch each other again on that chilly Thanksgiving night. No alcohol was necessary this time. Ferguson's unexpected use of the word *hankering* had thrust them back into a memory of that Thursday evening in August when the thing they had started had not been finished, and so it was that when Ferguson arrived at Evie's half of the two-family house on Warrington Place, they went upstairs to the bedroom, gradually removed their clothes, and made a long, happy night of finishing off what they had started at last.

IT WAS SERIOUS. Not a one-time fling to be forgotten in the morning— but the beginning of something, the first step of many steps to follow. Ferguson didn't care that she was older than he was, he didn't care if anyone knew about them, he didn't care if people talked. However *inappropriate* it might have been for a thirty-one-year-old woman to be carrying on with an eighteen-year-old boy, there was nothing the law could do about it, since Ferguson was past the age of consent and they were aboveboard and absolutely untouchable. If society looked upon what they were doing as wrong, then society could go on looking at them and lump it.

It wasn't just the sex, although the sex was a large part of it, as much for the still young Evie as for the sex-deprived Ferguson, who walked around with the permanent hard-on of all young men and couldn't get enough, the two of them trapped by the need to enfold themselves in each other and tangle up their arms and legs in frantic surges of carnal oblivion, florid, demonstrative sex that emptied them out and left them gasping for air, or else the long, slow arousals of touching skin as softly and delicately as possible and waiting until they couldn't wait anymore, the generosity of it all, the alternating sweetness and violence of it all, and because Ferguson's erotic history had been limited to only one other bed partner so far, the slender, light-boned Dana with her small breasts and narrow hips, the larger, more substantial Evie presented him with a new form of womanhood that was both thrilling and strange at first, then thrilling and not strange, then strange all over again because everything about sex was strange. That first of all, but by no means all of it. The bond of bodies. Bucking bodies and languid bodies, warm bodies and hot bodies, buttocks bodies, moist bodies, cock and pussy bodies, neck bodies and shoulder bodies, finger bodies and fingering bodies, hand and lip bodies, licking bodies, and always and ever face bodies, their two faces looking at each other both in and out of bed, and no, Evie's face was not beautiful, it could not be judged as even vaguely pretty by whatever standards were in force that year, too much nose, an angular Italian phiz with too many angles in it, but what eyes to look at him with, burning brown eyes that bored clear into him and never flinched or faked a feeling that wasn't there, and the charm of her slightly crooked two front teeth, which gave her the smallest hint of an overbite and turned her mouth into the sexiest mouth anywhere in America, and best of all he got to spend the night with her, which had not been possible with Dana more than two or three times, but now it was every time, and the prospect of waking up in the morning next to Evie helped him to fall into the profoundest, most blissful slumbers he had ever known.

They saw each other on the weekends, every weekend in New York until his grandfather returned from Florida in early April, and Ferguson's already split life was now spent jumping across an ever-growing void between campus and city, five nights a week in one place, two nights a week in the other, schoolwork and classes from Monday morning to Friday morning with no time for Mulligan because he was a Walt Whitman scholar and wasn't allowed to fuck up, and therefore it was imperative that he finish all Princeton obligations before he left for the city at noon on Friday (reading assignments, papers, studying for tests, discussing Zeno and Heraclitus with Howard), and then he would return to the other half of his double life in New York, which meant Evie from the moment she rang the doorbell on Friday between six and seven, Mulligan during the Friday hours before she showed up, Mulligan for four hours on Saturday and Sunday mornings as Evie corrected papers, read books, and prepared her classes for the week, then lunch and out into the city together, followed by Saturday nights with his friends or her friends or just the two of them at films, plays, concerts, or in the apartment rolling around on the bed, and the second half of their truncated Sundays as they returned to the quiet of the bedroom after brunch, talking or not talking until four, five, or six, when they would finally force themselves to put on their clothes and Evie would drive him down to Penn Station. That was always the worst part of it—saying good-bye, and then the train ride back to Princeton on Sunday evening. No matter how many times he made that trip, he never got used to it.

She was the only person who had read every story he had written in the past three years. She was the only person he had ever opened up to about the self-lacerating restrictions he had imposed on himself after Artie Federman's death. She was the only person who understood the depth of the bitterness he felt toward his father. She was the only person who fully grasped the nature of the havoc roiling inside him, the contradictory muddle of hard, unforgiving judgments and raging contempt for big-dollar American greed combined with an overall gentleness of spirit, his unstinting love for the people he cared about, his good-boy rectitude and out-of-step clumsiness with his own heart. Evie knew him better than anyone else. She knew how exceptionally odd he was and yet how breathtakingly normal he appeared to be, as if he were an extraterrestrial who had just landed in his flying saucer, she said to him one night back in July (before the incident with the doorbell, before they even suspected they would wind up going to bed together), a man from outer space dressed in the same clothes as any other twentieth-century Earthling, *the most dangerous spy in the universe*, and the exceptionally odd person with the normal exterior had been oddly comforted by her words, for that was precisely how he wanted to think of himself, and it was gratifying to think she was the only one who knew it.

They weren't as brave as he had been expecting them to be, however. The all-public, who-gives-a-damn approach to what they were doing could not work without certain exceptions, for it quickly became apparent that some people would have to be kept in the dark for their own good—and for Ferguson and Evie's good as well. In Ferguson's case, that meant his mother, and because of his mother, it also meant Dan, Amy, and Jim. In Evie's case, that meant her mother in the Bronx, her brother and his wife in Queens, and her sister and her husband in Manhattan. All of her relatives would be *scandalized*, Evie said, and while Ferguson didn't think his mother's response would be as strong as that, she was bound to be upset, or worried, or confused, and it wouldn't be worth the trouble to explain himself to her, since all his justifications would probably leave her only more upset, more worried, or more confused. With Evie's friends in Manhattan, on the other hand, there were no impediments to full exposure. They were actors, jazz musicians, and journalists, and they were all sophisticated enough not to care. The same held true for Ferguson's smaller collection of New York acquaintances (why would Ron Pearson care?), but Noah was a potential stumbling block, in that he was more than just a friend but Ferguson's cousin by marriage, and although it seemed unlikely that Noah would ever have a reason to talk to his father about his cousin's love life, there was always a chance that it could slip out at some unguarded moment while Mildred happened to be eavesdropping in the next room, but that was a chance he would have to take, Ferguson decided, since Noah's friendship was too important to him, and he trusted Noah enough to be able to count on his silence if he asked him to be silent, which Noah did, did without hesitation the moment he was asked, and as young Marx raised his right arm and solemnly promised *to keep his trap shut*, he congratulated Ferguson on having won the affections of an older woman. When Ferguson introduced them for the first time, Noah shook Evie's hand and said, The famous Mrs. Monroe at last. Archie's been talking about you for years, and now I see why. Some men have the hots for Marilyn, even though she's no longer with us, but for Archie it's always been Evelyn, and who can blame him for having the hots for you?

And who can blame me for having the hots for Archie? Evie said. It all works out rather beautifully, doesn't it?

Two weeks after that night, Evie opened the door of her soul and let Ferguson in.

It was another Saturday, another one of the good Saturdays in the middle of another one of their good weekends in New York, and they had just returned to the apartment on West Fifty-eighth Street from a small dinner with some of Evie's musician friends. Rather than go straight to the bedroom as they normally did after their Saturday night outings, Evie took Ferguson's hand and led him into the living room, saying there was something she wanted to talk to him about first, and so they sat down on the couch together, Ferguson lit up a Camel, passed the cigarette to Evie, who took one drag and gave it back to Ferguson, and then she said:

Something has happened to me, Archie. Something big. I was supposed to have my period on Monday, but it didn't come. Most of the time, I'm right on schedule, but every now and then I might be off by a

day or half a day, so I didn't think much about it, assuming it would
come on Tuesday, but nothing happened on Tuesday either. Exceptional.
Almost unprecedented. Deeply curious. In the past, that would be the
moment when I'd start to panic, wondering if I was pregnant or not,
playing out the grim possibilities in my head, since I've never wanted
to be pregnant, or at least I don't think I have, and I suppose the two
abortions prove that—one in my sophomore year at Vassar, one about a
year after Bobby and I were married. But now, and by now I mean Tuesday, four days ago, with my period two days late, for the first time in
my life I wasn't worried. What if I'm pregnant? I asked myself. Would
it matter? No, I answered myself, it wouldn't matter. It would be pretty
damned terrific. Never in my life, Archie—never once have I had that
thought and said those words to myself. Wednesday. Still no blood. Not
only was I not worried anymore, I felt on top of the world.

And? Ferguson asked.

And Thursday it was over. The whole world poured out of me, and
I'm still bleeding as if I'd been stabbed in the gut. I mean, you know that.
You slept with me last night.

Yes, there was a lot of blood. More than usual. Not that I cared, of
course.

Not that I cared either. But the important thing is this, Archie:
Something has happened to me. I'm different now.

Are you sure?

Yes, absolutely sure. I want to have a baby.

It took a while before Ferguson understood what she was talking
about, the mountain of unexplained particulars and daunting questions
such as who would be the father of that child, and how did she propose
to become a mother without being married, and, if she wasn't married
or living with someone, how could she go on teaching and be a mother
at the same time if she didn't have the money to pay for a nurse or baby-
sitter?

Evie deflected those questions by taking him on a short tour of her
inner life, with a heavy emphasis on the love and sex part of that life,
the boys and men she had fallen for over the years between girlhood
and now, the good and bad decisions she had made, the ephemeral
dalliances and longer commitments that had all come to nothing in the
end, the worst mistake being her impossible early marriage to Bobby
Monroe, which had lasted all of two and a half years, and the surpris-

ing thing about those passions and hopes and disappointments, Evie said, was that no one had ever made her happier than he did, her boy-man Archie, her irreplaceable Archie, and for the first time in her life she was with someone she felt she could trust, someone she could love without simultaneously dreading the moment when she would be slapped down for loving too hard or too much. No, Archie, she said, you're not like any of the others. You're the first man who isn't afraid of me. It's a remarkable thing, really, and I'm trying to live it as fully as I can, because deep down you know and I know that it isn't going to last.

Not last? Ferguson said. How can you say that?

Because it can't. Because it won't. Because you're still too young, and sooner or later we won't be right for each other anymore.

That was the nub of it, Ferguson realized, the anticipation of a time when they would no longer be together, a future time when all that was happening now would disappear and they would be turned into memory-ghosts living on in each other's minds, insubstantial beings without skin or bones or hearts, and that was why she was thinking about babies now and wanted one of her own—because of him, because she wanted him to be the father, a ghost-father who would bequeath his body to her child and go on living with her forever.

It made sense. And then again, it made no sense at all.

It wasn't anything urgent, she said, and it wasn't anything she wanted him to think about very often, simply that the possibility would be there now, a thing to tuck away in the back of their heads and then go on as before, and no, she wasn't asking him to take any responsibility, he wouldn't even have to sign the birth certificate if he didn't want to, it would be her job and not his, and thank God women didn't have to be married in order to have children, she said, and then she started to laugh, to let loose with the big laugh of someone who had made up her mind and was no longer afraid of anything.

THEY WENT ON as before. The only difference was that Evie left her diaphragm at home and Ferguson stopped buying condoms.

He wasn't disturbed by the thought of becoming a father, just as he hadn't been disturbed by the thought of becoming a husband when he proposed to Dana. What did disturb him was the thought of losing Evie. Now that she had made her pessimistic declaration about their eventual demise as a couple, he was determined to prove her wrong. However, if time should prove her right, then he would follow her example and try to make the most of the time they still had together by *living it as fully as he could.*

It was possible that he was no longer thinking clearly, but it didn't feel that way to Ferguson. His eyes were open, and the world was teeming around him.

Months passed.

He wrote the twenty-fourth chapter of *Mulligan's Travels*, an account of Mulligan's strenuous journey home from a country in the midst of a three-pronged civil war. Ferguson's book was finished, all one hundred and thirty-one double-spaced pages of it, but rather than burn the manuscript as he had been planning to do, he dug into his savings and shelled out the irrational sum of one hundred and fifty dollars to hire a professional typist to make three copies for him (an original plus two carbons), which he then gave as presents to Evie, Howard, and Noah. They all professed to like it. That reassured Ferguson, but he was sick of Mulligan by then and was already dreaming about his next project, a risky venture called *The Scarlet Notebook.*

Celia Federman was accepted by Barnard and NYU and would be starting Barnard in the fall, with the intention of majoring in biology. Ferguson sent her a bouquet of white roses. They still talked on the phone from time to time, but after Bruce and Evie came into their lives, there had been no more Saturdays in New York.

Howard and Ferguson decided to go on rooming together until the end of college. Next year, they would be taking their meals at the Woodrow Wilson Club, which was not an eating club but rather an anti-eating club for students who didn't want to join a club. Some of the smartest undergraduates ate there. The cozy dining room had about twenty small tables for four people each, which made it a kind of anti-cafeteria cafeteria, and one of the good things about it was that professors often came to give informal talks after dessert. Howard and Ferguson were planning to invite Nagle to discuss one of their best-loved fragments from Heraclitus: *If you do not hope, you will never stumble upon the unhoped for, which is sealed off and impenetrable.*

Noah informed him that he was planning to spend the summer working on his long-deferred idea of adapting *Sole Mates* into a short black-and-white film. When Ferguson told him not to waste his time on that juvenile rot, Noah said, Too late, Archibald, I've already written the script, and the sixteen-millimeter camera is on loan for a total of zero cents.

Jim was questioning his future in the Princeton Physics Department, and after months of *doubt and inner struggle* he had more or less decided to stop after his masters and become a high school science teacher. I'm not the hotshot I thought I was, he said, and I don't want to spend my life as a second-rate assistant working in someone else's lab. Besides, he and his girlfriend Nancy wanted to get married, and that meant he would have to find a real job with a real salary and become a full-fledged member of the real world. Ferguson and Jim postponed their plans to walk to Cape Cod, but when Easter vacation rolled around in April, they made the trek from Princeton to Woodhall Crescent on foot, about thirty-five miles in a straight line on the map but over forty on Jim's pedometer. Just to see if they could do it. Of course it rained that day, and of course they were soaked by the time they walked up the front steps of the house and rang the bell.

Amy joined SDS and found herself a new boyfriend, a fellow fresh-man from Brandeis who happened to come from Newark and also happened to be black. Luther Bond. What a good name, Ferguson thought, as Amy told it to him over the phone, but what about your father, he asked, does he know anything about it yet? No, of course not, Amy said, are you kidding? Don't worry, Ferguson said, Dan isn't like that, he won't care. Amy grunted. Don't bet on it, she said. And when do I get to meet him? Ferguson asked. Anytime you like, Amy said, any-where you like, just as long as the place isn't Woodhall Crescent.

His grandfather returned from Florida with a deep tan, a dozen more pounds around his middle, and a crazy look in his eyes, which led Ferguson to wonder what naughty things the old man had been up to with the lotus-eaters in the Sunshine State. Nothing he wanted to hear about, that much was certain, and because his grandfather was on the list of relatives who had to be kept in the dark about his affair with Evie, the moment Benjy Adler returned to his New York apartment, their New York idyll came to an end. West Fifty-eighth Street was off-limits now, and with no substitute apartment available to them anywhere in the city, the only solution was to forget New York and spend those days and nights at Evie's half-house in East Orange. It was a hard adjustment. No more plays or movies or dinners with friends, just the two of them together now for fifty uninterrupted hours every weekend, but what other choice did they have? They talked about renting a small studio apartment somewhere downtown, a cheap place that would give the city back to them without having to depend on wayward grandfathers or anyone else, but even cheap was more than they could afford.

THE DELAYED PERIOD in December, followed by clockwork blood flow in January, February, March, and April. Evie had told Ferguson not to think about it *very often,* but he suspected she was thinking about it a good deal more than very often, as many as fifty or sixty times a day, and after four months of no conception, of no sperm cell attaching itself to an ovum, of no zygote or blastula or embryo taking root in Evie's body, she was beginning to exhibit signs of frustration. Ferguson told her not to worry, that these things often took time, and to underscore his point he mentioned the two long years it had taken his mother to become pregnant with him. He was only trying to help, but the thought of those *two years* was more than Evie could handle, and she shouted back at him: Are you out of your mind, Archie? What makes you think we have *two years*? We probably don't have two months!

Four days later, she went to see her gynecologist for a thorough examination of her reproductive organs and to have blood drawn for detailed tests pertaining to her other organs as well. When the results came back on Thursday, she called Ferguson at Princeton and announced: I'm as healthy as an eighteen-year-old girl.

That begged the question: Was the nineteen-year-old Ferguson as healthy as an eighteen-year-old boy?

It can't be me, he said. It's not possible.

Nevertheless, Evie prevailed upon him to see a doctor—*just in case.*

Ferguson was scared. The idea of trying to plant a baby inside Evie was probably a foolish one, he admitted to himself, an act of unthinking love and misunderstood male pride that could lead to all sorts of wretched consequences in the long run, but whether he and Evie managed or didn't manage to have a baby together was not what concerned him now. It was his own life, his own life and his own future that were at stake. Ever since he was a small boy, ever since the moment when his young boy self had understood the mysterious fact that he was a transitional creature who was destined to grow up and become a man, he had assumed he would become a father one day, that he would eventually produce little Fergusons who would grow up to become men and women themselves, a daydream he had always taken for granted as a future reality because that was how the world worked, little people developed into big people who in turn brought more little people into the world, and once you were old enough to do that, that was what you did. Even now, as a world-weary nineteen-year-old philosopher and defender of obscure books, it was something he continued to look forward to with great relish.

NEVER HAD JERKING off been less enjoyable than on the day he went to Dr. Breuler's office on the outskirts of Princeton. Spilling his seed into a sanitized cup and then crossing his fingers that millions of potential babies were waltzing around in the slime. How many drunken sailors could dance on the head of a pin? How many pins did you need to hold yourself together?

The nurse scheduled a return visit for the following week.

When he showed up on the appointed day, Dr. Breuler said: Let's do it one more time, just to make sure we know what we're looking at.

The following week, when Ferguson returned for his third visit to the office, Dr. Breuler told him it was a condition that affected only seven percent of the male population, but a lower than normal sperm count seriously compromised a man's ability to father a child, that is, fewer than fifteen million sperm per milliliter of semen or a total count of fewer than thirty-nine million per ejaculate, and Ferguson's numbers were considerably below that.

Is there anything to be done? Ferguson asked.

No, I'm afraid not, Dr. Breuler said.

In other words, I'm sterile.

In the sense of not being able to produce children, yes.

It was time for Ferguson to go, but his body had begun to feel so heavy to him that he knew it would be impossible to lift himself out of the chair. He looked up and smiled wanly at Dr. Breuler, as if to apologize for not being able to move.

Don't worry, the doctor said. In all other respects, you're in perfect shape.

His life was only just getting started, Ferguson said to himself, his life hadn't even begun, and the most essential part of him was already dead.

The Fall of the House of Ferguson.

No one, not one other ever to follow him, no one now or ever until the end of time.

A fall to the rank of footnote in *The Book of Terrestrial Life,* a man forever after to be known as *The Last of the Fergusons.*

6.1

LATER ON, WHICH IS TO SAY ONE AND TWO AND THREE YEARS LATER, whenever Ferguson looked back and thought about the things that happened between the fall of 1966 and Amy's graduation at the beginning of June 1968, several events dominated his recollections, standing out vividly in spite of the time that had passed, whereas many others, if not most others, had been reduced to shadows: a mental painting composed of several areas bathed in an intense, clarifying light and other areas occluded by dimness, shapeless figures standing in murky brown corners of the canvas, and here and there splotches of all-black nothingness, the blackout dark of the black dormitory elevator.

The three other people who shared the apartment with them, for example, fellow students named Melanie, Fred, and Stu the first year, Alice, Alex, and Fred the second year, had no role to play in the story. They came and went, they read their books and cooked their meals, they slept in their beds and said hello when they popped out of the bathroom in the morning, but Ferguson barely took note of them and had trouble remembering their faces from one day to the next. Or the dreaded two-year science requirement, which he finally started tackling as a sophomore, enrolling in a course mockingly referred to as Physics for Poets and cutting nearly every class, completing his fake lab reports in a mad weekend rush with the help of one of Amy's math friends from Barnard—a matter of no importance. Even his decision not to join the managing board of the *Spectator* did not weigh heavily in the narrative. It was a question of the hours, nothing more than that, nothing to do with a lack of interest, but Friedman, Mullhouse, Branch, and the others were putting in fifty- and sixty-hour weeks at the paper, and that was more than Ferguson was willing to commit himself to. Not one member of the board had a girlfriend—no time for love. Not one of them was writing or translating poetry—no time for literature. Not one of them was on top of his course work—no time for studying. Ferguson had already decided to go on with journalism after he graduated from college, but for now he needed Amy and his poets and his seminars on Montaigne and Milton, so he compromised by staying on as a reporter and associate member of the board, reporting much during those years and doing his once-a-week stint as the night man, which entailed going to the office at Ferris Booth Hall and composing headlines for the articles that would be printed in tomorrow morning's paper, running the finished articles up to Angelo the typesetter on the fourth floor, retrieving the columns of type, pasting up the issue on boards, and then cabbing out to Brooklyn at around two A.M. to hand the boards to the printer, who would produce twenty thousand copies, which would be delivered to the Columbia campus by midmorning. It was a process Ferguson enjoyed taking part in, but neither that nor his decision not to join the board was of any significance in the long run.

What counted, on the other hand, was that both of his grandparents died during those years, his grandfather in December 1966 (heart attack) and his grandmother in December 1967 (stroke).

What also counted was the Six-Day War (June 1967), but it came and went too quickly to count for much, while the race riots that broke out in Newark the following month, which lasted no longer than the war in the Middle East had, changed everything forever. One minute, his parents were celebrating the victory of the tiny, gallant Jews over their gargantuan enemies, and the next minute Sam Brownstein's store on Springfield Avenue had been smashed and looted and Ferguson's parents were folding up their tent and escaping into the desert, not just leaving Newark and New Jersey behind them but going all the way down to southern Florida by the end of the year.

Another illuminated spot on the canvas: April 1968 and the explosion at Columbia, the revolution at Columbia, the *eight days that shook the world.*

All the rest of the light in the painting shone on Amy. Darkness above and below her, darkness behind her, darkness on either side of her, but Amy enveloped in light, a light so strong that it nearly made her invisible.

FALL 1966. AFTER attending more than a dozen SDS meetings, after taking part in a three-day hunger strike on the steps of Low Library in early November to protest the killing in Vietnam, after trying to get her points across in numerous conversations with her fellow members at the West End, the Hungarian Pastry Shop, and the College Inn, Amy was growing disenchanted. They don't listen to me, she said to Ferguson, as the two of them were brushing their teeth one night before going to bed. I stand up to speak, and they all look down at the floor, or else they interrupt and don't let me finish, or else they let me finish and don't say anything afterward, and then, fifteen minutes later, one of the guys stands up and says almost exactly what I just said, sometimes using the same words, and everyone applauds. They're bullies, Archie.

All of them?

No, not all of them. My friends from the ICV are okay, although I wish they'd back me more, but the ones from the PL faction are insufferable. Especially Mike Loeb, the leader of the pack. He cuts me off constantly, shouts me down, insults me. He thinks women in the movement should be making coffee for the men or handing out leaflets on rainy days, but otherwise we should keep our mouths shut.

Mike Loeb. He's been in a couple of my classes. Another boy from the Jersey suburbs, I'm sorry to say. One of those self-anointed geniuses who has an answer for everything. Mr. Certain in a plaid lumberjack shirt. A bore.

The funny thing is, he went to the same high school as Mark Rudd. Now they're together again in SDS, and they barely talk to each other.

Because Mark is an idealist and Mike is a fanatic.

He thinks the revolution is coming within the next five years.

Fat chance.

The problem is that the men outnumber the women by about twelve to one. We're too small, and it's easy to discount us.

Why not break away and form your own group?

You mean, quit SDS?

You don't have to quit. Just stop going to the meetings.

And?

And you become the first president of Barnard Women for Peace and Justice.

What a thought.

You don't like it?

We'd be marginalized. The big issues are all university issues, national issues, world issues, and twenty braless girls marching around with anti-war posters wouldn't have much of an effect.

What if there were a hundred of you?

There aren't. We just don't have enough people to get noticed. For better or worse, I think I'm stuck.

DECEMBER 1966. NOT only was the heart attack that killed Ferguson's grandfather unexpected (his cardiograms had been holding steady for years, his blood pressure was normal), but the manner of his death was an embarrassment to everyone in the family, a disgrace. It wasn't that his wife or daughters or sons-in-law or grandson were unaware of his penchant for skirt chasing, his long fascination with extramarital thrills, but not one of them suspected that the seventy-three-year-old Benjy Adler would go so far as to rent an apartment for a woman less than half his age and keep her as his full-time, live-in mistress. Didi Bryant was just thirty-four. She had been hired as a secretary at Gersh, Adler, and Pomerantz in 1962, and after she had been working there for eight months Ferguson's grandfather decided that he loved her, decided that no matter what the cost he must and would possess her, and when the sweet, curvy, Nebraska-born Didi Bryant told him she was willing to be possessed, the cost included the monthly rent for a one-bedroom apartment on East Sixty-third Street between Lexington and Park, sixteen pairs of shoes, twenty-seven dresses, six coats, one diamond bracelet, one gold bracelet, one pearl necklace, eight pairs of earrings, and one mink stole. The affair lasted approximately three years (quite happily, according to Didi Bryant), and then, on a frigid afternoon in early December, at an hour when Ferguson's grandfather was supposedly at his office on West Fifty-seventh Street, he walked over to Didi's place on East Sixty-third, climbed into bed with her, and suffered the immense coronary infarction that killed him just as he was ejaculating for the last time in his eventful, sloppily managed, mostly enjoyable life. *La petite mort* and *la grande mort* within ten seconds of each other—coming and going in the space of three short breaths.

It was, to be sure, an awkward business, a complex business. The horrified Didi pinned under the weight of her corpulent lover, staring at the top of his bald head and the few strands of hair that remained around the temples, which were dyed brown (O, the vanity of old men), extricating herself out from under the corpse and then calling for an ambulance, which conveyed her and the shrouded body of Ferguson's grandfather to Lenox Hill Hospital, where, at 3:52 P.M., Benjamin Adler was pronounced dead on arrival, and then the poor, shaken Didi had to call Ferguson's grandmother, who knew nothing about the young woman's existence, and tell her to come to the hospital right away because there had been an *accident*.

The funeral was restricted to the immediate family. No Gershes or Pomerantzes were invited, no friends, no business associates, not even Ferguson's great-aunt and great-uncle from California (his grand-mother's older brother, Saul, and his Scottish wife, Marjorie). The scandal had to be suppressed, and a large public gathering would have been too much for his grandmother to cope with, so just eight people made the trip out to the cemetery in Woodbridge, New Jersey, to attend his grandfather's burial: Ferguson and his parents, Amy, Great-aunt Pearl, Aunt Mildred and Uncle Henry (who had flown in from Berkeley the day before), and Ferguson's grandmother. They listened to the rabbi recite the Kaddish, they tossed dirt onto the pine box in the grave, and then they returned to the apartment on West Fifty-eighth Street for lunch, after which they repaired to the living room and spread out into three separate groups, three separate conversations that went on until it was well past dark: Amy on the sofa with Aunt Mildred and Uncle Henry, Ferguson's father and Great-aunt Pearl in the armchairs across from the sofa, and Ferguson at the little table in the alcove by the front windows with his mother and grandmother. For once, his grandmother did most of the talking. After all the years of sitting in silence while her husband held forth with his nonstop jokes and rambling stories, it was as if she were finally claiming her right to speak for herself, and what she said that afternoon astonished Ferguson, not only because the words them-selves were astonishing but because it was astonishing to learn how thoroughly he had misjudged her all his life.

The first astonishment was that she bore no resentment against Didi Bryant, whom she described as *that pretty girl in tears*. And how brave of her, his grandmother said, not to have run off and *disappeared into the night*, as most people in her situation would have done, but this girl was different, she had stuck around the lobby of the hospital until THE WIFE showed up and had not been embarrassed to talk about her affair with Benjy or how fond of him she had been or what a sad, sad thing it was that had just happened. Rather than blame Didi for Benjy's death, Ferguson's grandmother pitied her and called her *a good person*, and at one point, when Didi broke down and started to sob (this was the second astonishment), she had said to her: *Don't cry, dear. I'm sure you made him happy, and my Benjy was a man who needed to be happy.*

There was something heroic in that response, Ferguson felt, a depth of human understanding that overturned everything he had ever thought about his grandmother until that moment, and then she shifted slightly in her chair and looked directly at his mother, her eyes tearing up for the first time all day, and a moment later she was talking about things no one from her generation ever talked about, flatly asserting that she had failed her husband, that she had been a bad wife to him because the physical part of marriage had never interested her, she had found sexual intercourse painful and unpleasant, and after the girls were born she had told Benjy that she couldn't do it anymore, or only every now and then as a favor to him, and what could you expect, she asked Ferguson's mother, of course Benjy chased after other women, he was a man with *large appetites*, and how could she hold that against him when she had let him down and done such a miserable job in the bed department? In every other way she had loved him, for forty-seven years he was the only man in her life, *and believe me, Rose, not for one minute did I ever feel he didn't love me back.*

JUNE 1967. IT all came down to a question of money. When Ferguson's mother told him in late January that his father was covering the costs of Columbia and the apartment and the food, books, and extras allowance by cashing in portions of his life insurance policy every six months, Ferguson understood that he would have to start contributing something more than the minimum-wage crumbs he had been given as a bookstore clerk last summer, that he owed it to his parents to kick in whatever additional amounts he could earn as a gesture of good faith, of thanks.

Amy already had a job lined up for the summer. At the post-funeral lunch in his grandparents' apartment, she had spent several hours talking to Aunt Mildred and Uncle Henry. Henry the historian and Amy the history student had hit it off particularly well, and when Ferguson's uncle told her about the project he was planning to begin in June (a study of the American labor movement), Amy had jumped in with so many *interesting questions* (according to Henry) that she suddenly found herself being offered a summer job as a research assistant. The job was in Berkeley, of course, and now that Amy would be going there at the end of the spring semester, it naturally followed that Ferguson would go with her. All through the winter and early spring, they talked about it as their next big *foreign adventure*—another France, but this time traveling abroad in their own country. Train, plane, or bus, chancing it in the old Impala, hitchhiking, or one of those drive-away jobs to transport someone's car to another city: those were the options before them, and the trick was to figure out which one would cost the least. Still, it was essential that he find a job in Berkeley before he went out there, the whole project was contingent on his having work, and he couldn't afford to waste time looking for something after he arrived. Aunt Mildred promised to help, she assured him that jobs were plentiful and there would be no problem, but when he wrote to her at the end of March and again in the middle of April, her replies were so obscure, so devoid of details that he was almost certain she had forgotten to look for him, or hadn't yet started to look, or had no intention of looking until he was on his way to California. Then an opportunity presented itself to him in New York, a good opportunity, and in spite of the disappointment it caused him, he felt he couldn't turn it down without risking a summer with no job at all. Strangely enough, it was a job almost identical to Amy's, which somehow made the situation even worse, as if he had been turned into the butt of someone's warped idea of how to tell a bad joke. Ferguson's CC professor for the spring term had been commissioned to write a history of Columbia from its founding to the celebration of its two hundredth anniversary (1754 to 1954), and he was looking for a research assistant to help him *get the book off the ground*. Ferguson didn't have to apply for the post. Andrew Fleming offered it to him because he was impressed by the twenty-year-old's work in class and by his

ability to write—not just his academic papers but his news articles and
poetry translations as well. Ferguson was flattered by those generous
remarks, but it was the salary that clinched it, two hundred dollars a
week (funded by a grant from the university), which meant he would
accumulate over two thousand dollars by the time the fall semester
began, and just like that he wasn't going to California anymore. Little
matter that the tubby fifty-two-year-old Fleming was a life-long bachelor who took a serious interest in young men. Ferguson never doubted
that the professor had a crush on him—but it was nothing he couldn't
handle, and nothing to prevent him from accepting the job.

He wrote to Aunt Mildred one last time in early May, hoping that
something had finally turned up in Berkeley that would allow him to
back out of his handshake agreement with Fleming before he started
the job, but two weeks went by without an answer, and when he finally
splurged on the cost of a long-distance call to California, his aunt claimed
she hadn't received the letter. Ferguson suspected she was lying, but he
couldn't voice his suspicions without proof, and what difference did it
make anyway? Mildred hadn't set out to sabotage his plan, she was lazy,
that was all, she had let the matter slide, and now it was too late to do
anything about it, and his once doting aunt of the one and only Archie
had let him down.

Amy was miserable. Ferguson was in despair. The thought of being
separated from each other for two and a half months was too horrible
even to talk about, and yet neither one of them could see a way around
the problem. Amy said she admired him for *acting like a grown-up* (even
if he sensed that she was a little angry at him as well), and while Ferguson was tempted to ask her to cancel the trip and stay behind in New
York, he knew it would have been presumptuous and wrong of him to
do that, so he never asked. The Six-Day War broke out on June fifth, and
one day after it ended Amy took off for Berkeley on her own. Her parents had given her the money for a plane ticket, and Ferguson rode out
to the airport with them on the morning she left. An awkward, unhappy
farewell. No tears or grand gestures, but a long, solemn hug followed
by a promise to write to each other as often as possible. Back in his room
on West 111th Street, Ferguson sat down on the bed and looked at the
wall in front of him. He heard an infant crying in the next apartment,
he heard a man shouting *Fuck* at someone down on the sidewalk five
stories below, and all at once he realized that he had made the worst

mistake of his life. Job or no job—he should have gone with her and played out whatever hand he was dealt. That was how you were supposed to live, that was the leaping sort of life he wanted for himself, *a life that danced,* but he had chosen duty over adventure, responsibility to his parents over his love for Amy, and he hated himself for his cautiousness, for his stick-in-the-mud plodder's heart. Money. Always money. Always not enough money. For the first time in his life, he began to wonder how it would feel to have been born stinking rich.

Another summer in hot New York with the crazy people and the radios, listening to the snoring and farting of the subtenant in Amy's room next door as he lay in his bed at night, sweating, sweating through his shirts and socks every day by noon and walking down the streets with his fists clenched, a knifepoint mugging every other hour in the neighborhood now, four women raped in the elevators of their buildings, be prepared, keep your eyes open, and try not to breathe when you walked past a garbage can. Long days in the million-book Parthenon replica called Butler Library, taking notes on prerevolutionary Columbia, then known as King's College, and the living conditions of mid-eighteenth-century New York (pigs running through the streets, horse shit everywhere), the first college in the state, the fifth college anywhere in the country, John Jay, Alexander Hamilton, Gouverneur Morris, Robert Livingston, first chief justice of the Supreme Court, first secretary of the Treasury, author of the final draft of the U.S. Constitution, member of the five-man committee that composed the first draft of the Declaration of Independence, the Founding Fathers as young men, as boys, as toddlers running through the streets with the pigs and horses, and then home after five or six hours in musty Butler to type up his notes for Fleming, whom he met with twice a week in the air-conditioned West End, always there and never in Fleming's office or apartment, for even if the kind, decorous, deeply intelligent historian never laid a hand on Ferguson, his eyes were on him continually, searching for a sign of encouragement or some glance of reciprocal longing, and that was enough to contend with, Ferguson felt, since he liked Fleming and couldn't help feeling sorry for him.

Meanwhile, Amy was in hippie-land three thousand miles to the west, Amy was in the Garden of Eden, Amy was roaming down Telegraph Avenue in Berkeley during the Summer of Love, and Ferguson read and reread her letters as often as he could in order to go on

hearing her voice, carrying them to the library with him every morning to use as anti-boredom pills whenever his work threatened to put
him into a coma, and the letters he wrote back to her were light and
fast and as funny as he could make them, with no talk about the war or
the rancid smells in the streets or the women raped in elevators or the
gloom that had settled in his heart. *You seem to be having the time of your
life*, he wrote in one of the forty-two letters he sent to her that summer.
Back here in New York, I'm having the life of my times.

July 1967. In Ferguson's opinion, the saddest part of the sad Newark
riots was that nothing could have stopped them from happening.
Unlike most large events that occurred in the world, which also might
not have occurred if people had been thinking more clearly (Vietnam,
for example), Newark was unavoidable. Not to the extent of twenty-six
people killed, perhaps, or seven hundred people injured, or fifteen
hundred people arrested, or nine hundred businesses destroyed, or ten
million dollars in property damage, but Newark was a place where
everything had been going wrong for years, and the six days of violence that began on July twelfth were the logical outcome of a situation
that could be addressed only through violence of one sort or another.
That the war broke out when a black cab driver named John Smith
was arrested for illegally passing a police patrol car and then blud-
geoned by two white cops was not a cause so much as an effect. If it
hadn't been Smith, it would have been Jones. And if it hadn't been
Jones, it would have been Brown or White or Gray. In the event, it happened to be Smith, and when he was dragged into the Fourth Precinct
station house by arresting officers John DeSimone and Vito Pontrelli, a
rumor quickly spread among the residents of the large public housing
project across the street that Smith had been murdered. Not true, as it
turned out, but the deeper truth was that Newark's population was
more than fifty percent black now, and most of those two hundred and
twenty thousand people were poor. Newark had the highest percentage
of substandard housing in the country, the second-highest crime rate,
the second-highest infant mortality rate, and an unemployment rate
double the national average. The municipal government was all white,
the police department was ninety percent white, and nearly every construction contract was awarded to companies controlled by the Mob,

which thanked the city officials who helped them with generous kick-backs and refused to hire black workers because they didn't belong to the all-white unions. The system was so corrupt that City Hall was commonly referred to as the Steal Works.

Once upon a time, Newark had been a town where people made things, a town of factories and blue-collar jobs, and every object on earth had been manufactured there, from wristwatches to vacuum cleaners to lead pipes, from bottles to bottle brushes to buttons, from packaged bread to cupcakes to foot-long Italian salamis. Now the wood-stick houses were falling apart, the factories had shut down, and the white middle class was moving to the suburbs. Ferguson's parents had done that as long ago as 1950, and as far as he could tell, they were the only ones who had ever come back, but Weequahic wasn't really Newark, it was a Jewish town at the southwestern edge of an imaginary Newark, and everything had been tranquil there since the beginning of time. Seventy thousand Jews in one place, a splendid three-hundred-and-eleven-acre park designed by Olmsted, and a high school that produced more Ph.D.s than any other high school in the country.

Ferguson had been drinking beer at the West End on the evening of the twelfth, and when he returned to his apartment a few minutes after one o'clock, the telephone was ringing. He picked up and heard his father shouting into the receiver: Where the hell have you been, Archie? Newark is burning! They've smashed in the windows and looted the stores! The cops are blasting their guns, and your mother is out there on Springfield Avenue taking pictures for her goddamn paper! They've cordoned off the street, and I can't get in there! Come home, Archie! I need you here, and don't forget to bring your press card!

It was too late to think about going downtown to catch a bus from the Port Authority terminal, so Ferguson flagged a taxi on Broadway and told the driver to step on it, a phrase he had heard dozens of times in movies but had never once uttered himself, and while the trip cost him all but two of the thirty-four dollars in his wallet, he made it to the apartment house on Van Velsor Place in under an hour. Thankfully, the streets of the neighborhood were calm. The rioting had begun in the Central Ward and had later spread to parts of downtown, but the South Ward was still untouched. Even more reassuring, his mother had just come home, and his overwrought, semi-unhinged father was beginning to find his hinges again.

I've never seen anything like it, his mother said. Molotov cocktails, gutted stores, cops with their guns out, fires, frenzied people running all over the place—pure chaos.

Sam's store is gone, his father said. He called an hour ago and told me there's nothing left. Crazy, wild animals, that's what they are. Imagine burning down your own neighborhood. It's the stupidest thing I've ever heard of.

I'm going to bed, his mother announced. I'm all done in, and I have to be at the *Ledger* first thing tomorrow.

No more of this, Rose, his father said.

No more of what, Stanley?

No more war photography.

It's my job. I have to do it. One person in this family is already out of work because of tonight, and there's no way I'm not going to do it.

You'll get yourself killed.

No, I won't. I think it's nearly done now. Everyone was going home when I left. The party's over.

Or so she thought, and so thought many others as well, even the mayor, Hugh Addonizio, who shrugged off the disturbance as nothing more than *a few broken bottles*, but when rioting started up again the following night, she was back in the streets with her camera, and this time Ferguson was with her, carrying his press cards from both the *Montclair Times* and the *Columbia Spectator* in case he was stopped by the police and asked to identify himself. His father had spent the day with Sam Brownstein at his wrecked sporting goods establishment, assessing the damage, boarding up what had once been the front window with sheets of plywood, salvaging the few things that had been left behind, and he was still with Sam when Ferguson and his mother headed for Springfield Avenue after sundown. In his father's mind, Ferguson was there to protect his mother, but in Ferguson's mind he was there because he wanted to be there, since his mother didn't need to be protected as she went about her job of taking pictures, which she did with remarkable calm and discipline, he felt, so poised and concentrated on her work that it wasn't long before he realized that she in fact was the one who was protecting him. A large contingent of journalists and photographers had gathered in the Central Ward that night, people from the Newark papers, the New York papers, *Life* magazine, *Time* and *Newsweek*, the A.P., Reuters, the underground press, the black press, radio and television crews, and they mostly stuck together as they watched the tumult unfurl along Springfield Avenue. It was a disturbing thing to witness, and Ferguson openly admitted to himself that he was on edge, at times even frightened, but he was also stirred up and amazed, utterly unprepared for the explosiveness of the energy rippling through the street, the mixture of high emotion and reckless movement that seemed to fuse anger and joy into a feeling he had never encountered anywhere else, a new feeling that had yet to be given a name, and not only was it not crazy, as his father had said it was, it wasn't stupid either, for the black mob was systematically going after businesses owned by white people, many of them Jewish white people, and at the same time sparing businesses owned by black people, the storefronts with the words SOUL BRO written across them, and in that way they were telling the white man he was looked upon as an enemy invader and it was time for him to leave their country. It wasn't that Ferguson thought this was a good idea, but at least it made sense.

Again, the rioting eventually petered out, and again everyone went home, and this time it seemed to have ended for good, the second night of a two-night binge of destruction and anarchic release, but what no one in the departing crowd could have known then was that at twenty past two in the morning Mayor Addonizio had called Governor Richard Hughes and asked him to send in the National Guard and the New Jersey State Police. By daybreak, three thousand Guardsmen were rolling through the city in tanks, five hundred heavily armed state troopers were taking up their positions in the streets of the Central Ward, and for the next three days the Vietnam War came home to Newark, for if no Vietcong had ever called Muhammad Ali nigger, now the black people of Newark had been turned into the Vietcong.

Governor Hughes: "This is a criminal insurrection by people who say they hate the white man but who really hate America."

Barbed-wire checkpoints. A ten P.M. curfew for cars, everyone off the streets by eleven. The looting had stopped, and the exaltation of the first two nights had devolved into urban warfare, an all-out battle in which the weapons were rifles, machine guns, and fires. A white fire department captain named Michael Moran, thirty-eight years old, the father of six children, was shot and killed while standing on a ladder investigating an alarm on Central Avenue, and from that point on the Guard and the state police acted on the assumption that the city was infested with black snipers perched on rooftops aiming to gun down any whites they saw. That twenty-four of the twenty-six people killed during those days turned out to be black would seem to have disproved that assumption, but it allowed the Guard and the troopers to fire off thirteen thousand rounds of ammunition, shooting directly into the second-floor apartment of a woman named Rebecca Brown, for example, and killing her in what the *Star-Ledger* described as a "fusillade of bullets," or to blast twenty-three other bullets into the body of Jimmy Rutledge, or to shoot down twenty-four-year-old Billy Furr for the crime of taking a cold soda out of an already ransacked convenience store and handing it to a thirsty photographer from *Life* magazine.

Through it all, Ferguson's mother did what she could to go on taking her pictures, but she necessarily had to work by day, photographing the tanks and soldiers and the now demolished black businesses throughout the Central Ward, hundreds of pictures documenting whatever aspects of the conflagration she considered relevant, and because Ferguson's father had whipped himself into a panic about Rose's safety, he insisted on accompanying her wherever she went, which for those three days entailed sitting with her in the backseat of the old Impala as Ferguson drove his parents around the city, and then, as the curfew approached, dropping off the rolls of undeveloped film at the *Star-Ledger* building before returning to the apartment on quiet Van Velsor Place. Ferguson's admiration for his mother continued to grow throughout the horror of those days. That a forty-five-year-old woman who had spent her life as a studio portrait photographer and had started in journalism by shooting pictures of suburban garden parties could go out and do what she was doing now struck him as one of the most improbable human transformations he had ever seen. That was his one consolation, for everything else about that time made him sick, sick at heart, sick to his stomach, sick about the world he lived in, and it didn't help that his father ranted every night about *them*, the goddamned *schvartzes* and how much they hated *us*, the Jews, and this was the end, he declared, he would hate them back everlastingly from this moment forward, hate them furiously every minute until the day he died, and during one of those rants Ferguson became so disgusted that he lost his temper and told his father to shut up, which he had never done before in his life.

The troops pulled out on the seventeenth, and by the time the last tank left the city, the war was over.

Everything else was over as well, at least for the Jews of Weequahic, who seemed to be of one mind with Ferguson's father about what had happened, and within six months nearly every family in the area was gone, some of them moving to nearby Elizabeth, others heading to the suburbs of Essex and Morris Counties, and a neighborhood that had once been all Jews had no Jews in it anymore. How odd that most of the parents and grandparents of the black people who lived in Newark had come up from the South during the Great Migration between the wars, and now, because his mother's photographs of the riots had made a certain mark in the world and she had been offered a new job at the *Miami Herald*, his parents were trading places with their black neighbors and heading south themselves.

It was terrible to see them go.

FALL 1967. SOMETHING about the sunlight or the starlight or the moonbeams in California had brightened the color of Amy's hair and darkened the color of her skin, and she returned to New York with paler, blonder eyebrows and lashes and a more tawny glow radiating from her cheeks, arms, and legs, the gold-brown of a freshly baked muffin or a slice of warm, buttery toast. Ferguson wanted to eat her up. After two and a half months of celibate agony, he couldn't get enough of her, and because she too had starved herself for the entire summer, playing the role of what she called a *no-fun nun*, she was in an uncommonly arousable state, ready to give him as much as he was ready to give her, and Ferguson, who understood now that he had inherited most if not all of his grandfather's *large appetites*, was prepared to give her everything he had, which he did, and which Amy did with everything she had as well, and for three consecutive days after she came back to the apartment on West 111th Street, they camped out on the double bed in her room and reacquainted themselves with the unknown force that held them together.

Nevertheless, certain things had changed, and not all of them were to Ferguson's liking. For one thing, Amy had fallen in love with California, or at least the Bay Area part of California, and the girl who would never leave New York was now actively considering whether she should apply to law school at Berkeley for next year. Law was not the issue. Ferguson was all for her becoming a lawyer, which was something they had discussed many times in the past, a poor people's lawyer, an activist lawyer, a profession that would allow her to do more good in the world than someone who organized anti-war demonstrations or rent strikes against greedy, irresponsible landlords, since the war was bound to end one day (she hoped) and it would be far more satisfying to put greedy landlords in jail than to beg them to turn on the heat or exterminate the rats or get rid of the lead paint. By all means become a lawyer—but California, what was she talking about? Didn't she remember that he would still be in New York next year? Being apart for the summer had been bad enough, but a whole year of it would drive him crazy. And what made her assume he would want to follow her to California after he graduated? Couldn't she go to a sensible law school like Columbia or NYU or Fordham and stay on in the apartment with him? Why make everything so fucking complicated?

Archie, Archie, don't get carried away. It's only speculation at this point.

I'm stunned that you would even consider it.

You don't know what it's like out there. After two weeks, I stopped thinking about New York and was glad not to think about it. I felt I was home.

That's not what you used to say. New York is *it*, remember?

I was sixteen when I said that, and I'd never been to Berkeley or San Francisco. Now, as an old woman of twenty, I've changed my mind. New York is a stinkhole.

Granted. But not every part of it. We could always move to another neighborhood.

Northern California is the most beautiful place in America. As beautiful as France, Archie. Don't take my word for it if you don't want to. See it for yourself.

I'm kind of busy right now.

Christmas vacation. We could go out there during winter break.

Fine. But even if I think it's the best place in the world, that still won't solve the problem.

What problem?

The problem of one year apart.

We'll get through it. It won't be so hard.

I've just been through the loneliest, most wretched summer of my life. It was hard, Amy, very hard, so hard that I almost couldn't take it. A whole year would probably destroy me.

All right, it was hard. But I also think it was good for us. Being alone, sleeping alone, missing each other, and writing letters—I think it made us a stronger couple.

Ha.

I really do love you, Archie.

I know you do. But sometimes I think you love your future more than you love the idea of being with me.

DECEMBER 1967. THEY never made it out to California that winter because Ferguson's grandmother died, died from the same sort of abrupt inner explosion that had killed his grandfather the year before, and the trip had to be canceled so they could attend yet another burial ceremony in Woodbridge, New Jersey. Then followed a frantic week in which many hands took part in disposing of his grandmother's possessions and cleaning out her flat, which had to be accomplished in record time because Ferguson's parents were on the verge of moving to Florida, so everyone pulled together to chip in and help, Ferguson of course but also Amy, who wound up doing more than anyone else, and Nancy Solomon and her husband, Max, and Bobby George, who had been discharged from the army and was back in Montclair getting himself into shape for spring training, and even Didi Bryant, who had formed a friendship with Ferguson's grandmother after his grandfather's death and cried for her just as hard as she had cried for him (who in his right mind would ever contend that life made sense?), and Ferguson's mother needed the help because she was so distraught, shedding more tears that week than the sum total of tears Ferguson had seen her shed from his boyhood until now, and Ferguson too felt an overpowering sadness take hold of him, not just because he had lost his grandmother, which was sorrow enough, but also because he hated to see what was happening to the apartment, the slow dismantling of the rooms where one object after another was being wrapped up in newspapers and put into cardboard boxes, all the things that had been a part of his life since before he could remember being alive, the crummy little knickknacks he had played with on his hands and knees as a kid, his grandmother's ivory elephants and the green-glass hippopotamus, the yellowing lace doily under the telephone in the hall, his grandfather's pipes and empty humidors, which he had loved sticking his nose into for a deep whiff of the acrid tobacco smells left behind by long-vanished cigars, all gone now, forever gone now, and the worst of it was that his grandmother had been planning to go down to Florida with his parents and move into the new apartment in Miami Beach with them, and even though she had claimed to be looking forward to it (*You'll come down to visit me, Archie, and we'll go out for breakfast at Wolfie's on Collins Avenue and have scrambled eggs with lox and onions*), he suspected that the thought of leaving the apartment after so many years had terrified her, and perhaps she had willed herself to have the stroke because she simply couldn't face it.

The last thing on Ferguson's mind just then was the money, he who rarely stopped thinking and worrying about money in the day-to-day course of his own life had neglected to think about the question of estates and the financial consequences that followed from a person's death, but his grandfather had earned considerable gobs of money during his long years at Gersh, Adler, and Pomerantz, and even though large chunks of those gobs had been squandered on Didi Bryant and her predecessors, Ferguson's grandmother had inherited more than half a million dollars after her husband's death, and now that she herself had died, that money was passed on to her two daughters, Mildred and Rose, each of whom was given half according to the terms of the will, and once the estate taxes had been paid, Ferguson's aunt and mother were both two hundred thousand dollars richer than they had been before their mother's fatal stroke. Two hundred thousand dollars! It was such an outrageous sum that Ferguson laughed when his mother called from Florida in late January and told him the news, and then he laughed even harder when she announced that half of her half would be going to him.

Your father and I have gone over this very carefully, she said, and we think it's only fair that you should get something now. The number we came up with was twenty thousand. The other eighty we'll invest for you, so if and when you're ever in a spot where you might need to have some of it, the eighty will be more than eighty. You're a big boy now, Archie, and we figured twenty would be enough to get you through your last three semesters of college with a nice bit left over for the beginning of your so-called real life, a six- or eight-thousand dollar cushion, which will give you a chance to go for a job you really want rather than one you feel you have to take because you're desperate for money. Besides, this will make things easier for us old folks down in Miami Beach. Your father won't have to send you monthly checks anymore for your rent and allowance, he won't have to think about paying the tuition anymore, everything will be simpler for all of us, and from now on you'll be in charge.

What have I done to deserve this? Ferguson asked.

Nothing. But what did I do to deserve the money in the first place? Nothing. It's just the way it is, Archie. People die, and the world goes on, and whatever we can do to help each other out, well, that's what we do, isn't it?

JANUARY 1968. BECAUSE Amy was a person who never backed down after she had made up her mind about something, she stuck to her guns and sent off an application to Berkeley Law, and because Ferguson knew she was bound to get in and would decide to go there once they accepted her, even though she would also be accepted by Columbia and Harvard, he tried to comfort himself by thinking about the money, which would allow him to travel to California to see her for short visits, sometimes for long visits if she chose not to return to New York for Christmas and/or spring vacation, and in that way perhaps it would be possible to get through the year without feeling crushed by her absence. Not likely, he thought, but at least the money gave him a chance now, whereas before the money he had been utterly without hope.

Beyond that, the interesting thing about the money was how little it affected the outward circumstances of his life. He hesitated a bit less now about buying the books and records he wanted, he tended to replace worn-out clothes and shoes a bit more readily than he had in the past, and whenever he wanted to surprise Amy with a present (flowers mostly, but also books, records, and earrings), he could give in to the impulse without any second thoughts. Otherwise, not much had changed. He continued going to his classes and writing articles for the *Spectator* and translating French poems, and he kept on frequenting his usual inexpensive haunts—the West End, the Green Tree, and Chock Full o'Nuts—but on the inside, deep down in the submerged mental chamber where Ferguson lived alone in silent communion with his own consciousness, one thing was vastly different now. Thousands of dollars were sitting in his account at the First National City Bank on the corner of West 110th Street and Broadway, and just knowing they were there, even if he had no particular desire to spend them, relieved him of the obligation to think about money seven hundred and forty-six times a day, which in the end was just as bad if not worse than not having enough money, for those thoughts could be excruciating and even murderous, and not having to think them anymore was a blessing. That was the one true advantage of having money over not having money, he decided—not that you could buy more things with it but that you no longer had to walk around with that infernal thought bubble hanging over your head.

EARLY 1968. FERGUSON saw the situation as a series of concentric circles. The outer circle was the war and all that went with it: American soldiers in Vietnam, enemy combatants from the North and the South (Vietcong), Ho Chi Minh, the government in Saigon, Lyndon Johnson and his cabinet, U.S. foreign policy since the end of World War II, body counts, napalm, burning villages, hearts and minds, escalation, pacification, peace with honor. The second circle represented America, the two hundred million on the home front: the press (newspapers, magazines, radio, television), the anti-war movement, the pro-war movement, the Black Power movement, the counterculture movement (hippies and Yippies, pot and LSD, rock and roll, the underground press, Zap Comix, the Merry Pranksters, the Motherfuckers), the Hard Hats and the Love-It-or-Leave-It crowd, the empty air occupied by the so-called generation gap between middle-class parents and their children, and the vast throng of nameless citizens who would come to be known as the Silent Majority. The third circle was New York, which was almost identical to the second circle but more immediate, more vivid: a laboratory filled with examples of the aforementioned social currents that Ferguson could perceive directly with his own eyes rather than through the filter of written words or published images, all the while taking into account the nuances and particularities of New York itself, which was different from all the other cities in the United States, especially because of the enormous divide between rich and poor. The fourth circle was Columbia, Ferguson's temporary abode, the close-to-hand little world that surrounded him and his fellow students, the encompassing ground of an institution no longer walled off from the big world outside it, for the walls had come down and the outside was now indistinguishable from the inside. The fifth circle was the individual, each individual person in any one of the four other circles, but in Ferguson's case the individuals who counted most were the ones he knew personally, above all the friends he shared his life with at Columbia, and above all those others, of course, the individual of individuals, the dot at the center of the smallest of the five circles, the person who was himself.

Five realms, five separate realities, but each one was connected to the others, which meant that when something happened in the outer circle (the war), its effects could be felt throughout America, New York, Columbia, and every last dot in the inner circle of private, individual lives. When the war escalated in the spring of 1967, for example, half a million people marched in the streets of New York on April fifteenth to condemn the war and call for the immediate withdrawal of American troops from Vietnam. Five days after that, on the Columbia campus uptown, three hundred members of SDS showed up at John Jay Hall "to ask some questions" of the marine recruiters who had set up their tables in the lobby and were attacked by a charging gang of fifty jocks and NROTC boys, which led to a bloody scuffle of flying fists and bashed-in noses that had to be broken up by the police. The following afternoon, the largest demonstration at Columbia in over thirty years was held in the Van Am quadrangle between John Jay and Hamilton Halls as eight hundred members and supporters of SDS protested marine recruiting on campus and five hundred pro-marine jock hecklers threw eggs at them from the other side of the fence on South Field in their own counterdemonstration. Ferguson and Amy had both been involved in that hectic scene, she as a participant and he as a witness-reporter, and when he told her about his concentric circles theory that night at the West End, she smiled at him and said, But of course, my dear Holmes, how clever of you.

The point was that no one was happy on either side. The pro-war people were becoming more and more frustrated by Johnson's failure to win the war, and the anti-war people were becoming more and more frustrated by their failure to force Johnson to end the war. Meanwhile, the war continued to grow, five hundred thousand troops, five hundred and fifty thousand troops, and the bigger it became the more the outer circle pressed in on the other circles, squeezing them ever more tightly together, and before long the spaces between them had shrunk to the merest slivers of air, which was making it hard for the lone ones trapped in the center to breathe, and when a person can't breathe he starts to panic, and panic is something close to craziness, a feeling that you have lost your mind and are about to die, and by early 1968 Ferguson was beginning to feel that everyone had gone crazy, as crazy as the crazy people who talked out loud to themselves on Broadway, and bit by bit he had become as crazy as everyone else.

Then, in those early months of the new year, everything began to snap. The shock attacks by Vietcong sapper-commandos on more than a hundred South Vietnamese cities and towns during the Tet Offensive of January thirtieth proved that America could never win the war, even though American troops fought back and overwhelmed the enemy in every battle of the offensive, killing thirty-seven thousand Vietcong compared to the two thousand lost by the U.S., with tens of thousands of other Vietcong fighters either wounded or captured and half a million South Vietnamese civilians turned into homeless refugees. The message to the American public was that the North Vietnamese would never give up, that they would go on fighting until the last person in their country was dead, and how many more American soldiers would it take to destroy that country, would the five hundred thousand already there have to be increased to a million, to two million, to three million, and if so, would the destruction of North Vietnam not also mean the destruction of America? Two months later, Johnson appeared on television and announced that he would not be running for reelection in the fall. It was an admission of failure, an acknowledgment that public support for the war had eroded to such a point that his policies had been rejected, and Ferguson, who had admired the good Johnson of the War on Poverty and the Civil Rights Act and the Voting Rights Act and had loathed the bad Johnson of Vietnam, found himself in the uncomfortable position of feeling sorry for the president of the United States, at least for a minute or two as he tried to put himself in the head of Lyndon Johnson and experience the anguish he must have felt in deciding to abdicate his throne, and then Ferguson felt glad, both glad and relieved that LBJ would soon be gone.

Five days after that, Martin Luther King was assassinated in Memphis. Another bullet fired by an American nobody, another blow to the collective nervous system, and then hundreds of thousands of people ran out into the streets and started smashing windows and setting buildings on fire.

One hundred and twenty-eight Newarks.

The five concentric circles had merged into a single black disk.

It was an L.P. record now, and the song it kept playing was an old blues number called *Can't Take It No More, Sugar, 'Cause My Heart Hurts So Bad*.

SPRING 1968 (I). Amy was seldom around anymore. It was her last semester at Barnard, and because she had already fulfilled her academic requirements and had nearly enough points to graduate, her course load was exceptionally light that spring, which allowed her to spend most of her time doing political work with SDS. Until then, Ferguson's greatest worry had been Berkeley Law (which accepted her in early April, a few days after King was murdered in Memphis), but now he was afraid he would lose her before the summer began. Her positions had hardened during the crazy-making months of early sixty-eight, pushing her deeper into a stance of radical militancy and anti-capitalist fervor, and she could no longer laugh off their small differences of opinion, no longer understand why he didn't agree with her on all her points.

If you accept my analysis, she said to him one day, then you necessarily have to accept my conclusions.

No, I don't, Ferguson replied. Just because capitalism is the problem doesn't mean that SDS is going to make capitalism disappear. I'm trying to live in the real world, Amy, and you're dreaming about things that are never going to happen.

One example: Now that Johnson had withdrawn, Eugene McCarthy and Robert Kennedy were both running for the Democratic presidential nomination. Ferguson was distinctly unexcited and didn't support either one of them, but he paid close attention to their campaigns—especially to Kennedy's, since it was clear to him that McCarthy had no chance—for even if he was lukewarm about the New York senator, he felt that RFK was a better choice than discredited Humphrey, and any Democrat was preferable to Nixon or, even more troubling, Ronald Reagan, the governor of Amy's future state, who was even farther to the right than Goldwater. It wasn't that Ferguson felt any enthusiasm for the Democrats, but it was important to make distinctions, he told himself, important to recognize that there were bad things in this flawed world but also even worse things, and when it came to voting in an election, better to go for the bad over the worse. Amy refused to make those kinds of distinctions anymore. As far as she was concerned, the Democrats were all the same, each one a *sell-out liberal*, and she wanted no part of them, they were the ones who were responsible for Vietnam and all the other horrors America had visited upon the world, and a pox on them and everything they stood for, and if the Republicans happened to win, well, maybe that would be better for the country in the long run, because America would be turned into a fascist police state, and eventually the people would rise up against it, as if the people who had just elected the Republicans would want to overthrow them once they came to power, as if the people might not prefer to live in a fascist police state if it would lock up anti-American radicals like her.

The girl who had wept over the murder of John Kennedy in 1963 now saw his brother Robert as a tool of capitalist oppression. Ferguson was willing to shrug off such remarks as an excess of ideological enthusiasm, but by early April he too was coming under attack, and the political had suddenly become personal, too personal, too much about them rather than the ideas they were discussing. Ferguson wondered if Amy wasn't carrying on a secret dalliance with one of her SDS brethren, or if she and her Barnard pal Patsy Dugan weren't exploring the mysteries of Sapphic love together (she talked about Patsy a lot these days), or if she wasn't still irritated with him for not having gone to California with her last summer. No, not possible, he realized, none of those possibilities was even dimly possible, for it wasn't in Amy's nature to do things behind his back, and if she had fallen for someone else she would have told him about it, and if she still resented him for last summer it couldn't have been a conscious resentment, since that had been over and done with for months, and in the months after that there had been countless good times together, not to mention how glorious she had been in the sad days after his grandmother's death, taking up the slack from his nearly immobilized mother and orchestrating the apartment cleanout with the speed and precision of a Sandy Koufax fastball. Something had happened since then, however, and if it hadn't been caused by any of the usual causes, it also seemed impossible that it had been caused by a stupid disagreement about politics. He and Amy had always disagreed. One of the pleasures of living with her was the extent to which they disagreed and yet continued to love each other in spite of that. Their battles had always been fought about ideas, never about themselves, but now Amy had started going after him because his ideas didn't mesh with hers, because he was reluctant to jump into the revolutionary volcano with her, and therefore he had become a backward-thinking reactionary liberal, a pessimist, an ironist, an agenbite-of-inwit boy (meaning, he supposed, that he was too fond of Joyce and all things literary), a bystander, a dilettante, an old fogey, and a lump of shit.

From Ferguson's point of view, it all came down to one essential difference: Amy was a believer, and he was an agnostic.

One night when she was out late with her friends, no doubt arguing with Mike Loeb in a booth at the West End or plotting with Patsy Dugan about how to increase the female membership of SDS, Ferguson crawled into the bed in Amy's room, the same bed he had slept in for the better part of the past two years, and because he was especially tired that night, he fell asleep before Amy returned. When he woke the next morning, Amy was not in the bed beside him, and when he examined the plumped-up state of her pillow, he concluded that Amy had not come home and had spent the night somewhere else. Somewhere else turned out to be the bed in Ferguson's room next door, and when he walked into that room to look for a fresh set of socks and underwear, the noise of the creaking parquet floor woke her up.

What are you doing in here? Ferguson asked.

I felt like sleeping alone, she said.

Oh?

It felt good to sleep alone for a change.

Did it?

Yes, very good. I think we should keep on doing it for a while, Archie. You in your bed and me in my bed. What you might call a cooling-off period.

If that's what you want. It's not as though it's been very warm lately when we've slept together in the same bed.

Thank you, Archie.

You're welcome, Amy.

Thus commenced the so-called cooling-off period. For the next six nights, Ferguson and Amy slept alone in their own beds in their own rooms, neither one of them certain if they had come to the end or were merely taking a pause, and on the morning of the seventh day, April twenty-third, just hours after they climbed out of their separate beds and made their separate ways out of the apartment, the revolution began.

□ □ □

Spring 1968 (II). On March fourteenth, Ferguson and his *Spectator* comrades had elected Robert Friedman as their new editor in chief, the same March fourteenth on which Amy and her SDS comrades had voted in Mark Rudd as their new chairman, and from one instant to the next both organizations had changed. The paper continued to report the news as it always had, but its editorials became tougher and more outspoken, and Ferguson was pleased that Vietnam and black-white relations and Columbia's role in prolonging the war were now openly discussed, often pugnaciously discussed, as a matter of policy and conviction. With Students for a Democratic Society, the shift in tactics was even more striking. The national leadership had called for a move from "protest to resistance," and at Columbia the so-called Praxis Axis contingent had been replaced by the more confrontational Action Faction. Last year, the goal had been education and awareness, the timid gesture of approaching marine recruiters in order to "ask some questions," whereas now the aim was to provoke, to disrupt, to stir things up as often as possible.

One week after Rudd took over as chairman, the director of the New York headquarters of the Selective Service System, Colonel Paul B. Akst, came to the Columbia campus to deliver a talk at Earl Hall about recent modifications to the draft laws. One hundred and fifty people showed up, and as Akst stepped forward to begin his talk (a squat man bulging in full military garb), there was a commotion at the back of the auditorium. Several students dressed in army fatigues started playing a fife-and-drum rendition of "Yankee Doodle Dandy" while others waved around toy weapons. As if by reflex, a band of jocks leapt forward to quell, repel, and expel the pukes, and with everyone's attention diverted by the wrangling in back, someone sitting in the front row stood up and threw a lemon meringue pie in Colonel Akst's face. As in all good slapstick films, it was a direct hit. By the time the audience had turned around again, a side door had mysteriously opened, and the pie thrower and an accomplice had escaped.

That night, Amy told Ferguson that the pastry commando was an SDSer imported from Berkeley and that the accomplice was none other than Mark Rudd. Ferguson was highly amused. Too bad for the colonel, he thought, but no harm done, especially in light of the big harm being done by the war, and what a deft little frolic it had been. The Praxis Axis never would have dreamed of attempting a stunt like that (too frivolous), but the Action Faction was apparently not opposed to using levity as an instrument to make its political points. The administration was furious, of course, promising to "throw the book" at the mischief-maker if it turned out he wasn't a Columbia student and to suspend him if he was, but one week later the university found itself confronted by a more serious challenge than lemon meringue pies, and the guilty ones were never caught.

At that early stage of the drama, SDS was focusing its activities on two principal issues: the Institute for Defense Analyses and the ban against demonstrating and/or picketing inside university buildings, a new policy that had been initiated by President Grayson Kirk back in the fall. IDA had been set up by the Pentagon in 1956 as a conduit for enlisting the help of university scientists in weapons research for the government, but no one had been aware of Columbia's connection to the program until 1967, when two members of SDS found documents in the library stacks that referred to Columbia's membership in IDA, which had twelve university members in all, and now that faculty committees at Princeton and Chicago were recommending to the heads of their schools that they quit the program, students and faculty members at Columbia were asking their university to do the same, even though Kirk had been a member of the board for the past nine years, but how not to feel revulsion over the fact that IDA research had led to the development of chemical herbicides such as Agent Orange, which was being used to defoliate the jungles of Vietnam, or that the bloody tactic of "carpet bombing" was the result of IDA work on counterinsurgency techniques? In other words, Columbia was taking part in the war, it had *dirt on its hands* (as Amy often put it), and the only sensible action was to force it to stop. Not that the war would stop, but persuading Columbia to stop would constitute a small victory after so many large and small defeats. As for the ban on indoor demonstrations, the students argued that it was a violation of First Amendment rights, an unconstitutional act against the principle of free speech, and therefore Kirk's dictum was invalid.

For the past several weeks, SDS had been circulating a petition around campus demanding that Columbia withdraw from IDA, and now that fifteen hundred faculty members and students had signed it (among them Ferguson and Amy), SDS decided to confront both issues in a single action on March twenty-seventh, one week after the now forgotten pie-throwing caper. A group of one hundred students entered Low Library, the white domed building modeled on the Roman Pantheon that served as the university administrative center, and defied the injunction against indoor picketing and demonstrations by carrying placards with the words IDA MUST GO! written across them. Amy was there with the protesters, Ferguson was there in his capacity as witness-reporter, and for about half an hour the students wandered around the halls chanting slogans (one through a bullhorn), after which they went upstairs to the second floor and delivered the petition to a high-ranking university official, who assured them he would pass it on to President Kirk. The group then left the building, and the next day six of them were singled out for disciplinary measures, Rudd at the top of the list along with four others from the SDS steering committee, just six out of the hundred who had participated because, as one dean explained, they were the only ones who could be identified. For the next two weeks, the IDA 6 refused to meet with the dean, which was standard protocol for resolving disciplinary matters (a private discussion followed by what was supposed to be just punishment—as in most kangaroo courts), insisting instead that they be tried in an open hearing. The dean responded by telling them they would all be suspended if they didn't come to his office. On April twenty-second, they finally went in to see him but would not discuss their involvement with the IDA demonstration. Upon leaving the office, they were all put on disciplinary probation.

In the meantime, Martin Luther King had been murdered. Harlem did what Newark had done a year earlier, but Lindsay wasn't Addonizio and no National Guard or state police were called in to fire bullets at the demonstrators, and as Harlem burned just down the hill from Columbia, the craziness in the already crazy air on Morningside Heights was mounting into what Ferguson now felt had become a full-blown fever dream. On April ninth, the university shut down for the day in homage to King. Only one event was scheduled—a memorial service to be held at St. Paul's Chapel near the center of the campus, which wound up drawing a crowd of eleven hundred people—and just as university vice president David Truman was about to deliver his eulogy on behalf of the Columbia administration, a student dressed in a jacket and tie stood up from his seat in one of the front rows and walked slowly to the pulpit. Mark Rudd—again. The microphone was immediately turned off.

Speaking without notes, without amplification, without knowing how many people could hear him, Rudd addressed the crowd in a subdued voice. "Dr. Truman and President Kirk are committing a moral outrage against the memory of Dr. King," he said. "How can the leaders of the university eulogize a man who died while trying to unionize sanitation workers when they have, for years, fought against the unionization of the university's own black and Puerto Rican workers? How can these people praise a man who fought for human dignity when they steal land from the people of Harlem? And how can these administrators praise a man who preached nonviolent civil disobedience while disciplining its own students for peaceful protest?" He paused for a moment and then repeated his opening sentence. "Dr. Truman and President Kirk are committing a moral outrage against the memory of Dr. King. We will therefore protest this obscenity." Along with forty or fifty fellow protesters (both black and white, both students and non-students) Rudd then walked out of the chapel. Ferguson, who was sitting in one of the middle rows, silently applauded what had just happened. Well done, Mark, he said to himself, and bravo to you for having the guts to stand up and speak out.

Before Martin Luther King's assassination, there had been one group (SDS) and two issues (IDA and discipline) propelling left-wing political activity on campus. Then came a second group (SAS), and then came a third issue (the gym), and within two weeks of the King memorial, the big thing no one was expecting to happen, that no one had ever imagined could happen, was happening in all the unexpected and unimaginable ways that big things tend to happen.

The Columbia gym, which also went by the alternative name of Gym Crow, was to be built on one of the parcels of land in Harlem Rudd had accused Columbia of stealing, public land in this case, the dangerous, dilapidated, never-used-by-white-people Morningside Park, a steeply descending crag of rocks and dying trees that started at the top in Columbiaville and ended at the bottom in Harlemville. There was no question that the school needed a new gym. Columbia's basketball team had just won the Ivy League championship, it had entered the NCAA tournament ranked fourth in the country, and the current gym was more than sixty years old, too small, too worn out, no longer viable, but the contract the administration had negotiated with the city in the late fifties and early sixties was unprecedented. Two acres of the park would be leased to the university for the nominal sum of three thousand dollars a year, and Columbia would become the first private institution in New York history to build a structure on public land for its own private use. Down below at the Harlem end of the park, there would be a back entrance for members of the community leading to a separate gym-within-the-gym, which would occupy twelve and a half percent of the overall space. After pressure from local activists, Columbia agreed to augment the Harlem share to fifteen percent—with a swimming pool and a locker room thrown in for good measure. When H. Rap Brown came to New York for a community meeting in December 1967, the chairman of SNCC said: "If they build the first story, blow it up. If they sneak back at night and build three stories, burn it down. And if they get nine stories built, it's yours. Take it over, and maybe we'll let them in on the weekends." On February 19, 1968, Columbia went ahead and broke ground on the project. The next day, twenty people went to Morningside Park and put their bodies in front of bulldozers and dump trucks in order to stop work on the construction site. Six Columbia students and six neighborhood people were arrested, and a week later, when a crowd of a hundred and fifty turned out to protest the building of the gym, twelve more Columbia students were arrested. None of them was a member of SDS. Until then, the gym had not been an SDS issue, but now that the administration was refusing to reconsider its plans or even discuss the matter of reconsidering them, it quickly became one, and not only for SDS but for the black students on campus as well.

SAS (Students' Afro-American Society) had more than a hundred members, but until King's assassination it had not taken part in any overt political activities, concentrating instead on how to increase black enrollment in the college and talking to deans and department heads about adding courses on black history and culture to the undergraduate curriculum. As with every other elite college in America at the time, the black population at Columbia was minuscule, so sparse that Ferguson had only two black friends among his fellow undergraduates, two friends who were not close friends, which was true for most of his white acquaintances as well, who seemed to have no close black

friends either. The black students were isolated because of their numbers and doubly isolated because they kept to themselves, undoubtedly a bit lost and resentful in that white enclave of tradition and
power, more often than not looked upon as outsiders, even by the black
security guards on campus, who would stop them and ask to see their
IDs because young men with black faces could not have been Columbia students and therefore had no business being there. After King's
death, SAS elected a new board of radical leaders, some of them brilliant, some of them angry, some of them both brilliant and angry, and
all of them as bold as Rudd, that is, with enough confidence in themselves to be able to stand up and address a thousand as easily as they
talked to one, and for them the biggest issue was Columbia's relationship with Harlem, which meant that IDA and discipline could belong
to the white students but the gym was their affair.

Two days after the King memorial, Grayson Kirk went to the
University of Virginia to deliver a speech on the occasion of Thomas
Jefferson's two hundred and twenty-fifth birthday (tempestuous as
those days might have been, they were also thick with absurdities),
and there the former political scientist who sat on the boards of several
corporations and financial institutions, Mobil Oil, IBM, and Con Edi-
son among them, the president of Columbia University who had
succeeded Dwight D. Eisenhower after the general left Columbia to
become president of the United States, there for the first time Grayson
Kirk came out against the war in Vietnam, not because the war was
wrong or less than honorable, he said, but because of the damage it was
doing at home, and then he uttered the sentences that would soon find
their way back to the Columbia campus and add another dose of gasoline to the fire that was already starting to burn there: "Our young
people, in disturbing numbers, appear to reject all forms of authority,
from whatever source derived, and they have taken refuge in a turbulent and inchoate nihilism whose sole objectives are destruction. I know
of no time in our history when the gap between the generations has
been wider or more potentially dangerous."

On April twenty-second, the day the IDA 6 were put on probation,
SDS published a one-off four-page newspaper entitled *Up Against the
Wall!* in advance of the rally scheduled for noon the next day, which
was supposed to culminate in another indoor demonstration at Low

Library, where dozens or scores or hundreds would show their support for the IDA 6 by breaking the same rule that had gotten the 6 into trouble. One of the articles was written by Rudd, an eight-hundred-and-fifty-word letter addressed to Grayson Kirk in response to the remarks he had made at the University of Virginia. It ended with the following three short paragraphs:

Grayson, I doubt if you will understand any of this, since your fantasies have shut out the world as it really is from your thinking. Vice President Truman says the society is basically sound; you say the war in Vietnam was a well-intentioned accident. We, the young people, whom you so rightly fear, say that the society is sick and you and your capitalism are the sickness.

You call for order and respect for authority; we call for justice, freedom, and socialism.

There is only one thing left to say. It may sound nihilistic to you, since it is the opening shot in a war of liberation. I'll use the words of LeRoi Jones, whom I'm sure you don't like a whole lot: "Up against the wall, motherfucker, this is a stick-up."

Ferguson was appalled. After the eloquent speech Rudd had given at the King memorial, it made no sense that he should commit such a bad tactical blunder. That wasn't to say the substance of the text lacked merit, but the tone was obnoxious, and if SDS was trying to increase its support among the students, this kind of thing would only push them away. The article was an example of SDS talking to itself rather than reaching out to others, and Ferguson wanted SDS to win, for notwithstanding certain reservations about what was possible and not possible, he mostly stood behind the group and believed in its cause, but a noble cause demanded noble behavior from its advocates, something finer and more self-controlled than run-of-the-mill insults and cheap, adolescent shots. The pity of it was that Ferguson liked Mark Rudd. They had been friends since their freshman year (fellow New Jersey boys with almost identical backgrounds), and Mark had been impressive as chairman so far, so impressive that Ferguson had been blinded into thinking he could never make any mistakes, and now that he had slipped up with this *Dear Grayson* and *motherfucker* business, Ferguson was feeling let down, stranded in the awkward position of being against the ones who were against, which was a lonely place to be for a person who was also against the ones who were for.

Remarkably enough, Amy did not disagree with him. They were still in the midst of their two-bed cooling-off period and hadn't seen much of each other in the past several days, but when Amy came home from her SDS meeting on the night of the twenty-second, she too was feeling let down, not just because of the article, which she admitted was both *crude and childish*, but because only fifty to sixty people had come to Fayerweather Hall for the last meeting of the school year, whereas most of the gatherings in the past months had drawn two hundred or more, and she was afraid that SDS was losing ground, that nearly every inch of the ground it had won had now been lost, and tomorrow was going to be a disaster, she said, a feeble last stand that would end in failure and shut down SDS at Columbia for good.

She was wrong.

SPRING 1968 (III). Never before in the annals of. Never before so much as thought. The widening gyre, and all at once everyone turning within it. Nobodaddy doubled over with stomach cramps, the shits. Hotspur hopping, a shape with lion body and the head of a man, a horde. How who, who what, and all suddenly asking him: Why darkness & obscurity in all thy words and laws? The centre could not, the things could not, the horde could not not not do other than it did, but anarchy was not loosed, it was the world that loosened, at least for a time, and thus began the largest, most sustained student protest in American history.

Close to a thousand on the morning of. Two-thirds antis, gathered around the Sundial in the center of the campus, one-third anti-antis standing on the steps of Low, presumably to protect the building from assault, but also to smash and bash if it came to that. They had already published warnings, and the threat of fisticuffs had brought out a platoon of young professors prepared to break things up if necessary. Speeches to begin with, one by one the usual stuff, the SDS line, but SAS was there as well, the first integrated political rally at Columbia ever, and when Cicero Wilson mounted the Sundial to address the crowd, the newly elected president of SAS began by talking about Harlem and the gym, but moments later (Ferguson was shocked) he was attacking the white students. "If you want to know who they're talking about," he said, meaning racists, "you go look in a mirror—because you know nothing about black people."

Amy, who was standing in front, interrupted him and called out: "What makes you think there aren't white people on your side? What makes you think we aren't all in this together? We're your brothers and sisters, pal, and we'll be a hell of a lot stronger if you stand with us when we stand with you."

A bad beginning. Hats off to Amy for having spoken up, but a rocky start, and the confusion continued for some time. Low was impregnable. The doors had been locked, and no one was willing to break them down or start a fight with the security guards. Back to the Sundial, which was adorned with an inscription that read HORAM EXPECTA VENIET (Await the Hour, It Shall Come), but had the hour really come or was April twenty-third collapsing into yet one more missed opportunity? Another round of speeches, but everything had come to a standstill, and the energy of the crowd had evaporated. Just when it seemed that the rally was fizzling to its conclusion, however, someone yelled out, TO THE GYM SITE! The words struck with the force of a slap to the face, and suddenly three hundred students were running east down College Walk to Morningside Park.

Amy had underestimated the magnitude of the discontent, the epidemic of unhappiness that had spread through the ranks of the non-SDS majority on campus, most of whom seemed headed for nervous breakdowns as the unwinnable war thundered on and the Nobodaddies in the White House and Low Library kept speaking their dark words and issuing their obscure laws, and as Ferguson ran alongside the crowd that was running to the park, he understood that the students were possessed, that their souls had been taken over by the same fusion of anger and joy he had witnessed in the streets of Newark last summer, and as long as no bullets were fired, such a crowd could not be controlled. There were policemen in the park, but not enough of them to stop a gang of students from tearing down forty feet of the chain-link fence that surrounded the construction site as other students tussled with the outmanned guards, and there was David Zimmer, Ferguson noticed, and there was Zimmer's friend Marco Fogg, gentle Zimmer and even more gentle Fogg were in the gang attacking the fence, and for a moment Ferguson envied them, wishing he could join in and do what they were doing, but then the feeling passed and he held his ground.

Almost a battle, but not quite. Skirmishes, flare-ups, shoving

matches, cops against students, students against cops, students jumping cops, students kicking cops and pushing them into the dirt, one
Columbia boy hauled off in the middle of it (white, non-SDS), charged
with felonious assault, criminal mischief, and resisting arrest, and
when more cops began descending into the park with their billy clubs
out, the students left the site and headed back toward the campus.
Meanwhile, the other crowd of students—the ones who had stayed
behind—were now marching toward the park. The advancing group
and the retreating group met in the middle on Morningside Drive,
and when the retreaters told the advancers that their business in the
park was done, both groups walked back to the campus and reassembled at the Sundial. There were about five hundred of them at that point,
and no one knew what was going to happen next. An hour and a half
ago there had been a plan, but events had overpowered that plan, and
whatever happened next would have to be improvised. As far as Ferguson could tell, only one fact was clear: the crowd was still possessed—
and ready to do just about anything.

A few minutes later, most of them were on their way to Hamilton
Hall, where hundreds spilled into the lobby on the ground floor, a
mass of bodies crammed into that small space as jocks jostled and pukes
pushed back and more bodies poured in, everyone charged up and
confused, so confused that the first act of the campus rebellion was the
misguided, self-defeating error of locking the undergraduate dean in
his office and holding him hostage (a mistake that was rectified the
next afternoon when Henry Coleman was released), but still the students involved in the takeover of the building had the wherewithal to
form a steering committee composed of three members from SDS, three
from SAS, two from the College Citizenship Council, and one unaffili-
ated sympathizer and come up with a list of demands that set forth the
aims of the protest:

1. All disciplinary action now pending and probations already
imposed upon six students to be immediately terminated and a general
amnesty be granted to those students participating in this demonstration.

2. President Kirk's ban on demonstrations inside University buildings to be dropped.

3. Construction of the Columbia gymnasium in Morningside Park
cease at once.

4. All future disciplinary action taken against University students

be resolved through an open hearing before students and faculty which adheres to the standards of due process.

5. Columbia University disaffiliate, in fact and not merely on paper, from the Institute for Defense Analyses; and President Kirk and Trustee William A. M. Burden resign their positions on IDA's Board of Trustees and Executive Board.

6. Columbia University use its good offices to obtain dismissal of charges now pending against those participating in demonstrations at the gym construction site in the park.

The doors of the building remained open. It was early afternoon on a normal school day, and as Rudd later told Ferguson, the SDS contingent felt they couldn't afford to alienate the nonparticipating students by blocking their access to classes, which were still being held on the upper floors. They wanted to win those students over to their side, and it wouldn't have made sense to do something that would have turned the majority against them. The building wasn't "occupied" at that point, then, there was a sit-in taking place within the building, and as the day advanced and word got out about what was going on at Hamilton Hall, dozens of people who were not connected to the university began turning up, SDSers from other colleges, members of SNCC and CORE, representatives from various Peace Now organizations, and as those people arrived to lend their support, in came food, blankets, and other practical necessities for the people who would be spending the night in the building. Amy was one of those people, but Ferguson was busy taking notes and had no time to talk to her. He blew her a kiss instead. She smiled and waved back (one of the rare smiles she had given him in the past several weeks), and then he dashed off to the *Spectator* office in Ferris Booth Hall to write his article.

That night, the frail, short-lived alliance between SDS and SAS fell apart. The black students wanted to barricade the doors and shut everyone out of Hamilton until the six demands had been met. They were ready to make a stand, they said, and with talk circulating in the halls that guns had been smuggled into the building, the implication was that the stand they were talking about could be a violent one. It was five o'clock in the morning at that point, and hours of discussion had led to an impasse, the open door–closed door dispute could not be resolved, and now SAS was politely suggesting that SDS leave the building and occupy a building of its own. Ferguson understood the SAS position, but at the same time he found the split depressing and demoralizing, and he understood why SDS should have felt so hurt by the divorce. It was Rhonda Williams saying no all over again. It was his father saying all those repulsive things after the Newark riots. It was what the world had come to.

The irony was that without the SDS expulsion that morning, the rebellion at Columbia never would have spread beyond Hamilton Hall, and the story of the next six weeks would have been a different story, a much smaller story, and the big thing that eventually happened would not have been big enough for anyone to notice it.

In the minutes before dawn on April twenty-fourth, the banished SDSers broke into Low Library and barricaded themselves inside President Kirk's suite of offices. Sixteen hours later, one hundred students from the School of Architecture took control of Avery Hall. Four hours after that, at two A.M. on the morning of the twenty-fifth, two hundred graduate students locked themselves inside Fayerweather Hall. At one o'clock in the morning on the twenty-sixth, a spillover group from Low Library took over Mathematics Hall, and within hours two hundred students and non-student radicals were in charge of a fifth building. That same night, Columbia announced that it was acceding to Mayor Lindsay's request to suspend construction of the gym.

The university had shut down, and there was no activity on campus anymore that was not political activity. Low Library, Avery Hall, Fayerweather Hall, and Mathematics Hall were no longer a library and three halls but four communes. Hamilton Hall had been renamed Malcolm X University.

Nobodaddy's children were saying no, and still no one knew what was going to happen next.

Ferguson was scrambling. The five-day-a-week paper had become a seven-day-a-week paper, and there were articles to write, places to go to, people to talk to, meetings to attend, and all on little or no sleep, barely more than two or three hours a night, and all on little or no food but rolls, salami sandwiches, and coffee, coffee and a thousand cigarettes, but the scrambling was good for him, he realized, to be so busy and so exhausted had the double effect of keeping him awake and numb at the same time, and he needed to be awake in order to see the things that were happening around him and write about those events with the quickness and accuracy they demanded, and he needed to be numb in order not to think about Amy, who was all but lost to him now, all but gone, and even though he kept telling himself he would fight to win her back, do everything he could to prevent the unthinkable from happening, he knew that whatever they had been to each other in the past was not what they were now.

She was with the group in Low, one of the diehards. On the afternoon of the twenty-sixth, as Ferguson was rushing across the campus on his way to Mathematics Hall, he caught sight of her standing on the second-floor ledge just outside the window of Kirk's office. Standing to her right was Les Gottesman, who was no longer in the college but a student in the graduate English Department, and standing to her left was Hilton Obenzinger, Les's good friend, who was also Ferguson's friend, one of the stalwarts of the *Columbia Review*, and there was Amy standing between Les and Hilton with the sun shining down on her, a sun so strong that her impossible hair seemed ablaze in the afternoon light, and she looked happy, Ferguson thought, so damned happy that he wanted to weep.

SPRING 1968 (IV). What he was watching was a revolution in miniature, Ferguson decided, a revolution in a dollhouse. SDS's objective was to force a showdown with Columbia that would reveal the administration to be exactly what the group claimed it was (intransigent, out of touch with reality, a small piece in the large American picture of racism and imperialism), and once SDS had proved that to the rest of the students on campus, the ones in the middle would come over to their side. That was the point: to eliminate the middle, to create a situation that would thrust everyone into one camp or the other, the fors and the againsts, with no room left in between for waffling or moderation. *Radicalize* was the term used by SDS, and in order to achieve that goal they had to behave with the same stubbornness as the administration and never give an inch. There was intransigence on both sides, then, but because the students were powerless at Columbia, SDS's intransigence came across as a strength, while the intransigence of the administration, which held all the power, came across as a weakness. SDS was goading Kirk into using force to clear the buildings, which was the one thing everyone else wanted to avoid, but the spectacle of hundreds of policemen storming the campus was also the one thing that was bound to provoke horror and disgust in the ones who were still in the middle and turn them to the students' cause, and the dumb administration (which turned out to be even dumber than Ferguson had supposed—as dumb as the czar of Russia, as dumb as the king of France) fell right into the trap.

The administration stuck to its hard line because Kirk saw Columbia as a model for all other universities in the country, and if he caved in to the students' preposterous demands, what would happen elsewhere? It was the domino theory writ small, the same theory that had put half a million American soldiers in Vietnam, but as Ferguson had discovered in his first days of living in New York, dominoes was a game played on milk crates and folding tables by Puerto Ricans on the sidewalks of Spanish Harlem and had nothing to do with politics or the running of universities.

SDS, on the other hand, was making it up as it went along. Every day was packed with unexpected developments, every hour felt as long as a day, and to do what had to be done required absolute concentration as well as an openness of spirit found only in the best jazz musicians. As head of SDS, Mark Rudd became that jazz man, and the longer the occupation of the buildings went on, the more impressed Ferguson was by how fluidly Rudd adapted to each new circumstance, by how quickly he could think on his feet, by his willingness to talk about alternative approaches to each crisis as it came up. Kirk was rigid, but Rudd was loose and often playful, Kirk was a military band leader conducting John Philip Sousa numbers, but Rudd was onstage doing bebop with Charlie Parker, and Ferguson doubted that anyone else from SDS could have done a better job as spokesman for the group. By the night of April twenty-third, Ferguson had already forgiven Mark for the *Dear Grayson—motherfucker* fuck-up, which, by the by, had not offended people in the way he had thought it would—student-people, that is, pro-SDS and anti-administration students—which in turn had led Ferguson to ask himself what he knew about such things anyway, for not only had the words not offended people, they had become one of the rallying cries of the movement. It wasn't that Ferguson felt happy when he heard masses of students shouting out the phrase *Up against the wall, motherfucker!*, but it was clear to him that Mark had a better sense of what was going on than he did, which explained why Rudd was leading a revolution and Ferguson was only watching it and writing about it.

Swarms of people on the campus at all hours, even in the middle of the night, round-the-clock swarms for an entire week, then intermittent swarms during the month that followed, and whenever Ferguson thought about that time later, the chaos that began on April twenty-third and lasted until commencement day on June fourth, the swarms were always what came back to him first. Swarms of students and professors wearing different colored armbands, white ones for the faculty (who were trying to keep the peace), red ones for the radicals, green ones for the supporters of the radicals and the six demands, and blue ones for the jocks and right-wingers, who had named themselves the Majority Coalition and held angry, clamorous demonstrations to denounce the other demonstrations, launched an attack on Fayerweather Hall one night to evict the occupiers (they were repulsed after much pushing and shoving), and formed a successful blockade around Low on the final day of the sit-ins to prevent food from entering the building, which led to more shoving and punching and some bleeding scalps. As might have been expected from a university of Columbia's size (17,500 students counting all graduate and undergraduate divisions), the faculty was split into numerous factions, ranging from full support of the administration to full support of the students. Various suggestions were put forward, various committees were formed, a new approach to disciplinary procedures, for example, the tripartite commission, which advocated combined adjudication by equal numbers from the administration, faculty, and student body, and the bipartite commission, which advocated a panel of faculty and students only with no members from the administration, but the most active committee was the one that called itself the Ad Hoc Faculty Group, which was largely composed of younger professors, who held long and frantic meetings over the next days searching for a peaceful solution that would give the students most of what they wanted and get them out of the buildings without having to call in the police. All of their efforts failed. It wasn't that they didn't come up with some good ideas, but every one of those ideas was blocked by the administration, which refused to compromise or back down on any of the demands concerning discipline, and thus the faculty learned that they were just as powerless as the students were, that Columbia was a dictatorship, mostly benevolent until now but veering ever closer to absolutism, with no interest in reforming itself into anything that resembled a democracy. Students came and went, after all, faculty came and went, but the administration and the board of trustees were eternal.

Columbia wouldn't hesitate to call in the cops to drag the white students out of the buildings if necessary, but the black students in Hamilton Hall posed a more delicate and potentially more dangerous problem. If the police attacked them or handled them roughly while they were being arrested, the spectacle of white-on-black brutality could ignite the people of Harlem and send them rushing onto the campus in retaliation, and then Columbia would find itself at war with a vengeful black mob intent on ripping apart the university and burning Low Library to the ground. Given the anger in Harlem following Martin Luther King's murder, violence and destruction on such a massive scale was more than just an irrational fear, it was a distinct possibility. A police action to expel the trespassers in the five buildings was planned for the night of the twenty-fifth/twenty-sixth (the same night Mathematics Hall was taken), but when undercover plainclothesmen started banging their nightsticks on the heads of the white-armband professors gathered in front of Low to protect the demonstrators inside, Columbia backed off and canceled the operation. If this was what the Tactical Patrol Force would do against the whites, what were they not prepared to do against the blacks? The administration needed more time to negotiate with the SAS leaders in Hamilton so its faculty emissaries could work out a separate peace that would spare the university from a Harlem invasion.

As for the white students, the general feeling in the *Spectator* office was that SDS had already gained the upper hand on the two most important issues that had launched the protest, for it was almost certain now that the university would detach itself from IDA and that the gymnasium would never be built. The students in the occupied buildings could have walked out unharmed at that point and declared victory, but the four other demands were still on the table, and SDS refused to budge until all of them had been met. The most controversial item was the one about amnesty (*that a general amnesty be granted to the students participating in this demonstration*), which turned out to be something of a conundrum for most people on campus, even members of the *Spectator* staff, who were almost unanimously sympathetic to the occupiers in the buildings, for if, as SDS was claiming, the university was an illegitimate authority that had no right to punish them, how could they expect that same illegitimate authority to exonerate the protesters for what they were doing? As Mullhouse jokingly put it to Ferguson one afternoon in his pretend cowboy twang, It's a real doggone little head-scratcher, ain't it, Arch? Ferguson scratched his head in response and smiled. You're damned right it is, he said, and unless I'm mistaken, that's precisely what they want it to be. Their reasoning is absurd, but by holding out on a point they know they can't possibly win, they force the administration's hand.

To do what? Mullhouse asked.

To call in the cops.

You can't be serious. Nobody can be that cynical.

It's not cynicism, Greg. It's strategy.

Whether Ferguson was right or wrong, the cops were eventually called in at the close of the seventh day of the occupations, and at two-thirty in the morning on April thirtieth—an hour, as someone pointed out, when Harlem was asleep—the bust began. One thousand helmeted troops from the New York City riot police fanned out across the campus as a thousand onlookers stood in the chill and the damp of that eeri-est of all black nights while others swarmed and howled and chanted *No Violence!* at the police and the blue-bands cheered them on and the white-bands and the green-bands tried to block the T.P.F. from enter-ing the buildings, and the first thing Ferguson noticed was the animos-ity that existed between the police and the students, a mutual resentment that had nothing to do with the white-black antagonisms everyone had feared but white-white class hatred, the privileged students and the bottom-rung cops, who saw the Columbia boys and girls as rich, spoiled, anti-American hippie brats, and the professors who supported them were no better, pompous anti-war intellectual radicals, Reds, the ran-cid poisoners of young minds, so first they took care of evacuating Ham-ilton and getting the blacks out as smoothly as they could, and because there was no resistance from the proud, tightly organized students of Malcolm X University, who had voted not to resist and calmly let the police escort them through the tunnels under the building to the paddy wagons that were parked outside, not one punch was thrown at them, not one nightstick cracked down on any of their skulls, and Columbia, through no efforts of its own, managed to escape the wrath of Harlem. By then, the water supply to the other buildings had been shut off, and one by one the T.P.F. and their plainclothes undercovermen set about clearing Avery, Low, Fayerweather, and Math, where the occupying students were hurriedly reinforcing the barricades they had erected behind the doors, but each building had its own battalion of white-bands and green-bands in front of it, and they were the ones who got the worst of the pounding, the ones who were clubbed and punched and kicked as the cops plowed through them with crowbars to force open the locks and then charge in to bust up the barricades and arrest the students inside. No, it wasn't Newark, Ferguson kept telling himself as he watched the police go about their business, no shots were being fired and there-fore no one was going to be killed, but just because it wasn't as bad as Newark didn't mean it wasn't grotesque, for there was Alexander Platt, associate dean of the college, being punched in the chest by a cop, and there was philosopher Sidney Morgenbesser, he of the white sneakers and unraveling sweaters and zinging ontological quips, being banged over the head by a nightstick as he stood guard at the back entrance of Fayerweather Hall, and there was a young reporter from the *New York Times*, Robert McG. Thomas Jr., showing his press card as he mounted the stairs in Avery Hall and being ordered to quit the building, at which point he was slugged in the head by a cop using a pair of handcuffs as brass knuckles, then shoved down the stairs and hit with a dozen billy clubs as he tumbled to the bottom, and there was Steve Shapiro, a photographer from *Life* magazine, being punched in the eye by one cop as another cop smashed his camera, and there was a doctor from the volunteer first-aid crew dressed in doctor's whites being thrown to the ground, kicked, and dragged off to a paddy wagon, and there were doz-ens of male and female students being jumped by plainclothesmen hiding in the bushes and having their heads and faces clunked by saps, sticks, and pistol butts, dozens of students stumbling around with blood pouring from their scalps and foreheads and eyebrows, and then, after all the demonstrators in the buildings had been pulled out and carted away, a phalanx of T.P.F. warriors began systematically moving back and forth across South Field to clear the campus of the hundreds who remained, charging into crowds of defenseless students and pummel-ing them to the ground, and there were the mounted police on Broad-way going at full gallop after the lucky ones who had eluded the clubs in the campus assault, and there was Ferguson, trying to do his job as reporter for his humble student rag, being hit on the back of the head by a billy club wielded by yet another undercoverman dressed to look like a student, the same head that had been stitched up in eleven places four and a half years earlier, and as Ferguson fell to the ground from the impact of the blow, someone else stomped on his left hand with the heel of a boot or a shoe, the same hand that was already missing its thumb and two-thirds of its index finger, and when the foot came down on him Ferguson felt the hand must have been broken, which turned out not to be true, but how it hurt, and how quickly it swelled up afterward, and how much, from that moment on, he came to despise cops.

Seven hundred and twenty people arrested. Nearly one hundred and fifty injuries reported, with untold numbers of unreported injuries as well, among them the knocks that had been delivered to Ferguson's head and hand.

The editorial in that day's *Spectator* had no words in it—just the masthead followed by two blank columns bordered in black.

SPRING 1968 (V). On Saturday, May fourth, Ferguson and Amy finally sat down and talked. Ferguson was the one who insisted on it, and he made it clear to her that he didn't want it to be a conversation about his wounds or Amy's arrest with her fellow occupiers in Low, nor were they going to discuss the general strike against Columbia that had been declared on the evening of April thirtieth by a coalition of red-bands, green-bands, and moderates (the SDS strategy had worked) or dwell for a single moment on the big things that were starting to happen in their adored, fiercely remembered Paris, no, he said, for one night they would forget about politics and talk about themselves, and Amy reluctantly gave in, even though she could think about little else but the movement now, what she called *the euphoria of the struggle,* and *the electric awakening* that had transformed her after six days of communal living in Low.

In order to avoid a potential shouting match in the apartment, Ferguson suggested they go to a neutral site, a public site, where the presence of strangers would stop them from losing control of themselves, and because they hadn't been to the Green Tree in over two months, they decided to return to Yum City for what Ferguson supposed would be the last meal they ever had together for the rest of their lives. How happy Mr. and Mrs. Molnár were to see their favorite young couple walk through the door of the restaurant, and how accommodating they were when Ferguson asked for a rear corner table in the back room, the smaller, slightly elevated room that had fewer tables in it, and how kind they were to offer them a free bottle of Bordeaux to accompany their dinner, and how miserable Ferguson felt as he and Amy sat down for their last supper of all time, noting how perfectly apt it was that Amy should instinctively choose to sit in the chair with her back against the wall, meaning that she could look out and see the other people in the restaurant, while Ferguson instinctively sat down in the chair with his back to those other people, meaning that the only person he could see was Amy, Amy and the wall behind her, for that was who they were, he said to himself, that was who they had always been for the past four years and eight months, Amy looking out at others and he looking only at Amy.

They spent an hour and a half there, perhaps an hour and three-quarters, he was never sure exactly how long it was, and as the normally ravenous Amy picked at her food and Ferguson downed glass after glass of red wine, polishing off most of the first bottle himself and then order-ing another, they talked and fell silent, talked and fell silent again, and then talked and talked and talked, and soon enough Ferguson was being told they were finished, that they had outgrown each other and were moving in different directions now and therefore would have to stop living together, and no, Amy said, it wasn't anyone's fault, least of all Ferguson's fault, he who had loved her so hard and so well since their first kiss on the bench in that little Montclair park, no, it was simply that she could no longer bear the smothering confines of couplehood, she had to be free to push on alone, to go out to California unattached and unencumbered by anyone or anything and continue working for the movement, that was her life now and Ferguson had no place in it any-more, her wonderful Archie of the big soul and kind heart would have to get along without her, and she was sorry, so sorry, so immensely sorry, but that's the way it was now and nothing, not one thing in the whole wide world, could ever make it different.

Amy was crying by then, two streams of tears were falling down her face as she gently crucified the son of Rose and Stanley Ferguson, but Ferguson himself, who had far more reason to cry than she did, was too drunk to cry, not excessively drunk but drunk enough to feel no impulse to open the saltwater spigots, which was a fortunate thing, he felt, since he didn't want her last impression of him to be that of a destroyed man weeping his guts out in front of her, and therefore he summoned every bit of the strength he still had in him and said:

O, my best beloved Amy, my extraordinary Amy of the wild hair and shining eyes, my darling lover of a thousand transcendent naked nights, my brilliant girl whose mouth and body have done such wondrous things to my mouth and body over the years, the only girl who has ever slept with me, the only girl I have ever wanted to sleep with, not only am I going to miss your body every day for the rest of my life, but I will especially miss those parts of your body that belong only to me, that belong to my eyes and my hands and are not even known to you by yourself, the parts of you that you have never seen, the back parts that are invisible to you just as mine are to me, just as they are to each person who has a body of his or her own, beginning with your ass, of course, your deliciously round and shapely ass, and the backs of your legs with the little brown dots on them that I have worshipped for so long, and the lines engraved in your skin just behind your knees, in the place where the legs bend, how I have marveled at the beauty of those two lines, and then the hidden half of your neck and the bumps in your spine when you lean over and the lovely curve in the small of your back, which have belonged to me and only to me for all these years, and most of all your shoulder blades, darling Amy, the jut of your two shoulder blades, which have always reminded me of swan's wings, or the wings jutting from the back of the White Rock seltzer girl, who was the first girl I ever loved.

Please, Archie, Amy said. Please stop.

But I haven't finished.

No, Archie, please. I can't take it.

Ferguson was about to speak again, but before he could get his tongue into the proper position, Amy stood up from her chair, wiped away her tears with a napkin, and walked out of the restaurant.

MAY–JUNE 1968. THE next morning, Amy packed up her things, deposited them with her parents on West Seventy-fifth Street, and then spent her last month as a Barnard undergraduate camped out on the sofa in the living room of Patsy Dugan's apartment on Claremont Avenue.

Ferguson was more than exhausted now, more than numb, he was back in the dark dormitory elevator of the 1965 blackout, which could no longer be distinguished from the 1946–47 blackout when he was still in his mother's womb. He was twenty-one years old, and if he meant to have any kind of life in the future, he would have to be born all over again—a yowling neonate pulled from the darkness for another chance to find his way in the glare and shimmer of the world.

On May thirteenth, one million people marched through the streets of Paris. The whole country of France was in revolt, and where in God's name had de Gaulle gone to? One placard read: COLUMBIA-PARIS.

On the twenty-first, Hamilton Hall was occupied for a second time, and one hundred and thirty-eight people were arrested. That night, the battle on the Columbia campus between cops and students was bigger, bloodier, and even more savage than the one on the night of the seven-hundred-person bust.

After the May twenty-second issue, the *Spectator* ceased publication until the final issue of the semester on June third. That same day, Ferguson left New York to spend a month with his parents in Florida.

While he was in the air heading south, Andy Warhol was shot and almost killed by a woman named Valerie Solanas, who had written a manifesto entitled *SCUM* (Society for Cutting Up Men) and a play called *Up Your Ass*.

Two days after that, Robert Kennedy was shot in Los Angeles by a man named Sirhan Sirhan and killed at the age of forty-two.

Ferguson walked on the beach every evening at dusk, played tennis with his father on most mornings, ate lox and eggs at Wolfie's in honor of his grandmother, and spent the bulk of his time in the air-conditioned apartment working on his translations of French poems. On June sixteenth, not knowing where Amy was anymore, he sealed up one of those poems in an envelope and sent it off to her in care of her parents in New York. He couldn't write her a letter and wouldn't write her a letter, but the poem somehow managed to say most of the things he himself could no longer say to her.

THE PRETTY REDHEAD
BY GUILLAUME APOLLINAIRE

I stand here before you a man full of sense
Knowing life and as much of death as a living person can know
Having tasted the sorrows and joys of love
Having known at times how to get across his ideas

Knowing several languages
Having done his fair share of traveling
Having seen war in the Artillery and the Infantry
Wounded in the head trepanned under chloroform
Having lost his best friends in the nightmare of battle
I know as much as one man can know of both the ancient and
      the new
And without bothering myself about this war today
Between us and for us my friends
I judge this long quarrel between tradition and imagination
      As a dispute between Order and Adventure

You whose mouth is made in the image of God's mouth
A mouth that is order itself
Be gentle when you compare us
To those who are the perfection of order
We who are looking for adventure everywhere

We are not your enemies
We want to give you vast and strange kingdoms
Where the flowers of mystery are there for anyone to pluck
In those places there are new fires colors never seen
The chaos of a thousand optical illusions
Which must be made real

We want to explore kindness the enormous country where
      everything is silent
As well as time which can be chased away or summoned back
Pity for us who are always fighting at the frontiers
Of boundlessness and the future
Pity our mistakes pity our sins

Now summer is upon us the violent season
And my youth is as dead as the spring
O sun this is the time of burning Reason
      And I am waiting

To follow the sweet and noble form

She always takes so I alone can love her
She comes and draws me to her as iron filings to a magnet
     She has the charming look
     Of an adorable redhead

Her hair is made of gold it would seem
A beautiful flash of lightning that flashes on and on and on
Or those flames that waltz around
In wilting tea roses

But laugh laugh at me
Men from around the world especially people from here
For there are so many things I don't dare tell you
So many things you wouldn't let me say
Have pity on me

(translated by A. I. Ferguson)

6.2

6.3

THIRTY-NINE DAYS AFTER HE THREW FLEMING'S MONEY OUT THE
window, Ferguson typed the last pages of the final version of his
book. He had assumed he would start to feel all sorts of good things
about himself at that moment, but after a brief surge of elation as he
rolled the last five sheets of paper and carbon out of his typewriter,
those feelings soon went away, even the supposedly eternal good
feeling of having proved to himself that he was capable of writing a
book, that he was a person who finished what he started and not one of
those weak-willed pretenders who dreamed big dreams but never managed to deliver the goods, which was a human quality that pertained
to far more than just the writing of books, but after an hour or so Ferguson wasn't feeling much of anything but a kind of weary sadness,
and by the time he went downstairs for a pre-dinner drink with Vivian
and Lisa at six-thirty, his insides had gone numb.

Empty. That was the word for it, he said to himself, as he sat down
on the sofa and took his first sip of wine, the same *empty space* Vivian
had talked about when describing how she had felt after finishing her
own book. Not empty in the sense of standing alone in a room without
furniture—but empty in the sense of feeling hollowed out. Yes, that was
it, hollowed out in the way a woman was hollowed out after giving birth.
But in this case to a stillborn child, an infant who would never change
or grow or learn how to walk, for books lived inside you only as long
as you were writing them, but once they came out of you, they were all
used up and dead.

How long does the feeling go on? he asked Vivian, wondering if it was just a temporary crisis or the beginning of a plunge into full-blown melancholia, but before Vivian could answer him, live-wire Lisa jumped in and said, Not long, Archie. Only about a hundred years. Right, Viv?

There's one quick solution, Vivian said, smiling at the thought of those one hundred years. Start writing another book.

Another book? Ferguson said. I'm feeling so burned out right now, I'm not sure if I'll ever be able to *read* another book.

Nevertheless, Vivian and Lisa toasted Ferguson on having given birth to his baby, which might not have been alive for him, they said, but it was very much alive for them, and so much so, added Lisa (who hadn't read a single page of the book), that she would be willing to quit her law job if Ferguson promised to hire her as the nanny. Such was Lisa's sense of humor—her nonsensical sense of humor—but it tended to be funny because she herself was funny, and Ferguson laughed. Then he imagined Lisa strolling around Paris with a dead baby in a pram, and he laughed again.

The next morning, Ferguson and Vivian walked to the post office on the Boulevard Raspail, their local branch of the state-run PTT (Postes, Télégraphes et Téléphones), which in French was known as the Pay-Tay-Tay, the triple initials that tripped off the tongue so euphoniously that Ferguson never tired of repeating them, and once they had entered that sturdy edifice of communication services provided to the citizens of the French Republic and all others either traveling through or living in France, they airmailed a copy of Ferguson's manuscript to London. The envelope was not addressed to Aubrey Hull of Io Books but rather to a woman named Norma Stiles, who worked as a senior editor at Vivian's British publishing house (Thames & Hudson) and happened to be a friend of her younger T&H colleague Geoffrey Burnham, who in turn happened to be a close friend of Hull's. This was the way Vivian had chosen to submit the manuscript—through the intervention of her friend, who had assured her she would get to the manuscript *at once* and then pass it on to Burnham, who would then pass it on to Hull. Wasn't that unnecessarily complicated? Ferguson had asked Vivian when she proposed the idea to him. Wouldn't it be faster and simpler just to ship it off straight to Hull himself?

Faster, yes, Vivian had said, and simpler, too, but the odds of it being accepted would be close to nil, since *over-the-transom* submissions generally wind up in the *slush pile*—(both new terms to the uninitiated Ferguson)—and are almost always rejected without a proper reading. No, Archie, in this case the long way around is the better way, the only way.

In other words, Ferguson had said, two people have to like the book before it gets to the only person whose opinion matters.

I'm afraid so. Fortunately, those two people aren't dumb. We can count on them. The mystery is Hull. But at least there's a ninety-eight percent chance he'll read it.

So there they were on the morning of March 10, 1966, standing in line at the local Pay-Tay-Tay in the seventh arrondissement of Paris, and when their turn came, Ferguson marveled at how quickly and efficiently the little man behind the counter weighed the package on his gray metal scale, at how eagerly he slapped the postage onto the large brown envelope and then proceeded to pummel those red and green rectangles with his rubber stamp, canceling the multiple faces of Marianne to within an inch of her life, and suddenly Ferguson was thinking about the wild scene in *Monkey Business* when Harpo goes crazy stamping everything in sight, even the bald heads of the customs officials, and all at once he was flooded with a love for all things French, even the stupidest, most ridiculous things, and for the first time in several weeks he told himself how good it was to be living in Paris and how so much of what was good about it came from knowing Vivian and having her as a friend.

The cost of the airmail stamps was excessive, more than ninety francs when the insurance and the certified proof-of-delivery receipt were added in (close to twenty dollars, or one-fourth of his weekly allowance), but when Vivian reached into her bag to find the money to pay the clerk, Ferguson grabbed hold of her wrist and told her to stop.

Not this time, he said. It's my dead baby in there, and I'm the one who pays.

But Archie, it's so expensive . . .

I pay, Viv. At the Pay-Tay-Tay, I'm the one who pays.

Okay, Mr. Ferguson, as you wish. But now that your book is about to fly off to London, promise me you'll stop thinking about it. At least until there's a reason to start thinking about it again. All right?

I'll do my best, but I'm not making any promises.

□ □ □

THE SECOND PHASE of his life in Paris had begun. With no book to work on anymore and no need to continue going to the language classes at the Alliance Française, Ferguson was no longer bound by the rigid daytime schedule of the past five months. Except for his studies with Vivian, he was free to do whatever he wanted now, which above all meant that he had the time to go to movies on weekday afternoons, to write longer and more frequent letters to the people who counted most for him (his mother and Gil, Amy and Jim), to look for an indoor or outdoor court somewhere so he could start playing basketball again, and to make inquiries about rounding up some potential students for private English lessons. The basketball question wasn't resolved until the beginning of May, and he never managed to find any students, but he did send off a steady flow of letters and saw a staggering number of films, for good as New York had been as a place for watching movies, Paris was even better, and in the next two months he added one hundred and thirty entries to his loose-leaf binder, so many new pages that the original binder from New York now had a French brother.

That was the only writing he did throughout the first part of the spring—letters, aerograms, and postcards to America and a growing stack of one- and two-page synopses and shorthand observations of films. While working on the final revisions of his book, he had also been thinking about the essays and articles he wanted to write afterward, but now he realized those thoughts had been fueled by the adrenaline driving him to finish the book, and once the book was finished, the adrenaline was gone and his brain was kaput. He needed a little pause before he started up again, and consequently all through the early weeks of spring he was content to jot down ideas in the pocket-sized notebook he carried around with him on his walks, to sketch out possible arguments and counterarguments on various subjects while sitting at the desk in his room, and to come up with more examples for the piece he wanted to write about children in films, the representation of childhood in films, from the stinging switch whacks delivered to Freddie Bartholomew's rump by Basil Rathbone in *David Copperfield* to Peggy Ann Garner walking into the barbershop to retrieve her dead father's shaving mug in *A Tree Grows in Brooklyn*, from the hard slap to Jean-Pierre Léaud's head in *The 400 Blows* to Apu and his sister sitting first in a field of reeds to watch the train rush by and then perched in the hollow of a tree as rain pours down on them in *Pather Panchali*, the single most beautiful and devastating image of children Ferguson had ever encountered on film, an image so stark and dense with meaning that he had to restrain himself from crying every time he thought of it, but that essay and the other essays were all on hold for the time being because he was still so spent from working on his miserable little book that he scarcely had the energy to sustain a sequence of thoughts for more than twenty or thirty seconds without forgetting the first thought by the time he came to the third.

In spite of his joke about not being sure if he would ever be able to read another book, Ferguson read many books that spring, more books than he had read at any time in his life, and as his studies with Vivian moved forward, he felt more and more engaged in what they were doing together, more fully in it because Vivian herself seemed more confident, more comfortable in her role as teacher. So one by one they marched through six more plays by Shakespeare along with plays by Racine, Molière, and Calderón de la Barca, then tackled the essays of Montaigne as Vivian introduced him to the word *parataxis* and they discussed the power and speed of the prose and explored the mind of the man who had discovered or revealed or invented what Vivian called *the modern mind*, and then it was on to three solid weeks with the Knight of the Sad Countenance, who did for Ferguson at age nineteen what Laurel and Hardy had done for him as a boy, that is, conquer his heart with an all-embracing love for an imaginary being, the early seventeenth-century fumbler-visionary-madman who, like the movie clowns Ferguson had written about in his book, *never gave up*: ". . . and for a long while, stumbling here, falling there, flung down in one place and rising up in another, I have been carrying out a great part of my design . . ."

The books on Gil's list but also books about film, histories and anthologies in both English and French, essays and polemics by André Bazin, Lotte Eisner, and the New Wave directors before they started making their own films, the early articles of Godard, Truffaut, and Chabrol, a rereading of Eisenstein's two books, the musings of Parker Tyler, Manny Farber, and James Agee, studies and meditations by old venerables such as Siegfried Kracauer, Rudolf Arnheim, and Béla Balázs, every issue of *Cahiers du Cinéma* from cover to cover, sitting in the British Council Library reading *Sight & Sound*, waiting for his subscription copies of *Film Culture* and *Film Comment* to arrive from New York, and then, after reading in the morning from eight-thirty to twelve, the afternoon excursions to the Cinémathèque just across the river, only one franc for a ticket with his old student card from the Riverside Academy, which the ticket taker never even glanced at to see if the card was still valid, the first and biggest and best film archive anywhere in the world, founded by the fat, obsessive, Quixote-like Henri Langlois, the film man of all film men, and how curious it was to watch rare British films with Swedish subtitles or silent films with no musical accompaniment, but that was the Langlois Law, NO MUSIC, and although it took Ferguson some time to adjust to an all-silent screen and a theater with no sounds in it but the coughs and sneezes of the crowd and an occasional crackling from the projector, he came to appreciate the power of that silence, for it often happened that he *heard* things while watching those films, the slamming of a car door or a glass of water being put down on a table or a bomb exploding on a battlefield, the silence of the silent films seemed to produce a frenzy of auditory hallucinations, which said something about human perception, he supposed, and how people experienced things when they were emotionally involved in the experience, and when he wasn't going to the Cinémathèque, he was off to La Pagode, Le Champollion, or one of the theaters on the rue Monsieur-le-Prince or on or behind the Boulevard Saint-Michel near the rue des Écoles, and then, most helpful to furthering his education, there was the surprise discovery of Action Lafayette, Action République, and Action Christine, the triumvirate of Action houses that showed nothing but old Hollywood films, the black-and-white studio fare of a bygone America that few Americans remembered anymore, the comedies, crime stories, Depression dramas, boxing pictures, and war movies from the thirties, forties, and early fifties that had been cranked out by the thousands, and so rich were the possibilities offered to him that Ferguson's knowledge of American films greatly increased after he moved to Paris—just as his love of French films had been born at the Thalia Theater and the Museum of Modern Art in New York.

Meanwhile, Fleming was after him, Fleming was desperate to apologize, Fleming was bending over backward to make up for the night of the money and the tears, and for many days after that night he called Vivian's apartment at least once a day to talk to Ferguson, but when

Celestine slipped the messages under the door of Ferguson's room, Ferguson would tear them up and not call back. Two straight weeks of unanswered calls, and then the calls stopped and the letters and notes began. Please, Archie, let me prove to you that I'm not the person you think I am. Please, Archie, allow me to be your friend. Please, Archie, I've met so many interesting students here in Paris, and I would love to introduce them to you so you can begin making friends with people your own age. Three straight weeks of two or three letters a week, all of them unanswered, all of them torn up and thrown away, and then, finally, the letters stopped as well. Ferguson prayed that was the end of it, but there was always the possibility he would run into Fleming at another dinner somewhere or accidentally bump into him on the street, and therefore the story wouldn't be officially over until Fleming went back to America in August, which was still months away.

The nights continued to be gruesome, with no bed partner or kissing mate of either sex to pull him out of his isolation, but better to be alone with no one to touch than to be touched by a man like Fleming, he said to himself, even if it wasn't Fleming's fault for being who he was, and then Ferguson would switch off the light, lower his head onto the pillow, and lie in the dark remembering.

THE INDUSTRIOUS AND efficient PTT, which did the same work in France that was divided among three entities in America (the U.S. Post Office, Western Union, and Ma Bell), saw to it that the mail was delivered twice a day, once in the morning and once in the afternoon, and because Ferguson's address was the same as Vivian's address, his letters and packages made their initial landing in the downstairs apartment. Once they arrived, the good Celestine would carry them upstairs, slipping the letters under the door of Ferguson's room or knocking on the door to hand him the things that were too large to fit through that narrow space—his American film magazines, for example, or the books Gil and Amy occasionally sent him. At ten past nine on the morning of April eleventh, as Ferguson sat in his room reading Calderón de la Barca's *Life Is a Dream* (*La Vida es Sueño*), he heard the familiar light tread of Celestine's feet on the stairs, then the creaking floorboards in the corridor as she approached his room, and a moment later a slim white envelope was lying on the floor just inches from his feet. British postage. A business envelope with a printed return address in the upper left-hand corner that read: Io Books. Fully expecting bad news, Ferguson bent down, picked up the letter, and then delayed opening it for six or seven minutes, long enough to begin asking himself why he was so scared of something he had already told himself didn't matter.

It took another thirty or forty seconds for him to understand that the bad news he had been expecting was in fact good news, that for an advance of four hundred pounds against royalties it was Io's *enthusiastic intention* to publish *How Laurel and Hardy Saved My Life* sometime in March or April of the following year, but not even the affirmative response from Aubrey Hull could convince him that anyone would truly want to accept his book, so Ferguson concocted a story to explain the letter by silently accusing Vivian of having put up the money to pay for the publication herself, no doubt buying off Hull in one of those sinister backroom deals that had included writing another check for many thousands of pounds to pay for more Io Books in the future. Not once since he had moved to Paris had he ever been angry at Vivian, not once had he ever spoken a harsh word to her or suspected her of being anything less than honest and kind, but this was taking kindness too far, he said to himself, this was turning kindness into a form of humiliation, and on top of that it was deeply and revoltingly dishonest.

By nine-thirty, he was downstairs in Vivian's apartment, thrusting Hull's letter at her and demanding that she own up to what she had done. Vivian had never seen Ferguson in such a foul temper. The young man was beside himself, fuming with outrageous, paranoiac visions of devious plots and vile deceptions, and as Vivian later told him, only two possible reactions occurred to her as she stood there watching him fall apart: either slap him across the face or laugh. She chose to laugh. Laughter was the slower of the two solutions, but within ten minutes she had managed to persuade the proud, overly sensitive, pathologically self-doubting Ferguson that she had played no role in the acceptance of his book and had not sent Hull a farthing, a sou, or a single red dime.

Believe in yourself, Archie, she said. Show some swagger. And for God's sake, don't ever accuse me of anything like that again.

Ferguson promised he wouldn't. He felt so ashamed of himself, he said, so mortified by his *inexcusable tantrum,* and the worst part of it was that he had no idea what had gotten into him. Crazy, that's what it was, pure craziness, and if it ever happened again, she should forget about laughing and slap him across the face.

Vivian accepted his apology. They made up. The storm had passed, and a short time later they even went into the kitchen together to celebrate the good news by having a second breakfast of mimosas and little crackers topped with caviar, but good as Ferguson was beginning to feel about the good news in Hull's letter, his mad outburst continued to trouble him, and he wondered if that scene with Vivian wasn't an early warning sign of an eventual crack-up.

For the first time in his life, he was beginning to feel a little afraid of himself.

ON THE FIFTEENTH, a second letter arrived from Hull announcing that he would be coming to Paris on Tuesday the nineteenth. The Io man apologized for being *so terribly last-minute about the trip*, but if Ferguson happened to be unengaged that afternoon, he would welcome the chance to meet him. He suggested a twelve-thirty lunch at Fouquet's, where they could discuss plans for the book, and if the conversation needed to be extended beyond lunch, his hotel was right around the corner off the Champs-Élysées, and they could pop over there and continue. One way or the other, Ferguson could accept or decline by leaving word with the concierge at the George V. All good wishes, etc.

Based on what Vivian had learned from her friend Norma Stiles, whose knowledge was based on what she had learned from her co-worker Geoffrey Burnham, what Ferguson knew about Aubrey Hull was limited to these facts: thirty years old, married to a woman named Fiona and the father of two small children (ages four and one), a graduate of Oxford's Balliol College (where he had met Burnham), the son of a wealthy chocolate and biscuit manufacturer, a quasi–black sheep (a gray sheep?) who liked to travel in artistic circles and had a good nose for literature, a serious publisher but also known as a *party person* and a bit of an *eccentric*.

The vagueness of that portrait led Ferguson to imagine Hull as one of those pompous British gentlemen who showed up frequently in American films, the snide and snooty fellow with a ruddy face and a penchant for mocking, under-the-breath remarks that were supposed to be amusing but never were. Perhaps Ferguson had been watching too many films, or perhaps his instinctive fear of the unknown had taught him to expect the worst in all new situations, but the truth was that not only did Aubrey Hull not have a ruddy face or a snide disposition, he turned out to be one of the most affectionate and lovable human beings Ferguson had ever run across in his travels through life.

So small, so much a miniaturized sort of man, just five foot three and every one of his features miniaturized in proportion as well: small head, small face, small hands, small mouth, small arms and legs. Bright blue eyes. The creamy-white complexion of a person who lived in a sunless, rain-soaked country, and a crown of curly hair that fell somewhere between red and blond on the spectrum, the shade of hair Ferguson had once heard someone call *ginger*. At a loss for words when they shook hands and sat down for lunch at Fouquet's on the afternoon of the nineteenth, Ferguson forced himself to try to make conversation by witlessly telling Hull that he was the first person he had ever met with the name Aubrey. Hull smiled and asked Ferguson if he knew what the name meant. No, Ferguson said, he had no idea. *The ruler of the elves*, Hull said, and so comical and unexpected was that answer to Ferguson that he had to struggle to push back the laugh that was gathering in his lungs, a laugh that could have been misconstrued as an insult, he realized, and why would he risk insulting the man who had accepted his book within the first two minutes of their first meeting? But still—how apt it was, how perfectly fitting that this little man should be the ruler of the elves! It was as if the gods had walked into Aubrey's house the night before he was born and had instructed his parents on the name they should give their child, and now that Ferguson's head was filing up with images of elves and gods, he looked at his publisher's small, handsome face and wondered if he wasn't sitting in the presence of a mythical being.

Until that day, Ferguson had known nothing about how publishing houses operated or what they did to promote their books. Other than designing and printing them, he had assumed the principal job was to get them reviewed in as many newspapers and magazines as possible. If the reviews were good, the book was a hit. If the reviews were bad, the book was a flop. Now Aubrey was telling him that the reviews were only one element in the process, and as the ruler of the elves elaborated on what some of the other elements were, Ferguson grew more and more interested, more and more amazed by what would be happening to him when his book was published. A trip to London for one thing. Interviews with the daily and weekly press, interviews with reporters from the BBC, perhaps even an appearance on *live telly*. An evening event at a small theater, where Ferguson would read passages from his book to the audience and then sit down for a conversation about the book with a sympathetic journalist or fellow writer. And—still to be worked out, but what a pleasant prospect if it did work out—a Laurel and Hardy night at the NFT or some other cinema with Ferguson on stage to introduce the films.

Ferguson in the limelight. Ferguson with his picture in the paper. Ferguson with his voice on the radio. Ferguson onstage reading to a hushed crowd of devoted fans.

How could anyone not want that?

The point is, Aubrey was saying, your book is so damned good that it deserves the whole bloody treatment. No one is supposed to write books at nineteen. It just isn't heard of, and my bet is that people are going to be fucking bowled over by it, just as I was, just as Fiona was, just as everyone on my staff was.

Let's hope so, Ferguson said, trying to keep a lid on his excitement so as not to get carried away by Aubrey's words and end up making a fool of himself. But how good he was beginning to feel now. Doors were opening. One by one, Aubrey was opening doors for him, and one by one there would be new rooms for him to enter, and the thought of what he would find in those rooms filled him with happiness—more happiness than he had felt in months.

I don't want to exaggerate, Aubrey said (probably meaning that he did), but even if you dropped dead tomorrow, *How Laurel and Hardy Saved My Life* would live on forever.

What a strange sentence, Ferguson replied. It could be the strangest sentence I've ever heard.

Yes, it was rather odd, wasn't it?

First I'm dropping dead, then I'm saving my life, and then I'm living on forever, even though I'm supposed to be dead.

Very odd indeed. But delivered from the heart and meant as a sincere compliment.

They looked at each other and laughed. Something was beginning to rise to the surface, something strong enough to make Ferguson suspect that Aubrey was coming on to him, that his jolly, ginger-headed lunch companion was the same kind of two-way person he was and had been down this road many times before. He wondered if Aubrey's dick was as small as the rest of him, and then, starting to think about his own dick, he asked himself if he would ever have a chance to find out.

You see, Archie, Aubrey continued, I've come to the conclusion that you're a person apart from most other people, a special person. I sensed that when I read your manuscript, but now that I've met you face to face, I'm convinced of it. You're your own man, and because of that you're a thrilling person to be with, but also because of that you're never going to fit in anywhere, which is a good thing, I believe, since you'll be able to go on being your own man, and a man who is his own man is a better man than most men, even if he doesn't fit in.

Actually, Ferguson said, putting forth his best and biggest smile as he plunged into the seduction game Aubrey seemed to have started, I try to fit it in wherever I can . . . with whomever I can.

Aubrey grinned back at him after that obscene retort, heartened to know that Ferguson understood every nuance of the situation. That's what I mean, he said. You're open to all experiences.

Yes, Ferguson replied, very open. To one and all.

One and all in this case meant the one who was sitting across from him in the posh and pleasingly clamorous Fouquet's, the thoroughly engaging Aubrey Hull, a man who had dropped out of nowhere and was going to do everything in his power to transform Ferguson's life by turning his book into a success, the charming and flirtatious Aubrey Hull, a most desirable and intoxicating sort of man whose pretty little mouth Ferguson so urgently wanted to kiss, and then, after Aubrey had thrown back another glass or two of wine, the supposed eccentric started calling Ferguson a bonny boy and a lovely lad, a good lad, a fine lad, which wasn't eccentric so much as endearing and arousing, and by the time they finished their lunch it was all out in the open, with no more mysteries to ponder or questions to be asked.

Ferguson sat down on the bed in the fifth-floor room of the Hôtel George V and watched Aubrey take off his suit jacket and tie. It had been so long since he had been with anyone he cared about, so long since any-one had touched him or had wanted to touch him without first talking about money that when the ruler of the elves walked over to the bed, climbed into his lap, and put his arms around Ferguson's fully clothed torso, Ferguson shivered. Then he was kissing the pretty little mouth and shuddering up and down the entire length of his body, and as their tongues met and the embrace tightened, Ferguson remembered the words he had said to himself years earlier while riding on the bus to Boston to see his beloved Jim: *the gates of heaven.* Yes, that was how it felt to him now, and after the rooms he had visited in his mind during lunch, the rooms he had walked into as Aubrey had stood there opening one door after another for him, now another door was opening and he and Aubrey were walking into the room together. Earthbound men. A bed in a Paris hotel named after an English king. An Englishman and an American on that bed in their bare, earthbound flesh. *Au-delà.* The French word for the hereafter. The next world breathing inside them in the here and now of this one.

The dick was as small as he had imagined it would be, but as with all the rest of Aubrey, it was fit to the proportions of his miniaturized frame and was no less pretty than his pretty little mouth or any other part of him. The important thing was that Aubrey knew what to do with what he had. At thirty, he was far more experienced in bed and body matters than the boys Ferguson had slept with in the past, and because he was a companionable lover with no odd or unsavory inclinations and no guilt about his passion for fucking and being fucked by boys, he was at once more subtle and more aggressive than Andy Cohen and Brian Mischevski had been, at once more confident in himself and more generous, a darling person who enjoyed doing it as much as he enjoyed having it done to him, and the hours he spent with Ferguson that afternoon and evening were surely the best and most satisfying hours of Ferguson's life in Paris so far. One week earlier, Ferguson had feared he was heading for a crack-up. Now his brain was bulging with a thousand new thoughts, and his body was at rest.

TEN DAYS AFTER traveling to the next world in the arms of his English publisher, Ferguson put his arms around his mother and asked her to forgive him. She and Gil had just landed in Paris. The *New York Herald Tribune* had shut down and died on April twenty-fourth, and with Gil temporarily unemployed until the fall, when he would begin his new career as a professor at the Mannes College of Music, Ferguson's mother and stepfather had decided to go on the honeymoon they still hadn't taken after six and a half years of marriage. One week in Paris to start with. Then Amsterdam, Florence, Rome, and West Berlin, which Gil had last seen six months after the end of the war in late 1945. They were planning to spend their time looking at Dutch and Italian art, and then Gil would show Ferguson's mother the places where he had lived as a boy.

Ferguson had finished typing the three copies of his book on March ninth. One copy was now sitting on the top shelf of the bookcase in his room in Paris, another copy was sitting on Aubrey's desk in London, and the third had been sent to his parents' apartment on Riverside Drive in New York. Two weeks after the manuscript had made its way across the ocean, Ferguson had received a letter from Gil. That was normal, since his mother wasn't much of a letter writer and nine-tenths of the correspondence he sent to the two of them jointly was answered solely by Gil, sometimes with a short P.S. from his mother at the end (*I miss you so much, Archie!* or *A thousand kisses from your Ma!*) and sometimes not. The early paragraphs of Gil's letter had been full of positive comments about the book and the *outstanding job* he had done in balancing *the emotional content of the story with the physical and phenomenological data* and how impressed he was by Ferguson's *rapid growth and improvement as a writer*. By the fourth paragraph, however, the tone of the letter had begun to change. *But dear Archie,* Gil had written, *you must realize how profoundly the book has upset your mother and how difficult it was for her to read it. Of course, reliving such hard days from the past would be difficult for anyone, and I don't fault you for having made her cry (I shed some tears myself), but there were a few spots where you might have been a bit too honest, I'm afraid, and she was stunned by the intimacy of the details you revealed about her. In looking over the manuscript again, I would say that the most offensive passage falls on pp. 46–47, in the middle of the section about the grim summer the two of you spent at the Jersey shore, locked in that little house together watching television from early in the morning to late at night and hardly ever setting foot on the beach. Just to refresh your memory: "My mother had always smoked, but now she smoked without interruption, consuming four and five packs of Chesterfields per day, rarely bothering to use matches or lighters anymore because it was simpler and more efficient to light the next cigarette with the burning tip of the last one. As far as I knew, she had seldom drunk alcohol in the past, but now she drank six and seven shot glasses of straight vodka every evening, and by the time she put me to bed at night her voice would be slurred and her eyelids would be half-closed over eyes that could no longer bear to look at the world. My father had been dead for eight months by then, and every night that summer I would climb under the warm and rumpled top sheet of my bed and pray that my mother would still be alive in the morning." This is rough stuff, Archie. Perhaps you should consider cutting it out of the final version or at least modifying it to some degree—to spare your mother the pain of having that wretched interval of her life exposed to public view. Stop and think about it for a moment, and you'll understand why I'm asking you to do this . . .* Then came the final paragraph: *The good news is that the Trib is about to croak, and I'll soon be out of a job. Once that happens, your mother and I will be off to Europe—most likely by the end of April. We can talk about it then.*

But Ferguson hadn't wanted to wait until then. The matter was too disturbing to be put off until the end of April, for now that Gil had lifted those sentences out of the book and isolated them from the surrounding material, Ferguson understood that he had been too harsh and deserved the scolding his stepfather had given him. It wasn't that the passage was untrue, at least from the perspective of his eight-year-old self as remembered by his older self while he had been writing the book. His mother had been smoking too much that summer, she had been drinking straight shots of vodka and not taking care of the house, and he had been alarmed by the listlessness and passivity that had taken hold of her, at times even frightened by her numbed withdrawal from him as he sat beside her building sand castles on the beach and she looked out at the waves. The sentences Gil had transcribed in his letter depicted Ferguson's mother at her lowest ebb, at the very bottom of her descent into grief and confusion, but the whole point had been to contrast that lost summer with what had happened to her after they returned to New York, which had marked her return to photography and the beginning of a new life, the invention of Rose Adler. It seemed that Ferguson had made too much of the contrast, however, infusing his little-boy fears and misapprehensions of adult behavior into a situation that had been less dire than he had imagined (there had been some vodka, according to what his mother had told Gil, but only two bottles over the forty-six days they had spent in Belmar), and therefore Ferguson had sat down after finishing the letter and had written contrite one-page responses to both his mother and his stepfather, apologizing for any upset he might have caused them and promising to delete the offending passage from the book.

So there he was now on the morning of April twenty-ninth standing in the lobby of the Hôtel Pont Royal with his arms around his jet-
lagged mother asking her to forgive him. Outside, rain was pounding
down on the streets, and as Ferguson settled his chin onto his mother's
shoulder, he looked through the front window of the hotel and saw an
umbrella go flying out of a woman's hand.

No, Archie, his mother said, I don't need to forgive you for anything.
You need to forgive me.

Gil was already standing in line at the front desk, waiting his turn
to hand over their passports, sign the register, and check them into the
hotel, and while he went about that tedious business, Ferguson led his
mother to a bench in a corner of the lobby. She looked worn out from
the trip, and if she wanted to go on talking to him as he supposed she
did, it would be easier for her to do it sitting down. Worn out, Ferguson
added to himself, but no more than anyone else would have been after
traveling for twelve or thirteen straight hours, and looking just fine,
he thought, with scarcely an iota of difference between now and the
last time he had seen her six and a half months ago. His beautiful
mother. His beautiful, somewhat exhausted mother, and how good it
felt to be looking at her face again.

I've really missed you, Archie, she said. I know you're a big person
now, and you have every right to live wherever you want, but this is the
longest we've ever been apart, and it's taken some getting used to.

I know, Ferguson said. It's been the same for me.

But you're happy here, aren't you?

Yes, most of the time. At least I think I am. Life isn't perfect, you
know. Not even in Paris.

That's a good one. Not even in Paris. Not even in New York either,
for that matter.

Tell me, Ma. Why did you say what you said a couple of moments
ago—before we came over here and sat down?

Because it's true, that's why. Because it was wrong of me to make
such a fuss.

I don't agree. What I wrote was cruel and unfair.

Not necessarily. Not from where you were sitting as an eight-year-
old boy. I'd managed to hold it together while you were going to school,
but then it was vacation time, and I didn't know what to do with myself

anymore. A mess, Archie, that's what I was, an unholy mess, and it must have been a bit scary for you to be around me then.

That's not the point

No, you're wrong. It is the point. You remember *Jewish Wedding*, don't you?

Of course I do. Mean old cousin Charlotte and her bald, myopic husband, Mr. What's-His-Name.

Nathan Birnbaum, the dentist.

It's been about ten years, hasn't it?

Almost eleven years. And I still haven't talked to them again in all that time. You understand why, don't you? (*Ferguson shook his head.*) Because they did to me what I almost did to you.

I don't follow.

I took pictures of them that they didn't like. Pretty good pictures, I thought. Not the most flattering pictures in the world, but good pictures, interesting pictures, and when they refused to let me publish them, I let Charlotte and Nathan disappear from my life because I thought they were a pair of fools.

What does that have to do with *Laurel and Hardy*?

Don't you get it? You took a picture of me in your book. Lots of pictures, actually, dozens and dozens of them, and most of them were very flattering, some of them so flattering that I was almost embarrassed to read those things about myself, but along with all the flattering pictures there were one or two that showed me in a different light, an unflattering light, and when I read those parts of the book I felt hurt and angry, so hurt and angry that I talked to Gil about it, which I shouldn't have done, and then he wrote that letter to you, which made you feel so bad, bad because I know the last thing you would ever want to do is hurt me, and when you wrote those little letters back to us, I felt I'd done you a wrong turn. Your book is an honest book, Archie. You told the truth in every sentence of it, and I don't want you to revise anything or delete anything for my sake. Are you listening to me, Archie? *Don't change a word.*

The week passed quickly. Vivian suspended their study sessions for the length of the visit, and although Ferguson carried on with several hours of reading in the morning, he met up with his mother and Gil every afternoon for lunch and then remained with them until it was time to come home and go to bed. Many things had changed in the months since he had left New York, and yet everything was essentially the same. Gil had finished his book on Beethoven after seven years of work, and he seemed to have no regrets about giving up the pressures of reviewing and journalism for the quieter life of teaching music history at Mannes. Ferguson's mother continued to make portraits of well-known people for magazines and was slowly assembling a new book about the anti-war movement at home (she was vehemently pro-anti). She took the small Leica and several rolls of film with her everywhere they went during those days, snapping picture after picture of the protest signs that had gone up all over Paris (U.S. OUT OF VIETNAM, YANKEE GO HOME, À BAS LES AMERLOQUES, LE VIETNAM POUR LES VIETNAMIENS) along with numerous shots of Paris street scenes and a couple of rolls of just Ferguson and Gil, both singly and together. The three of them looked at paintings in the Louvre and the Jeu de Paume, they went to the Salle Pleyel for a performance of Haydn's *Mass in Time of War* (Ferguson and his mother both thought it was *extraordinary*, but Gil answered their enthusiasm with a pained smile, which meant it hadn't been up to snuff for him), and one night after dinner Ferguson coaxed them into traveling to the Action Lafayette for a ten o'clock screening of Mervyn LeRoy's *Random Harvest*, a film they all agreed had enough horseshit in it to fill up four stables, but, as Ferguson's mother pointed out, how enjoyable it was to watch Greer Garson and Ronald Colman pretending to be in love.

Needless to say, Ferguson told them about the letter from Io Books. Needless to say, his mother said she would be glad to donate a negative of *Archie* for the cover. Needless to say, Ferguson took them upstairs and showed them his room on the sixth floor. Needless to say, his mother and Gil reacted differently to what they saw. His mother gasped and said: Oh, Archie, is it really possible? Gil, on the other hand, clapped him on the shoulder and said: Anyone who can make a go of it in here has my full and enduring respect.

Other matters were not so simple or pleasant for Ferguson, however, and several times throughout the week he found himself in the uncomfortable position of having to hold things back from them or having to tell them lies. When his mother asked if he had met any *nice girls*, for example, he made up a story about a brief flirtation with an attractive Italian student named Giovanna who had been in his language class at the Alliance Française. It was true that Giovanna had been in the class, but other than two thirty-minute conversations in the café around the corner from the school, nothing had developed between them. Nor had anything developed between him and Béatrice, the *highly intelligent* French girl who worked as an assistant at the Galerie Maeght and was supposedly someone he had dated for a *month or two*. Yes, Béatrice worked for the gallery, and they had sat next to each other at a Maeght *vernissage* dinner back in December, flirting in a mild, unfocused sort of way, but when Ferguson called to ask her out, she turned him down with the excuse that she was engaged to be married, something she hadn't bothered to mention at the dinner. No, he couldn't talk to his mother about girls because there hadn't been any girls except for the five overweight and underweight hookers he had found in the streets of Les Halles, and he wasn't about to talk to her about them, nor was he was going to break her heart by talking about Aubrey and how excited he had been when the ruler of the elves had pushed his stiffened cock deep into his ass. She could never know any of those things about him. There were zones of his life that had to be walled off from her and guarded with utmost vigilance, and because of that they could never be as close to each other as they had once been, as he still wanted them to be. That wasn't to say he hadn't lied to her in the past, but he was older now and the circumstances were different, and yet even as he walked around Paris with her and rejoiced in how happy she looked, rejoiced in how fully she continued to stand behind him, those days were tinged with sadness as well, a feeling that some essential part of him was on the verge of melting away and disappearing from his life forever.

There were three dinners with Vivian that week, two in restaurants and one at the apartment on the rue de l'Université, a small dinner with just the four of them and no other guests, not even Lisa, who normally came to all of Vivian's parties. Ferguson was a bit surprised when he was told that Lisa wouldn't be joining them, but then he thought about it for a couple of minutes and understood that Vivian was protecting herself, which was exactly what he would have done if he had been in her place. Like him, she had a dirty secret to hide from the world, and even though Gil was an old friend, he apparently knew nothing about the complicated marriage she had built with Jean-Pierre and nothing about what she had been up to since Jean-Pierre's death and therefore could not be exposed to the spectacle of dining with Vivian's new female bed partner. Shades of Aunt Mildred and the cowgirl in Palo Alto four years ago, Ferguson said to himself, but with this crucial difference: even at fifteen, he hadn't cared and hadn't been shocked, but while the fifty-two-year-old Gil might have thought he wouldn't care, he almost certainly would have been shocked.

As the four of them sat around the dining room table that evening, Ferguson was comforted to see how well Vivian and his mother got along, how rapidly they had turned into friends after just a few encounters, but the two women were bound together now because of Gil and their admiration for each other (how many times had Vivian talked about his mother's *exceptional photographs*?) and also because of him, his mother's displaced son now living under Vivian's roof, and again and again since coming to Paris his mother had told him how grateful she was to Vivian for taking care of him and studying with him and giving him *so much*, and at the dinner that night she was saying those things directly to Vivian herself, thanking her for watching over her *rascal of a boy*, and yes, Vivian said, *That imp of yours can be quite a handful at times*, the two of them teasing him because they both knew he could take it and didn't mind, for not only did he not mind but he actually enjoyed being teased by them, and in the middle of that lighthearted, anti-Archie mockathon, it occurred to him that Vivian had a better grasp of who he was now than his mother did. Not only had she worked on the manuscript of his book with him, not only were they plowing their way through the one hundred most important works in Western literature together, but she knew everything about his split-in-two inner self and was, undoubtedly, the most trusted confidant he had ever had. A second mother? No, not that. No need for more mothers at this late date. But what? More than a friend, less than a mother. His female twin, perhaps. The person he would have become if he had been born a girl.

On the last day, he stopped by the Hôtel Pont Royal to see them off. The city was at its best and most beautiful that morning, a bright blue sky overheard, the air warm and clear, good smells floating out of the neighborhood *boulangeries*, pretty girls in the streets, honking cars, farting mopeds, the whole glorious, Gershwinian dazzle of Springtime in Paris, the Paris of a hundred cornball songs and Technicolor movies, but the fact was that it truly was glorious and inspiring, it truly was the best place on earth, and yet as Ferguson walked from the apartment house on the rue de l'Université to the hotel on the rue Montalembert, even as he took note of the sky and the smells and the girls, he was struggling against the immense weight that had fallen upon him that morning, the dumb and childish dread of having to say good-bye to his mother. He didn't want her to go. A week hadn't been long enough, even if a part of him knew he would be better off with her gone, that bit by bit he always turned into a baby again when he was with her, but now the ordinary sadness of another farewell had mutated into a premonition that he would never see her again, that something was going to happen to her before they had another chance to be together and that this good-bye would be their last one. A ridiculous thought, he said to himself, the stuff of feebleminded romantic fantasies, a surge of adolescent angst in its most embarrassing form, but the thought was in him now and he didn't know how to get rid of it.

When he arrived at the hotel, he found his mother in a whirling state of hustle and excitement, wrapped up in the moment with no time to talk about dark premonitions of fatal diseases and deadly accidents, for on this particular morning she was going to the Gare du Nord, she was going to Amsterdam, she was on her way out of Paris to another city, another country, another adventure was about to begin, and there were satchels and suitcases to be loaded into the trunk of the taxi, there were last-minute peeks into her handbag to make sure she had Gil's stomach tablets with her, there were tips to be handed out and doormen and bellhops to thank and say good-bye to, and after giving her son a quick and ebullient farewell hug, she turned to head for the cab, but just as Gil opened the door for her and she was about to climb into the backseat, she turned around and blew Ferguson a big, smiling kiss. Be a good boy, Archie, she said, and suddenly the bad feeling he had been carrying around with him since early in the morning went away.

As he watched the taxi disappear around the corner, Ferguson decided he was going to ignore his mother's wishes and cut the passage from the book.

THE BAD FEELING vanished, but as events would prove ten months later, Ferguson's premonition had not been wrong. The farewell hug he exchanged with his mother on May sixth was the last time they ever touched each other, and once she climbed into the backseat of the taxi and Gil shut the door, Ferguson never saw her again. They spoke to each other on the telephone, one call on the night of his twentieth birthday in March 1967, but after Ferguson hung up the receiver, he never heard her voice again. His premonition had not been wrong, but neither had it been exactly on the mark. The deadly accident or disease that Ferguson had imagined would strike down his mother did not happen to her but to him, in his case a traffic accident that occurred during his visit to London to celebrate the publication of his book, which meant that after he said good-bye to his mother in Paris on May 6, 1966, he had three hundred and four days to live.

Mercifully, he was not aware of the cruel plan the gods had devised for him. Mercifully, he did not know he was destined to have such a brief entry in *The Book of Terrestrial Life*, and therefore he went on living as if there were thousands of tomorrows in front of him rather than just three hundred and four.

Two days after his mother and Gil left for Amsterdam, Ferguson backed out of going to a party with Vivian and Lisa when he found out that Fleming had been invited. It had been more than three months since the night of the money and the tears, and he had long since absolved Fleming of any blame for his part in the misunderstanding. It was the memory of what he had allowed himself to do with Fleming that continued to haunt him, the conviction that it had been his own fault, all his fault, and because Fleming hadn't forced him to do anything he hadn't said he was willing to do, how could he hold Fleming responsible for what had happened? It wasn't Fleming, it was himself, his own shame, the memory of his own greed and degradation that had prompted him to rip up Fleming's letters and not return his calls, but even if he bore no grudge against Fleming now, why would he ever want to see him again?

At breakfast in the kitchen the following morning, Vivian told him about someone she had met at the party, which had been thrown in the courtyard garden of Reid Hall, Columbia University's outpost in Paris, a young man of twenty-five or twenty-six who had made a strong impression on her, she said, someone she thought Ferguson would like just as much as she had. A Canadian from Montreal with a white Québécquoise mother and a black American father originally from New Orleans, a person by the name of Albert Dufresne (Al-bear Du-frenn) who had graduated from Howard University in Washington, where he had played on *the basketball team* (something Vivian supposed would interest Ferguson, which it did), and who had moved to Paris after his father's death, where he was working on *his first novel* (another thing

Vivian supposed would interest Ferguson, which it did), and now that
she had captured his attention, he asked her to tell him more.

Such as?

Such as, what is he like?

Intense. Intelligent. Engaged—as in *engagé*. Not a big sense of humor,
I'm sorry to report. But very alive. Captivating. One of those burning
young men who wants to turn the world upside down and reinvent it.

Unlike me, for example.

You don't want to reinvent the world, Archie, you want to understand the world so you can find a way to live in it.

And what makes you think I'd get along with this person?

A fellow scribbler, a fellow basketball player, a fellow North American, a fellow only child, and even though his father died only a couple
of years ago, a fellow fatherless boy, since his old man absconded when
Albert was six and went back to live in New Orleans.

What did the father do?

Jazz trumpet, and according to his son, a hard-drinking, dyed-in-
the-wool, lifelong son of a bitch.

And the mother?

A fifth-grade schoolteacher. Just like my mother.

You must have had a lot to talk about.

I should also say that Mr. Dufresne cuts a fine figure, a most unusual
figure.

How so?

Tall. About six-one or six-two. Lean and muscular, I would guess,
although he was standing there with his clothes on, of course, so I can't
be more precise. But he seems to be an ex-athlete who's managed to keep
himself in shape. Says he still plays *hoops* whenever he can.

That's good. But I fail to see what's unusual about it.

It's his face, I think, the striking qualities of his face. Not only was
his father black, but there's Choctaw blood in there, too, he told me, and
when you mix that up with his white mother's genes, he comes across
as a light-skinned black person with somewhat Asiatic features, Eur-
asian features. A remarkable skin color, I found, with a glowing, cop-
pery cast to it, skin that's neither dark nor pale, Goldilocks's *just right*, if
you know what I mean, such lovely skin that I kept wanting to touch
his face while I was talking to him.

Handsome?

No, I wouldn't go that far. But nice-looking. A face you want to look at.

And what about his . . . his innermost inclinations?

I can't say for sure. Usually, I can tell right off, but this Albert is something of a puzzle. A man for other men, I'd presume, but a manly sort of man who doesn't want to broadcast his attraction to other men.

A macho queer.

Perhaps. He mentioned James Baldwin a few times, if that means anything. He loves Baldwin above all American writers. That's why he came to Paris, he said, because he wanted to *follow in Jimmy's footsteps*.

I love Baldwin, too, and I agree that he's the best American writer, but just because he happens to swing toward men doesn't prove anything about the men who like his books.

Exactly. In any case, I talked about you quite a bit, and Albert seemed mightily impressed when I told him about your book, maybe even a little envious. Nineteen, he kept saying. Nineteen, and already about to be published, and there he was in his mid-twenties still grinding away at the first half of his first novel.

I hope you told him it was a short book.

I did. A very short book. And I also mentioned that you've been dying to play basketball. Believe it or not, he lives on the rue Descartes in the fifth, and right across the street from his building there's an outdoor court. The fence is always locked, he says, but it's easy to climb over it, and no one has ever given him any trouble about going in and playing there.

I've walked past that court a dozen times, but the French are so strict about locks and keys and regulations, I assumed I'd be deported if I tried to go in.

He said he'd like to meet you. Are you interested?

Of course I am. Let's have dinner with him tonight. There's that little Moroccan restaurant you like so much, the one just off the Place de la Contrescarpe, La Casbah, and the rue Descartes is right up the hill from there. If he doesn't have other plans, maybe he could join us for a platter of *couscous royale*.

DINNER AT LA Casbah that night with Vivian, Lisa, and the stranger, who showed up fifteen minutes late, looking just as Vivian had described him with that remarkable skin of his and his intense, confident bearing. No, not a person given to small talk or cracking jokes, but he was capable of smiling and even laughing when he felt there was something to laugh about, and whatever hard thing had been locked up inside him was softened by the gentleness of his voice and the curiosity in his eyes. Ferguson was sitting directly across from him. He could see the whole of his face front-on, and while Vivian had probably been right to call it a less than handsome face, Ferguson found it beautiful. No thank you, Albert said, when the waiter tried to pour some wine into his glass, and then he looked at Ferguson and explained that he was *off the stuff for now*, which seemed to suggest he had been on it earlier, no doubt more than he should have been, an admission of a weakness, perhaps, and coming from such a restrained, self-possessed figure as Albert Dufresne, Ferguson welcomed it as a sign that the man was human, after all. Again the gentle, evenly modulated voice, which reminded Ferguson of how much he had enjoyed listening to his father's voice when he was a boy, and with the bilingual Albert, who spoke with a small trace of a Canadian accent when he spoke French and a small trace of a French accent when he spoke his idiomatic North American English, Ferguson found himself experiencing a similar if not wholly identical sort of pleasure.

A meandering conversation that went on for two hours, with Lisa more subdued than Ferguson had ever seen her, contributing only a couple of funny interjections instead of a hundred, as if she were under the spell of the stranger and understood that her antics would have struck the wrong note with him, but how relaxed Albert seemed to be with Vivian, who had that effect on most people, of course, although in this case the effect might have been enhanced because there was something about her that echoed some quality of his mother, a person he was *very close to,* he said, the white mother of this black man with his despised lout of a dead black father, how complicated it must have been, Ferguson realized, and how much heavy baggage Albert must have been carrying with him, and then they were on to New York and the year and a half he had spent in Harlem after graduating from college, followed by the decision to come to France because America was *a mass grave* for every black person who lived there, especially for a black person like him (meaning a man-man person like him, Ferguson wondered, or was he referring to something else?), and then they were all talking about the long history of black American writers and artists who had come to live in Paris, the *nude and numinous* Josephine Baker, as Albert put it, and Richard Wright, Chester Himes, Countee Cullen, and Miles Davis in the arms of Juliette Gréco, Nancy Cunard in the arms of Henry Crowder, and Albert's heroic Jimmy, who had been so rudely insulted by not being asked to speak at the March on Washington three years ago, he said, but with Bayard Rustin already on the list of speakers *maybe they figured one black fag was enough* (the evidence was mounting), and then Ferguson jumped in and started talking about *Giovanni's Room*, which in his *humble, heartfelt opinion* was one of the bravest, most elegantly written books he had ever read (a comment that received an approving nod from Albert), and a moment later, as so often happened with dinner conversations, they were on to another subject and the two of them were talking about basketball, the Boston Celtics, and Bill Russell, which led Ferguson to ask Albert the same question he had asked Jim many years before, Why is Russell the best when he's not even good?, to which Albert replied: But he is good, Archie. Russell could score twenty-five points a game if he wanted to. It's just that Auerbach doesn't need him to do that. He wants him to be the conductor of the team, and as we all know, a conductor doesn't play an instrument. He stands up there with his baton and leads the orchestra, and even though it looks simple, if there were no conductor to do that job, the musicians would go off-key and hit all the wrong notes.

The evening ended with an invitation. If Ferguson wasn't busy tomorrow afternoon, he could come over to Albert's place at around four-thirty for a friendly game of one-on-one on his "private court" across the street from his building on the rue Descartes. Ferguson told Albert that he hadn't played in months and was bound to be rusty, but yes, he said, he would love to.

Thus Albert Dufresne entered Ferguson's life. Thus the man who would come to be known alternately as Al Bear and Mr. Bear joined the regiment as Ferguson's comrade-in-arms for the next battle in the never-ending Bore War against the Pains of Human Existence, for unlike the two-way Aubrey Hull, who was contentedly married to his one-way Fiona and an adoring father to his two young offspring, the single, one-way Al Bear, whose innermost inclinations tilted toward the Aubreys of this world rather than the Fionas, was available for full-time combat duty, and because he lived in the same city as Ferguson, full-time meant nearly every day, at least for the time the battle lasted.

The unexpected developments of their first afternoon together, beginning with the rough, contentious games of one-on-one as the out-of-practice ex–Commando-in-Chief crashed the boards against the nimble, ex–point guard Mr. Bear, their bodies banging against each other as they tussled for loose balls and tried to block shots, three close games with twenty or thirty fouls in each one of them and the laughable twist that white-boy Ferguson could outjump black-boy Dufresne, and although Ferguson wound up losing all three games because his outside shot was horrendously off, it was clear that they were more or less evenly matched, and once Ferguson rounded into form again, Albert would have to play his hardest to keep up with him.

Climbing over the chain-link fence afterward, both of them exhausted, breathing hard, drenched in salty, sticky sweat, and then walking across the street and going up to Albert's third-floor apartment. The order and cleanliness of the two rooms, the wall of four hundred books in the larger one with the bed and the armoire in it, the desk and the Remington typewriter in the smaller room with the pages of Albert's novel in progress piled up in a neat stack, the light coming through the windows in the tidy, sit-down kitchen with its wooden table and four wooden chairs, and more light coming through the windows in the white tiled bathroom. Not the kinds of showers one took in America, but the handheld showers of France, standing or sitting in the tub and spraying oneself with what Ferguson called *telephone nozzles*, and because Ferguson was the guest, Albert kindly offered him first crack at washing up, so into the bathroom Ferguson went, where he kicked off his sneakers, removed his damp and smelly socks, shorts, and T-shirt, turned on the water, and stepped into the deep, squarish tub. An all-over dousing with the telephone nozzle held up in his right hand and water splashing down on his head, and with the noise of the water in his ears and his eyes closed to protect them from the hot liquid darts, he did not hear Albert knock on the door and did not see him enter the bathroom a moment later.

A hand was touching him on the back of his neck. Ferguson dropped his arm, let go of the showerhead, and opened his eyes.

Albert still had his shorts on, but everything else had come off.

I assume you're okay with this, he said to Ferguson, as the hand traveled down Ferguson's back and settled on his ass.

More than okay, Ferguson said. If it hadn't happened, I would have walked out of here one sad and disappointed customer.

Albert put his other hand around Ferguson's waist and pulled his body toward him. You're such a marvelous boy, Archie, he said, and I certainly wouldn't want you to walk out of here disappointed. In fact, it would be much better for both of us if you stayed, don't you think?

The afternoon turned into the evening, the evening turned into the night, the night turned into the morning, and the morning turned into another afternoon. As far as Ferguson was concerned, this was it, the once-in-a-lifetime big-bang love, and for the next two hundred and fifty-six days he lived in another country, a place that was neither France nor America nor anywhere else, a new country that had no name, no borders, and no cities or towns, a country with a population of two.

That wasn't to say that Mr. Bear was an easy person to get along with or that Ferguson didn't go through some rough patches during those eight-plus months of sex, camaraderie, and conflict, for the baggage his new friend carried was indeed a heavy burden on him, and no matter how young or brilliant or sure of himself Albert appeared to be when he stepped out into the world, his soul was old and weary, and old and weary souls could be bitter at times, and angry at times, most especially against the souls of the ones who did not feel that same bitterness and anger. Loving as Albert was on most days, frequently with a tenderness and a warmth that overwhelmed Ferguson and made him think there was no better person in the world than the warm and tender man lying beside him in bed, Albert was also proud and competitive and given to making harsh moral judgments about others, and it didn't help that the young one's book was going to be published while the older one was still working on his, and it didn't help that Ferguson's boyish sense of humor was often at odds with Albert's sour righteousness, the giddy splurges of madcap ideas that would come rushing out of him in moments of postcoital happiness, such as the suggestion that they shave off all the hair on their bodies, buy wigs and women's clothes, and then go out to a restaurant or a party and see if they could pull off the gag by passing as real women. *Ar-shee*, Ferguson said, imitating Celestine's pronunciation of his name, *and wouldn't it be interesting if I could actually be a she for one night?* Albert's irritable response: *Don't be stupid*, he said. *You're a man. Be proud of being a man and forget about this drag-queen nonsense. If you want to change who you are, try being a black person for a day or two and see what happens to you then.* Or else, after a particularly rewarding session in bed, Ferguson's proposal that they get into the business of posing naked together for gay porno magazines, full-color feature spreads of the two of them kissing and giving each other blow jobs and fucking each other in the ass with close-ups of the cum spurting out of their cocks, wouldn't that be a blast, Ferguson said, and just think of the money they could make.

Where's your dignity? Albert shot back at him, once again failing to realize that Ferguson was joking. And why all this talk about money? You might not get much from your parents, but Vivian takes care of you pretty damned well, it seems to me, so why talk about humiliating your-self for a handful of extra francs?

That's just it, Ferguson said, leaving behind his whimsical fantasy to address something real, something that had been preoccupying him for the past couple of months. Vivian takes such good care of me, I'm beginning to feel like a moocher, and I don't like that feeling, at least not anymore I don't. There's something wrong about taking so much from her, but I'm not allowed to work in this country, as you well know, so what am I supposed to do?

You could always hustle your ass in queer bars, Albert said. Then you'd get a real taste of what it feels like to live in the mud.

I've already thought about that, Ferguson answered, remembering the night of the money and the tears. I'm not interested.

As the younger of the two by seven years, Ferguson was the junior partner in the affair, the little one following the lead of the big one, which was the role he felt better suited to play, for nothing felt better to him than the feeling of living under Albert's protection, of not having to be the responsible one or the one who was supposed to have figured everything out, and by and large Albert did protect him, and by and large he did take care of him exceedingly well. Albert was the first per-son he had ever known who shared his double but unified passion for the mental and the physical, the physical being first of all sex, the primacy of sex over all other human activities, but basketball and working out and running as well, running in the Jardin des Plantes, push-ups, sit-ups, squats, and jumping jacks on the court or in the apartment, and the ferocious, bruising games of one-on-one, which were challenging and fulfilling in themselves but also served as an elab-orate kind of erotic foreplay, because now that he knew Albert's body so well, it was hard not to think about the naked body hidden under Albert's shorts and T-shirt as he moved around on the court, the splendid and deeply loved particulars of Mr. Bear's physical self, and the mental being not just the functions and cognitive efforts of the brain but the study of books, films, and works of art, the need to write, the essential business of trying to understand or reinvent the world, the obligation to think about oneself in relation to others and to reject the enticement of living just for one's self, and when Ferguson discovered that Albert cared about films as well as books, that is, cared about them as much as he himself now cared about books, they fell into the habit of going to films together on most evenings, all kinds of films because of Ferguson's eclectic tastes and Albert's willingness to follow him into any theater he chose, but of the many films they saw none was more important to them than the new film by Bresson, *Au Hasard Balthazar*, which opened in Paris on May twenty-fifth and which they sat through together on four consecutive nights, a film that roared into their hearts and heads with the fury of a divine revelation, Dostoyevsky's *Idiot* transformed into a tale about a donkey in rural France, the downtrodden and cruelly dealt with Balthazar, emblem of human suffering and saintly forbearance, and Ferguson and Albert couldn't get enough of it because each one of them saw the story of his own life in Balthazar's story, each one of them felt he was Balthazar while watching the film play on-screen, and so they went back three more times after the first time, and by the end of the last showing Ferguson had taught himself how to replicate the piercing, discordant sounds that burst from the donkey's mouth at crucial moments in the film, the asthmatic keening of a victim-creature struggling for the next breath, a horrible sound, a heartbreaking sound, and from then on, whenever Ferguson wanted to tell Albert that he was down in the dumps or aching over some injustice he had seen in the world, he would dispense with words and do his imitation of Balthazar's atonal, in-and-out double screech, the *bray from beyond*, as Albert called it, and because Albert himself was incapable of letting go to that extent and therefore could not join in, every time Ferguson became the suffering donkey, he felt he was doing it for both of them.

Similar tastes in most things, similar responses to books and films and people (Albert adored Vivian), but as far as their writing went, they had fallen into a standoff because neither one of them could find the courage to show his work to the other. Ferguson wanted Albert to read his book, but he was reluctant to force it on him, and since Albert never asked to see it, Ferguson held back and said nothing, nor did he share any news with him about the copyedited manuscript Aubrey had sent from London, the decision to use his mother's photograph on the cover, or the selection of ten Laurel and Hardy stills and ten other stills from movies released in late 1954 and 1955 (among them Marilyn Monroe in *There's No Business Like Show Business*, Dean Martin and Jerry Lewis in *Artists and Models*, Kim Novak and William Holden in *Picnic*, Marlon Brando and Jean Simmons in *Guys and Dolls*, and Gene Tierney and Humphrey Bogart in *The Left Hand of God*). Nor did he say a word about the first-pass galleys, the second-pass galleys, or the bound galleys after they showed up in early July, late July, and early September, and not once did he mention the letter he received from Aubrey telling him that Paul Sandler at Random House in New York (Ferguson's ex-uncle Paul) would be copublishing an American edition of the book one month after it was released in England.

When Ferguson asked Albert if he could have a look at the first half of his novel in progress (a bit more than two hundred pages, apparently), Albert said it was still *too rough* and that he couldn't show it to anyone until it was finished. Ferguson said he understood, which in fact was true, since he hadn't shown his book to anyone until it was finished either, but at least maybe he could tell him what the title was. Albert shook his head, claiming the book didn't have one yet, or rather that he was toying with three different possibilities and still hadn't decided which one he preferred, an answer that could have been true or could have been a polite evasion. The first time Ferguson had stepped into Albert's study, the manuscript had been sitting on the desk near the Remington typewriter, but after that day the manuscript had disappeared, no doubt into one of the drawers of the large wooden desk. On several occasions during the months they spent together, Ferguson found himself alone in the apartment while Albert was out on an errand somewhere in the neighborhood, which meant he could have gone into the study and pulled out the manuscript from the drawer it was hiding in, but Ferguson never did that because he didn't want to be the kind of person who did those sorts of things, who betrayed the trust of others and broke promises and acted underhandedly when no one was watching, for taking a look at Albert's manuscript would have been just as bad as stealing it or burning it, an act of such repugnant disloyalty that it would have been unforgivable.

Albert kept his book a secret, but in other ways he was surprisingly unwithheld, at times even eager to talk about himself, and in their first weeks together Ferguson came to know many things about his past. Abandoned by his father at six, just as he had told Vivian on the night they met at Reid Hall, but then, after seventeen years of no contact, remembered in his father's will, remembered to the tune of sixty thousand dollars, enough money to live on in Paris for five years or more with nothing to worry about except his novel. His closeness to his mother, who had been booted out of her strict Roman Catholic family after marrying a black man, and even after the black man left and the family was willing to forgive and forget, his strong, spirited mother had stayed booted out on purpose because she wasn't willing to forgive or forget. Montreal, a city not devoid of black people and mixed-race people, a city where Albert had thrived as a pup, a top boy in sports, a top boy in school, but by mid-adolescence the growing knowledge that he was *different* from most boys whether black or white or mixed and the fear that his mother would find out, which Albert felt would have devastated her, and so he had left Montreal at seventeen for college in America at all-black Howard in mostly black Washington, a fine school but a rotten place to live, and bit by bit during his first year down there he had come undone. First booze, then cocaine, then heroin, the big crash into apathetic confusion and enraged certainty, a lethal mixture that sent him limping back to Montreal and into the arms of his mother, but better to be a drug-addict son than a faggot-son, he reasoned, and then she dragged him off to the Laurentian Mountains for the summer and locked him up in a barn for what she called the Miles Davis Cure, four straight days of vomiting and shitting and screaming, the shaking and wailing grotesqueries of cold-turkey detox, the brutal confrontation with his own pathetic nothingness and the puny god who refused to watch over him, and then his mother led him out of the barn and sat with him quietly for the next two months as he learned how to eat again and think again and stop feeling sorry for himself. Back to Howard in the fall, and from that day on not a drop of wine, beer, or booze, not a whiff of grass or a snort of coke, clean for the past eight years but still frightened to his bones that he would lapse and die an O.D. death, and when Albert told Ferguson that story on the third day they were together, Ferguson resolved to stop drinking in Albert's presence, he who took such pleasure in alcohol and enjoyed drinking wine almost as much as he enjoyed having sex would no longer drink with dear Mr. Bear, and no, it wasn't fun, it wasn't fun at all, but it was necessary.

TEN DAYS AFTER that third day, Ferguson started writing again. His original plan had been to tiptoe back into it by looking over some of his old high school articles to see if anything could be salvaged from them, but after a close examination of the piece on John Ford's non-Westerns, which he had once felt was the best essay he had written, he found it crude and wanting, not worth thinking about anymore. He had come so far since then, and why go back when everything in him was crying out to go forward? He had accumulated enough good examples to begin writing the article about the representation of childhood in films, and the ever-evolving "Junkyards and Geniuses" had been given the simpler, more direct title of "Films and Movies," a distinction that would allow him to explore the often fuzzy line between art and entertainment, but in the middle of his deliberations about which piece to write first, something new had come up, something big enough to encompass both of those ideas, and Ferguson was ready to dig in.

Gil had sent a letter from Amsterdam along with a package of books, pamphlets, and postcards from the Anne Frank House at Prinsengracht 263, which he and Ferguson's mother had visited on their last day in the city. It was a museum now, Gil wrote, and the public could climb the stairs up to the Secret Annex and stand in the room where young Anne Frank had written her diary, and because he remembered how taken Ferguson had been with that book when he'd read it with his eighth-grade English class at the Riverside Academy, *swept up in it to such a degree that you confessed to having a "gigantic crush" on Anne Frank and once went so far as to say you were "madly in love with her," I thought the enclosed material would interest you. I know there's something unseemly about the fetishization of this poor girl,* Gil continued. *After the bestselling book, and then the play and the movie, Anne Frank has been turned into the kitsch representative of the Holocaust for the non-Jewish population in America and elsewhere, but one can't blame Anne Frank for that, Anne Frank is dead, and the book she wrote is a fine piece of work, the work of a budding writer with genuine talent, and I must say that your mother and I were both deeply moved by our visit to that house. After you told us about the essay you're planning to write about children in films, I couldn't help thinking of you when I* *looked at the pictures Anne had taped onto a wall in the Secret Annex, cutouts* *from newspapers and magazines of Hollywood stars—Ginger Rogers, Greta* *Garbo, Ray Milland, the Lane sisters—which led me to buy you the book of her* *writings not connected to the diary,* Tales from the House Behind. *Take a* *look at the story "Dreams of Movie Stardom," a wish-fulfillment fantasy about a* *seventeen-year-old European girl named Anne Franklin (Anne Frank did not* *live to be seventeen) who writes to Priscilla Lane in Hollywood and is eventu-* *ally invited to spend her summer vacation with the Lane family. A long trip by* *air across the ocean, then across the American continent, and once she lands in* *California, Priscilla takes her to the Warner Bros. studio, where the girl is photo-* *graphed and tested—and winds up with a job modeling tennis outfits. What a* *delirium! And remember, too, Archie, the photograph that Anne F. pasted into* *her diary with the caption "This is a photograph of me as I wish I looked all the* *time. Then I might have a chance of getting into Hollywood." The slaughter of* *millions, the end of civilization, and a little Dutch girl destined to die in a camp* *is dreaming of Hollywood. You might want to think about this.*

That became Ferguson's next project, an essay of as yet undetermined length entitled "Anne Frank in Hollywood." Not only would he
write about children *in* films, he would write about the effect of films
on children, especially Hollywood films, and not just American children
but children from around the world, for he remembered having read
somewhere about the young Satyajit Ray in India writing a fan letter to
juvenile star Deanna Durbin in California, and by using Ray and Anne
Frank as his principal examples, he would also be able to explore the
art-entertainment divide he had been thinking about ever since he'd
started thinking about films. The lure of entering a parallel world of
glamour and freedom, the desire to align oneself with the larger-than-
real and better-than-real stories of others, the self levitating out of itself
and leaving the earth behind. Not an insignificant subject, and in Anne
Frank's case, a matter of life and death. Movies and films. His once
beloved Anne, his still beloved Anne, trapped in the Secret Annex and
longing to go to Hollywood, dead at fifteen, murdered in Bergen-Belsen
at age fifteen, and then Hollywood made a movie about the last years
of her life and turned her into a star.

You have no idea how precious these things are to me, Ferguson wrote to
his stepfather, thanking him for the letter and the books. *They've crys-* *talized my thoughts and given me a new way into what I want to write about*

next. Serious. Because of you, the thrust of the thing has been lifted up to a new level of seriousness, and I can only hope I have it in me to do it justice. Tennis outfits. Barbed-wire villages watched over by machine guns. Greta Garbo laughing for the first time. Romping on the beaches of California as a typhoid epidemic breaks out in the capital of Mud. Time for cocktails, everyone. Time for the lime pits, my starved little dying children. How can we love one another anymore? How can we go on thinking our selfish thoughts anymore? You were there, Gil, you saw it firsthand and breathed in the smells, and yet you've given your life to music. Impossible to tell you how much I admire you and love you.

BEING WITH ALBERT meant not being with Albert for the bulk of the daylight hours. Albert on the rue Descartes adding words to his novel, Ferguson in his *chambre de bonne* reading the books on Gil's list and working on his essay, and then at around five o'clock Ferguson would put down his pen and walk over to Albert's place, where they sometimes played basketball and sometimes didn't, and depending on whether they did or didn't, afterward they would walk down to the noisy market on the rue Mouffetard and shop for dinner, or else not shop for dinner and go to a restaurant later, and because Ferguson couldn't afford to eat in restaurants, Albert would pay for his share of the check (he was consistently generous with money and again and again would tell Ferguson to *eat up and forget about it*), and then, after going or not going to a movie (usually going), they would return to the third-floor apartment across from the basketball court and crawl into bed together, except on the evenings when Albert came to dinner at Vivian's apartment and would spend the night in Ferguson's little room on the sixth floor.

Ferguson imagined it would go on forever, and if not forever a long time, many more months and years of time, but after two hundred and fifty-six days of living in that enthralling routine, the thing he had been dreading about his mother on the morning he'd said good-bye to her in May weirdly and unexpectedly happened to Albert's mother. A telegram at seven A.M. on January twenty-first while the two of them were still asleep in Albert's bed on the rue Descartes, the concierge knocking loudly on the door and saying, *Monsieur Dufresne, un télégramme urgent pour vous*, and all of a sudden they were both climbing out of bed and jumping into their clothes, and then Albert was reading the telegram, the blue telegram with the black news that his mother had tripped and fallen down a flight of stairs in her Montreal apartment house and was dead at the age of sixty. Albert said nothing. He handed the telegram to Ferguson and continued to say nothing, and by the time Ferguson had finished reading the telegram, which ended with the words COME HOME AT ONCE, Albert had begun to howl.

He left for Canada at one in the afternoon that same day, and because there were many complicated family matters and financial matters to attend to while he was there, and because he decided to go down to New Orleans after he buried his mother to *find out more about his father's life*, as he put it in a letter to Ferguson, he wound up staying on the other side of the world for two months, and because Ferguson had only forty-three days left to live on the day of Albert's departure from Paris, they never saw each other again.

FERGUSON WAS CALM. He knew that Albert would be coming back at some point, and meanwhile he would forge on with his work and take advantage of Albert's absence to resume his old habit of drinking wine at dinner, glass after glass of drunk-making wine if necessary, for even though he was calm, he was also worried about Albert, who had been hammered by the telegram and had seemed half-deranged when they'd hugged good-bye at the airport, and what if he couldn't hold it together and stumbled into using again? Stay calm, he said to himself, and have another glass of wine, stay calm and keep pushing forward. The Anne Frank essay was more than a hundred pages long by now and had grown into a book, another book that would take at least another year to finish, but then it wasn't January anymore, it was February, and with the publication of *Laurel and Hardy* just one month away, he was beginning to find it hard to concentrate.

Aubrey had not returned to Paris since his brief visit in April, but he and Ferguson had written to each other a couple of dozen times over the past ten months. So many large and small details to go over concerning the book, but also jocular and affectionate allusions to the hours they had spent together in the fifth-floor room of the Hôtel George V, and even though Ferguson had written that he was more or less *shacked up* with someone in Paris, the ruler of the elves remained undaunted and was fully prepared for a repeat performance or several performances during his author's upcoming visit to London. That seemed to be how things worked in the no-woman world Ferguson was traveling in now. As Albert had once explained to him, the fidelity rules in force for men and women did not apply to men and men, and if there was any advantage to being an outlaw queer over a law-abiding married citizen, it was the liberty to bonk at will with whomever you wished whenever you wished—as long as you didn't hurt the feelings of your number one. But what did that mean, exactly? Not telling your number one that you had been with someone else, Ferguson supposed, and if Albert was bonking someone or several someones on his peregrinations through North America, Ferguson wouldn't want to know about it, nor would he say anything to Albert if he wound up bonking Aubrey in London. No, not *if*, he said to himself, but *when*, when and where and how many times during the days and nights he would be in England, for even though he loved Albert, he found Aubrey irresistible.

The plan was to release the book on March sixth, a Monday. Ferguson would celebrate his twentieth birthday in Paris on the third, then take the boat train from the Gare du Nord on the night of the fourth and arrive at Victoria Station on the morning of the fifth. In his most recent dispatches, Aubrey had confirmed that interviews and events had been lined up as promised, including the Laurel and Hardy evening at the National Film Theatre, a program of shorts that would bring together the twenty-minute *Big Business*, the twenty-one-minute *Two Tars*, the twenty-six-minute *Blotto*, and the thirty-minute howler of the century, *The Music Box*, and once the NFT's decision was passed on to him, Ferguson spent a full week composing one-page introductions to each of the four films, panicked by the thought of freezing up in front of the audience if he tried to wing it onstage without notes, and because he wanted his little texts to be charming and witty as well as informative, it took many hours of writing and rewriting before he was even remotely satisfied with the results. But what fun that night was going to be—and what a thoughtful and generous thing Aubrey had done for him—and then, just twenty-four hours after he finished the introductions, two advance copies of the book arrived in the afternoon mail on Wednesday, February fifteenth, and for the first time in Ferguson's experience of the world, the past, the future, and the present were one. He had written the book, and then he had waited for the book, and now the book was in his hands.

He gave one of the copies to Vivian, and when she asked him to sign it for her, Ferguson laughed and said, I've never done this before, you know. Where am I supposed to sign it, and what am I supposed to say?

The title page is the traditional spot, Vivian said. And you can say whatever you like. If you can't think of anything, just sign your name.

No, that won't do. I have to say something. Give me a minute, all right?

They were in the living room. Vivian was sitting on the sofa with the book in her lap, but instead of sitting down beside her, Ferguson began pacing back and forth in front of her, and after a couple of backs and forths he left the area around the sofa and walked to the farthest wall in the room, turned right and walked to the next wall, then turned right again and walked to the next wall after that, and then he turned around and walked back to the sofa, where he finally sat down next to Vivian.

Okay, he said, I'm ready. Give me the book and I'll sign it for you.

Vivian said: I think you're the strangest, funniest person I've ever known, Archie.

Yeah, that's me. A genuine laugh riot. Mr. Ha-Ha in a purple clown suit. Now give me the book.

Vivian handed him the book.

Ferguson found the title page and reached into his pocket for a pen, but just as he was about to begin writing, he paused, turned to Vivian, and said, It's going to be short. I hope you don't mind.

No, Archie, I don't mind. Not in the least.

Ferguson wrote: *For Vivian, Beloved friend and savior—Archie.*

The earth spun around sixteen more times, and on the evening of March third they celebrated his twentieth birthday with a small dinner at the apartment. Vivian had offered to invite as many others as he wished, but Ferguson had said no others, thank you, he wanted to *keep it in the family*, which meant the two of them along with Lisa and the absent Albert, who was wandering around the South trying to track down members of his father's family, and even though Ferguson knew it was ridiculous, he asked Vivian if they could set a place for Albert, in the same spirit as the place that was set for Elijah at Passover, and Vivian, who didn't think it was ridiculous, asked Celestine to set the table for four. A moment later, she decided to increase the number to six so that Ferguson's mother and stepfather could be included as well.

He had two days to live, and it was the last time he would ever talk to them, but the phone call had been arranged in advance, and one hour before he sat down to dinner with Vivian and Lisa on the night of the third, his mother and Gil rang from New York to wish him a happy birthday and good luck on his trip to London. Ferguson told Gil that he would be carrying along *Our Mutual Friend* with him (the ninety-first book on the list), which would keep him company on the two long trips across the Channel (eleven hours each), but he doubted he would have much time for it in London because his schedule had become so crowded there. In any case, there would be only nine books left after this one, and he and Vivian were planning to get through all of them by the end of May, but what a pleasure it was to be living inside that Englishman's *teeming brain*, he remarked, and after he and Professor Vivian had polished off number one hundred, he wanted to catch up on all the Dickens novels he still hadn't read.

Then his mother came on and started talking to him about the weather. England was a wet place, she said, and he should remember to carry an umbrella with him at all times and wear his raincoat and perhaps even buy a pair of rubbers to protect his shoes and feet. On any other day, Ferguson would have felt annoyed. She was talking to him as if he were a seven-year-old child, and normally he would have brushed her off with a groan or laughed her off with some droll and acerbic comment, but on this particular day he didn't feel annoyed but amused, both warmed and amused by the unending motherness that continued to burn inside her. Of course not, Ma, he said. I won't go anywhere without my umbrella. I promise.

As it happened, Ferguson left his umbrella on the train after he arrived in London on the morning of the fifth. He hadn't meant to lose it, but in the scramble to gather up his belongings and rush out onto the platform to look for Aubrey, the umbrella had been forgotten. And yes, rain was falling on the city that morning, just as his mother had predicted it would, for England was indeed a wet place, and the first thing that struck Ferguson about it were the smells, the assault of new smells that entered his body the instant he left the air of his compartment for the air of the station, smells that were altogether unlike the smells in Paris and New York, a harsher, more stinging atmosphere charged with the mingled emanations of damp woolen jackets and

burning coal and moistened stone walls and the smoke of Player's cigarettes with their too-sweet Virginia tobacco in contrast to the bluntness
of Gauloises and the toasty fragrances of Luckys and Camels. A different world. Everything utterly different, and because it was still early
March and not yet spring, a new sort of chill in the bones.

And then Aubrey was smiling at him and throwing his little arms
around Ferguson's body, declaring that the bonny boy had alighted at
last and what a good week it was going to be for both of them. Off to
the cabstand outside, where they huddled together under the dome of
Aubrey's black umbrella and waited their turn, talking first about how
happy they were to see each other again, but a few moments later Aubrey
the publisher was telling Ferguson the author that the first reviews of
the book had started coming in over the past days and that they had all
been good except for one, an excellent piece in the *New Statesman*, a rave
in the *Observer*, but nothing less than good with any of the others except
for the pissy nonsense in *Punch*. How nice, Ferguson said, understanding how much those opinions meant to Aubrey, but he himself felt
curiously detached from it all, as if the reviews had been written about
someone else's book, another person with the same name as his, perhaps, but not the person who was stepping into a London taxi for the
first time, one of the fabled black elephant cars he had seen in so many
films over the years and which turned out to be even bigger than he
had imagined, another British thing that was different from American
and French things, and how enjoyable it was to be sitting in the huge
area in back listening to Aubrey rattle off the names of magazine editors and reviewers he knew nothing about and who were no more real
to him than walk-on characters in an eighteenth-century play. Then
the cab took off and started heading toward the hotel, and suddenly it
was no longer enjoyable but disconcerting and even a bit scary. The
steering wheel was on the wrong side of the car, and the driver was
driving on the wrong side of the road! Ferguson knew perfectly well
that the English did it that way, but he had never experienced it himself, and by force of long habit and a lifetime of built-in reflex reactions,
his first ride through the London streets had him flinching every time
the driver made a turn or another car approached them from the opposite direction, and again and again he had to close his eyes for fear they
would crash.

A safe landing at Durrants Hotel at 26 George Street (W1), not far from the Wallace Collection and St. James's Roman Catholic Church. Durrants as in *currants*, and Aubrey said he had chosen it for Ferguson because it was so quintessentially British and respectable, not Mod London but an example of what he called Plod London, with a wood-paneled bar on the ground floor that was so stodgy and spectacularly arcane that C. Aubrey Smith was a regular there, even though he had been dead for twenty years.

And besides, the ruler of the elves continued, the beds are *ever so comfortable*.

You and your dirty mind, Ferguson said. No wonder we get along so well.

Birds of a feather, my young Yankee friend. With dandy doodles in our pants and a fine pair of ponies to take us to town.

Aubrey helped Ferguson check in, but then he had to rush off and go home. It was Sunday, the nanny's day off, and he had promised to stay with Fiona and the children until teatime, at which point he would return to the hotel for a pony ride and then take Ferguson out to dinner.

Fiona can't wait to meet you, he said, but it won't happen until tomorrow, alas.

As for me, I can't wait until you come back this afternoon. When is teatime, by the way?

For our purposes, anywhere between four and six. You can rest up until then. Those Channel crossings can be brutal on the system, and you must be feeling fried—or at least sautéed.

Believe it or not, I managed to sleep on the train, so I'm good. Uncooked, as it were. Raw and fresh and raring to go.

After Ferguson unpacked, he returned to the ground floor and went into the dining room for breakfast, which was still being served at ten o'clock, and had his first taste of English cuisine, a platter that consisted of one sunny-side-up egg (greasy but delicious), two undercooked rashers of bacon (slightly repellent but delicious), two pork sausages, a thoroughly cooked cooked tomato, and two thick slices of homemade white bread slathered with Devonshire butter that was better than any butter he had ever tasted. The coffee was undrinkable, so he switched to a pot of tea, no doubt the strongest tea anywhere in Christendom, which he had to dilute with hot water before he could get it down his throat, and then he thanked the waiter, stood up from his chair, and trotted off to the gents' for a long, unhappy session with his rumbling bowels.

He wanted to go out for a walk, but the mild rain that had been falling earlier had turned into a downpour, and rather than go upstairs and lock himself in his room, he decided to visit the famous wood-paneled bar and look for the ghost of C. Aubrey Smith.

The bar was empty at that hour, but no one seemed to mind when he asked if he could sit in there for a while as he waited for the weather to clear (sun was forecast for the afternoon), and because the porter was so friendly about it when he asked the question, Ferguson decided that he liked the English and found them to be a noble, generous people, not stiff in the way the French could be, not angry in the way Americans could be, but good-natured and calm, a tolerant folk who accepted the foibles of their fellow men and didn't butt in or condemn you for speaking with the wrong accent.

So Ferguson sat down in the vacant wood-paneled bar and mused about the English for a while, in particular about C. Aubrey Smith and the nice but unimportant fact that he, the most English of all English gentlemen, the very embodiment of England for American audiences in countless Hollywood films, had been another ruler of the elves, in this case the elves of Movieland, and before long Ferguson had pulled out the little notebook he carried around in his jacket pocket and was writing down the names of British actors who had worked in California and, to a degree Ferguson had never considered until that morning, had helped create what the world now thought of as *American movies*. So many names, and so many films with those names on the list of credits, and as Ferguson wrote them down off the top of his head, or rather plucked them out from within his head as each one occurred to him, he included the titles of the movies he had seen those names act in and was astonished by how many there were, an avalanche of films and more films and more and more films, too many films, finally, an appalling number of films, and no doubt there were many others he had forgotten as well.

To begin with the first name on his list, the inevitable Stan, partner of Ollie, born Arthur Stanley Jefferson in the town of Ulverston in 1890 and then taken to America in 1910 with the Fred Karno Company as Charlie Chaplin's understudy, more than eighty films seen with Stan

Laurel in them, more than fifty with Chaplin, and at least twenty with C. Aubrey Smith (including *Queen Christina, The Scarlet Empress, The Lives of a Bengal Lancer, China Seas, Little Lord Fauntleroy, The Prisoner of Zenda*), and hundreds more with Ronald Colman, Basil Rathbone, Freddie Bartholomew, Greer Garson, Cary Grant, James Mason, Boris Karloff, Ray Milland, David Niven, Laurence Olivier, Ralph Richardson, Vivian Leigh, Deborah Kerr, Edmund Gwenn, George Sanders, Laurence Harvey, Michael Redgrave, Vanessa Redgrave, Lynn Redgrave, Robert Donat, Leo G. Carroll, Roland Young, Nigel Bruce, Gladys Cooper, Claude Rains, Donald Crisp, Robert Morley, Edna May Oliver, Albert Finney, Julie Christie, Alan Bates, Robert Shaw, Tom Courtenay, Peter Sellers, Herbert Marshall, Roddy McDowall, Elsa Lanchester, Charles Laughton, Wilfrid Hyde-White, Alan Mowbray, Eric Blore, Henry Stephenson, Peter Ustinov, Henry Travers, Finlay Currie, Henry Daniell, Wendy Hiller, Angela Lansbury, Lionel Atwill, Peter Finch, Richard Burton, Terence Stamp, Rex Harrison, Julie Andrews, George Arliss, Leslie Howard, Trevor Howard, Cedric Hardwicke, John Gielgud, John Mills, Hayley Mills, Alec Guinness, Reginald Owen, Stewart Granger, Jean Simmons, Michael Caine, Sean Connery, and Elizabeth Taylor.

The rain stopped at two, but the sun didn't come out. Instead, the cloudy sky filled with more clouds, clouds so thick and voluminous that they started to sag, slowly descending from their customary place in the heavens until they touched the ground, and when Ferguson finally stepped out of the hotel for a short walk around the neighborhood, the streets were a labyrinth of fog. Never had he been given so little to see in what was supposedly still the daytime, and he puzzled over how the English could go about their business in these sodden, vaporous murks, but then again, he said to himself, the English were probably on intimate terms with clouds, for if he had learned nothing else from Dickens, it was that the clouds in the sky over London came down for frequent visits among the people, and on a day such as this one it looked as if they had brought along their toothbrushes and were planning to spend the night.

It was a few minutes past three. Ferguson decided he should start walking back to the hotel to prepare himself for Aubrey's return, which could be as early as four or as late as six, but he wanted to be ready at four in the hope that Aubrey would be able to detach himself from his family early rather than late. A bath or a shower first, and then he would

put on the birthday presents Vivian had bought for him in Paris last
week, the new pants and the new shirt and the new jacket that made
him look like *a million bucks,* she had said, and he wanted to look like a
million bucks for Aubrey in his new clothes, and then the clothes would
come off and they would climb onto the bed to do what they had done
at the Hôtel George V, and no, he wouldn't feel guilty about it, he said
to himself, he would enjoy it, and as far as Albert was concerned he
would console himself by imagining that Mr. Bear was doing the same
thing with someone else and enjoying it just as much as he was, and as
he walked along thinking about Aubrey and Albert and the differences
between them, not only the physical differences between light and dark
and large and small but the mental differences and cultural differences
and the differences between their outlooks on life, the somber depths
of Albert's heart as opposed to Aubrey's whimsical good cheer, Ferguson marched on in the direction of the hotel, suddenly shifting his
thoughts to the interview he would be doing with someone from the
Telegraph tomorrow morning at ten, the first interview of his life, and
even though Aubrey had told him not to worry and *just relax and be himself,* he couldn't help feeling a little worried, and what did it mean to
be himself anyway, he wondered, he had several selves inside him,
even many selves, a strong self and a weak self, a thoughtful self and an
impulsive self, a generous self and a selfish self, so many different selves
that in the end he was as large as everyone or as small as no one, and if
that was true for him, then it had to be true for everyone else as well,
meaning that everyone was everyone and no one at the same time, and
with that thought bouncing around in his head he came to the intersection of Marylebone High Street and Blandford Street, at the spot where
Marylebone turned into Thayer just around the corner from the hotel
on George, and even though the fog was pressing in and wrapping itself
around him, Ferguson could make out the blinking red traffic light
looming in the blur, a blinking red light that was the equivalent of a stop
sign, so Ferguson stopped and waited for a car to pass, and because he
was lost in his reveries about everyone and no one, he turned his head
and looked to the left, that is, did what he had always done when crossing streets throughout his life, the reflexive, automatic look to the left
to make sure no car was coming, forgetting that he was in London and
that in English towns and cities one was supposed to look to the right
and not to the left, and therefore he did not see the maroon British Ford

sweeping around the bend on Blandford, so he stepped off the curb and started to cross the street, not understanding that the car he hadn't seen had the right of way, and when the car slammed into Ferguson's body, it hit him so hard that he went flying into the air, as if he were an airborne human missile launched into space, a young man on his way to the moon and the stars beyond, and then he reached the top of his trajectory and started to come down, and when he touched bottom his head landed on the edge of the curb and he cracked his skull, and from that moment on every future thought, word, and feeling that would have been born inside that skull was erased.

The gods looked down from their mountain and shrugged.

W ILY, IRRESPONSIBLE NOAH MARX, WHO HAD GIVEN HIS WORD
not to show the manuscript of *Mulligan's Travels* to anyone but
his father and stepmother, broke that word by lending his copy to
twenty-four-year-old Billy Best, a prose writer and Columbia dropout
who earned his living as the superintendent of a four-story walk-up
building on East Eighty-ninth Street between First and Second Avenues, a working-class subsection of Yorkville known as the Rhinelander
District. Two years earlier, Billy had founded a small publishing house
of mimeographed books called Gizmo Press, a noncommercial, anti-
commercial operation that had released about a dozen works so far,
among them volumes of poetry by Ann Wexler, Lewis Tarkowski, and
Tulsa-born Ron Pearson, who had given the author of *Mulligan's Travels*
a copy of John Cage's *Silence* back in October. In those days before the
advent of cheap offset printing, mimeo was the only form of book and
magazine production available to the young, penniless writers of New
York, and far from being a sign of obscurity or a one-way path to terminal neglect, having your work published in mimeo by a house such as
Gizmo Press was considered a badge of honor. The print runs averaged
around two hundred copies. The titles and illustrations on the cardboard covers were drawn in black and white by Billy's downtown
artist friends (most often by Serge Grieman or Bo Jainard, fluid and
inventive draftsmen whose cover work helped set the tone of mid-
sixties graphic design, the look of the moment, which was bold and
unadorned and tried not to take itself too seriously), and even if there

was something ragged and improvisational about books printed on eight-and-a-half-by-eleven-inch typing paper, the contents were unsmudged and readable, as clear as any offset or letterpress book. Billy's wife, Joanna, prepared the stencils on her large office-sized Remington in single-spaced pica characters with unjustified right-hand margins when the work was in prose, and then the stencils were fed into the mimeograph machine in Billy's workroom and run off on both the recto and verso of each page, collated by a group of friends and volunteers, and put together with saddle-stitch binding (staples). Most of the copies were given away for free, that is, sent off or handed to fellow writers and artists, and the remaining fifty or so were distributed to the handful of Manhattan booksellers who believed in the next generation of American newness, and for a young person to walk into the Gotham Book Mart or the Eighth Street Bookshop and see his mimeo book among the recent offerings of poetry and fiction was to understand that he was beginning to exist as a writer.

Ferguson should have been furious with his cousin for having gone behind his back and shown the book to someone without permission, but he wasn't. Noah had run into Billy Best at a Lower East Side gathering in mid-May, one month after Ferguson had finished the manuscript and one week after his third and final visit to Dr. Breuler. Noah had started talking to Billy about his cousin's work, Billy had expressed an interest in seeing it, and by the last week in May Noah was on the telephone with Ferguson letting the cat out of the bag. Sorry, sorry, he said, he knew he wasn't supposed to have shown the manuscript around, but he had gone ahead and done it anyway, and now that Billy had been *floored* by *Mulligan's Travels* and wanted to publish it, Ferguson wasn't going to be dumb enough to try to prevent that from happening, was he? No, Ferguson said, he was all for it, and then he thanked Noah for his help, which launched them into a conversation that lasted for about half an hour, and after they hung up Ferguson understood that it made no difference if he thought the book should be burned and forgotten, he needed the book now because his life was over, and publishing it would perhaps be a way to trick himself into thinking he still had a future, even if no more Fergusons would ever be a part of that future, and how fitting it was that he had chosen to publish his work under the name of a murdered man, his paternal grandfather Isaac, felled by two bullets in a Chicago leather-goods warehouse in 1923, the man who was supposed to have been Rockefeller but wound up being Ferguson, father of a father who had vanished from his son's life and grandfather of a grandson who would never live to become a father himself.

Billy Best became a good friend and a devoted publisher of Ferguson's early books, but Noah Marx was the best man there was, and whenever Ferguson tried to imagine who he would have been without him, his mind would shut down and refuse to give an answer.

Nimble Joanna managed to convert the one hundred and thirty-one double-spaced pages of the manuscript into fifty-nine single-spaced pages by eliminating the blanks that preceded each chapter head of Mulligan's twenty-four journeys and starting the new journeys on the same pages as the old, which reduced the better part of a year's work to thirty sheets of paper—thin enough to be stapled together without difficulty. Instead of using Bo Jainard or Serge Grieman to design the cover, Ferguson asked Billy if Howard Small could take a shot at it, and because Howard produced such a good drawing (Mulligan sitting at a desk and writing one of his reports in a room crammed with artifacts and souvenirs from his adventures), he too became a part of the Gizmo family and went on contributing covers and illustrations until the press folded in 1970. Fifty-nine pages on thirty sheets of paper—which meant that the last page of the book was empty. Billy asked Ferguson if he would like to write a biographical note about himself to fill that emptiness, and after thinking about it for close to a week, Ferguson submitted the following two sentences:

Nineteen-year-old Isaac Ferguson can often be found wandering the streets of New York. He lives elsewhere.

NO MORE EVIE. No more visits to the half-house in East Orange after the last visit to Dr. Breuler's office in Princeton. Ferguson could no longer bring himself to face her. He had let her down and destroyed her hopes, and he didn't have the courage to look her in the eyes and tell her he would never be the phantom father of the illusory baby she had invented to hold them together in some future world when circumstances would at last have driven them apart. What a tangled business it was. How badly they had both deceived themselves, and now that the words of a doctor had put an end to their deluded aspirations, Ferguson picked up the phone and announced that end as any other coward would have done it, not even daring to sit down in her presence and talk it out and perhaps come to the conclusion that it wasn't the worst tragedy in the world and that they could go on in spite of it. Evie was shocked by his callousness. Too bad and all that, she said, and I really do feel sorry for you, Archie, but what does it have to do with us?

Everything, he said.

No, you're wrong, she replied, it makes no difference, and if you don't understand what I'm saying to you now, then you're not the person I thought you were.

Ferguson was fighting back tears on the other end of the line.

We weren't going to last much longer, Evie continued, and maybe I was a fool to drag you into this pregnancy talk, but damnit, Archie, I've given you everything I have, and at least you owe me the decency of saying good-bye to me in person.

I can't, Ferguson said. If I came to see you, I'd break down and cry, and I don't want you to see me cry.

Would that be so terrible?

It would be for me. Worse than anything.

Grow up, Archie. Try acting like a man.

I am trying.

Not hard enough.

I'll try harder, I promise. The important thing is that I'll never stop loving you.

You already have. You're so sick of us, you don't even want to look at me anymore.

That's not true.

Stop lying, please. And while you're at it, Archie, please, from the bottom of my heart, go fuck yourself, too.

On Wednesday, May twenty-fifth, two weeks after that hellish conversation with Evie, Noah called with the news that Billy Best wanted to publish *Mulligan's Travels*. Ferguson and Billy talked on the twenty-fifth and arranged to meet each other on Saturday, the twenty-eighth, and consequently Ferguson did not remain in Princeton that weekend to study for finals with Howard as he had planned but went to New York on Friday as usual, but having told his grandfather he would not be coming that weekend, and then having forgotten to tell his grand-

father that in fact he would be coming, he caught his grandfather
by surprise, and the surprise he caused his grandfather was only one
one-hundredth as big as the surprise he caused himself.

As far as he knew, he was the only other person who had a key to
the apartment. Now that he and Evie were quits, Ferguson had come
back twice for solo weekend stays in his grandfather's spare bedroom,
and on both of those Friday afternoons he had let himself into a quiet
apartment, walking in to discover his grandfather sitting on the sofa in
the living room reading the sports pages of the *Post*, but this time when
he slipped the key into the lock and opened the door, he heard voices
coming from the living room, perhaps two or three voices, he couldn't
tell how many, but none of them his grandfather's voice, and once he
was inside the first thing he heard distinctly was a man's voice saying,
That's right, Al, put your cock in her now, and then another man's voice
was saying, *And just when he does that, Georgia, remember to take hold of
Ed's hard-on and put it in your mouth.*

There was a short hallway between the front door and the entrance
to the living room, and as Ferguson tiptoed past the closed door of the
spare bedroom to his right and then past the narrow galley kitchen that
was also to his right, he came to the end of the wall and was standing
at the edge of the living room, and what he saw in there was his grandfather sitting next to a man operating a sixteen-millimeter camera, three
light stands burning brightly at what must have been a thousand watts
each, another man in the middle of the room with a clipboard under
his arm, and three naked people on the sofa, a woman and two men,
a dead-eyed woman of about thirty with bleached-blond hair, large
breasts, and a flaccid, protruding stomach, and two nearly indistinguishable men (perhaps twins), chunky, hairy beasts with tumescent
cocks and woolly butts carrying out the instructions of the director and
the cameraman.

Ferguson's grandfather was smiling. That was the most jarring element in the whole sordid picture—the smile on his grandfather's face
as the old man watched the woman and the two men sucking and fucking on the sofa.

The director was the first one who saw him, a small young punk in
his mid-twenties wearing jeans and a gray sweatshirt, the one who had
been talking through the action because they weren't recording sound,
which no doubt would be added in later as a series of histrionic moans

and groans during the postproduction of this cheapest of cheap cinematic endeavors, and when the young director spotted Ferguson standing in the hall just outside the living room, he said: Who the hell are
you?

No, Ferguson said, who the hell are *you*, and what do you think
you're doing?

Archie! his grandfather yelled out, as the smile vanished and turned
into a look of fear. You told me you weren't coming this weekend!

Well, I changed my plans, Ferguson said, and now I think these
people should get their asses out of this apartment.

Calm down, sport, the director said. Mr. Adler is our producer.
He's the one who invited us here, and we're not leaving until we finish
shooting the film.

I'm sorry, Ferguson said, as he walked over to the naked people on
the couch, but the fun is over for today. Put on your clothes and get out.

As he reached for the woman's hand to pull her up and get her on
her way, the director rushed toward him from behind and wrapped his
arms around Ferguson's torso, pinning his arms against his sides. One
of the naked twins then jumped up from the sofa and threw his right
fist into Ferguson's stomach, a painful jab that so incensed the embat-
tled Ferguson that he broke free of the small director and tossed him to
the floor. The woman said: For crying out loud, you assholes. Stop this
shit and let's get on with it.

Before it could develop into a genuine brawl, Ferguson's grandfather stepped in and said to the director, Too bad, Adam, but I think
we should call it a day. This boy is my grandson, and I need to have a
word with him. Call me tomorrow and we'll figure out the next step.

Within ten minutes, the director, the cameraman, and the three
actors were gone. Ferguson and his grandfather were in the kitchen by
then, sitting across from each other at opposite ends of the table, and
the moment Ferguson heard the door bang shut, he said: You stupid old
man. I'm so disgusted with you, I don't ever want to see you again.

His grandfather wiped his eyes with a handkerchief and looked
down at the table. The girls mustn't know, he said, meaning his two
daughters. If they ever found out, it would kill them.

You mean it would kill you, his grandson said.

Don't say a word, Archie. Promise me that.

Ferguson, who had never even considered telling his mother or

Aunt Mildred what he had seen that day, refused to make any promises, even though he knew he would never tell anyone.

I'm so lonely, his grandfather said. All I wanted was a little fun.

Some fun. Throwing your money into a third-rate porn flick. What's
wrong with you, anyway?

It's harmless. No one gets hurt. Everyone has a good time. What's
wrong with that?

If you need to ask that question, then you're beyond hope.

You're so hard, Archie. How did you ever get to be so hard?

Not hard. Just shocked, and a little sick to my stomach.

They can't ever know. As long as you promise not to tell them, I'll
do anything you want.

Just stop, that's all. Shut down the film and never do it again.

Look, Archie, what if I gave you some money? Would that help? I
know you don't want to stay here with me anymore, but if you had some
money, you could go out and find yourself another apartment in New
York. You'd like that, wouldn't you?

Are you trying to bribe me?

Call it what you want. But if I gave you five . . . six . . . no, let's say . . .
ten thousand dollars . . . that would help you out a lot, wouldn't it? You
could rent your own little apartment somewhere and spend the summer writing instead of working at that job you told me about. What was
it again?

Junk removal.

Junk removal. What a waste of time and energy.

But I don't want your money.

Of course you do. Everyone wants money. Everyone needs money.
Think of it as a gift.

As a bribe, you mean.

No, as a gift.

FERGUSON TOOK THE money. He accepted his grandfather's offer with
a clear conscience because in point of fact it wasn't a bribe but a gift,
since he never would have said a word to his mother or Aunt Mildred
anyway, and if his grandfather was so flush that he could afford to write
a check for ten thousand dollars, better that the money should go to his
grandson than to finance another woebegone fuck-film. But what a jolt

it had been to walk in on that bizarre scene, and how crazy and perverse his grandfather was becoming in his old age—widowed and alone
with no restraints on him anymore, free to indulge himself in any
debauched whim that caught his fancy, and what further embarrassment would be coming tomorrow? Ferguson still loved his grandfather, but he had lost all respect for him and perhaps even despised
him now, enough never to want to stay in the apartment again and yet
not half as much as he despised his father, who was altogether gone
from his life now, gone for reasons that largely had to do with money,
and there he was gladly accepting money from his grandfather and
shaking his hand to thank him for it. Another complicated business,
another daunting fork in the road, and just as Lazlo Flute had found out
in *Right, Left, or Straight Ahead?*, whatever choice he made was bound to
be the wrong one.

Nevertheless, ten thousand dollars was a monumental sum in 1966,
a bundle beyond imagining. With small apartments in run-down New
York neighborhoods renting for less than a hundred dollars a month,
sometimes for as little as fifty or sixty, Ferguson would be able to find
something for his escapes from Princeton and still have enough to live
on during the summers without having to work at summer jobs. It wasn't
that he had been dreading the prospect of hauling junk in the interim
between his freshman and sophomore years. He knew from his high
school summers with Arnie Frazier and Richard Brinkerstaff that menial
work had numerous satisfactions to offer and that one could learn valuable lessons about life in the process, but there were many years of that
sort of work still in front of him, and the chance to take a pause from
heavy lifting during his time in college was an unanticipated lucky
break. All because he had walked in on his grandfather and caught him
with his pants down. A revolting discovery, yes, but how not to laugh
about it at the same time? And he who would have kept his lips sealed
until the last breath in his body had exited his lungs was rolling in a
pile of hush money. If you couldn't laugh at that, there was something
wrong with you, something not quite right in your head.

Ferguson went out for a dinner of pizza and beer with Noah in the
Village, then spent the night on the floor of his cousin's NYU dorm room,
and the next day, when he traveled uptown to meet Billy Best, more
startling things kept on happening to him. Billy was so relaxed and
genial, so effusive in his praise of Ferguson's book, which he called the

weirdest fucking shit he had read in a long time, that the young author again silently thanked his cousin for having put him in touch with this person, who resembled no other person he had ever known. Billy was both a working-class roughneck and a sophisticated avant-garde writer, born and raised on the block where he still lived, super of his building because he had inherited the job from his father, a street-savvy native son who watched over the neighborhood like a sheriff in a Hollywood Western, but also the author of a complex, hallucinatory novel in progress set during the French and Indian Wars called *Crushed Heads* (Ferguson adored the title), and to listen to his publisher's melodious New York Irish-American tenor voice made him feel as if the very bricks of the buildings on East Eighty-ninth Street were vibrating with words. On top of that, Billy's pregnant wife, Joanna, spoke with the same voice he did, down-to-earth and welcoming, a legal secretary by day, typist–stencil cutter for Gizmo Press by night, she was the one who would be working on Ferguson's book as her baby grew inside her, bringing Ferguson's baby to life even if it was only a book and he would never have anything to do with the production of real babies, and when Joanna and Billy asked him to stay for dinner on that first Saturday night of their new friendship, Ferguson mentioned that he would be looking for an apartment in the coming days, just as soon as the check in his wallet had cleared, and because Billy and Joanna knew everything that went on in their small neighborhood, they tipped him off about an apartment six doors down the block, a one-room studio that went on the market just days after their first meal together, and that was how Ferguson wound up renting his third-floor digs on East Eighty-ninth Street for seventy-seven dollars and fifty cents a month.

His first year at Princeton was coming to an end. Howard would be taking off for the summer to work on his aunt and uncle's dairy farm in southern Vermont, and although Ferguson had been invited to join him in that bucolic venture, the half-destroyed ex-lover of Evie Monroe, who had simultaneously become the half-resurrected author of the soon-to-be-published *Mulligan's Travels*, had already backed out of his junk-removal job and was planning to spend the summer working on his next writing project, *The Scarlet Notebook*. Amy would be down in the city for those months as well (working as an editorial assistant for a trade magazine called *Nurses Digest*), and so would her new boyfriend, Luther Bond, who had found a spot filling in for someone in the Coming Events department at the *Village Voice*. Celia Federman, on the other hand, would be far away, profiting from the reward her parents had given her for graduating early from high school: a two-month trek through Europe with her twenty-year-old cousin Emily. As predicted, Bruce-the-boyfriend, a.k.a. the Human Buffer Zone, was a thing of the past. Celia promised to write Ferguson exactly twenty-four letters, which she instructed him to keep in a special box labeled *Federman's Travels*.

Noah would be gone, too, unexpectedly and at the last minute gone, up to northern Massachusetts to take part in the Williamstown Theatre Festival, which he had tried out for on a whim because the girl he was pursuing had wanted to try out, but while she was turned down without a single callback, Noah wasn't, and now he would be acting in two different plays over the summer (*All My Sons* and *Waiting for Godot*) and the plan to do a film version of *Sole Mates* was put on the shelf again. Ferguson was relieved. More than that, he was happy for Noah, who had always been the best actor onstage whenever he had seen him perform, which must have been seven or eight times over the years, and however much Noah wanted to become a filmmaker, Ferguson was convinced he had the stuff to become a top-of-the-line actor, not just in comedies, which he already excelled at, but in dramas, too, although perhaps not in tragedies, at least not the fifty-ton classics in which men plucked out their eyes and mothers boiled their children and Fortinbras entered as the curtain eased down slowly on a mass of bloody corpses. Ferguson also felt that Noah could have made people piss in their pants if he ever decided to do stand-up, but each time he had suggested it to him, Noah had frowned and said, *Not for me*. But he was wrong, Ferguson thought, dead wrong to resist, and one evening he had even gone to the trouble of sitting down and trying to write some jokes for Noah, just to get him started, but jokes were hard, so hard they were almost impossible, and except for some of the tennis matches he had done with Howard earlier in the year, he seemed to have no talent for them. Writing droll sentences in a story was one thing, but coming up with unforgettable, punch-out zingers required a different sort of brain from the one that had been planted in Ferguson's skull.

Amy had been linked to Luther Bond since the beginning of May. Now it was June, and according to Ferguson's most recent telephone conversation with her, his aggressive, battling stepsister still hadn't found the nerve to tell her father or stepmother about the new man in her life. That disappointed Ferguson, who had always admired Amy for her guts, even though he had sometimes wanted to strangle her as well, and the only reason he could come up with to account for her hesitation was not that her boyfriend happened to be black but that he was militantly black, a Black Power person who stood even farther to the left than Amy, a large, menacing figure in a black leather jacket with a black beret sitting atop his Afro—just the sort of man to frighten Amy's gentle, live-and-let-live father into a month-long panic attack.

Then the couple came down from Boston and moved into their summer sublet on Morningside Heights. That same evening, they met Ferguson for a drink at the West End Bar, and when Ferguson shook Luther Bond's hand for the first time, the cartoon he had drawn in his head exploded into a thousand worthless fragments. Yes, Luther Bond was black, and yes, he had the firm handshake of a physically strong person, and yes, there was a stubborn sort of determination in his eyes, but when those eyes looked into Ferguson's eyes, Ferguson understood that they were looking not at an enemy but at a potential friend, someone he was earnestly hoping he would like, and if Luther wasn't the belligerent, hate-filled terrorist of the cartoon, then what was wrong with Amy, and why in the world had she not told her father about him?

He would have to talk to her about that in private and do what he could to pound some sense into her, but for now he had to focus on Mr. Bond himself in order to figure out what kind of person he was. Not a big person, that much was clear, but an average person of five-nine or so, roughly the same height as Amy, and if hair was any indication of a person's political beliefs, then Luther's modest Afro suggested he was on the left but not the far left, as opposed to the large Afros worn by the Black Is Beautiful people, and as for his face, well, it was awfully handsome, Ferguson thought, so good-looking as to verge on *cute*, if such an adjective could be applied to men, and as Ferguson studied that face, he understood why Amy had been attracted to Luther and was still attracted to him after six weeks of talk and steady sex, but putting aside those superficial things for a moment, the extraneous details of how tall or how short and hair lengths and cuteness quotients, the more important thing Ferguson was discovering about Luther was that he had a sharp sense of humor, something Ferguson valued in people because he was so bereft of verbal wit himself, which was why he gravitated toward people like Noah Marx and Howard Small and Richard Brink-erstaff, all of whom could talk circles around him, and when Luther told Ferguson that his roommate at Brandeis had been a fellow freshman named Timothy Sawyer, in other words *Tim Sawyer*, Ferguson laughed, and then he asked Luther if Tim bore any resemblance to Tom, but Luther said no, he reminded him more of that other character in the Murk Twang book, Hick Funn.

That was funny. Murk Twang and Hick Funn were genuinely funny, the same kinds of two-in-one things Howard would blurt out in his inspired moments, and the fact that Amy laughed made it even funnier, no doubt much funnier, because the volume of her laughter meant she had been caught off balance, which proved she had never heard Luther say those things before, which in turn proved that Luther hadn't come up with his distorted versions of Mark Twain and Huck Finn last month or last year and had not been going around repeating them to his friends, no, he had invented them on the spot, right there at the West End Bar, and Ferguson appreciated a mind that was quick enough and clever enough to deliver a pair of such delicious puns, or, as he wanted to say out loud but didn't, such *pungent puns*. Instead, he laughed along with his snorting stepsister and then asked Mr. Bond if he could buy him another beer.

Ferguson had already been given some information about Luther's background and the odd path he had traveled from the Central Ward of Newark to Brandeis University in New England, things Amy had mentioned to him on the phone such as the seven years Luther had spent at the Newark Academy, one of the top private schools in the area, not paid for by Luther's cab-driver father or his housemaid mother but by his mother's employers, Sid and Edna Waxman, a wealthy couple from South Orange whose only son had been killed in the Battle of the Bulge, an uncommon duo of grieving souls who had fallen in love with Luther when he was a little boy, and now that Luther had won his scholarship to Brandeis, the Waxmans were doing the same thing for his younger brother, Septimus (Seppy), and how about them apples, Amy had said to Ferguson on the phone, a rich Jewish family and a struggling black family united forever in the Disunited States of America—Ha!

Ferguson was therefore up on the fact that Amy's boyfriend had attended the Newark Academy when the three of them sat down for drinks at the West End, and before long the conversation came around to Newark itself, then Newark and basketball, a sport that Luther and Ferguson had both played in high school, and because the words *Newark* and *basketball* had unexpectedly occurred in the same sentence, Ferguson brought up the Newark gym where he had played in the triple-overtime game when he was fourteen, and the moment he said the words *triple overtime*, Luther leaned forward, made a wordless, indecipherable noise somewhere in the back of his throat, and said: I was there.

So you remember what happened, Ferguson said.

I'll never forget it.

Were you playing in the game?

No, sitting in the stands waiting for your game to be over so mine could begin.

You saw the half-court shot.

The longest swish on record. At the buzzer.

And afterward?

Yes, that too. As if it was yesterday.

Kids were pouring out of the stands and I got punched, punched hard as I was running out of the gym, punched so hard that it went on hurting for hours.

It was probably me.

You?

I punched someone, but I don't know who it was. All white people look the same, right?

I was the only person on my team who got punched. It had to be me. And if it was me, it had to be you.

Amy said: The once stable earth is wobbling out of orbit. Tidal waves are rushing across the Seven Seas, volcanoes are wiping out cities. Or am I just imagining things?

Ferguson smiled briefly at Amy and then turned back to Luther. Why did you do it? he asked.

I don't know. I didn't know then, and I still can't explain it now.

It shook me up, Ferguson said. Not the punch, but the reason for the punch. The madness in the gym, the hatred.

It built up slowly, but by the third tie score it was starting to get ugly in there. Then came the swish, and everyone snapped.

Until that morning, I was your average American numskull boy. A person who believed in progress and *the search for a better tomorrow*. We'd cured polio, hadn't we? Racism was going to be next. The civil rights movement was the magic pill that was going to turn America into a color-blind society. After that punch, after *your* punch, I suddenly got a lot smarter about a whole lot of things. I'm so smart now, I can't think about the future without feeling sick. You changed my life, Luther.

For what it's worth, Luther said, that punch changed me, too. The feelings of the crowd got inside me that morning, and the anger of the crowd became my anger. I wasn't thinking for myself anymore, I was letting the crowd think for me, so I lost control when the crowd lost control, and I ran down onto the court and did that dumb thing. Never again, I said to myself. From now on, I'm the one who's in charge of me. Christ. White people were sending me to school, weren't they? What did I have against white people?

Just wait, Amy said. You've been lucky so far.

I know, Luther replied. Plan A: Work to become a lawyer like Thurgood Marshall, work to become the first black mayor of Newark, work to become the first black senator from New Jersey. But if that doesn't turn out, there's always Plan B: Buy myself a machine gun and follow the words of Malcolm. *By any means necessary*. It's never too late, right?

Let's hope not, Ferguson said, as he raised his glass and nodded in assent.

Luther laughed. I like this stepbrother of yours, he said to Amy. He tickles my funny bone—and knows how to take a punch. His arm might have hurt that day, but what about my hand? I thought my knuckles were broken.

THE SCARLET NOTEBOOK was going to be difficult, far and away the most challenging work he had ever attempted, and Ferguson had serious doubts about whether he could pull it off. A book about a book, a book that one could read and also write in, a book that one could enter as if it were a three-dimensional physical space, a book that was the world and yet of the mind, a conundrum, a fraught landscape filled with beauties and dangers, and little by little a story would begin to develop inside it that would thrust the fictitious author, F., into a confrontation with the darkest elements of himself. A dream book. A book about the immediate realities in front of F.'s nose. An impossible book that could not be written and would surely devolve into a chaos of random, unconnected shards, a pile of meaninglessness. Why attempt to do such a thing? Why not simply invent another story and tell it as any other writer would? Because Ferguson wanted to do something different. Because Ferguson was no longer interested in telling mere stories. Because Ferguson wanted to test himself against the unknown and see if he could survive the struggle.

First Entry. In the scarlet notebook there are all the words that have yet to be spoken and all the years of my life before I bought the scarlet notebook.

Second Entry. The scarlet notebook is not imaginary. It is a real notebook, no less real than the pen in my hand or the shirt on my back, and it is lying in front of me on my desk. I bought it three days ago in a stationery store on Lexington Avenue in New York City. There were many other notebooks for sale in the store—blue notebooks, green notebooks, yellow notebooks, brown notebooks—but when I caught sight of the red one, I heard it call out to me and speak my name. The red was so red that the color was in fact *scarlet*, for it burned as brightly as the A on Hester Prynne's frock. The pages inside the scarlet notebook are of course white, and there are many of them, more pages than a person could possibly count in the hours between dawn and dusk on a long midsummer day.

Fourth Entry. When I open the scarlet notebook, I see the window I am looking through in my mind. I see the city on the other side of the window. I see an old woman walking her dog, and I hear the baseball game playing on the radio in the apartment next door. Two balls, two strikes, two men out. *Here comes the pitch.*

Seventh Entry. When I turn the pages of the scarlet notebook, I often see things I thought I had forgotten, and suddenly I find myself back in the past. I remember old telephone numbers of vanished friends.

I remember the dress my mother was wearing on the day I graduated from elementary school. I remember the date of the signing of the Magna Carta. I even remember the first scarlet notebook I ever bought. That was in Maplewood, New Jersey, many years ago.

Ninth Entry. In the scarlet notebook there are cardinals, red-winged blackbirds, and robins. There are the Boston Red Sox and the Cincinnati Red Stockings. There are roses, tulips, and poppies. There is a photograph of Sitting Bull. There is the beard of Erik the Red. There are left-wing political tracts, boiled beets, and hunks of raw steak. There is fire. There is blood. Included also are *The Red and the Black*, the Red Scare, and *The Masque of the Red Death*. This is only a partial list.

Twelfth Entry. There are days when a person who owns a scarlet notebook must do nothing but read it. On other days, it is necessary for him to write in it. This can be troublesome, and on some mornings when I sit down to work I am not certain which activity is the correct one to pursue. It seems to depend on which page you have come to at that moment, but as the pages are unnumbered, it is difficult to know in advance. That explains why I have spent so many fruitless hours staring at blank pages. I feel I am supposed to find an image there, but when nothing materializes after my efforts, I am often gripped by panic. One episode was so demoralizing to me that I was afraid I would lose my mind. I called my friend W., who also owns a scarlet notebook, and told him how desperate I was. "Those are the risks of having a scarlet notebook," he said. "Either you give in to your despair and wait for it to pass or you burn your scarlet notebook and forget you ever had it." W. might have a point, but I could never do that. No matter how much pain it causes me, no matter how lost I sometimes feel, I could never live without my scarlet notebook.

Fourteenth Entry. On the right-hand pages of the scarlet notebook a soothing, crepuscular light appears at various moments during the day, a light similar to the one that falls on wheat and barley fields at dusk in late summer, but more glowing somehow, more ethereal, more restful to the eye, whereas the left-hand pages give off a light that makes one think of a cold afternoon in winter.

Seventeenth Entry. The startling discovery last week that it is possible to enter the scarlet notebook, or rather that the notebook is an instrument for entering imagined spaces so vivid and tangible that they take on the appearance of reality. It is not just a collection of pages for reading and writing words, then, it is a *locus solus*, a microscopic slit in the universe that can expand to allow a person through if he presses the scarlet notebook against his face and breathes in the smells of the paper with his eyes closed. My friend W. has warned me how dangerous it can be to go off on these impromptu excursions, but now that I have made my discovery, how can I resist the urge to slide into those other spaces every now and then? I pack a light lunch, throw some things into a small overnight bag (a sweater, a collapsible umbrella, a compass), and then telephone W. to let him know I'm about to take off. He worries about me constantly, I'm afraid, but W. is much older than I am (he turned seventy on his last birthday), and perhaps he has lost his feel for adventure. Good luck, he says to me, *you moron*, and then I laugh into the phone and hang up. Until now, I have not been gone for more than two or three hours at a stretch.

Twentieth Entry. In the scarlet notebook, I am happy to report, there is a violent curse against each and every person who has ever wronged me.

Twenty-third Entry. Not everything in the scarlet notebook is what it seems to be. The New York that dwells inside it, for example, does not always correspond to the New York of my waking life. It has happened to me that while walking down East Eighty-ninth Street and turning the corner onto what I was expecting to be Second Avenue, I have found myself on Central Park South near Columbus Circle. Perhaps this is because I know those streets more intimately than any others in the city, having just settled into an apartment on East Eighty-ninth Street at the beginning of the summer and having gone to Central Park South hundreds of times since the beginning of my life to visit my grandparents, whose apartment building on West Fifty-eighth Street also has an entrance on Central Park South. This geographical synapse would suggest that the scarlet notebook is a highly personal instrument for each person who owns one and that no two scarlet notebooks are alike, even if their covers all look the same. Memories are not continuous. They jump around from place to place and vault over large swaths of time with many gaps in between, and because of what my stepbrother calls this *quantum effect*, the multiple and often contradictory stories to be found in the scarlet notebook do not form a continuous narrative. Rather, they tend to unfold as dreams do—which is to say, with a logic that is not always readily apparent.

Twenty-fifth Entry. On every page of the scarlet notebook, there is my desk and everything else in the room where I am sitting now. Although I have often been tempted to take the scarlet notebook with me on my walks through the city, I have not yet found the courage to remove it from my desk. On the other hand, when I go off into the scarlet notebook itself, I always seem to have the scarlet notebook with me.

So began Ferguson's second swim across the lake, his Walden Pond of solitary word-work and seven to ten hours of desk time per day. It would turn into a long and messy splash, with frequent submersions and ever more exhausted arms and legs, but Ferguson had an inborn talent for jumping into deep and perilous waters when no lifeguards were around, and given that such a book had never been written or even dreamed of by anyone before him, Ferguson had to teach himself how to do what he was doing in the process of doing it. As seemed to be the case with everything he wrote now, he discarded more material than he kept, whittling down the 365 entries he composed between early June and mid-September 1966 to 174, which filled one hundred and eleven double-spaced typewritten pages in the ultimate draft, making his second novella-length book slightly shorter than the first, and when it was boiled down further on Gizmo's single-spaced stencils, the text came to fifty-four pages, an even number that absolved Ferguson of the onerous responsibility of having to write another autobiographical note about himself.

HE ENJOYED LIVING in his small hush-money apartment, and all through his first summer there in 1966, as Joanna worked on the typing of *Mulligan's Travels* and Ferguson sweated out the pages of *The Scarlet*

Notebook, he continued to think about the ten thousand dollars and how slyly and underhandedly his grandfather had explained the "gift" to his daughter Rose, calling her at home the very next day, which was the same day Ferguson had met Billy and Joanna Best for the first time, to tell her he had started his own informal equivalent of the Rockefeller Foundation, i.e., the Adler Foundation for the Promotion of the Arts, and had just bestowed a ten-thousand-dollar award on his grandson to encourage his progress as a writer. What a colossal mound of bullshit, Ferguson thought, and yet how interesting that a man who had been shamed into tears and had written out a check to cover up his guilt could turn around the next day and start bragging about what he had done. Crazy, stupid old man, but when Ferguson talked to his mother from Princeton the following Monday, he had to suppress his laughter as she reported what her father had said to her, the incredible phoniness of it all, the show-off self-aggrandizement of his unparalleled generosity, and when his mother said, Just think, Archie—first the Walt Whitman Scholarship and now this amazing gift from your grandfather—Ferguson replied, I know, I know, I'm the luckiest man on the face of the earth, consciously repeating the words Lou Gehrig had spoken at Yankee Stadium after he found out he was dying from the disease that would eventually be named after him. Sitting pretty, Ferguson's mother said. Yes, that was it, sitting pretty, and what a grand and beautiful world it was if you didn't stop to look at it too closely.

A MATTRESS ON the floor, a desk and a chair found on a nearby sidewalk and hauled up to the room with Billy's help, some pots and pans bought for nickels and dimes at a local Goodwill Mission store, sheets, towels, and bedding donated by his mother and Dan as *housewarming gifts*, and a second typewriter bought secondhand at Osner's typewriter shop on Amsterdam Avenue to avoid having to lug a machine from Princeton to New York and then back to Princeton every Friday and Sunday, an Olympia manufactured in West Germany circa 1960 with an even finer and faster touch than his dependable, deeply loved Smith-Corona. Frequent dinners with the Bests, frequent dinners with Amy and Luther, occasional get-togethers with Ron Pearson and his wife, Peg, and solo expeditions for early dinners at the Ideal Lunch Counter on East Eighty-sixth Street, the eating hole with a sign over the door that read: SERVING GERMAN FOOD SINCE 1932 (a significant date that established *no connection* with what happened in Germany the following year), and how Ferguson liked to chow down on those heavy, lump-in-the-stomach dishes, Königsberger Klopse and Wiener schnitzel, and to hear the large, muscular waitress behind the counter shout into the kitchen with her thick accent, *Vun schnitzel!*, which never failed to evoke memories of Dan and Gil's dead father, that other crazy grandfather in the tribe, Jim and Amy's cantankerous, crackpot *Opa*. The luckiest man on the face of the earth also had the good fortune to meet Mary Donohue that summer, Joanna's twenty-one-year-old younger sister, who was spending those months with the Bests and working in an office before heading back to Ann Arbor for her senior year, and because the plump, jovial, sex-mad Mary took a shine to Ferguson, she often came to his apartment at night and crawled into bed with him, which helped diminish the constant longing he still felt for Evie and turn his thoughts from the vile thing he had done to her by cutting it off without a proper good-bye. Mary's soft and abundant flesh—a good place to drown in and forget who he was, to throw off the burden of being himself—and the sex was good because it was simple and transitory, sex without strings, without delu-sions, without hope for anything more lasting than it was.

Ferguson's initial plan was to barge in and settle the Amy-Luther problem himself, to go behind their backs in the same way Noah had done with his manuscript and call his mother to tell her what was going on and ask how she thought Dan would react to the news. Then he reexamined that approach and concluded he didn't have the right to deceive his stepsister or act without her consent, so one evening in the middle of June, as Ferguson, Bond, and Schneiderman sat in the West End inhaling and imbibing another round of cigarettes and beers, the son of Rose asked the stepdaughter of Rose if she would allow him to speak to his mother on her behalf in order to *get this nonsense over with*. Before Amy could respond, Luther leaned forward and said, Thanks, Archie, and a moment later Amy said more or less the same thing, Thank you, Arch.

Ferguson called his mother the next morning, and when he told her why he was calling, his mother laughed.

We already know about this, she said.

You know? How can you possibly know?

From the Waxmans. And also from Jim.

Jim?

Yes, Jim.

And how does Jim feel about it?

He doesn't care. Or rather he does care, because he likes Luther so much.

And what about Dan?

A bit shocked at first, I would say. But I think he's over it now. I mean, Amy and Luther aren't planning to get married, are they?

I have no idea.

Marriage would be tough. Tough for both of them, a tough, tough road if they ever decided to do that, but also tough for Luther's parents, who are none too pleased about this little romance to begin with.

You've talked to the Bonds?

No, but Edna Waxman says the Bonds are worried about their son. They think he's been around white people too much, that he's lost the sense of his own blackness. The Newark Academy, now Brandeis, and always everyone's darling, the white people's darling. Too gentle and accommodating, they say, *no chip on his shoulder*, and yet, at the same time, they're so proud of him and so grateful to the Waxmans for helping them out. It's a complicated world, isn't it, Archie?

And how do you feel about all this?

My mind is still open. I won't know what I think until I've had a chance to meet Luther. Tell Amy to call me, okay?

I will. And don't worry. Luther's a good guy, and tell Edna Waxman to tell the Bonds not to worry either. Their son does have a chip on his shoulder. It's just not a big one, that's all. The right length of chip, I'd say, a chip that suits him well.

One month and one week later, Ferguson, Mary Donohue, Amy, and Luther were on their way north in the old Pontiac, heading for the farm in southern Vermont where Howard Small was spending the summer, and on that same Friday in another car, Ferguson's mother and Amy's father along with Ferguson's aunt and stepuncle were heading toward Williamstown, Massachusetts, where the five undergraduates would be joining up with them the following evening to watch Noah perform as Lucky in *Waiting for Godot*. Pigs and cows and chickens, the stench of manure in the barn, wind rushing down the green hills and swirling through the valley below, and broad-shouldered Howard tramping beside the New York foursome as they toured the grounds of his aunt and uncle's sixty-acre spread on the outskirts of Newfane. How happy Ferguson was to see his college pal again, and how good it was that the aunt and uncle had no prissy qualms about the coed sleeping arrangements (Howard had put his foot down and forced them to accept—or else), and now that the business between Amy and her father concerning Luther had been resolved, how relaxed everyone was that weekend, far from the hot cement and steaming fumes of New York as Amy galloped around a meadow on a chestnut stallion, a memorable image that Ferguson would go on savoring for years afterward, but nothing was more memorable than the performance on Saturday evening in Williamstown, just fifty miles from the farm, the play that Ferguson had read in high school but had never seen mounted onstage, which he had reread earlier that week to prepare himself for the production, but nothing as it turned out could have prepared him for what he saw that night, Noah with his wig of long white hair hanging under his bowler hat and the rope around his neck, the abused slave and bearer of burdens, the dunce, the mute clown who falls and totters and stumbles, such finely choreographed steps, the shuffling, torporous, snap-to surges forward and back, dozing off on his feet, the unexpected kick delivered to Estragon's leg, the unexpected tears that fall down his face, the contorted, pathetic dance he does when ordered to dance, the whip and the bags up and the bags down again and again, Pozzo's stool folded and unfolded again and again, it didn't seem credible that Noah could do such things, and then, in the first act, the famous speech, the Puncher and Wattman speech, the quaquaquaqua speech, the long harangue of unpunctuated scholarly gibberish, and Noah flew into it as if in a trance, such an impossible display of breath control and complex verbal rhythm, and Jesus Christ, Ferguson said to himself, Jesus fucking Christ as the words flew out of his cousin's mouth, and then the other three onstage jumped him and pounded him and smashed his hat, and Pozzo brandished the whip again, and once again it was *Up! Pig!*, and off they went, exiting the stage as Lucky crashed in the wings.

After the bows and the applause, Ferguson took Noah in his arms and embraced him so tightly that he almost broke his ribs. Once Noah was able to breathe again, he said: I'm glad you liked it, Archie, but I think I've done a better job in most of the other performances. Knowing you were in the audience, and my father, and Mildred, and Amy, and your mother—well, you get the idea. Pressure, man. Real pressure.

The New York quartet drove back to the city on Sunday night, and the next morning, July twenty-fifth, the poet Frank O'Hara was struck by a dune buggy on a Fire Island beach and killed at the age of forty. As word of the accident spread among the writers, painters, and musicians of New York, a great lamentation rose up throughout the city, and one by one the young downtown poets who had worshipped O'Hara broke down and wept. Ron Pearson wept. Ann Wexler wept. Lewis Tarkowski wept. And uptown, on East Eighty-ninth Street, Billy Best punched a wall so hard that his fist went straight through the Sheetrock. Ferguson had never met O'Hara, but he knew his work and admired it for its effervescence and freedom, and though he didn't break down or put his fist through a wall, he spent the next day rereading the two books of O'Hara's that he owned, *Lunch Poems* and *Meditations in an Emergency*.

I am the least difficult of men, O'Hara had written in 1954. *All I want is boundless love.*

TRUE TO HER word, Celia sent Ferguson precisely twenty-four letters during her two months of travel abroad. Good letters, he felt, well-written letters, with many observant remarks about her experiences in Dublin, Cork, London, Paris, Nice, Florence, and Rome, for not unlike her brother, Artie, Celia knew how to look at things carefully, with more patience and curiosity than most people did, as displayed in this sentence about the Irish countryside in one of her early letters, which set the tone for everything that followed: *A green treeless land dotted with gray stones and black rooks flying overhead, a stillness in the heart of all things, even when the heart is beating and the wind has begun to blow.* Not bad for a future biologist, Ferguson thought, but friendly as the letters were, there was nothing intimate or revealing about them, and when Celia returned to New York on August twenty-third, one day after Mary Donohue kissed him good-bye and returned to Ann Arbor, Ferguson had no idea where he stood with her. He meant to find out as quickly as possible, however, for now that Celia was seventeen and a half, the ban against physical contact had been lifted. Love was a contact sport, after all, and Ferguson was looking for love now, he was *ready for love*, to use the words from the old number in *Singin' in the Rain*, and for all the old reasons and all the new ones as well, he was hoping to find that love in the arms of Celia Federman. If she would have him.

She was dumbfounded by the bareness of his apartment when she came to visit on the twenty-seventh. The desk was fine, the mattress was fine, but how could he keep his clothes in a cardboard box in the closet and not have a bag or a basket for dirty laundry and just throw his socks and undies on the bathroom floor? And why not get a bookcase instead of piling up books against the wall? And why no pictures? And why eat at his desk when there was room for a small kitchen table in the corner? Because he wanted as few things as possible, Ferguson said, and because he didn't care. Yes, yes, Celia said, she was acting like a middle-aged woman from the suburbs and he was roughing it as a bohemian renegade in the jungles of Manhattan, she got all that, and it wasn't her concern, but didn't he want to make it just a little bit nicer?

They were standing in the middle of the room with sunlight pouring in on them, sunlight pouring in through the windows and onto Celia's face, the illuminated face of a seventeen-and-a-half-year-old girl of such beauty that Ferguson was stunned by the sight of her, stunned into silence and awe and trembling uncertainty, and as he went on looking at her, looking and looking at her because he was unable to look at anything else, Celia smiled and said, What's wrong, Archie? Why are you staring at me like that?

I'm sorry, he said. I can't help it. It's just that you're so beautiful, Celia, so astonishingly beautiful, I'm beginning to wonder if you're real.

Celia laughed. Don't be absurd, she said. I'm not even pretty. Just your average workaday girl.

Who's been feeding you that crap? You're a goddess, the queen of all earth and every city in heaven.

Well, it's nice that you think so, but maybe you should have your eyes checked, Archie, and get a pair of glasses.

The sun shifted in the sky, or a cloud passed in front of it, or Ferguson was beginning to feel embarrassed by his gushing pronouncement, but four seconds after Celia said those words the subject of her looks was no longer on the table, the subject was once again the table Ferguson didn't have, the bookcase he didn't have, the bureau he didn't have, and if it meant so much to her, he said, maybe they could borrow Billy's hand truck and go out looking for furniture on the streets, it was the tried and true method of decorating apartments in Manhattan, and with the rich people on the Upper East Side throwing out good stuff every day, all they had to do was walk a few blocks south and a few blocks west, where they were bound to find something on the sidewalk that would meet with her approval.

I'm game if you are, Celia said.

Ferguson was game, but before they left there were a couple of things he wanted to show her, and then he led Celia over to his desk, where he pointed to a small wooden box with the words *Federman's Travels* written on it, and once she had absorbed the significance of that box and the loyalty to their friendship it demonstrated, Ferguson opened the bottom right-hand drawer of the desk, pulled out a copy of the Gizmo Press edition of *Mulligan's Travels*, and handed it to her.

Your book! Celia said. It's been published!

She looked down at Howard's cover, ran her hand softly over the drawing of Mulligan, thumbed briefly through the mimeographed pages inside, and then, inexplicably, let the book drop to the floor.

Why did you do that? Ferguson asked.

Because I want to kiss you, she said.

A moment later, she put her arms around him and pressed her mouth against his, and all at once his arms were around her, and their tongues were inside each other's mouths.

It was their first kiss.

And it was a real kiss, which gladdened Ferguson's heart greatly, for not only did the kiss offer the promise of more kisses in the days ahead, it proved that Celia was in fact real.

THERE HAD BEEN no contact with his father in over a year. Ferguson rarely thought about him now, and whenever he did, he noticed that the rage he had once felt against him had subsided into a dull indifference, or perhaps into nothing, a blank in his head. He had no father. The man who had once been married to his mother had vanished into the shadows of an alternate world that no longer intersected with the world his son lived in, and if the man was not yet certifiably dead, he had gone missing a long time ago and would never be found at any time in the future.

Three days before he left for Princeton to begin his sophomore year, however, as Ferguson sat in the living room of the house on Woodhall Crescent watching a Mets game with his stepbrother, Jim, and Jim's fiancée, Nancy, the prophet of profits unexpectedly jumped onto the TV screen in a between-innings commercial. Sporting thick sideburns with a touch of gray in them, and decked out in a natty, fashionable suit (color unknown since it was a black-and-white TV), he was announcing the opening of a new Ferguson's outlet in Florham Park and hammering away at the *low prices*, the *low, low prices you can afford*, and come on over and check out the new RCA color televisions and the stupefying bargains that would be available next weekend when the store opened for business. How deftly and confidently he was making his pitch, Ferguson said to himself, assuring the audience how much their anguished, monotone lives would be enhanced by shopping at Ferguson's, and for a man *who had never learned how to talk*, as his mother had once put it, he was doing a hell of a good job of talking now, and how relaxed and comfortable he looked in front of the camera, how pleased with himself, how perfectly in charge of the moment, and as he waved his arm and smiled, gesturing to the invisible masses to *come on in and save a bundle*, a quartet of unaccompanied soprano and tenor voices trilled brightly in the background: *Prices never lower / Spirits never higher / At Ferguson's, Ferguson's, Fer-gu-son's!*

Two thoughts appeared in Ferguson's mind after the commercial ended, the one forming so quickly after the other that they were almost simultaneous:

1) That he should stop watching baseball games on television, and 2) That his father was still hovering around the edges of his life, not yet fully effaced, still there in spite of the distance between them, and perhaps another chapter of the story still had to be written before the book could finally be closed.

UNLESS HE TOOK a crash course in ancient Greek and learned the language in a single academic year, there would be no more classes with Nagle. But Nagle was still his faculty adviser, and for reasons that had everything to do with his father, or perhaps nothing to do with his father, Ferguson continued to look to Nagle for validation and encouragement, wanting to impress the older man by doing top-quality work in his courses, by exhibiting proof of the soundness of character demanded from the participants in the Walt Whitman Scholars Program, but most of all by winning the professor's support for the fiction he was writing, a sign that he was fulfilling the promise Nagle had seen in him after reading *Eleven Moments from the Life of Gregor Flamm*. At their first one-on-one conference of the fall semester, Ferguson handed Nagle a copy of the Gizmo Press edition of *Mulligan's Travels*, ambivalent and fearful that he had jumped into publishing his work too soon, worried that Nagle would regard the mimeo book as the overly ambitious act of a young writer who wasn't ready to be published, doubly worried that Nagle would read the book and find it awful, delivering another one of the punches Ferguson dreaded so much even as he longed for kisses from the people he admired, but Nagle accepted the book that first afternoon with a friendly nod and a few words of congratulations, knowing nothing about the contents, of course, but at least not condemning Ferguson for having rushed into premature publication and the inevitable regret and embarrassment that would follow from such an ill-conceived show of arrogance, and as Nagle held the book in his hands and studied the black-and-white illustration on the cover, he mentioned how good he thought the drawing was. Who's H.S.? he asked, pointing to the abbreviated signature in the lower right-hand corner, and when Ferguson said it was Howard Small, his Princeton roommate, Nagle's dour mien sent forth one of its unaccustomed smiles. Hard-working Howard Small, he said. Such a good student, but I had no idea he could draw so well. You boys are quite a pair, aren't you?

At their next sit-down in the professor's office three days later, when they were supposed to decide which courses Ferguson would be taking that semester, Nagle began by pronouncing his verdict on *Mulligan's Travels*. It didn't matter that Billy, Ron, and Noah had all warmly embraced the book, nor did it matter that Amy, Luther, and Celia had responded with enthusiastic kisses (in Celia's case, genuine physical kisses), and forget that Uncle Don and Aunt Mildred had taken the trouble to call on the phone and shower him with flattering comments for close to an hour or that Dan and his mother and the departed Evie Monroe and the departed Mary Donohue had all told him how good they thought it was, Nagle's opinion was the one that counted most because he was the only objective observer, the only one not tied to Ferguson by friendship or love or familial bonds, and a negative word from him would undercut and perhaps even demolish the accumulated positive words from the others.

Not bad, he said, using the phrase he tended to fall back on when he liked something rather well but with certain reservations. An advance from your previous work, he continued, tautly written, a fine and subtle music in the sentences, absorbing to read, but stark, raving mad, of course, an inventiveness bordering on mental-breakdown territory, and yet, for all that, the texts are funny when you mean for them to be funny, dramatic when you mean for them to be dramatic, and clearly you've read Borges by now and have learned some lessons from him about how to walk the line between what I would call fiction and speculative prose. Some silly, sophomoric ideas, I'm afraid, but that's what you are, Ferguson, a sophomore, so we won't dwell on the book's weaknesses. If nothing else, you've convinced me you're making progress, which suggests you're going to continue to make more progress as time goes on.

Thank you, Ferguson said. I scarcely know what to say.

Don't turn mute on me now, Ferguson. We still have to discuss your plans for the semester. Which brings me to the question I've been meaning to ask you. Have you changed your mind about registering for one of the creative writing workshops?

No, not really.

It's a good program, you know. One of the best anywhere.

I'm sure you're right. I just feel I'll be happier gutting it out on my own.

I understand your reservations, but at the same time I think it would help you. And then there's the matter of Princeton, of being a part of the Princeton community. Why, for example, haven't you submitted any of your work to the *Nassau Literary Review*?

I don't know. It never occurred to me.

Do you have anything against Princeton?

No, not at all. I love it here.

No second thoughts, then?

None whatsoever. I feel blessed.

As he went on talking to Nagle and the two of them mapped out his curriculum for the fall, Howard was in their dorm room reading *The Scarlet Notebook*, which Ferguson had pronounced D.O.A. one week earlier, *yet another corpse expelled from my shit-infested brain*, as he had said to Howard when he handed him the manuscript, but Howard was used to Ferguson's torments and self-doubts by then and paid them no heed, confident in the strength of his own intelligence to draw his own independent conclusions, and by the time Ferguson walked into the room after his conference with Nagle, Howard had finished the book.

Archie, he said. Have you ever read Wittgenstein?

No, not yet. He's one of many on my *not-yet* list.

Good. Or rather, get a load of this, *mein Herr.*

Howard picked up a blue book with Wittgenstein's name on the cover, opened it to whatever page he was looking for, and read out loud to Ferguson: *And it also means something to talk about "living in the pages of a book."*

How true, how true, Ferguson said. And then, bringing himself to attention and giving a stiff military salute, he added: Thank you, Ludwig!

You see where I'm going with this, don't you?

Not really.

The Scarlet Notebook. I just finished reading it about ten minutes ago.

"How I Spent My Summer Vacation." Remember those things we had to write as kids? Well, that's how I spent my summer vacation. Living in the pages of that monstrosity . . . that abortion of a book.

You know how much I loved *Mulligan*, right? This one is deeper and better and more original. A breakthrough. And I hope to God you let me do the cover for it.

What makes you think Billy will want to publish it?

Don't be an idiot. Of course he'll want to publish it. Billy discovered you, and he thinks you're a genius, his bright-eyed baby genius, and wherever you go, that's where he'll want to go, too.

Now you tell me, Ferguson said, beginning to crack a smile. I just got the lowdown on *Mulligan* from Nagle. Good and not good. Sophomoric but fun. Written by a madman who should be put in a straitjacket. A step forward, but still a long way to go. I happen to agree with him.

You shouldn't listen to Nagle, Archie. He's a brilliant professor—of Greek. We both love him, but he isn't qualified to judge your work. He's stuck *back there*, and you're what's going to happen *next*. Not tomorrow maybe, but definitely the day after tomorrow.

So began Ferguson's second year in black squirrel heaven, with a pep talk from his roommate, Howard Small, who was just as important a friend to him now as Noah and Jim were, an indispensable part of what was keeping him alive, and however exaggerated Howard's comments about his work might have been, he was correct to assume that Billy would want to publish his new book, and because Joanna was seven-and-a-half months pregnant and too close to having her baby to type up the stencils, Billy did the job himself, so that one week before little Molly Best came into the world on November ninth, Ferguson's second little book was in print.

It was a better year than the first one had been, with fewer anxieties and inner stumbles, with a more solid sense of belonging to the place where fortune had willed him to be, the year of Anglo-Saxon poems and Chaucer and the gorgeous, alliterative verses of Sir Thomas Wyatt (. . . *as she fleeth afore / Fainting I follow* . . .), the year of protesting the Vietnam War by joining in the demonstrations against Dow Chemical at the Engineering Quad with Howard and his other friends from the Woodrow Wilson Club to denounce the manufacturer of napalm, of settling into his more amply decorated New York weekend apartment and strengthening his friendships with Billy, Joanna, Ron, and Bo Jainard, of appearing as an extra in Noah's first film, a seven-minute short entitled *Manhattan Confidential* in which Ferguson could be glimpsed at a back table in a low-life bar reading Spinoza in French, and the year of working on *The Souls of Inanimate Things*, a sequence of thirteen meditations on the objects in his apartment that he finished at the end of May. It was also the year when his grandfather died the strange and ignominious death that no one in the family wanted to talk about, the culmination of a week-long gambling binge in Las Vegas during which he lost over ninety thousand dollars at roulette and then suffered a heart attack while making love (or trying to make love) to two twenty-year-old hookers in his room. In the seventeen months since his wife's death, Benjy Adler had blown more than three hundred and fifty thousand dollars and was put in his grave as a pauper by the Jewish burial society run by the Workmen's Circle, an organization he had joined in 1936, back in the days when he had been reading the novels of Jack London and still thought of himself as a socialist.

THEN THERE WAS Celia, first and last there was Celia, for that was the year when Ferguson fell in love, and the most perplexing thing about it was that no one but his mother saw in her what he did. Rose judged her to be *a magnificent girl*, but all the others were confused. Noah called her a *gawky stalk* from Westchester, the female version of her ghosty-boy brother but with darker skin and a more attractive face, a Barnard geek who would spend her life in a white lab coat studying rats. Jim thought she was good-looking but too young for Ferguson, not yet fully evolved. Howard admired her intelligence but wondered if she wasn't too conventional for Ferguson, a bourgeois goody-good who would never understand how little he cared about what everyone else seemed to care about. Amy weighed in with a single word: Why? Luther called her a work in progress, and Billy said: Archie, what are you doing?

Did he know what he was doing? He thought he did. He had thought so when Celia put down the dollar bill in front of the old man at Horn & Hardart's. He had thought so when she insisted on *no more fake-brother stuff* while walking from Grand Central to the automat. And he had thought so when she dropped his book to the floor and declared she wanted to kiss him.

How many kisses had followed that first kiss over the ensuing months? Hundreds of them. Thousands of them. And the unexpected discovery on the night of October twenty-second, when they lowered themselves onto the mattress in Ferguson's room and made love for the first time, that Celia was no longer a virgin. There had been the aforementioned Bruce in the spring of her last year of high school, and there had been two American travelers on her tour of Europe with her cousin Emily, an Ohioan in Cork and a California boy in Paris, but rather than feel disappointed by the knowledge that he wasn't her first one, Ferguson was heartened by it, encouraged that she was adventurous and open and had a carnal appetite strong enough to push her into taking risks.

He loved her body. He found her naked body so beautiful that he could barely speak the first time she took off her clothes and lay down beside him. The impossible smoothness and warmth of her skin, her slender arms and legs, the curving cheeks of her round, clutchable ass, her small, upright breasts and dark, pointed nipples, he had never known anyone as beautiful as she was, and what the others couldn't understand was how happy it made him to be with her, to run his hands over the body of the person he now loved more than any person he had ever loved. If the others couldn't get that, too bad for them, but Ferguson wasn't about to ask the minstrel boys to unpack their violins and lay it on thick with the schmaltz. One violin was enough, and as long as Ferguson could hear the music it was playing, he would go on listening to it by himself.

More important than the others or what the others thought was the simple fact of the two of them, and now that they had advanced to the next stage, there was the ever more urgent need to understand precisely what was going on. Was his burgeoning love for Celia still connected to Artie's death, he asked himself, or had her brother finally been dropped from the equation? That was how it had started, after all, back in the days of the New Rochelle dinners when the world had split in half and the arithmetic of the gods had provided him with a formula to glue it together again: fall in love with his dead friend's sister, and henceforth the earth would continue to revolve around the sun. The mad calculations of an overheated adolescent mind, of an angry, grieving mind, but however irrational the numbers might have been, he had hoped he would eventually fall for her, and if and when he did, he had also hoped she would fall for him, and now that both of those things had happened, he didn't want Artie to be involved in it anymore, for the things that had happened had mostly happened on their own, starting with the day in New York when he saw a compassionate girl pull a dollar from her purse and give it to a broken-down old man, with that same girl one year later standing in the light of his apartment and overpowering him with the force of her beauty, with twenty-four letters from foreign countries stashed away in a wooden box, with an excited girl dropping his book to the floor and wanting to kiss him, none of which had anything to do with Artie, and yet now that he and Celia had fallen for each other, Ferguson had to admit that it felt good and right that she was the one he was with and no one else, even if something in him cringed at the thought of that *good and right*, because now that he loved Celia he understood how sick his desire for her had been in the first place, to look upon a living, breathing person and turn her into a symbol of his campaign to rectify the injustices of the world, what had he been thinking, for God's sake, and how much better it would be if Artie were out of it for good now. No more ghosts, Ferguson said to himself. The dead boy had brought him together with Celia, but now that he had done his job, it was time for him to go away.

Never a word to her about any of that, and as 1966 turned into 1967 it was remarkable how little they talked about her brother, how determined they both were to avoid the subject and get on with the business of being just two so the invisible third would not be standing between them or floating above them, and as the months rolled on and their connection tightened and Ferguson's friends gradually came round and began to accept her as a permanent part of the landscape, he realized there was one necessary act still in front of him before the spell could be broken. It was spring by then, and having celebrated their double March birthdays on the third and sixth of the month, they were now twenty and eighteen years old, and one Saturday afternoon in the middle of May, one week after Ferguson had written the final paragraph of *The Souls of Inanimate Things*, he traveled across town to Morningside Heights, where Celia was ensconced in her dormitory room at Brooks Hall working on two end-of-the-year term papers, which meant that weekend would be different from most other weekends and would not include their customary walks and talks and nighttime explorations in Ferguson's bed, but he had called Celia at ten o'clock that morning and asked if he could "borrow her" for thirty or forty minutes later in the day, and no, he said, not for *that*, although he dearly wished it could be *that*, but rather to do something for him that would be both simple and unstrenuous and yet, at the same time, of utmost importance to their future happiness together. When she asked him what that thing was, he said he would tell her later.

Why so mysterious, Archie?

Because, he said. Just because, that's why.

As he traveled along the edge of Central Park on the crosstown bus, his right hand was in the pocket of his spring jacket, and the fingers of that hand were wrapped around a pink rubber ball, which he had bought that morning at a candy and cigarette store on First Avenue, a commonplace pink rubber ball manufactured by the Spalding Company and widely referred to in New York as a *spaldeen*. That was Ferguson's mission on that bright afternoon in the middle of May: to walk into Riverside Park with Celia and have a catch with her, to renounce the vow he had taken in the silent depths of his misery six years ago and have done with his obsession at last.

Celia smiled when he told her what the thing of utmost importance was, giving him a look that seemed to suggest she knew he was playing a joke or had something else up his sleeve and was still hiding it from her, but she was happy to be liberated from her room, she said, and what better way to pass the time than by having a catch in the park?

Celia was doubly up for it because she was an athletic girl, an excellent swimmer, a decent tennis player, and a not-bad shooter of baskets, and having observed her on the tennis court a couple of times, Ferguson knew she could catch a ball and didn't throw the way girls usually did, with the arm cocked at the elbow, but more or less as boys did, with a thrust from the shoulder of a fully extended arm. He pressed his lips against her face and thanked her for coming along. No matter how much he might have wanted to, he could never tell her why they were doing this.

As they headed for the park, mysterious bursts of sweat began spilling from Ferguson's pores, his stomach began to throb, and it was becoming more and more difficult to fill his lungs with air. Dizzy. So dizzy that he took hold of Celia's arm to maintain his balance as they walked down the sharp incline of West 116th Street and shuffled toward Riverside Drive. Dizzy and scared. He had made the promise to himself when he was still a boy, and since then it had been one of the burning forces in his life, a test of will and inner strength and sacrifice to a holy cause, solidarity across the chasm between the living and the dead, honoring the dead by saying no to something beautiful from this world, and to break that promise now wasn't easy for him, it was hard, harder than anything he could think of, but it had to be done, had to be done now, for noble as his sacrifice had been, it had also been crazy, and he didn't want to be crazy anymore.

They crossed Riverside Drive, and once their feet were touching the grass in the park, Ferguson took the ball out of his pocket.

Back up a little bit, Celia, he said to her, and after the smiling Celia had bounced back until they were standing about twelve feet apart, Ferguson raised his arm and threw her the ball.

THE SUMMER PROMISED great things for everyone in his circle. Or so it appeared when the summer began, and why mention the disasters of July and August when the chronology calls for the high hopes of June to come first in the reckoning? For Ferguson and his friends, it was a time when everyone seemed to be rushing along in the same direction, when everyone stood on the brink of doing something unheard of, some extraordinary thing that none of them had ever imagined would be possible. In far-off California, the summer of 1967 had been declared the

Summer of Love. Back home on the East Coast, it began as the Summer of Exaltations.

Noah was returning to Williamstown for another season of acting (Chekhov, Pinter) and was hard at work on the script for his second little film, which would be less little than the first one had been, a sixteen-minute talkie with the working title of *Tickle My Feet*. On top of that, he had found himself a new girlfriend in the person of frizzy-headed, large-breasted Vicki Tremain, a fellow NYUer from the class of '69 who had memorized more than a hundred poems by Emily Dickinson, smoked pot as compulsively as other people smoked cigarettes, and had aspirations to become the first woman to traverse the twenty-six blocks between Washington Square and the Empire State Building by walking on her hands. Or so she said. She also said she had been raped repeatedly by Lyndon Johnson over the past four years and that Marilyn Monroe wouldn't have killed herself if she had married Henry Miller instead of Arthur Miller. Vicki was a young woman with a rich sense of humor and a keen awareness of the absurdities of life, and Noah was so bowled over by her that his legs wobbled whenever she came near him.

Amy and Luther would not be coming down to New York again. They had found an apartment in Somerville, and while Luther took supplementary courses at Harvard, Amy would be spending the next two and a half months as an assembly-line worker at the Necco factory in Cambridge. Ferguson remembered Necco wafers from his childhood, in particular the bad-weather battles he had fought with them at Camp Paradise, all the boys cooped up in the cabin and flinging those hard little disks of candy at one another as rain poured down on the roof, but then Rosenberg caught one just below the eye and Necco wafer wars were banned. An interesting choice, Ferguson said to Amy on the phone, but why factory work, and what was it all about? Politics, she said. Members of SDS had been asked to find jobs in factories that summer to help spread the anti-war movement to the working class, which was still mostly pro-war at that point. Ferguson asked whether she thought it would do any good. She had no idea, Amy said, but even if the inside-agitator stuff didn't pan out, it would be a good experience for her, a chance to learn something about American labor conditions and the people who did the laboring. She had read a hundred books on the subject, but a summer at the Necco factory was bound to teach her a lot more. Full immersion. Hands-on, practical knowledge. Rolling up her sleeves and plunging in. Right?

Right, Ferguson said, but promise me one thing.

What?

Don't eat too many Necco wafers.

Oh? And why is that?

They're bad for your teeth. And don't throw them at Luther. If properly aimed, they can be turned into deadly weapons, and Luther's health is of great importance to me, since I want to go to a baseball game with him this summer.

All right, Archie. I won't eat them, and I won't throw them. I'll just make them.

Jim had completed his masters in physics at Princeton and would be marrying Nancy Hammerstein in early June. They had already signed a lease on a two-bedroom apartment in South Orange, a third-floor flat in the building that stood on the corner of South Orange Avenue and Ridgewood Road, one of the rare apartment buildings in a town largely made up of one-family houses, and they would be moving in after they returned from their camping-trip honeymoon in the Berkshires. Jim had been offered a job teaching physics at West Orange High School and Nancy would be teaching history at Montclair High, but they had chosen to live in South Orange because Jim still had many friends there, and with babies on the not-too-distant horizon, it made sense to be in the same town as the future grandparents of those children. What a thought that was, Ferguson said to himself: he an uncle, Amy an aunt, and his mother and her father bouncing a pair of grandkids on their knees.

Howard was going back to the farm in Vermont, not to milk cows and repair barbed-wire fences as he had in the past but to put his four semesters of ancient Greek to good use by translating the written fragments and recorded utterances of Democritus and Heraclitus into English, the two pre-Socratic thinkers who were commonly referred to as the Laughing Philosopher and the Weeping Philosopher. Howard had discovered an amusing passage in an early text by John Donne that he was planning to insert as an epigraph to the project: *Now among our wise men, I doubt not but many would be found who would laugh at Heraclitus weeping, none which weep at Democritus laughing.* But even as Howard wrestled with his versions of D. (*Action begins with boldness: chance rules the end*) and H. (*The way up and the way down are one and the same*), he was pursuing his T.M. project as well, the work of illustrating the sixty best tennis matches he and Ferguson had come up with over the past two years, for Howard was one of those fluky beings who felt at home with both words and images and was happiest when living in both realms simultaneously, and beyond those jobs of translating and drawing, his chief objective that summer was to spend as many hours as he could with Mona Veltry, his childhood friend from Brattleboro who in recent months had been elevated to the status of girlfriend, lover, intellectual companion, and possible future wife. Before saying good-bye to each other at Princeton on the day following the last day of finals, Howard had extracted a promise from Ferguson to come to Vermont for two long visits that summer, perhaps even three.

Billy was closing in on the end of his long, four-hundred-page novel and was planning to release *The Souls of Inanimate Things* by mid-August. Ron and Peg Pearson were expecting their first child, and Ron, Ann, and Lewis, who had been talking about the idea for over a year, had found a wealthy backer in Ann's mother's first husband's ex-wife to help them launch a new publishing house, Tumult Books, a small press that would bring out six or seven books a year, standard-dimension hardcovers with sewn bindings and traditional typography printed by the same presses that churned out books for other New York publishers. Mimeo was far from dead, but alternative solutions were slowly becoming available because some of the penniless writers from lower Manhattan had figured out where the pennies were.

As for Celia, she too would be summering in Massachusetts along with Noah, Amy, and Luther, not with them in a literal sense but bound for the village of Woods Hole at the tip of Cape Cod's western peninsula to work as an intern at the Marine Biological Laboratory. Not rats, as Noah had forecast back in the fall, but mollusks and plankton, and although Celia was technically too young for such a position, her Barnard biology professor, Alexander Mestrovic, had been so impressed by her intelligence and innate feel for the micro-nuances of cellular life that he had urged her to accompany him to Massachusetts for the genetics research project he would be participating in there, hoping the opportunity to observe the professors and advanced graduate students go about their business would acclimate her to the rigors of lab work, which in turn would help prepare her for a future in science.

Celia was reluctant to go. She wanted to find a job in the city and live with Ferguson over the summer, which was precisely what he wanted as well, but no, he said, she couldn't turn Mestrovic down, his invitation was an honor of such magnitude that she would regret not going for the rest of her life, and fear not, he added, he had access to a car and would be spending much time in Vermont and Massachusetts over the coming months, visiting Howard, Noah, Amy, and Luther in Newfane, Williamstown, and Somerville, and Woods Hole would be the prime destination on all his jaunts north, he would visit her as often as she could stand it, and please, he said to her, don't be ridiculous, you have to accept, and so she did accept, and one morning smack in the middle of the Six-Day War, she kissed Ferguson good-bye and off she went.

There was little question that he would be lonely, but it wouldn't be an unbearable loneliness, he felt, not with the chance to see her a couple of times every month, not with the extended visits to Howard's farm, and now that his last little book was behind him, the slate was blank again. More than eight months had been put into dreaming up those peculiar meditations on household objects and the imagined lives they had led before he picked them off the street, the nutty excursus on the broken toaster and whether a broken toaster could still be called a toaster if it could no longer function as a toaster and if not whether it needed to be given another name, reflections on lamps, mirrors, rugs, and ashtrays along with stories about the imagined people who had owned them and used them before they wound up in his apartment, such a daunting if not pointless thing to have done, and now there was one more little book for Billy to make two hundred copies of and hand out to their friends. The last chapter of the Gizmo Period, as Ferguson would later come to think of it, three small works of dubious merit, no doubt flawed and stunted but never lackluster or predictable, at times even effulgent, so perhaps not the out-and-out failures he often took them to be, and because Billy and the others were behind what he did, perhaps good enough to have established him as someone with a possible future, the potential for a possible future, in any case, and having spent the past two-plus years composing that trio of frantic warm-up exercises, Ferguson understood that the first phase of his apprenticeship had come to an end. He needed to move on to something else now. Above all, he said to himself, he needed to slow down and start telling stories again, to work his way back into a world populated by minds other than his own.

He wrote nothing during the first three weeks of summer vacation. There was Jim and Nancy's wedding in Brooklyn on June tenth, there were the splendid days with Celia in Woods Hole from the sixteenth to the eighteenth, but mostly he walked around the city and killed time, making an effort to keep his eyes fixed on the things in front of him as the still unanswered letter from Dana Rosenbloom sat in his pocket. New York was crumbling. The buildings, the sidewalks, the benches, the storm drains, the lampposts, the street signs were all cracked or broken or falling apart, hundreds of thousands of young men were fighting in Vietnam, the boys of Ferguson's generation were being shipped off to be killed for reasons no one had fully or adequately justified, the old men in charge had lost hold of the truth, lies were the accepted currency of American political discourse now, and every roach-infested, piss-poor coffee joint up and down the length of Manhattan had a neon sign in the window that read: THE BEST CUP OF COFFEE IN THE WORLD.

Dana was married, six months pregnant, and both *happy and fulfilled* according to her letter. Ferguson was glad for her. Knowing what he now knew about himself, it was clear that she had done well to avoid marrying a man incapable of fathering children, but much as he wanted to write back to congratulate her, other parts of her letter had disturbed him, and he was still searching for a way to answer her. The exultant tone of her comments about the war, the smug certainties of military conquest, the tribalism of Hebrew warriors vanquishing their myriad foes. The West Bank, Sinai, East Jerusalem, all under Israeli control now, and yes, it had been a great and surprising victory, and of course they were feeling proud of themselves, but no good would come of it if Israel persisted in occupying those territories, Ferguson felt, it would only lead to more trouble down the road, but Dana couldn't see that, perhaps no one in Israel could look at the situation from the outside, they had been trapped inside their fear for so long and now they were dancing inside their newly won power, and because Ferguson didn't want to upset Dana with his opinions, which could have been wrong opinions for all he knew, he kept putting off the letter he wanted to write.

Six days after he returned from Woods Hole, he went out for another one of his rambles through the city, and as he walked past a vacant lot cluttered with abandoned refrigerators, headless dolls, and smashed-up high chairs, an unbidden phrase surged up in his mind, four words that came to him as if from nowhere and then continued to repeat themselves as he went on walking, *the capital of ruins,* and the more he thought about those words, the more convinced he became that they were the title of his next piece of work, a novel this time, his first attempt at a novel, a grave and pitiless book about the broken country he lived in, a descent into a much darker register than anything that had come before it, and even as he walked along the sidewalk that afternoon, it was beginning to take shape inside him, the story of a doctor named Henry Noyes, whose name was stolen from pre-med student William Noyes, Ferguson's freshman-year suitemate at Brown Hall, but a name that was pronounced as if it were the word *noise* and yet broke down into the words *no* and *yes* when you separated the second and third letters was the inevitable choice, the only choice that answered the needs of the story. *The Capital of Ruins.* It would take Ferguson two years to finish that two-hundred-and-forty-six-page novel, but one day before he set off for Howard's farm in Vermont, on June 30, 1967, he sat down and wrote the first version of the first paragraph of what he would come to regard as his first real book.

He remembered the first outbreak thirty-five years ago, the rash of inexplicable suicides that had stunned the city of R. during the winter and spring of 1931, that terrible stretch of months when close to two dozen young people between the ages of fifteen and twenty had put an end to their own lives. He had been young then himself, just fourteen years old, a freshman in high school, and he would never forget hearing the news that Billy Nolan was dead, never forget the tears that had poured out of him when he was told that beautiful Alice Morgan had hanged herself in the attic of her house. Most of them hanged themselves thirty-five years ago, leaving behind no note or explanation, and now it was starting again, four deaths in March alone, but this time the young people were killing themselves by asphyxiation, gassing themselves to death as they sat in idling cars parked inside locked garages. He knew there would be more deaths, that more young people would vanish before the epidemic came to an end, and he took those disasters personally, for he was a doctor now, general practitioner Henry J. Noyes, and three of the four newly dead children had been his patients, Eddie Brickman, Linda Ryan, and Ruth Mariano, and he had brought all three of them into the world with his own hands.

THEY WERE ALL supposed to gather at Howard's farm between five and six o'clock on Saturday, July first. Celia would be coming from Woods Hole in the used Chevy Impala her parents had bought for her in May, Schneiderman and Bond from Somerville in the 1961 Skylark the Waxmans had given Luther as a going-away present when he left for his freshman year of college, and Ferguson from the house on Woodhall Crescent, where he had to go early that morning to fetch the old Pontiac. The plan was to spend Saturday night at the farm, eat breakfast there the following morning, and then drive over to Williamstown to watch Noah strut the boards as Konstantin in the Sunday matinee of *The Seagull*. After that, Celia would return to Woods Hole, Amy and Luther would return to Somerville, and Ferguson, Howard, and Mona Veltry would go back to the farm. Ferguson had an open invitation to remain there as long as he wished. He imagined he would stick around for about two weeks, but nothing was definite, and perhaps he would camp out there for the rest of the month, with trips to Woods Hole on the weekends.

Everyone made it to Vermont at the appointed hour, and because Howard's aunt and uncle were visiting friends in Burlington that evening, and because no one was in the mood for cooking, the three couples decided to go out for dinner at a place called Tom's Bar and Grill, a run-down watering hole on Route 30 about three-quarters of a mile from the center of Brattleboro. The six of them crammed into Howard's station wagon after a couple of rounds of beer at the farm, a small guzzle in the kitchen because the Vermont drinking age was twenty-one and they wouldn't be allowed to have any beer at Tom's, and because one round had not been enough, they didn't leave until close to nine o'clock, and by nine o'clock on a Saturday night Tom's was generally in a state of near chaos, with loud country music thumping on the jukebox and the slosh-heads at the bar well into their umpteenth round of liquid refreshments.

It was a rough working-class and farmer crowd, no doubt a predominantly right-wing, pro-war crowd, and when Ferguson walked in with his little band of left-wing college friends, he immediately understood

that they had come to the wrong place. There was something about
the men and women sitting at the bar, he felt, something about them that
seemed to want trouble, and the pity was that he and his friends had
to sit within eyeshot of that bar because there were no free tables in the
back room. What was it, he kept asking himself, as a friendly waitress
showed up to take their orders (Hi, kids. What'll it be?), wondering if
the sour looks aimed in their direction had anything to do with his longish hair and Howard's somewhat longer hair, or with Luther's modest
Afro, or with Luther himself because he was the only black person anywhere in sight, or with the elegant, upper-crust prettiness of the three
girls, even though Amy was working in a factory that summer and
Mona's parents could have been at one of the tables in the other room
that night, and then, as Ferguson studied the people at the bar more
closely, some of whom had their backs turned to them, he realized that
most of the looks were coming from two guys at the end, the ones sitting along the right plank of the three-sided bar, the ones with the
unobstructed view of their table, two guys in their late twenties or
early thirties who could have been woodcutters or auto mechanics or
professors of philosophy from all Ferguson could tell, which was just
about nothing beyond the obvious fact that they looked displeased, and
then Amy did something she must have done several hundred times in
the past year, she snuggled up against Luther and kissed him on the
cheek, and suddenly Ferguson understood what was making the philosophers angry, not that a black person had entered their all-white
domain but that a young white woman was touching a young black man
in public, *snuggling up against his body and kissing him*, and when you factored in all the other aggravations they had been dealt that night, the
college boys with the long hair, the fresh-faced college girls with their
long legs and beautiful teeth, the flag burners and draft-card burners
and the whole brigade of anti-war hippie snots, and then added in the
number of beers they had consumed in the hours they had been sitting
there, no fewer than six apiece and perhaps as many as ten, it wasn't
strange or even remotely surprising that the larger of the two philosophy professors should have lifted himself off his barstool, walked over
to their table, and said to Ferguson's stepsister:

Cut that out, girl. Stuff like that ain't allowed in here.

Before Amy could collect her thoughts and answer him, Luther said:
Butt out, mister. Get lost.

I'm not talking to you, Charlie, the philosopher replied. I'm talking to *her*.

To emphasize his point, he pointed his finger at Amy.

Charlie! Luther said, with a loud, theatrical guffaw. That's a good one. You're the Charlie, mister, not me. *Mister Charlie* himself.

Ferguson, whose chair was closest to the standing philosopher, decided to stand up and give him a lesson in geography.

I think you're a little confused, he said. We're not in Mississippi, we're in Vermont.

We're in *America*, the philosopher rejoined, turning his attention to Ferguson now. Land of the free and home of the brave!

Free for you but not for them, is that it? Ferguson asked.

That's it, Charlie, the philosopher said. Not for them if they're going to carry on like that in public.

Like what? Ferguson said, with a sarcastic edge in his voice, which turned the words *like what* into something that resembled *fuck off*.

Like this, asshole, the philosopher said.

And then he punched Ferguson in the face and the fight began.

IT WAS ALL so idiotic. A barroom brawl with a drunken racist itching for a fight, but after the first punch had been thrown, what else could Ferguson do but punch back? Fortunately, the philosopher's friend did not jump in on the action, and while Howard and Luther both tried to break it up, they didn't succeed quickly enough to prevent Tom from calling the cops, and for the first time in his life Ferguson was arrested, handcuffed, and driven off to a police station to be booked, fingerprinted, and photographed from three different angles. The night-court judge fixed bail at one thousand dollars (one hundred dollars in cash), which Ferguson posted with help from Howard, Celia, Luther, and Amy.

Cuts above both eyes, the outer edge of his right eyebrow gone for good, an aching jaw, blood trickling down his checks, but nothing broken, whereas the man who had attacked him, a thirty-two-year-old plumber named Chet Johnson, emerged from the combat with a fractured nose and spent the night at Brattleboro Memorial Hospital. At the arraignment on Monday morning, he and Ferguson were both charged with assault, disorderly conduct, and destruction of private property (a chair and some glasses had been broken in the scuffle), and the trial date was set for Tuesday, July twenty-fifth.

Before the Monday arraignment, the grim Sunday at the farm with Noah's play forgotten and everyone sitting around the living room discussing what had happened the night before. Howard blamed himself. He never should have dragged them off to Tom's, he said, and Mona backed him by asserting her own guilt in the affair: I should have known better than to let you walk into that redneck crazy house. Celia talked at length about what she called Ferguson's *incredible bravery*—but also about how scared she had been when the fight started, the horrific violence of that first punch. Amy ranted for a while, cursing herself for not having stood up to that *ugly, bigoted slob*, galled by the panic she had felt when he thrust out his finger and pointed it at her, and then, unlike the Amy Ferguson had known for so many years, she put her hands over her face and started to cry. Luther was the angriest among them, the most bitter, the one most incensed by the confrontation, and he excoriated himself for having let Archie bear the brunt of it instead of pushing him out of the way and using his own black fist to slug the bastard in the mouth. Howard's aunt and uncle, already thinking about the next step, talked about finding a good lawyer to handle Ferguson's case. By the middle of the afternoon, Amy the Bold had regained enough clarity of mind to call the house on Woodhall Crescent and tell her father about *the mess* Archie was in. She passed the receiver to Ferguson, and when his confused and anxious mother came on, he told her not to worry, the situation was under control and there was no need for them to drive up to Vermont. But how could he be sure of anything, he asked himself as he spoke those words, and what on earth was going to happen to him?

Days passed. A supposedly good young lawyer from Brattleboro named Dennis McBride would be defending him. Celia would be coming back to the farm every weekend because Ferguson wasn't allowed to leave the state of Vermont until the trial was over, assuming it didn't end with the court putting him in prison for a month or three months or a year when the gavel of judgment came down on him. All sorts of money would have to be shelled out in order to stop that from happening, more dollars from the dwindling pile of ten thousand dollars his now dead grandfather had given him the year before, but at least he had the money and didn't have to ask his mother and Dan for help. Then it was July twelfth, and as he listened to his mother tell him the news over the phone, he found it difficult to imagine what she was talking about. In the midst of his small private struggles, a big public nightmare was spreading through the streets of Newark, and the city where he had spent the first years of his life was burning to the ground.

Race war. Not race riots, as the newspapers were telling everyone, but a war between the races. National Guardsmen and New Jersey state troopers firing their guns to kill, twenty-six dead in those days of havoc and bloodshed, twenty-four of one color and two of the other, not to speak of the hundreds if not thousands who were beaten and injured, among them the poet and playwright LeRoi Jones, citizen of Newark and former close friend of the late Frank O'Hara, dragged from his car as he drove around to examine the wreckage in the Central Ward, taken to a local precinct house, locked in a room, and beaten so badly by a white cop that Jones thought he was going to die. The cop who did the beating had once been his friend in high school.

According to Amy, no one in the Bond family had been touched. Luther had sat out the war in Somerville, sixteen-year-old Seppy was traveling around Europe with the Waxmans, and Mr. and Mrs. Bond had managed to avoid the bullets and billy clubs and fists. One hallelujah among a thousand wails of grief and horror and disgust. Ferguson's hometown had become the capital of ruins, but all four Bonds were alive.

Living through all that as he prepared to defend his own life in court. Eight days until his trial when the war in Newark ended, a second six-day war to accompany the Six-Day War in Dana's Israel, and whether the combatants understood it or not, both sides in both wars had lost, and as Ferguson made his daily trips into Brattleboro to consult with his lawyer and prepare their case, he wondered if he wasn't about to lose everything as well, wondered and worried to such a point that his insides seemed to be unraveling, the coiled tubes of guts and bowels were coming undone, and sooner or later they would burst through his stomach and splatter onto Main Street in Brattleboro, where a hungry dog would come to lap them up and then give thanks to the all-powerful dog-god for the munificence of his blessings.

McBride was steady and calm and *cautiously optimistic*, knowing that his client had not been the aggressor on the night in question, and with five witnesses to back up his story, five *reliable witnesses* who were all attending major universities and colleges, their testimony was bound to outweigh the probable false testimony from Chet Johnson's inebriated friend, Robert Allen Gardiner.

Ferguson was told that the judge who would be presiding over his case was a graduate of Princeton from the class of 1936, which meant that William T. Burdock had been a fellow student and perhaps friend of Ferguson's scholarship benefactor, Gordon DeWitt. It was impossible to know if that was a good thing or a bad thing. Given that the case would not be settled by a jury, that the decision would be entirely in Judge Burdock's hands, Ferguson hoped it was a good thing.

On the night of the twenty-second, three days before the trial was scheduled to begin, Luther called the farm and asked to speak to *Archie*. As Howard's aunt handed the phone to Ferguson, a fresh wave of fear rumbled through his insides. What now? he asked himself. Was Luther calling to tell him he wouldn't be able to show up in court on Tuesday?

Nothing like that, Luther said. Of course I'm going to testify. I'm your star witness, aren't I?

Ferguson exhaled into the phone. I'm counting on you, he said.

Luther paused for a moment on the other end of the line. Then it turned into a long moment, much longer than Ferguson had been expecting. Static reverberated through the wires, as if Luther's silence was not a silence but the clamor of the thoughts thrashing around in his mind. At last he said: Do you remember Plan A and Plan B?

Yes, I remember. Plan A: Play along. Plan B: Don't play along.

That's it—in a nutshell. Now I've come up with Plan C.

Are you telling me there's another alternative?

I'm afraid so. The farewell-and-good-luck alternative.

What does that mean?

I'm calling you from my parents' apartment in Newark. Do you have any idea what Newark looks like these days?

I've seen the pictures. Whole blocks destroyed. Burned out, gutted buildings. The end of one part of the world.

They're trying to kill us, Archie. It's not just that they want to lock us out, they want us dead.

Not everyone, Luther. Only the worst ones.

The ones in power. The mayors and the governors and the generals. They want to wipe us out.

What does that have to do with Plan C?

Until now, I've been willing to play along, but after what happened last week, I don't think I can do that anymore. Then I look at Plan B and start gasping for breath. The Panthers are a force now, and they're doing exactly what I thought I would be doing if Plan A failed. Buying guns to defend themselves, taking action. They look strong now, but they're not. White America won't stand for what they're doing, and one by one they're going to be mowed down and killed. What a stupid way to die, Archie—for nothing. So forget Plan B.

And Plan C?

I'm getting out. Pulling up stakes, as they used to say in the old cowboy movies. I'll be driving up to Vermont for your trial on Tuesday, and when the trial is finished, I won't be going south to Massachusetts, I'll be heading north to Canada.

Canada. Why Canada?

First, because it isn't the United States. Second, because I have a bunch of relatives in Montreal. Third, because I can finish college at McGill. I was accepted there out of high school, you know. I'm sure they'll want me again.

I'm sure they will, but it takes time to transfer, and if you drop out of school for the fall term, you'll be drafted.

Maybe so, but what difference does it make if I'm never coming back?

Never?

Never.

And what about Amy?

I asked her to come with me, but she said no.

You understand why, don't you? It has nothing to do with you.

Probably not. But just because she stays down here, that doesn't mean she can't come up and visit me. It's not the end of the world, after all.

No, but it probably means the end of you and Amy.

Maybe that's not such a bad thing. We weren't going to last in the long run. In the short run, I think we've been trying to prove a point. If not to ourselves, then to everyone else. And then that schmuck walked over to our table the other night and threatened us. We've made our point, but who wants to live in a world that forces you to stare down the haters who spend their lives staring at you? Life is hard enough as it is, and I'm exhausted, Archie, just about at the end of my rope.

□ □ □

THERE WERE TWO parts to what happened next, the good first part and the less than good second part. The first part was the trial, which went more or less as McBride had predicted it would. Not that Ferguson wasn't scared throughout most of the proceedings, not that his intestines weren't threatening to unravel again during the two and a half hours he spent in the courtroom, but it helped that his mother and stepfather were there along with Noah, Aunt Mildred, and Uncle Don, and it helped that his friends were such precise, articulate witnesses, first Howard, then Mona, then Celia, then Luther, and finally Amy, who gave a vivid account of how frightened she had been by Johnson's menacing words and gestures before the first punch was thrown, and it also helped that when Johnson took the stand he openly confessed to being drunk on the night of July first and couldn't remember what he had or hadn't done. Nevertheless, Ferguson felt McBride committed a tactical error by making him talk so much about college during his testimony, not only asking him what he did for a living (student) but where he attended school (Princeton) and under what conditions (as a Walt Whitman Scholar) and what his grade point average was (three point seven), for even if those answers made a noticeable impression on Judge Burdock, they were irrelevant to the matter at hand and could have been seen as putting unfair pressure on him. In the event, Burdock found Johnson guilty of instigating the brawl and ordered him to pay a heavy fine of one thousand dollars, whereas Ferguson, the first-time offender, was acquitted of the assault charge and ordered to pay fifty dollars in damages to Thomas Griswold, the owner of Tom's Bar and Grill, to cover the costs of a new chair and six new drinking glasses. It was the best possible outcome, the utter and permanent removal of the weight he had been carrying around on his back, and as Ferguson's friends and family gathered around him to celebrate the victory, he thanked McBride for his good work. Perhaps the man had known what he was doing, after all. The Princeton brotherhood. If the myth was true, then every Princeton man was bound together with every other Princeton man across the generations, in death as well as in life, and if Ferguson was indeed a Princeton man, as he supposed he was by now, then what man could argue that the Tiger hadn't saved his skin?

Not long after they left the courthouse, as all eleven of them strolled out into the parking lot to search for their cars, Luther came up from behind Ferguson, put his arm around his shoulder and said, Take good care of yourself, Archie. I'm off.

Before Ferguson could answer him, Luther abruptly turned around and began heading in the opposite direction, walking quickly toward his green Buick, which was parked near the exit at the front of the lot. Ferguson said to himself: So that's how you do it. No tears, no grand gestures, no tender hugs of farewell. Just sit your ass down in your car and drive away, hoping for a better life in the next country. Admirable. But then again, how could you say good-bye to a country that didn't exist for you anymore? It would have been like trying to shake hands with a dead man.

As Ferguson watched the grown-up version of the fourteen-year-old punching boy climb into the car, Amy suddenly sprinted into view. The engine kicked over, and at the last second, just as Luther was putting the Skylark into drive, she yanked open the passenger door and hopped in with him.

They drove off together.

That didn't mean she was intending to stay with him in Canada. It only meant that letting go was hard, too hard for now.

THE SECOND PART of what happened next had everything to do with Gordon DeWitt and the myth of the Princeton brotherhood.

The Walt Whitman Scholars luncheon was held each year during the first week of the fall semester, and Ferguson had attended two of them so far, once as a freshman and once as a sophomore. Standing up to take a bow as one of the original four the first year, standing up to take another bow when the ranks expanded to eight the second year, a three-course chicken lunch in the faculty club dining room punctuated by short addresses from university president Robert F. Goheen and other Princeton officials, hopeful, idealistic remarks about young American manhood and the future of the country, precisely what one would have expected to hear at such gatherings, but Ferguson had been impressed by some of the things DeWitt had said at the first of those affairs, or at least by the awkward and sincere way in which he had said them, not only about how he believed that *every boy deserved a chance, no matter how humble his background* but also about his own memories of coming to Princeton as a public high school kid from a poor family and how *out of place* he had felt in the beginning, which had struck a chord in the still out-of-place Ferguson, who at the time he heard those words had been on campus for just three days. The next year, DeWitt had stood up and delivered an almost identical speech—but with one fundamental addition. He had mentioned the war in Vietnam, emphasizing the obligation of all Americans to pull together in the effort to *push back the tide of communism* and harshly attacking the growing numbers of young people and *deluded anti-American leftists* who were against the war. DeWitt stood with the hawks, but what else could one expect from a Wall Street sharpshooter who had made millions serving in the trenches of American capital-ism? On top of that, he was a graduate of the same university that had educated John Foster Dulles and his brother Allen, the two men who had invented the Cold War as secretary of state and director of the C.I.A. under Eisenhower, and if not for what those two had done in the fifties, America wouldn't have been fighting against North Vietnam in the sixties.

Still and all, Ferguson was happy to accept DeWitt's money, and in spite of their political differences, he rather liked the man himself. Short and compact, with thick eyebrows, clear brown eyes, and a square jaw, he had pumped Ferguson's hand vigorously the first time they met, wishing him *all the luck in the world* as he embarked on his *collegiate adventure,* and the second time, when Ferguson's first-year performance had become a matter of record, DeWitt had called him by his first name. *Keep up the good work, Archie,* he had said, *I'm very proud of you.* Ferguson was one of his boys now, and DeWitt took a keen interest in his boys and was following their progress closely.

The morning after the trial, Ferguson said good-bye to his friends in Vermont and drove back to New York. The enervations of the past three weeks had worn him down and left him with much to think about. The violent scene in the bar, the violence in Newark, the strong, tactile memory of the handcuffs pressing against his wrists, the ache in his stomach during the trial, Luther's sudden but not impetuous deci-sion to make a new life for himself in Montreal, and Amy, poor, ravaged Amy sprinting madly toward the car. There was his book to think about as well, the book he was hoping he would be able to write, and bit by bit he settled in again and began to take comfort from his room and his desk and his long talks on the phone with Celia at night. On August eleventh, his mother called to tell him that a letter from the Walt Whitman Scholars Program had turned up in the mail that afternoon. Did he want her to read it to him over the phone or should she forward it to East Eighty-ninth Street? Assuming it was nothing of any importance, most likely a message from Mrs. Tommasini, the program's secretary, with information about the date and time of the upcoming September luncheon, Ferguson told his mother not to waste her breath and to send it on to him the next time she had to stop in at the post office. A full week went by before the letter made it to New York, but on the morning of the day it arrived, Friday, August eighteenth, Ferguson left for Woods Hole on a Trailways bus (the Pontiac was in the shop for minor repairs), and consequently it was not until he returned from his visit with Celia on Monday the twenty-first that Ferguson opened the envelope and received his second punch to the face that summer.

The letter wasn't from Mrs. Tommasini but from Gordon DeWitt, a one-paragraph letter from the founder of the Walt Whitman Scholars Program in which Ferguson was told that a number of distressing facts had recently been brought to his attention (DeWitt's attention) by a former Princeton classmate, Judge William T. Burdock of Brattleboro, Vermont, concerning a barroom fight in which he (Ferguson) had been responsible for breaking a man's nose, and although legally he had been judged to have acted in self-defense, morally he had behaved in a most reprehensible manner, since there was no defense for his having entered such an unsavory establishment in the first place, and the mere fact that he had been there cast alarming doubts on his ability to assess right from wrong. As Ferguson well knew, all participants in the Walt Whitman Scholars Program had to sign a character oath in which they promised to act as gentlemen in any and all situations, to take it upon themselves to become models of good conduct and civic virtue, and because Ferguson had failed to keep the promise he had made, it was his sad duty (DeWitt's sad duty) to inform him that his scholarship had been revoked. Ferguson could remain at Princeton as a student in good standing if he chose to remain, but his tuition and room-and-board fees would no longer be funded by the Program. Regretfully but sincerely yours . . .

FERGUSON PICKED UP the phone and dialed the number of DeWitt's Wall Street office. Sorry, the secretary said, Mr. DeWitt is traveling in Asia and won't be back until September tenth.

No use calling Nagle. Nagle and his wife were in Greece.

Was it possible to cover the costs himself? No, not possible. He had written a check to McBride for five thousand dollars, and his account now stood at just over two thousand. Not enough.

Ask his mother and Dan to pay for it? No, he didn't have the heart to do that. His mother's calendar and datebook project was finished now, and Phil Costanza, Dan's Tommy the Bear collaborator for the past sixteen years, had been flattened by a stroke and would probably never work again. Not the best moment to be asking for favors.

Throw in his two thousand and ask them to make up the difference? Perhaps. But what about next year, when the two thousand would be gone?

Throwing in the two thousand would also mean having to give up the apartment. A gruesome thought: no more New York.

And yet, if he didn't go back to Princeton, he would lose his student deferment. That would mean the draft, and because he would refuse to serve if and when he was called up, the draft would mean jail.

Another college? A less expensive college? But which one, and how in the world could he swing a transfer with so little time left?

He had no idea what to do.

One thing was certain: they didn't want him anymore. They had decided he was no good and had kicked him out.

$$\boxed{7.1}$$

AFTER HE RETURNED FROM FLORIDA, HE PACKED UP HIS THINGS AND moved four blocks south to an apartment on West 107th Street between Broadway and Amsterdam Avenue. Two rooms plus kitchen for the extravagant yet wholly affordable sum of one hundred and thirty dollars a month (there were benefits to having money in the bank), but even though he preferred living without roommates and was glad to have left behind the haunted interiors of West 111th Street (a necessary act), sleeping alone was difficult. The top pillow was either too firm or too soft, the bottom pillow was either too flat or too lumpy, and every night the sheets scratched his arms or twisted themselves around his legs, and with no Amy beside him anymore to lull him into drowsiness with the placid motions of her breathing, his muscles couldn't relax, his lungs refused to slow down, and he couldn't stop his mind from running at a speed that churned out fifty-two thoughts per minute, one for every card in the deck. How many cigarettes smoked at two-thirty in the morning? How many glasses of red wine drunk past midnight to quell the jitters and induce his eyes to shut? Neck-aches nearly every morning. Stomach cramps in the afternoon. Shortness of breath in the evening. And morning, noon, and night: a heart that beat too fast.

It wasn't about Amy anymore. He had spent the summer reconciling himself to the fact of their separation, to the inevitability of their splitting apart for good, and he no longer blamed her or even blamed himself. They had been moving in opposite directions for close to a year, and sooner or later the filament that had been holding them together was bound to snap. Snap it did, and so big and so powerful was the snap that it had shot her clear across the country. California. The calamity of distant California, and since the beginning of May, not a single word from her or about her—a zero as large as a hole in the sky.

At his strongest moments, he could tell himself that it was all for the best, that the person Amy had become was no longer a person he could live with or want to live with, and therefore he should regret nothing. At his weakest moments, he missed her, missed her in the same way he had missed his two severed fingers after the crash, and now that she was gone, it often felt as if another part of his body had been stolen from him. When he stood in the middle ground between strongest and weakest, he prayed that someone else would come along to occupy the other half of his bed and cure him of his insomnia.

New digs, the dream of a new love, the long summer of work on his translations that persisted through the fall, winter, and spring, the somatic troubles caused by the loss of his old love and/or his current state of mind that eventually landed him in the emergency room at St. Luke's Hospital with twenty-seven daggers in his gut (not the burst appendix he had thought it was but an attack of gastritis), the ongoing mayhem in Vietnam coupled with numerous other shocks that occurred throughout the latter half of 1968 and the first half of 1969—they were all part of Ferguson's story—but for now attention must be drawn to the war he was fighting against the symbolic figure of Nobodaddy, the character invented by William Blake who stood in Ferguson's mind as the representative of the irrational men who had been put in charge of running the world. By mid-September, when he went back to Columbia for his last year of college, he was feeling disillusioned and bitter about most things, among them the things he had discovered concerning the manipulations of the American press, and now he was reconsidering whether he wanted to join the ranks of that fraternity after he left college, whether the decision he had made back in high school to become a professional journalist was still worth making in light of the corruption and dishonesty he had witnessed firsthand during the days of the Columbia revolt last spring. The *New York Times* had lied. The so-called paper of record, the supposed bastion of ethical, unbiased reporting, had faked its story about the police intervention on April thirtieth and had published an account of the events that was written *before those events ever took place.* A. M. Rosenthal, the deputy managing editor of the *Times,* had been tipped off by someone in the Columbia administration about the impending bust several hours before the T.P.F. showed up in the neighborhood, and with the knowledge that one thousand troops would be called in, the lead story on the front page of the early morning edition on April thirtieth announced that those one thousand men had cleared the occupied buildings of the demonstrating students and had arrested seven hundred of them on charges of criminal trespass (a number that had been plugged in at the last minute, after the article had been written), but not one word about what had really happened, not one word about the bloodshed and violence, not one word about the battered students and professors, and not one word about how the police had used handcuffs and nightsticks to pound one of the *Times'* own reporters in Avery Hall. In the next morning's paper, the front-page lead again failed to mention the police riot that had taken place on campus during the bust, although there was a modest story about alleged acts of police brutality hidden on page 35: LINDSAY ORDERS REPORT ON POLICE. The third paragraph of the article contended that "police brutality in such a situation is hard to define, as the remarks of dozens of Columbia students suggest. To an experienced antiwar or civil rights demonstrator, yesterday morning's police action on the Columbia campus was, for the most part, relatively gentle." The sadistic beating of *Times* reporter Robert McG. Thomas Jr. was not mentioned until the eleventh paragraph.

Dozens of students. But which students, Ferguson wanted to know, and what were their names? And who were the experienced veterans of the anti-war and civil rights movements who had been roughed up by the police at earlier demonstrations? No undergraduate working for the *Columbia Daily Spectator* would have been allowed to publish such a piece, not without providing direct quotations along with the identities of the students who had made those comments, if indeed any of them had been made. Was this a news story, Ferguson asked himself, or an editorial posing as a news story? And what, pray tell, was the definition of the word "gentle"?

Another front-page article on May first was written by Rosenthal himself, a curiously disjointed, rambling mélange of sorrows, impressions, and angry disbelief. "It was 4:30 in the morning," the first paragraph began, "and the president of the university leaned against the wall of the room. This had been his office. He passed a hand over his face. 'My God,' he said, 'how could human beings do a thing like this?' . . . He wandered about the room. It was almost empty of furniture. The desks and chairs had been smashed, broken and shoved into adjoining rooms by the occupying students . . ."

On page 36 of that same morning's edition of the *Times*, another article told of the damage done to various rooms and offices by the occupiers of Mathematics Hall. Shattered windows, an overturned cabinet of library index cards, dismembered desks and chairs, cigarette burns on carpets, tipped-over filing cabinets, broken doors. "A secretary, returning to the building for the first time since it was seized last Thursday night, looked about disgustedly. 'They're just pigs,' she said."

The pigs, however, were not the students who had occupied the buildings but the police who had gone into the buildings after the bust. They were the ones who had smashed the desks and chairs, the ones who had tossed streams of dripping black ink against the walls, who had ripped open five- and ten-pound bags of rice and sugar and scattered their contents around offices and classrooms and had dumped broken jars of tomato paste onto floors, desks, and filing cabinets, the ones who had punched out windows with their clubs and nightsticks. If their aim was to discredit the students, the strategy worked, for within hours of that second police rampage scores of photographs attesting to the damage were circulated around the country (the ink-splattered wall was especially popular) and the young rebels were turned into an uncivilized pack of hooligans and thugs, a gang of barbarians whose sole purpose was to destroy the most sacred institutions of American life.

Ferguson knew the real story because he had been one of the *Spectator* reporters assigned to investigate the charges of vandalism against the occupying students, and what he and his fellow reporters had discovered—through sworn affidavits from members of the faculty—was that no ink had been on the walls when a contingent of professors toured the empty Math building at seven o'clock on the morning of April thirtieth. After they left, only police and press photographers had been allowed to enter the building, and when the professors returned later in the day, they found the walls covered with ink. Ditto for the desks, chairs, filing cabinets, windows, and packages of food. In good condition at seven A.M., pillaged and destroyed by noon.

It didn't help that the publisher of the *New York Times*, Arthur Ochs

Sulzberger, was a member of the Columbia board of trustees. Nor that William S. Paley, head of the CBS television network, and Frank Hogan, the Manhattan district attorney, sat on the board as well. Unlike many of his friends, Ferguson was not in the habit of looking for conspiracies to account for the shrouded operations of Nobodaddy's henchmen, but how not to wonder that America's most influential newspaper had willfully distorted its coverage of the events at Columbia and that the most influential television network had invited Columbia president Grayson Kirk to appear on *Face the Nation* but never asked one of the student leaders to give the other side of the story. As for the question of law enforcement, Ferguson and his fellow students on Morningside Heights were all aware of what the police had done both during and after the bust, but no one else seemed terribly interested.

Case closed.

FERGUSON WALKED BACK onto the Columbia campus that September feeling crushed and demoralized. A state of depletion and spent resolve as the August outrages continued to echo inside him, Soviet tanks crossing into Czechoslovakia to exterminate the Prague Spring, Daley calling Ribicoff a motherfucking dirty Jew at the Democratic Convention in Chicago as twenty-three thousand local, state, and federal cops gassed and pummeled young demonstrators and journalists in Grant Park, the mob crying out in unison, *The whole world is watching!*, and then Ferguson began his senior year with New York in yet another crisis, the deranged spectacle of public school teachers going out on strike to contest community control of the School Board in Ocean Hill–Brownsville, yet one more clash between blacks and whites, race hatred in its ugliest, most suicidal form, blacks against Jews, Jews against blacks, more poison to fill the air as the world turned its eyes to the Olympics that were about to begin in Mexico City, where police battled a horde of thirty thousand protesting students and workers, killing twenty-three of them and arresting thousands, and then, in early November, the twenty-one-year-old Ferguson voted for the first time, and America elected Richard Nixon as its new president.

All during the first six months of that last school year, he felt as if he had been trapped inside a stranger's body and could no longer recognize himself when he looked at his face in the mirror, which was also true of the thoughts he was thinking whenever he looked inside his head, since they were mostly the thoughts of a stranger as well: cynical thoughts, splenetic thoughts, disgusted thoughts that had nothing to do with the person he had once been. Eventually, a man would come down from the north and help cure him of his bitterness, but that didn't happen until the first day of spring, and the fall and winter were hard on Ferguson, so hard that his body broke down and he wound up in the emergency room.

If he wasn't going to be a journalist anymore, then it made no sense to go on reporting for the *Spectator*. For the first time in years, he would be able to crawl out of his glass monastery and rub shoulders with the world again, not as a chronicler of other people's actions but as the hero of his own life, however troubled and confused that life might have been. No more reporting, but nothing so drastic as a total break, since he loved the people he worked with there (if he respected any journalists in America now, it was Friedman and the other *Spectator* boys), so rather than cut all ties to the paper, he relinquished his spot as an associate member of the board and turned himself into an occasional reviewer of books and films, which meant that he handed in about one longish piece every month, speculations on such divergent topics as the posthumous poems of Christopher Smart and Godard's newest film, *Weekend*, which Ferguson argued was the first instance on record of what he called *public Surrealism*, as opposed to the *private Surrealism* of Breton and his followers, for the two and a half days from Friday afternoon to Sunday night, commonly referred to as *the weekend*, made up approximately one-third of the week in industrial and post-industrial societies such as France and America, just as the seven or eight hours an individual spent in bed every night constituted about one-third of that person's life, the dreamtime of private men and women in parallel to the dreamtime of the society they lived in, and Godard's anarchic, blood-spattered film of smashed-up cars and cannibalistic sex was nothing if not the exploration of a mass nightmare, which was just the sort of thing that spoke most deeply to Ferguson now.

Hilton Obenzinger and Dan Quinn were appointed the new editors in chief of the *Columbia Review*, David Zimmer and Jim Freeman were the new associate editors, and Ferguson became one of nine on the literary board. Two issues per year as in the past, but now money had been raised to set up something called the Columbia Review Press, which would allow them to publish four small books in addition to the two issues. When the thirteen gathered for their inaugural meeting at Ferris Booth Hall in mid-September, there was little argument about the first three titles on the list. Poems by Zimmer, poems by Quinn, and a collection of stories by Billy Best, an ex–Columbia student who had dropped out five years earlier but was still in touch with various members of the *Review*. The fourth book posed a problem. Jim and Hilton both begged off, saying they didn't have enough strong work to fill sixty-four pages, perhaps not even forty-eight pages, and then, during a pause in the discussion, Hilton unwrapped a one-pound package of ground beef, bunched it up in his hands, rose from his chair, and flung it with great force against a wall, shouting the word *Meat!* as it smacked against the surface and stuck there for a few seconds before it slid down to the floor. Such was Hilton's brave Dada spirit, and such was the spirit of that year, when the best minds on campus understood that the most important questions could be answered only by *off-the-wall* non sequiturs, in contrast to the *up-against-the-wall* tactics of the previous spring, and once everyone had applauded Hilton for his lesson on the finer points of logic, Jim Freeman looked at Ferguson and said, What about your translations, Archie? Do you have enough of them to make a book?

Not quite, Ferguson said, but I did a lot of work over the summer. Can we wait until the spring?

By unanimous vote it was decided that a small anthology of Ferguson's twentieth-century French poets would be the fourth and final book published that year. When Ferguson reminded them that it was illegal to publish translations without buying the rights to the originals, no one seemed to care. Quinn pointed out that the edition would be limited to five hundred copies, most of which would be given away for free, and if a French publisher happened to come to New York and stumble across Ferguson's book on a shelf in the Gotham Book Mart, what could he do about it? They would all be gone by then, scattered far and wide across the country and no doubt across other countries as well, and why would anyone bother to go after them for a couple of hundred dollars?

I'm with Dan, Zimmer said. Fuck money.

For the first time in what must have been weeks, if not months, Ferguson laughed.

Then they voted again, just to make it official, and one by one all thirteen members of the *Columbia Review* board repeated Zimmer's words: *Fuck money.*

Jim and Hilton set a cutoff date of April first for handing in the finished manuscript, which would give them enough time to print the book before they all graduated in June, and as the months pushed on, Ferguson often wondered what would have happened to him if Jim Freeman hadn't asked his question, for with each month that passed, it was becoming more and more clear to him that the deadline was saving his life.

Those poems were his refuge, the one small island of sanity where he didn't feel estranged from himself or at odds with Everything That Was, and even though he had finished many more translations than he had let on at the meeting, no fewer than a hundred pages so far, perhaps a hundred and twenty, he forged on with his versions of Apollinaire, Desnos, Cendrars, Éluard, Reverdy, Tzara, and the others, wanting to accumulate an abundance of material to work with when the time came to pare down the selection to the fifty or sixty pages the press could afford to publish, a dissonant book that would dart around from the brokenhearted cries of *The Pretty Redhead* to the mad, musical tumbling act of Tzara's *Approximate Man*, from the discursive rhythms of Cendrars's *Easter in New York* to the lyric grace of Paul Éluard:

> Do we reach the sea with clocks
> In our pockets, with the noise of the sea
> In the sea, or are we the carriers
> Of a purer and more silent water?
>
> The water rubbing against our hands sharpens knives.
> The warriors have found their weapons in the waves
> And the sound of their blows is like
> The rocks that smash the boats at night.
>
> It is the storm and the thunder. Why not the silence
> Of the flood, for we have dreamt within us
> Space for the greatest silence and we breathe
> Like the wind over terrible seas, like the wind
>
> That creeps slowly over every horizon.

So Ferguson had his extracurricular jobs of translating and reviewing, each of them alternately and often simultaneously both a struggle and a pleasure for him, the pleasure of the struggle to get it right, the frustrations of not getting it right more often than he should have, the poems that defeated him and could not be rendered into acceptable English after two dozen stabs at them, the failure of his piece on the effect of listening to different kinds of music as sung by different kinds of female voices (Janet Baker, Billie Holiday, Aretha Franklin) because in the end it was impossible to write about music, he decided, at least impossible for him, but still he managed to produce some articles that were less than awful enough to hand in and publish, and still the pile of translations continued to grow, and in the midst of all that there were the classes he was taking as well, mostly seminars in English and French literature at that point because he had fulfilled all his academic requirements except one, science, the abominable two-year science requirement that was an utter waste of time and effort in his opinion, but he discovered there was a course designed for lunkheads like himself, Introduction to Astronomy, which apparently no one failed because the professor was against flunking non-science students in science, and even if you never showed up for any of the classes, all you had to do was take a multiple-choice exam at the end of the year, a test you could not fail even if you failed to beat the guess-work odds and scored only ten percent, so Ferguson registered for that lunkhead course in celestial mathematics, but because he was living in a stranger's body and didn't know who he was anymore, and because he felt nothing but contempt for the rulers of Columbia and the point-less subjects they were forcing him to study against his will, he went into the college bookstore at the beginning of the first semester and stole the astronomy textbook, he who had never stolen anything in his life, who had worked at Book World during the summer after his fresh-man year and had caught six or seven students in the act of stealing books and had thrown them out of the store, now he was a book thief himself, slipping a ten-pound hardcover under his jacket and calmly walking toward the exit and out into the sunshine of Indian summer, now he was doing things he never would have done in the past, behaving as if *he were no longer himself,* but then again, perhaps this was the person he had become now, for the truth was that he didn't feel guilty about pinching the book—he didn't feel anything about it at all.

Too many nights at the West End, too many nights getting plastered with Zimmer and Fogg, but Ferguson craved the company and the talk, and on the nights when he went into the bar alone there was always the off chance of running into a girl who was just as lonely as he was. Off chance rather than chance because he was so dreadfully inexperienced when it came to such matters, having spent close to five years of his youth and early adulthood with one girl, the eternally departed Amy Schneiderman, who had loved him and then not loved him and had tossed him aside, and now he was starting from the bottom again, a beginner in the art of amorous conquest, knowing next to nothing about how to approach someone and start a conversation, but a tipsy Ferguson was more charming than a sober Ferguson, and three times during his first three months back at Columbia, when he had tippled enough to overcome his shyness but was not too far gone to have lost control of his thoughts, he wound up in bed with a woman, once for an hour, once for several hours, once for the whole night. All of the women were older than he was, and on two of those three occasions he was the one who was approached rather than the other way around.

The first occasion was a disaster. He had enrolled in a graduate seminar on the French novel, the only undergraduate in a class with two graduate-student men and six graduate-student women, and when one of those women turned up at the West End in the third week of September, he walked over to her and said hello. Alice Dotson was twenty-four or twenty-five, not unattractive or unwilling but plump and awkward, perhaps not accustomed to the protocols of casual sex, perhaps even more shy than he was, and when he found himself in her arms later that night, her body looked and felt so different from Amy's that he was thrown by the unfamiliarity of it all, and then, to compound his confusion, she was far more passive in bed than the ardent and spirited Amy had been, and as Ferguson went about the job of trying to copulate with her, his mind kept wandering from the task at hand, and even though Alice seemed to be enjoying herself in a mild, dreamy sort of way, he couldn't finish what he had started, which was something that had never happened in all his years with Amy, and the pleasant tumble he had been looking forward to was turned into a wretched hour of impotence and shame. Nor was he ever allowed to forget that blow to his masculine pride, since the class met for two hours every Monday and Thursday, and twice a week for the rest of the year there was Alice Dotson sitting around the table with the other students, doing her best to ignore him.

The second occasion left no scars but taught him a valuable lesson. A thirty-one-year-old secretary of pleasing but unremarkable aspect came into the West End one night with the express purpose of picking up a student. She called herself Zoe (last name never given), and when she fixed her eyes on the solitary Ferguson, she sat down next to him at the bar, ordered a Manhattan, and began talking about the World Series currently in progress between the Cardinals and the Tigers (she was pulling for St. Louis because she had been raised in Joplin, Missouri). After three or four sips of her drink, she tested the waters by placing her hand on Ferguson's thigh, and because he was susceptible to provocations of that sort, he responded by kissing her on the back of the neck. Zoe downed the rest of her Manhattan, Ferguson polished off his beer, and then they climbed into a taxi and headed for her place on West Eighty-fourth Street, exchanging no more than six or seven words as they pawed and kissed each other in the back. It was all rather impersonal, he supposed, but her lithe body moved in ways that excited Ferguson, and after they reached her apartment, the sorry organ that had let him down so cruelly with Alice Dotson had no trouble finishing what it had started with Zoe No-Name. It was his first one-night stand. Or almost a night, in that there was a first round followed by a second round, but after the second round ended at two o'clock, Zoe asked Ferguson to leave, assuring him they would both feel better about it in the morning if they didn't spend the rest of the night together. He didn't know what to think. Fun while it had lasted, he said to himself, but sex without feeling had its decided limitations, and as he walked back to his apartment in the windy autumn night, he realized that it hadn't been worth it.

The third occasion was memorable, the one good thing that happened to him during those long, empty months. Although the West End was essentially a student hangout, there were a number of regulars who had stopped being students or had never been students, the oddball dreamers and drunks who sat alone in booths plotting the overthrow of imaginary governments or were having one last round before they took another crack at A.A. or reminisced about the old days when Dylan Thomas used to sit at the bar reciting his poems. Among those regulars was a young woman Ferguson had met all the way back at the

beginning of his freshman year, a slender, long-legged beauty from Lub-
bock, Texas, named Nora Kovacs, someone he had always felt attracted
to but had never even flirted with because of Amy, a most unusual girl
who had come up north to attend Barnard in 1961, had dropped out in
the middle of her first semester, and had remained in the neighborhood
ever since, foul-mouthed, raunchy, go-fuck-yourself Nora, who had
drifted into the profession of removing her clothes in front of strangers,
a striptease artist who toured far-flung outposts of American industry to
enhance the lives of the womanless men who worked in oil fields, ship-
yards, and mills, a well-paid performer who would vanish from New
York for a couple of months to bounce around Alaska or the Gulf Coast
of Texas, but she would always come back to claim her seat at the bar of
the West End, where she went nearly every night to chat with anyone
who happened to be sitting next to her, talking about her adventures
on the road and sounding off about the dimwitted Nobodaddies who
were destroying the universe. Ferguson didn't know her well, but over
the years they had had five or six long conversations together, and
because Ferguson had once helped her out on a matter of considerable
importance, there was a special bond between them, even if they weren't
close friends. It went back to a night during his freshman year when he
had gone into the West End without Amy and had spent four hours talking one-on-one with Nora in a side booth. She was about to go off on
her first stripping tour, she had told him, and she needed to come up
with a stage name for herself, since she sure as hell wasn't going to hawk
her wares as Nora LuAnn Kovacs. In a sudden flash of inspiration, Ferguson had said: *Starr Bolt*. Hot damn, Nora had said back to him, hot
diggity damn, Archie, you're a genius, and perhaps for that one moment
he had been a genius, for *Starr Bolt* was a name that radiated glamour,
freedom, and sexual power, the essential qualities every stripper needed
to rise to the top, and whenever he had run into Nora over the ensuing
years, she had always thanked him for turning her into what she playfully called the *Queen of the Hinterlands*.

Ferguson liked Nora because he was attracted to her, or he was
attracted to her because he liked her, but he also understood that Nora
was a mess, that she drank too much and took too many drugs, that she
had evolved into what the guardians of virtue would have called a trol-
lop or a slut, a young woman traveling down a fast road to rack and
ruin, too outspoken for her own good, too comfortable in the gorgeous

body God had given her for no other purpose than to test the morale of weak men and wavering sinners, a woman who fucked whomever she pleased and openly talked about her cunt, her clit, and the pleasures of having a hard cock rammed up her ass, but at the same time Ferguson found her to be one of the more intelligent members of the West End crowd, a girl with a warm heart and kind impulses, and even though he suspected she wouldn't live past thirty or thirty-five, he felt nothing but affection for her.

He hadn't seen her in months, perhaps not for half a year, but there she was one night in early November, just a couple of days after Nixon had defeated Humphrey, which had further darkened the already dark mood that had enveloped Ferguson that fall, and when he sat down next to her at the bar, Nora laughed one of her big laughs and planted a kiss on his left cheek.

They talked for about an hour, covering a number of vital subjects such as the arrest of Nora's ex-boyfriend for selling drugs, Amy's definitive exit from Ferguson's life, the disappointing announcement (for Ferguson) that Nora would be leaving for Arizona the next morning, and the curious fact that while Nora had been *jiggling her boobs in Nome* (a phrase he vowed never to forget), she had managed to *keep abreast* (Nora's joke) of what had been going on at Columbia last spring by reading issues of the *Spectator*, which had been sent to her every day from New York by her friends Molly and Jack. As a consequence, she had read all of Ferguson's articles about the occupation of the buildings, the police bust, the strike, and everything else.

The news might have been slow in getting to Alaska, but his articles were *damned good*, she said to him, *fucking terrific, Archie*, and after he thanked her for the compliment, he told her that he had retired from reporting. Perhaps permanently, he said, perhaps temporarily, he wasn't sure yet, but one thing he was sure of was that he didn't know what to think anymore, that his brain had been bled dry and that shit (thank you, Sal Martino) was everywhere.

Nora said she had never seen him looking so low.

I'm lower than low, Ferguson answered. I've just reached the ninety-third sub-basement, and the elevator is still going down.

There's only one solution, Nora said.

A solution? Out with it—please—at once.

A bath.

A bath?

A nice warm bath, with the two of us in it together.

Never had a proposal been so graciously offered to him, and never had Ferguson been so pleased to accept.

Twenty-five minutes later, as Nora turned on the faucets of the tub in her apartment on Claremont Avenue, Ferguson told her that God had indeed given her a glorious body, but more important than that, He had also given her a sense of humor, and even though she would be leaving for Arizona in the morning, Ferguson wished he could marry her now, and even though he knew he couldn't marry her now or at any time in the future, he wanted to spend every minute of the next eleven hours with her, to be with her every second until she walked onto the plane, and now that she was being so nice to him, he wanted her to know that he loved her for it and would go on loving her for the rest of his life, even if he never saw her again.

Come on, Archie, Nora said. Kick your clothes into the corner and climb in. The bath is full, and we don't want the water to get cold, do we?

NOVEMBER. DECEMBER. JANUARY. February.

He was still in college but already finished with college, limping his way to the end as he pondered what to do with himself after they handed him his degree. First of all, there would be the matter of letting Nobodaddy peer into his anus and examine his testicles, of coughing the obligatory cough and taking a written test that would prove whether he was intelligent enough to die for his country. The draft board would be summoning him for his army physical sometime in June or July, but he wasn't worried about that because of his two absent fingers, and now that the pro-war Quaker with a secret plan to end the war was sitting on his throne and talking about *troop reductions*, Ferguson doubted the military would be desperate enough to start filling its regiments with one-thumbed soldiers. No, the problem wasn't the army, the problem was what to do after the army rejected him, and among the dozens of things he had already decided against was graduate school. He had considered it for three or four minutes over Christmas break with his parents in Florida, but just saying the words out loud had made him

understand how deeply the thought of spending one more day of his
life in a university revolted him, and now that February was about to
turn into March, the deadline for sending off applications had passed.
Teaching school was another option. A push was being made to enlist
recent college graduates to teach in poor neighborhoods around the
city, the black and Latino slums of upper and lower Manhattan, the
tumbledown wards of the outer boroughs, and at least there would
be something honorable about doing that for a couple of years, he told
himself, trying to educate the kids from those disintegrating barrios
and in the process no doubt learning as much from them as they would
ever learn from him, Mr. White Boy doing his small bit to make things
better rather than worse, but then he would come back to earth and
think about his inability to talk in front of people when more than five
or six strangers were in the room, the paralyzing self-consciousness
that made it a torture for him to stand up and speak in public, and how
could he manage a classroom of thirty or thirty-five ten-year-olds if no
words ever came out of his mouth? He wouldn't be capable of doing it.
Even if he wanted to do it, it wouldn't be possible for him.

He had already dismissed journalism, but sometime around the second or third week of February, he began to wonder if he hadn't been
too hasty, for even if the big-time establishment press was no longer
worth thinking about, there were other branches of journalism to consider. The anti-establishment press, otherwise known as the alternative
press or the underground press, had been growing stronger in the past
year or so, and with the *East Village Other*, Liberation News Service, and
the *Rat* all in bloom, not to mention several dozen independent weeklies in cities outside New York, rags so wild and unconventional that
they made the *Village Voice* look as stodgy as the old *Herald Tribune*, perhaps there was something to be said for working at one of those places.
At least they were against all the things Ferguson was against and for
many of the things he was for, but there were a number of drawbacks
to be examined as well, including the problem of low pay (he wanted
to support himself with his work and not have to dig too deeply into
his grandmother's fund) and the greater problem of writing exclusively
for people on the left (his hope had always been to change people's
thinking, not just confirm what they already thought), which would
hardly put him in the Panglossian position of living in the best of all

possible worlds, but in a world where *best* and *possible* seldom appeared together in the same sentence, a possible job he could live with and not feel tainted by was surely better than no job at all.

A. I. Ferguson, ace reporter for the *Weekly Blast*, the Amerikan bible of malcontents and vitiated Faustians, the paper of record for the chosen few.

If nothing else, it was a subject that demanded some careful thought.

So Ferguson went on thinking for the next fifteen or twenty days, and then came the Night of the Daggers, which fell just past midnight on March 10, 1969, one week after his twenty-second birthday and four days after he had gone to Jim Freeman's apartment on West 108th Street and handed him the finished manuscript of *The Pretty Redhead and Other Poems from France*, a too-large selection he had told Jim to cut down in any way he saw fit, and as Ferguson paced the rooms of his own apartment on the night of the tenth, composing a long, introspective letter to Nora Kovacs in his head, he felt a sharp twinge in the lower part of his abdomen, one of many that had plagued him in recent months, but rather than subside after ten or twelve seconds as most twinges did, this one was followed by a second, more powerful twinge, which hurt so much that it no longer qualified as a twinge but as genuine pain, and a moment after that second stab the assault had begun, the daggers in his gut, the twenty-seven spears that left him writhing on the bed for close to two hours, and the longer the pain went on, the more likely it seemed that his appendix or some other organ was rupturing inside his body, which so frightened him that he willed himself to stand up, put on his coat, and stagger off to the emergency room at St. Luke's Hospital seven and a half blocks away, Ferguson clutching his stomach and grunting loudly as he wobbled forward in the night, stopping every so often to cling to a lamppost when he felt in danger of falling to the ground, but for all that no one on Amsterdam Avenue seemed to notice he was there, no one bothered to come up to him and ask if he needed help, not one person among the eight million in New York was the least bit interested in whether he lived or died, and then he waited for an hour and a half until he was called into a room where a young doctor spent fifteen minutes asking him questions and probing his belly, after which Ferguson was told to go back to the waiting room, where he went on sitting for another two hours, and when it became clear that his appendix was not going to explode that night, the doctor saw him again and prescribed pills, telling him to stay away from spicy foods, to avoid whiskey and other hard drinks, to shun grapefruits, to stick to the blandest diet possible for the next two or three weeks, and if another attack should occur during that time, he would do well to have another person accompany him to the hospital, and as Ferguson nodded at the doctor's sound and helpful instructions, he asked himself: But what person, and who in the world would be there for him the next time he thought he was going to die?

HE STAYED IN bed for four days drinking weak tea and nibbling on crackers and slices of dry toast, and seven days after he was well enough to go out again, a man named Carl McManus came down from upstate New York to talk to the departing members of the *Spectator* staff. The editorial board of Friedman, Branch, Mullhouse, and the others had already finished its March-to-March one-year term and had handed the paper over to the new board, and Ferguson, the occasional freelance critic, had already written the last article he would ever publish in the *Spectator*, a somber, admiring review of George Oppen's latest collection of poems, *Of Being Numerous*, which had come out on March seventh, three days before the Night of the Daggers. The irony was that he was the only one of the seniors who was still toying with the idea of going into journalism. The overworked, mind-blasted Friedman was planning to hibernate in one of the public school teaching jobs that had scared off Ferguson, Branch was going to med school at Harvard, Mullhouse was staying at Columbia to do graduate work in history, but they all came to the meeting because McManus had written a letter to Friedman back in the spring praising the work of the *Spectator* staff during the "Troubles," and praise from Carl McManus meant something to them. The executive editor of the *Rochester Times-Union* had been editor in chief of the *Spectator* in 1934, and in the thirty-plus years since then he had gone to Spain to cover the Spanish Civil War, had gone to Asia to cover the Pacific front in World War II, and had stayed at home to cover the Red Scare in the late forties and the civil rights movement in the fifties and early sixties. A long stint of editorial work with the *Washington Post* after that, and now, as of a year and a half ago, the head man at the *Times-Union*, where he had found his first job after graduating from Columbia in the thirties. Not quite a legend (he had never published a book and rarely appeared on radio or TV) but a known personage, a man with a large enough reputation to have lifted the spirits of the exhausted *Spectator* crew when his letter arrived in early May.

A Brooklyn accent, a broad Irish face with protruding ears, a body that could have belonged to an ex-linebacker or longshoreman, alert blue eyes and a mop of graying reddish hair, long enough to suggest an interest in keeping pace with the times or else the hair of a man who had forgotten to go to the barbershop for his next haircut. Informal. More at ease with himself than most men, and a good resonant laugh when Mullhouse proposed they all go down to the Lion's Den on the first floor, the student snack bar that served, in Mullhouse's riff on the familiar New York phrase, *the worst cup of coffee in the world.*

Seven people sitting around a brown Formica table, six students in their early twenties and the fifty-six-year-old man from Rochester, who got straight to the point and told them he had come back to Columbia in search of recruits. Several positions were about to open up at his paper, and he wanted to fill them with what he called *fresh blood, hungry kids who would bust their asses for him* and turn a decent operation into a good one, a better one, and because he was already familiar with their work and knew what they were capable of, he was willing to hire three of them on the spot. That is, he added, if anyone was crazy enough to want to move to Rochester, New York, where the winds that gusted off Lake Ontario in winter could *freeze the snot in your nose and turn your legs into popsicle sticks.*

Mike Aronson asked him why he was talking to them and not to anyone from the School of Journalism, or was he planning to stop in there, too?

Because, McManus said, the experience gained from four years of work at the *Spectator* is more valuable than one year in a graduate program. The story you covered last spring was a big, complicated business, one of the biggest college stories in years, and every one of you sitting at this table did a good job, in some cases a remarkable job. You've been through the fire, you've all been tested, and I know what I'll be getting if any of you chooses to join up.

Then Branch raised the far more important issue of the *New York Times*. What did McManus think of their reporting about Columbia last spring, and why would any of them ever want to work for the main-stream press when all they did was print lies?

They broke the rules, McManus said, and I'm just as angry about it as you are, Mr. Branch. What they did bordered on the monstrous, the unforgivable.

Much later, when Ferguson had a chance to reflect on what happened that afternoon, to think about why he did what he did and to ask himself what the consequences of not doing it would have been or not have been, he understood that everything turned on the word *monstrous*. A lesser, more prudent man would have said *irresponsible*, or *shoddy*, or *disappointing*, none of which would have had the smallest effect on Ferguson, only *monstrous* carried the full force of the indignation he had been walking around with for the past months, an indignation that was apparently shared by McManus, and if the two of them felt the same way about that one thing, then they must have felt the same way about other things as well, and if Ferguson still had any interest in working for a daily paper or in finding out whether journalism was the solution for him or not, then perhaps it wouldn't be such a bad idea to brave the winds of the frozen north and accept the offer from McManus. It was only a job, after all. If it didn't work out, he could always move on and try his hand at something else.

Count me in, Ferguson said. I think I'm willing to give it a shot.

There were no other takers. One by one Ferguson's friends all bowed out, one by one they all shook McManus's hand and said good-bye, and then it was just the two of them, Ferguson and his future boss, and because McManus's plane wasn't scheduled to leave until seven o'clock, Ferguson decided to cut his class on English Romantic poetry and suggested they walk across the street to the West End, where they could continue the conversation in more pleasant surroundings.

They found a spot in one of the front booths, ordered two bottles of Guinness, and after some brief words about Columbia *then* and Columbia *now*, McManus started to fill him in on the geography of the place where he would be going, talking with refreshing bluntness about the dying world of northwestern New York, the only part of the country where the population was going down, he said, nowhere more drastically than in Buffalo, which had lost nearly one hundred thousand people in the past decade, *once glorious Buffalo*, as he put it, not without

a touch of mock blarney in his voice, the jewel of the old canal and shipping culture, now a half-empty wasteland of ruined and abandoned
factories, derelict houses, boarded-up, caved-in structures, a bombed-
out city never touched by bombs or war, and then, moving beyond dismal Buffalo, he took Ferguson on a short tour of some of the other cities
in the region, choosing his epithets carefully as he touched on sad-sack
Syracuse, anemic Elmira, ugly Utica, hapless Binghamton, and ragged
Rome, which had never been the capital of any empire.

You make it sound so . . . so enticing, Ferguson said. But what about
Rochester?

Rochester was a bit different, McManus said, a better brand of
decline, a place that was falling more slowly than the others, and therefore still more or less solid, at least for now. A city of three hundred
thousand in a metropolitan area of about one point two million, which
accounted for the *Times-Union*'s circulation of two hundred and fifty
thousand copies per day. A minor league town, of course, but not a two-
bit minor league town, with the Triple-A Red Wings feeding the Baltimore Orioles a high-protein diet of Boog Powells, Jim Palmers, and Paul
Blairs, home of Eastman Kodak, Bausch & Lomb, Xerox, and the indispensable French's mustard, companion to every American hot dog since
1904, which made it a city where most people had jobs in businesses that
weren't about to head down south or go abroad. On the other hand, in
spite of the sailboats and country clubs, the splendid film archive and
decent philharmonic orchestra, the good university and even better
music school, which was one of the best in the world, there were the
gambling, prostitution, and extortion rackets controlled by Frank
Valenti and the Mob as well as vast zones of poverty and crime, the
rough black slums that housed fifteen to twenty percent of the population, many of those people struggling or out of work or doing drugs,
and in case Ferguson had forgotten (Ferguson hadn't forgotten), there
had been the three days of rioting in the summer of 1964, one week after
the riots in Harlem, three dead, two hundred stores looted and damaged, a thousand arrests, and then Rockefeller had called in the National
Guard to put an end to it, the first time on record that the Guard had
breached the walls of a northern city.

At that point, Ferguson mentioned Newark, Newark in the summer
of 1967, and how it had felt to stand with his mother on Springfield
Avenue during the night of the broken glass.

So you know what I'm talking about, McManus said.

I'm afraid so, Ferguson replied.

Chilly springs, McManus continued, lovely summers, tolerable autumns, brutal winters. You'll see George Eastman's name everywhere you turn, but remember that Frederick Douglass and Susan B. Anthony lived in Rochester, too, and even Emma Goldman put in time there organizing sweatshop workers at the end of the last century. Also—and this is very important—whenever you're in a down mood and feel you might want to kill yourself, go for a walk in Mount Hope. It's one of the biggest and oldest public cemeteries anywhere in America and still the most beautiful spot in the city. I often go there myself, especially when I have an urge to think deep thoughts and smoke long, fat cigars. It never fails to clarify and sometimes even illuminate. The resting ground of three hundred thousand departed souls.

Three hundred thousand people above ground in Rochester, Ferguson said, and three hundred thousand below. What our good friend might have called *fearful symmetry*.

Or the marriage of heaven and hell.

So began the first conversation between Ferguson and Carl McManus, the warm-up to the two hours they spent together at the West End discussing the kinds of stories he would be writing for the paper, the initiation period of local reportage that would eventually lead to state and national events if he panned out, which McManus thankfully seemed to accept as a foregone conclusion, the salary he would be given to start with (low, but not to the point of dire struggle or heart-wrenching misery), detailed information about the staff and the running of the paper, and the more they talked the more pleased Ferguson became with the decision he had made, his instinctive *count me in* as an answer to the word *monstrous*, and now that he was getting to know McManus a little bit, he understood he would learn much by working for this man, that unlikely Rochester was in fact a good and plausible move, and as he held up his left hand and showed it to McManus (who was the first stranger who had ever asked him how he had lost his fingers), he said: I'm hoping this keeps the draft board off my back so I can take the job.

Don't worry about the draft board, McManus said. You've already signed up with me, and no man can serve in two armies at the same time.

□ □ □

LITTLE BY LITTLE, his heartbeat slowed down that spring and the daggers withdrew from his belly. He bought himself a new pair of down pillows, continued to avoid grapefruits, and took three more baths with Nora. He corrected the proofs of his book. He ordered a three-month subscription to the *Times-Union* and began following day-to-day life in Rochester. Asked to join the newly formed, whimsically named Columbia Poem Team, he traveled to Sarah Lawrence and Yale with Obenzinger, Quinn, Freeman, and Zimmer to give joint readings to the students (speaking in public was impossible but reading from his typed-up translations was not), high-energy events followed by considerable drinking and laughter and (at Sarah Lawrence) a ninety-minute conversation with a stunning coed named Delia Burns whom he desperately wanted to kiss but didn't. He wrote the final papers for his literature seminars and managed not to oversleep on the morning of the astronomy exam. There were one hundred questions with five possible answers for each, and since Ferguson had attended only one lecture and had never opened the text book, he circled the *A*'s through *E*'s at random and was heartened to score eighteen percent, which was good enough to earn a passing grade of D+. Then, to round off his small act of almost invisible rebellion, he returned to the college bookstore and sold the book back to them, thus sticking it to them twice. They gave him six dollars and fifty cents for it. Ten minutes later, as he walked down Broadway toward his apartment on West 107th Street, a panhandler approached him and asked for a dime. Rather than give a dime, Ferguson thrust the whole six dollars and fifty cents into the man's open palm and said, Here you are, sir. A gift from the trustees of Columbia University. With my compliments.

His book was published on May twelfth in a fine soft-covered edition of seventy-two pages that gave him much pleasure to look at and hold in his hands in the hours after it was lifted out of a cardboard box in the *Review* office, and within one week he had given away all but five of his twenty author's copies to friends and relatives. The cover was illustrated with a reproduction of the well-known photograph of Apollinaire from the First World War, the one that showed the head of Wilhelm Apollinaris de Kostrowitzky wrapped in bandages following the operation to repair the shrapnel wound to his temple: the poet as martyr, the modern age born in the mud of the trenches, France in 1916, America in 1969, both trapped in never-ending wars that devoured their young. Three copies were consigned to the Gotham Book Mart, another three to the Eighth Street Bookshop, and six to the paperback den on campus. Inestimable Zimmer, Ferguson's closest, most admired friend among the people in his class, reviewed the book for the *Spectator* and said nothing but kind things about it, excessively kind things. "The works in this assemblage of poems from France should not be looked on as mere translations but as English poems in their own right, a valuable contribution to our own literature. Mr. Ferguson has the ear and the heart of a true poet, and I for one will be going back to these magnificent works again and again as the years roll on."

Excessively kind. But such a person was young David Zimmer, who would soon be facing the big question all of them would be facing the instant they left Morningside Heights. In Zimmer's case, the dilemma expressed itself in a rhyme. Yale or jail. A four-year fellowship to do graduate work in literature at Yale or two to five years of jail if they wound up drafting him into the army. Yale or jail. What a neat little ditty that was, and what a world Nobodaddy had wrought.

It wasn't going to be hard to say good-bye to Columbia, which was living through another round of protests and demonstrations in the spring of 1969, events that Ferguson was willing himself to ignore for reasons of pure self-preservation, but he would miss his friends and some of his professors, he would miss not being able to further the education he had received from Nora on the handful of nights they had spent together, and he would miss the hopeful boy who had come there in the fall of 1965, the boy who had slowly vanished over the past four years and would never be found again.

ON THE SAME morning in mid-June that Ferguson coughed the cough and took the written exam at the draft-board building on Whitehall Street, Bobby George and Margaret O'Mara were joined in holy wedlock at St. Thomas Aquinas Catholic Church in Dallas, Texas, where Bobby was the starting catcher for Baltimore's Double-A ball club, which happened to be the same day (according to a letter Ferguson received from his Aunt Mildred) that the still silent and permanently decamped Amy attended the SDS national convention in Chicago, a rancorous meeting that devolved into an angry clash over tactics and ideology between the PL faction and the group that would come to be known as the Weathermen, which led to the crack-up and sudden, shocking demise of SDS as a political organization. Uncle Henry and Aunt Mildred had kept in sporadic contact with Amy during her first year of law school, and Mildred wrote to her former one and only to tell him that Amy had decided *to turn her back on the delusions of revolutionary activism and devote herself to the more realistic cause of women's rights.* The moment of revelation occurred when a man named Chaka Wells, the deputy minister of information for the Chicago Black Panthers, stood up to attack the PL and for no discernible reason started talking about the women in SDS by using the term "pussy power" and saying that "Superman was a punk because he never even tried to fuck Lois Lane," a sentiment echoed a few minutes later by another Black Panther, Jewel Cook, who declared that he was for "pussy power" as well and that "the brother was only trying to say to you sisters that you have a strategic position in the revolution: prone." It was a tired old joke by then, one that Amy had heard dozens of times in the past years, but that day in Chicago she finally had had enough, and instead of joining forces with the Weathermen, the break-off faction that included ex-Columbia students Mike Loeb, Ted Gold, Mark Rudd, and others, all of whom had been expelled from Columbia at the end of the spring term last year, she stood up from her seat and walked out of the convention center. As Aunt Mildred put it at the end of her letter, lapsing into the patronizing Aunt Mildred tone she often resorted to when talking about other people: *I thought you should know about this, Archie, even if the two of you are no longer a couple. It seems to me that our Amy is finally beginning to grow up.*

Bobby George says *I do.* Ferguson sticks out his left hand and shows it to a U.S. Army doctor. Amy walks out of the Chicago Coliseum and quits the movement for good. Was it possible that all three of those things happened at the same instant? Ferguson would have liked to have thought so.

Even more interesting: by the time Ferguson moved to Rochester at the beginning of July, Bobby had already been promoted to the Triple-A Red Wings of the International League. In a city where Ferguson knew absolutely no one, how improbable was it that his oldest friend should be there with him, not for the long haul, perhaps, but at least until the end of the summer and the close of the baseball season, the early months of adjustment and settling in, Bobby and his bride Margaret, two people he had known forever, pretty Maggie O'Mara with her short flowered dresses and drooping socks sticking out her tongue at rough-and-tumble, mouth-breathing Bobby George in the kindergarten class with Mrs. Canobbio in Montclair, now the still pretty but sophisticated and opinionated twenty-two-year-old Margaret with her degree in business management from Rutgers and the ever-amiable, powerhouse Bobby climbing the ladder to the major leagues, an unlikely union, Ferguson felt, not anything he would have predicted, but the mere fact that Bobby had persuaded Margaret to marry him must have meant that after two years in the army and a year and a half as a professional ball player, he was finally beginning to grow up as well.

As for Amy, it was none of his business now, which meant he shouldn't have cared about what she was doing or not doing with herself, but Ferguson did care, he could never fully bring himself not to care, and as the months went on, he felt more and more relieved by her decision not to join the Weathermen in Chicago. Their old friends from Columbia had gone insane. The intractable power of the great Oblivious One had thwarted their idealistic impulses and crushed their ability to think rationally anymore, and through a long series of wrong assumptions and wrong conclusions and wrong decisions based on those wrong assumptions and wrong conclusions, they had worked themselves into a corner where they were left with no choice but to believe that an army of one or two hundred middle-class ex-students with no followers and no support anywhere in the country could lead a revolution that would bring down the American government. That government was destroying its young by shipping off the poorest and least educated ones to fight in the war that was supposedly ending but wasn't ending while the privileged young were destroying themselves. Eight and a half months after Amy walked out of the Chicago convention, her old friend from Columbia SDS, Ted Gold, along with his fellow Weathermen Diana Oughton and Terry Robbins, were blown up and killed in a townhouse on West Eleventh Street in New York when one of them connected the wrong wire to a pipe bomb they were building in the basement. Oughton's body was so thoroughly obliterated that the sole means of identifying her came from the print on a severed finger found in the rubble. There was nothing left of Robbins. His skin and bones had dematerialized in the fire caused by the detonation of the gas mains, and his death was confirmed only after the Weathermen sent out word that he had been there with the two others.

FERGUSON DROVE UP to Rochester in the old Impala on July first, but his job at the *Times-Union* wouldn't be starting until August fourth. Five weeks to acclimate himself to his new surroundings, to hunt for an apartment and transfer his money to a local bank, to hang out with Bobby and Margaret, to wait for his new classification from the draft board, to see Kennedy's promise fulfilled as he watched a pair of American astronauts walk on the surface of the moon, to carry on with the project he had started in New York of translating the poems of François Villon, and to get New York out of his system. The largest, least expensive apartment he could find was in a run-down neighborhood called South Wedge, a cluster of blocks on the east side of town not far from the Genesee River. McManus's beloved Mount Hope was just a few steps away, as were the University of Rochester and a large grassy terrain called Highland Park, where the annual lilac festival was held every spring. Prices were low in that part of the world, and for eighty-seven dollars a month he took possession of the entire top floor of a three-story wooden house on Crawford Street. The house itself wasn't much to look at, with its cracked ceilings and rickety staircase, its overclogged storm gutters and yellow paint peeling on the façade, but Ferguson had three furnished rooms and a kitchen all to himself, and the light that poured through the windows in the afternoon was so much better for his mental health than the darkness of West 107th Street that he was willing to overlook the house's flaws. The owners lived in the apartment on the ground floor, and even though Mr. and Mrs. Crowley's weakness for vodka often led them to bicker at night, they were never less than cordial with Ferguson, which was also true of Mrs. Crowley's unmarried younger brother, Charlie Vincent, the World War II vet who occupied the middle apartment and lived on monthly disability payments, an agreeable sort who seemed to do little else but smoke, cough, and watch television, along with suffering through an occasional bad night when he would call out in his sleep, shouting *Stuart! Stuart!* at the top of his voice, so loud and so panicked that Ferguson could hear him through the floorboards upstairs, but who could blame Charlie for reliving his past from time to time when his guard was down, and how not to pity the teenage boy who had been sent off to fight in the Pacific twenty-six years ago and had come home to Rochester with a head full of nightmares?

As it turned out, Bobby and Margaret had to leave town before there was a chance to do much hanging out together. Ferguson had one dinner with them, he managed to see Bobby play in one game for the Red Wings, but the team was on the road when he arrived on July first, and four days after Bobby returned to Rochester on the tenth, the Orioles catcher broke his hand in a collision with a New York Yankee at home plate. After batting .327 in his first three weeks of Triple-A, Bobby was called up to join the roster of first-place Baltimore, and if he could hold his own against American League pitching, it was unlikely he would ever work in the minors again. Impossible not to feel happy for him, impossible not to exult in his promotion—and yet, hard as it was for Ferguson to admit to himself, impossible not to feel glad they were moving away.

It had nothing to do with Bobby. Bobby was still the same old Bobby, an older, more experienced, more reflective Bobby, but still the bighearted boy who was incapable of thinking a bad thought about anyone, Ferguson's most constant and loving friend, the one who loved him more than anyone else ever had, including Amy, especially including Amy, and how alive Bobby was on the night of their one dinner in Rochester at the Crescent Beach Hotel, hugging Margaret every fourteen seconds and talking about the old days in Montclair, the glory days of their sophomore year when Ferguson's hand was still intact and they were on the team together, the youngest starters on that conference-winning 16-and-2 team, the team that had pulled off *the play*. Of course Bobby had to talk about *the play* because he never tired of talking about it, and when Ferguson asked him to tell the story again for Margaret's benefit, Bobby smiled, kissed his wife on the cheek, and launched into his account of that May afternoon six years ago. This is how it was, he said. We're down one–nothing to Bloomfield in the last inning. One man out and two men on, Archie at third and Caleb at second, Caleb Williams, Rhonda's older brother, and then Fortunato comes up and Coach Martino signals for the bunt, two taps to the brim of his cap and then he takes off the cap and scratches his head, that was the signal, the only time he ever gave it, not just a bunt for a suicide squeeze to bring in one run but a *double* suicide squeeze to bring in two. No one in history had ever thought of that play, but Sal Martino invented it because he was a baseball genius. A tough play to execute because you need to have a fast runner on second, but Caleb was extra fast, the fastest runner on the team, and so the pitch comes in and Fortunato lays down a good bunt, a slow little dribbler to the right of the mound. By the time the pitcher gets to it, Archie is already crossing the plate to tie the score. Figuring there's nothing else to do, the pitcher throws to first, and Fortunato is out by three or four steps. But what the pitcher doesn't realize is that Caleb started running at the same time Archie did, just as he was going into his windup, and by the time the first baseman catches the ball, Caleb is three-quarters of the way home. Everyone on Bloomfield is shouting to the first baseman, *Throw the ball! Throw the ball!*, so he throws the ball home, but the throw is late, a hard throw right into the catcher's glove, but it's a couple of seconds too late, and Caleb slides in with the winning run. A cloud of dust, and Caleb is jumping to his feet with his arms in the air. Victory out of loss, a big win from a squiggly little nothing of a teeny-tiny bunt. I've never seen anything like it. I've played in hundreds of games since then, but that was the best and most exciting thing I've ever seen on a baseball field, my number one all-time moment. Two runs, boys and girls, and the ball didn't travel more than thirty feet.

No, the problem wasn't Bobby, who was in the full flower of his inimitable Bobbyness by then, the problem was Margaret, the same Margaret who had developed a crush on Ferguson when she was seven years old, who had written him an unsigned love letter when she was twelve, who had made eyes at him throughout high school and had actively rejoiced at Anne-Marie Dumartin's return to Belgium, who had been the one girl he had been tempted by during his four and a half months apart from Amy in their senior year, who had been the one whose mouth his tongue would have entered if not for Bobby's infatuation with her, who had mocked him as Cyrano when he had tried to intercede on Bobby's behalf, the dull but intelligent and achingly attractive Margaret who for reasons he could not fathom was now the wife of his oldest friend, for Ferguson was fairly stunned by how little attention she paid to Bobby's monologue about the double suicide squeeze, by how she kept looking at him across the table and not at her husband while her husband spoke, *eating him up with her eyes*, as if she were telling him, yes, I've been married to this kind, softheaded lummox for a month now, but I'm still dreaming about you, Archie, and how could you possibly have rejected me for all those years when in fact we were made for each other from the start, and here I am, take me, and damn the consequences because all along I've always wanted only you. Or so Ferguson gathered from the way she looked at him in the restaurant of the Crescent Beach Hotel, and the truth was that he was aroused by her, as a solitary, celibate, unloved bachelor searching for love as a stranger in a new town, how could he not have been aroused by the looks she was giving him, and who knew if he wouldn't have capitulated to her that summer if she and Bobby hadn't left for Baltimore, since there would have been countless opportunities for them to see each other alone, all the nights when Bobby would have been on the road playing games in far-off Louisville, Columbus, and Richmond, and how many times would he have accepted her invitations to come to dinner at her apartment, how many bottles of wine would they have drunk together, surely his resistance would have weakened at some point, yes, that was what her eyes were telling him as they sat across from each other at the hotel restaurant, *give in, please give in, Archie,* and because Ferguson understood that he might not have been strong enough to keep his hands off her if she had stayed, he was more than happy to see her go.

LAST YEAR, THE concentric circles had fused into a solid black disk, an L.P. record with a single blues song playing on Side A. Now the record had been turned over, and the song on the flip side was a dirge called *Lord, Thy Name Is Death.* The melody entered Ferguson's head just days after he started his job at the *Times-Union,* and as the first bar floated in from California on August ninth with the words *Charles Manson* and the *Tate-LaBianca murders,* it wasn't long before it modulated into the suicide on Halloween night of young Marshall Bloom, cofounder of Liberation News Service, which Ferguson had seriously considered joining straight out of college, which segued by the middle of fall into a verse about Lieutenant William Calley and the My Lai massacre in South Vietnam, and then, as the last year of the 1960s went into its final month, the Chicago police belted out a loud staccato refrain by shooting and killing Black Panther Fred Hampton as he lay asleep in his bed, and two days after that, as the Rolling Stones mounted the stage at Altamont to sing the rest of the song, a crew of Hells Angels jumped a young black man waving a gun in the crowd and stabbed him to death.

Woodstock II. The flower children and the heavies. And behold how quickly the day hath melted into night.

Bobby Seale strapped to a chair with a gag in his mouth by order of Judge Julius Hoffman as the original Eight were turned into the Seven.

The Weathermen launching a kamikaze attack against two thousand Chicago cops during the Days of Rage in October, Ferguson's old school pals girded in football helmets and goggles, jockstraps and cups bulging on the outside of their pants, poised to do battle with chains, pipes, and clubs. Six of them were shot, hundreds were carted off in paddy wagons. To what end? "To bring the war home," they shouted. But since when had the war ever not been at home?

Four days after that: Vietnam Moratorium Day. Millions of Americans said yes, and for twenty-four hours nearly everything in America stopped.

One month to the day after the Day: Seven hundred and fifty thousand people marched on Washington to end the war, the largest political demonstration ever seen in the New World. Nixon watched a football game that afternoon and told the country it wouldn't make any difference.

At the Weathermen gathering that December in Flint, Michigan, Bernardine Dohrn extolled Charles Manson for having killed "those pigs," meaning the pregnant Sharon Tate and the others who had died with her in the house. One of Ferguson's old pals from Columbia stood up and said: "We're against everything that's 'good and decent' in honky America. We will burn and loot and destroy. We are the incubation of your mother's nightmare."

Then they went into hiding and never appeared in public again.

And there was Ferguson, back in his role as the smallest dot at the center of the smallest circle, no longer surrounded by Columbia and New York but by the *Times-Union* and Rochester. As far as he could tell, it had been a fairly even trade, and now that he was in the clear (his 4-F notice arrived three days before he started work), the job was his as long as he could prove he deserved it.

There were two dailies in Rochester. Both of them were owned by the Gannett Publishing Company, but each one had a different purpose, a different editorial doctrine, and a different outlook on life. In spite of its name, the morning *Democrat and Chronicle* was solidly Republican and pro-business, whereas the afternoon *Times-Union* was more in the liberal camp, especially now that McManus was in charge. Liberal was better than conservative, of course, even if it was finally just another term for *middle of the road*, which was hardly where Ferguson stood on any political issue of the moment, but for the time being he was content to be where he was, writing stories for McManus and not for the *East Village Other*, the *Rat*, or L.N.S., which had gone through such a violent split that it had broken into two separate organizations, the hardline Marxists in New York City and the counterculture dreamers on a farm in western Massachusetts, which was where Marshall Bloom had killed himself, just twenty-five years old and now dead from carbon monoxide poisoning, and with that death Ferguson had begun to lose faith in the closed-off world of far-left journalism, which at times seemed to have gone just as insane as the splinter groups from defunct SDS, and now that the *Los Angeles Free Press* was publishing a regular column written by Charles Manson, Ferguson wanted no part of that world anymore. He hated the right, he hated the government, but now he hated the false revolution of the far left as well, and if that meant having to work for a middle-of-the-road paper like the *Rochester Times-Union*, then so be it. He had to start somewhere, and McManus had promised to give him a real chance—if and when he proved himself.

It was a rough initiation. He was put on the city desk, the youngest of several reporters working under a man named Joe Dunlap, who correctly or incorrectly saw Ferguson as McManus's fair-haired boy, his hotshot Ivy League protégé, the chosen one among the newcomers to the staff, and consequently Dunlap made a point of being hard on Ferguson, for it was the rare article Ferguson handed in to him that was not extensively rewritten, not just the leads and the slant of the stories but often the words themselves, always to the detriment of the piece as a whole, Ferguson felt, making his articles worse rather than better, as if Dunlap's editorial axe was an instrument not for pruning but for chopping down trees. McManus had warned him about that during their first talk at the West End and had instructed him never to complain. Dunlap was a boot-camp sergeant out to break his spirit, and as a raw buck private Ferguson had to do what he was told, keep his mouth shut, and not allow his spirit to be broken, no matter how many times he would be tempted to punch Dunlap in the face.

Other people were less difficult to work with, some of them downright pleasant in fact, people who little by little began to count as friends,
among them Tom Gianelli, a chunky, balding photographer from the
Bronx who often went out on stories with Ferguson and could imitate
the voices of two dozen Hollywood actors and actresses to near perfection (his Bette Davis was sublime), and Nancy Sperone, a recent graduate from the University of Rochester who had landed a spot on the
Women's Page and was going for an advanced degree in after-hours
flirting, which helped get him through the early adjustment period
without having to sleep alone every night, and Vic Howser from sports,
who was tracking Bobby's progress with the Orioles and responded no
less happily than Ferguson did when Bobby went two for four in his
one World Series start against the Mets, and beyond the people he was
coming to know and like at the paper there was the paper itself, the big
building and the hundreds of employees who worked there every day,
editors and movie critics, receptionists and telephone operators, obitu-
ary writers and fishing columnists, reporters typing up stories at their
desks, copyboys running around from floor to floor, and the huge,
on-site printing press down below, cranking out a new paper every
morning in time to hit the streets by noon, and despite the grumpy,
butchering Dunlap, who had emerged as the second coming of Edward
Imhoff, Ferguson enjoyed being part of that complex swarm of bustling
bodies and never regretted the decision he had made.

No regrets, but even though Nancy Sperone was an unencumbered
single woman, which had not been the case with the tempting but off-
limits Margaret O'Mara George, Ferguson knew from the start that she
was not the answer. Nevertheless, he went on going out with her and
sleeping with her during his first nine months in Rochester, which was
the first time in his life he had entered into a less than passionate, off-
and-on affair with a woman he was fond of but could never bring himself to love. The native-born Nancy showed him around town by
introducing him to one of Rochester's famous Friday Night Fish Fries,
dragged him to a joint called Nick Tahou Hots to indulge in another
Rochester dish known as the Garbage Plate (an experience Ferguson
swore he would never repeat for as long as he lived), and sat through
several old movies with him at the Eastman House archive, among them
Bresson's *A Man Escaped* and Kazan's 1945 sob-a-thon *A Tree Grows in
Brooklyn*, which induced both of them to shed the requisite oceans of

blubbering, nonsensical tears. Nancy was bright and companionable, an earnest reader of books and a talented journalist who had joined the *Times-Union* as another one of McManus's *new wave of kids*, a dark-eyed brunette with short hair and a large, round face (her Little Lulu face, as Nancy called it), a bit on the heavy side, perhaps, but sexy enough to make Ferguson long for her body whenever they were apart for more than a week or ten days. It wasn't Nancy's fault that he couldn't love her, but neither was it Ferguson's fault that Nancy was looking for a husband and he had no interest in looking for a wife. In mid-December, when he went down to Florida for a short weekend visit with his parents, he understood that he and Nancy were going nowhere, but still he went on seeing her for another four months after he returned, muddling along as previously until Nancy found a new man who wanted to marry her, which was a good thing, Ferguson decided, since all through the months of not being able to love Nancy Sperone there had been the dawning awareness that after one full year and the better part of another year with no Schneiderman in sight, he still hadn't recovered from losing Amy. He was still mourning her absence—as if hanging on in the aftermath of a divorce, perhaps even a death, and there was nothing to be done about it except to keep hanging on until he didn't feel it anymore.

Almost a year had gone by since he had last been with his parents, and now that they had fully settled into the alien world of southern Florida, they had turned into creatures of the sun, tanned and healthy-looking ex-northerners living and working in the Land of No Snow, advocates of long walks on sand-covered patches of earth (his mother) and outdoor tennis every morning from January through December (his father), and yes, Ferguson was glad to see them again, but they had both changed in the gap between visits, and those changes were the first things he noticed when they picked him up at the airport early Friday evening. Not so much his mother, perhaps, who was still rushing around with her photography work at the *Herald* and liked nothing better than to talk newspaper talk with her son, but she had been trying to quit smoking in the past six months and had put on weight, perhaps ten or twelve pounds, which made her look different somehow, both older and younger at the same time, if such a thing was possible, whereas his father, who was nearing fifty-six and still strong because of his daily tennis routine, nevertheless struck Ferguson as slightly diminished, with grayer, more thinned-out hair and a slight limp when he had to walk for more than fifty or a hundred yards (a pulled muscle, or else permanently aching feet), no longer the numb and silent Dr. Manette toiling away at his workbench but a clerk in the classifieds department at the *Herald*, a job he professed to enjoy and even love, but it had turned him into a lowly Bob Cratchit, and Ferguson couldn't help thinking of what a long, slow fall it had been from 3 Brothers Home World to this.

The best day of the Friday-to-Sunday visit was the last day, when they went out for a large, unhurried brunch at Wolfie's on Collins Avenue, the good smells of fresh onion rolls and smoked fish flooding the room as the three of them ate lox and eggs in honor of Ferguson's grandmother, whom they talked about at length, along with Ferguson's grandfather and the now vanished Didi Bryant, but mostly his mother asked him questions about Rochester and the *Times-Union*, wanting to know *everything about everything*, and Ferguson told them nearly everything he could, failing to mention his involvement with Nancy Sperone because it probably wouldn't have sat well with his father, the mere thought of his boy going around with an Italian Catholic girl no doubt would have upset him, leading to some bitter *us-versus-them* remarks about *schvartzes* and *shiksas* (words that Ferguson hated, two of the ugliest words in the Yiddish lexicon), and so he left Nancy out of it and talked about McManus and Dunlap instead, about Bobby George hitting his first big-league home run in Boston last July and now just four months away from becoming a father, about some of the articles he had written and the tawdry, beaten-up apartment where he lived, which led his mother to ask the question all mothers ask their children, whether those children are small, piss-in-the-pants tykes or twenty-two-year-old college graduates:

Are you okay, Archie?

I sometimes wonder what I'm doing there, Ferguson said, but I think I'm all right, still feeling my way for now, more or less okay, more or less happy with the job, but one thing is clear, one thing you can be absolutely certain about: I'm not going to spend the rest of my life in Rochester, New York.

THREE-ALARM FIRES. THE twentieth anniversary of an unsolved murder case. Anti-war activity at the local colleges and universities. The breakup of a ring of dog snatchers. A fatal traffic accident on Park Ave-

nue. The establishment of a new tenant association in the black neighborhoods on the west side of town. For five months Ferguson toiled as
a lowly cub reporter under the suspicious gaze of Joe Dunlap, and then
McManus pulled him off the city beat and handed him something big.
Apparently, Ferguson had passed the test. Not that he had ever known
the precise nature of the test or by what standards McManus had been
judging him, but however it had happened, one could only conclude that
the boss now felt he had graduated to the next level.

On the morning after Christmas, McManus summoned Ferguson
to his office and told him about a thought that had been turning
around in his mind lately. The sixties were just about done, he said,
there was less than a week to go before the big ball dropped, and what
did Ferguson think about writing a series of articles on the past ten
years and how they had affected American life? Not a chronological
approach, not a time-line summary of major events, but something
more substantial than that, a sequence of twenty-five-hundred-word
stories on various pertinent subjects, the war in Vietnam, the civil
rights movement, the growth of the counterculture, developments in
art, music, literature, and film, the space program, the contrasting tonal-
ities among the Eisenhower, Kennedy, Johnson, and Nixon administra-
tions, the nightmare assassinations of prominent public figures, racial
conflict and the burning ghettos of American cities, sports, fashion,
television, the rise and fall of the New Left, the fall and rise of right-
wing Republicanism and hard-hat anger, the evolution of the Black
Power movement and the revolution of the Pill, everything from politics to rock and roll to changes in the American vernacular, the portrait of a decade so dense with tumult that it had given the country
both Malcolm X and George Wallace, *The Sound of Music* and Jimi
Hendrix, the Berrigan brothers and Ronald Reagan. No, it wouldn't be
the usual kind of reportage, McManus continued, it would be a look
back, a way of reminding *Times-Union* readers where they had been
ten years ago and where they were now. That was one of the advantages of working for an afternoon paper. More leeway, more time to
dig around and investigate, more opportunities to run feature-length
stories. But it couldn't be just a dry rehash. He wasn't looking for an
academic history but articles with some bite to them, and for every
book and back-issue magazine Ferguson read for his research,
McManus wanted him to talk to five people. If he couldn't get hold of

Muhammad Ali, then he should track down his trainer and corner-
man, Angelo Dundee, and if he couldn't get through to Andy Warhol,
then he should call Roy Lichtenstein or Leo Castelli. Primary sources.
The ones who did the doing or were close by when something happened. Was he making himself clear?

Yes, he was making himself clear.

And what did Ferguson think?

I'm all for it, Ferguson said. But how many pieces do you want, and
how long do I have to write them?

About eight or ten, I would imagine. And roughly two weeks to
write each one, give or take. Is that enough?

If I give up sleeping for a while, I suppose it will be. Do I hand them
in to Mr. Dunlap?

No, you're finished with Dunlap. You'll be working directly with me
on this.

And where and how do I begin?

Go back to your desk and come up with fifteen or twenty ideas.
Subjects, titles, musings, whatever seems most urgent to you, and then
we'll figure out an overall plan.

I can't tell you how much this means to me.

It's a job for a young person, Archie, and you're the youngest one I
have. Let's see what happens.

Ferguson put everything he had into the articles because his entire
future at the paper depended on them. He wrote and rewrote, he
whipped through more than a hundred books and close to a thousand
magazines and newspapers, and not only did he talk on the phone to
Angelo Dundee, Roy Lichtenstein, and Leo Castelli but to dozens of
other people as well, assembling a chorus of voices to accompany the
texts he wrote on the good-old-bad-old days of recently vanished yore,
eight twenty-five-hundred-word stories that covered politics, presidents,
and the pandemonium of social dissent, along with excursions into the
music of John Berryman's Dream Songs, the slow-motion massacre at the
end of Bonnie and Clyde, and the spectacle of half a million American
children dancing in the mud one weekend on a farm in New York State
just two hundred and fifty miles south of Rochester. By and large,
McManus was satisfied with the results and edited his work only lightly,
which was the most gratifying part of the exercise for Ferguson, but the
boss was also pleased that the articles elicited scores of letters from the

public, most of them positive, with comments such as "A big thanks to A. I. Ferguson for leading us on a walk down Memory Lane," but with a fair share of negative comments as well, attacks on Ferguson's "pinko views of our great country" that stung a little, he had to admit, even though he had been expecting worse. What he hadn't been expecting was how much hostility he would feel from some of the young reporters on the staff, but that was how the game worked, he supposed, every man for himself in the scrum to grab the ball, and as Nancy pointed out each time he published another piece, their resentment only proved how well he was doing his job.

There were supposed to be ten articles in the series, but Ferguson had to stop just as he was preparing to tackle the ninth one (on long hair, miniskirts, love beads, and white leather boots—the novelties of mid- and late-sixties fashion) when another hammer blow was delivered from beyond. The anti-war movement had been relatively quiet in recent months. The gradual withdrawal of American troops, the so-called Vietnamization of the war, and the new draft lottery system had all contributed to the lull in activity, but then, in the final days of April 1970, Nixon and Kissinger abruptly expanded the war by invading Cambodia. American opinion was still divided down the middle, roughly half for and half against, which meant that half the country supported the action, but the other half, the ones who had been marching against the war for the past five years, saw this *strategic incursion* as the end of all hope. They took to the streets by the hundreds of thousands, massive demonstrations were organized on college campuses, and on one of those campuses in Ohio, nervous, badly trained young National Guardsmen fired live ammunition at the students, a three-second fusillade that wound up killing four and wounding nine, and so horrified were most Americans by what happened at Kent State that they spontaneously opened their mouths and sent forth a collective howl that spread across the entire land. Early the next morning, May fifth, McManus dispatched Ferguson and his photo partner Tom Gianelli to the University of Buffalo to report on the demonstrations there, and suddenly he was no longer investigating the recent past but living in the Now again.

The school had gone through weeks of fractious conflict in late February and early March, but even the more subdued eruption after Kent State was much wilder than anything Ferguson had seen at Columbia, especially on the second day he was there, a wintry Buffalo day in mid-spring, with snow on the ground and ice winds blasting in off Lake Erie. No buildings were occupied, but the atmosphere was more charged and potentially more dangerous as close to two thousand students and professors were attacked by helmeted riot police carrying guns, clubs, and tear-gas rifles. Rocks were thrown, bricks were thrown, the windows of police cars and university buildings were smashed, heads and bodies were smashed, and once again Ferguson found himself dead center between two warring mobs, but it was scarier this time because the Buffalo students were more willing to fight than the Columbia students had been, some of them so incensed and out of control that Ferguson felt they might have been willing to die. Whether he was a journalist or not, he was just as exposed as they were, and much as he had been swept up into it two years earlier with the blows to his head and hand, this time he was teargassed along with everyone else, and as he pressed a wet handkerchief against his stinging eyes and vomited his lunch onto the pavement, Gianelli took hold of his arm and pulled him away to look for a spot where the air would be more breathable, and a couple of minutes later, when they had come to the corner of Main Street and Minnesota Avenue just off campus, Ferguson removed the wet handkerchief from his face, opened his eyes, and saw a young man throw a brick through the window of a bank.

Within another day or two, three-quarters of the colleges and universities in America were on strike. More than four million students joined in the protest, and one by one every college and university in Rochester shut down for the rest of the academic year.

The day after Ferguson filed his Buffalo story, he had a brief talk with McManus at the front entrance of the *Times-Union* building. Staring out at the traffic as they smoked their cigarettes, they both reluctantly acknowledged that there would be no point in publishing any more articles about the sixties. Eight had been enough, and the ninth and tenth were no longer necessary.

AFTER NANCY SPERONE found her new man in the early days of the student strike, Ferguson squandered the next six months pursuing two different women who were not worth the effort of pursuing and shall remain nameless because they are not worth the effort of naming. Ferguson was beginning to grow restless, feeling that perhaps he had had enough of Rochester after a year and a half in that minor league city, wondering if he shouldn't try his luck somewhere else with another paper or perhaps leave journalism altogether and try to earn his living as a translator, for however much he still enjoyed the pressures of high-speed composition, wrestling with Villon's fifteenth-century French was ultimately more satisfying to him, and even though time was scarce, he had polished off a not-bad first rendering of *The Legacy* and was halfway into a preliminary version of *The Testament*, not that he could ever feed himself by translating poetry, of course, but a fat book of prose every now and then might help cover the bills, and if nothing else, even if he did stay in Rochester for a while longer, wouldn't it make sense to leave the crummy, roach-infested dump on Crawford Street and move to a better place?

It was January 1971, February 1971, the darkest, coldest days of the year in that glum hibernal outpost, a time when only glum things could be expected to happen, a time of death fantasies and daydreams about living in the tropics, but just as Ferguson was beginning to think he should bury himself under a pile of quilts and remain in bed for the next three months, his job at the *Times-Union* became interesting again. The circus was back in town. The lions and tigers were roaring, a crowd was gathering under the large tent, and Ferguson hastily jumped back into his tightrope walker's costume and scrambled up the ladder to take his spot on the platform.

After the Kent State shootings, he had been reassigned to the national desk and was now working under a man named Alex Pittman, a young editor with good instincts and a more tolerable disposition than Dunlap's. Ferguson had handed in dozens of stories to Pittman over the long weeks between May and February, but nothing as compelling as the two big stories that broke in the first half of the new year, which curiously enough turned out to be two versions of the same story: tying up loose ends from the fifties and sixties because someone had been brave enough to steal classified government documents and release them to the public, which meant that even if the sixties were chronologically over, they weren't over and were in fact just beginning— all over again. On March eighth, an unknown group of invisible activists calling themselves the Citizens' Commission to Investigate the F.B.I. broke into the small, two-man government office in the oddly named town of Media, Pennsylvania, and swiped more than a thousand secret documents. By the next day, those documents had been sent to various news organizations across the country, exposing the F.B.I.'s covert spy operation, COINTELPRO (Counter-Intelligence Program), which had been started by J. Edgar Hoover in 1956 to harass the fourteen or twenty-six Communists still left in America and then had expanded to include members of black civil rights organizations, anti–Vietnam War organizations, Black Power organizations, feminist organizations, and over two hundred organizations from the New Left, among them SDS and the Weathermen. Not just spying on them but infiltrating their ranks with informants and *agents provocateurs* to disrupt and discredit them, and just like that the nuthouse fears of sixties activists were turning out to be true, Big Brother had indeed been watching, and Nobodaddy's craziest, most loyal soldier had been behind it all, squat little J. Edgar Hoover, who had amassed so much power during his forty-seven years in office that presidents quaked when he knocked on their door. The documents revealed hundreds of crimes and hundreds of low blows to smear the names of innocent people, but none lower than the job he had done on Viola Liuzzo, who was the subject of one of Ferguson's articles, the Detroit housewife with five children who had gone down to Alabama for the Selma-Montgomery march and for the simple act of opening her car door and giving a lift to a black man had been murdered by a group from the Klan, one of the murderers being Gary Thomas Rowe, "an acknowledged F.B.I. informant," and then Hoover had had the temerity to write a letter to Johnson telling him that Mrs. Liuzzo had been a member of the Communist Party and had abandoned her children in order to have sex with black men from the civil rights movement, a bogus accusation that suggested she had been an enemy of the people and therefore someone who had deserved to die.

Three months after the COINTELPRO scandal, the Pentagon Papers were published in the *New York Times*, and Ferguson worked on that story as well, including the story behind the story of how Daniel Ellsberg had smuggled the papers out of the building and given them to *Times* reporter Neil Sheehan, the once abhorred *New York Times* perhaps atoning for the lies it had printed in sixty-eight by taking the risk of going public with classified documents, a bright moment for American journalism, as Pittman, McManus, and Ferguson all agreed, and suddenly the lies of the American government were standing naked in front of the entire world, the things that had never been reported anywhere in the press, the secret bombings of Cambodia and Laos, the coastal raids on North Vietnam, but beyond that and before that the thousands of pages delineating the step-by-step process by which something that had once seemed to make sense had collapsed into utter senselessness.

THEN THE CIRCUS left town again, and Ferguson fell into the arms of Hallie Doyle, a twenty-one-year-old student from Mount Holyoke with a summer job at the paper, the first woman he had met since moving north who might have had the power to break the Amy-spell at last, a deeply intelligent and insightful person who had been raised in the Roman Catholic Church but was no longer part of it because she didn't believe that virgins could be mothers or that dead men could climb out of their graves, yet she lived with an inner certainty that the meek would inherit the earth, that virtue was its own reward, and that not doing unto others what you didn't want them to do unto you was a more sensible way to conduct your life than struggling to follow the precepts of the golden rule, which forced human beings to turn themselves into saints and led to nothing but guilt and unending despair.

A sane person, perhaps even a wise one. A small but not diminutive person of five-four or five-five with a lean, quick-moving body, a pair of granny glasses perched on her nose, and intensely yellow hair, so blond as to create the impression of a fully grown Goldilocks, but attractive as that golden hair was to Ferguson, the mystery was in Hallie's face, which was both a plain face and a pretty face, by turns dull and sparkling, a face that changed aspect with the slightest turn or tilt of her head, now a Goldilocksian mouse, now a stunning White Rock girl, now bland and almost featureless, now radiant and arresting, an unremarkable Irish mug that could, in a single blink, transform itself into the most ravishing countenance ever beheld this side of a movie screen. What was he to make of such a conundrum? Nothing, Ferguson decided, nothing at all, since the only answer was to go on looking at her in order to feel the more and more pleasant sensation of being permanently off balance.

She had grown up in Rochester and was back in town for the

summer to sell her family's house on East Avenue, which had become redundant after her science-writer parents moved to San Francisco earlier in the year. The job at the *Times-Union* had been obtained through the help of an old family friend and was nothing but a way to kill the time more efficiently than by doing nothing—along with a chance to earn some extra cash into the bargain.

A temporary newsroom assistant for the summer, but in her real life a dual English-biology major who would be starting her senior year in the fall. A budding poet with a long-range plan to go to medical school, then push on to become a psychiatrist, and finally to train as a psychoanalyst, all of which was impressive enough, but what impressed Ferguson even more was how she had spent the two summers before this one: living in New York and answering telephones at a suicide hotline on East Fourth Street and Avenue A.

In other words, he said to himself, when he had been listening to the record spin out the lurid, demoralizing verses of *Lord, Thy Name Is Death*, Hallie had been working to save lives. Not everything all at once, as Amy and so many others believed, but one by one by one. Talk to a man on the telephone and gradually convince him not to pull the trigger of the gun he is pointing at his head. Talk to a woman the next night and slowly persuade her not to down the bottle of pills clenched in her hand. No impulse to reinvent the world from the bottom up, no acts of revolutionary defiance, but a commitment to doing good in the broken world she belonged to, a plan to spend her life helping others, which was not a political act so much as a religious act, a religion without religion or dogma, a faith in the value of the one and the one and the one, a journey that would begin with medical school and then continue for however long it took to complete her psychoanalytic training, and while Amy and a host of others would have argued that people were sick because society was sick and helping them adjust to a sick society would only make them worse, Hallie would have answered, Please, go ahead and improve society if you can, but meanwhile people are suffering, and I have a job to do.

Not only had Ferguson met the *next one*, but as the summer went on he asked himself if he hadn't found the *One* who would blot out all others for the rest of his days on this wretched, beautiful earth.

She moved into the Crawford Street rathole with him in early July, and because it was an especially hot summer that year, they pulled down the window shades and turned into nudists whenever they were indoors. Outdoors, on weekday nights and weekend days and nights, they went to twelve movies together, attended six Red Wings games, played tennis four times (the ultra-athletic Hallie consistently beat him two sets to one), took walks in Mount Hope Cemetery, sat in Highland Park reading each other's poems and translations until Hallie broke down in tears one Sunday afternoon and declared that her work was no good (no, not no good, Ferguson said to her, *still developing*, although there seemed little doubt that she had a more promising future in medicine than in literature), went to four classical concerts at the Eastman School of Music, Bach, Mozart, Bach, and Webern, and ate numerous dinners in all manner of restaurants both decent and atrocious, but no dinner was more memorable than the one they had at Antonio's on Lake Avenue, where the meal was accompanied by nonstop music from a man named Lou Blandisi, who billed himself as the Corny Accordionist from Little Italy and seemed to know every song that had ever been written, from American pop standards to Irish jigs to klezmer from the Pale.

More to the point: by the first days of August they had both uttered the decisive three-word sentence several dozen times each, the three words that seal the deal and announce there is no turning back, and by the end of the month they were both starting to think long-term, permanent thoughts about the future. Then came the inevitable good-bye, and as Ferguson's love drove off for her last year of college in South Hadley, Massachusetts, he wondered how he was going to survive without her.

September eighth. The summer was over and done with now. The kids were yelling under his bedroom window early in the morning again, and overnight the Rochester air had taken on the vivid, beginning-of-the-year feel of freshly sharpened pencils and stiff new shoes—the scent of childhood, the deep-in-the-bone memories of way back when. Sad Monsieur Solitaire, who had been pining for his absent Hallie every hour over the past ten days, returned to his rathole at four-thirty that afternoon, and within one minute of his arrival, before he had managed to unload the brown paper bag with the makings of his dinner in it, the telephone rang. Pittman calling from his office at the *Times-Union*. Pittman with a tone of urgency in his voice. Pittman telling him that "something was brewing at Attica," the state prison fifty miles southwest of Rochester, and he was assigning Ferguson and Gianelli to go there early tomorrow morning to talk to Vincent Mancusi, the superintendent of the prison, "to find out what was going on." The interview had already been arranged for nine o'clock, Gianelli would be picking him up at seven, and while it was still just a little mess at this point, it could turn out to be a big one, so "keep your eyes and ears open, Archie, and stay out of trouble."

There had been two large disturbances at New York prisons in the past year, one at upstate Auburn and the other at the Tombs in Manhattan, rugged, physical confrontations between prisoners and guards that had led to scores of indictments and additional punishments. Leaders from both uprisings—most of them black, all of them committed to some form of revolutionary politics—had been transferred to Attica in order to "weed out the troublemakers," and now that Black Panther George Jackson had been gunned down and killed at San Quentin Prison in California during a supposed attempt to escape with *a gun stashed inside the Afro wig he was wearing* (some people actually believed that), the inmates at the overcrowded New York prisons were beginning to make noise again. Sixty percent of the 2,250 prisoners at Attica were black, one hundred percent of the guards were white, and not only was Ferguson not looking forward to his first visit to a maximum-security correctional facility, he was dreading it. He was glad Gianelli would be going with him, the one-hour drive would be pleasant enough as Tom talked to him in the voices of Cary Grant and Jean Harlow and rattled on about the National League pennant race, but once they got there and walked into the prison, they would be stepping into hell.

Ferguson didn't want it anymore. He was burned out and ready to give up, and after telling himself he was finished half a dozen times in the past eight or nine months and then not doing anything about it, this time he wasn't going to back down. He had come to the end of what he could endure. Enough of Rochester, enough of the paper, enough of having to live with his eyes permanently fixed on the dark world of meaningless wars and lying governments and spying undercover cops and angry, hopeless men trapped in dungeons built by the state of New York. It wasn't teaching him anything anymore. Again and again he kept learning the same lesson, and by now he knew the story by heart even before he sat down to write it. *Rien ne va plus*, as the gamblers in Monte Carlo were told when the wheel was about to spin again. No more bets. He had put his money on number zero and had lost, and now it was time to get out.

He would go to the prison with Gianelli in the morning, he would do the interview with the warden, who would probably tell him everything was *under control*, and if he asked to have a look around and perhaps talk to one or two of the prisoners, he would doubtless be turned down for *security reasons*. Then he would write whatever story he was able to write and hand it in to Pittman. But that would be the last one. He would tell Pittman he was through and shake his hand good-bye. After that, he would go to McManus's office and thank Carl for having given him the chance to work there, shake his hand and thank him for the privilege of having known him, but he wasn't cut out for this kind of work anymore, he would say, the job was killing him now and he was all washed up, and then he would thank his boss again for being the good man he was and walk out of the building for the last time.

Five o'clock. He picked up the phone and dialed Hallie's number in Massachusetts, but no one answered after fourteen rings, not even Hallie's roommate to tell him Hallie was out for the evening and wouldn't be back until eleven or twelve.

Hallie's blue eyes looking at him as he looked at her crawling toward him on the bed. Hallie's fierce little white body pressing up against him. Tell me some of the things you like best, she had once asked him, and he had answered her with a silly, punning joke: *The seals in Central Park, the ceiling in Grand Central Station, and the convenience of using self-sealing envelopes. Sí, sí, sí*, she had responded. Or perhaps she was saying *See, see, see*.

At times she laughed so hard that her face turned red.

If he wasn't going to live in Rochester anymore, where did he want to go? Massachusetts to begin with. South Hadley, Massachusetts, to talk things out with her and come up with some kind of plan. Perhaps rent an apartment somewhere in the neighborhood and work on Villon while she went to school. Or else do that for a while as he decompressed and learned how to become human again and then fly off to Paris with her over Christmas break. Or else wander around Europe on his own and see as much as he could in a month or two months or four months. No, not four months. That would be too long, he wouldn't be able to stand it. A little apartment in Amherst or some other town. That might be a good solution for the time being, and then off to Europe together for a couple of months after she graduated in June. Anything was possible. By dipping into his grandmother's fund whenever the urge came over him, all things would be possible this year.

Six o'clock. Scrambled eggs, ham, and two slices of buttered toast for dinner—along with four glasses of red wine.

Luy qui buvoit du meilleur et plus chier
Et ne deust il avoir vaillant ung pigne

Seven o'clock. He was sitting at his desk now and looking at those two lines from Villon's *Testament*. Roughly meaning: He who drank the best and most expensive wines / And didn't have enough to buy a comb. Or: And couldn't afford the price of a comb. Or: And didn't have the cash to buy a comb. Or: And lacked the dough to spring for a comb. Or: And was too broke to splurge on a comb. Or: And didn't have the bread to pop for a comb.

Nine o'clock. He called Massachusetts again. Twenty rings this time, but again there was no answer.

It wasn't just a new love but a new kind of love, a new way of being with someone that translated into a new way of being himself, a better way because of who and what and how she was with him, the way of being himself he had always aspired to but had never managed to accomplish in the past. No more bouts of morose introspection, no more journeys into the bogs of brooding self-torment, no more turning against himself, which was a weakness that had always made him less than he should have been. GUINNESS GIVES YOU STRENGTH said the signs on the walls in bars. Hallie gave him strength. GUINNESS IS GOOD FOR YOU said the signs on the walls in bars. There was no doubt that Hallie Doyle was good for him.

A quarter to eleven. Ferguson went into the bedroom, wound the clock, and set the alarm for six A.M. Then he returned to the living room, picked up the phone, and called Hallie again.

There was no answer.

IN THE APARTMENT directly below Ferguson's, Charlie Vincent turned off the television, stretched his arms, and rose from the couch. The tenant upstairs was climbing into bed, the good-looking boy who had been sleeping with the pretty blonde all through the summer, such nice, friendly kids they were, always with a pleasant word on the stairs or in front of the mailboxes, but now the girl was gone and the boy was sleeping alone again, which was too bad in a way, since he had enjoyed listening to the bed shake upstairs and hearing the boy's grunts and the girl's yelps and moans, such good sounds they were, so satisfying to the ear and every other part of him, always wishing he could have been upstairs in the bed with them, not as he was now but in the old body he used to have when he was young and pretty himself, the years, the years, how many long years ago had that been, and even if he couldn't go upstairs to be with them or watch them from a chair in a corner of their room, listening to them and imagining them had been almost as good, and now that the boy was alone there was something good about that, too, such a lovely boy with his broad shoulders and sympathetic eyes, what he wouldn't give to hold that naked boy in his arms and cover his body with kisses, so Charlie Vincent turned off the television and shuffled from the living room to his bedroom in order to listen to the bed creak as the boy tossed around on the mattress and settled in for the night. It was dark in the room now. Charlie Vincent took off his clothes, lay down on the bed, and thought about the boy as he fiddled with himself until his breath grew short and the warmth spread through him and the job was done. Then, for the fifty-third time since that morning, he lit one of his long, unfiltered Pall Malls and began to puff . . .

7.2

7.3

Aunt Mildred saved him from the worst of it. Pulling strings, asserting her authority as chairman of the English Department, cutting through spool after spool of red tape, threatening to quit in protest if the director of admissions didn't bend to her will, arguing her case over two hour-long meetings with the newly installed, antiwar president Francis F. Kilcoyne, a man known for his compassion and high moral principles, Professor Adler wrangled a spot for Ferguson as a fully matriculating student at Brooklyn College one week before the first semester of his junior year began.

When Ferguson asked her how she had managed to pull off such an incredible stunt, Mildred said: I told them the truth, Archie.

The truth being that he had come to the defense of a black friend under threat from a white bigot and had been exonerated for his actions in court, which would suggest that his Walt Whitman Scholarship at Princeton had been revoked unfairly and he deserved a place at Brooklyn, not only because his grade point average ranked him in the top ten percent of his class but because the loss of the scholarship would bar him from continuing at Princeton for lack of funds, and if he was not enrolled in another college by the beginning of the fall semester, he would lose his student deferment on top of losing his scholarship and find himself subject to the military draft. As an opponent of the war in Vietnam, he would refuse to join the army if called upon to serve, which likely would result in a prison term for resisting

816 PAUL AUSTER

the Selective Service laws, and wasn't it Brooklyn College's duty to save this promising young man from such a dark and pointless outcome?

It had never occurred to him that his aunt had it in her to take such a forceful stand about anything, least of all about him or anyone else in the family, but on August twenty-first, less than an hour after calling DeWitt's office and being told the great man was traveling abroad, he had turned to Aunt Mildred out of desperation—not because he was expecting her to do anything for him but because he needed advice, and with Nagle off on a Mediterranean island sifting through pre-Hellenic pottery shards, she was the only one who could give it to him. Uncle Don picked up the phone that day on the fourth ring. Mildred was out doing some errands, he said, and wasn't expected back for another hour or so, but Ferguson couldn't wait an hour, his insides were jammed up with dread and disbelief as he continued to swallow down the words of DeWitt's letter, so he barfed out the whole thing to Don, who was shocked and outraged and sufficiently furious to tell Ferguson that DeWitt should be drawn and quartered for what he had done, but even in those early moments of the crisis, when Ferguson was still in no condition to think, Don was feeling his way toward a solution, wondering how to finagle an opening that would get Ferguson into another college before time ran out on them, meaning it was *his idea* to begin with, but once Mildred returned to the apartment and talked to Don, it quickly became her idea as well, and when she called back Ferguson forty-five minutes later, she told him not to worry because she was going to *handle everything.*

It made all the difference to have her on his side. The hot and cold Aunt Mildred, the kind and cruel Aunt Mildred, the inconstant, not-so-friendly sister of her sister Rose, the somewhat encouraging but mostly distracted stepmother of Don's son Noah, the goodwilled but essentially unengaged aunt of her only nephew now seemed to be telling her sister's son that she cared about him far more than he had ever suspected. She had told Ferguson how she had managed to get him into Brooklyn College, but when he asked her why she had bothered to go to all that trouble for him in the first place, the ferocity of her answer startled him: I have tremendous faith in you, Archie. I believe in your future, and over my dead body was I going to allow anyone to take that future away from you. Let Gordon DeWitt go fry an egg. We're people of the Book, and people of the Book have to stick together.

Queen Esther. Mother Courage. Mother Jones. Sister Kenny. Aunt Mildred.

The first and most important thing to be said about going to Brooklyn College was that the tuition was free. In a rare display of political wisdom, the city fathers of New York had declared that the boys and girls of the five boroughs were entitled to an education at an annual cost of no dollars, which not only helped advance the principles of democracy and proved how the greater good might be served when municipal tax revenues were put into the correct hands, it offered tens of thousands, hundreds of thousands, and over the years millions of New York boys and girls the opportunity to receive an education most of them would not otherwise have been able to afford, and Ferguson, who could no longer afford the high cost of Princeton, thanked those long-dead city fathers every time he strode up the concrete steps of the Flatbush Avenue subway station and walked onto the Midwood campus. More than that, it was a good college, an excellent college. A minimum high school average of 87 was required for admission along with passing a stringent entrance exam, which meant there was no one in any of his classes who had performed under a B+ level, and with most of them in the 92-to-96 range, Ferguson was surrounded by highly intelligent people, many of them smart enough to qualify as brilliant. Princeton had had its share of brilliant students as well, but also a certain percentage of deadwood legacy boys, whereas Brooklyn consisted of both boys and girls (thankfully) and carried no dead wood. Everyone came from the city, of course, roughly twice the number of students as at Princeton, where the undergraduate population had come from every part of the country, but Ferguson was a die-hard New Yorker now and staunchly pro-city, and just as he had relished the companionship of his New York friends at Camp Paradise when he was a boy, he took pleasure in being with his high-strung, argumentative fellow New Yorkers at B.C., where the student body might have been less geographically diverse than at Princeton but was more humanly diverse in its teeming jumble of ethnicities and cultural backgrounds, with hordes of Catholics and Jews, a refreshing number of black and Asian faces, and since most of them were the grandchildren of Ellis Island immigrants, the odds were better than even that they were the first ones in their families ever to attend college. On top of that, the campus was a model of sound architectural design, not at all what Ferguson had been expecting, a cozy twenty-six acres as compared to the five hundred acres at Princeton, but just as attractive to his eyes, with elegant Georgian buildings filling the landscape instead of imposing Gothic towers, grassy quadrangles studded with elms, and a lily pond and garden to visit in the lulls between classes, with no dormitories, no eating clubs, and no football madness. It was an altogether different way of going to college, with anti-war politics replacing sports as the principal obsession on campus, the demands of academic work pushing out most extracurricular pastimes, and, best of all, the chance to go home to his apartment on East Eighty-ninth Street when his work for the day was done.

The subway rides from Yorkville in Manhattan to Midwood in Brooklyn and then back again every Monday through Thursday were so long that Ferguson managed to do most of the reading for his courses while sitting on the train. He didn't register for Aunt Mildred's class on the Victorian novel because he thought his presence in the room might be a burden on her, but when Uncle Don came back as a guest lecturer in the spring to teach his biennial one-semester course on the art of biography, Ferguson signed up for it. Don delivered a dense, rapid-fire mini-lecture at the start of each class and then opened things up for general discussion, a somewhat awkward, scattershot kind of teacher, Ferguson supposed, but never dull or ponderous, always up to the challenge of thinking on his feet, both humorous and deadpan as he was under most circumstances elsewhere, and what a range of books he had them read that spring, Plutarch, Suetonius, Augustine, Vasari, Montaigne, Rousseau, and Dr. Johnson's bizarre, sexed-up chum James Boswell, who confessed in his journals that he would interrupt his writing in mid-sentence to go out into the London streets and make rumpty-rumpty with as many as three different whores in a single night, but the most enthralling part of that class for Ferguson was finally reading Montaigne for the first time, and now that he had been exposed to the Frenchman's intractable, lightning-bolt sentences, he had found a new master to accompany him on his own travels through the Land of Ink.

So it was that a bad thing had been transformed into a good thing. A knockout punch from Gordon DeWitt that theoretically should have flattened him, but just as Ferguson was beginning to fall, a dozen people jumped into the ring and caught him in their arms before his body hit the canvas, Aunt Mildred first and most significantly as the strongest of the body catchers, but also quick-thinking Uncle Don, and one by one all the others who gathered around him when they were told about the punch, Celia, his mother and Dan, Noah, Jim and Nancy, Billy and Joanna, Ron and Peg, and Howard, who talked to Nagle the morning after Ferguson's ex–academic adviser returned to Princeton, and then Nagle himself, who wrote an uncommonly warm letter after Howard broke the *disturbing news* to him about the scholarship, offering to help in any way he could and suggesting that perhaps Susan could swing something for him at Rutgers, how much that letter meant to Ferguson, Nagle reaching out to him as a friend and taking his side over DeWitt's, and the long telephone conversation with Amy and Luther in Montreal, coupled with the alarming turn that led to Howard's breakup with Mona Veltry, a fierce verbal spat about which one of them had been responsible for leading the group to Tom's Bar and Grill, each one blaming the other until they lost control of themselves and their big love died as rapidly as a sick flower dies with the first frost, and then, no more than days after that, Luther abruptly put an end to it with Amy, pushing her out the door and demanding that she go back to America, and there was Ferguson's dazed and grieving stepsister telling him that Luther had done it for *her own good*, and Please, Archie, she said, my dear, crazy brother, don't do anything stupid like running off to Canada, just hold your ground and hold your breath and pray that something good turns up, which was precisely what happened because of Mother Courage Mildred, and despite the havoc he lived through in those days of uncertainty, Ferguson felt so deeply loved by the people he loved that winning the Walt Whitman Scholarship turned out to have done less for his morale than losing it.

THE WORLD WAS churning. All things everywhere were in flux. The war was boiling in his blood, Newark was a dead city on the other side of the river, lovers were going up in flames, and now that Ferguson had been granted his reprieve, he was back inside his book about Dr. Noyes and the dead children of R. Two hours starting at six o'clock every morning from Monday to Thursday, and then as many hours as possible from Friday to Sunday, in spite of the ever-mounting load of schoolwork, which he had to plow through diligently in order to repay his debt to Mildred, who would have been disappointed in him if he slacked off and failed to do well. Montaigne; Leibniz; Leopardi; and Dr. Noyes. The world was falling apart, and the only way not to fall apart with it was to keep his mind fixed on his work—to roll out of bed every morning and get down to business, whether the sun chose to come up that day or not.

The free tuition was a blessing, but there were still a number of money problems to be dealt with, and for the first weeks of the fall semester Ferguson struggled to come up with a plan that would not include help from his mother and stepfather. The scholarship had covered room and board as well as tuition, which had allowed him to stuff his face at no charge three times a day five days a week, five days that could have been seven days if he hadn't insisted on spending the other two days in New York, but now that he was in the city and only in the city, he had to pay for all his meals and groceries, which was something he could no longer afford to do, not after shelling out five thousand dollars to the Brattleboro lawyer and being left with just over two thousand in the bank. He figured he could muddle along on about four thousand a year, which would provide him with enough crumbs to sustain a lowly sort of church mouse existence, but two thousand wasn't four thousand, and he still had only half of what he would need. True to form, Dan offered to make up the difference with a monthly allowance, which Ferguson reluctantly agreed to because he had no choice in the end, knowing the only alternative was to take a part-time job somewhere (assuming he could find one), which would make it impossible to go on with his book. He said yes because he had to say yes, but just because he was thankful to Dan for the two hundred dollars a month, that didn't require him to feel happy about the arrangement.

In early November, help came from an unexpected source, which directly or indirectly could be traced back to his own past but at the same time had nothing to do with him. Others were responsible for giving him the money he needed, money he hadn't earned but had nevertheless worked for without any intention of earning money, for just as a writer couldn't know whether he was about to be mauled or embraced, he couldn't know whether the hours he spent at his desk would lead to something or nothing. All along, Ferguson had assumed nothing, and therefore he had never spoken the words *writing* and *money* in the same breath, thinking only sellouts and Grub Street hacks dreamed about money while doing their work, thinking money would always have to come from somewhere else in order to feed his compulsion for filling up white rectangles with row after row of descending black marks, but at the preposterously unadvanced age of twenty Ferguson learned that *always* did not mean *always* but just *most of the time*, and at those rare times when the somber expectations of *always* were proved to be wrong, the only proper response was to thank the gods for their random act of benevolence and then return to the somber expectations of *always*, even if one's first encounter with the principle of *most of the time* thundered in the bones with the force of a holy benediction.

Tumult Books, the legitimate, non-mimeo press that had been launched by Ron, Lewis, and Anne in the spring, released its first batch of publications on November fourth: two collections of poems (one by Lewis, the other by Anne), Ron's translations of Pierre Reverdy, and Billy's 372-page epic, *Crushed Heads*. The angel of the enterprise, Anne's mother's first husband's ex-wife, an effusive woman in her mid-forties named Trixie Davenport, threw a large party at her Lexington Avenue duplex to celebrate the event, and Ferguson, along with nearly every-one else he knew, was invited to the Saturday night bash. He had never felt comfortable in crowds, the crush of too many bodies crammed together in enclosed spaces tended to make him dizzy and mute, but that night was different for some reason, perhaps because he felt so good for Billy after all the years he had put into writing his book, or perhaps because he found it amusing to see the scruffy, impoverished, down-town poets and painters mixing with the East Side swells, but whether it was for one of those reasons or both of them, he felt glad to be there that night, standing next to the beautiful, somewhat intimidated Celia, who wasn't much of a crowd person herself, and as Ferguson turned around and surveyed that packed and noisy scene, he saw John Ash-bery alone in a corner puffing on a Gitane, Alex Katz sipping a glass of white wine, Harry Mathews shaking the hand of a tall, redheaded woman in a blue dress, Norman Bluhm laughing as he put someone in a pretend hammerlock, and there was dapper, frizzy-haired Noah stand-ing with voluptuous, frizzy-haired Vicki Tremain, and there was How-ard talking to none other than Amy Schneiderman, who had come down to New York for the weekend, and ten minutes after Ferguson arrived, there was Ron Pearson elbowing his way toward him, and a moment later Ron was putting his arm around his shoulder and guiding him out of the room because *he wanted to talk to him about something.*

They made their way upstairs, walked down a corridor, turned left down another corridor, and slipped into an empty room with a couple of thousand books in it and six or seven paintings hanging on one of the walls. *Something* turned out to be a business proposition, if a minute, bound-to-be-unprofitable operation such as Tumult Books could be called a business. As Ron explained it, the triumvirate in charge of running the press had voted to include Ferguson on next year's list by gathering together his three Gizmo titles and publishing them as a single book. According to their calculations, it would come out to around 250 or 275 pages, and they could have it ready sometime in the next eight to twelve months. What did he say to that?

I don't know, Ferguson said. Do you think those books are good enough?

We wouldn't be making the offer if we thought they were bad, Ron said. Of course they're good enough.

And what about Billy? Doesn't he have to give his permission?

He already has. Billy's all in behind it. He's with us now, and he wants you to be with us, too.

What a guy. *I grapple with my groots and shoot down the grovelers and medicine men with my trusted blunderbuss.* No one has ever written a cooler sentence than that.

I should also mention the money.

What money?

We're trying to act like real publishers, Archie.

I don't understand.

A contract, an advance, royalties. Surely you've heard of those things.

Vaguely. In some other world where I don't happen to live.

Three books in one book, published in an edition of three thousand copies. We thought a two-thousand-dollar advance would have a nice asymmetrical ring to it.

Don't joke, Ron. Two thousand would save me. No more begging on street corners, no more handouts from people who can't afford to hand out money, no more midnight sweats. Please tell me you're not pulling my leg.

Ron smiled one of his thin, minimal smiles and sat down in a chair. The standard procedure is to get half when you sign the contract, he continued, and the other half when the book is published, but if you need the full amount up front, I'm sure that can be arranged.

How can you be sure?

Because, Ron said, pointing to a Mondrian on the opposite wall, Trixie can do anything she wants.

Yes, Ferguson replied, as he turned around and looked at the canvas, I suppose she can.

There's just one last thing to discuss. A title, an overall title for the three books. There's no rush, but Anne came up with one at the meeting that we all thought was pretty funny. Funny because you're still so shockingly young and new to the world that we sometimes ask ourselves if you still wear diapers.

Only at night, but I don't need them during the day anymore.

Mr. Sloppy Pants walks around in clean undies now.

Most of the time, in any case. And what did Anne suggest?

Collected Works.

Ah. Yes, it's pretty funny all right, but also . . . what's the word I'm looking for? . . . a bit *funereal*. As if I'd been embalmed and was about to set off on a one-way trip to the past tense. I think I'd prefer something a little more hopeful.

It's your book. You're the one who gets to decide.

How about *Prolusions*?

As in those early works by Milton?

That's right. "A literary composition of a preliminary or preparatory nature."

We know what the word means, but will anyone else know?

If they don't, they can look it up.

Ron removed his glasses, rubbed down the lenses with a handkerchief, and then put them back on. After a small pause, he shrugged and said: I'm with you, Archie. Let them look it up.

Ferguson walked back into the party feeling stunned and weightless, as if his head were no longer attached to his body. When he tried to tell Celia the good news, the din of voices circling around them was so intense that she couldn't hear what he was saying to her. Never mind, Ferguson said, as he squeezed her hand and kissed her on the neck, I'll tell you later. Then he looked out at the throng of vertical people gathered in the room and saw that Howard and Amy were still talking to each other, standing quite close now, each one leaning into the other and entirely absorbed in their conversation, and as he watched how his stepsister and former roommate were looking at each other it dawned on Ferguson that they could be turning into an item, that with Mona and Luther both gone and no doubt forever gone for both of them, it made sense for Howard and Amy to be exploring the possibilities, and how curious it would be if Howard wound up inserting himself into the tangled, mixed-up tribe of overlapping clans and lineages to become an honorary member of the Schneiderman-Adler-Ferguson-Marx traveling vaudeville team, which would turn his friend into an unofficial brother-in-law, and what an honor that would be, Ferguson said to himself, welcoming Howard into the inner circle and giving him advice on how to duck when Amy started throwing Necco wafers at his head, the extraordinary Amy Schneiderman, the girl he had wanted so badly that it still hurt to think about what might have happened but never did.

HE HAD ENOUGH money to live on for a year, and for the first five months of that year Ferguson managed to hold himself together by sticking to his plan. Only four things mattered to him now: writing his book, loving Celia, loving his friends, and going back and forth to Brooklyn College. It wasn't that he had stopped paying attention to the world, but the world was no longer simply falling apart, the world had caught fire, and the question was: What to do or not to do when the world was on fire and you didn't have the equipment to put out the flames, when the fire was in you as much as it was around you, and no matter what you did or didn't do, your actions would change nothing? Stick to the plan by writing the book. That was the only answer Ferguson could come up with. Write the book by replacing the real fire with an imaginary fire and hope the effort would add up to something more than nothing. As for the Tet Offensive in South Vietnam, as for Lyndon Johnson's abdication, as for the murder of Martin Luther King: watch them as carefully as he could, take them in as deeply as he could, but other than that, nothing. He wasn't going to fight on the barricades, but he would cheer for the ones who did, and then he would return to his room and write his book.

He understood how shaky that position was. The arrogance of it, the selfishness of it, the *art above all else* flaw in his thinking, but if he

didn't hold fast to his argument (which probably wasn't an argument
so much as an instinctive reflex), he would be giving in to a counter-
argument that posited a world in which books were no longer necessary,
and what moment could be more important for the writing of books
than a year when the world was on fire—and you were on fire with it?

Then came the first of the two big blows that crashed down on him
that spring.

At nine o'clock in the evening on April sixth, two days after the
murder of Martin Luther King, as real fires were burning in half the
cities in America, the telephone rang in Ferguson's apartment on East
Eighty-ninth Street. Someone named Allen Blumenthal wanted to talk
to Archie Ferguson, and was that Archie Ferguson on the line now? Yes,
Ferguson said, trying to remember where he had heard the name Allen
Blumenthal, which seemed to set off a distant bell in some far corner
of his memory . . . Blumenthal . . . Blumenthal . . . and then the jolt of
recognition arrived at last: Allen Blumenthal, the son of Ethel Blumenthal, the woman his father had been married to for the past three years,
Ferguson's unknown stepbrother, sixteen at the time of the wedding
and therefore nineteen now, just two years younger than Ferguson—
Celia's age.

You know who I am, don't you? Blumenthal asked.

If you're the Allen Blumenthal I think you are, Ferguson said, then
you're my stepbrother. (*A pause to let the magnitude of the word sink in.*)
Hello, stepbrother.

Blumenthal didn't laugh at Ferguson's mild but friendly joke, nor
did he waste any time in getting down to business. At seven o'clock that
morning, while playing a round of prework tennis on an indoor court
at the South Mountain Tennis Center with his boyhood friend Sam
Brownstein, Ferguson's father had collapsed and died of a heart attack.
The funeral would be held the day after tomorrow at Temple B'nai Abraham in Newark, and Blumenthal was calling on his mother's behalf to
invite Ferguson to attend the service, which would be officiated by Rabbi
Prinz, and then to accompany the family to the cemetery in Woodbridge
for the burial, after which (if Ferguson was so inclined) he could join
them at the house in Maplewood. What should Blumenthal tell his
mother? Yes or no?

Yes, Ferguson said. Of course I'll be there.

Stanley was such a wonderful guy, the unknown stepbrother said, as his voice began to wobble into another register. I can't believe this has happened.

Ferguson heard the air catch in Blumenthal's throat, and suddenly the boy was sobbing . . .

There were no tears for Ferguson, however. For a long time after he hung up the phone, he couldn't feel anything but an immense weight bearing down on his head, a ten-ton stone immobilizing him all the way down to his ankles and the soles of his feet, and then bit by bit the weight turned inward and was supplanted by horror, horror crawling up through his body and humming in his veins, and after the horror, an invasion of darkness, darkness within him and around him and a voice in his head telling him the world was no longer real.

Fifty-four. And not one glimpse of him since that grotesque TV commercial eighteen months ago. Prices never lower, spirits never higher. Imagine: dropping dead at fifty-four.

Not once in all the years of their struggles and silences had Ferguson ever wished for such a thing or imagined it could happen. His non-smoking, nondrinking, eternally fit and athletic father was going to live to an advanced old age, and somehow or other, at some point in the decades still to come, he and Ferguson would have found a way to purge the rancor that had grown between them, but that assumption had been based on the certainty that there were many more years ahead of them, and now there were no more years, there was not even a day or an hour or the smallest fraction of a second.

Three years of unbroken silence. That was the worst part of it now, those three years and no chance to undo the silence anymore, no death-bed farewells, no premonitory illness to prepare him for the blow, and how strange it was that ever since he had signed the contract for his book Ferguson had been thinking more and more about his father again (because of the money, he suspected, proof that there were people in the world willing to give him money for the no-account work of writing make-believe stories), and in the past month or so Ferguson had even been considering the possibility of sending his father a copy of *Prolusions* when the book was published in order to show him that he was getting by, getting along *on his own terms*, and also (perhaps) as an opening-round gesture that might have led to some future reconciliation, wondering if his father would respond or not, wondering if he would toss out the book or sit down and write him a letter, and if

he did respond, then writing back to him and arranging to meet somewhere to have it out once and for all, honest and open with each other
for the first time, no doubt cursing and shouting at each other throughout most of it, and whenever Ferguson played out that scene in his head,
it generally wound up in a bloody fistfight, with the two of them pounding each other until they were too tired to hold up their arms anymore.
It was also possible that he might not have sent the book in the end, but
at least he had been thinking about it, and surely that meant something,
surely that was a sign of hope, for even punches would have been
better than the blank standoff of the past three years.

Going to the synagogue. Going to the cemetery. Going to the house
in Maplewood. The nullity and futility of it all: meeting Ethel and her
children for the first time, and the discovery that they were real people
with arms and legs and faces and hands, the distraught widow doing
what she could to hold herself upright through the ordeal, not the cold
person of the wedding photograph in the *Star-Ledger* but a thoughtful,
unpretentious woman who had fallen for his father and married him,
almost certainly a patient, giving wife, perhaps in some ways a better
wife for his father than the fast-moving, independent Rose had been,
and after receiving a kiss on the cheek from their mother, shaking hands
with Allen and Stephanie, who clearly had loved Stanley more than
Stanley's biological son ever had, Allen finishing his first year at Rutgers
and intending to major in economics, which must have pleased his
father, a sensible boy with his head in the real world, unlike the disappointing real son who mostly dwelled on the moon, and beyond his
father's second family, Ferguson found himself with members of his first
family as well, the aunts and uncles from California, Joan and Millie,
Arnold and Lew, not seen since the early days of Ferguson's childhood, and what struck him most about those long-lost relatives was
the curious fact that while the brothers did not look terribly alike, each
in his different way bore a strong resemblance to his father.

For some reason, Ferguson stayed on in the house longer than he
should have, the old Castle of Silence where he had been held prisoner
for seven years and had written the story about the shoes, for the most
part standing alone in a corner of the living room and not saying much
to the several dozen strangers who were there, neither wanting to be
there himself nor willing to leave, accepting condolences from various
men and women after they were informed that he was Stanley's son,

nodding thanks, shaking hands, but still too stunned to do anything more than agree with them about how shocked and stunned they were by his father's sudden, shocking death. His aunts and uncles made an early exit, the weeping, overwrought Sam Brownstein and his wife, Peggy, headed for the door, but even after most of the other guests filed out toward the end of the afternoon, Ferguson still wasn't ready to call Dan and ask to be picked up (he was planning to spend the night at the house on Woodhall Crescent) because the reason why he had stayed so long he now understood was to have a chance to talk to Ethel in private, and when she walked up to him a couple of minutes later and asked if they could go off somewhere together to talk alone, he was comforted to know that she had been thinking the same thought as well.

It was a sad conversation, one of the saddest conversations in the history of his life so far, sitting with his unknown stepmother in the TV nook of the newly refurbished basement as they shared what they knew about the enigma that had been Stanley Ferguson, a man Ethel admitted had been *all but unreachable* to her, and how sorry Ferguson felt for that woman as he watched her convulse in tears, then pull herself together for a while, then collapse again, the shock of it, she kept saying, the shock of a fifty-four-year-old man running at full speed into a brick wall of death, the second husband she had buried in the past nine years, Ethel Blumberg, Ethel Blumenthal, Ethel Ferguson, for two decades a sixth-grade teacher in the Livingston public schools, mother of Allen and Stephanie, and yes, she said, it made perfect sense that they had adored Stanley because Stanley had been exceedingly good to them, for after much study on the subject of Stanley Ferguson she had come to the conclusion that he was generous and kind to strangers but closed off and impenetrable with the ones he should have been most intimate with, his wife and children, in this case his one child, Archie, since Allen and Stephanie were no more than distant outsiders to him, a pair of children equivalent to the son and daughter of a third cousin or the man who washed his car, which had made it easy for him to be kind and generous to them, but what about you, Archie, Ethel asked, and why did so much resentment build up between the two of you over the years, so much bitterness that Stanley refused to allow me to meet you and blocked you from our wedding, even though he kept on saying he had *nothing against you* and was—to use his words—*content to wait it out.*

Ferguson wanted to explain it to her, but he knew how difficult it would be to delve into the thousand nuanced particulars of the *long twi-light struggle* that had lasted the better part of his life, so he boiled it down to one simple and comprehensible statement:

I was waiting for him to contact me, he was waiting for me to contact him, and before either one of us was willing to budge, time ran out.

Two stubborn fools, Ethel said.

That's it. Two fools locked in their stubbornness.

We can't change what happened, Archie. It's over and done with now, and all I can say is I hope you won't go on tormenting yourself about it any more than you already have. Your father was an odd man, but not a cruel or vindictive man, and even though he made things hard on you, I believe he was on your side.

How can you know that?

Because he didn't cut you out of his will. As far as I'm concerned, it should have been a much larger amount, but according to what your father told me, you have no interest in being the co-owner of a chain of seven appliance stores. Is that right?

None whatsoever.

I'm still convinced he should have left you a lot more, but one hundred thousand dollars isn't too bad, is it?

Ferguson didn't know what to say, so he went on sitting in his chair and said nothing, answering Ethel's question by shaking his head, meaning no, one hundred thousand dollars wasn't too bad, even though he wasn't sure at that point if he wanted to accept it or not, and now that there was nothing more to be said, Ethel and Ferguson went back upstairs, where he called his stepfather and told him he was ready to be picked up. When Dan's car appeared in front of the house fifteen minutes later, Ferguson shook hands with Allen and Stephanie and said good-bye to them, and as Ethel walked him to the door, she told her dead husband's son that he should expect a call from Kaminsky the lawyer about his inheritance sometime within the next week or two, and then Ferguson and Ethel hugged each other good-bye, a hard, fervent embrace of solidarity and affection as they promised to stay in touch with each other from now on, even though they both knew they never would.

In the car, Ferguson lit his fourteenth Camel of the day, cracked open the window, and turned to Dan. *How was his mother doing?* That was the first question he asked as they made their way to Woodhall Crescent, the peculiar but necessary question about his mother's state of mind after learning that her ex-husband and spouse for eighteen years and the father of her son had abruptly and unexpectedly left this world, for in spite of their angry divorce and the uninterrupted silence that had existed between them since the divorce, it must have come as a jolt to her just the same.

The word *jolt* says it all, Dan replied. Which accounts for the tears, I think, and the astonishment, and the sorrow. But that was two days ago, and by now she's more or less come to terms with it. You know how it is, Archie. Once a person dies, you start to feel different things about that person, no matter what trouble there might have been in the past.

So you're saying she's all right.

Don't worry. Before I left, she asked me to ask you if you knew anything about your father's will. Her brain is working again, which suggests the tears are finished. *(Momentarily turning his eyes from the road to look at Ferguson.)* She's a lot more concerned about you than she is about herself. As am I, for that matter.

Rather than talk about the deadness and confusion in his own brain, Ferguson told Dan about the one hundred thousand dollars. He assumed the six-figure number would impress him, but the normally unriled and devil-may-care Dan Schneiderman was distinctly unimpressed. For a man of Stanley Ferguson's wealth, he said, one hundred thousand was the bare minimum, and anything lower than that would have been *obnoxious*.

Still and all, Ferguson countered, it was a hell of a lot of money.

Yes, Dan agreed, it was a veritable mountain.

Ferguson then explained that he still hadn't decided what he wanted to do about it, whether to accept the money for himself or give it away, and while he was thinking it over he wanted Dan and his mother to hold on to it for him, and if they should ever want to use some of it for themselves while he was still making up his mind, then they should feel free to do that, with his blessings.

Don't be an ass, Dan said. The money's yours, Archie. Put it in your own account and spend it on yourself—any way you want. Your war with your father is over now, and you don't have to go on fighting it after he's dead.

You could be right. But I have to make that decision myself, and I still haven't made it. In the meantime, the money goes to you and my mother for safekeeping.

All right, give us the money. And when we get it, the first thing I'm going to do is write you a check for five thousand dollars.

Why five thousand?

Because that's what you'll need to live on for the summer and your last year of college. It used to be four thousand, but now it's five. You've heard of inflation, haven't you? Not only is the war killing people, it's also starting to kill the economy.

But if I decide I don't want to keep the money, it won't be a hundred thousand anymore, it will be ninety-five thousand.

Not after a year it won't. Interest is at six percent these days. By the time you graduate from college, the ninety-five thousand will be a hundred thousand again. It's what we call *invisible money*.

I never knew you were such a schemer.

I'm not. You're the schemer, Archie, but unless I do a little scheming myself, I won't be able to keep up with you.

THE NEXT BIG blow that spring was losing Celia.

First Cause: By the time Aunt Mildred pulled Ferguson out of the burning house and found him new shelter at Brooklyn College, it had been one year since he and Celia had put their arms around each other and ventured their first kiss. Love had followed from that kiss, a big love that now dwarfed all other loves from the past, but in that year he had also learned how complicated loving Celia could be. When it was just the two of them alone together, Ferguson felt they were mostly in harmony, mostly able to overcome the differences that sometimes flared up between them by shedding their clothes and crawling into bed, and the bond of copious, lustful copulations kept them united even when they were at odds about how to live or what they imagined they were living for. Ferguson and Celia both had strong opinions on the matters that concerned them most, but those matters were often different matters in that Ferguson was preparing himself for a future in art and Celia was preparing herself for a future in science, and even though they both professed to admire what the other did (Ferguson had no doubt that Celia was enthusiastic about his work, Celia had no doubt that Ferguson was in awe of her *immense academic brain*), they couldn't be all things to each other all the time.

Rebuttal: A gap between them, but not so broad a gap as to thwart their efforts to bridge it. Celia read books, listened to music, and merrily trotted off to movies and plays with Ferguson, and Ferguson himself was studying biology that year, needing one more science course to fulfill his requirement, but making that course biology because of her, in order to master the rudiments of the language she spoke, and, as he explained to Celia, to immerse himself more deeply in his book, which they both understood could be written only by penetrating the Noyesian realm of physical bodies, the tissues and bones of the ill and healthy bodies his man had been treating for more than twenty years as a medical doctor. Beyond helping him with the work for his biology class, Celia also took it upon herself to arrange interviews for him with pre-med students from Barnard and Columbia, with young interns at St. Luke's, Lenox Hill, and Columbia Presbyterian, and an invaluable four-hour meeting with her own family doctor since childhood, Gordon Edelman from New Rochelle, a compact, round-chested man who calmly walked Ferguson through the history and day-to-day routines of his practice, the dramas he had confronted over the years, and even talked for a while about Celia's brother's early death, explaining that Artie *did not present* symptoms of an aneurysm and consequently was not subjected to the dangerous procedure of an angiograph, which was the only method for examining a living brain in 1961, as opposed to the more reliable procedure of picking apart a dead brain during an autopsy. *Did not present.* In other words, there was nothing anyone could have done, and then the day arrived when the vessel broke and the doctor's words were scrambled into three different words that carried an altogether different meaning: *No longer present.*

Because of his novel, Ferguson was also making the bleak but necessary journey through the literature of suicide, and in order to keep pace with him, Celia read some of those books as well, beginning with philosophical, sociological, and psychological essays and studies by Hume, Schopenhauer, Durkheim, and Menninger, then numerous accounts from the distant past and near present, Empedocles and his mythic leap into the flames of Mount Etna, Socrates (hemlock), Mark Antony (sword), the mass suicide of Jewish rebels at Masada, Plutarch's description of Cato's self-murder in *Parallel Lives* (plucking out his own bowels in front of his son, his doctor, and his servants), the disgraced boy genius Thomas Chatterton (arsenic), the Russian poet Marina Tsvetaeva (hanging), Hart Crane (jumping off a ship into the Gulf of Mexico), George Eastman (a gunshot to the heart), Hermann Göring (cyanide), and, most pertinent of all, the opening sentences from *The Myth of Sisyphus*: "There is but one truly serious philosophical problem, and that is suicide. Judging whether life is or is not worth living amounts to answering the fundamental question of philosophy."

F: What do you think, Celia? Is Camus right or wrong?

C: Probably right. But then again . . .

F: I agree with you. Probably right, but not necessarily.

Not all things all the time, but more than enough things to make a decent go of it, perhaps a splendid and lasting go, but they were still just eighteen and twenty when the school year began, and one of the good things they shared was the double conviction that work came before pleasure and that neither of them had any aptitude for domestic life. Even if Ferguson's apartment on East Eighty-ninth Street had been big enough for two rather than one, they never would have considered living together, not because they were too young for the rigors of steady cohabitation but because they were both essentially loners and needed long stretches of time alone in order to do their work. For Celia, that meant her studies at Barnard, where she was excelling not only in science and math but in all her subjects, which put her firmly in the grind camp, an obsessive, round-the-clock grind who had joined up with four other Barnard grind-girls for her sophomore year and was living in a large, gloomy dump on West 111th Street, an apartment she teasingly referred to as the Cloister of Perpetual Stillness. For Ferguson, the exigencies of work were no less demanding, the taxing double job of trying to do his best at Brooklyn College while trying to write his novel, which was advancing slowly because of that, but one more good thing about the obsessive Celia was how deeply attuned she was to his obsessions, and several times that year, on the Fridays and Saturdays and Sundays when they had made plans to see each other and Ferguson found himself on a sudden roll with his book, she didn't take offense when he called her at the last minute to cancel the date, telling him to *forge on* and *write his heart out* and *not to worry*. That was the crux of it, he realized, the comrade spirit that set her apart from everyone else he had known, for there was never any doubt that she was disappointed by those last-minute calls but had the guts (the strength of character) to pretend she wasn't.

Second Cause: A mostly harmonious meeting of minds and bodies when it was just the two of them alone together, but whenever they stepped out into the world and mixed with other people, life became problematic. Beyond the four girls she shared her apartment with, Celia had few close friends, perhaps no close friends, and therefore the bulk of their infrequent socializing consisted of floating in and out of Ferguson's world, which was mostly an alien world to Celia, a world she tried to understand but couldn't. She had no difficulties with the older generation and felt warmly treated by Ferguson's mother and stepfather, she enjoyed herself at the two dinners they had with Aunt Mildred and Uncle Don, but Noah and Howard both rubbed her the wrong way, Noah because she found his sarcastic, nonstop jesting unbearable and Howard because she felt wounded by his polite indifference to her. She got along well enough with Amy and Jim's wife, Nancy, but the ever-expanding circle of Ferguson's poet and painter friends bored her and repelled her in equal measure, and it saddened Ferguson to see how unhappy she looked whenever they spent an evening with Billy and Joanna, who were as close to him as blood relations now, a sadness that turned into both guilt and irritation when he watched her sit through another one of his long, meandering talks about poets and writers with Ron, Lewis, or Anne, and even less did she comprehend why her noble, deep-thinking Archie found it so much fun to go to trashy Joan Crawford movies with Bo Jainard and his friend Jack Ellerby, those slender fey boys who sometimes kissed each other in the darkness of the balcony and never stopped laughing, they all laughed too much, she said, not one person in the crowd ever took anything seriously, they were sloppy, floppy, loosey-goosey starvelings with no aim in life except to prowl the margins of life and make art that no one wanted to see or buy, and yes, Ferguson admitted, perhaps that was true, but they were his boys and girls, his gallant, unembittered fellow outcasts, and because none of them was quite fit for this world, a burst of laughter now and then showed they were doing the best they could under the circumstances.

Rebuttal: By the beginning of the new year (1968), Ferguson under-

stood that he could no longer subject Celia to his disreputable companions, some of whom were blatant homosexuals, some of whom were
addicts and drunks, some of whom were emotionally disturbed crip-
ples under psychiatric care, and even if some of them were contentedly
married parents of young children, no matter how hard he tried to bring
her into that small society of cracked-in-the-head monomaniacs, she
would always resist it, and rather than go on punishing her for the sin
of wanting to accompany him when he sought out the company of
others, he would absolve her of the obligation to be with any others who
were not to her liking. He knew it was a step in the wrong direction,
that cutting her off from that part of his life would open a permanent
space between them, but he didn't want to run the risk of losing Celia,
and how else could he hold on to her except by liberating her from those
unhappy evenings with his friends?

The next time she slept over at his place, he picked up on something
she said and then moved in on the subject as delicately as he could. They
were lying in bed together, sharing one of his Camels after a richly satisfying hour under and on top of the sheets and down comforter, talking about nothing of any importance, or perhaps not talking at all (he
couldn't remember), perhaps just looking at each other, as they tended
to do at such moments, each one filled up with the other and yet prolonging the moment by running their hands up and down and over the
other's naked skin, no words other than Ferguson telling her how beautiful she was, if indeed he was saying that much, but he remembered
that Celia's eyes were closed and she was humming to herself, a soft
little tuneless sound that resembled a purr, languorous, long-limbed,
panther-woman Celia lounging on her side and whispering to him in a
throaty voice: I love it when we're like this, Archie. Just the two of us
on our island together with the waves of the city splashing outside.

Me, too, Ferguson said. That's why I'm proposing a moratorium, a
ban on any more contact with the outside.

Are you saying we should lock ourselves in this room and never
go out?

No, we can go out. But just the two of us. No more running around
with other people.

That's fine with me. What do I care about other people?

There's just one problem. (A pause to puff and think about how to say it
without upsetting her.) We'll have to start seeing each other a bit less often.

Why would we want to do that?

Because the people you don't care about are not people I don't care about.

And which people are we referring to?

The ones I've forced down your throat. Billy Best, Howard Small, Noah Marx, Bo Jainard—the whole lot of unacceptables.

I'm not against them, Archie.

Maybe not, but you're not for them either, and I don't see why you should have to put up with them anymore.

Are you saying this for me or for you?

For both of us. It kills me to see you go into those funks of yours.

I know you're trying to be nice, but you think I'm a twit, don't you? An uptight, bourgeois noodlehead.

That's right. A girl with straight A's and an invitation to go back to Woods Hole for the summer must be a twit and a noodlehead.

But they're your friends. I don't want to let you down.

They're my friends, but there's nothing that says they have to be your friends.

It's kind of sad, don't you think?

Not really. It's just a new arrangement, that's all.

I'm talking about *less,* about seeing each other less often.

If the quality of that less is more than the more we have now, then less will compensate for all the miserable hours I've spent watching you suffer with those people, and less will end up trumping more, less in fact will *be* more.

They settled into a new rhythm of weekends only, two late afternoons, evenings, and nights per weekend, either Friday and Saturday, Friday and Sunday, or Saturday and Sunday, except on those rare Fridays, Saturdays, or Sundays when Ferguson called to cancel at the last minute, which left him free to associate with one or more of the unacceptables on the weekend night that was not shared with Celia, not to mention the weekday nights when he was not overburdened with schoolwork, the roughly one night in four when he had dinner with Billy and Joanna at their place down the street, talking about writers, politics, movies, painters, and sports as they took turns holding and playing with one-year-old Molly, big-brother Billy Best, who had believed in Ferguson before anyone else and was his only prose-writer friend in the fish tank of poets where he was swimming now, the only one with an ear for prose who could follow his arguments about why Flannery O'Conner and Grace Paley were bolder, more inventive stylists than Bellow, Updike, or any other American man except perhaps Baldwin, and in that way Ferguson managed not to lose contact with the Bests or Noah or Howard or the Tumult trio or any of the other necessary ones who kept him anchored to the world. Yes, it was a little sad, as Celia had put it, but after a month and then another month of the new arrangement, he felt they were beginning to do better, breathing less fitfully because there were fewer distractions and exasperations to contend with, and yet Ferguson also knew there was much work still to be done, that the small problem he had solved was nothing compared to the big problem of hiding too much of himself from her, and unless he found the strength to open up to Celia and tell her everything she needed to be told about him, he would eventually destroy their future and end up with nothing.

Third Cause: It could be argued that the entire affair had been built on a false premise. It wasn't that Ferguson had lied to Celia, but he had persisted in withholding the truth from her about the primacy of Artie's death in the love-equals-divine-justice formula, and even though he felt he had largely surmounted that problem with the game of catch in Riverside Park last spring, which had evolved into one-on-one games of wiffleball with Celia throughout the summer, both in Woods Hole and on the farm in Vermont, especially during the grim weeks before his trial when those festive, laughing games had momentarily kept him from thinking about his day of reckoning in court, he still hadn't said a word to her about any of it. The mad, six-year-long fixation had come to an end, but if he was cured now or even just partially restored to health, why hadn't he summoned the courage to tell Celia about the abnegations he had imposed on himself as a tribute to his dead A.F. twin? Because he was scared. Because he feared she would judge him insane and want nothing to do with him anymore.

Even worse, there was his inability to tell her about his *condition*, to reveal the secret of his abnormal birth as the progeny of a male donkey and a female horse, the braying jack who had mounted the comely mare in a New Jersey barn one night in the summer of 1946 and had impregnated her with a mule, Ferguson the Talking Mule, who was a creature who could sire no offspring and therefore fell into the category of genetic dud, and so crushing was that truth to Ferguson, so damaging to the phallic certainties of his male self, he could never bring himself to share it with Celia, which meant that he allowed her to go through the needless exercise of taking birth-control precautions every time they went to bed together, never once telling her there was no point in inserting her diaphragm because making love with him guaranteed that she would never have to worry about becoming pregnant.

An inexcusable error. Cowardice on such a grand scale that it turned him into the one thing he had vowed never to become: dishonorable.

Rebuttal: There was no rebuttal. In Ferguson's mind, however, the possibility that Dr. Brueler's diagnosis had been wrong continued to give him hope. Until and unless he consulted another doctor, the inexcusable would remain excusable because there was always a small chance that birth control was necessary, and he didn't want Celia to know the shameful truth of his condition until he was one hundred percent certain of it. All he had to do was go to another doctor and have himself tested again—but he was too afraid to go, too afraid to find out, and he kept putting it off.

Conclusion: Two and a half weeks after his father's death, when the fire of the moment spread its flames to the Columbia campus, Celia put on a green armband and helped the cause by making sandwiches for the students inside the buildings, one of several dozen volunteers in the Ferris Booth Hall Chow Brigade. Not the red armband of the activists but the green band of sympathizers and supporters, a reasonable position for someone who took no part in campus politics and devoted all her energies to studying for her classes, but Celia had political opinions, and even if she wasn't cut out for the front-line actions of manning barricades and occupying university buildings, those opinions were strong enough to put her on the side of the students against the administration, no matter what qualms she might have had about the students' tactics and no matter how often she cringed when she heard a hundred or five hundred voices shouting *Up against the wall, motherfucker!* As Ferguson saw it, Celia was acting in accord with the fundamental principles of the Federman Bill of Rights, the same impulse that had prompted her to put down the dollar in front of the old man at the automat when she was sixteen, and now that she was nineteen, nothing had changed. She called him at his apartment on the night of the twenty-third, and as Ferguson listened to her describe what had happened at Columbia that day, the noon rally at the Sundial in the middle of the campus, the attack on the gym construction site in Morningside Park, and then the takeover of Hamilton Hall by a coalition of SDS and SAS, white students and black students working in concert to shut down the university, he started to laugh—partly out of surprise, he imagined, but mostly out of happiness. When he hung up the phone, he understood that it was the first good laugh he had produced since before the evening he had picked up the same phone and talked to Allen Blumenthal.

At one o'clock on Friday afternoon (the twenty-sixth), he decided to suspend work on his novel for the rest of the day and head crosstown to check out what was happening at Columbia. It was too late to call Celia, who was undoubtedly with her fellow sandwich makers in the Chow Room at Ferris Booth Hall, but it wasn't going to be difficult to find her, and once he managed to tear her away from her platters of ham, bologna, and precut slices of packaged bread, they could walk around the campus together and see what was going on. As the crosstown bus traveled up Madison Avenue, he fell into the same conversation he seemed to have with himself every time he went to Morningside Heights: What if he had gone to Columbia instead of Princeton? And if he had gone there, how would his life have been different from the one he was leading now? No Brooklyn College for one thing. No East Eighty-ninth Street for another. No walking in on his grandfather's porn movie for yet another. No ten thousand dollars, no Nagle, and no Howard Small—which would have meant no barroom fight in Vermont, no trial, no miraculous rescue by Aunt Mildred, no imaginary tennis matches, and no romance between Howard and Amy, which had turned into a hot romance that showed no signs of cooling off anytime soon. The same three books with Gizmo, however, although the second and third would have been slightly different books. And the same roles for Mary Dono-hue, Evie Monroe, and Celia. But if he had gone to Columbia, would he be sitting in one of the occupied buildings with the protesting students now or would his life have put him on this same crosstown bus that was traveling along the northern edge of Central Park on its way to Morningside Heights?

The situation had altered since the twenty-third. The black-white alliance had broken apart, but four more buildings had been taken over by students, and the chairman of SDS, the acknowledged leader of the rebellion, happened to be one of Ferguson's old friends from high school, Mark Rudd. Yes, Mike Loeb was part of it too—Amy's ex-tormentor, ergo

Ferguson's ex-friend—but according to what Celia had heard, Loeb was just another one of the SDSers taking part in meetings at Mathematics Hall, whereas Rudd was in charge, the SDS spokesman and instigator-in-chief, and he and Ferguson had always gotten along well, sitting in many of the same English, French, and history classes together, going out on double dates with their almost identically named girlfriends, Dana and Diana, and cutting school together one morning to run off to New York, where they visited the Stock Exchange on Wall Street in order to see *capitalism in action*, and how fitting and oddly funny it was that Mark, who had taught him how to drive a standard-shift car in the spring of their junior year, which had allowed Ferguson to operate Arnie Frazier's Chevy van and spend another summer as a mover of large, heavy objects, was now leading a student rebellion and had his picture in the paper every day.

As it happened, Ferguson didn't quite make it to Columbia that afternoon. The number 4 crosstown bus traveled from the East Side to the West Side along 110th Street, alternatively known as Cathedral Park-way in the blocks between Central Park West and Riverside Drive, and when the bus reached the corner of Broadway and 110th, Ferguson jumped off and began walking north toward the campus on 116th Street, but in order to get to where he was going, he first had to go by the block where Celia lived, West 111th between Broadway and Amsterdam, and curiously enough, as he passed 111th and plodded on toward the next corner, he unexpectedly caught sight of Celia herself, Celia in a flowing blue skirt and pink blouse, about half a block ahead of him and also walking north, no doubt on her way to the Chow Room at Ferris Booth Hall. The fact that Celia wasn't alone did not disturb him, even though the person she was with was not one of her Barnard roommates but a man, in this case a twenty-two-year-old man named Richard Smolen, whom Ferguson recognized as one of the Columbia pre-med students he had talked to back in October when Celia had been setting up inter-views for him as an aid to writing his novel, and because Smolen was from New Rochelle and had played on baseball and basketball teams with Artie as a boy, Celia had known him all her life, and why would Ferguson feel the slightest envy or apprehension to discover that Celia was walking uptown with an old friend? He quickened his pace in order to catch up with them, but before he could get within shouting distance, Celia and Richard Smolen stopped in the middle of the sidewalk, threw their arms around each other, and began to kiss. It was a passionate kiss, a prolonged kiss, a lustful kiss of pure and uncontrollable desire, and from all Ferguson could gather as he stood on the sidewalk not twenty feet from where they were embracing, it was a kiss of love.

If it was love, one could only assume they had just emerged from Celia's apartment, where they had spent the past however many hours rolling around on Celia's bed, and now that they had put their clothes back on and were walking north to Columbia to make sandwiches for the students in the occupied buildings, the afterglow of their lust binge was burning so brightly that they couldn't keep their hands off each other and were still hungry for more.

Ferguson turned around and began walking south.

Epilogue: He didn't call, and she didn't call until Monday—to tell him about Smolen (which was old news to him by then) and to call it quits. A silent weekend, during which he concluded that he was to blame for the disaster and that Smolen wasn't the cause of his troubles so much as a symptom of them, and because he had been dishonest with her from the start, he deserved to be dumped. Celia the beautiful. Celia and the manifold deliriums of touching Celia and folding her body into his. But sex wasn't enough. It seemed unimaginable to have arrived at that thought, but sex wasn't enough, and nearly everything else about them had been wrong. He had willed himself to love her, but he had never loved anything but the idea of loving her, which wasn't love but a form of gross and unforgivable stupidity, so let her go off with her handsome pre-med boy, he said to himself, let her walk with her future heart specialist and current heartthrob back into the whirlwind at Columbia, for the fire was still spreading, and the time had come for Ferguson to let her whirl out of his life and go to the next place without him.

IN THE MONTHS that followed, no more central characters in *The Ferguson Story* dropped dead on tennis courts or anywhere else, and no more loves were found or lost or even contemplated. A slow, dreary summer with his novel as he began writing the second of the two parts, locked up in his studio apartment for most of the day with no one to see at night except for Billy and Joanna down the block and Noah, who was in town working as an actor in his first professional film, but Noah was both busy and exhausted and had little time for him except on the weekends.

Everyone else was gone, either camped out in family bungalows or rented shacks in upstate New York and New England or following the low-budget trail through various cities and countrysides in western Europe. As always, Howard was at his aunt and uncle's farm in Vermont, but this time Amy was with him, and the two of them were already discussing plans for life after college, which would begin in just one year, and assuming Howard managed to avoid the draft, they were both thinking about graduate school, Howard in philosophy and Amy in American history, the ideal choice being Columbia, where they could live together in an apartment on Morningside Heights and become citizens of New York. Again and again, Howard and Amy asked Ferguson to visit them in Vermont, and again and again Ferguson invented an excuse not to make the trip. Vermont was a haunted place for him, he said, and he still didn't know if he was quite ready to go back there, or he was too wrapped up in his novel to think of leaving New York, or he had come down with a summer cold and wasn't up to traveling, but even as he said those things (which were partly true) the greater truth was that now that he had lost Celia, Amy was in his thoughts again, the eternally lost and beloved Amy who had never wanted him and never would, and to expose himself to the spectacle of her happiness with his unofficial brother-in-law was more than he could have handled just then. It wasn't that he had stopped thinking about Celia that summer, but she climbed into his head less often than he had imagined she would, and as the first hot month turned into the second hot month, he was beginning to feel almost glad they were no longer together, as if a spell had been broken and he was back to being himself and not some fabricated or deluded vision of himself, whereas Artie was with him again in the summer heat, Artie's death and his father's death, those were the memories he dwelled on most as he sat in his hot little room bleeding out the words of his book, and once the matter of his inheritance had been settled at the end of April (not a standard bequest, as it turned out, but the funds from a life insurance policy that circumvented the need to pay any death taxes), he had taken the five thousand dollars from Dan and now watched in morbid wonder as month by month the ninety-five thousand inched its way back to the original one hundred thousand. Invisible money, Dan had said. Ferguson called it *ghost money.*

He was writing a book about death, and on some days he felt the book was trying to kill him. Every sentence was a struggle, every word in every sentence could have been a different word, and as with all the other things he had written in the past three years, he was turning out roughly four pages for every page he kept. Still and all, he had one hundred and twenty-two finished pages by the beginning of the summer, and half the story had been told. A plague of suicides that is now coming to the end of its third month, during which the city of R. has buried twenty-one of its children, an alarming number for a provincial town of ninety-four thousand inhabitants, and Dr. Noyes has been in the thick of it from the start, working with two dozen fellow doctors, a dozen psychiatrists, and close to thirty priests and ministers to ward off the next suicide, but in spite of their intense collective effort, which entails long interviews and counseling sessions with every young person in the city, nothing they do provides the smallest bit of help, and by now the doctor is questioning whether the countless hours they are putting in to end the scourge have only prolonged it, whether isolating a problem and holding it up to public view month after month after month doesn't keep the problem alive rather than solve it, thereby tempting the vulnerable ones to solve their own problems in ways they might not have thought of on their own, and so the children of R. go on killing themselves as before, and bit by bit the staunch Dr. Noyes is coming undone. That was where Ferguson had left off when he took his final exams and wrote his end-of-the-term course papers in June, and as he felt his way back into the story during the early weeks of the summer, he already knew how it was going to end, but helpful as it was to know that, knowing was not doing, and getting to the end would mean little unless he managed to do it right. The problems facing the young people of Noyes's city are at once eternal and of the moment, a combination of biological destiny and contingent historical facts. The adolescent upheavals of first loves and broken loves, the daily fear of being singled out for expulsion by the herd, the fear of pregnancy, the trauma of real pregnancy and too-early motherhood, the thrills of excess (driving too fast, drinking too much), ennui, contempt for parents, adults, and everyone in charge, melancholy, loneliness, and the pain of the world (*Weltschmerz*) pressing on the heart even as sunlight pours down upon them—the old, never-ending torments of being young—but for the ones most at risk, the seventeen- and eighteen-year-old boys, there is the threat of Vietnam looming before them the instant they leave school, the incontestable reality of the American moment, for few high school graduates go on to college from the blue-collar city of R., where the end of high school means the beginning of adult life, and now that sixty-four coffins containing the bodies of dead U.S. soldiers have been shipped back home and buried in local cemeteries over the past three years, now that the limbless and eyeless older brothers of those boys have landed in the wards of the nearby V.A. hospital in W., the patriotic fervor that swept through R. in the summer of 1965 has turned to revulsion and dread by the spring of 1968, and the war being fought by the American government on the other side of the world is no longer a war any of those boys is willing to fight in. To die for nothing as their brothers did, as their cousins did, as their friends' brothers did seems to mock the principles of life itself, and why were they born, they ask themselves, and what are they doing on this earth if it is only to give away their lives for nothing before they have even begun to live? Some maim themselves by shooting off fingers and toes in order to flunk their army physicals, but others prefer the less bloody solution of gassing themselves to death in idling cars enclosed within their parents' locked garages, and as often as not, if the boy happens to have a girlfriend, the girl and the boy will be sitting in the car together, wrapped in each other's arms as the fumes slowly carry out their work. In the beginning, Noyes is appalled by these senseless deaths and does everything he can to stop them, but as time goes on his thoughts start moving in a different direction, and by the fourth or fifth month, he is infected by the contagion himself. What Ferguson was proposing to do with the story after that was to follow Noyes through the various steps that will lead him to take his own life at the end of the book, the enormous sympathy he develops for the young people in his charge, the conversations with more than two hundred and fifty boys and girls that convince him the city is not going through a medical crisis but a spiritual crisis, that the question is not death or a desire for death but a loss of hope in the future, and once Noyes understands that they are all living in a world without hope, Ferguson was planning to put him together with one of the young people he has been counseling for the past months, a seventeen-year-old girl named Lily McNamara, whose twin brother Harold has already killed himself, and the no longer married and childless Dr. Noyes will take Lily into his house for a week or a month or half a year and try to talk the plain, stubborn, inarticulate girl into giving up her thoughts of death. It will be his last stand, a last effort to push back his own desire to succumb, and when he fails to turn her back to life, he will follow her into the garage, shut the doors and windows, and then climb into the car with her and turn on the ignition . . .

Seventy-four slowly written and rewritten pages between mid-June and mid-September, and two weeks after he started riding the subway back and forth to Brooklyn again, his collected works were published by Tumult Books. After such a hard summer, *Prolusions* sprang up out of the earth as unexpectedly as the first crocus in early spring. A flash of purple bursting through the mud and blackened snow on the chilly ground, a beautiful spear of color in an otherwise colorless world, for the dust jacket of *Prolusions* was indeed purple, the shade of purple called mauve, the color Ferguson and Ron had selected out of the numerous colors available to them, an austerely designed typographical cover with his name and the title in black bordered by a thin white rectangle, a glancing nod to the Gallimard covers in France, elegant, so very elegant, Ferguson thought, and when he held a copy of the book in his hands for the first time, he experienced something he had not been prepared for: a thunderbolt of exaltation. Not dissimilar to the exaltation he had felt after winning the Walt Whitman Scholarship, he realized, but with this difference: the scholarship had been taken away from him, but the book would always be his, even if no more than seventeen people ever read it.

There were reviews. For the first time in his life, he was bussed and slapped in public, thirteen times over the next four months by his reckoning, long, medium, and short reviews in newspapers, magazines, and literary quarterlies, five satisfying tongue kisses, a friendly pat on the back, three punches to the face, one knee to the balls, one execution by firing squad, and two shrugs. Ferguson was both a genius and an idiot, both a wonder boy and a supercilious oaf, both the best thing that had happened this year and the worst thing that had happened this year, both brimming with talent and utterly devoid of it. Nothing had changed since the Hank-Frank rumpus with Mrs. Baldwin and the contravening opinions of Aunt Mildred and Uncle Don half a century ago, the push and pull of positive and negative, the endless standoff in the courtrooms of judgment, but try as he did to ignore both the good and the bad that were said about him, Ferguson had to admit that the stings went on

stinging long after the kisses had worn off, that it was harder to forget
being attacked as "a frantic, out-of-control hippie who doesn't believe
in literature and wants to destroy it" than it was to remember being
praised as "a bright new kid on the block." Fuck it, he said to himself,
as he filed away the reviews in the bottom drawer of his desk. If and
when he ever published another book, he would stop up his ears with
candle wax, cover his eyes with a blindfold, strap his body to the mast
of a ship, and then ride out the storm until the Sirens could no longer
touch him.

Not long after the book came out, Mary Donohue came back in.
Celia had been gone for five months at that point, and the solitary, sex-
starved Ferguson was more than interested to hear from Joanna that her
sister had recently broken up with her boyfriend of the past eighteen
months, and if Ferguson had any wish to see Mary again, Joanna would
be more than happy to invite both of them to dinner one night in the
coming days or weeks. Mary was all done with Michigan now and
was back in New York studying law at NYU, fifteen or twenty pounds
slimmer, according to Joanna, and she was asking him because Mary
had asked her, and if Ferguson was willing, it appeared Mary would be
willing, too, and so it was that Ferguson and Mary started seeing each
other again, that is, started sleeping together again as in the old days
back in the summer of 1966, and no, it wasn't love, it would never be
love, but in some ways it was even better than love, friendship, friendship pure and simple, with immense quantities of admiration on both
sides, and so deeply had Ferguson come to trust Mary by the second
month of their second affair that she was the one he chose to unburden
himself to about Celia, opening up for the first time about the Artie
business, the baseball business, and the shameful diaphragm business,
telling her what he had never been able to tell anyone else, and when
he had marched to the end of that wretched tale of silence and deceit,
he turned away from her, looked at the wall, and said: What's wrong
with me?

Being young, Mary replied. That's the only thing that was ever
wrong with you. You were young, and you thought the thoughts of an
undeveloped young person with a big heart and an overdeveloped case
of youthful idealism. Now you're not so young anymore, and you've
stopped thinking that way.

Is that all?

That's all. Except for the other thing, which has nothing to do with being young. You should have told her, Archie. What you did was . . . how can I say this without hurting your feelings . . . ?

Reprehensible.

Yes, that's the word for it. Reprehensible.

I wanted to marry her, you see, or at least I thought I wanted to marry her, and if I'd told her we would never be able to have children, she probably would have turned me down.

Still. It was wrong not to say anything about it.

Well, I've told you, haven't I?

It's not the same with me.

Oh? And why is that?

Because you don't want to marry me.

Who knows if I do or don't? Who knows if you do or don't? Who knows anything?

Mary laughed.

At least you can stop taking the Pill now, Ferguson continued.

You're not the only man in New York, you know. What happens if I stumble out one night, bump into Señor Magnifico, and get swept off my feet?

Just don't tell me about it, that's all I ask.

In the meantime, Archie, you should go to another doctor—just to make sure.

I know, Ferguson said, I know I should, and I will, someday soon, of course I'll go, someday soon, I promise.

NINETEEN SIXTY-NINE WAS the year of the seven conundrums, the eight bombs, the fourteen refusals, the two broken bones, the number two hundred and sixty-three, and the one life-changing joke.

1) Four days after Richard Nixon was installed as the thirty-seventh president of the United States, Ferguson wrote the last sentence of *The Capital of Ruins*. The first draft was done, the long-labored-over first draft, which had been through so many revisions by then that it probably could have counted as the ninth or tenth draft, but Ferguson still wasn't satisfied with the manuscript, not fully satisfied at any rate, feeling there was more work to be done before he could declare it finished, so he held on to the book for another four months, tinkering

and refining, cutting and adding, replacing words and sharpening sentences, and when he sat down to type up the final, final version in early June, he was in the middle of his final exams at Brooklyn College and almost ready to graduate.

There was only one publisher Ferguson knew, only one publisher he wanted to publish with, and now that he had completed his novel, how pleasant it would have been to hand over the manuscript to his friends at Tumult Books, who again and again had told him they would go on publishing his work *forever*. But things had changed in the past several months, and the still developing young company, which had brought out twelve books since its birth in the summer of 1967, was on the verge of extinction. The twice-married Trixie Davenport, the sole financial backer of the small but not invisible press, had married for a third time in April, and her new husband, Victor Krantz, who seemed to have no visible occupation beyond managing Trixie's investments, was not a lover of art (except for the art produced by dead painters such as Mondrian and Kandinsky) and advised the Tumult angel to stop throwing her money away on "useless causes" such as Tumult Books. Thus the plug was pulled. All contracts for future books were canceled, copies not already in bookstores or in the distributor's warehouse were to be remaindered, and those not remaindered were to be pulped. In the nine months since it had been published, *Prolusions* had sold 806 copies. Not so many, perhaps, but by Tumult standards a decent showing, the fourth-best seller on the list after Anne's book of erotic poems (1,486), Billy's *Crushed Heads* (1,141), and Bo's racy diaries about downtown queer life after dark (966). In late May, Ferguson bought one hundred dred copies of his own book for two dollars each, stored the boxes in the basement of the house on Woodhall Crescent, and then returned to New York that same evening to attend a crowded party at Billy's place, where all who had worked for or published with Tumult Books along with their wives, husbands, girlfriends, and boyfriends gathered to curse the name of Victor Krantz and get themselves snockered. Even sadder, now that Joanna was pregnant again and Billy was working as a furniture mover to bring more money into the household, there was the inevitable moment when Billy stood up on a chair in the middle of the party and announced the end of Gizmo Press, but at least, Billy said, shouting drunkenly as the veins bulged in his neck, at least I'm going to carry on until I've published all the books and pamphlets I promised

I would, because *I'm A Person Who Honors His Commitments!*, a pointed reference to the pulled plugs at Tumult, and everyone applauded and praised Billy for being *a man of his word* as Joanna stood next to him with tears rolling down her cheeks and Mary stood next to Joanna with her arm around her sister's shoulder, and then Mary took out a handkerchief and started dabbing off the tears from Joanna's face, and Ferguson, who was standing close by and watching the scene carefully, loved Mary for doing that.

On Billy's advice, Ferguson found himself a literary agent to handle the business of setting him up with a new publisher. Her name was Lynn Eberhardt, and needless to say she was Billy's agent as well (not because Billy had finished another book but because she was hoping to sign up *Crushed Heads* with a paperback house now that Tumult had stopped breathing), and Ferguson was heartened by her response to *The Capital of Ruins*, which she called a brilliant *anti-war novel* in the letter she wrote accepting him as a client, and then, two days later on the phone, described it as *a Bergman movie transplanted to America and rendered into words*. Ferguson had mixed feelings about Bergman's films (he liked some and didn't like others), but he understood that Lynn considered it to be a high compliment and thanked her for her generous remark. Lynn was young and enthusiastic, a small, pretty woman with blond hair and bright rouged lips who had struck out on her own about one year earlier, and as a young, independent agent with no former clients in her stable, she was on a mission to find the best of the new young writers, and at twenty-two years and three months old, Ferguson was nothing if not young. Then she started sending out the manuscript to the New York publishers on her list, and one by one the rejections started coming in. It wasn't that any of those publishers thought Ferguson's book was bad or unworthy or didn't show signs of what one of them called "a remarkable talent," but the unanimous judgment was that *The Capital of Ruins* was so flagrantly *uncommercial* that even if they paid an advance of fifty dollars or no advance at all, they would have a hard time earning back the costs of printing the book. By the end of the year, after traveling through the mailrooms and offices of fourteen publishing companies, the manuscript had received fourteen rejection letters.

Fourteen straight punches, and every one of them hurt.

Don't worry, Lynn said. I'll think of something.

2) The four youngest members of the tangled-up clan graduated from their respective colleges in early June, Amy from Brandeis, Howard from Princeton, Noah from NYU, and Ferguson from his rural retreat near the Flatbush subway stop in Midwood, and now that the commencement exercises were over, all four of them had commenced their journeys into the future.

After spending the bulk of his adolescence and all of his youth preparing for a life in film, Noah had bushwhacked Ferguson and the others by reversing course and declaring his intention to stick to the theater from now on. Film acting was a mug's game, he said, a stop-and-start mechanized sham that couldn't compare to the real sham of performing in front of a live audience with no retakes or editor's scissors to save your skin. He had directed three little films of his own and had acted in three others, but now he was saying good-bye to celluloid and heading off to study three-dimensional acting and directing at the Yale School of Drama. Why more school? Ferguson asked him. Because I need more training, Noah said, but if it turns out that I don't, I'll quit the program, come back to New York, and move in with you. It's an awfully small place, Ferguson said. I know that, Noah answered, but you won't mind sleeping on the floor, will you?

More school for Noah, as not expected, and more school for Amy and Howard, as already promised and planned. Columbia for both of them, along with the splendors of unmarried conjugal life as Amy worked for a Ph.D. in American history, but Howard had backed off from philosophy and would be studying in the Classics Department, where he could delve ever more deeply into the gnomic utterances of the pre-Socratics and not have to waste his time on the doltish Anglo-American analyticals currently in fashion. Wittgenstein yes, but Quine gave him a headache, he said, and reading Strawson was like chewing glass. Ferguson understood how much Howard adored his old Greeks (the Nagle influence had been profound, far more lasting on Howard than it had been on him), but Ferguson couldn't help feeling a little disappointed by his friend's decision, for it seemed to him that Howard was better suited to art than to scholarship, and he wanted him to push on dangerously with his pens and pencils and try to make a go of it with his drawings, living off the hand that was already more skilled than the professional hand of Amy's father, and after the covers he had done for Billy and the cartoons he had published in the *Princeton Tiger* and the sidesplitting tennis matches and the dozens of other marvels he had zipped out over the years, Ferguson at last confronted Howard and asked him why school and not art? Because, his old roommate said, art is too easy for me, and I'm never going to get any better at it than I am now. I'm looking for something that will test me, a discipline to push me beyond where I think I can go. Does that make sense, Archie? Yes, it made sense, perhaps a good deal of sense, but still Ferguson was disappointed.

As for Ferguson himself, there had never been any question of more school. Enough was enough, he announced to the other members of the clan, and sometime late that spring he found himself a job, which was precisely the sort of job his father would have disapproved of, a job that was no doubt causing him to turn over in his grave now, but Fritz Mangini, the smartest and most reliable of Ferguson's friends at Brooklyn College, had a father who ran a contracting company, and one of the services that company contracted for was painting apartments, and when Fritz told Ferguson his father was looking for another painter to join the crew that summer, Ferguson met with Mr. Mangini in his office on Desbrosses Street in lower Manhattan and was hired. It wasn't a regular five-day-a-week job as most jobs were but a job-to-job situation with pauses in between, which would suit his purposes well, he figured, working for a week or two and then not working for a week or two, and the periods when he was on would generate enough money for him to eat and pay the rent during the periods when he was off. Now that he had graduated from college, he therefore was both a writer and a housepainter, but because he had just finished his first novel and was not yet prepared to begin something else (his brain was exhausted and he had run out of ideas), he was mostly a housepainter.

Amy would be marching forward with no obstacles in front of her, but the plans of the three others were contingent on what happened to them during and after their army physicals, which were scheduled to take place that summer, Howard's in mid-July, Noah's in early August, and Ferguson's in late August. In the event they were called up, Howard and Noah had each decided to follow Luther Bond's example and go north to Canada, but Ferguson, who was more stubborn and hotheaded than they were, had decided he would be willing to risk going to prison. The pro-war faction had names for people like them—*draft dodgers, cowards, traitors to their country*—but the three friends would not have objected to fighting for America in a war they felt to be just, since none of them was a pacifist who believed in opposing all wars, they were opposed only to this war, and in that they considered it to be morally indefensible, not just a political blunder but an act of criminal madness, they were enjoined by their patriotic duty to resist taking part in it. Howard's father, Noah's father, and Ferguson's stepfather had all been soldiers in World War II, and their sons and stepson admired them for having fought in the battle against fascism, which they considered to have been a just war, but Vietnam was something different, and how comforting it was for everyone in the large, tangled-up tribe to know that the three veterans of that other war stood by their sons and step-son in opposing this war.

The Battle of Hamburger Hill, Operation Apache Snow in the A Shau Valley, and the Battle of Binh Ba in Phuoc Tuy Province. Those were some of the names and places drifting back from Vietnam in the weeks before and after the three of them graduated from college, and as they prepared for their visits to the draft board in Newark (Howard) and the one on Whitehall Street in Manhattan (Noah and Ferguson), both Howard and Noah consulted doctors about imaginary ailments they hoped would earn them a classification of either 4-F (unfit for military service) or 1-Y (fit for military service, but only in cases of utmost urgency), which would spare them from having to move to Canada. Howard suffered from allergies to dust, grass, ragweed, goldenrod, and other airborne pollens during the spring and summer (hay fever), but his sympathetic, anti-war doctor wrote a letter declaring that he also suffered from asthma, a chronic disease that might or might not have warranted Howard a medical exemption. Noah went armed with a letter as well, a statement from the anti-war psychoanalyst he had been visiting twice a week for the past six months attesting to his patient's neurotic fear of open spaces (agoraphobia), which in times of undue stress blossomed into full-blown paranoia, and which, when coupled with his latent homosexual tendencies, made it impossible for him to function normally in all-male environments. When Noah pulled out the letter and showed it to Ferguson, he shook his head and laughed. Look at me, Archie, he said. I'm a danger to society. An out-and-out lunatic.

Do you think the doctor believes any of this junk? Ferguson asked.

Who can say? Noah replied. Then, after a brief pause, he let out another laugh and said: Probably.

In his own best interests, Ferguson supposed he should have gone to a doctor himself and done something similar to what Howard and Noah had done, but as the reader will have observed by now, Ferguson did not always act in his own best interests. On Monday morning, August twenty-fifth, he appeared at the induction center on White- hall Street with no letter to present to the army medical staff about any real or imagined physical or mental complaints. It was true that he had suffered from hay fever as a child himself, but he seemed to have outgrown it in recent years, and the one condition he did have, which had condemned him to the status of talking mule, was irrelevant to the matter at hand.

He wandered through the building in his white underpants, accompanied by a mob of other young men walking around in their white underpants. White young men, brown young men, black young men, and yellow young men—all of them in the same boat. He took the written exam, his body was measured, weighed, and scrutinized, and then he went home, wondering what would happen to him next.

3) Ho Chi Minh died on September second at the age of seventy- nine. Ferguson, who was on his fourth job for Mr. Mangini since the start of the summer, heard the news on the radio as he stood on a lad- der painting the kitchen ceiling of a three-bedroom apartment on Cen- tral Park West between Eighty-third and Eighty-fourth Streets. Uncle Ho was dead, but nothing would change because of that, and the war would go on until the North conquered the South and the Americans were booted out. That much was certain, he said to himself, as he dipped his brush into the can for another swipe at the ceiling, but many other things were not. Why the letter announcing the date of his physi- cal had been sent to him a full month after Howard and Noah had been sent theirs, for example, or why Howard had already been given his new classification from the board in Newark (1-Y) but after an equivalent length of time Noah still had heard nothing from the board in Manhattan. It was all so arbitrary, it seemed, a system that func- tioned with two independent hands, each one unaware of what the other was doing as they performed their separate tasks, and now that the physical was behind him, it was unclear how long he would have to wait.

He was preparing himself for the worst, and throughout the summer and into the fall he thought endlessly about prison, about being locked up against his will and having to submit to the capricious rules and commands of his jailers, about the threat of being raped by one or more of his fellow prisoners, about sharing a cell with a violent, shiv-toting con serving out a seven-year sentence for armed robbery or a hundred years for murder. Then his mind would drift off from the present and he would start thinking about *The Count of Monte Cristo*, the book he had read as a twelve-year-old boy, the falsely accused Edmond Dantès held captive for fourteen years in the Château d'If, or *Darkness at Noon*, the novel he had read in the eighth grade, with the two imprisoned men in adjoining cells tapping out coded messages to each other on the walls, or the inordinate number of prison movies he had watched over the years, among them *Grand Illusion*, *A Man Escaped*, *I Am a Fugitive from a Chain Gang*, Dreyfus on Devil's Island in *The Life of Emile Zola*, *Riot in Cell Block 11*, *The Big House*, *20,000 Years in Sing Sing*, and *The Man in the Iron Mask*, another Dumas story in which the evil twin brother is choked to death by his own beard.

Jittery, darting thoughts hatched in the dual incubators of uncertainty and steadily growing panic.

Summer had always been a time of intense work for him, but that summer Ferguson accomplished little except to read the first four rejection letters that came in for *The Capital of Ruins*. One month after Ho Chi Minh's death, the number was up to seven.

4) Throughout the summer and fall of that year, as Ferguson put in his hours for Mr. Mangini and pondered the uncertain future that lay before him, a man was setting off bombs around New York City. Sam Melville, or Samuel Melville, had been born Samuel Grossman in 1934, but he had changed his name in honor of the man who wrote *Moby-Dick*, or else in honor of the French film director Jean-Pierre Melville, who himself had been born Jean-Pierre Grumbach, or else in honor of no one and for no reason at all, except perhaps to disassociate himself from his father and his father's name. An independent Marxist allied to the Weathermen and the Black Panthers but essentially working on his own (sometimes with an accomplice or two, most often not), Melville planted his first bomb on July twenty-seventh, damaging the structure of Grace Pier on the New York waterfront, an installation owned by the United Fruit Company, the age-old exploiter of down-

trodden peasants in Central and South America. On August twentieth, he attacked the Marine Midland Bank Building; on September nineteenth, the offices of the Department of Commerce and the Army Inspector General in the Federal Office Building on lower Broadway. Subsequent targets included the Standard Oil offices in the RCA Building, the headquarters of Chase Manhattan Bank, and, on November eleventh, the General Motors Building on Fifth Avenue, but the following day, when Melville went to bomb the Criminal Courts Building on Centre Street, where the Panther 21 trial was being held, he made the error of choosing an F.B.I. informant as his accomplice and was nabbed on the spot. He wound up in the Tombs in April 1970, where he organized a strike among the prisoners, which led to his transfer to Sing Sing in July, where he organized another prison strike, which led to another transfer in September to one of the maximum-security facilities in upstate New York, Attica.

By all accounts, Melville's growing radicalism had been spurred by the events at Columbia in the spring of 1968. On the night of the April thirtieth bust, the thirty-four-year-old ex–plumbing designer turned up on campus to lend his support to the students, and in the mayhem of one thousand swarming T.P.F. grunts and seven hundred arrested students and the innumerable assaults on the green-bands and white-bands, Melville urged the students to push back and fight the police. With a small gang of protesters, he started hauling fifty-gallon garbage cans made of tempered, vulcanized steel to the roof of Low Library to drop down on the cops below. The younger students were afraid, not at all prepared to take part in such a reckless action, and scattered into the night. Before long, Melville was discovered by the police and dragged into another building, where they pounded him with clubs and left him tied to a chair. Some days after that, he joined up with the local Community Action Committee (C.A.C.), a group opposed to Columbia's policy of evicting poor tenants from university-owned buildings, and at one of the C.A.C. demonstrations in front of the St. Marks Arms on West 112th Street, he was arrested along with several other members of the group.

Columbia had lit the fire in him, and by the next year he had begun his bombing campaign throughout the city. So skillfully did he pull off the first attacks that he remained at large for three and a half months, undetected and untraceable. The tabloids called him the Mad Bomber.

Ferguson had never met Sam Melville and had no idea who he was until his arrest on November twelfth, but their stories crossed with the fourth and most destructive of the eight bombings, crossed in such a way as to alter the direction of Ferguson's life, for it was all but certain that the fit and healthy college graduate would have been classified 1-A by his draft board, which would have opened the path to a trial in federal court and a term in federal prison, but when Melville blew up the Army Induction Center on Whitehall Street in early October, Ferguson still had not received any word about his classification, and when no word came for the rest of that month, nor any word throughout November, Ferguson cautiously advanced the theory that his army records had been destroyed by Melville's bomb, that he was, as he liked to say to himself, *off the books.*

In other words, if Ferguson was indeed off the books, then Sam Melville had saved his life. The so-called Mad Bomber had saved his life along with the lives of hundreds if not thousands of others, and then Melville had sacrificed his own life by going to prison *for them.*

5) Or so Ferguson imagined, or so he hoped, or so he prayed was true, but whether he was off the books or not, there was still one more bridge to cross before the matter could be settled. Nixon had changed the law. The Selective Service System would no longer be depending on the entire pool of American men between eighteen and twenty-six to fill the ranks of the army but only on some of them, the ones who would be assigned the lowest numbers in the new draft lottery, which would be held on Monday, December first. Three hundred and sixty-six possible numbers, one for every day of the year including leap year, one for the birthday of every young man in the United States, a blind draw of numbers that would tell you whether you were free or not free, whether you were going off to fight or staying home, whether you were going to prison or not going to prison, the whole shape of your future life to be sculpted by the hands of General Pure Dumb Luck, commander of urns, coffins, and all national graveyards.

Absurd.

The country had been transformed into a casino, and you weren't even allowed to roll the dice for yourself. The government would be rolling them for you. Anything below eighty or a hundred would spell danger. Anything above would spell: *Thank you, massuh.*

The number for March third was 263.

No exaltation this time, no thunderbolt or electric current in his veins, no purple crocus jutting through the blackened snow, but a sudden feeling of calm, perhaps even resignation, perhaps even sadness. He had been ready to do the defiant thing he had promised to do, and now he didn't have to do it anymore. He didn't even have to think about it anymore. Stand up and breathe, stand up and move around, stand up and take in the world, and as Ferguson stood up and breathed and moved around and took in the world, he understood that he had been living in a state of paralysis for the past five months.

Father, he said to himself, my strange, dead father, your boy will not be going to live behind bars. Your boy is free to go wherever he wants. Pray for your boy, father, just as he prays for you.

Ferguson sat back down at his desk and scanned the newspaper for June sixteenth, Noah's birthday.

Number 274.

And then Howard's, which was January twenty-second.

Number 337.

Late the following afternoon, Noah hitched a ride down from New Haven, and at seven o'clock Ferguson and Howard met him at the West End to begin the evening with a round of drinks before going off to a celebratory Chinese dinner at the Moon Palace, just two blocks south on Broadway. Feeling comfortable in their front corner booth, however, they lingered at the West End and never made it to the restaurant, dining on their favorite bar's abominable pot roast and noodles and then staying on until two-thirty in the morning as they slurped down vast quantities of alcohol in several of its best known forms, mostly scotch for Ferguson, mediocre blended scotch that led him on a bumpy ride to the nethermost bowels of drunkenness, but until he dissolved into a slurry, blotto, double-visioned torpor and was lugged by his two wobbling companions back to Howard and Amy's apartment on West 113th Street, where he spent the early morning hours passed out on the sofa, he remembered that Howard and Noah had ganged up on him at one point and had criticized him for a number of things, some of which he could still remember, some of which he couldn't, but among those he could remember were the following:

□ He was a fool for not touching the money his father had left him.

□ With help from the money he still hadn't touched, he should wave good-bye to America, cross the Atlantic, and spend a minimum of one year in Europe. He had yet to go anywhere in his sorry little life and needed to start traveling *now*.

☐ Forget that Mary Donohue had found her Señor Magnifico and was talking about marriage, for even though Mary was a remarkable woman and had held Ferguson together through some rough times, they had no future together because he wasn't what she wanted or needed and had nothing to offer her.

☐ Twelve rejections from New York publishers was nothing to lose any sleep over, and even if the book was rejected by twelve more publishers, it would eventually be published by someone, and the only thing that mattered now was to start thinking about his next book . . .

As Ferguson remembered it, he had agreed with them on all their points.

6) Because he was a conscientious employee, and because he didn't want to let down his fellow crew members by coming in late, Ferguson showed up for work the next morning at nine sharp. He had slept for four and a half hours on Howard and Amy's couch, and after drinking three cups of black coffee at Tom's Restaurant on the corner of Broadway and 112th Street, he walked over to the job site on Riverside Drive between Eighty-eighth and Eighty-ninth Streets, a gigantic four-bedroom apartment he had started painting a few days earlier with Juan, Felix, and Harry. The air was freezing that morning, and Ferguson was badly hungover, with bloodshot eyes, a cracked head, and an iffy gut, stumbling downtown with his face buried in his scarf, which began to reek of the booze still permeating his breath. Juan said: What happened to you, man? Felix said: You look wasted, kid. Harry said: Why don't you go home and sleep it off? But Ferguson didn't want to go home and sleep it off, he was perfectly fine and had come to work, but one hour later, as he stood on a tall, expandable ladder painting yet another kitchen ceiling, he lost his balance and fell to the floor, breaking his left ankle and his left wrist. Harry called for an ambulance, and after the doctor at Roosevelt Hospital had set the bones and put the wrist and ankle in plaster casts, he looked over his work and commented: A hard fall, young man. You're lucky you didn't land on your head.

7) Ferguson spent the next six weeks at the house on Woodhall Crescent, gorging himself on his mother's good cooking as his bones knit together again, playing gin rummy with Dan in the evenings after

dinner, sitting around the living room with the two Schneiderman men on the nights when the Knicks games were on television, his mother and the pregnant Nancy off by themselves in the kitchen talking about the mysteries of womanhood, home life, the comforts and pleasures of being at home for a little while as he took his *compulsory breather* (Dan's words) or simply *took stock* (his mother's words) and thought about what he was going to do next.

Mary was gone, soon to be married to an intelligent señor named Bob Stanton, a thirty-one-year-old assistant district attorney from Queens, someone far more settled than Ferguson would ever be, not an unwise decision, he felt, but nevertheless an ache that would require more time to mend than his broken bones would, and with Mary gone now there was nothing to hold him in New York, nothing that compelled him to go on working as a housepainter for Mr. Mangini, for Howard and Noah had finally talked some sense into him on the night of their drunken binge, and he had reversed his thinking about his father's money, reluctantly agreeing with them that not to accept it would be an insult. His father was dead, and dead men couldn't defend themselves anymore. Whatever angers had built up between them over the years, his father had included him in his will, which meant he had wanted Ferguson to take the one hundred thousand dollars and use it in any way he saw fit, with the understanding that fit in this case meant living off the money in order to go on writing, surely his father must have known that, Ferguson reasoned, and the truth was there was little anger left in him now, the more his father went on being dead the less anger he felt, so little now after a year and a half that it was almost entirely gone, and the space that had once held the anger was now filled with sorrow and confusion, sorrow and confusion and regret.

It was a lot of money, enough money to live on for years if he spent it carefully, and Howard and Noah had done well to emphasize the importance of that money, wisely counseling patience on the matter of Ferguson's rejected novel (which Lynn Eberhardt finally found a home for in early February when she sent it to Columbus Books, a small, intrepid, against-the-grain San Francisco publisher that had been in operation since the 1950s), but most of all understanding that the money would allow Ferguson to take the step that would do him the most good in his present circumstances, and as he languished in the house on Woodhall Crescent and looked into the blur of possibilities the money had offered him, he gradually came round to his friends' point of view: the moment had come to get out of America and see something of the world, to leave the fire behind him and go somewhere else—anywhere else.

Ferguson dithered and mulled for the next two weeks, one by one reducing the plethora of anywheres from five to three to one. Language would have to have the last word, but even though they spoke English in England and English in Ireland, he doubted he would be happy living in one of those dank, wet-weather places. It rained in Paris, too, of course, but French was the only other language he could speak and read with tolerable proficiency, and since he had never heard anyone say a single negative word about Paris, he decided to take his chances there. As a warm-up, he would go to Montreal for a short visit with Luther Bond, who was alive and well in his new country, having talked his way into McGill around the same time Ferguson had entered Brooklyn College, and now that he had graduated, he was working as an apprentice reporter for the *Montreal Gazette* and living with a new girlfriend, Claire, Claire Simpson or Sampson (Luther's handwriting was often hard to decipher), and Ferguson was itching to go north, itching to go east, itching to be gone.

He figured he would be walking freely on his ankle again by the end of January, which would be more than enough time to vacate the apartment on East Eighty-ninth Street and prepare himself for the big move.

Then, on January first, as Ferguson was about to take the first bite of his first breakfast of the new decade, his mother told him the joke.

IT WAS AN old joke, apparently, one that had been circulating in Jewish living rooms for years, but for some unaccountable reason it had escaped Ferguson's notice, somehow or other he had never been in one of those living rooms when someone had been telling it, but on that New Year's Day morning of 1970 his mother finally told it to him in the kitchen, the classic story about the young Russian Jew with the long, unpronounceable name who arrives at Ellis Island and begins chatting with an older, more experienced *Lantsman*, and when the young one tells the old one his name, the old one frowns and says a name that long and unpronounceable won't do the job for his new life in America, he needs to change it to something shorter, something with a nice American ring to it. What do you suggest? the young one asks. Tell them you're Rockefeller, the old one says, you can't go wrong with that. Two hours go by, and when the young Russian sits down to be interviewed by an immigration official, he can no longer dredge up the name the old man advised him to give. Your name? the official asks. Slapping his head in frustration, the young man blurts out in Yiddish, *Ikh hob fargessen (I've forgotten)!* And so the Ellis Island official uncaps his fountain pen and dutifully records the name in his ledger: Ichabod Ferguson.

Ferguson liked the joke, and he laughed hard when his mother told it to him over breakfast in the kitchen, but when he limped upstairs to his bedroom afterward, he found himself unable to stop thinking about it, and with nothing to distract him from his thoughts, he kept on thinking about the poor immigrant for the rest of the morning and into the early afternoon, at which point the story was released from the domain of jokes to become a parable about human destiny and the endlessly forking paths a person must confront as he walks through life. A young man is suddenly torn into three young men, each one identical to the others but each with a different name: Rockefeller, Ferguson, and the long, unpronounceable X that has traveled with him from Russia to Ellis Island. In the joke, he ends up as Ferguson because the immigration official doesn't understand the language he is speaking. That was already interesting enough—to have a name forced on you because of someone's bureaucratic error and then to go on bearing that name for the rest of your life. Interesting, as in *bizarre* or *funny* or *tragic.* A Russian Jew transformed into a Scottish Presbyterian with fifteen strokes from another man's pen. And if the Jew is taken for a Protestant in white, Protestant America, if every person he encounters automatically assumes he is someone other than who he is, how will that affect his future life in America? Impossible to say exactly how, but one can assume it will make a difference, that the life he will lead as Ferguson will not be the same one he would have led as the young Hebrew X. On the other hand, young X was not opposed to becoming Rockefeller. He accepted his older compatriot's advice about the need to choose another name, and what if he had remembered that name instead of letting it slip out of his mind? He would have become a Rockefeller, and from that day forth people would have assumed he was a member of the richest family in America. His Yiddish accent would have fooled no one, but how would that have prevented people from assuming he belonged to another branch of the family, one of the subsidiary foreign branches that could trace its bloodlines directly back to John D. and his heirs? And if young X had had the wherewithal to remember to call himself Rockefeller, how would that have affected his future life in America? Would he have had the same life or a different life? No doubt a different life, Ferguson said to himself, but in what ways it was impossible to know.

Ferguson, whose name was not Ferguson, found it intriguing to imagine himself having been born a Ferguson or a Rockefeller, someone with a different name from the X that had been attached to him when he was pulled from his mother's womb on March 3, 1947. In point of fact, his father's father had not been given another name when he arrived at Ellis Island on January 1, 1900—but what if he had?

Out of that question, Ferguson's next book was born.

Not one person with three names, he said to himself that afternoon, which happened to be January 1, 1970, the seventieth anniversary of his grandfather's arrival in America (if family legend was to be believed), the man who had become neither Ferguson nor Rockefeller and had been gunned down in a Chicago leather-goods warehouse in 1923, but for the purposes of the story Ferguson would begin with his grandfather and the joke, and once the joke was told in the first paragraph his grandfather would no longer be a young man with three possible names but one name, neither X nor Rockefeller but Ferguson, and then, after telling the story of how his parents met, were married, and he himself was born (all based on the anecdotes he had heard from his mother over the years), Ferguson would turn the proposition on its head, and rather than pursue the notion of one person with three names, he would invent three other versions of himself and tell their stories along with his own story (more or less his own story, since he too would become a fictionalized version of himself), and write a book about four identical but different people with the same name: Ferguson.

A name born out of a joke about names. The punch line to a joke about the Jews from Poland and Russia who had boarded ships and come to America. Without question a Jewish joke about America—and the enormous statue that stood in New York Harbor.

Mother of exiles.

Father of strife.

Bestower of misbegotten names.

He was still traveling the two roads he had imagined as a fourteen-year-old boy, still walking down the three roads with Lazlo Flute, and all along, from the beginning of his conscious life, the persistent feeling that the forks and parallels of the roads taken and not taken were all being traveled by the same people at the same time, the visible people and the shadow people, and that the world as it was could never be more than a fraction of the world, for the real also consisted of what could have happened but didn't, that one road was no better or worse than any other road, but the torment of being alive in a single body was that at any given moment you had to be on one road only, even though you could have been on another, traveling toward an altogether different place.

Identical but different, meaning four boys with the same parents, the same bodies, and the same genetic material, but each one living in a different house in a different town with his own set of circumstances. Spun this way and that by the effect of those circumstances, the boys would begin to diverge as the book moved forward, crawling or walking or galloping their way through childhood, adolescence, and early manhood as more and more distinct characters, each one on his own separate path, and yet all of them still the same person, three imaginary versions of himself, and then himself thrown in as Number Four for good measure, the author of the book, but the details of the book were still unknown to him at that point, he would understand what he was trying to do only after he started doing it, but the essential thing was to love those other boys as if they were real, to love them as much as he loved himself, as much as he had loved the boy who had dropped dead before his eyes on a hot summer afternoon in 1961, and now that his father was dead as well, this was the book he needed to write—for them.

God was nowhere, he said to himself, but life was everywhere, and death was everywhere, and the living and the dead were joined.

Only one thing was certain. One by one, the imaginary Fergusons would die, just as Artie Federman had died, but only after he had learned to love them as if they were real, only after the thought of seeing them die had become unbearable to him, and then he would be alone with himself again, the last man standing.

Hence the title of the book: *4 3 2 1.*

□ □ □

SO ENDS THE book—with Ferguson going off to write the book. Loaded down with two heavy suitcases and a knapsack, he left New York on February third and traveled by bus to Montreal, where he spent one week with Luther Bond, and then he climbed onto a plane and headed across the ocean to Paris. For the next five and a half years, he lived in a two-room flat on the rue Descartes in the fifth arrondissement, working steadily on his novel about the four Fergusons, which grew into a much longer book than he had imagined it would be, and when he wrote the last word on August 25, 1975, the manuscript came to a total of one thousand one hundred and thirty-three double-spaced typed pages.

The most difficult passages for him to write were the ones that recounted the deaths of his beloved boys. How hard it was to conjure up the storm that killed the thirteen-year-old youth of the shining countenance, and how anguished he felt as he wrote down the details of the traffic accident that ended the life of the twenty-year-old Ferguson-3, and after those two necessary but horrendous obliterations, nothing caused him more pain than having to tell of Ferguson-1's death on the night of September 8, 1971, a passage he put off writing until the last pages of the book, the account of the fire that consumed the house in Rochester, New York, when Charlie Vincent, Ferguson-1's downstairs neighbor, fell asleep while smoking one of his Pall Malls in bed, igniting himself along with the sheets and blankets that covered him, and as the flames sprinted across the room, they eventually rose up and touched the ceiling, and because the wood in that old house was dry and crumbling, the fire burst through the ceiling and set the floor of the upstairs bedroom ablaze, and so rapidly did the fire advance upon the sleeping twenty-four-year-old journalist, translator, and lover of Hallie Doyle, that the entire room was burning before he had a chance to spring from the bed and crawl out the window.

Ferguson took a pause. He stood up from the desk, pulled out a cigarette from his shirt pocket, and walked around and back and forth between the two rooms of the small flat, and once he felt his mind was clear enough to start again, he returned to the desk, sat down in the chair, and wrote the final paragraphs of the book:

If Ferguson-1 had lived through the night, he would have woken the next morning and traveled to Attica with Gianelli, and for the next five days he would have written articles about the uprising at the prison, the mass takeover by more than a thousand men that shut down the facility as the strikers took thirty-nine guards hostage in order to press their demands for reform. There was little doubt that Ferguson-1 would have been heartened by the solidarity among the inmates. Nearly everyone in the racially divided prison stood together in backing the demands, and for the first time anyone could remember, black prisoners, white prisoners, and Latino prisoners were all on the same side. The other side budged a little, but not enough to offer any hope. They rejected the demand for amnesty, they rejected the demand to replace the prison superintendent, and they rejected the admittedly impossible demand to give the rebels safe passage out of the country, even after the Algerian government promised to accept them all. Four days of grinding, unsuccessful negotiations between the inmates and Department of Correctional Services commissioner Russell Oswald, and for four straight days Governor Rockefeller refused to come to the prison to help the two sides reach a settlement. Then, on September thirteenth, Rockefeller's mystifying command to take back the prison by force. At 9:46 A.M., the battalion of corrections officers and New York State troopers poised on top of the prison's outer walls opened fire on the men down in the yard, killing ten of the hostages and twenty-nine prisoners, among them Sam Melville, who was hunted down and executed at point-blank range minutes after the barrage of rifle fire had stopped. In addition to those thirty-nine deaths, three hostages and eighty-five inmates were wounded. The yard was awash in blood.

In the immediate aftermath of the attack, word spread that the inmates had slit the throats of the ten murdered captives, but the following day in Rochester, when the Monroe County medical examiner looked over the bodies of the ten dead guards, he affirmed that not one of them had been killed by knife wounds. They had all been shot by their fellow officers. In a *New York Times* story written by Joseph Lelyveld on the fifteenth, a relative of one of the slain guards, Carl Valone, viewed the body and later said: "There was no slashing. Carl was not even touched. He was killed by a bullet that had the name Rockefeller on it."

Nelson Rockefeller represented the liberal wing of the Republican Party, and until the Attica massacre he had always been seen as a man of moderation and good sense, but in May 1973 he again confounded the world when he pushed a series of laws through the New York State legislature that stipulated minimum penalties of fifteen years to life in prison for selling two ounces or more of heroin, morphine, opium, cocaine, or cannabis or for possessing four ounces or more of those same substances. The so-called Rockefeller Drug Laws were the most punitive ever imposed by any state in the country.

Perhaps he was still dreaming of becoming president and wanted to show how tough he was to the tough, law-and-order camp of the American public, but much as he had always wanted to become the leader of the Free World, he had failed to win his party's nomination after running for president in 1960, 1964, and 1968, losing out to Nixon, Goldwater, and again to Nixon, but when the disgraced Nixon resigned from office in 1974, his vice president, Gerald Ford, who himself had been appointed after the resignation of the disgraced Spiro Agnew, took over as the new president and appointed Nelson Rockefeller to become his vice president, making them the only two men in American history to hold their offices without being elected by the American people, and so it was, on December 19, 1974, after a 287-to-128 vote in the House of Representatives and a 90-to-7 vote in the Senate, that Nelson Rockefeller was sworn in as the forty-first vice president of the United States.

He was married to a woman named Happy.